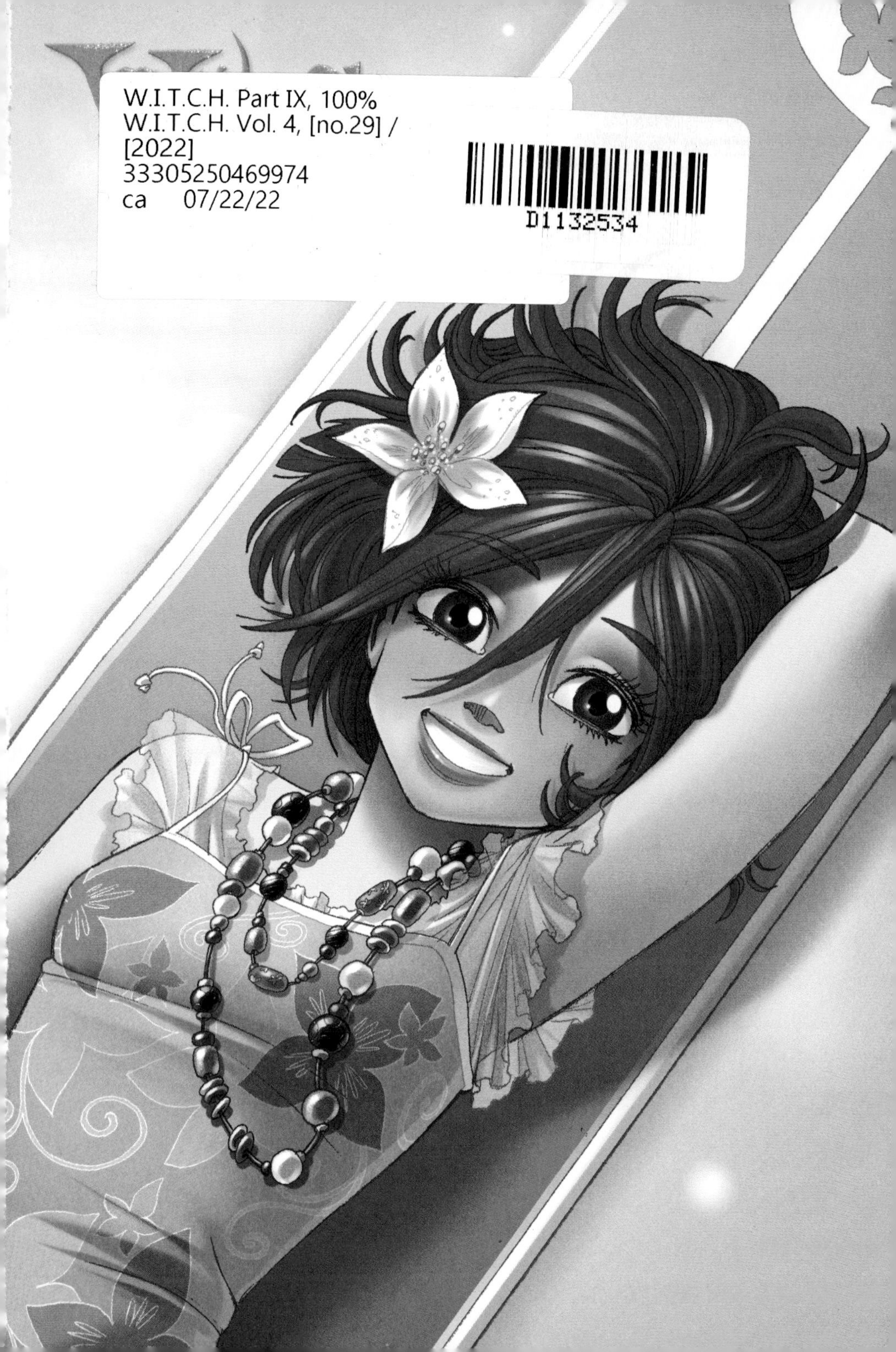

W.i.t.c.h.

Will   Irma   Taranee   Cornelia   Hay Lin

Part IX.
100% W.I.T.C.H.
Volume 4

CONTENTS

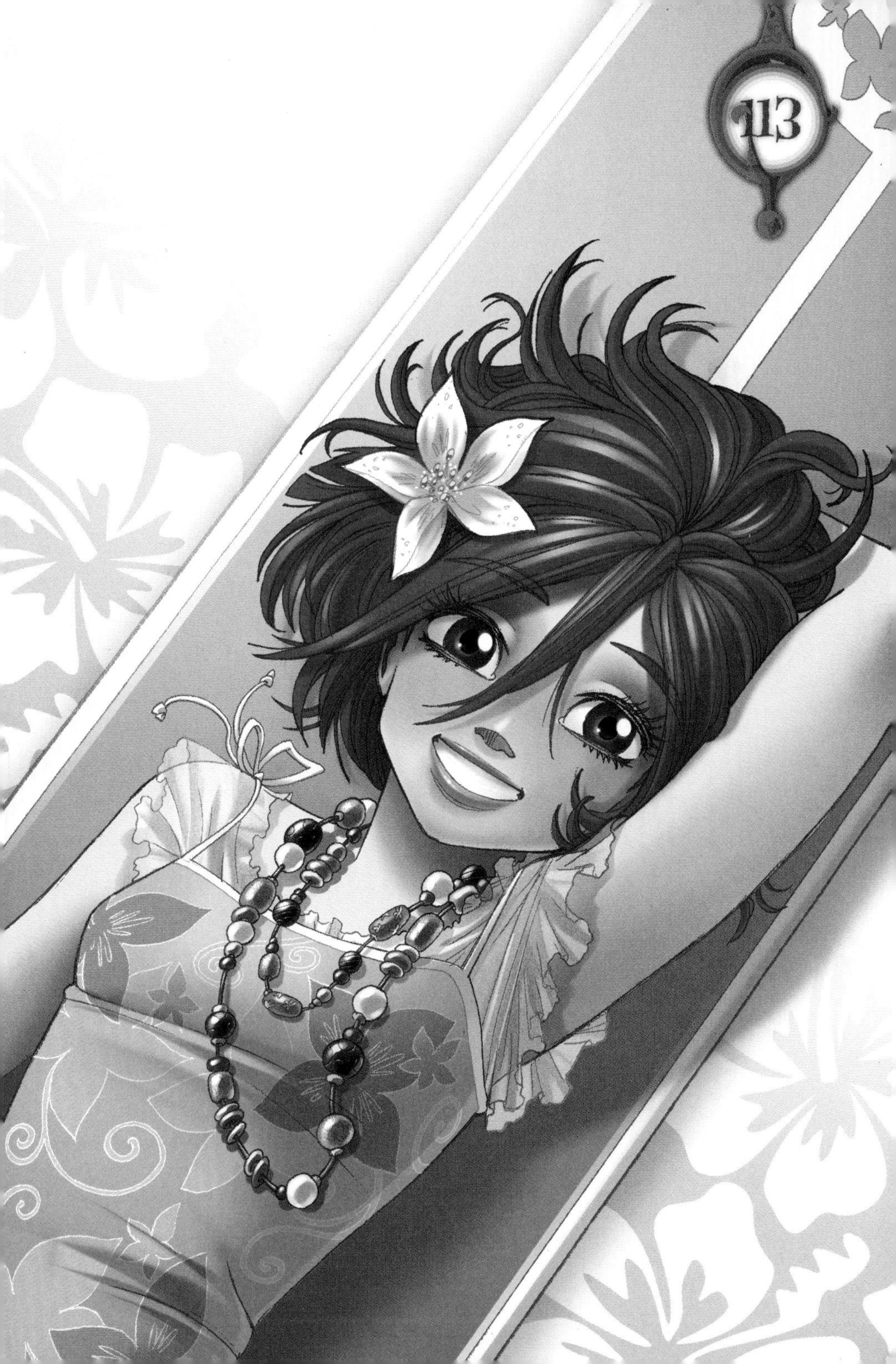
113

Will   Irma   Taranee   Cornelia   Hay Lin

The Long Kiss

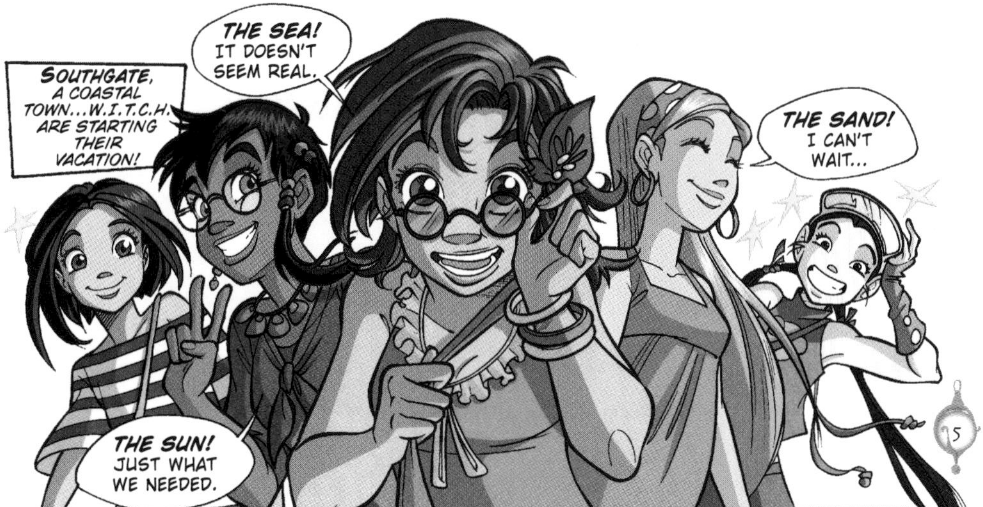
SOUTHGATE, A COASTAL TOWN... W.I.T.C.H. ARE STARTING THEIR VACATION!
THE SEA! IT DOESN'T SEEM REAL.
THE SAND! I CAN'T WAIT...
THE SUN! JUST WHAT WE NEEDED.

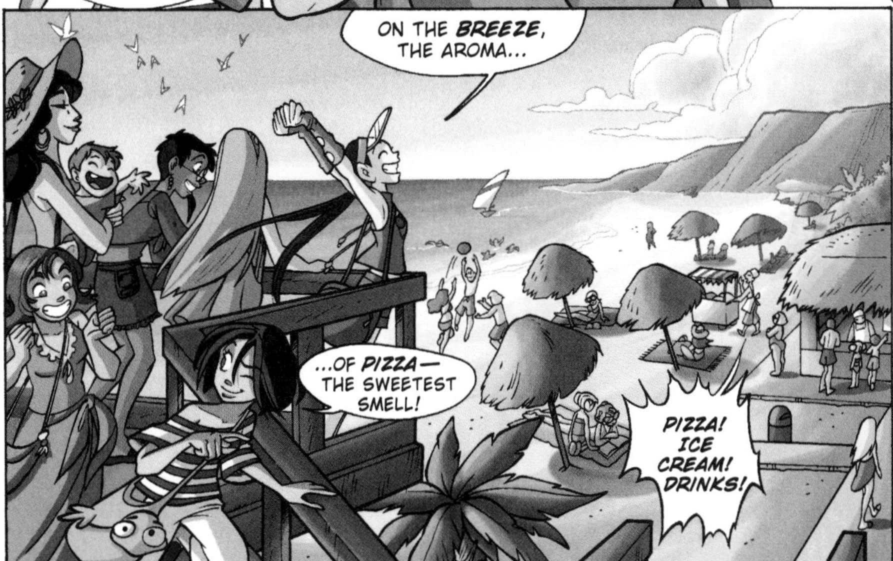
ON THE BREEZE, THE AROMA...
...OF PIZZA— THE SWEETEST SMELL!
PIZZA! ICE CREAM! DRINKS!

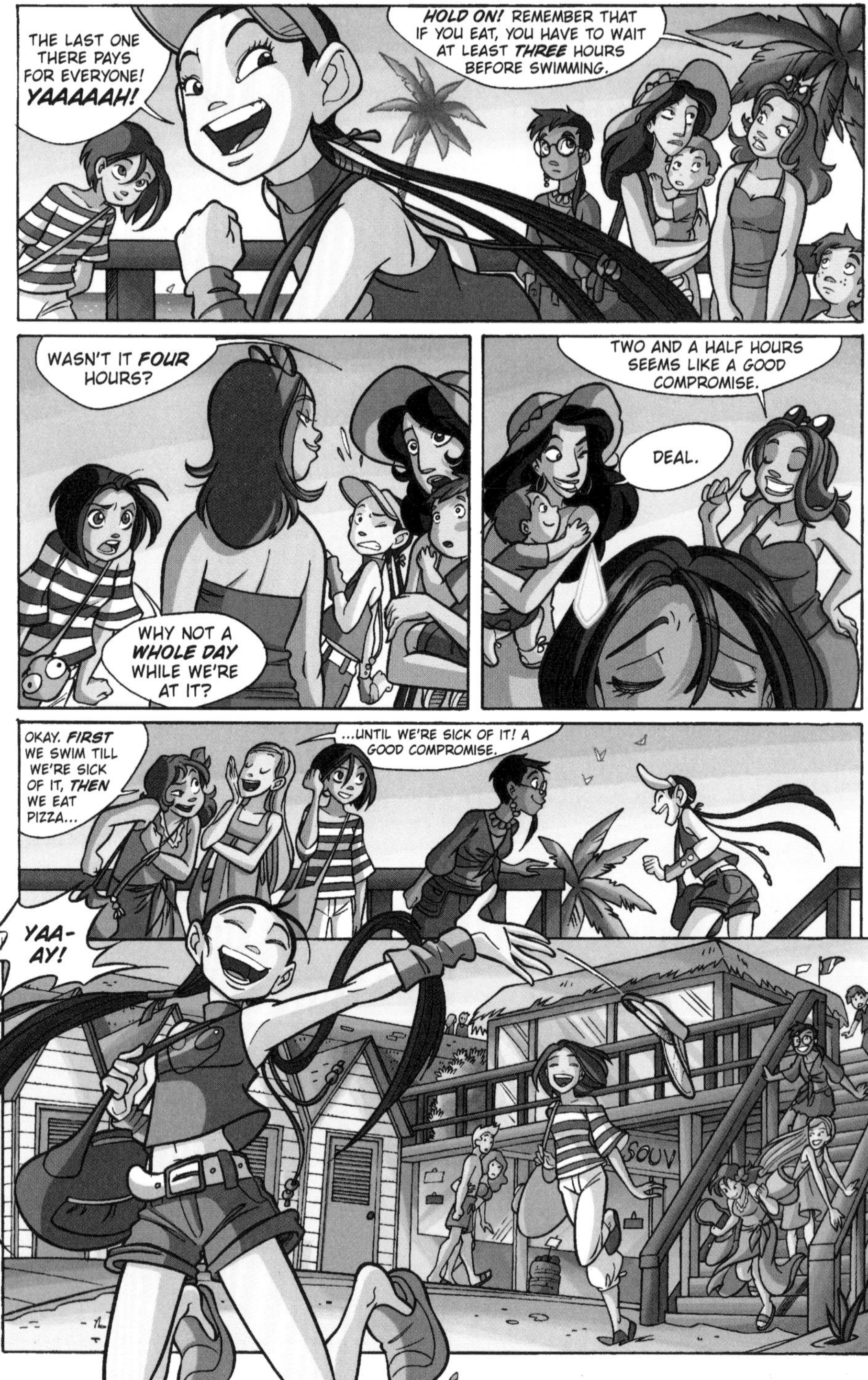

THE LAST ONE THERE PAYS FOR EVERYONE! YAAAAAH!
HOLD ON! REMEMBER THAT IF YOU EAT, YOU HAVE TO WAIT AT LEAST THREE HOURS BEFORE SWIMMING.
WASN'T IT FOUR HOURS?
WHY NOT A WHOLE DAY WHILE WE'RE AT IT?
TWO AND A HALF HOURS SEEMS LIKE A GOOD COMPROMISE.
DEAL.
OKAY. FIRST WE SWIM TILL WE'RE SICK OF IT, THEN WE EAT PIZZA...
...UNTIL WE'RE SICK OF IT! A GOOD COMPROMISE.
YAA-AY!
SOUV

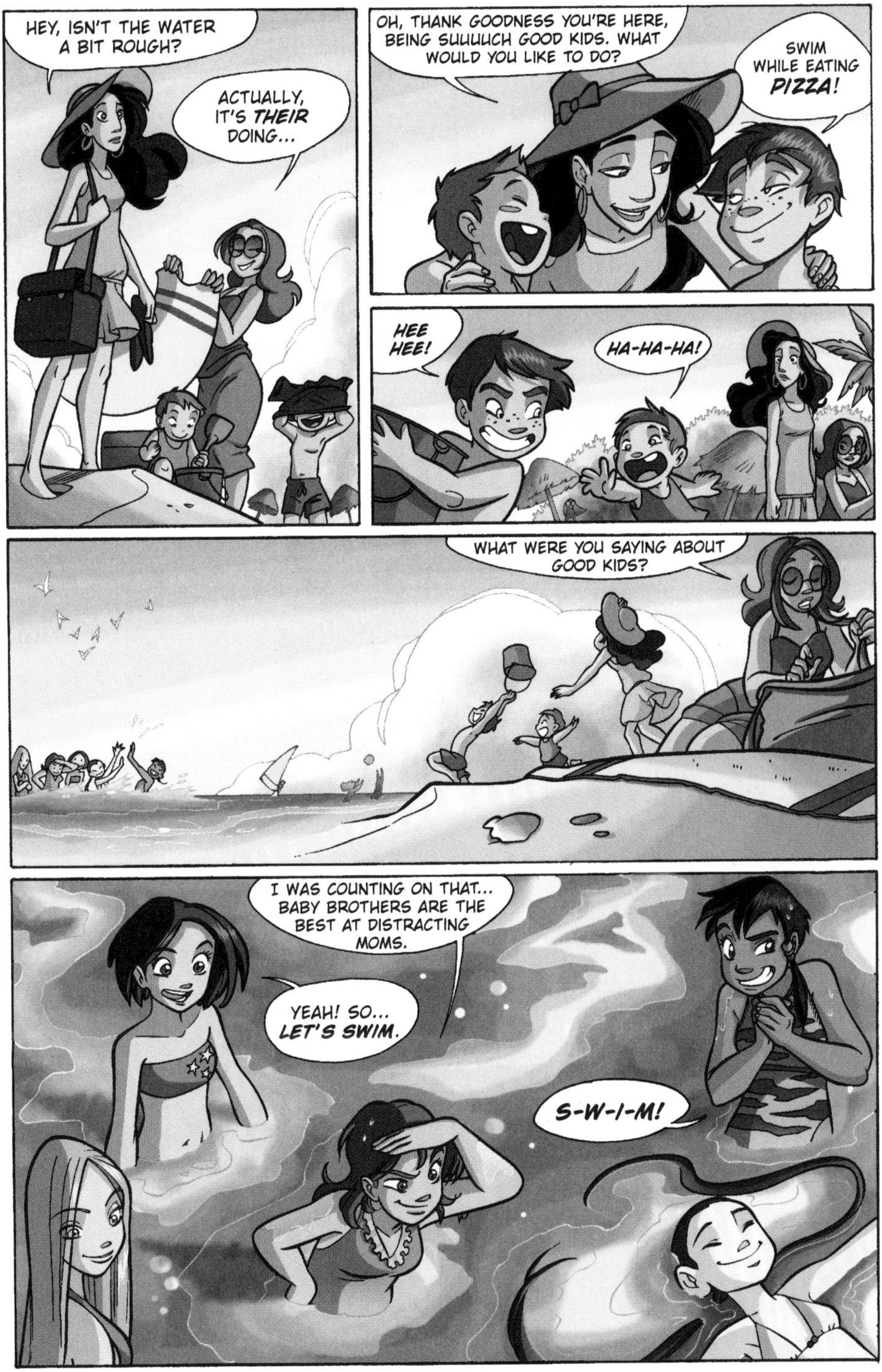
HEY, ISN'T THE WATER A BIT ROUGH?
ACTUALLY, IT'S THEIR DOING...
OH, THANK GOODNESS YOU'RE HERE, BEING SUUUUCH GOOD KIDS. WHAT WOULD YOU LIKE TO DO?
SWIM WHILE EATING PIZZA!
HEE HEE!
HA-HA-HA!
WHAT WERE YOU SAYING ABOUT GOOD KIDS?
I WAS COUNTING ON THAT... BABY BROTHERS ARE THE BEST AT DISTRACTING MOMS.
YEAH! SO... LET'S SWIM.
S-W-I-M!

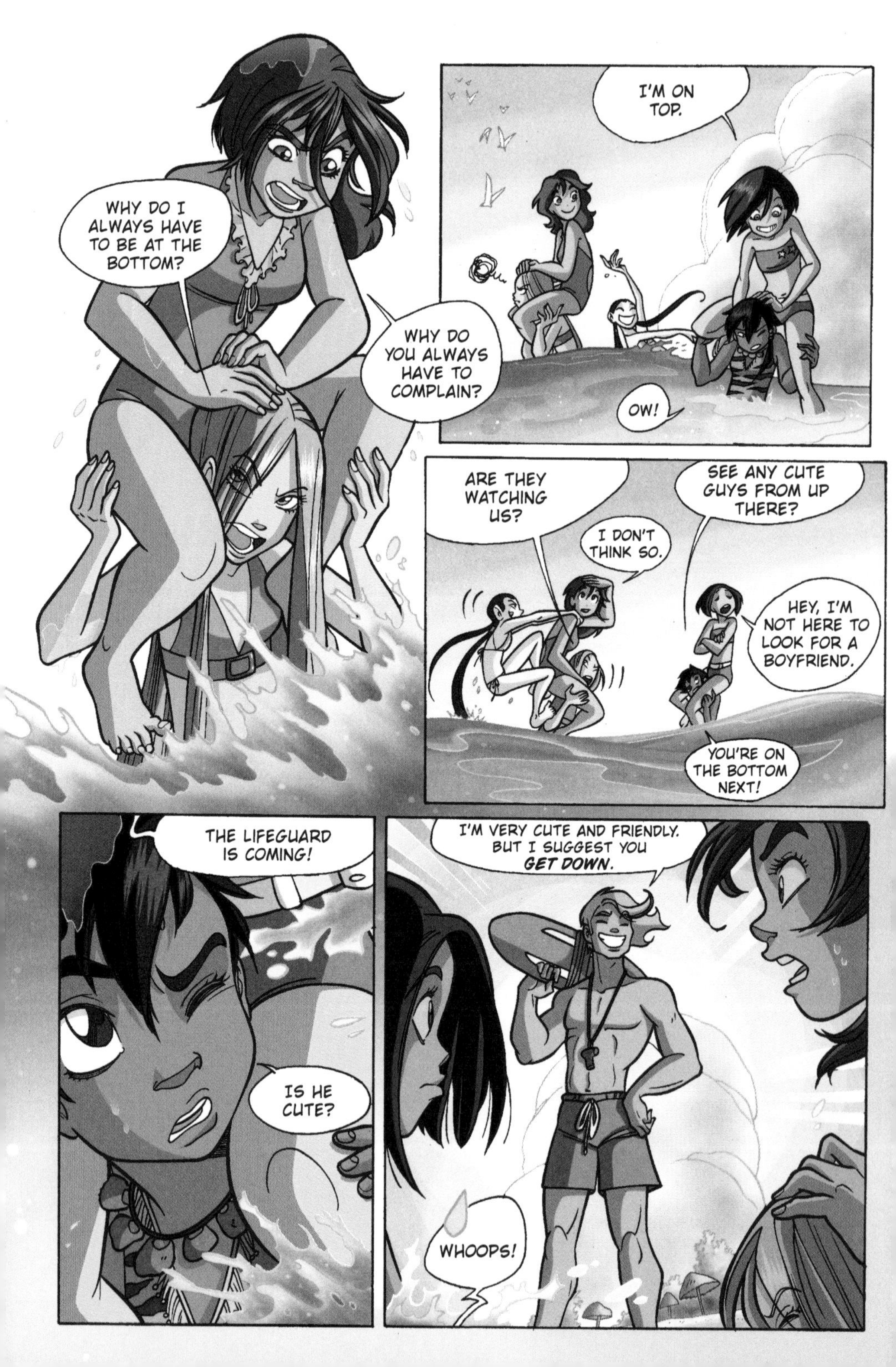
WHY DO I ALWAYS HAVE TO BE AT THE BOTTOM?
WHY DO YOU ALWAYS HAVE TO COMPLAIN?
I'M ON TOP.
OW!
ARE THEY WATCHING US?
I DON'T THINK SO.
SEE ANY CUTE GUYS FROM UP THERE?
HEY, I'M NOT HERE TO LOOK FOR A BOYFRIEND.
YOU'RE ON THE BOTTOM NEXT!
THE LIFEGUARD IS COMING!
IS HE CUTE?
I'M VERY CUTE AND FRIENDLY. BUT I SUGGEST YOU **GET DOWN**.
WHOOPS!

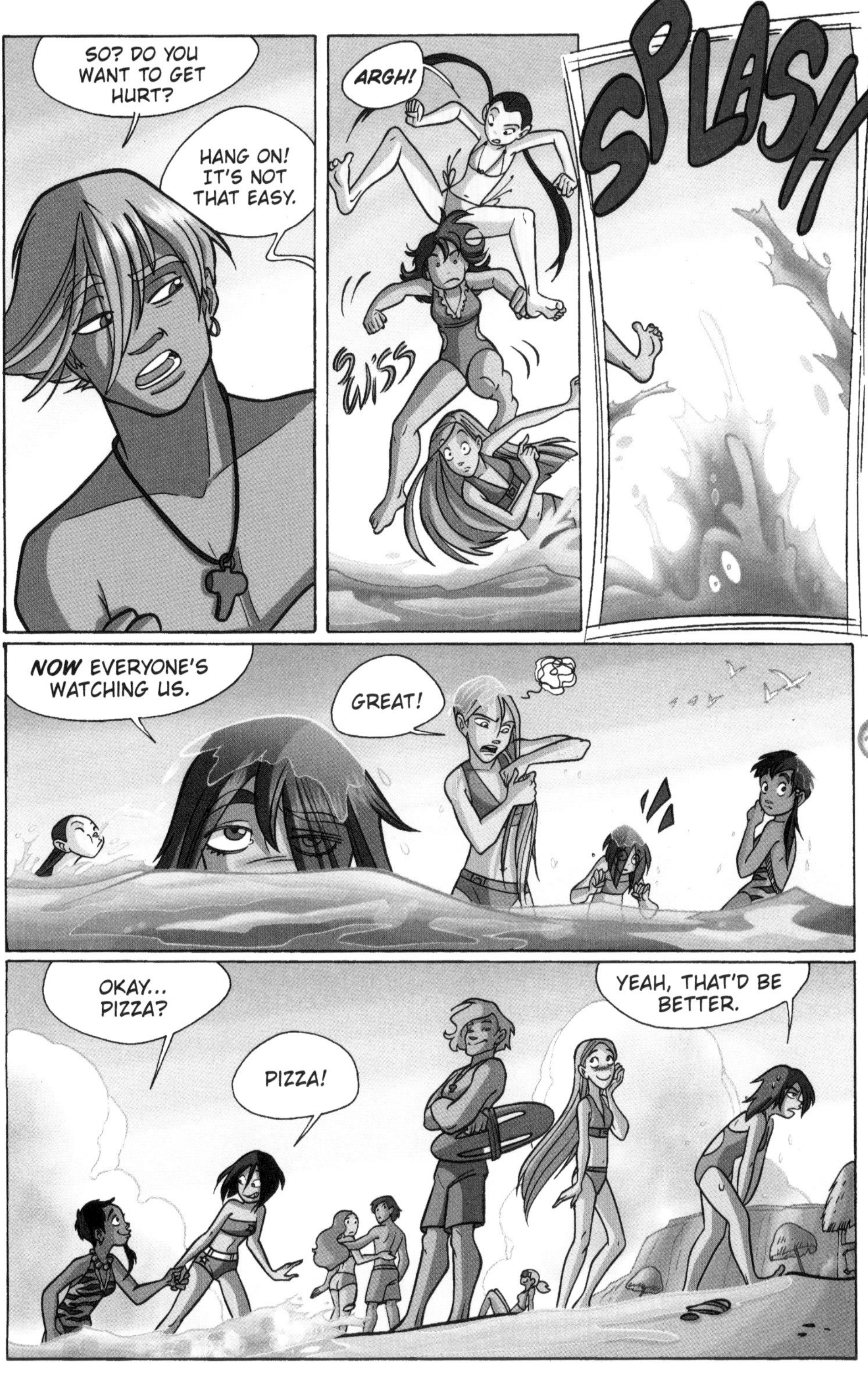
SO? DO YOU WANT TO GET HURT?
HANG ON! IT'S NOT THAT EASY.
ARGH!
SWISS
SPLASH
NOW EVERYONE'S WATCHING US.
GREAT!
OKAY... PIZZA?
PIZZA!
YEAH, THAT'D BE BETTER.

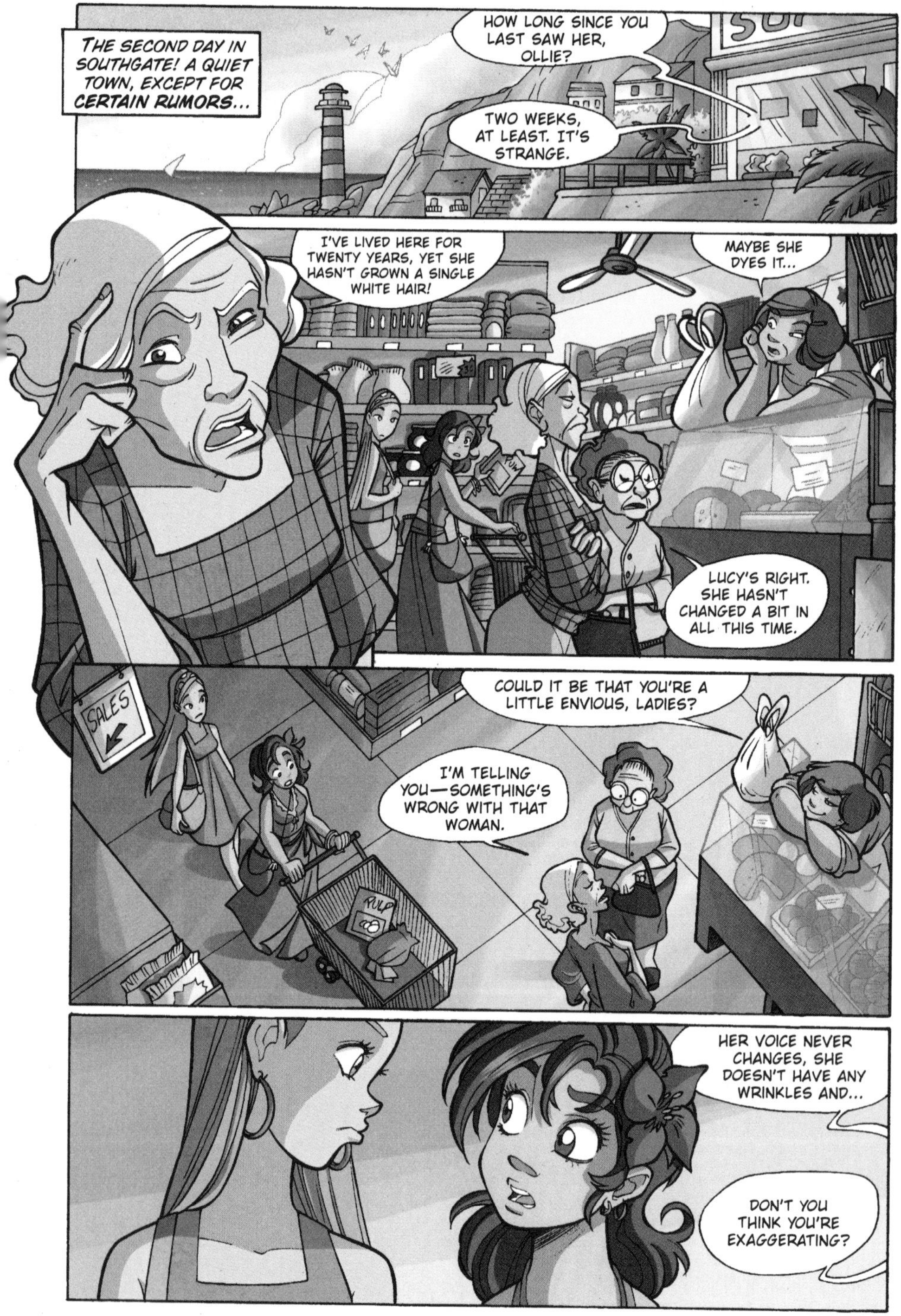
THE SECOND DAY IN SOUTHGATE! A QUIET TOWN, EXCEPT FOR CERTAIN RUMORS...
HOW LONG SINCE YOU LAST SAW HER, OLLIE?
TWO WEEKS, AT LEAST. IT'S STRANGE.
I'VE LIVED HERE FOR TWENTY YEARS, YET SHE HASN'T GROWN A SINGLE WHITE HAIR!
MAYBE SHE DYES IT...
LUCY'S RIGHT. SHE HASN'T CHANGED A BIT IN ALL THIS TIME.
SALES
COULD IT BE THAT YOU'RE A LITTLE ENVIOUS, LADIES?
I'M TELLING YOU—SOMETHING'S WRONG WITH THAT WOMAN.
HER VOICE NEVER CHANGES, SHE DOESN'T HAVE ANY WRINKLES AND...
DON'T YOU THINK YOU'RE EXAGGERATING?

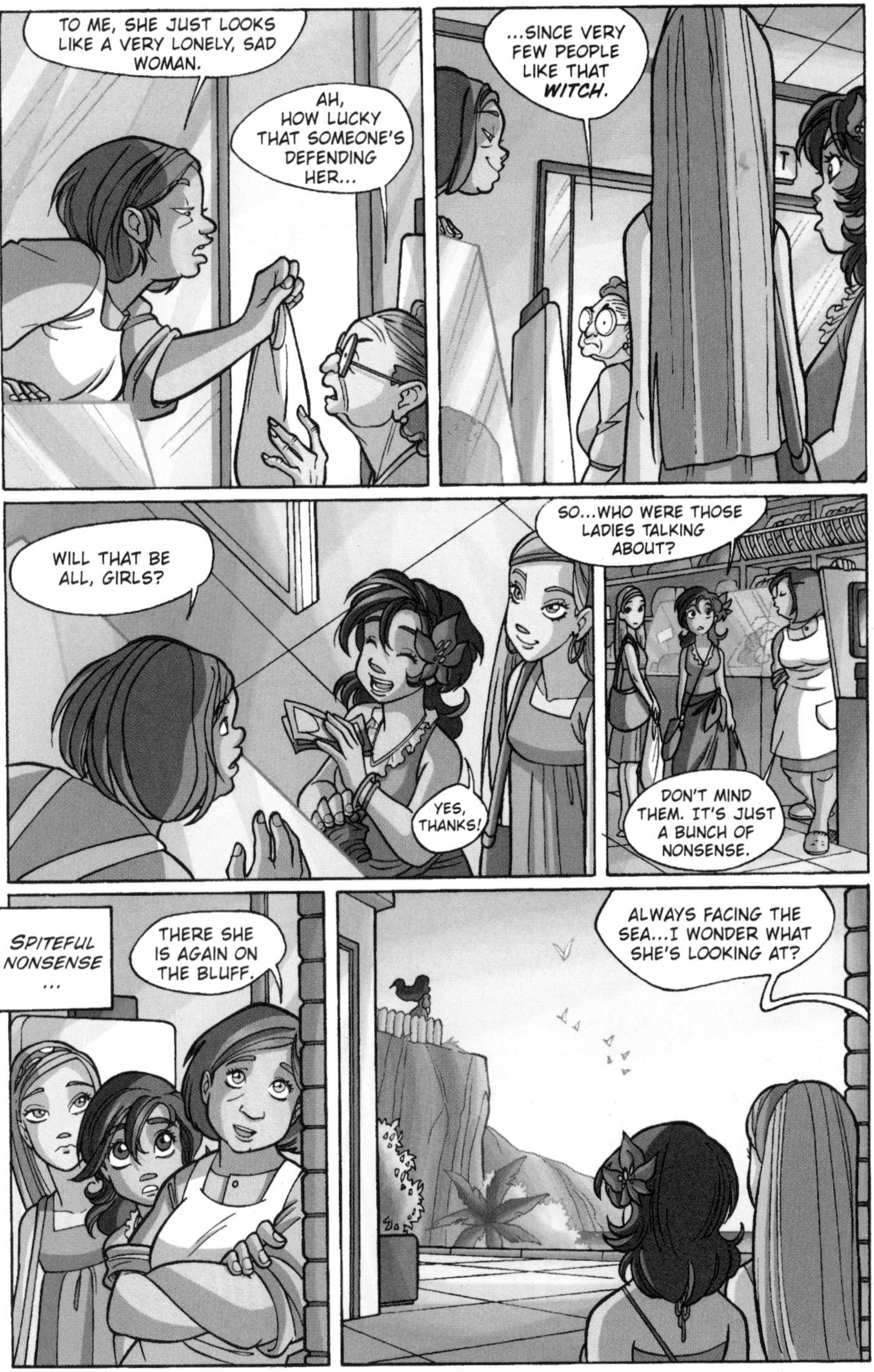
TO ME, SHE JUST LOOKS LIKE A VERY LONELY, SAD WOMAN.
AH, HOW LUCKY THAT SOMEONE'S DEFENDING HER...
...SINCE VERY FEW PEOPLE LIKE THAT WITCH.
WILL THAT BE ALL, GIRLS?
YES, THANKS!
SO...WHO WERE THOSE LADIES TALKING ABOUT?
DON'T MIND THEM. IT'S JUST A BUNCH OF NONSENSE.
SPITEFUL NONSENSE ...
THERE SHE IS AGAIN ON THE BLUFF.
ALWAYS FACING THE SEA...I WONDER WHAT SHE'S LOOKING AT?

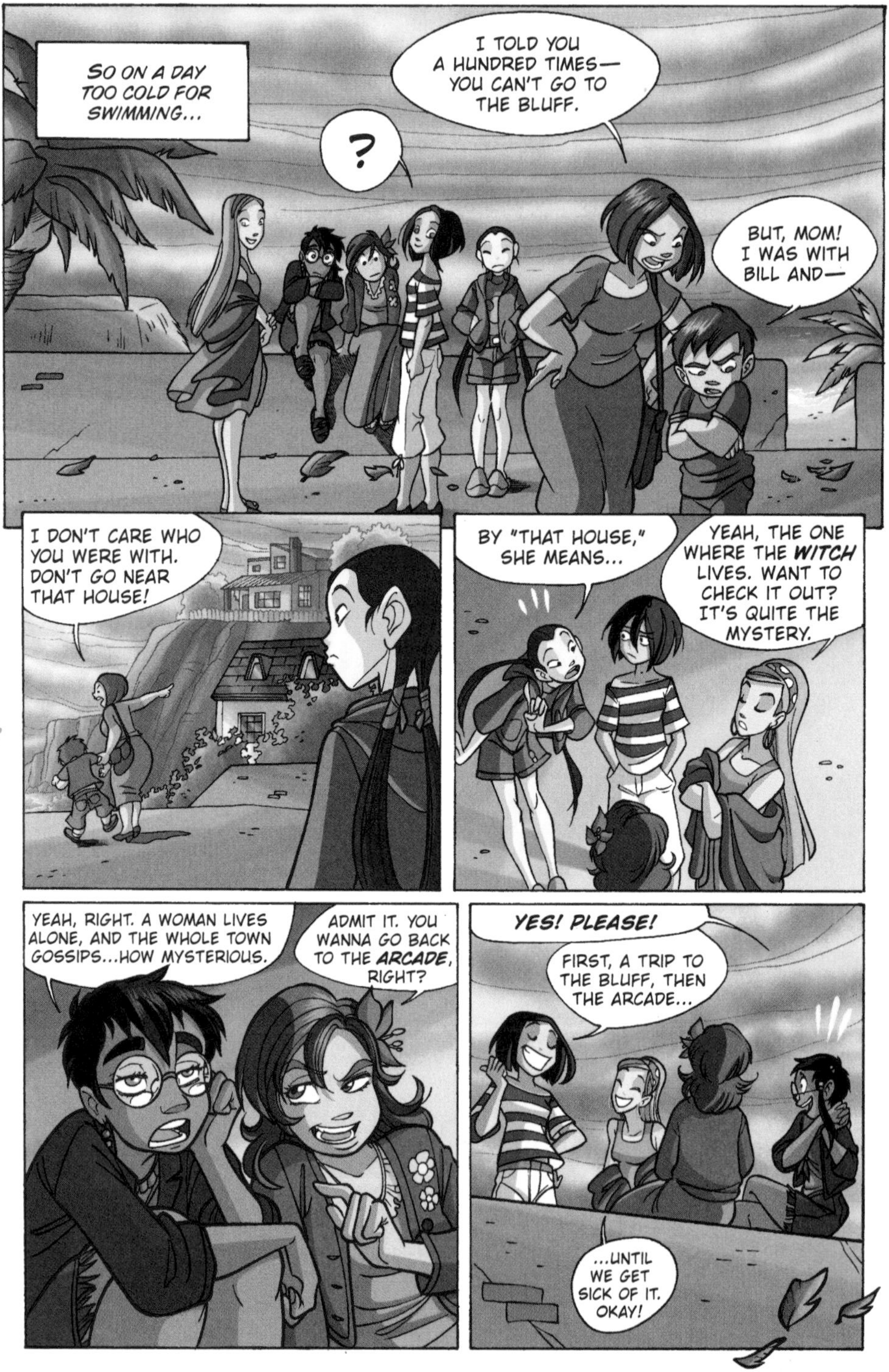
SO ON A DAY TOO COLD FOR SWIMMING...
?
I TOLD YOU A HUNDRED TIMES— YOU CAN'T GO TO THE BLUFF.
BUT, MOM! I WAS WITH BILL AND—
I DON'T CARE WHO YOU WERE WITH. DON'T GO NEAR THAT HOUSE!
BY "THAT HOUSE," SHE MEANS...
YEAH, THE ONE WHERE THE WITCH LIVES. WANT TO CHECK IT OUT? IT'S QUITE THE MYSTERY.
YEAH, RIGHT. A WOMAN LIVES ALONE, AND THE WHOLE TOWN GOSSIPS...HOW MYSTERIOUS.
ADMIT IT. YOU WANNA GO BACK TO THE ARCADE, RIGHT?
YES! PLEASE!
FIRST, A TRIP TO THE BLUFF, THEN THE ARCADE...
...UNTIL WE GET SICK OF IT. OKAY!

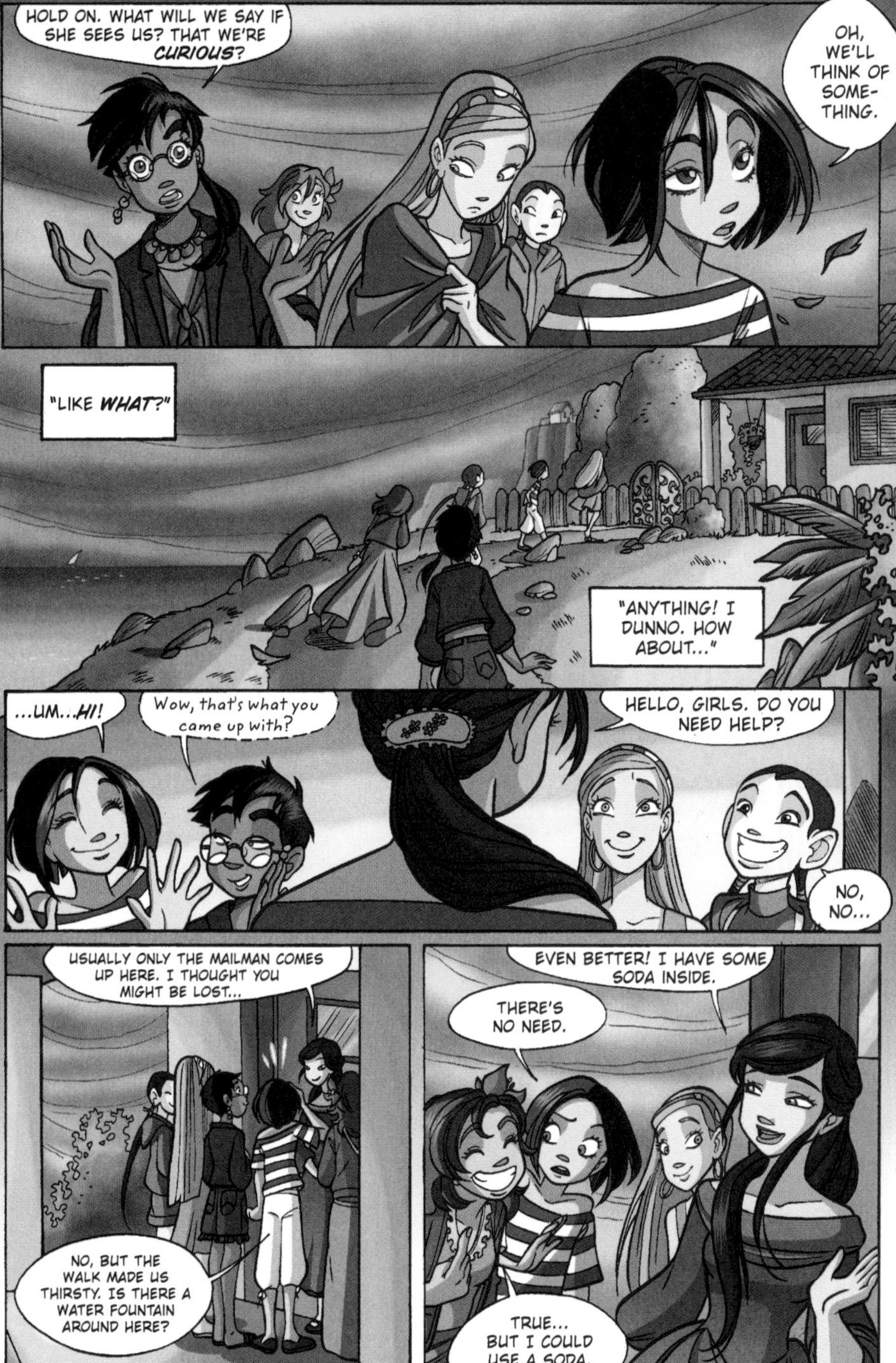
HOLD ON. WHAT WILL WE SAY IF SHE SEES US? THAT WE'RE *CURIOUS*?
OH, WE'LL THINK OF SOME-THING.
"LIKE *WHAT*?"
"ANYTHING! I DUNNO. HOW ABOUT..."
...UM...*HI!*
Wow, that's what you came up with?
HELLO, GIRLS. DO YOU NEED HELP?
NO, NO...
USUALLY ONLY THE MAILMAN COMES UP HERE. I THOUGHT YOU MIGHT BE LOST...
NO, BUT THE WALK MADE US THIRSTY. IS THERE A WATER FOUNTAIN AROUND HERE?
EVEN BETTER! I HAVE SOME SODA INSIDE.
THERE'S NO NEED.
TRUE... BUT I COULD USE A SODA.

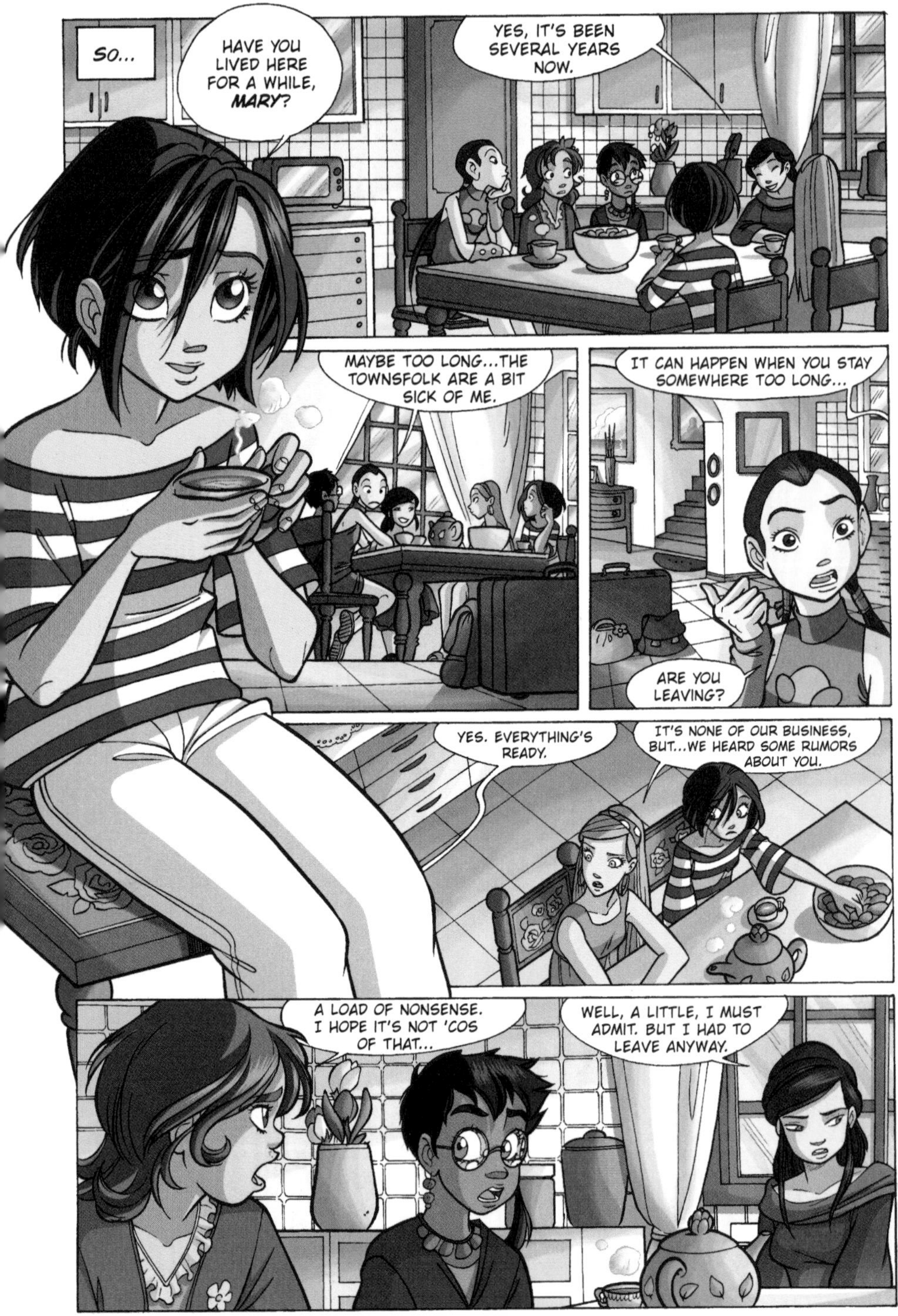
SO...
HAVE YOU LIVED HERE FOR A WHILE, MARY?
YES, IT'S BEEN SEVERAL YEARS NOW.
MAYBE TOO LONG...THE TOWNSFOLK ARE A BIT SICK OF ME.
IT CAN HAPPEN WHEN YOU STAY SOMEWHERE TOO LONG...
ARE YOU LEAVING?
YES. EVERYTHING'S READY.
IT'S NONE OF OUR BUSINESS, BUT...WE HEARD SOME RUMORS ABOUT YOU.
A LOAD OF NONSENSE. I HOPE IT'S NOT 'COS OF THAT...
WELL, A LITTLE, I MUST ADMIT. BUT I HAD TO LEAVE ANYWAY.

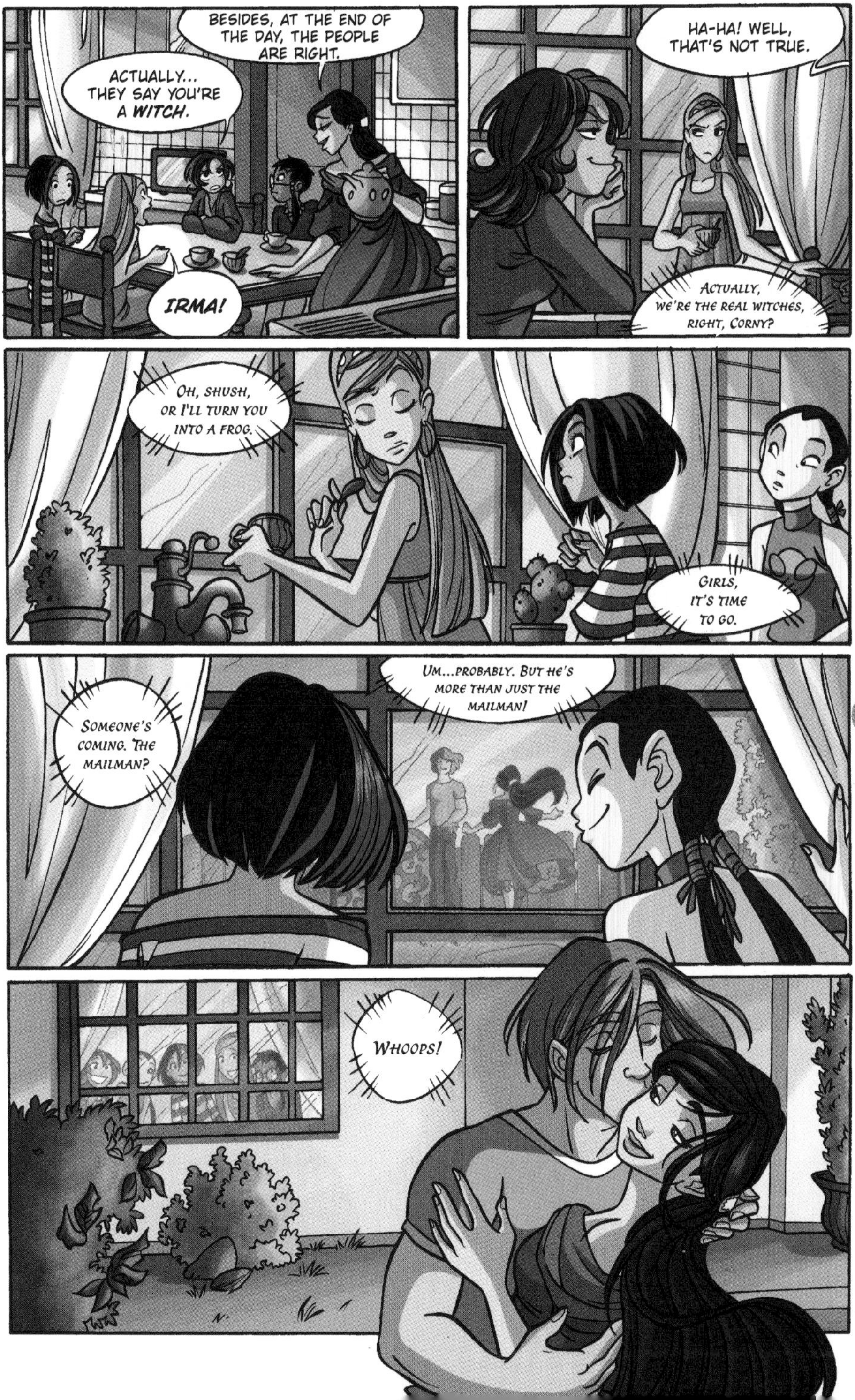
Actually... they say you're a witch.
Besides, at the end of the day, the people are right.
Irma!
Ha-ha! Well, that's not true.
Actually, we're the real witches, right, Corny?
Oh, shush, or I'll turn you into a frog.
Girls, it's time to go.
Someone's coming. The mailman?
Um...probably. But he's more than just the mailman!
Whoops!

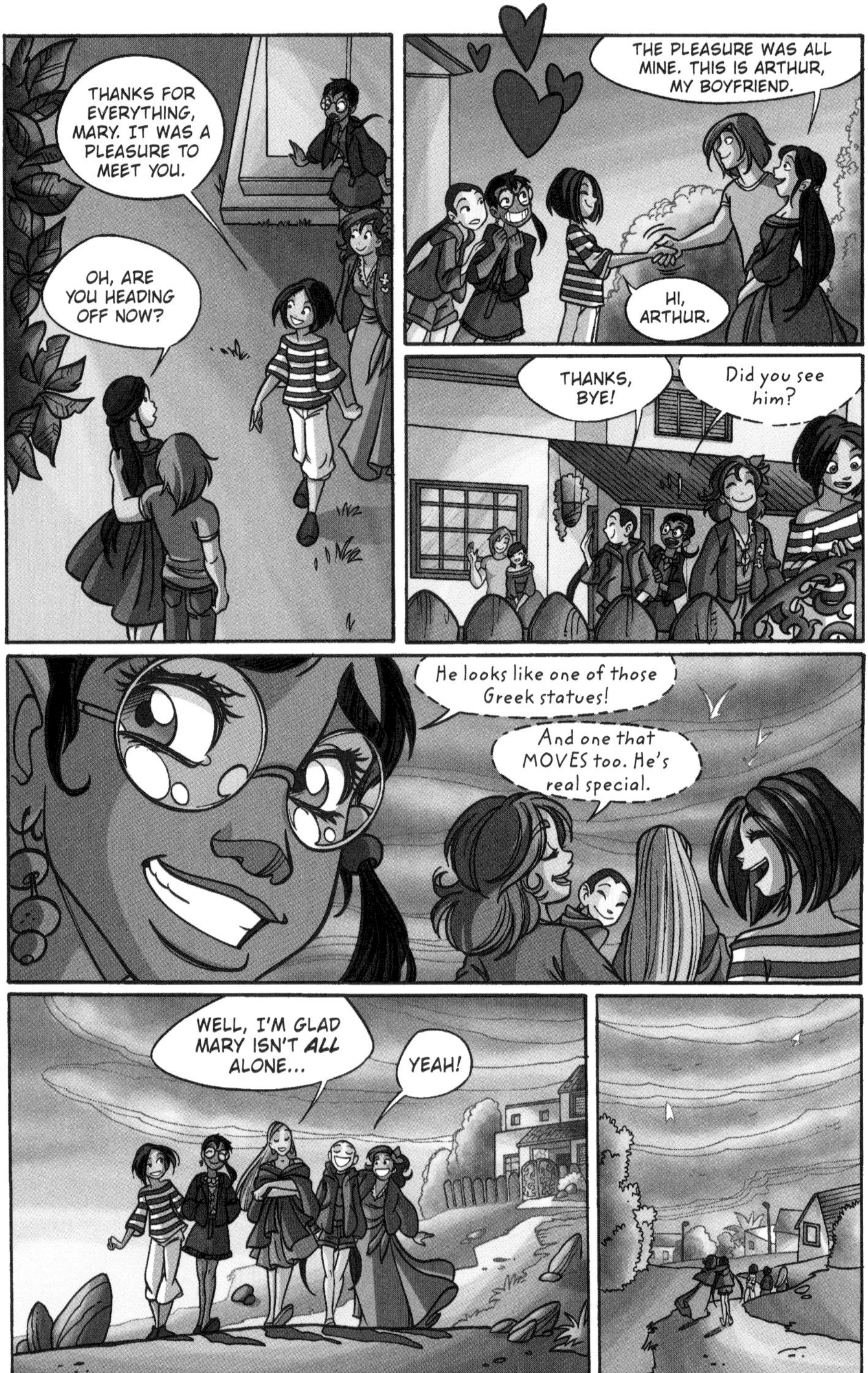

THANKS FOR EVERYTHING, MARY. IT WAS A PLEASURE TO MEET YOU.
OH, ARE YOU HEADING OFF NOW?
THE PLEASURE WAS ALL MINE. THIS IS ARTHUR, MY BOYFRIEND.
HI, ARTHUR.
THANKS, BYE!
Did you see him?
He looks like one of those Greek statues!
And one that MOVES too. He's real special.
WELL, I'M GLAD MARY ISN'T ALL ALONE...
YEAH!

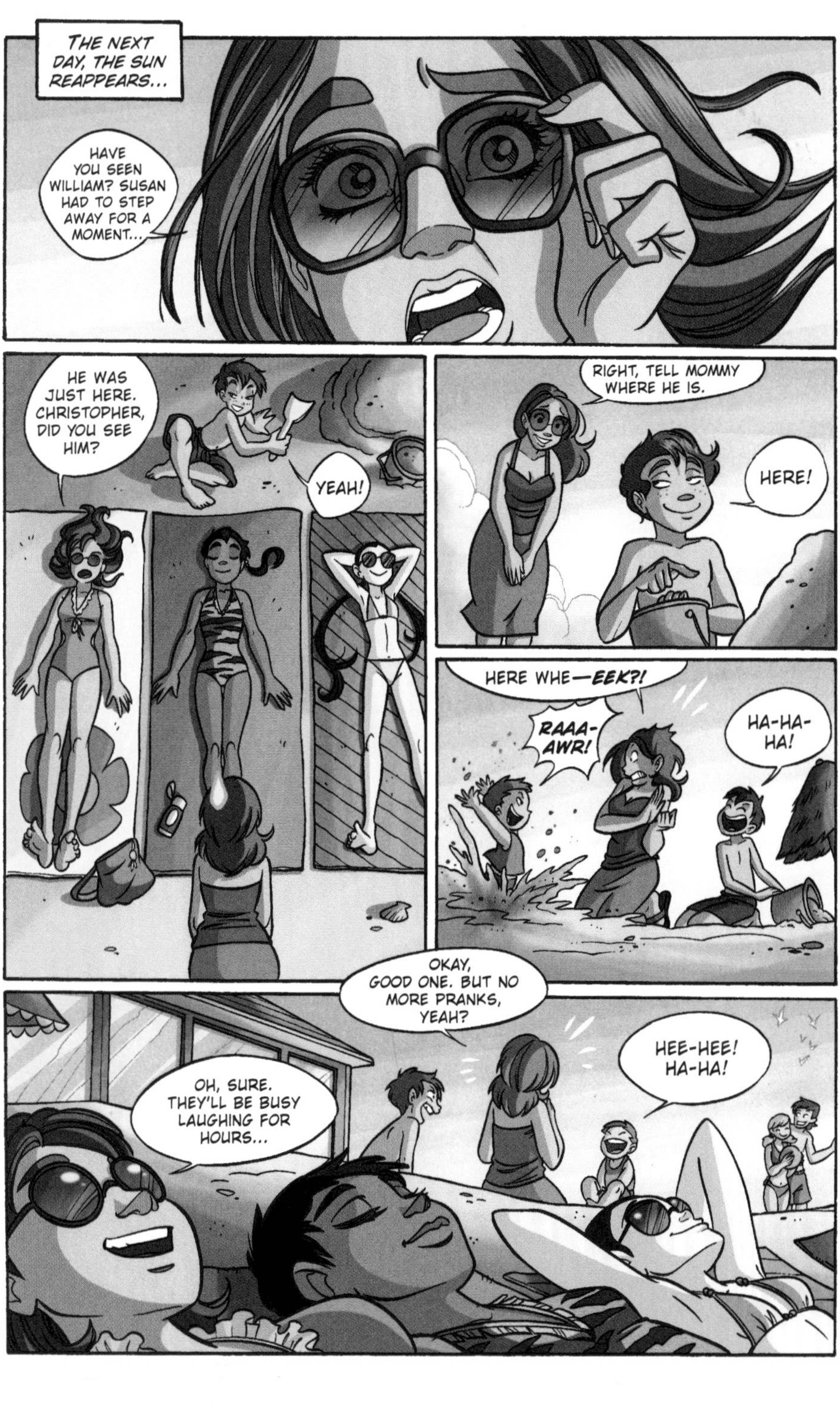
THE NEXT DAY, THE SUN REAPPEARS...
HAVE YOU SEEN WILLIAM? SUSAN HAD TO STEP AWAY FOR A MOMENT...
HE WAS JUST HERE. CHRISTOPHER, DID YOU SEE HIM?
YEAH!
RIGHT, TELL MOMMY WHERE HE IS.
HERE!
HERE WHE—**EEK?!**
RAAA-AWR!
HA-HA-HA!
OKAY, GOOD ONE. BUT NO MORE PRANKS, YEAH?
OH, SURE. THEY'LL BE BUSY LAUGHING FOR HOURS...
HEE-HEE! HA-HA!

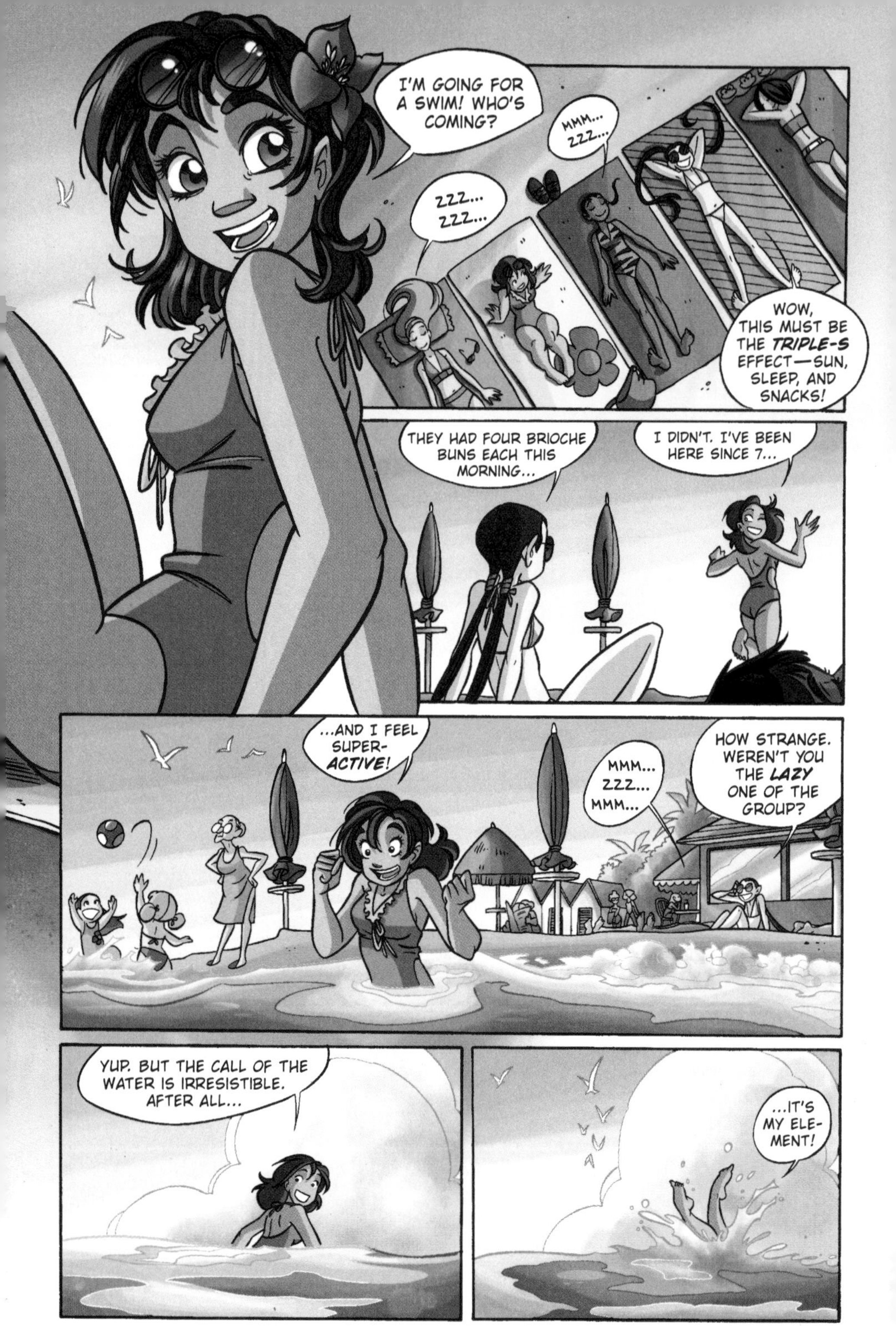
I'M GOING FOR A SWIM! WHO'S COMING?
ZZZ... ZZZ...
MMM... ZZZ...
WOW, THIS MUST BE THE ***TRIPLE-S*** EFFECT—SUN, SLEEP, AND SNACKS!
THEY HAD FOUR BRIOCHE BUNS EACH THIS MORNING...
I DIDN'T. I'VE BEEN HERE SINCE 7...
...AND I FEEL SUPER-***ACTIVE***!
MMM... ZZZ... MMM...
HOW STRANGE. WEREN'T YOU THE ***LAZY*** ONE OF THE GROUP?
YUP. BUT THE CALL OF THE WATER IS IRRESISTIBLE. AFTER ALL...
...IT'S MY ELEMENT!

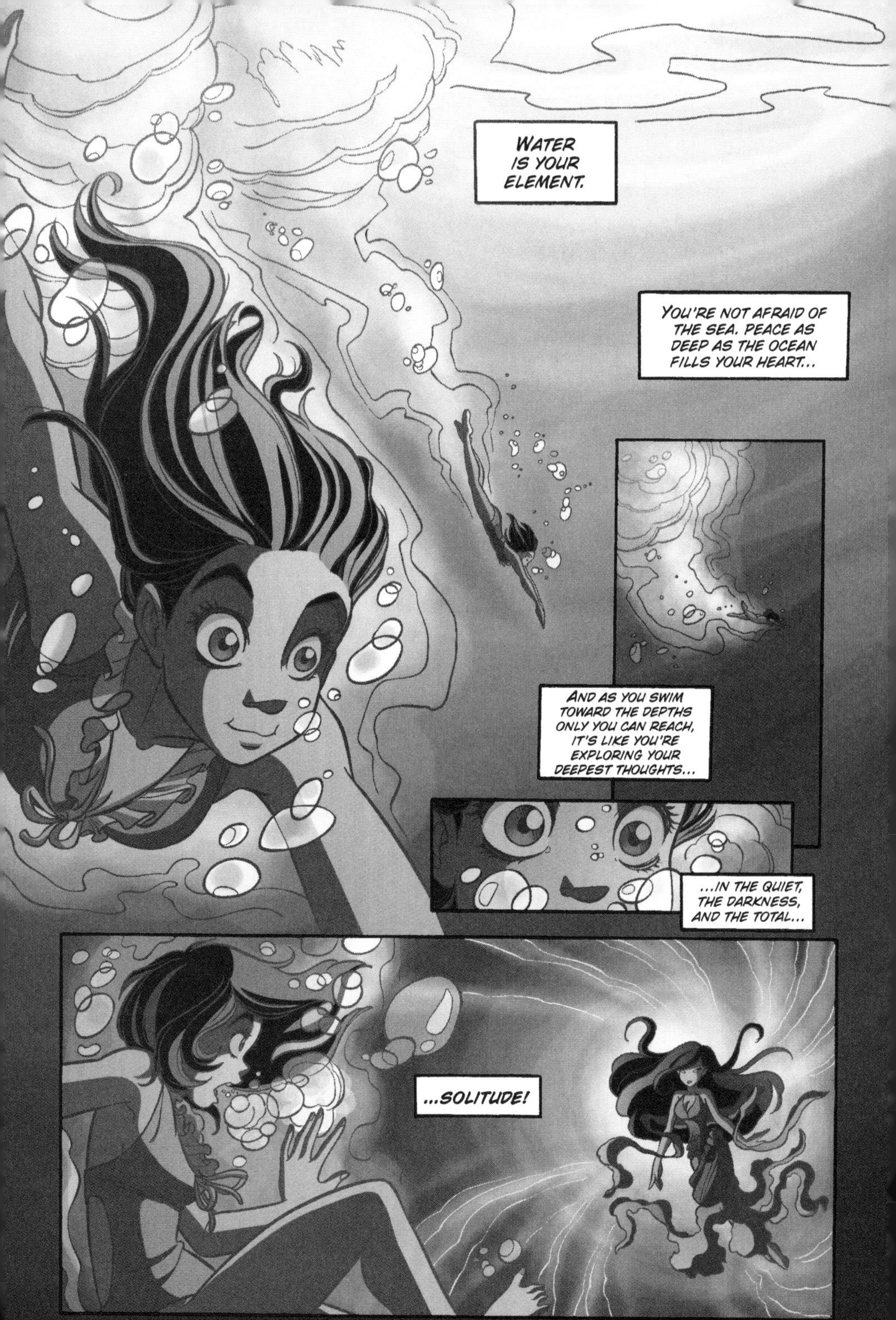
WATER IS YOUR ELEMENT.
YOU'RE NOT AFRAID OF THE SEA. PEACE AS DEEP AS THE OCEAN FILLS YOUR HEART...
AND AS YOU SWIM TOWARD THE DEPTHS ONLY YOU CAN REACH, IT'S LIKE YOU'RE EXPLORING YOUR DEEPEST THOUGHTS...
...IN THE QUIET, THE DARKNESS, AND THE TOTAL...
...SOLITUDE!

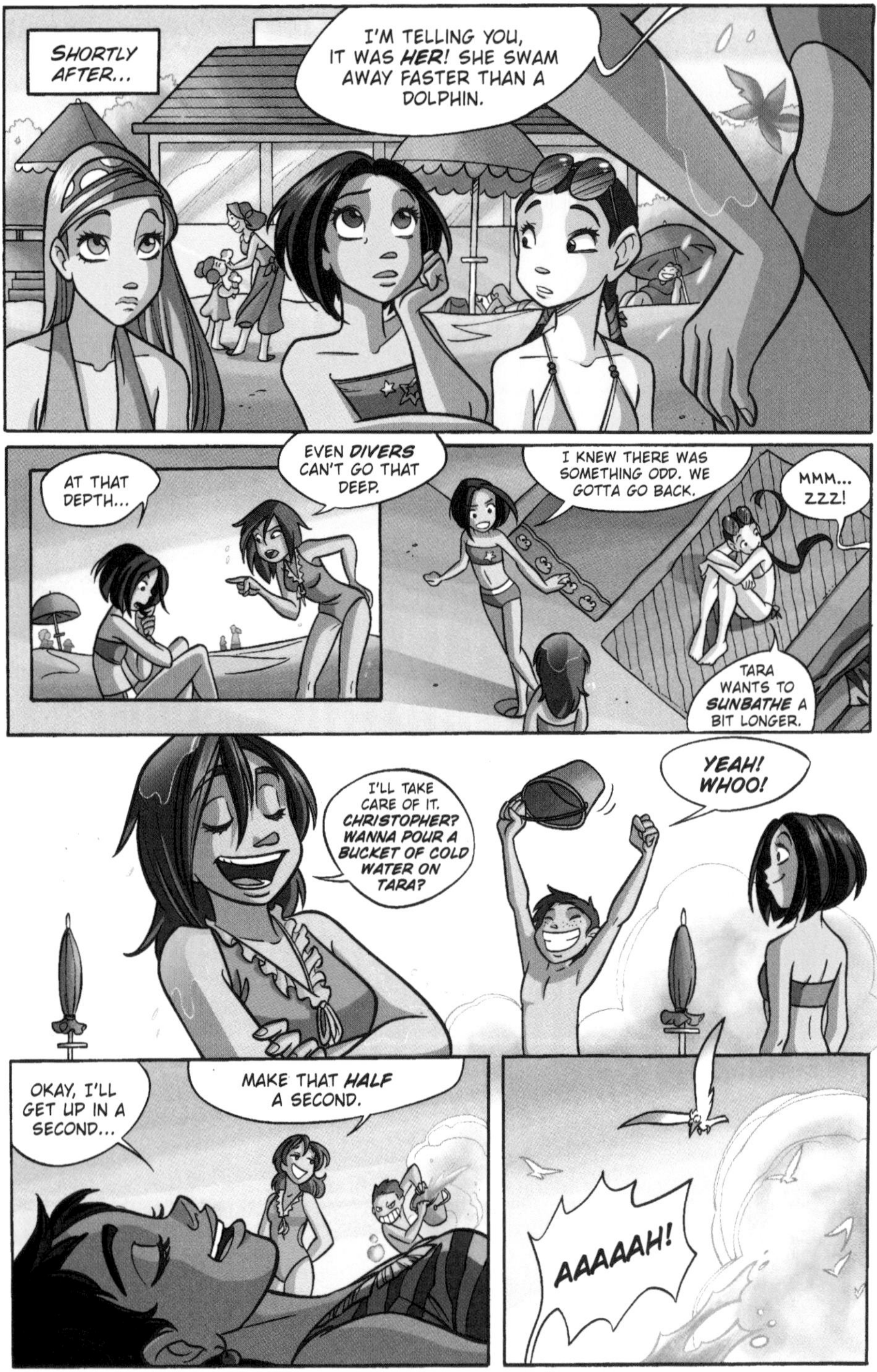
SHORTLY AFTER...
I'M TELLING YOU, IT WAS HER! SHE SWAM AWAY FASTER THAN A DOLPHIN.
AT THAT DEPTH...
EVEN DIVERS CAN'T GO THAT DEEP.
I KNEW THERE WAS SOMETHING ODD. WE GOTTA GO BACK.
MMM... ZZZ!
TARA WANTS TO SUNBATHE A BIT LONGER.
I'LL TAKE CARE OF IT. CHRISTOPHER? WANNA POUR A BUCKET OF COLD WATER ON TARA?
YEAH! WHOO!
OKAY, I'LL GET UP IN A SECOND...
MAKE THAT HALF A SECOND.
AAAAAH!

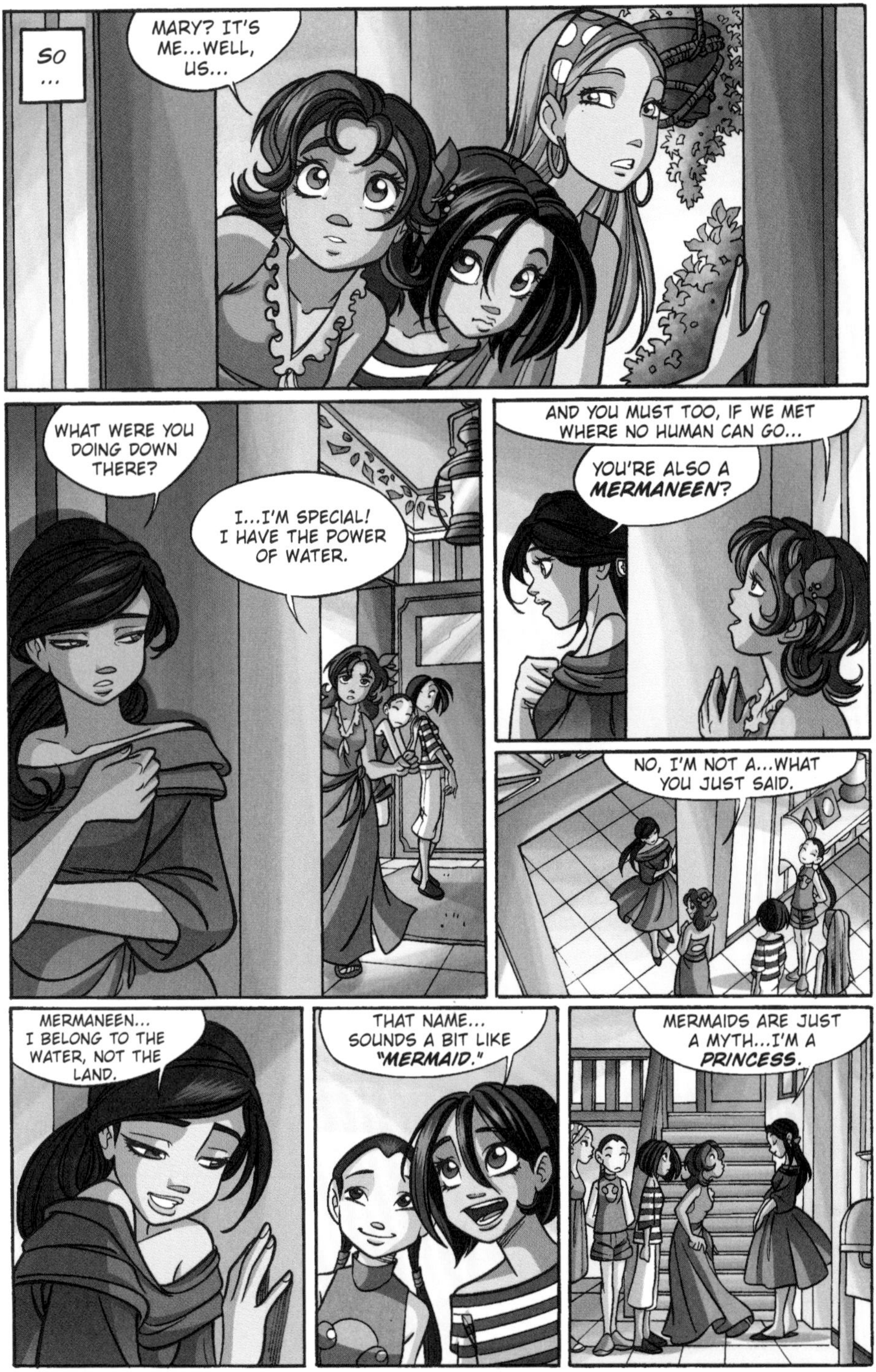
SO ...
MARY? IT'S ME...WELL, US...
WHAT WERE YOU DOING DOWN THERE?
I...I'M SPECIAL! I HAVE THE POWER OF WATER.
AND YOU MUST TOO, IF WE MET WHERE NO HUMAN CAN GO...
YOU'RE ALSO A **MERMANEEN**?
NO, I'M NOT A...WHAT YOU JUST SAID.
MERMANEEN... I BELONG TO THE WATER, NOT THE LAND.
THAT NAME... SOUNDS A BIT LIKE **"MERMAID."**
MERMAIDS ARE JUST A MYTH...I'M A **PRINCESS**.

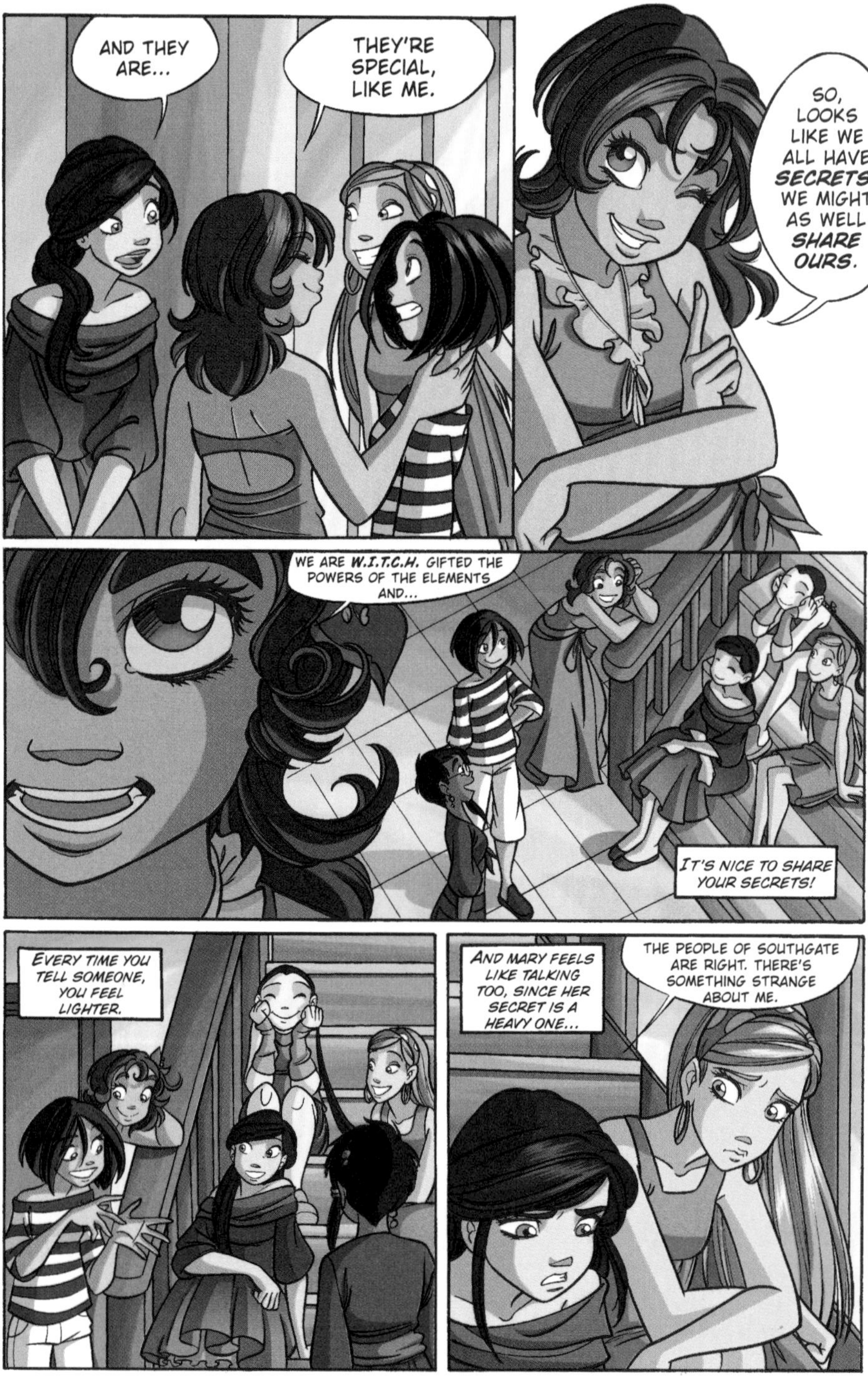

AND THEY ARE...
THEY'RE SPECIAL, LIKE ME.
SO, LOOKS LIKE WE ALL HAVE SECRETS. WE MIGHT AS WELL SHARE OURS.
WE ARE W.I.T.C.H. GIFTED THE POWERS OF THE ELEMENTS AND...
IT'S NICE TO SHARE YOUR SECRETS!
EVERY TIME YOU TELL SOMEONE, YOU FEEL LIGHTER.
AND MARY FEELS LIKE TALKING TOO, SINCE HER SECRET IS A HEAVY ONE...
THE PEOPLE OF SOUTHGATE ARE RIGHT. THERE'S SOMETHING STRANGE ABOUT ME.

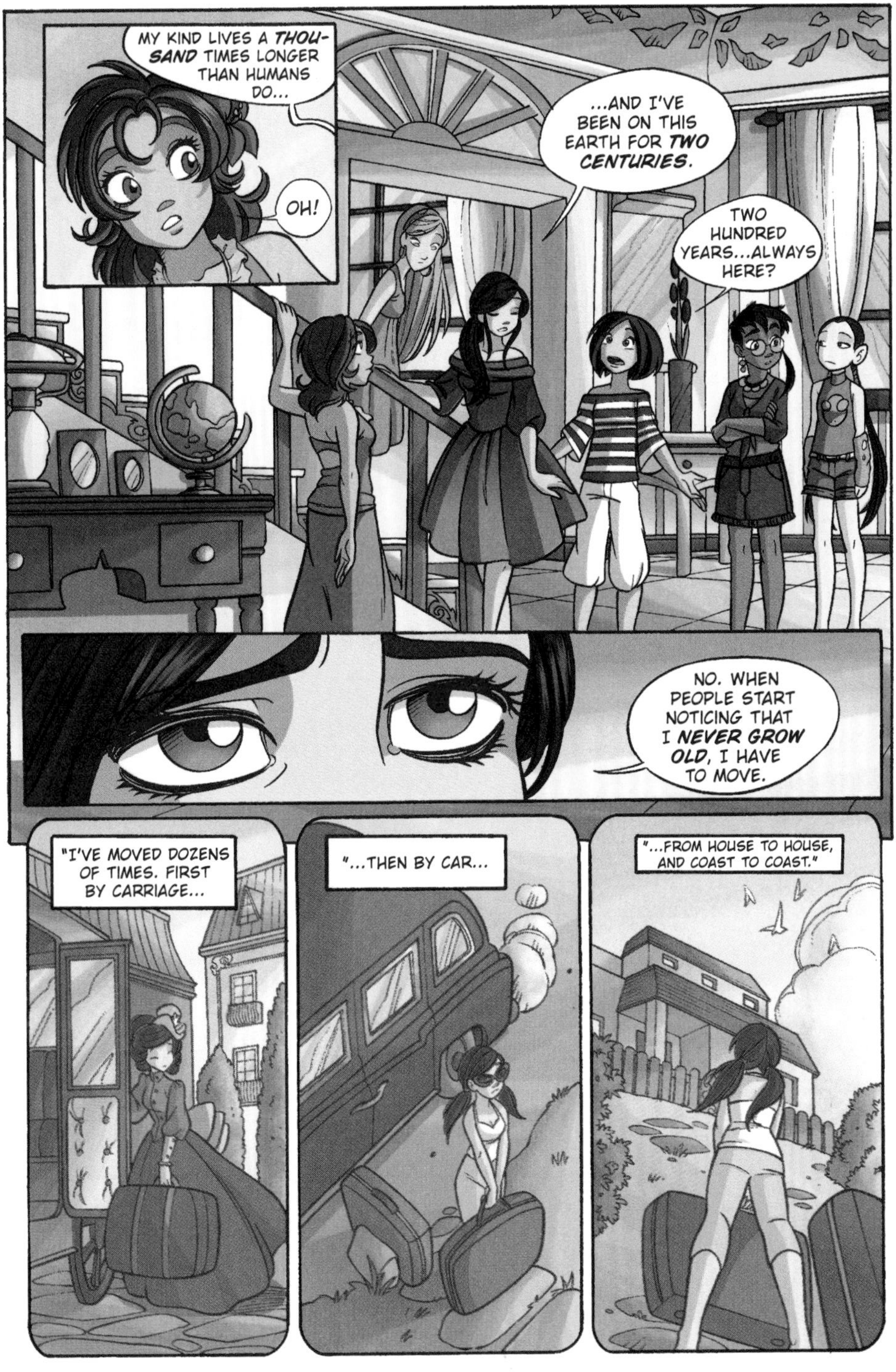

MY KIND LIVES A THOUSAND TIMES LONGER THAN HUMANS DO...
OH!
...AND I'VE BEEN ON THIS EARTH FOR TWO CENTURIES.
TWO HUNDRED YEARS...ALWAYS HERE?
NO. WHEN PEOPLE START NOTICING THAT I NEVER GROW OLD, I HAVE TO MOVE.
"I'VE MOVED DOZENS OF TIMES. FIRST BY CARRIAGE...
"...THEN BY CAR...
"...FROM HOUSE TO HOUSE, AND COAST TO COAST."

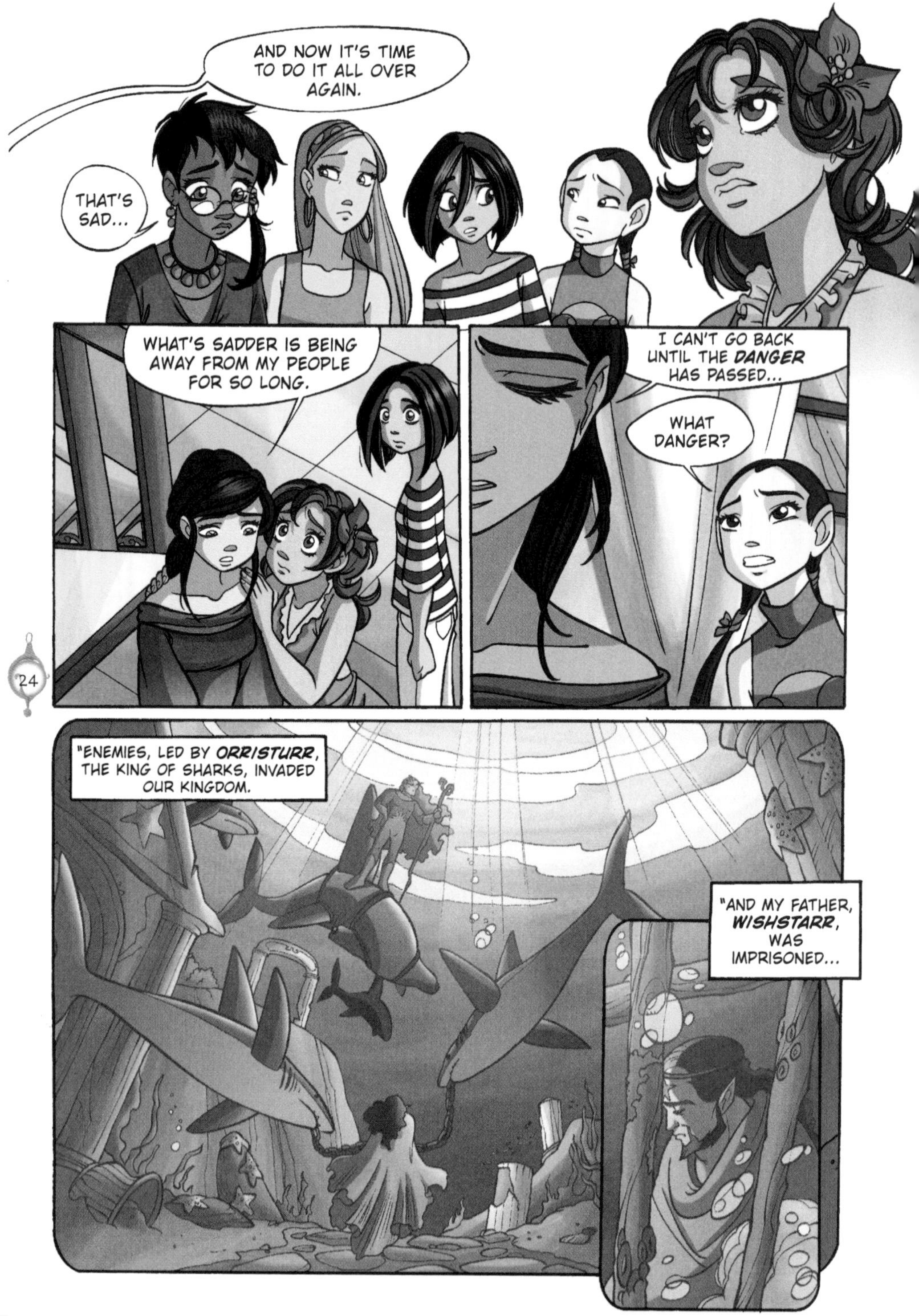
AND NOW IT'S TIME TO DO IT ALL OVER AGAIN.
THAT'S SAD...
WHAT'S SADDER IS BEING AWAY FROM MY PEOPLE FOR SO LONG.
I CAN'T GO BACK UNTIL THE DANGER HAS PASSED...
WHAT DANGER?
"ENEMIES, LED BY ORRISTURR, THE KING OF SHARKS, INVADED OUR KINGDOM.
"AND MY FATHER, WISHSTARR, WAS IMPRISONED...

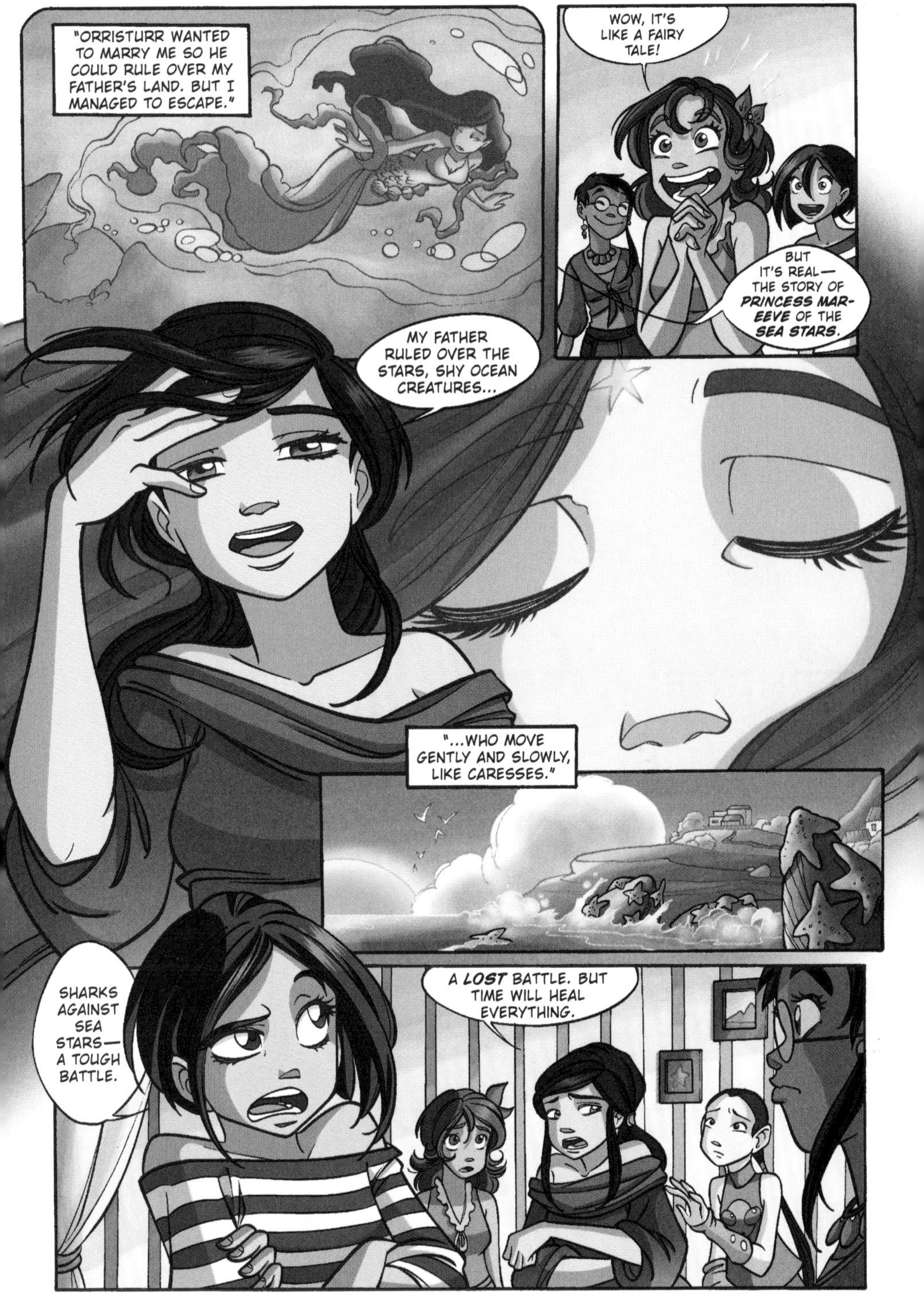
"ORRISTURR WANTED TO MARRY ME SO HE COULD RULE OVER MY FATHER'S LAND. BUT I MANAGED TO ESCAPE."
WOW, IT'S LIKE A FAIRY TALE!
BUT IT'S REAL— THE STORY OF PRINCESS MAREEVE OF THE SEA STARS.
MY FATHER RULED OVER THE STARS, SHY OCEAN CREATURES...
"...WHO MOVE GENTLY AND SLOWLY, LIKE CARESSES."
SHARKS AGAINST SEA STARS— A TOUGH BATTLE.
A LOST BATTLE. BUT TIME WILL HEAL EVERYTHING.

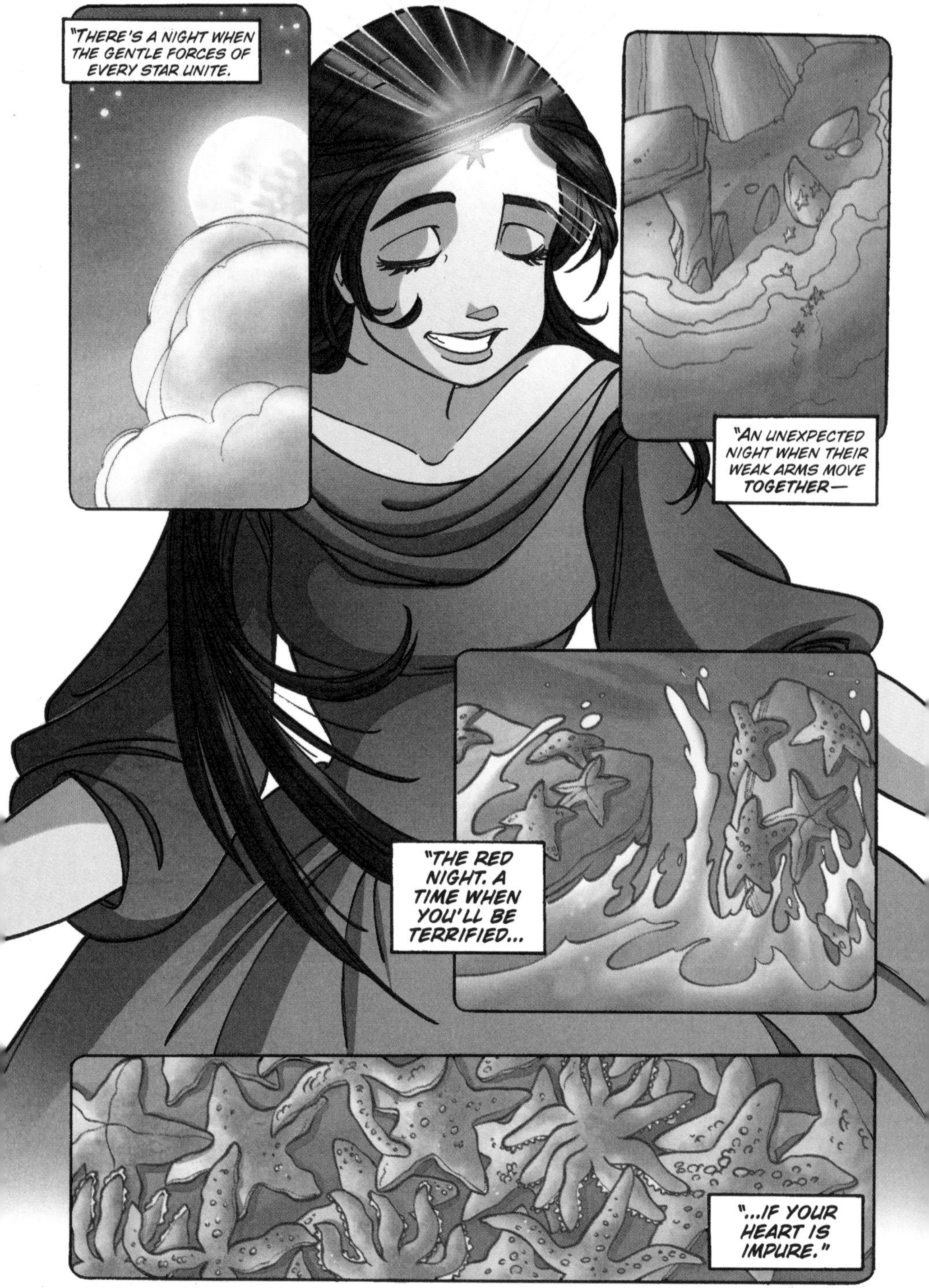
"THERE'S A NIGHT WHEN THE GENTLE FORCES OF EVERY STAR UNITE.
"AN UNEXPECTED NIGHT WHEN THEIR WEAK ARMS MOVE TOGETHER—
"THE RED NIGHT. A TIME WHEN YOU'LL BE TERRIFIED...
"...IF YOUR HEART IS IMPURE."

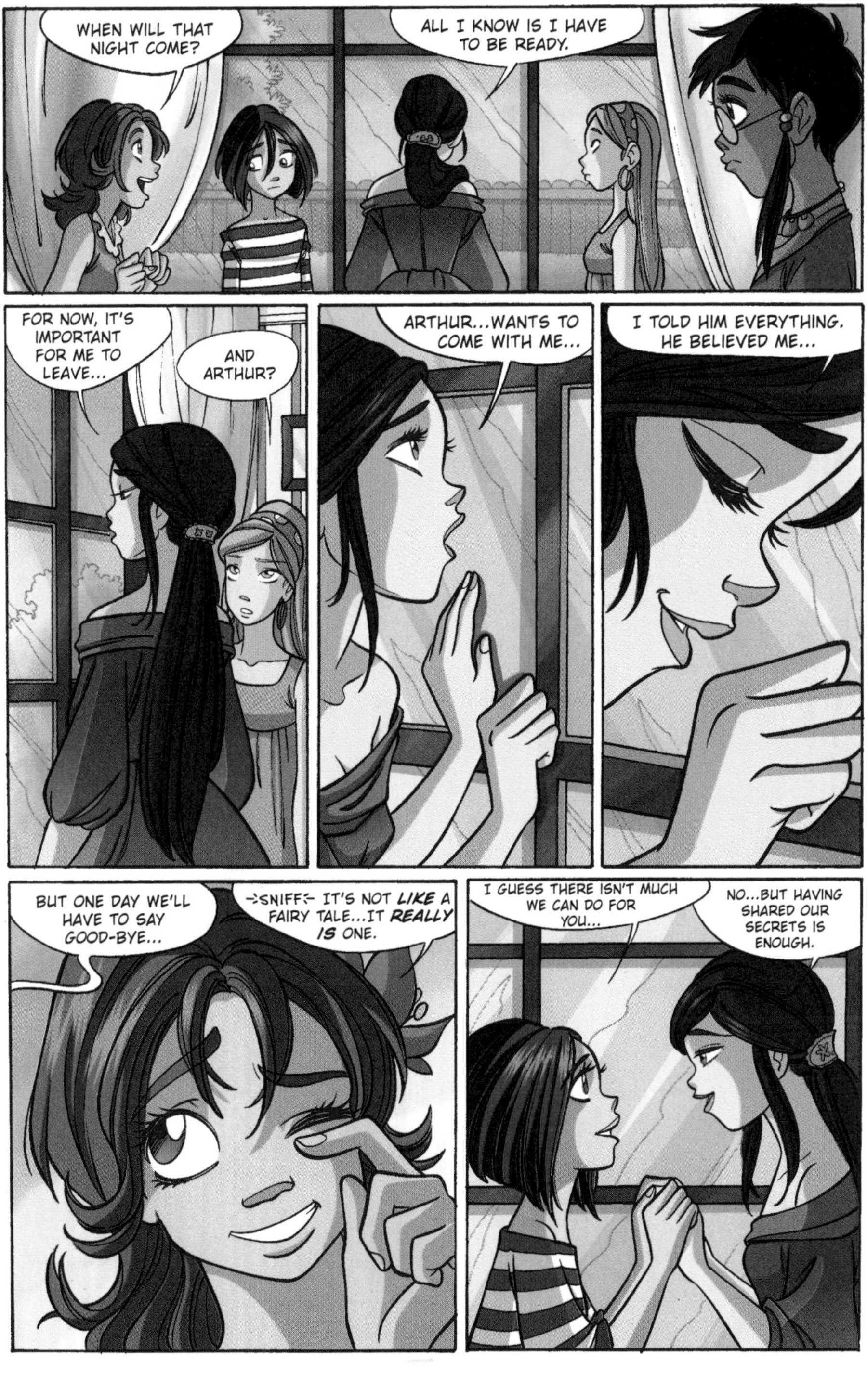
WHEN WILL THAT NIGHT COME?
ALL I KNOW IS I HAVE TO BE READY.
FOR NOW, IT'S IMPORTANT FOR ME TO LEAVE...
AND ARTHUR?
ARTHUR...WANTS TO COME WITH ME...
I TOLD HIM EVERYTHING. HE BELIEVED ME...
BUT ONE DAY WE'LL HAVE TO SAY GOOD-BYE...
SNIFF IT'S NOT *LIKE* A FAIRY TALE...IT *REALLY IS* ONE.
I GUESS THERE ISN'T MUCH WE CAN DO FOR YOU...
NO...BUT HAVING SHARED OUR SECRETS IS ENOUGH.

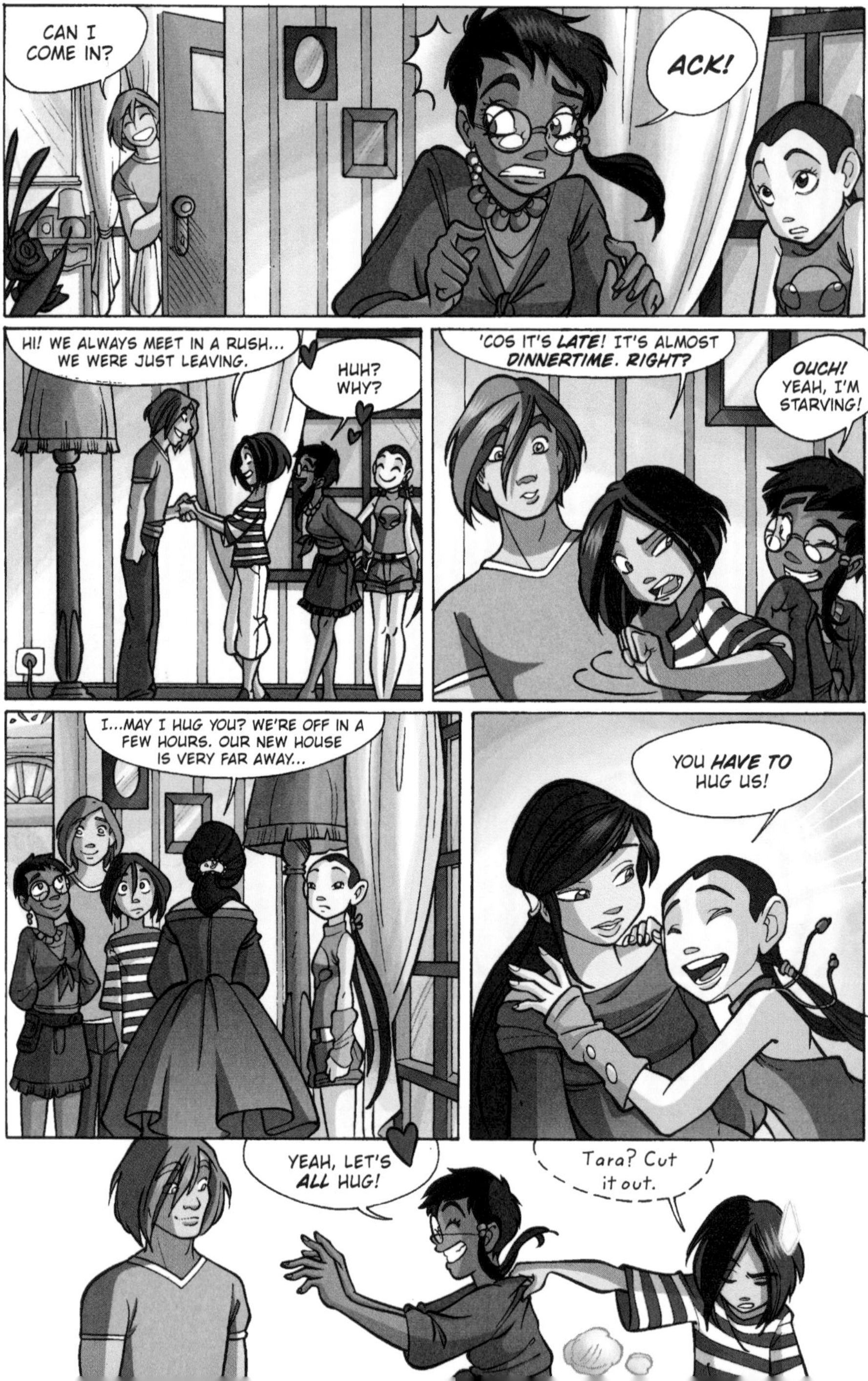
CAN I COME IN?
ACK!
HI! WE ALWAYS MEET IN A RUSH... WE WERE JUST LEAVING.
HUH? WHY?
'COS IT'S LATE! IT'S ALMOST DINNERTIME. RIGHT?
OUCH! YEAH, I'M STARVING!
I...MAY I HUG YOU? WE'RE OFF IN A FEW HOURS. OUR NEW HOUSE IS VERY FAR AWAY...
YOU HAVE TO HUG US!
YEAH, LET'S ALL HUG!
Tara? Cut it out.

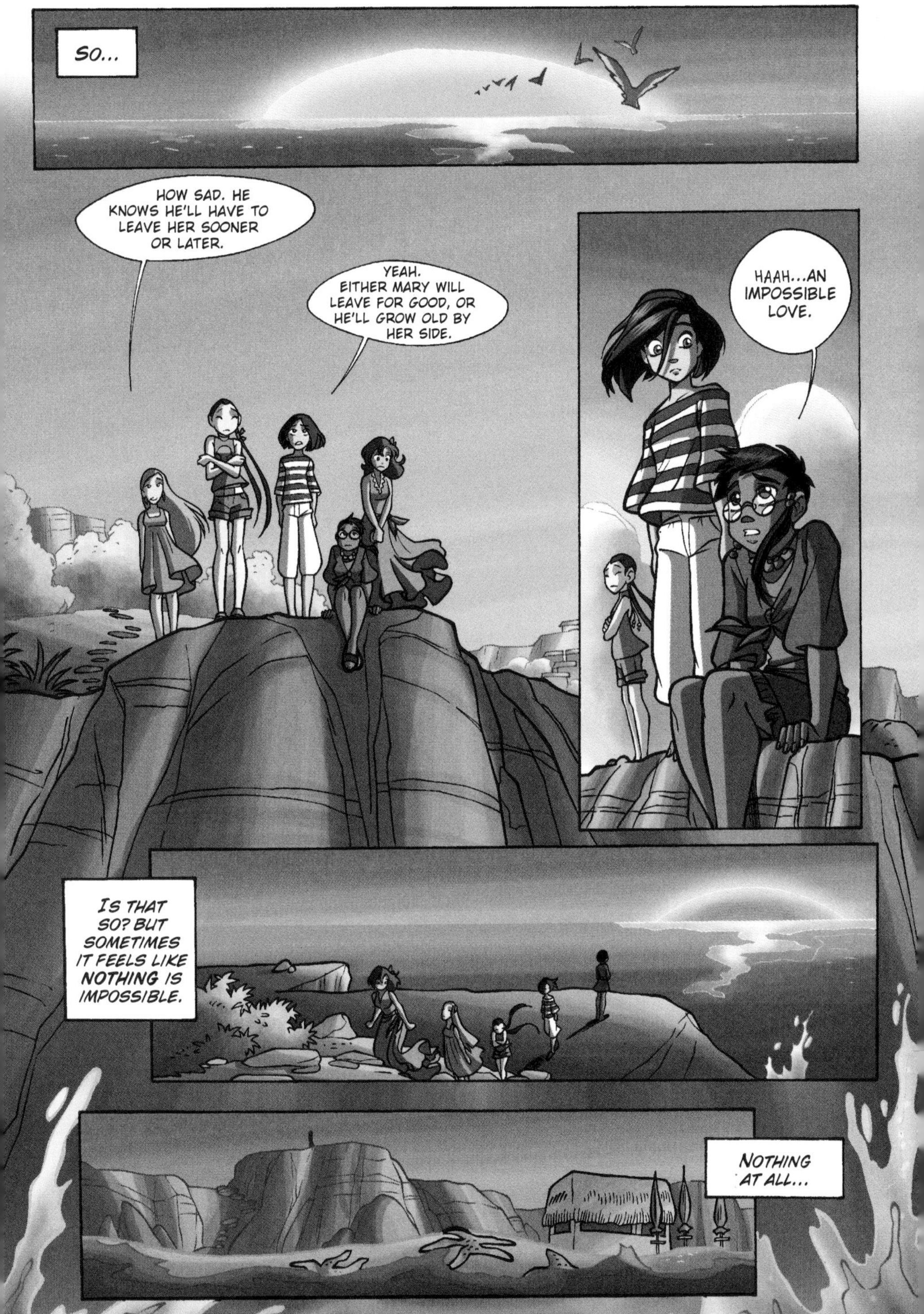
SO...
HOW SAD. HE KNOWS HE'LL HAVE TO LEAVE HER SOONER OR LATER.
YEAH. EITHER MARY WILL LEAVE FOR GOOD, OR HE'LL GROW OLD BY HER SIDE.
HAAH...AN IMPOSSIBLE LOVE.
IS THAT SO? BUT SOMETIMES IT FEELS LIKE NOTHING IS IMPOSSIBLE.
NOTHING AT ALL...

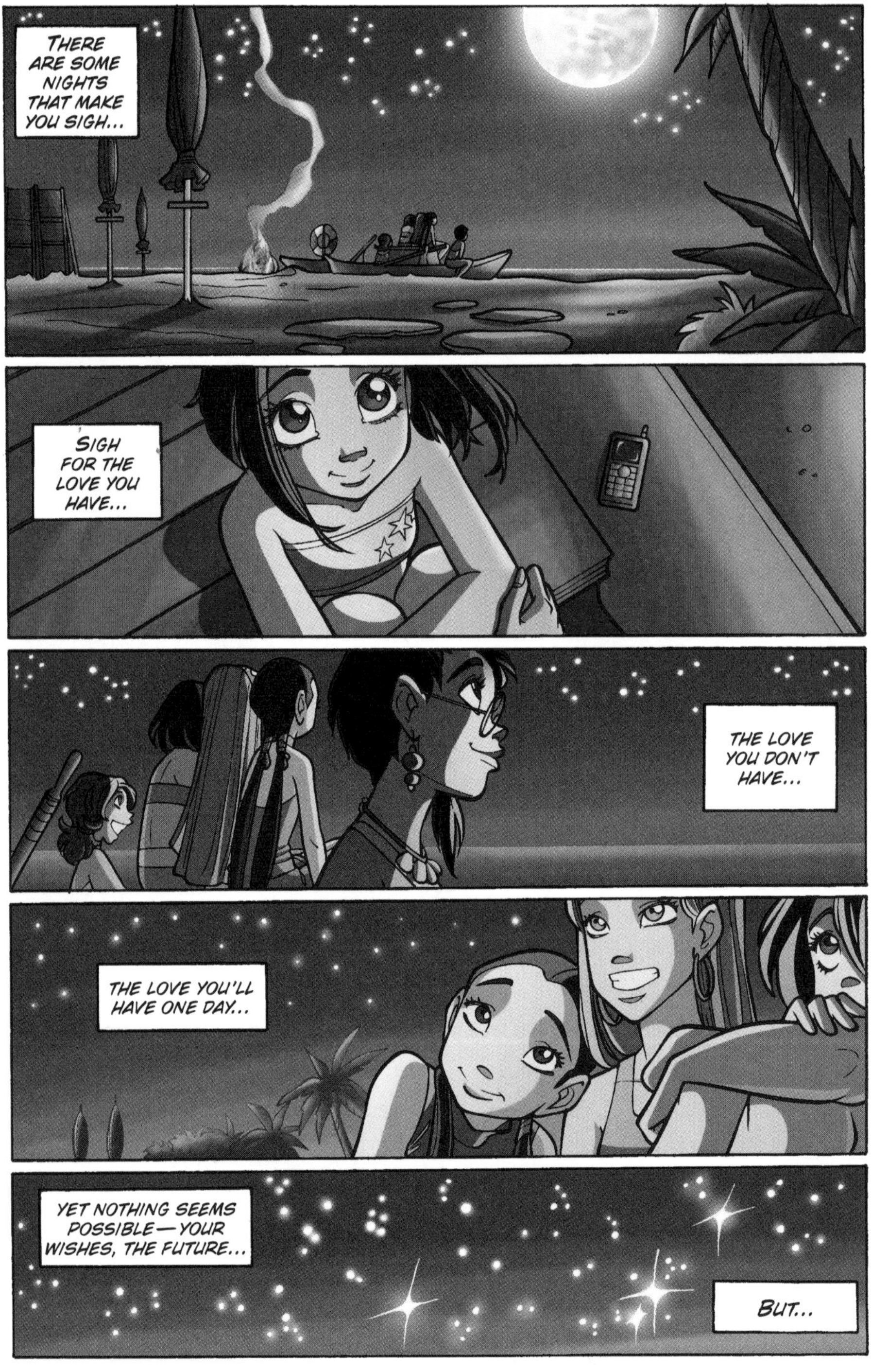
THERE ARE SOME NIGHTS THAT MAKE YOU SIGH...
SIGH FOR THE LOVE YOU HAVE...
THE LOVE YOU DON'T HAVE...
THE LOVE YOU'LL HAVE ONE DAY...
YET NOTHING SEEMS POSSIBLE—YOUR WISHES, THE FUTURE...
BUT...

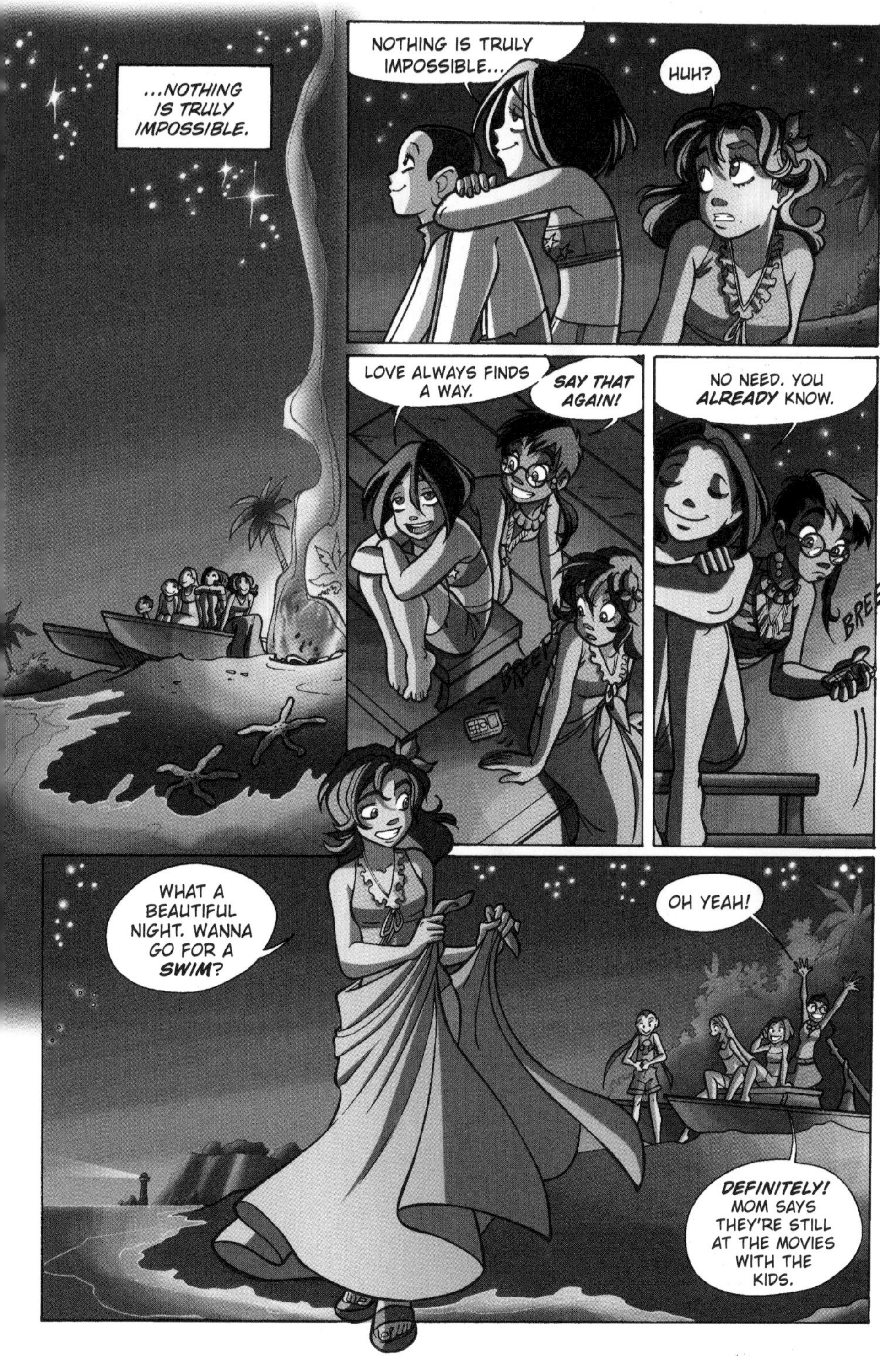
...NOTHING IS TRULY IMPOSSIBLE.
NOTHING IS TRULY IMPOSSIBLE...
HUH?
LOVE ALWAYS FINDS A WAY.
SAY THAT AGAIN!
BREEP
NO NEED. YOU ALREADY KNOW.
BREEP
WHAT A BEAUTIFUL NIGHT. WANNA GO FOR A SWIM?
OH YEAH!
DEFINITELY! MOM SAYS THEY'RE STILL AT THE MOVIES WITH THE KIDS.

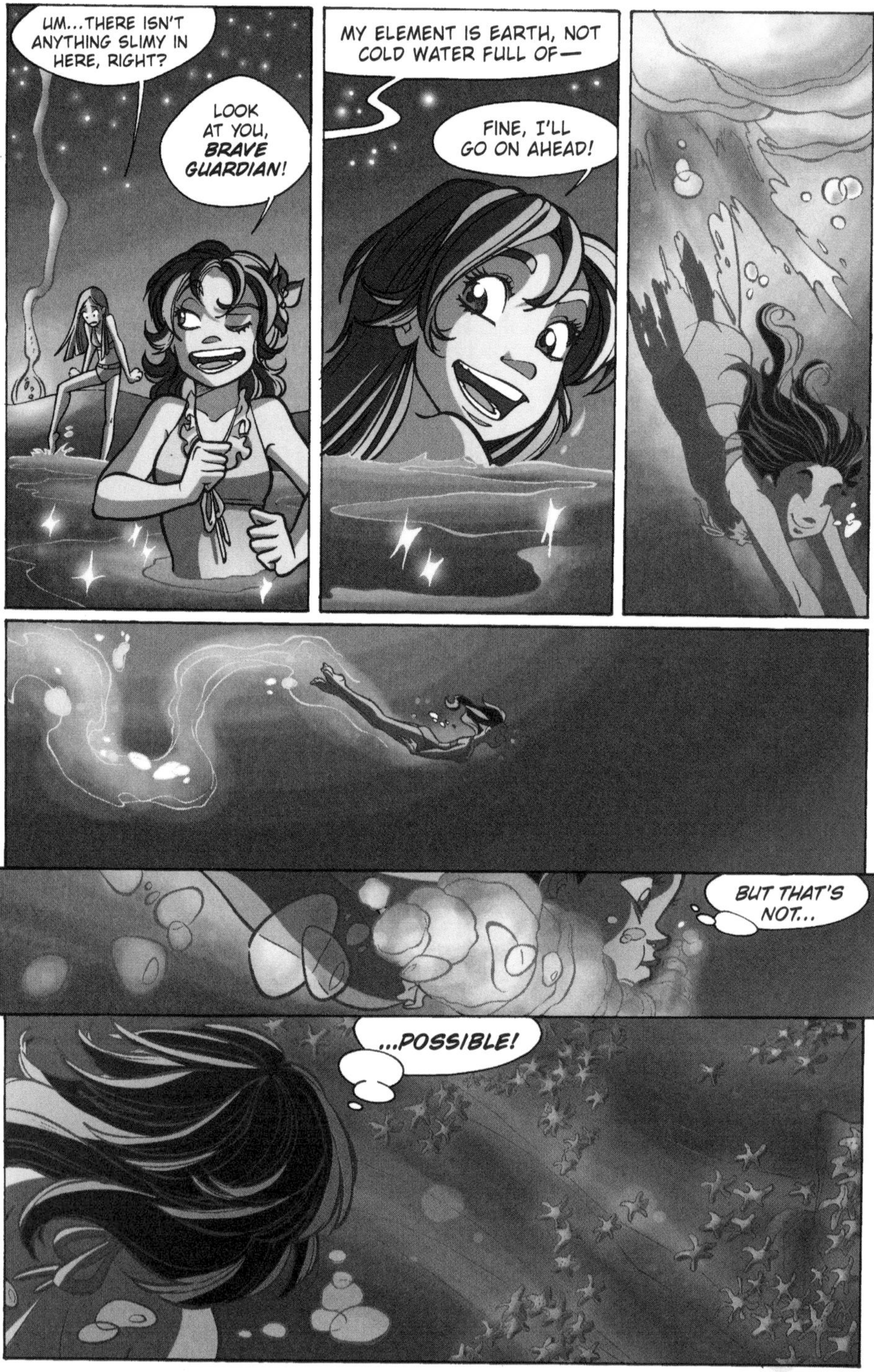
UM...THERE ISN'T ANYTHING SLIMY IN HERE, RIGHT?
LOOK AT YOU, BRAVE GUARDIAN!
MY ELEMENT IS EARTH, NOT COLD WATER FULL OF—
FINE, I'LL GO ON AHEAD!
BUT THAT'S NOT...
...POSSIBLE!

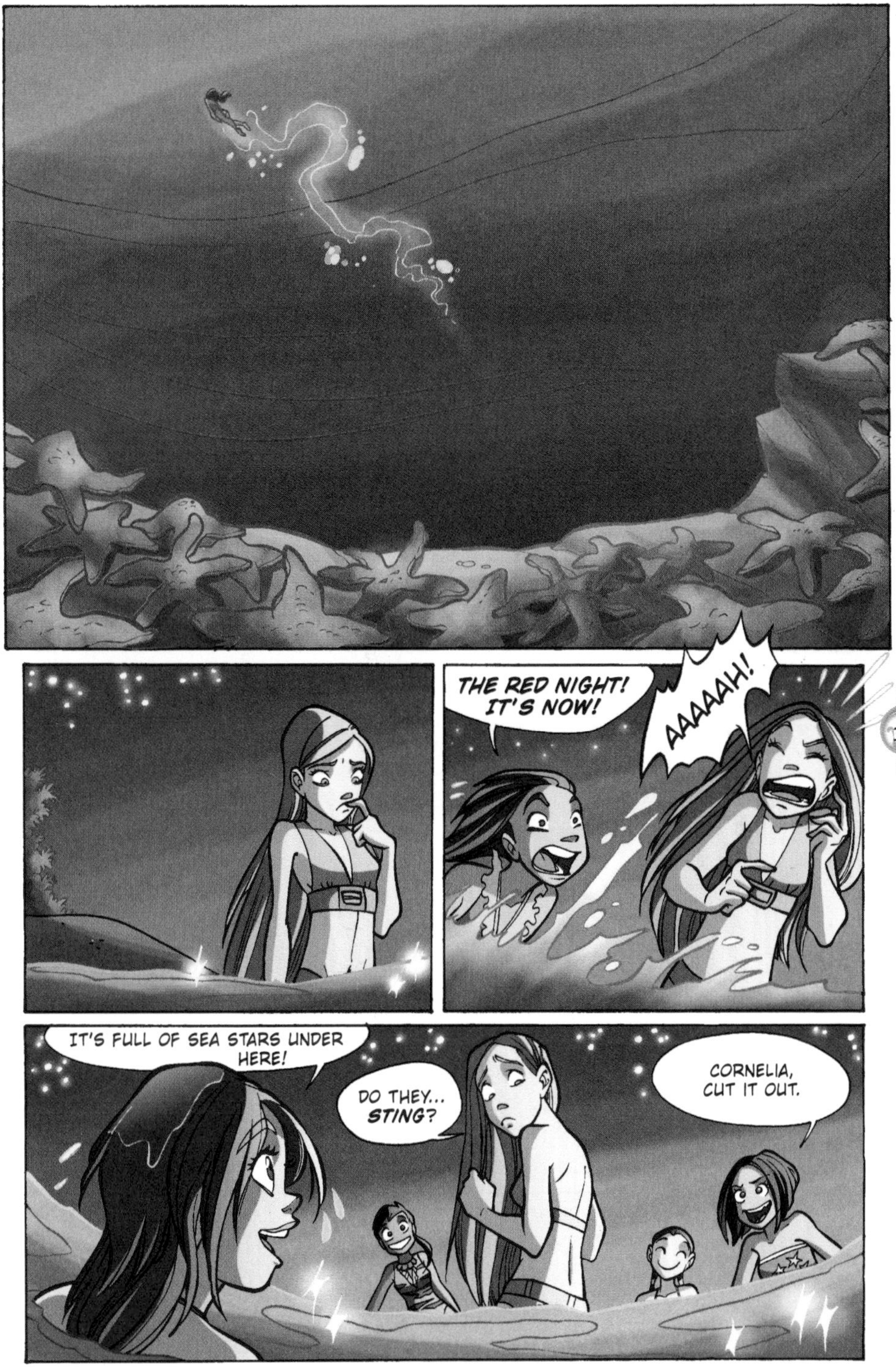

THE RED NIGHT! IT'S NOW!
AAAAAH!
IT'S FULL OF SEA STARS UNDER HERE!
DO THEY... *STING*?
CORNELIA, CUT IT OUT.

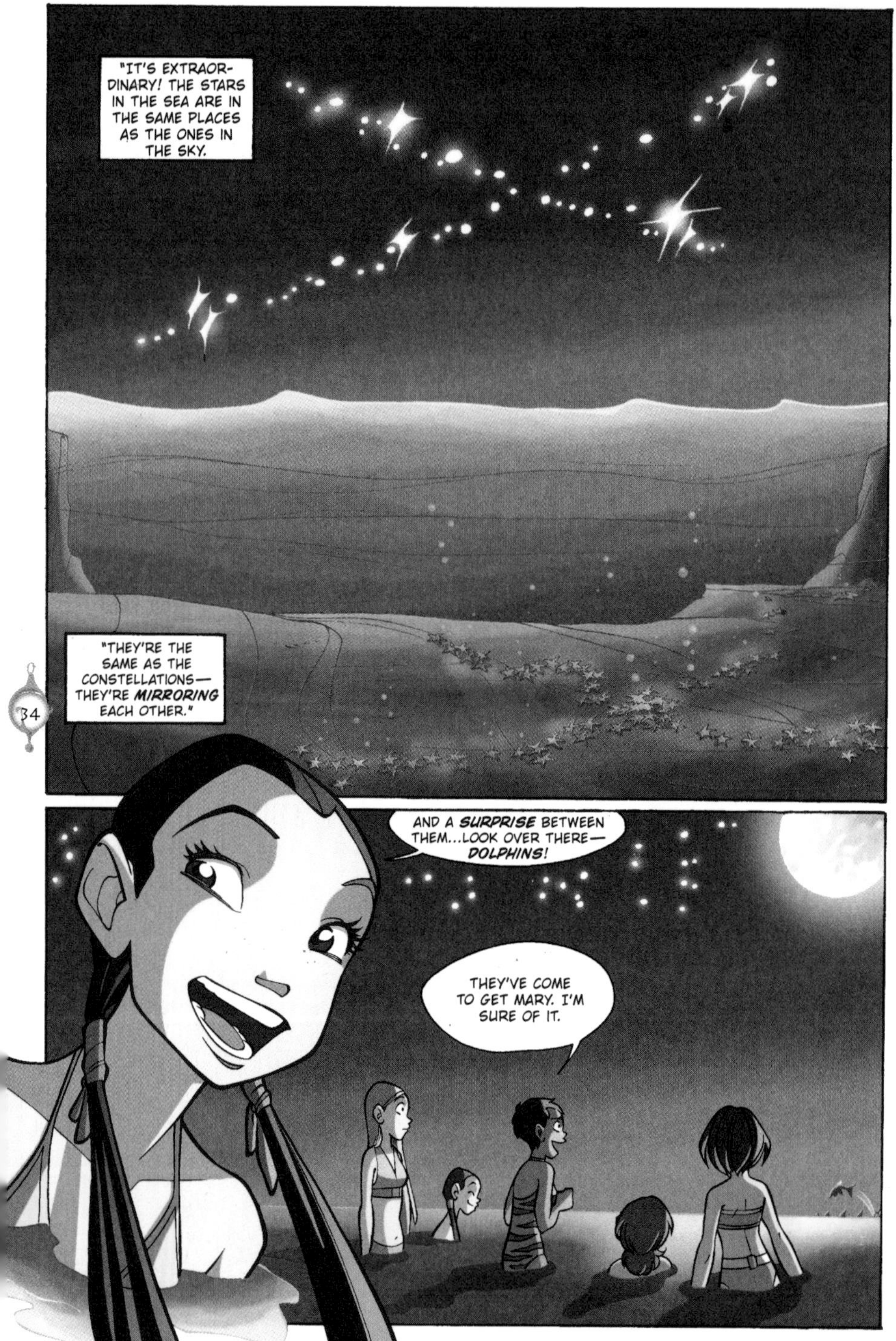
"IT'S EXTRAORDINARY! THE STARS IN THE SEA ARE IN THE SAME PLACES AS THE ONES IN THE SKY.
"THEY'RE THE SAME AS THE CONSTELLATIONS—THEY'RE MIRRORING EACH OTHER."
AND A SURPRISE BETWEEN THEM...LOOK OVER THERE—DOLPHINS!
THEY'VE COME TO GET MARY. I'M SURE OF IT.

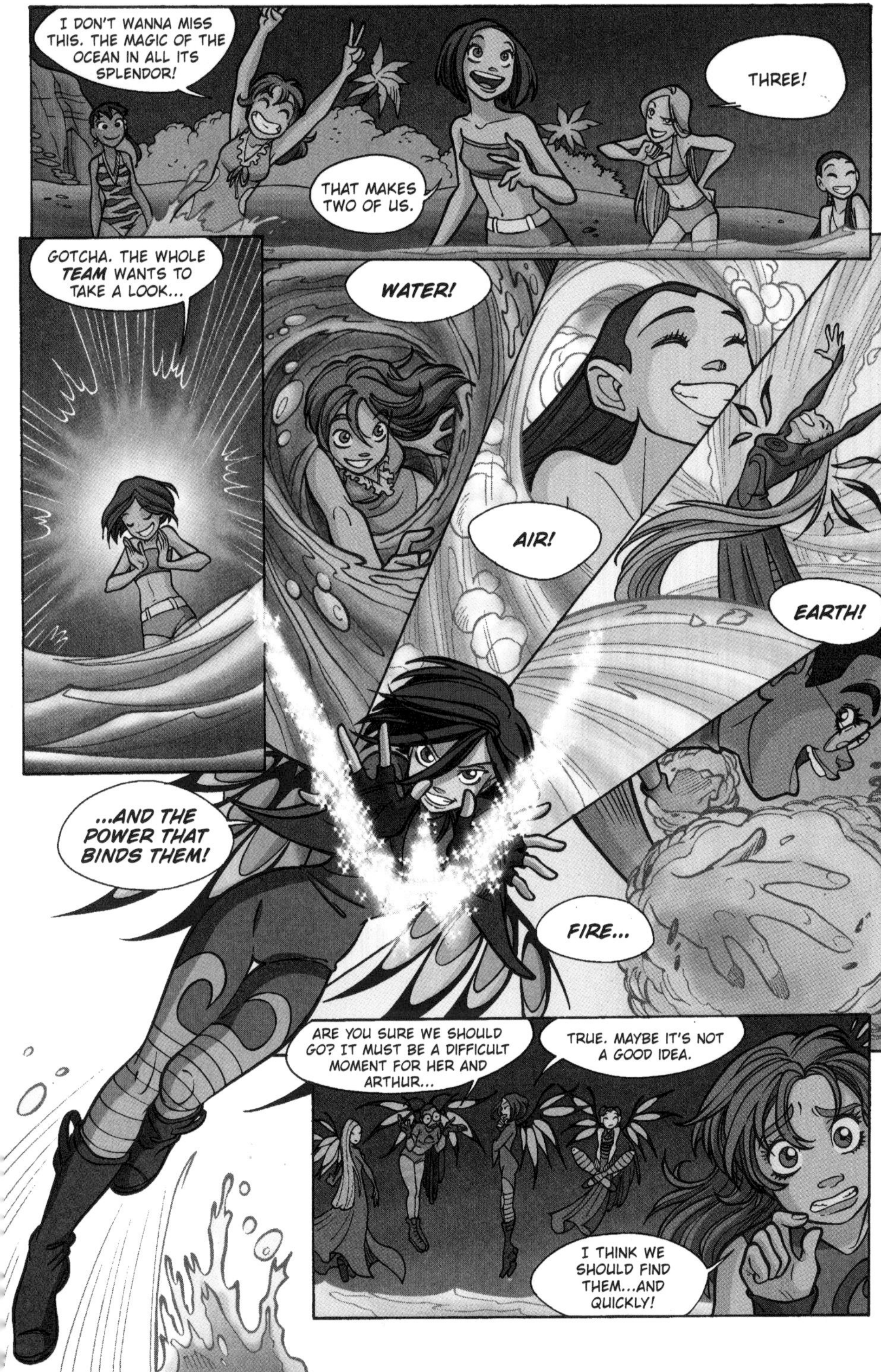
I DON'T WANNA MISS THIS. THE MAGIC OF THE OCEAN IN ALL ITS SPLENDOR!
THAT MAKES TWO OF US.
THREE!
GOTCHA. THE WHOLE TEAM WANTS TO TAKE A LOOK...
WATER!
AIR!
EARTH!
FIRE...
...AND THE POWER THAT BINDS THEM!
ARE YOU SURE WE SHOULD GO? IT MUST BE A DIFFICULT MOMENT FOR HER AND ARTHUR...
TRUE. MAYBE IT'S NOT A GOOD IDEA.
I THINK WE SHOULD FIND THEM...AND QUICKLY!

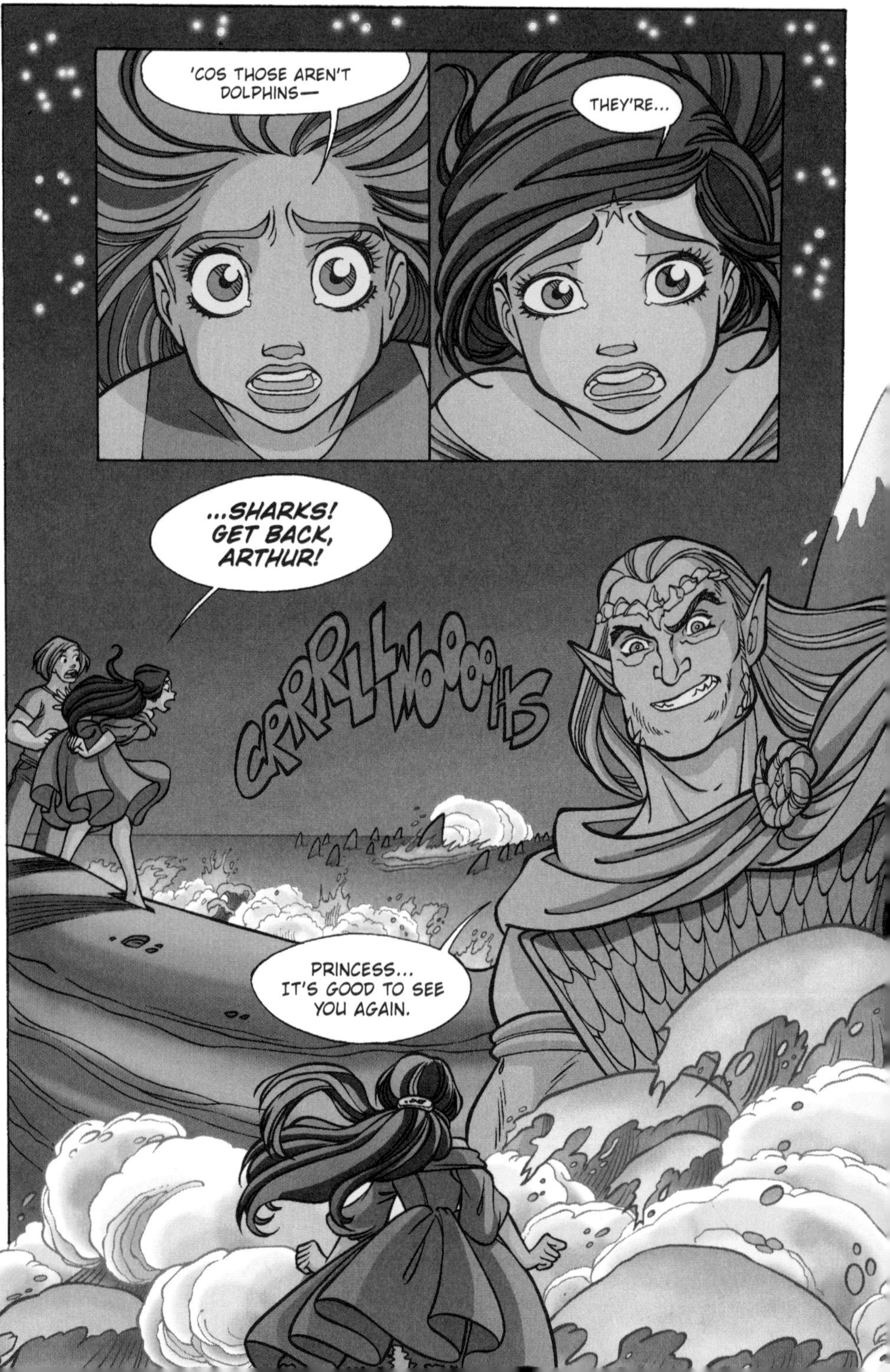
'COS THOSE AREN'T DOLPHINS—
THEY'RE...
...SHARKS! GET BACK, ARTHUR!
CRRRLLWOOOOHS
PRINCESS... IT'S GOOD TO SEE YOU AGAIN.

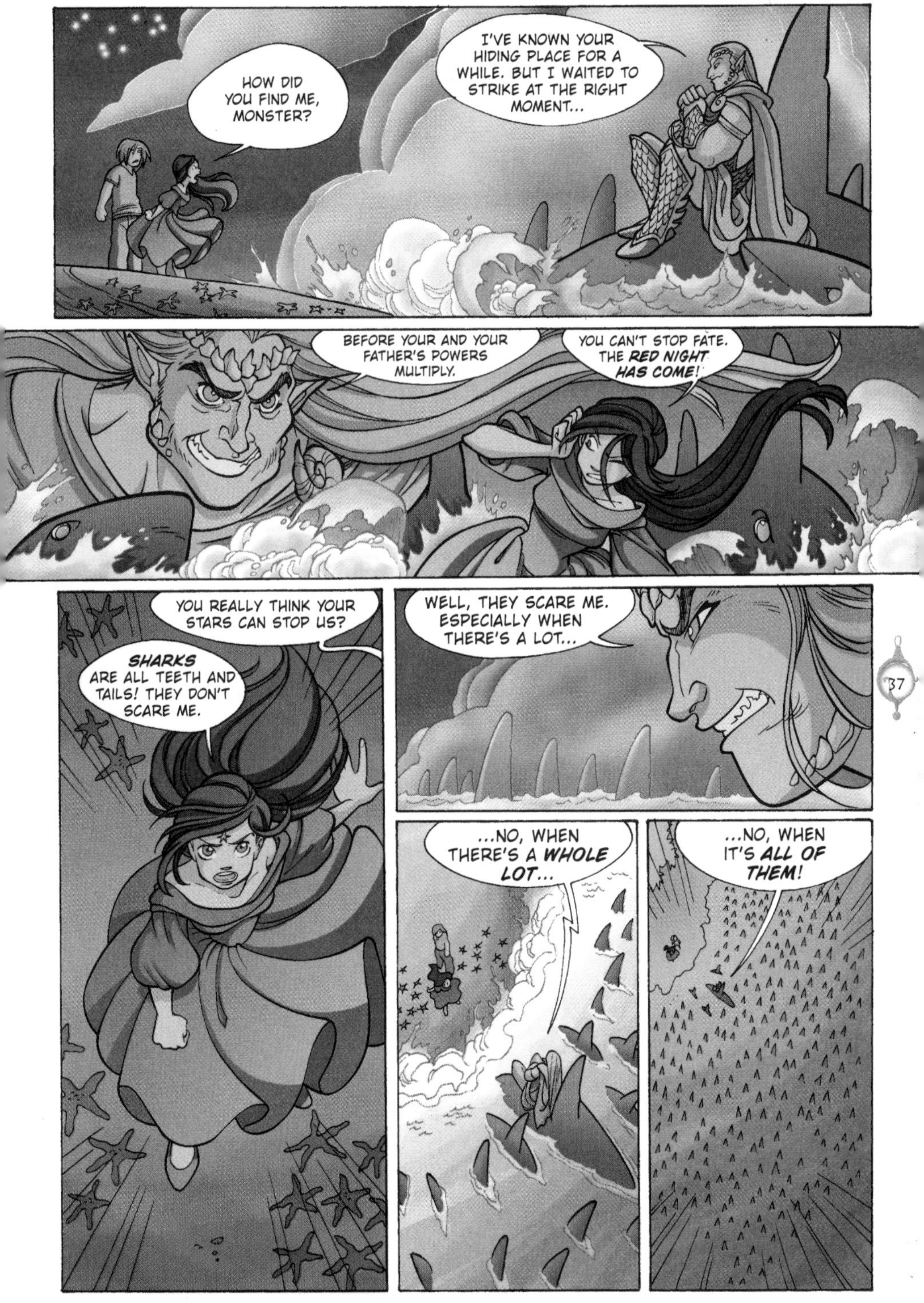
HOW DID YOU FIND ME, MONSTER?
I'VE KNOWN YOUR HIDING PLACE FOR A WHILE. BUT I WAITED TO STRIKE AT THE RIGHT MOMENT...
BEFORE YOUR AND YOUR FATHER'S POWERS MULTIPLY.
YOU CAN'T STOP FATE. THE **RED NIGHT HAS COME**!
YOU REALLY THINK YOUR STARS CAN STOP US?
SHARKS ARE ALL TEETH AND TAILS! THEY DON'T SCARE ME.
WELL, THEY SCARE ME. ESPECIALLY WHEN THERE'S A LOT...
...NO, WHEN THERE'S A **WHOLE LOT**...
...NO, WHEN IT'S **ALL OF THEM**!

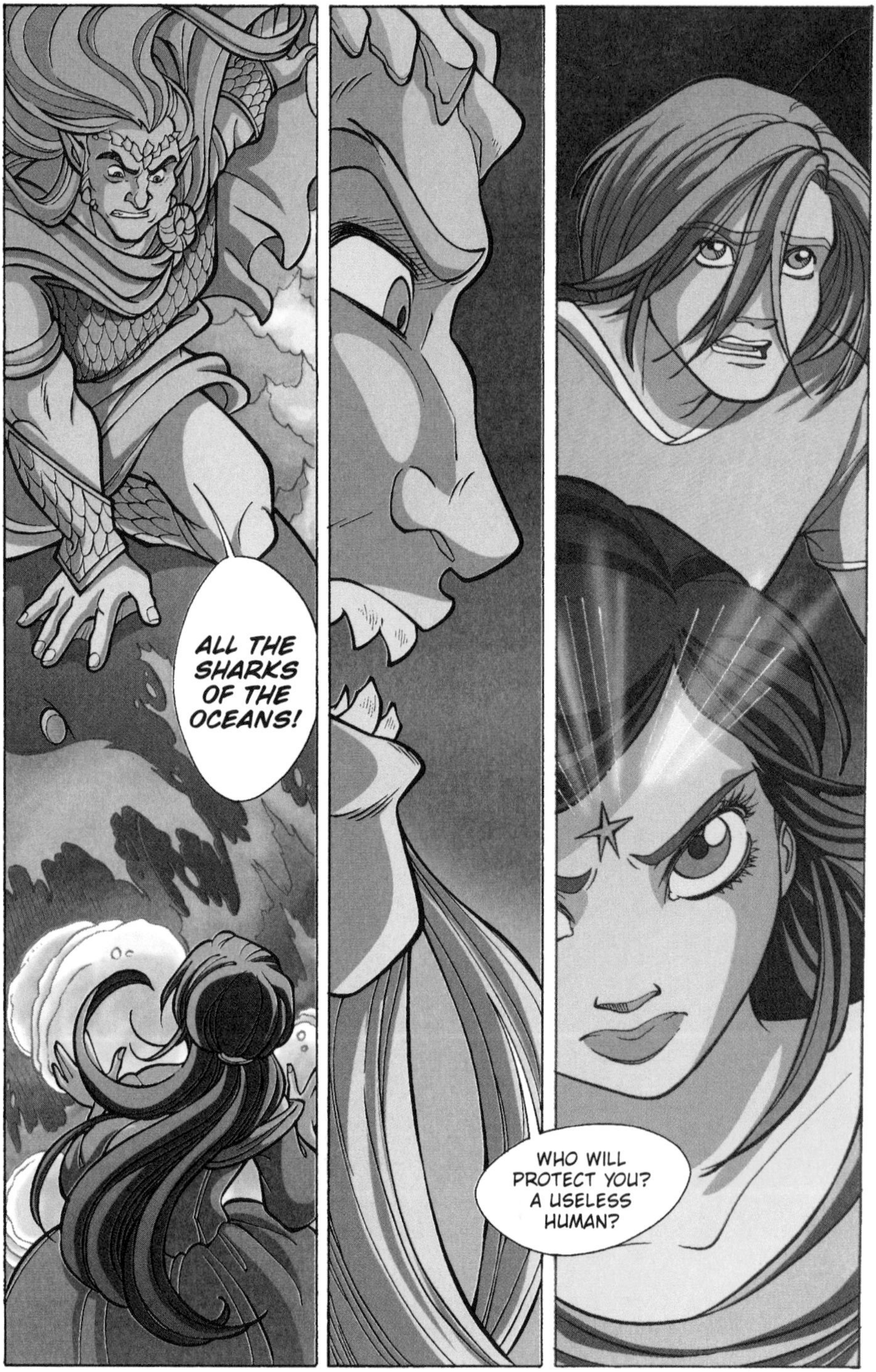
ALL THE SHARKS OF THE OCEANS!
WHO WILL PROTECT YOU? A USELESS HUMAN?

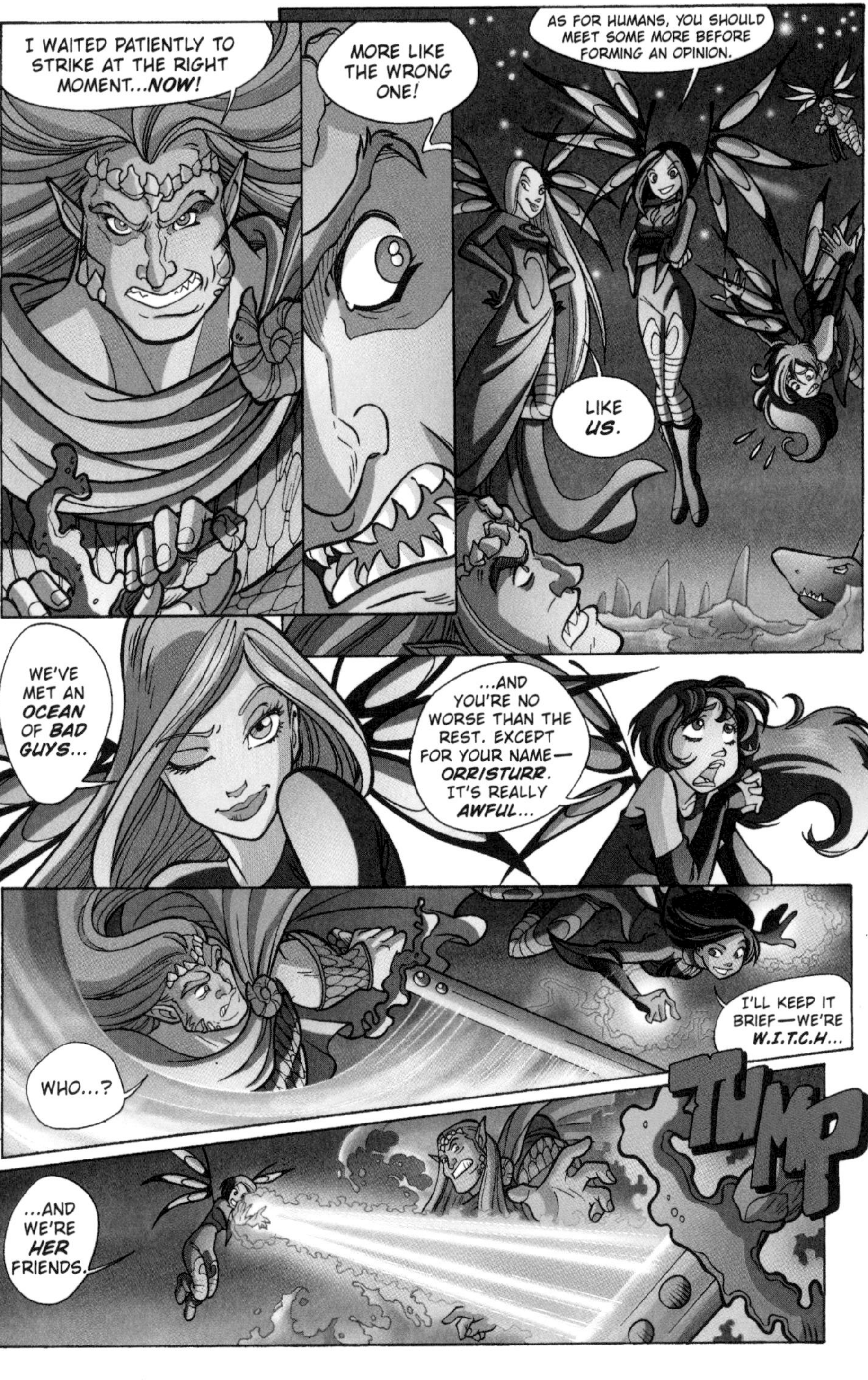
I WAITED PATIENTLY TO STRIKE AT THE RIGHT MOMENT...NOW!
MORE LIKE THE WRONG ONE!
AS FOR HUMANS, YOU SHOULD MEET SOME MORE BEFORE FORMING AN OPINION.
LIKE US.
WE'VE MET AN OCEAN OF BAD GUYS...
...AND YOU'RE NO WORSE THAN THE REST. EXCEPT FOR YOUR NAME—ORRISTURR. IT'S REALLY AWFUL...
WHO...?
I'LL KEEP IT BRIEF—WE'RE W.I.T.C.H...
TUMP
...AND WE'RE HER FRIENDS.

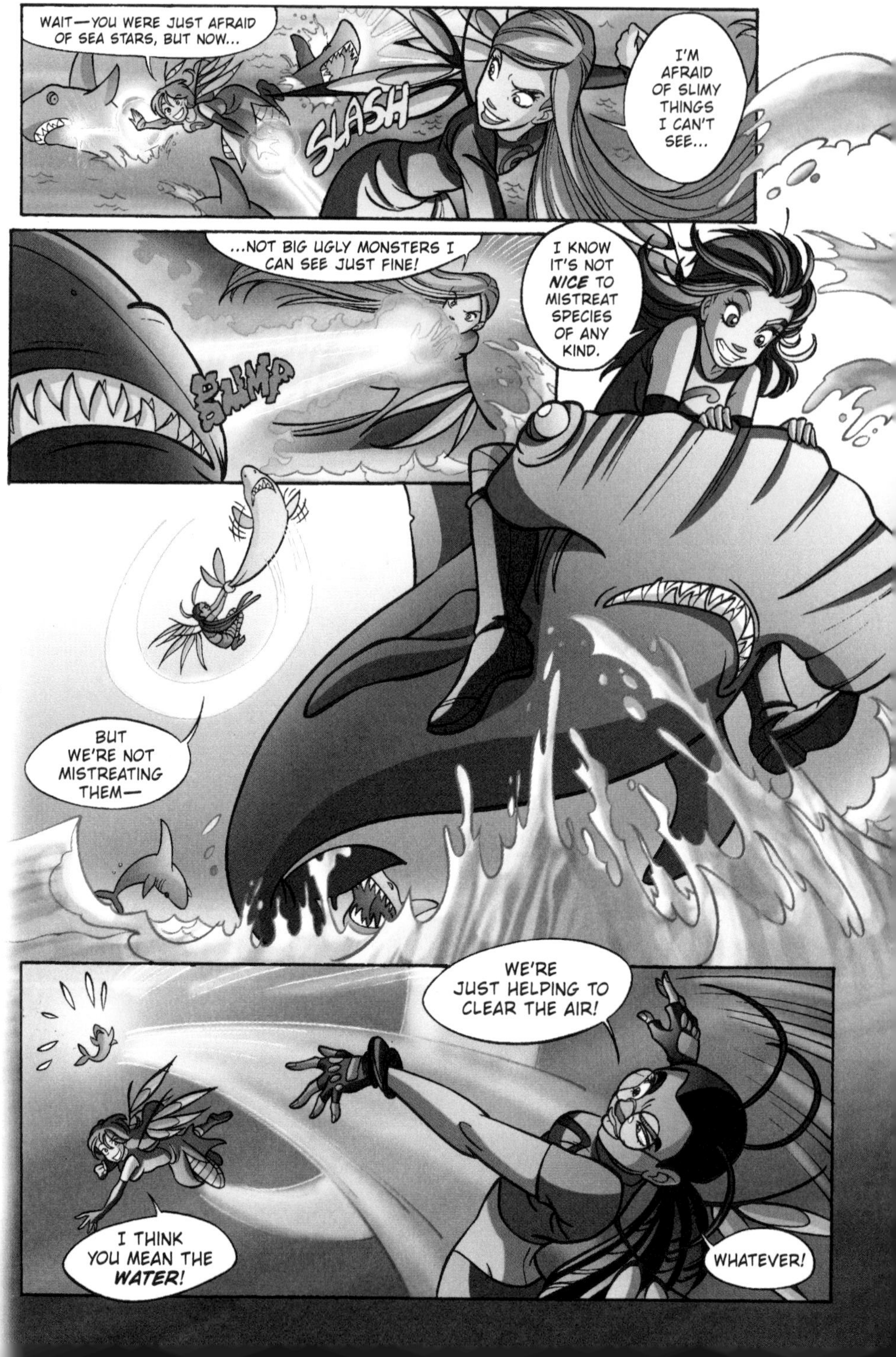
WAIT—YOU WERE JUST AFRAID OF SEA STARS, BUT NOW...
SLASH
I'M AFRAID OF SLIMY THINGS I CAN'T SEE...
...NOT BIG UGLY MONSTERS I CAN SEE JUST FINE!
BUMP
I KNOW IT'S NOT NICE TO MISTREAT SPECIES OF ANY KIND.
BUT WE'RE NOT MISTREATING THEM—
WE'RE JUST HELPING TO CLEAR THE AIR!
I THINK YOU MEAN THE WATER!
WHATEVER!

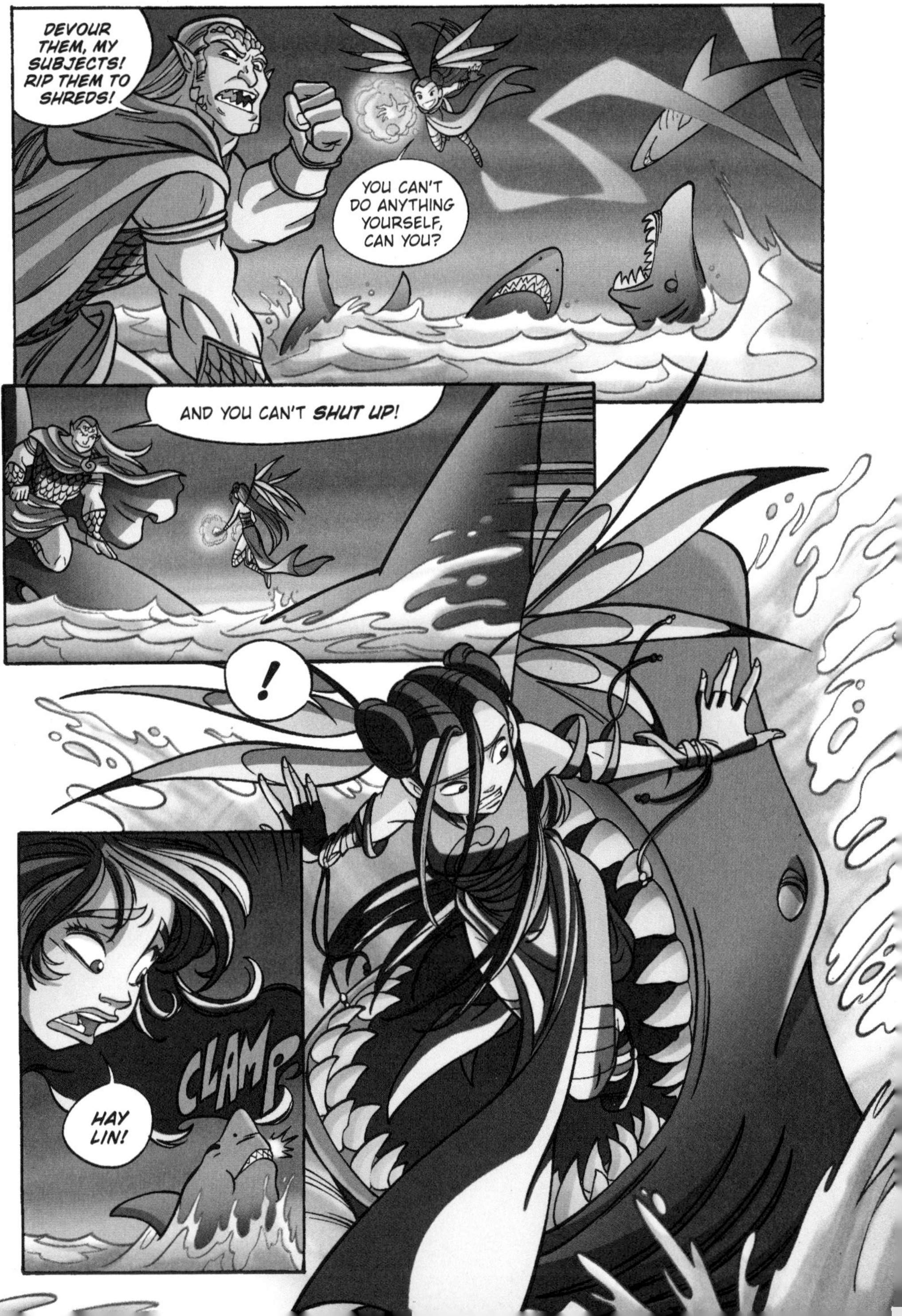
DEVOUR THEM, MY SUBJECTS! RIP THEM TO SHREDS!
YOU CAN'T DO ANYTHING YOURSELF, CAN YOU?
AND YOU CAN'T SHUT UP!
!
CLAMP
HAY LIN!

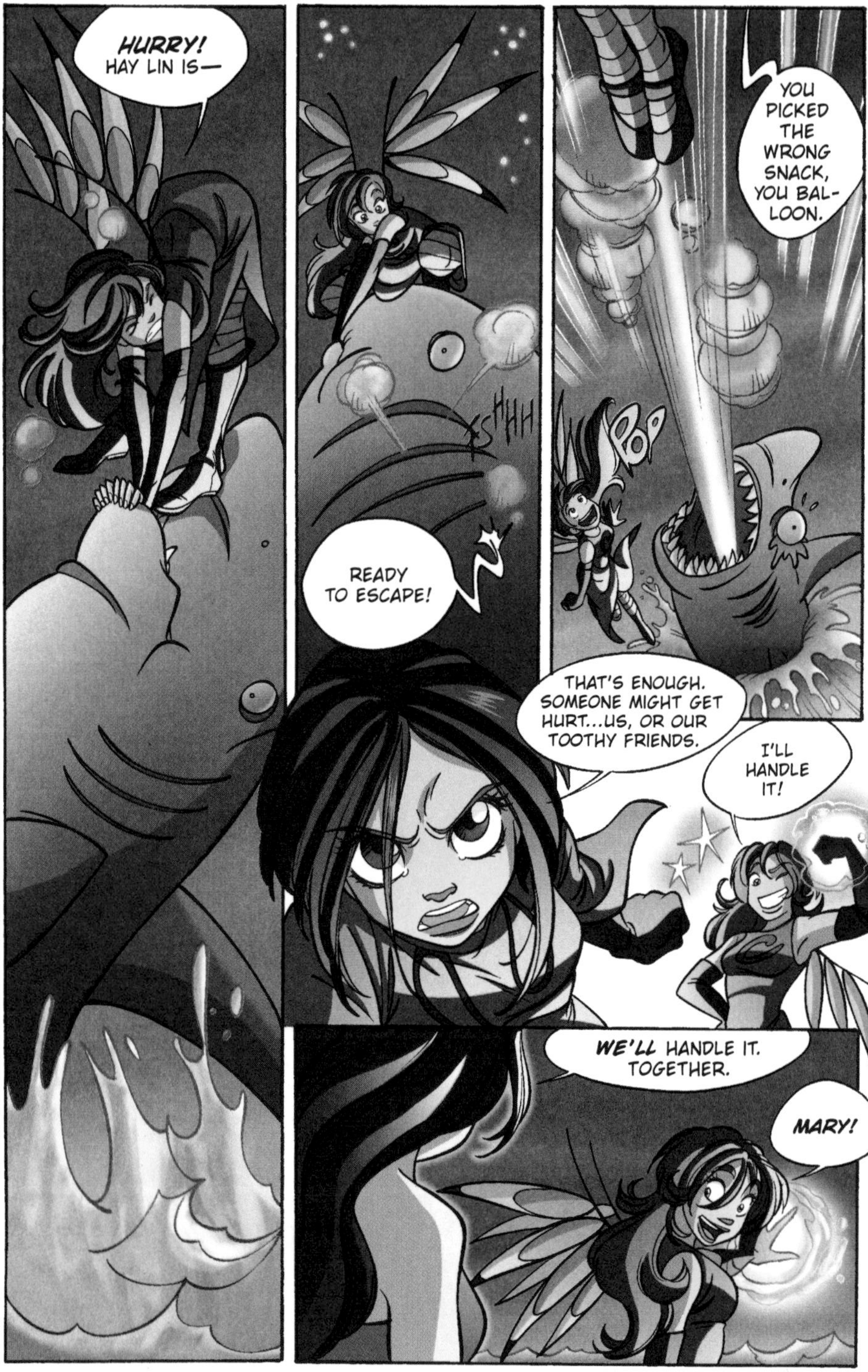

HURRY!
HAY LIN IS—
READY TO ESCAPE!
FSHHH
YOU PICKED THE WRONG SNACK, YOU BAL-LOON.
POP
THAT'S ENOUGH. SOMEONE MIGHT GET HURT...US, OR OUR TOOTHY FRIENDS.
I'LL HANDLE IT!
WE'LL HANDLE IT. TOGETHER.
MARY!

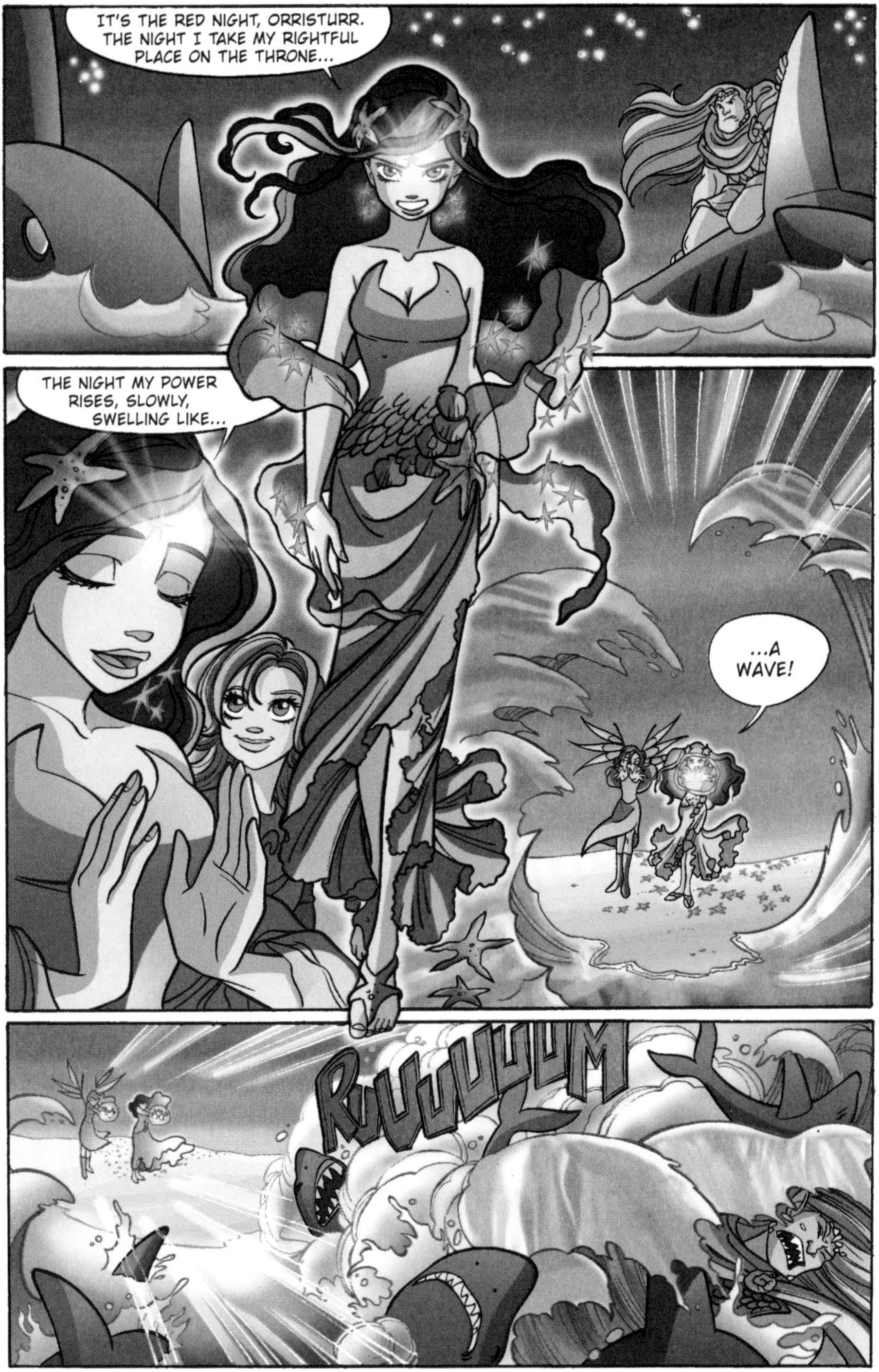

IT'S THE RED NIGHT, ORRISTURR. THE NIGHT I TAKE MY RIGHTFUL PLACE ON THE THRONE...
THE NIGHT MY POWER RISES, SLOWLY, SWELLING LIKE...
...A WAVE!
RUUUUUUM

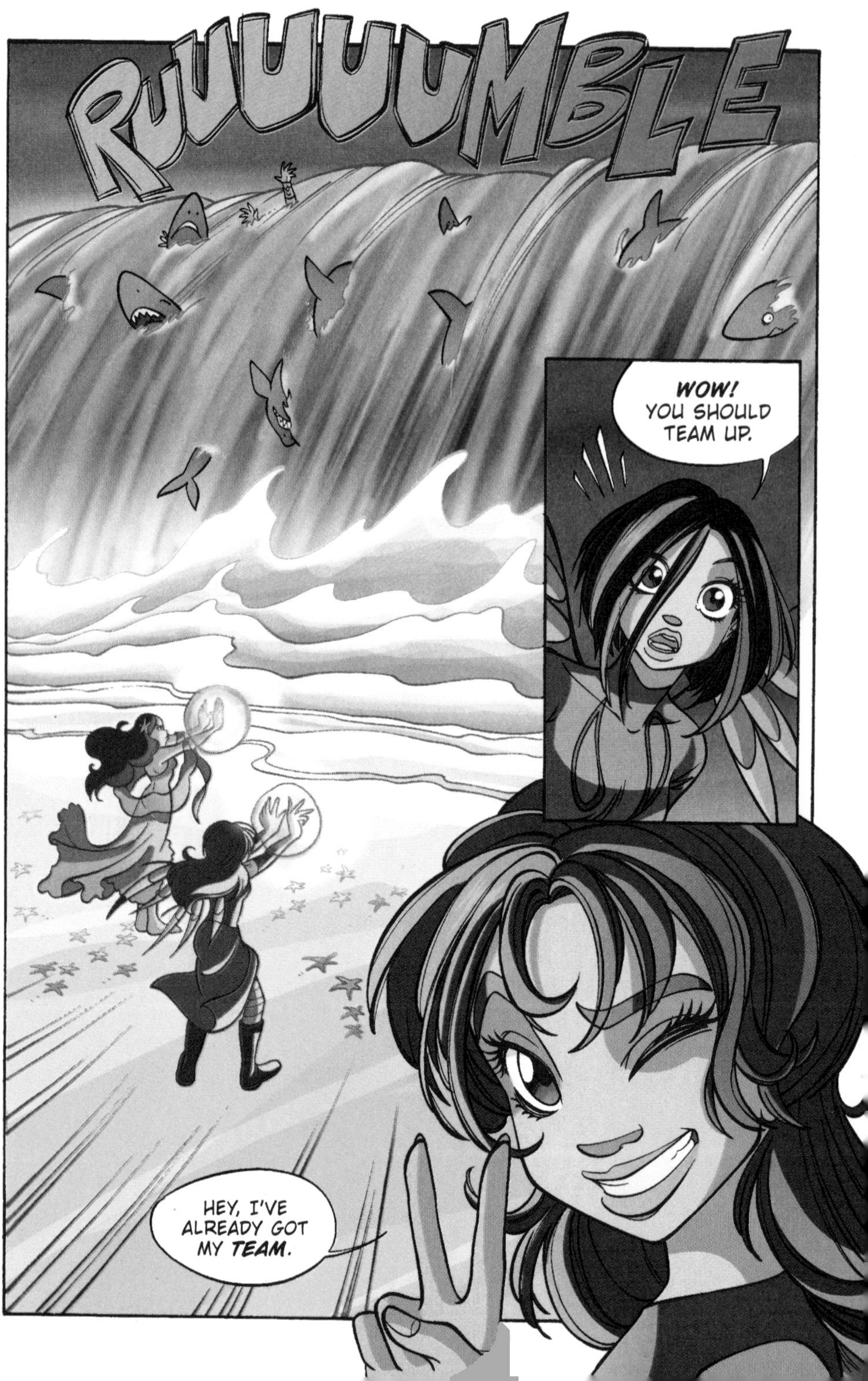
RUUUUUMBLE
WOW! YOU SHOULD TEAM UP.
HEY, I'VE ALREADY GOT MY TEAM.

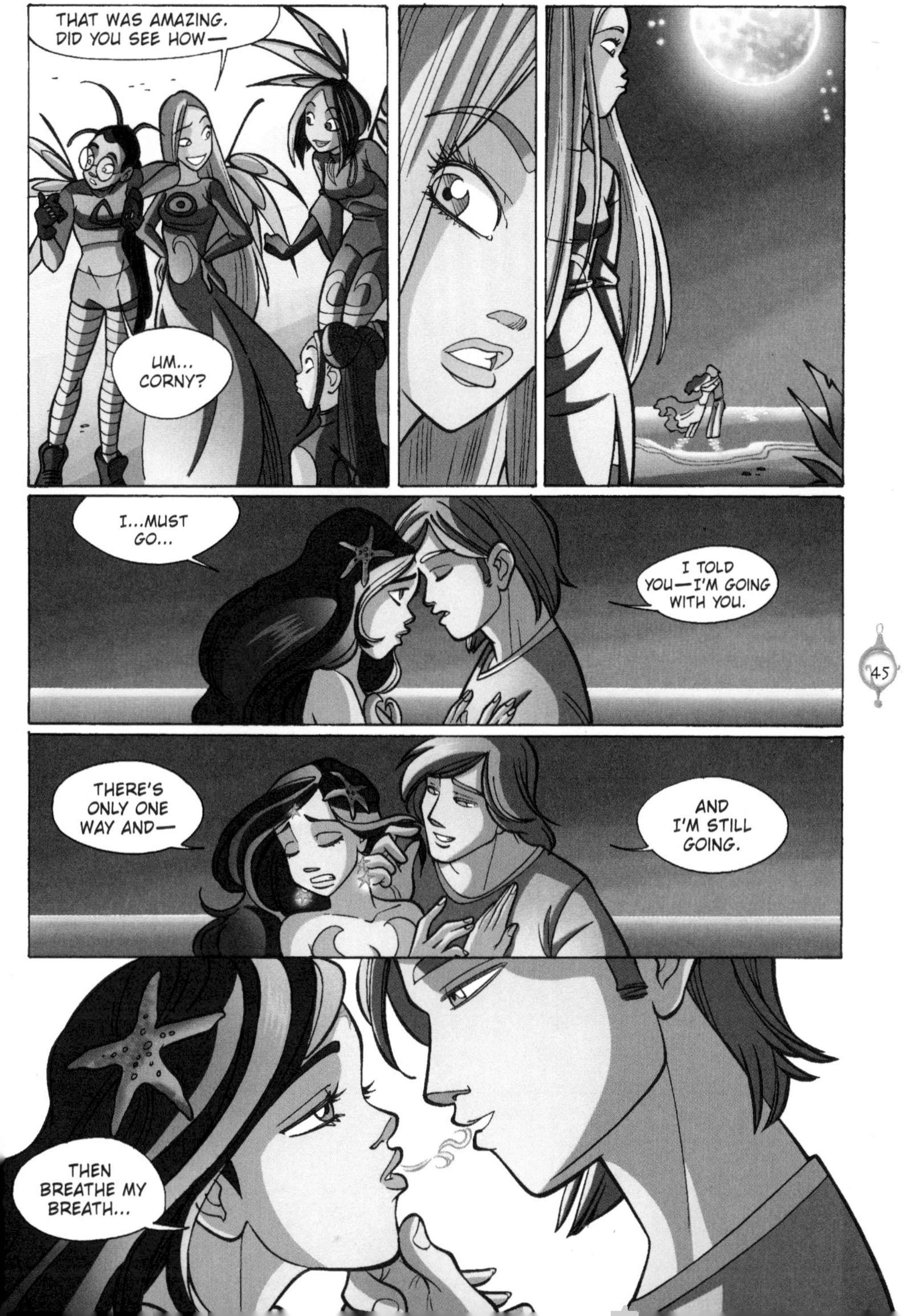
THAT WAS AMAZING. DID YOU SEE HOW—
UM... CORNY?
I...MUST GO...
I TOLD YOU—I'M GOING WITH YOU.
THERE'S ONLY ONE WAY AND—
AND I'M STILL GOING.
THEN BREATHE MY BREATH...

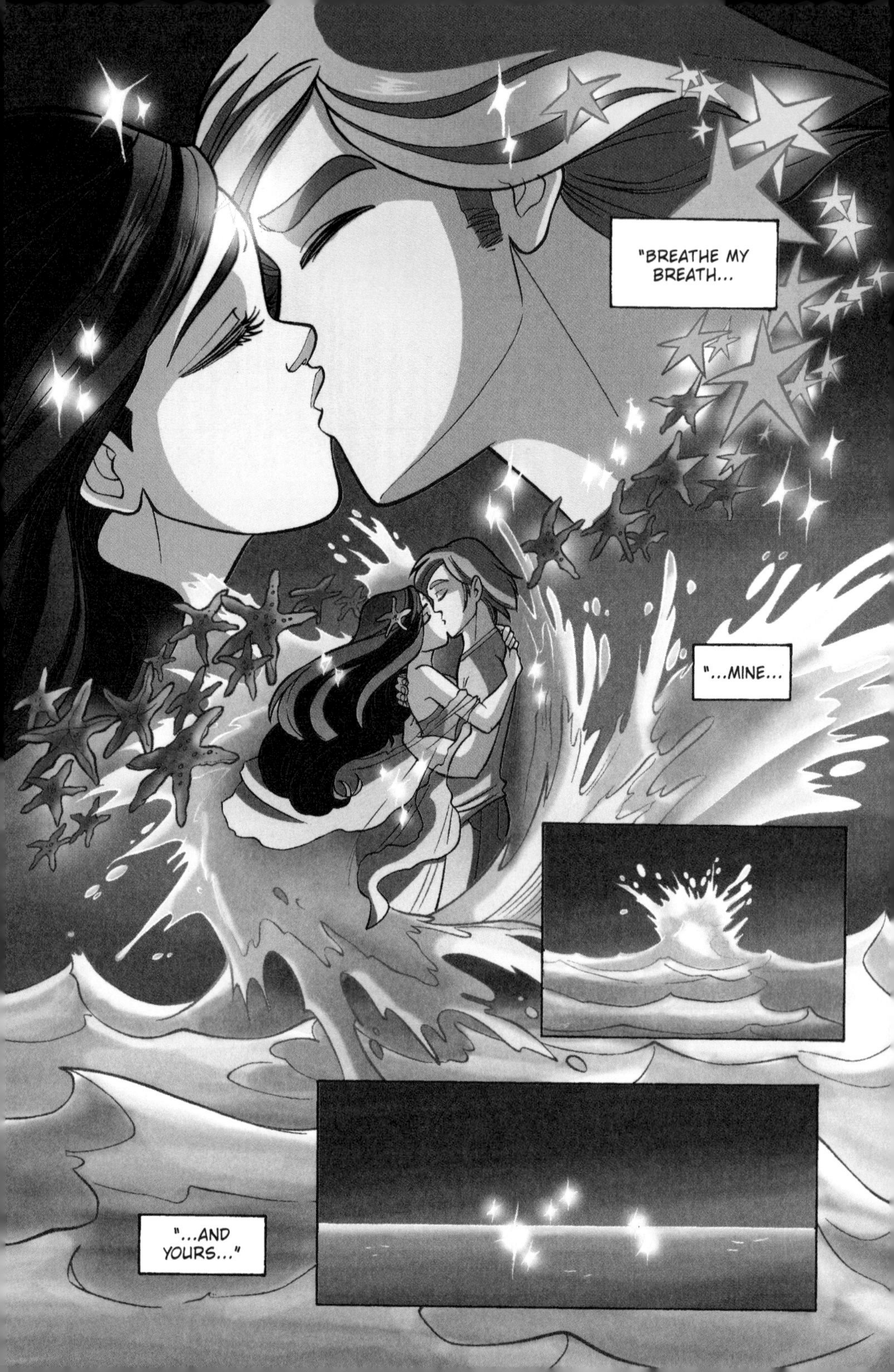
"BREATHE MY BREATH...
"...MINE...
"...AND YOURS..."

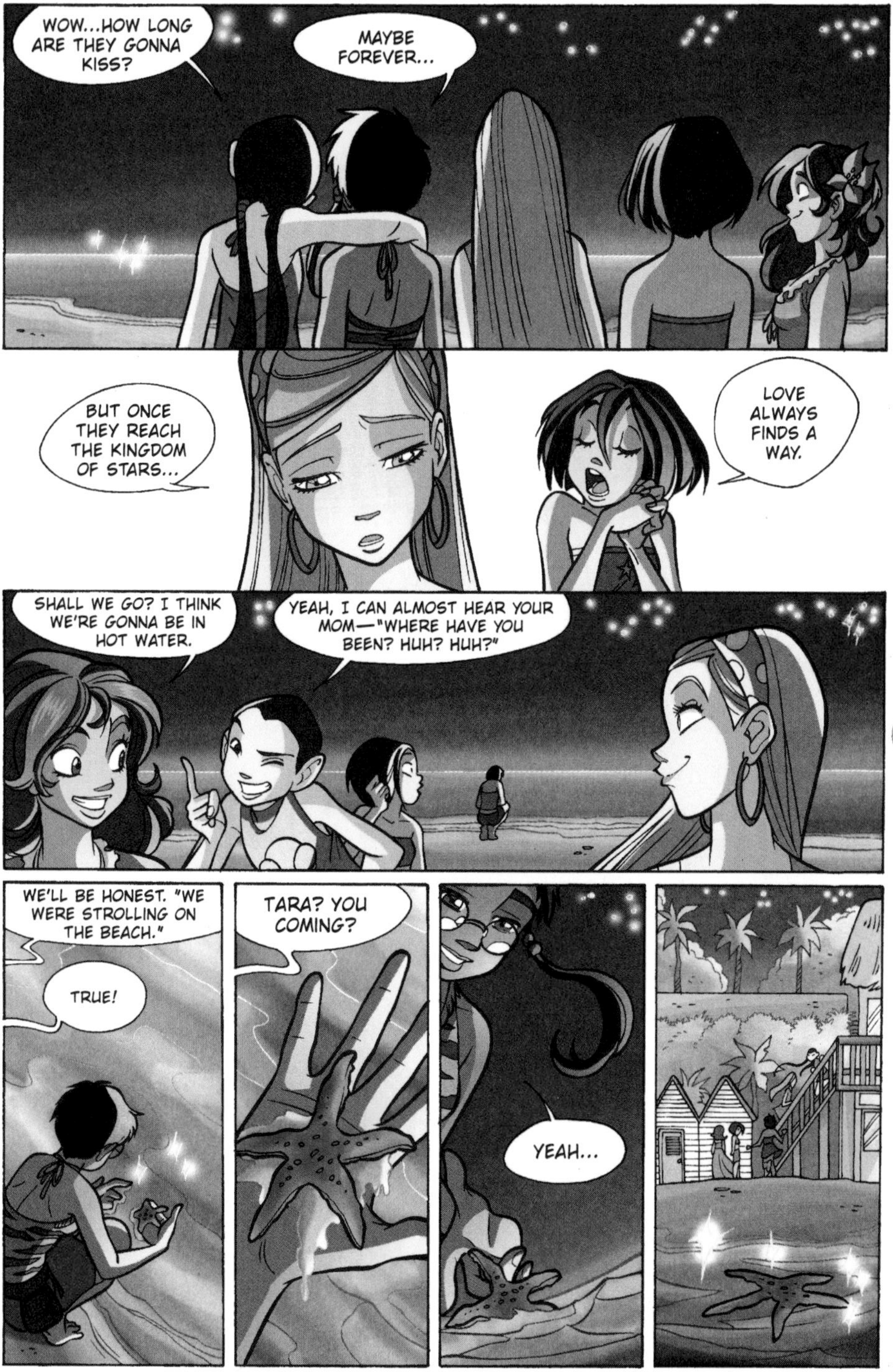
WOW...HOW LONG ARE THEY GONNA KISS?
MAYBE FOREVER...
BUT ONCE THEY REACH THE KINGDOM OF STARS...
LOVE ALWAYS FINDS A WAY.
SHALL WE GO? I THINK WE'RE GONNA BE IN HOT WATER.
YEAH, I CAN ALMOST HEAR YOUR MOM—"WHERE HAVE YOU BEEN? HUH? HUH?"
WE'LL BE HONEST. "WE WERE STROLLING ON THE BEACH."
TRUE!
TARA? YOU COMING?
YEAH...

SO...

HOLD IT. THAT'S *PERFECT!*

C'MON, MOM. THE SAND IS SUPER-HOT.

OKAY, OKAY. SMILE! ONE...

...TWO... AND...

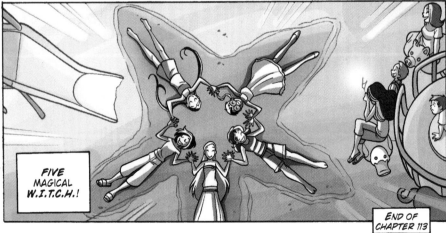

FIVE MAGICAL *W.I.T.C.H.!*

END OF CHAPTER 113

114

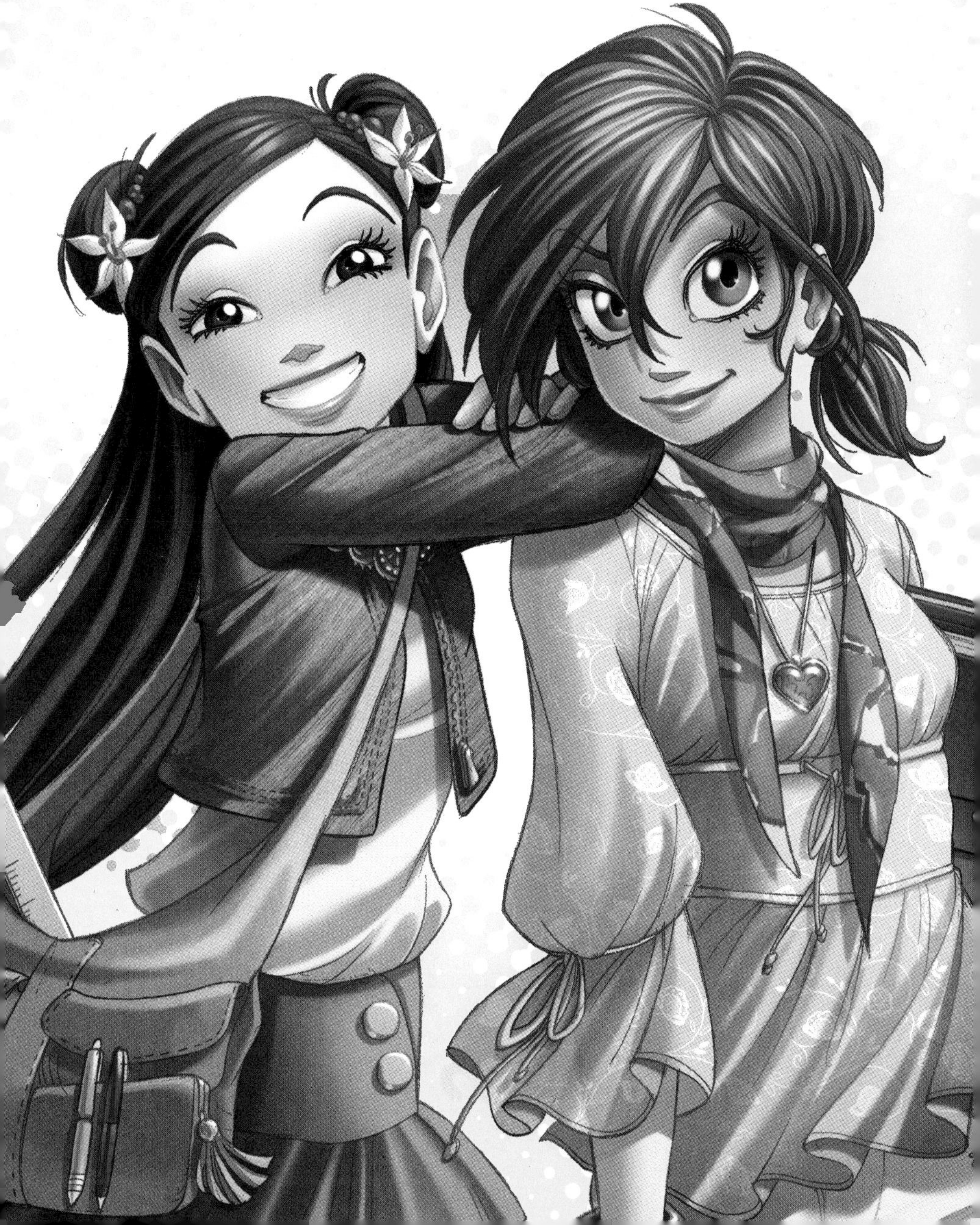

W.i.t.c.h.

Will Irma Taranee Cornelia Hay Lin

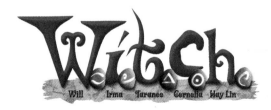

Back to School

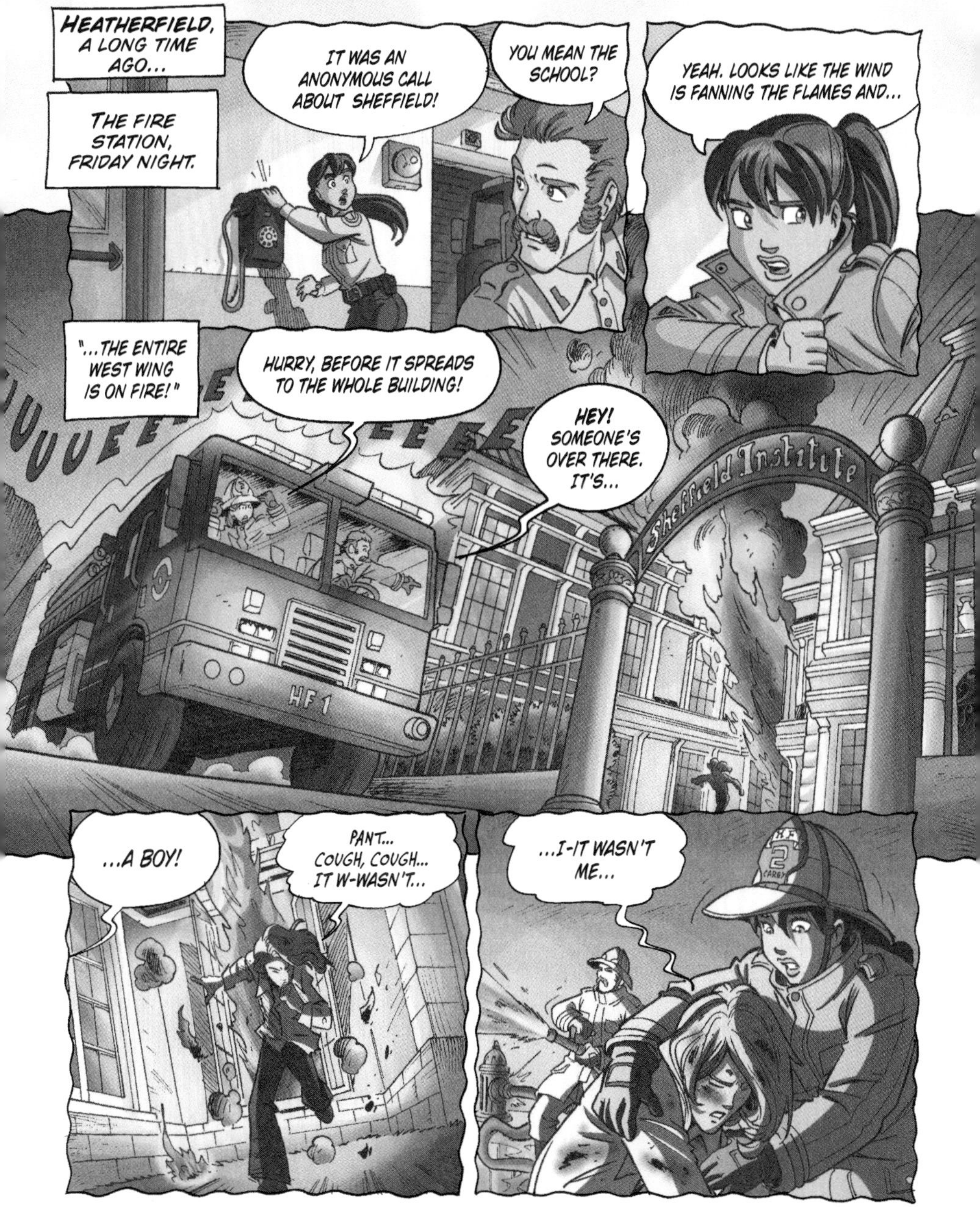
HEATHERFIELD, A LONG TIME AGO...
THE FIRE STATION, FRIDAY NIGHT.
IT WAS AN ANONYMOUS CALL ABOUT SHEFFIELD!
YOU MEAN THE SCHOOL?
YEAH. LOOKS LIKE THE WIND IS FANNING THE FLAMES AND...
"...THE ENTIRE WEST WING IS ON FIRE!"
HURRY, BEFORE IT SPREADS TO THE WHOLE BUILDING!
UUUEEEEEEEEEEE
HEY! SOMEONE'S OVER THERE. IT'S...
Sheffield Institute
HF 1
...A BOY!
PANT... COUGH, COUGH... IT W-WASN'T...
...I-IT WASN'T ME...

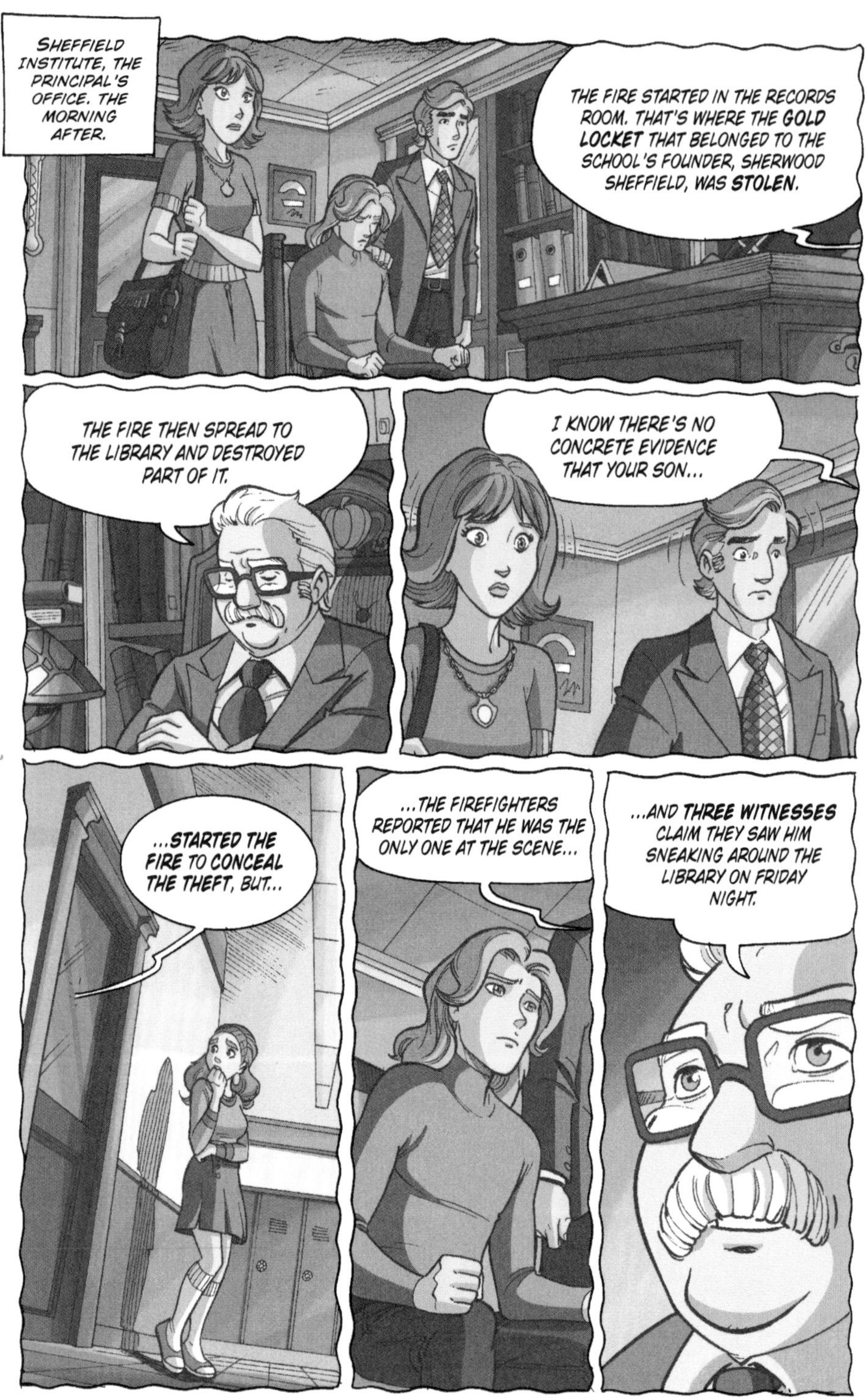
SHEFFIELD INSTITUTE, THE PRINCIPAL'S OFFICE. THE MORNING AFTER.
THE FIRE STARTED IN THE RECORDS ROOM. THAT'S WHERE THE GOLD LOCKET THAT BELONGED TO THE SCHOOL'S FOUNDER, SHERWOOD SHEFFIELD, WAS STOLEN.
THE FIRE THEN SPREAD TO THE LIBRARY AND DESTROYED PART OF IT.
I KNOW THERE'S NO CONCRETE EVIDENCE THAT YOUR SON...
...STARTED THE FIRE TO CONCEAL THE THEFT, BUT...
...THE FIREFIGHTERS REPORTED THAT HE WAS THE ONLY ONE AT THE SCENE...
...AND THREE WITNESSES CLAIM THEY SAW HIM SNEAKING AROUND THE LIBRARY ON FRIDAY NIGHT.

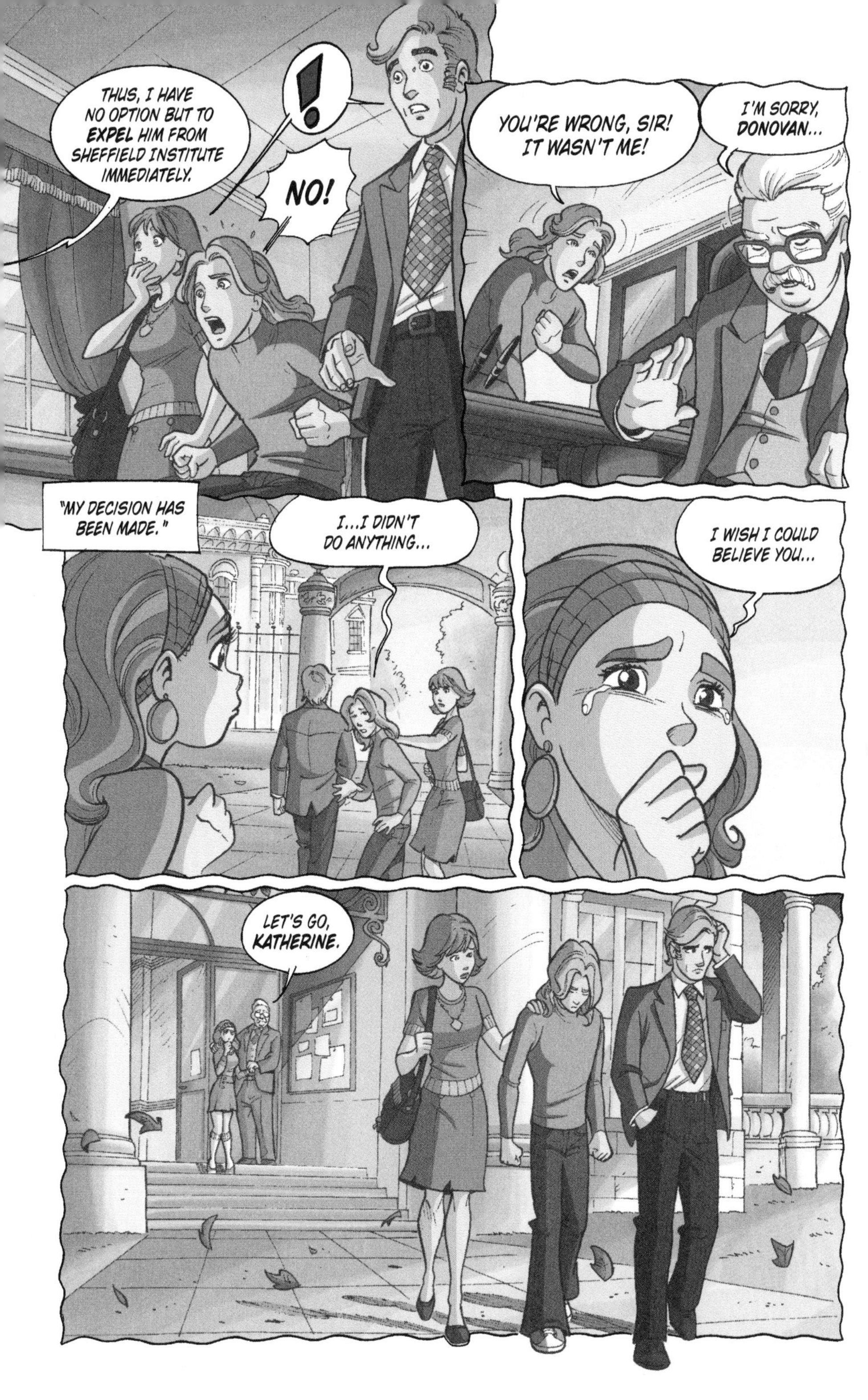
THUS, I HAVE NO OPTION BUT TO EXPEL HIM FROM SHEFFIELD INSTITUTE IMMEDIATELY.
!
NO!
YOU'RE WRONG, SIR! IT WASN'T ME!
I'M SORRY, DONOVAN...
"MY DECISION HAS BEEN MADE."
I...I DIDN'T DO ANYTHING...
I WISH I COULD BELIEVE YOU...
LET'S GO, KATHERINE.

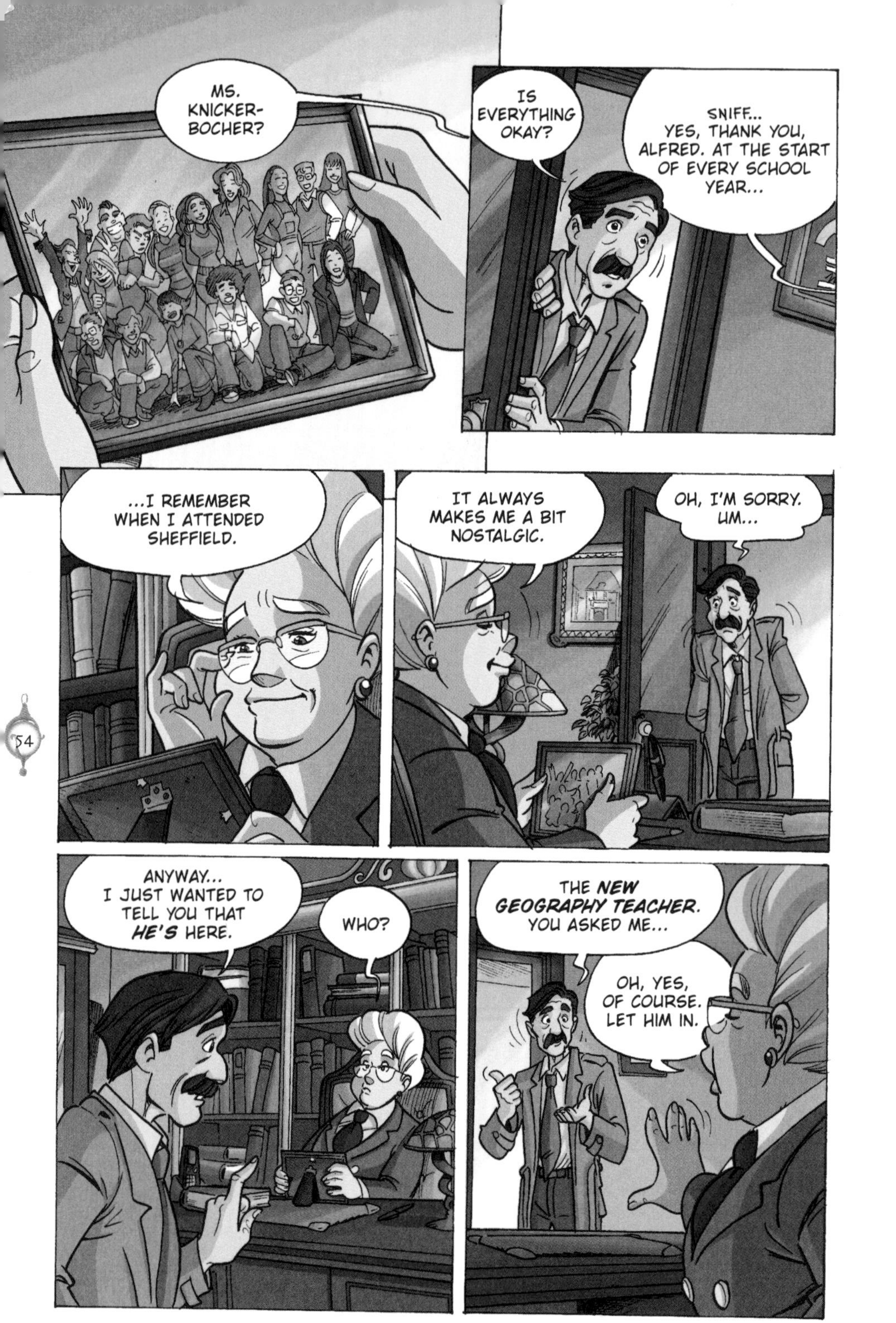
MS. KNICKER-BOCHER?
IS EVERYTHING OKAY?
SNIFF... YES, THANK YOU, ALFRED. AT THE START OF EVERY SCHOOL YEAR...
...I REMEMBER WHEN I ATTENDED SHEFFIELD.
IT ALWAYS MAKES ME A BIT NOSTALGIC.
OH, I'M SORRY. UM...
ANYWAY... I JUST WANTED TO TELL YOU THAT ***HE'S*** HERE.
WHO?
THE ***NEW GEOGRAPHY TEACHER***. YOU ASKED ME...
OH, YES, OF COURSE. LET HIM IN.

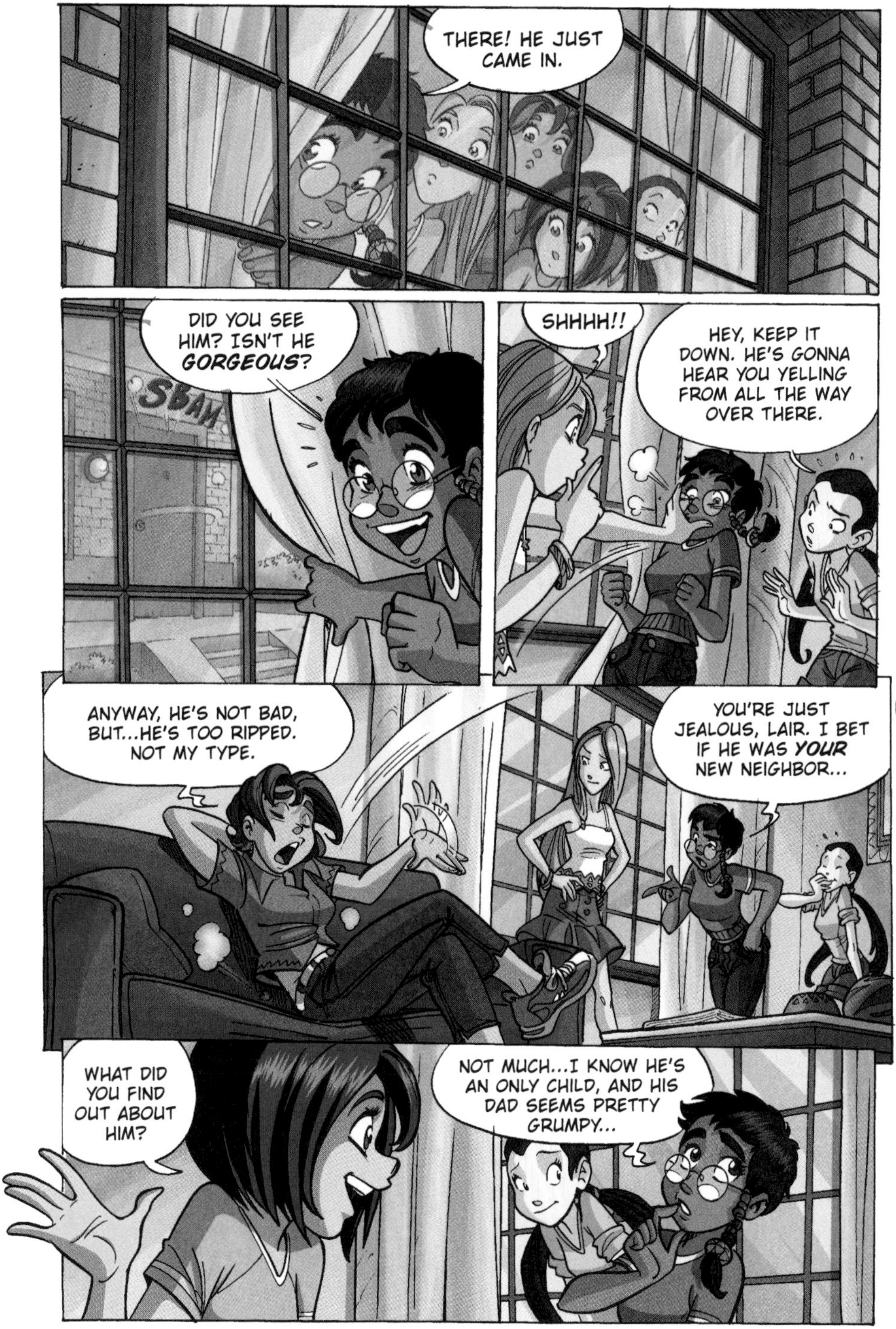
THERE! HE JUST CAME IN.
DID YOU SEE HIM? ISN'T HE GORGEOUS?
SBAM
SHHHH!!
HEY, KEEP IT DOWN. HE'S GONNA HEAR YOU YELLING FROM ALL THE WAY OVER THERE.
ANYWAY, HE'S NOT BAD, BUT...HE'S TOO RIPPED. NOT MY TYPE.
YOU'RE JUST JEALOUS, LAIR. I BET IF HE WAS *YOUR* NEW NEIGHBOR...
WHAT DID YOU FIND OUT ABOUT HIM?
NOT MUCH...I KNOW HE'S AN ONLY CHILD, AND HIS DAD SEEMS PRETTY GRUMPY...

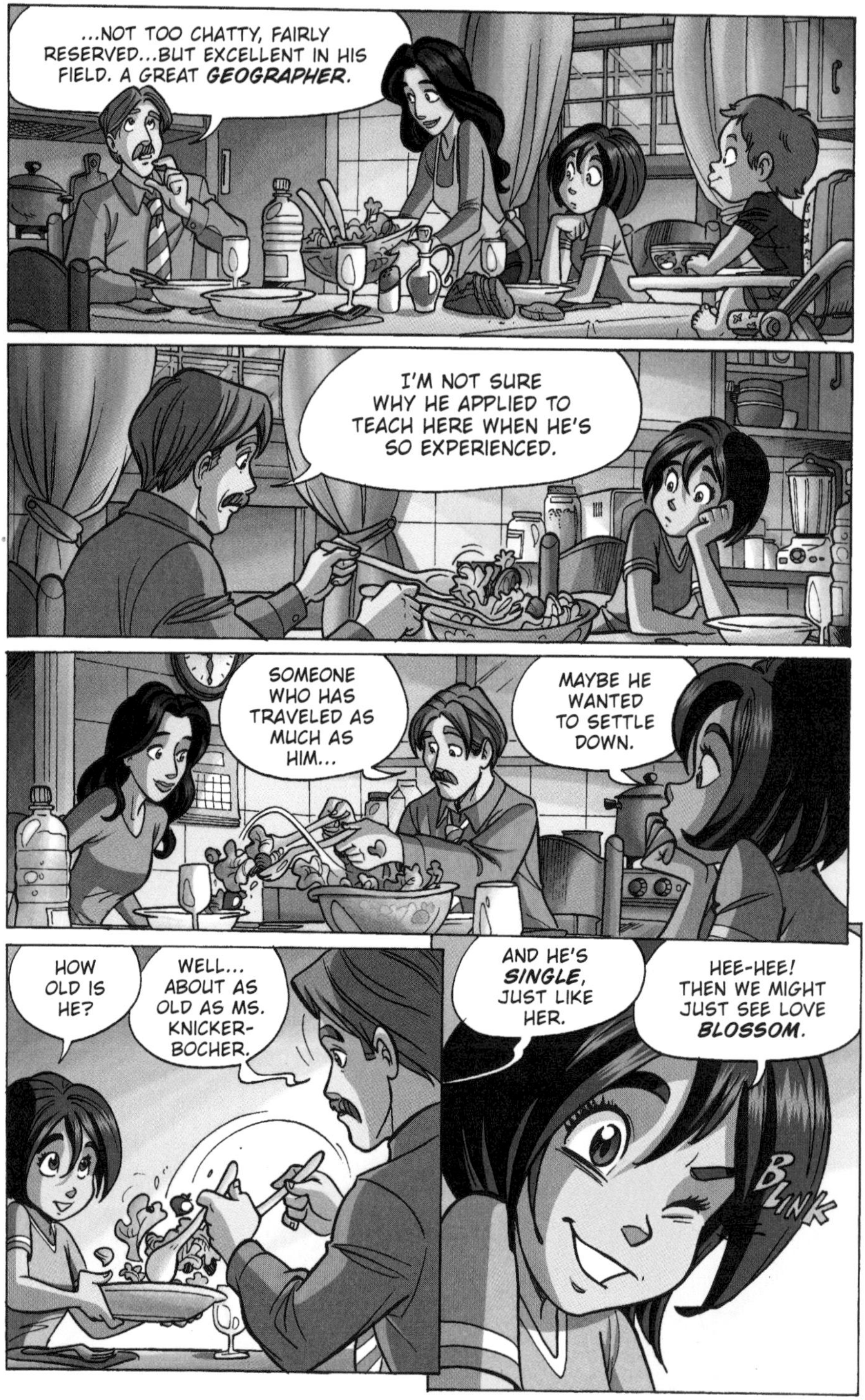

...NOT TOO CHATTY, FAIRLY RESERVED...BUT EXCELLENT IN HIS FIELD. A GREAT **GEOGRAPHER**.
I'M NOT SURE WHY HE APPLIED TO TEACH HERE WHEN HE'S SO EXPERIENCED.
SOMEONE WHO HAS TRAVELED AS MUCH AS HIM...
MAYBE HE WANTED TO SETTLE DOWN.
HOW OLD IS HE?
WELL... ABOUT AS OLD AS MS. KNICKER-BOCHER.
AND HE'S **SINGLE**, JUST LIKE HER.
HEE-HEE! THEN WE MIGHT JUST SEE LOVE **BLOSSOM**.
BLINK

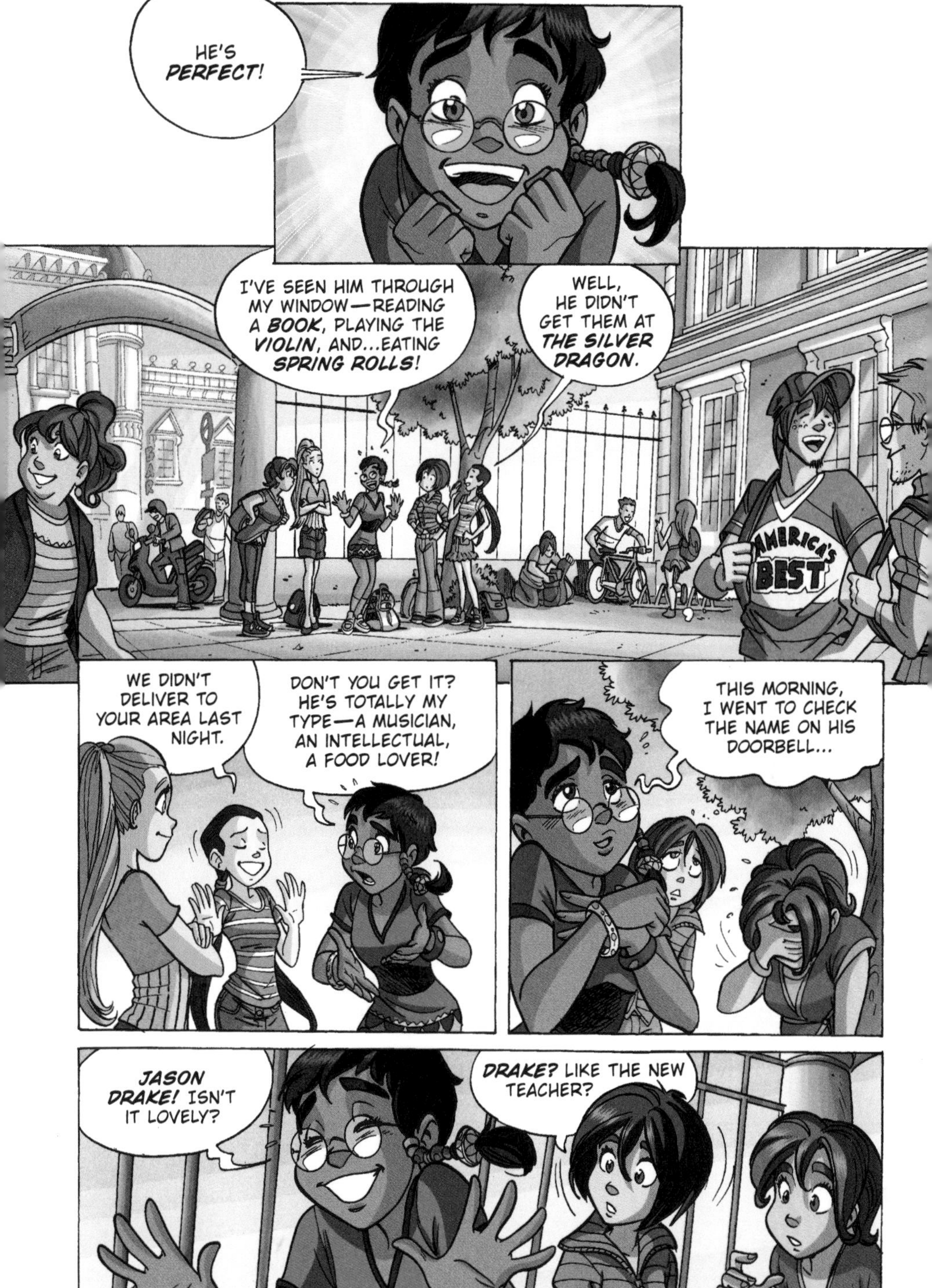
HE'S *PERFECT!*
I'VE SEEN HIM THROUGH MY WINDOW—READING A *BOOK*, PLAYING THE *VIOLIN*, AND...EATING *SPRING ROLLS!*
WELL, HE DIDN'T GET THEM AT *THE SILVER DRAGON*.
AMERICA'S BEST
WE DIDN'T DELIVER TO YOUR AREA LAST NIGHT.
DON'T YOU GET IT? HE'S TOTALLY MY TYPE—A MUSICIAN, AN INTELLECTUAL, A FOOD LOVER!
THIS MORNING, I WENT TO CHECK THE NAME ON HIS DOORBELL...
JASON DRAKE! ISN'T IT LOVELY?
DRAKE? LIKE THE NEW TEACHER?

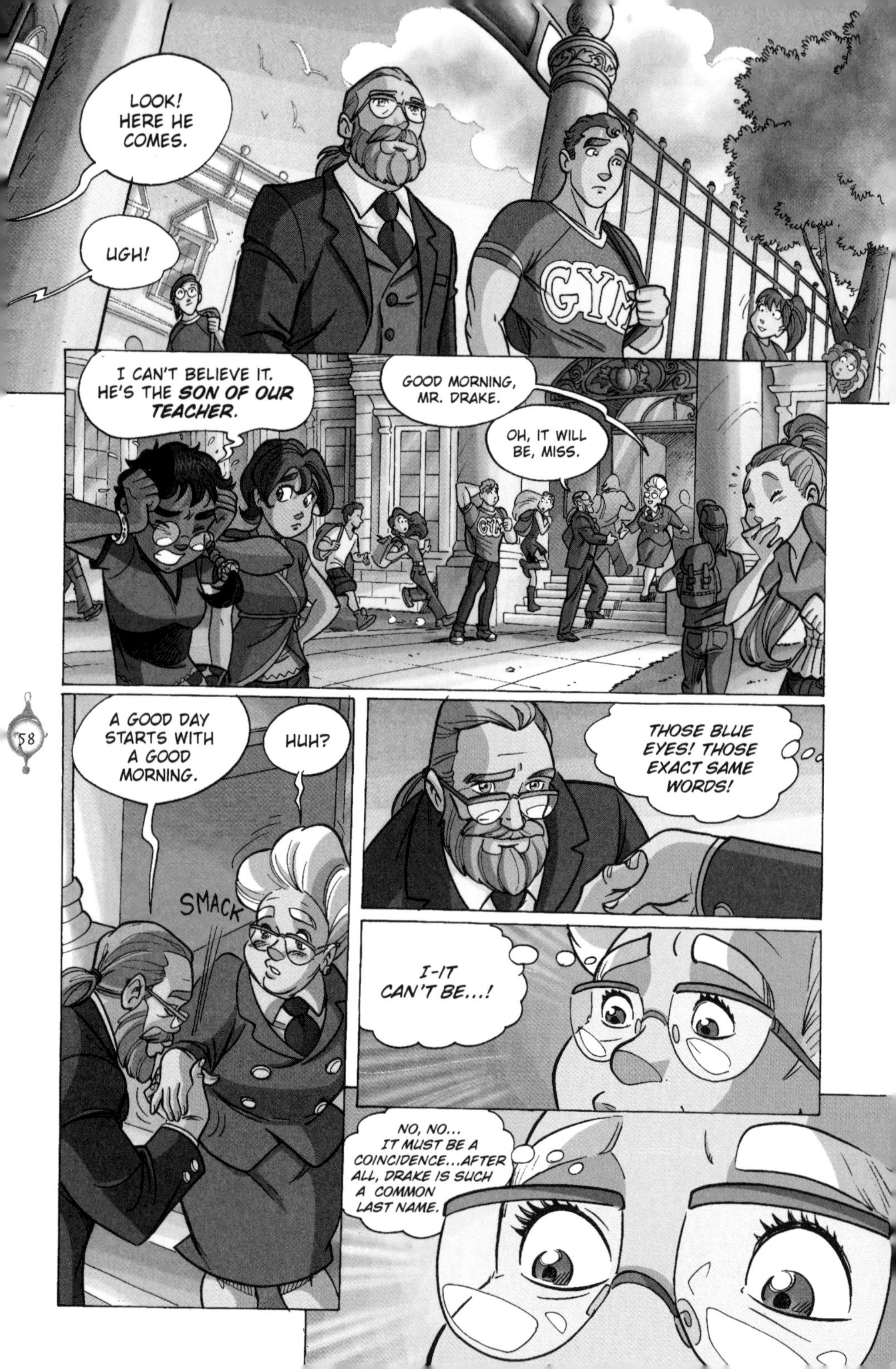
LOOK! HERE HE COMES.
UGH!
I CAN'T BELIEVE IT. HE'S THE SON OF OUR TEACHER.
GOOD MORNING, MR. DRAKE.
OH, IT WILL BE, MISS.
A GOOD DAY STARTS WITH A GOOD MORNING.
HUH?
SMACK
THOSE BLUE EYES! THOSE EXACT SAME WORDS!
I-IT CAN'T BE...!
NO, NO... IT MUST BE A COINCIDENCE...AFTER ALL, DRAKE IS SUCH A COMMON LAST NAME.

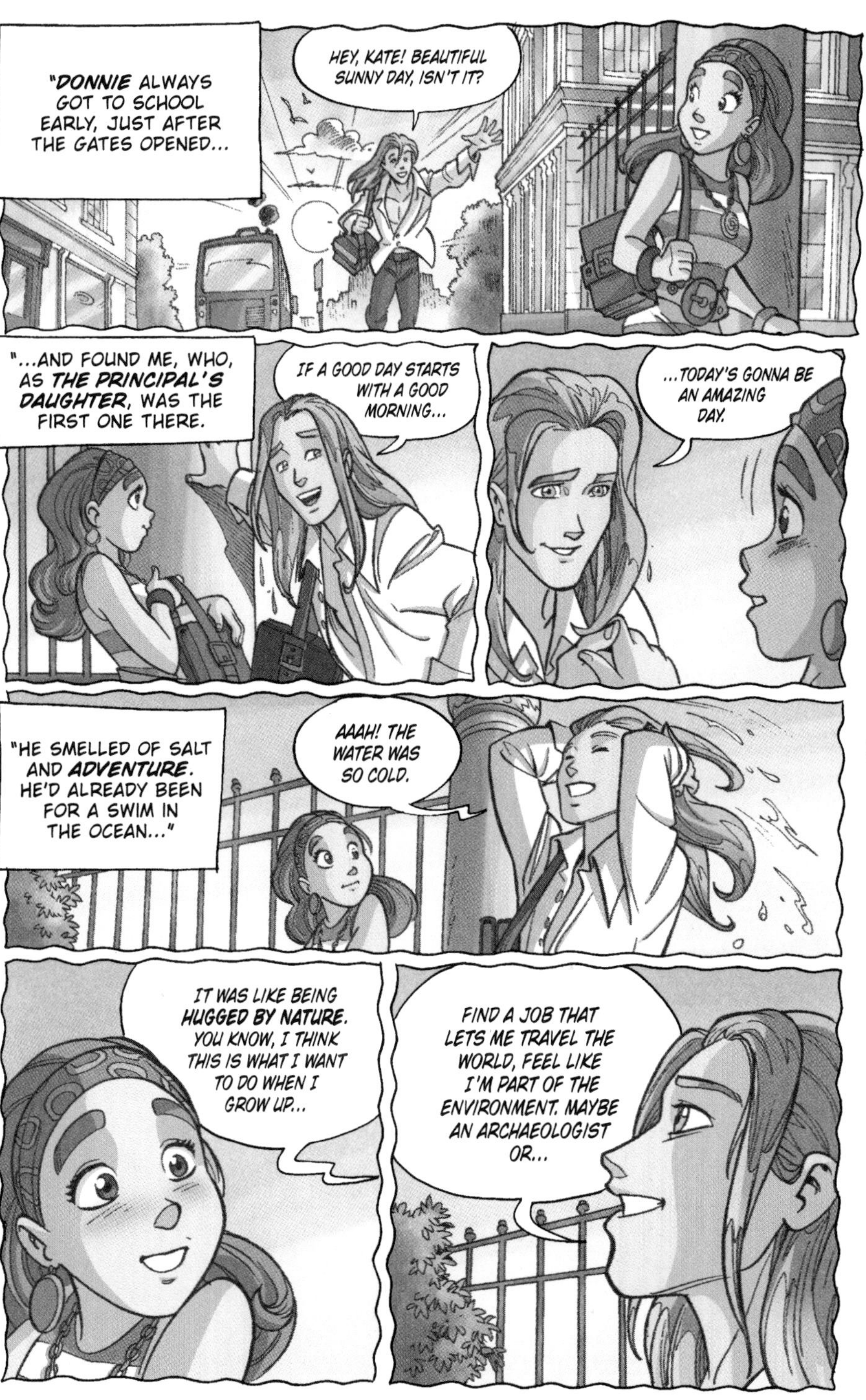
"DONNIE ALWAYS GOT TO SCHOOL EARLY, JUST AFTER THE GATES OPENED...
HEY, KATE! BEAUTIFUL SUNNY DAY, ISN'T IT?
"...AND FOUND ME, WHO, AS THE PRINCIPAL'S DAUGHTER, WAS THE FIRST ONE THERE.
IF A GOOD DAY STARTS WITH A GOOD MORNING...
...TODAY'S GONNA BE AN AMAZING DAY.
"HE SMELLED OF SALT AND ADVENTURE. HE'D ALREADY BEEN FOR A SWIM IN THE OCEAN..."
AAAH! THE WATER WAS SO COLD.
IT WAS LIKE BEING HUGGED BY NATURE. YOU KNOW, I THINK THIS IS WHAT I WANT TO DO WHEN I GROW UP...
FIND A JOB THAT LETS ME TRAVEL THE WORLD, FEEL LIKE I'M PART OF THE ENVIRONMENT. MAYBE AN ARCHAEOLOGIST OR...

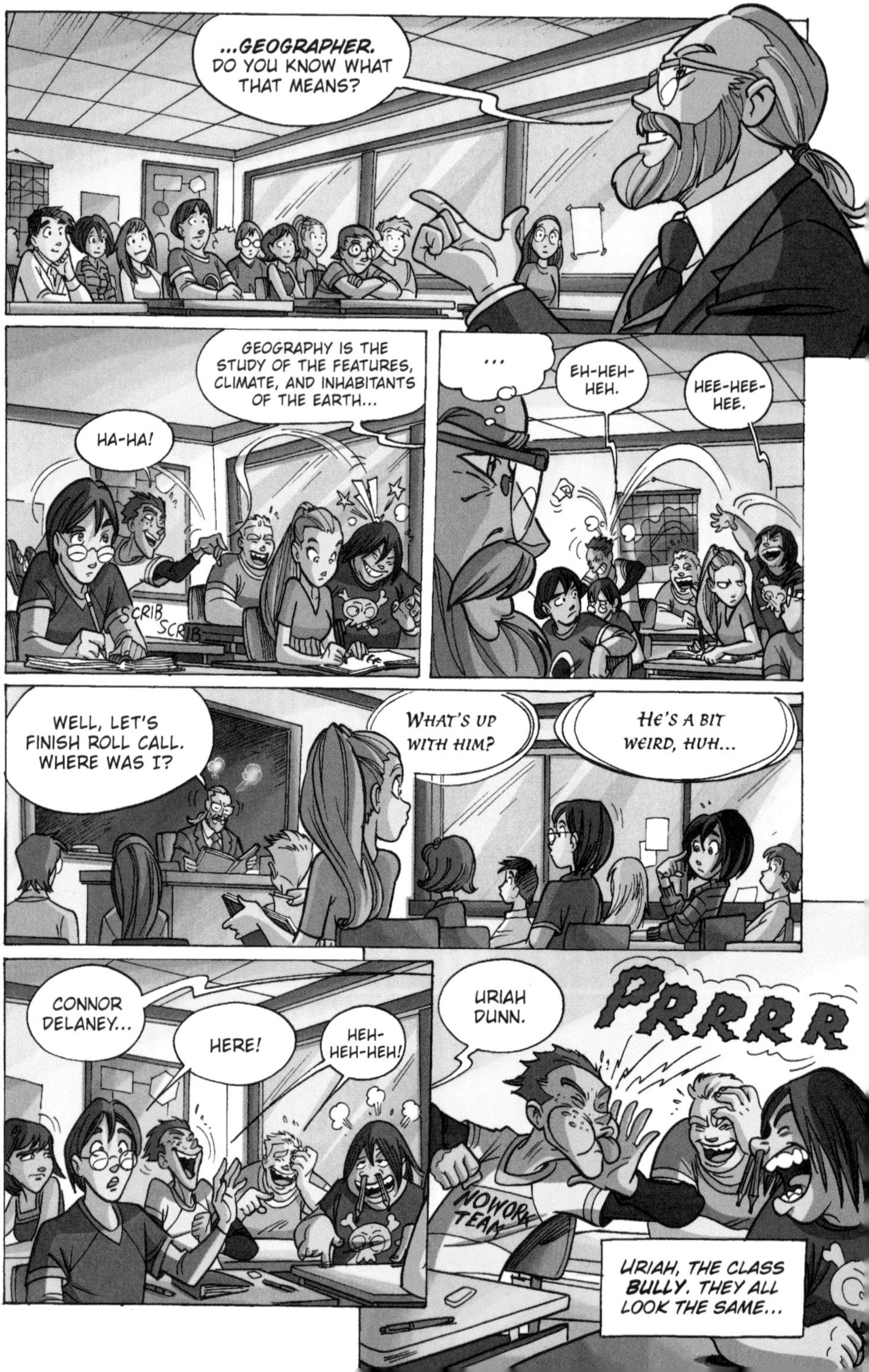
...GEOGRAPHER. DO YOU KNOW WHAT THAT MEANS?
GEOGRAPHY IS THE STUDY OF THE FEATURES, CLIMATE, AND INHABITANTS OF THE EARTH...
HA-HA!
SCRIB SCRIB
...
EH-HEH-HEH.
HEE-HEE-HEE.
WELL, LET'S FINISH ROLL CALL. WHERE WAS I?
WHAT'S UP WITH HIM?
HE'S A BIT WEIRD, HUH...
CONNOR DELANEY...
HERE!
HEH-HEH-HEH!
URIAH DUNN.
PRRRR
NOWORK TEAM
URIAH, THE CLASS BULLY. THEY ALL LOOK THE SAME...

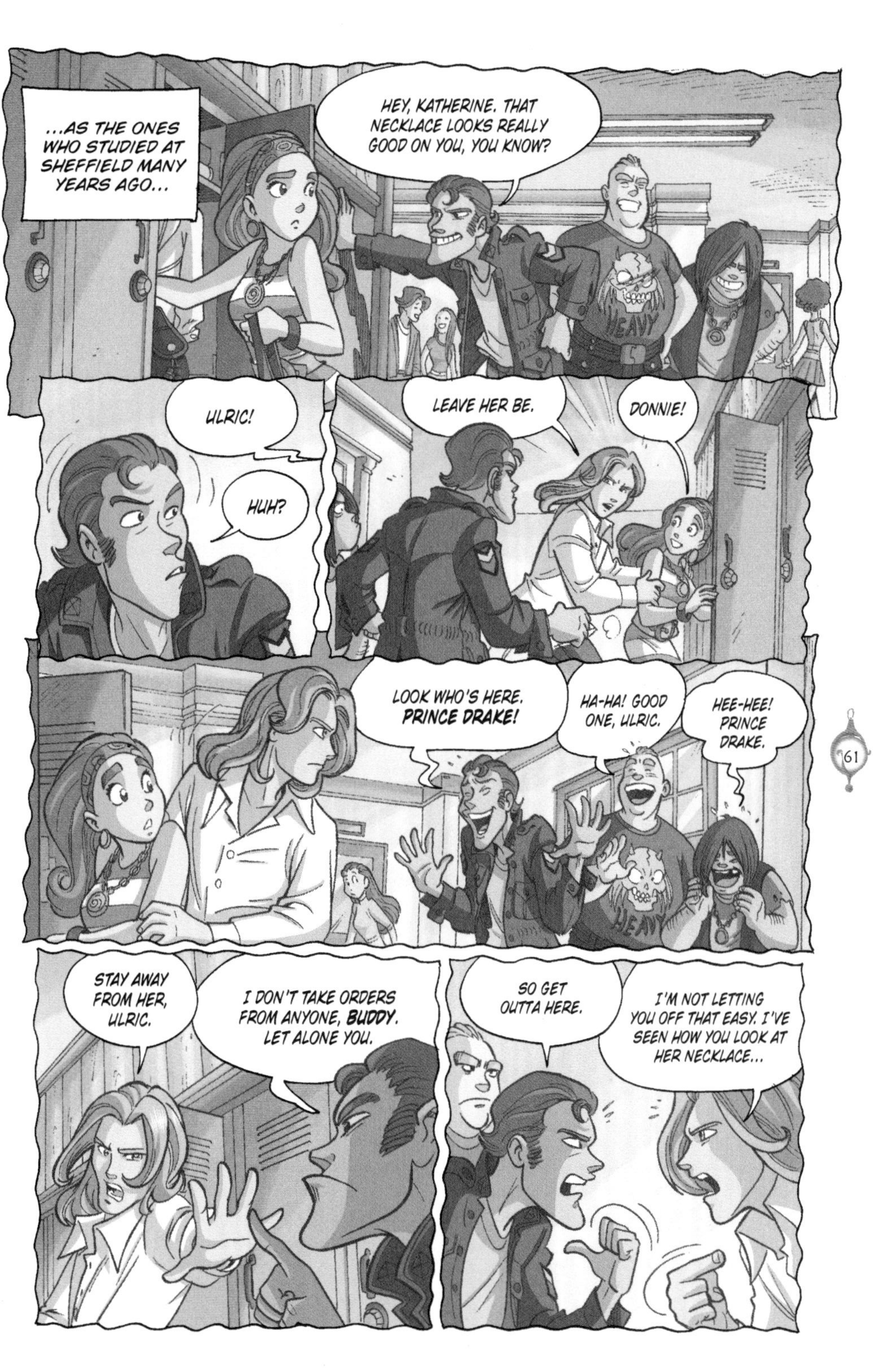
...AS THE ONES WHO STUDIED AT SHEFFIELD MANY YEARS AGO...
HEY, KATHERINE. THAT NECKLACE LOOKS REALLY GOOD ON YOU, YOU KNOW?
HEAVY
ULRIC!
HUH?
LEAVE HER BE.
DONNIE!
LOOK WHO'S HERE. **PRINCE DRAKE!**
HA-HA! GOOD ONE, ULRIC.
HEE-HEE! PRINCE DRAKE.
HEAVY
STAY AWAY FROM HER, ULRIC.
I DON'T TAKE ORDERS FROM ANYONE, **BUDDY**. LET ALONE YOU.
SO GET OUTTA HERE.
I'M NOT LETTING YOU OFF THAT EASY. I'VE SEEN HOW YOU LOOK AT HER NECKLACE...

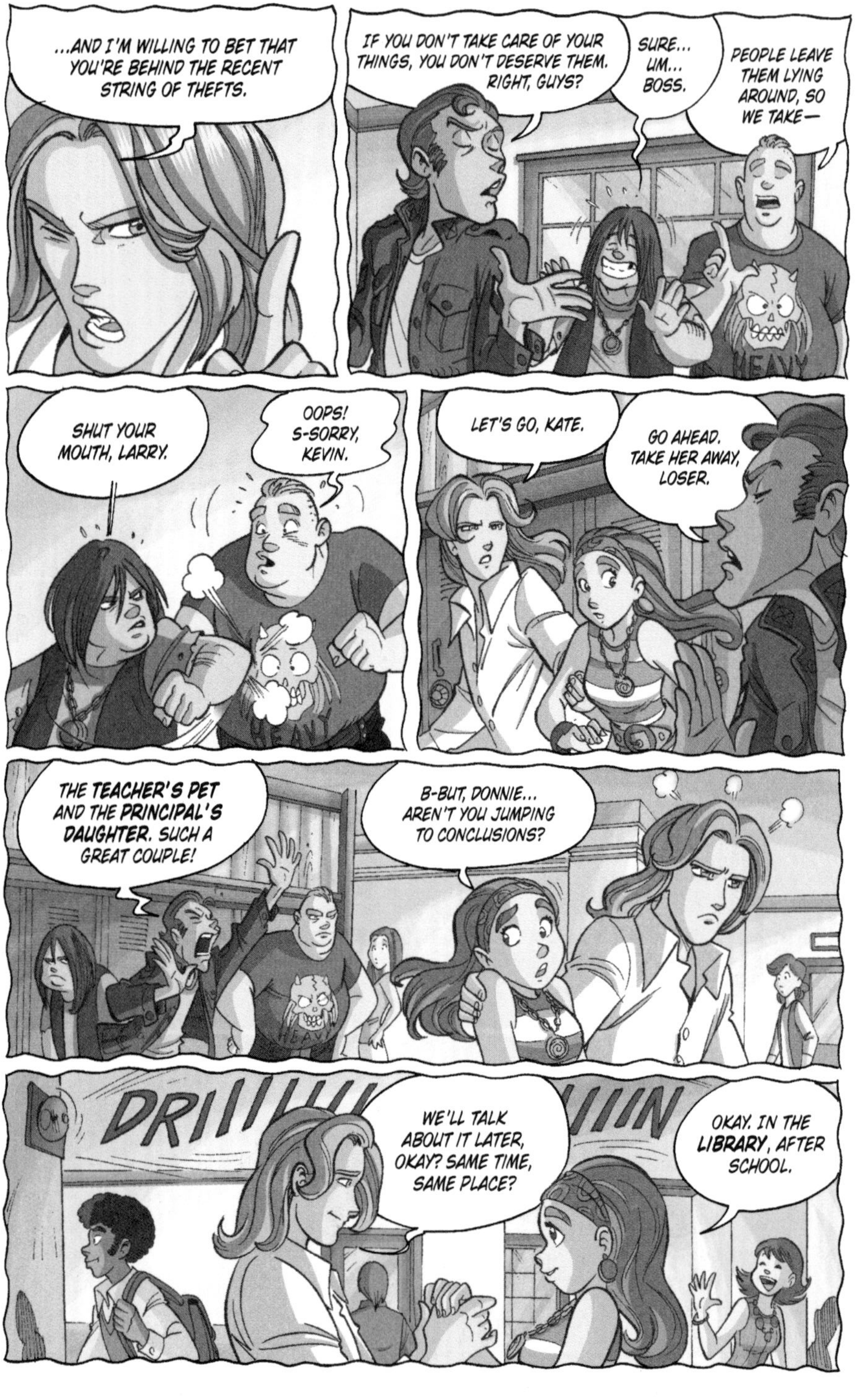
...AND I'M WILLING TO BET THAT YOU'RE BEHIND THE RECENT STRING OF THEFTS.
IF YOU DON'T TAKE CARE OF YOUR THINGS, YOU DON'T DESERVE THEM. RIGHT, GUYS?
SURE... UM... BOSS.
PEOPLE LEAVE THEM LYING AROUND, SO WE TAKE—
SHUT YOUR MOUTH, LARRY.
OOPS! S-SORRY, KEVIN.
LET'S GO, KATE.
GO AHEAD. TAKE HER AWAY, LOSER.
THE TEACHER'S PET AND THE PRINCIPAL'S DAUGHTER. SUCH A GREAT COUPLE!
B-BUT, DONNIE... AREN'T YOU JUMPING TO CONCLUSIONS?
DRIIIIIIIIIIIIIIN
WE'LL TALK ABOUT IT LATER, OKAY? SAME TIME, SAME PLACE?
OKAY. IN THE LIBRARY, AFTER SCHOOL.

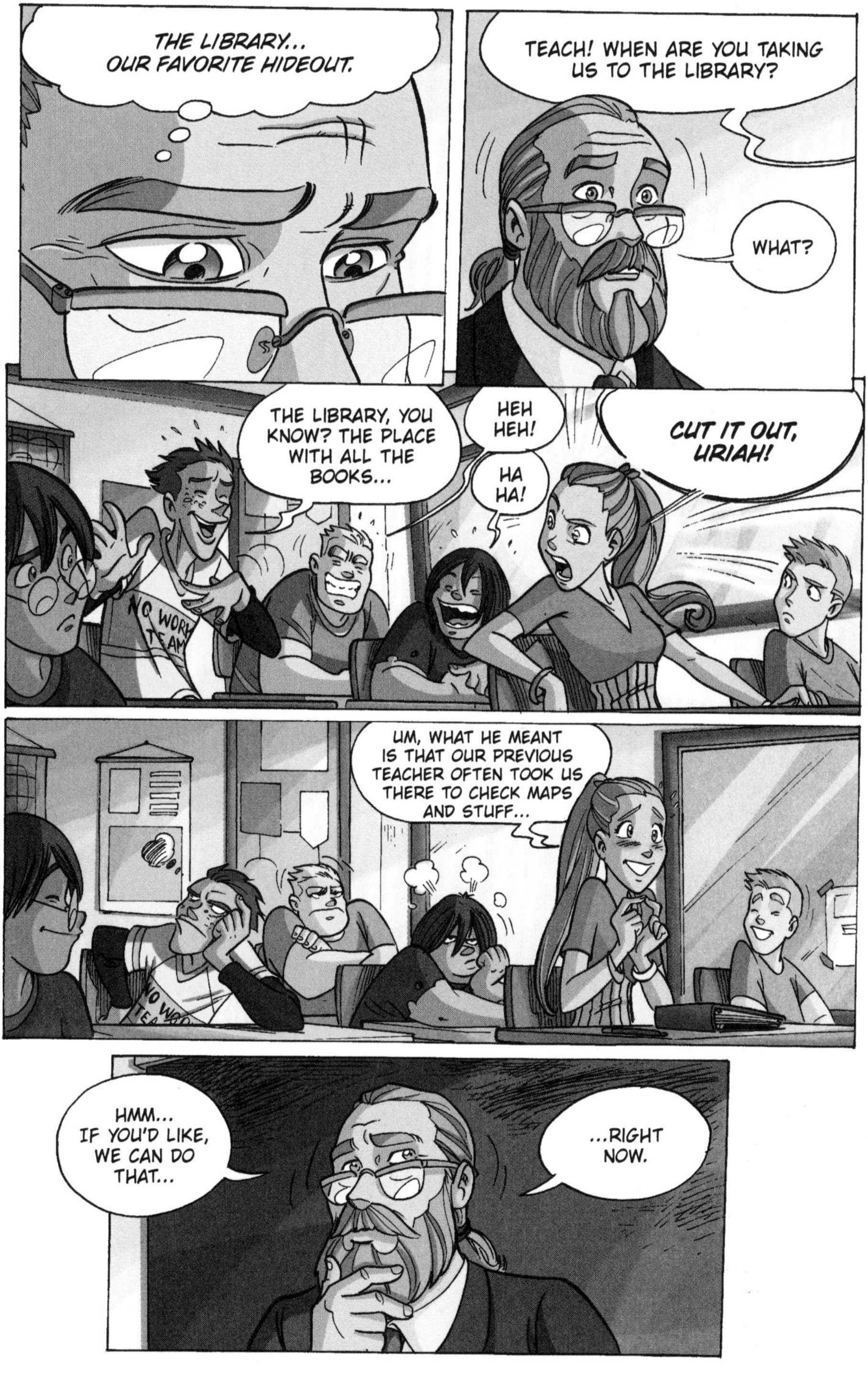
THE LIBRARY... OUR FAVORITE HIDEOUT.
TEACH! WHEN ARE YOU TAKING US TO THE LIBRARY?
WHAT?
THE LIBRARY, YOU KNOW? THE PLACE WITH ALL THE BOOKS...
HEH HEH!
HA HA!
CUT IT OUT, URIAH!
NO WORK TEAM
UM, WHAT HE MEANT IS THAT OUR PREVIOUS TEACHER OFTEN TOOK US THERE TO CHECK MAPS AND STUFF...
HMM... IF YOU'D LIKE, WE CAN DO THAT...
...RIGHT NOW.

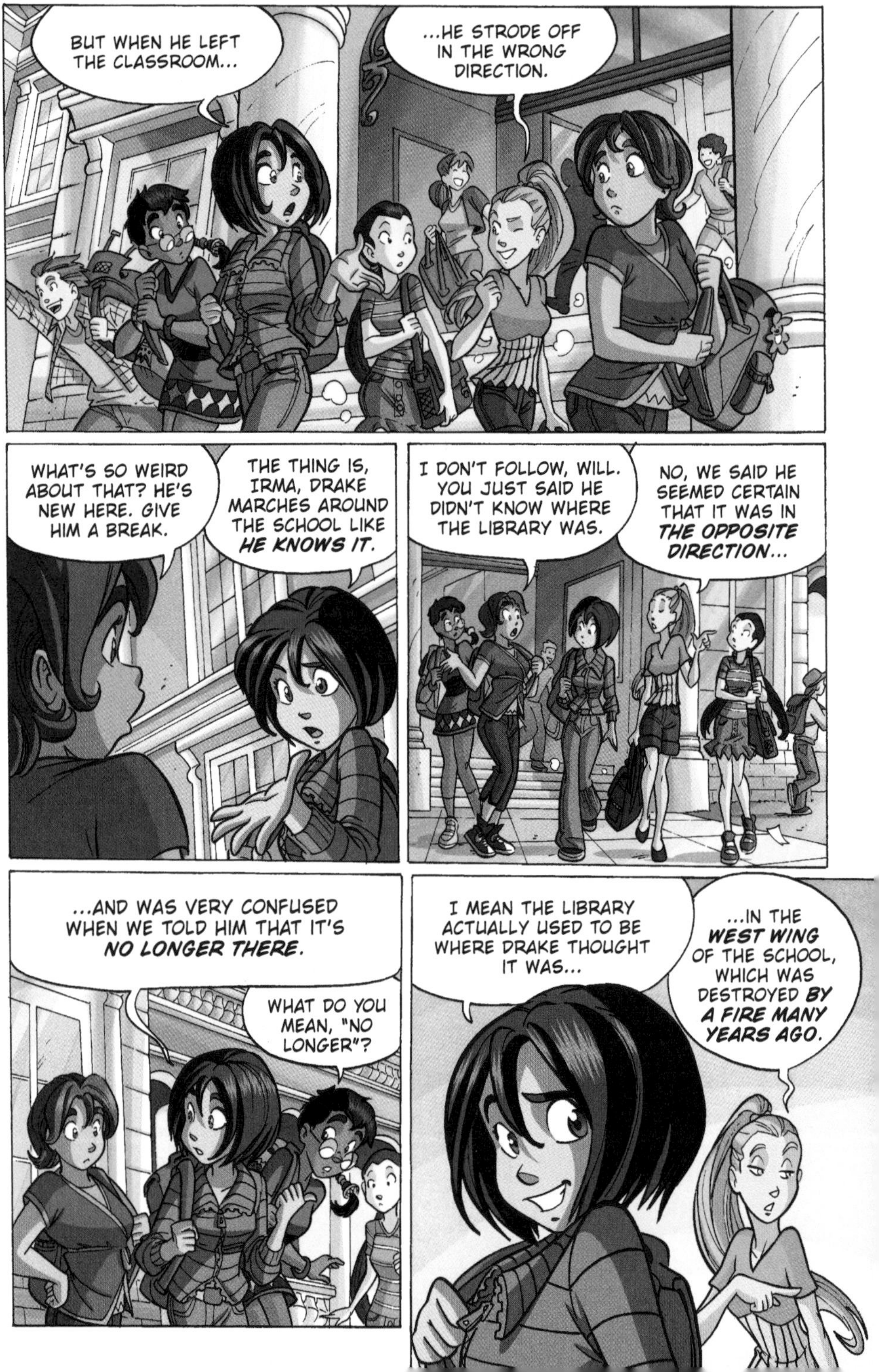
BUT WHEN HE LEFT THE CLASSROOM...
...HE STRODE OFF IN THE WRONG DIRECTION.
WHAT'S SO WEIRD ABOUT THAT? HE'S NEW HERE. GIVE HIM A BREAK.
THE THING IS, IRMA, DRAKE MARCHES AROUND THE SCHOOL LIKE *HE KNOWS IT*.
I DON'T FOLLOW, WILL. YOU JUST SAID HE DIDN'T KNOW WHERE THE LIBRARY WAS.
NO, WE SAID HE SEEMED CERTAIN THAT IT WAS IN *THE OPPOSITE DIRECTION*...
...AND WAS VERY CONFUSED WHEN WE TOLD HIM THAT IT'S *NO LONGER THERE*.
WHAT DO YOU MEAN, "NO LONGER"?
I MEAN THE LIBRARY ACTUALLY USED TO BE WHERE DRAKE THOUGHT IT WAS...
...IN THE *WEST WING* OF THE SCHOOL, WHICH WAS DESTROYED *BY A FIRE MANY YEARS AGO*.

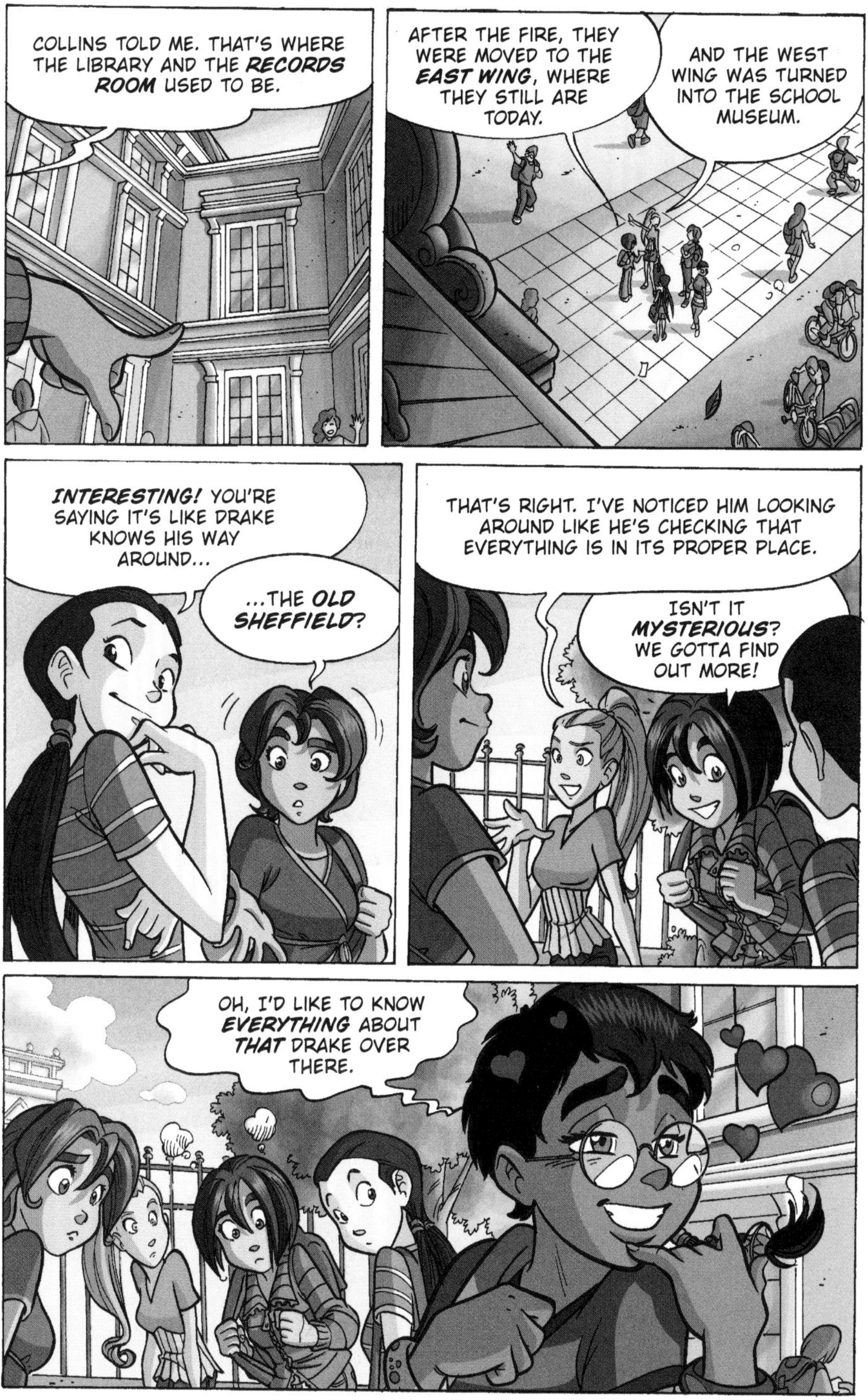
COLLINS TOLD ME. THAT'S WHERE THE LIBRARY AND THE RECORDS ROOM USED TO BE.
AFTER THE FIRE, THEY WERE MOVED TO THE EAST WING, WHERE THEY STILL ARE TODAY.
AND THE WEST WING WAS TURNED INTO THE SCHOOL MUSEUM.
INTERESTING! YOU'RE SAYING IT'S LIKE DRAKE KNOWS HIS WAY AROUND...
...THE OLD SHEFFIELD?
THAT'S RIGHT. I'VE NOTICED HIM LOOKING AROUND LIKE HE'S CHECKING THAT EVERYTHING IS IN ITS PROPER PLACE.
ISN'T IT MYSTERIOUS? WE GOTTA FIND OUT MORE!
OH, I'D LIKE TO KNOW EVERYTHING ABOUT THAT DRAKE OVER THERE.

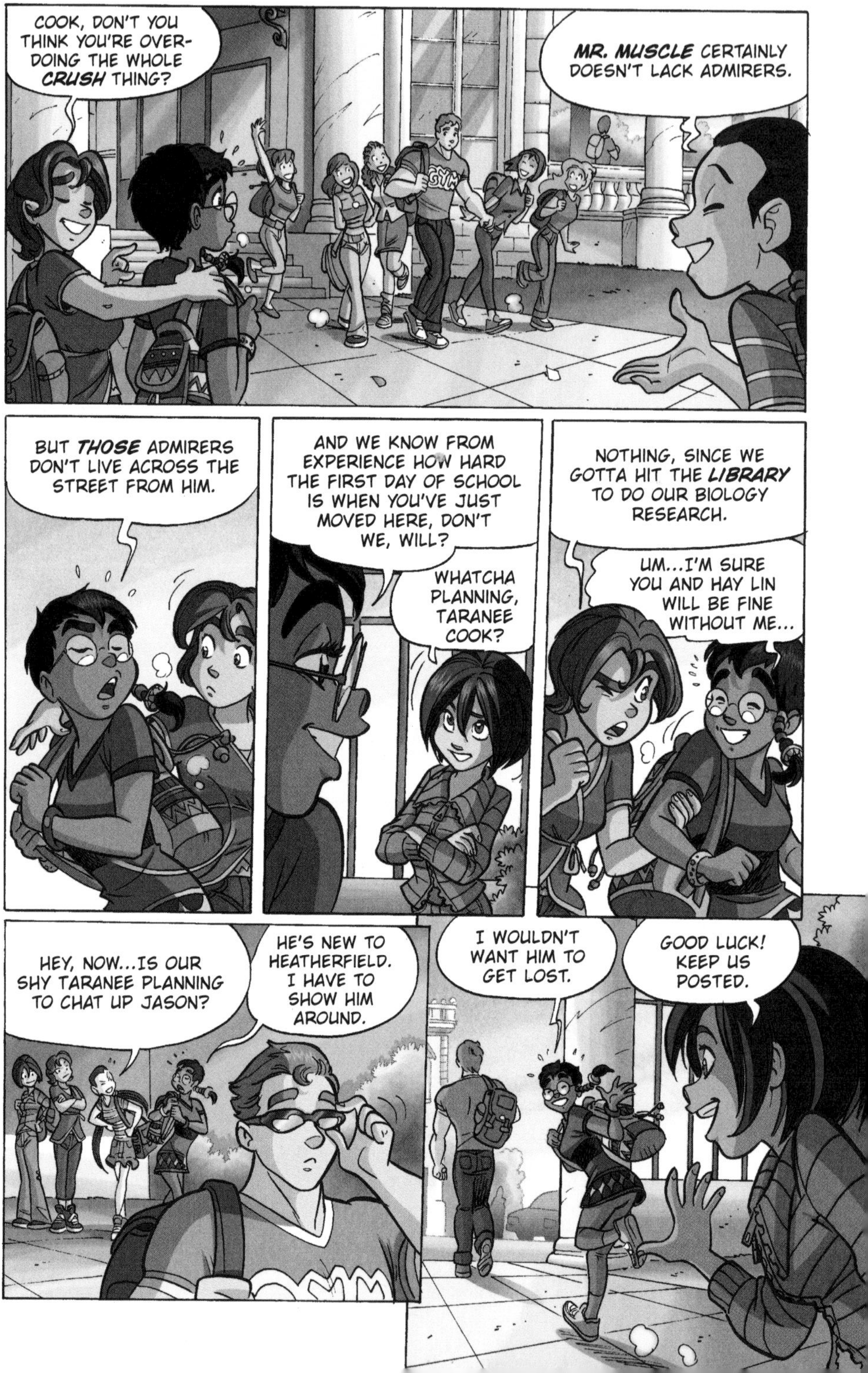
COOK, DON'T YOU THINK YOU'RE OVER-DOING THE WHOLE CRUSH THING?
MR. MUSCLE CERTAINLY DOESN'T LACK ADMIRERS.
BUT THOSE ADMIRERS DON'T LIVE ACROSS THE STREET FROM HIM.
AND WE KNOW FROM EXPERIENCE HOW HARD THE FIRST DAY OF SCHOOL IS WHEN YOU'VE JUST MOVED HERE, DON'T WE, WILL?
WHATCHA PLANNING, TARANEE COOK?
NOTHING, SINCE WE GOTTA HIT THE LIBRARY TO DO OUR BIOLOGY RESEARCH.
UM...I'M SURE YOU AND HAY LIN WILL BE FINE WITHOUT ME...
HEY, NOW...IS OUR SHY TARANEE PLANNING TO CHAT UP JASON?
HE'S NEW TO HEATHERFIELD. I HAVE TO SHOW HIM AROUND.
I WOULDN'T WANT HIM TO GET LOST.
GOOD LUCK! KEEP US POSTED.

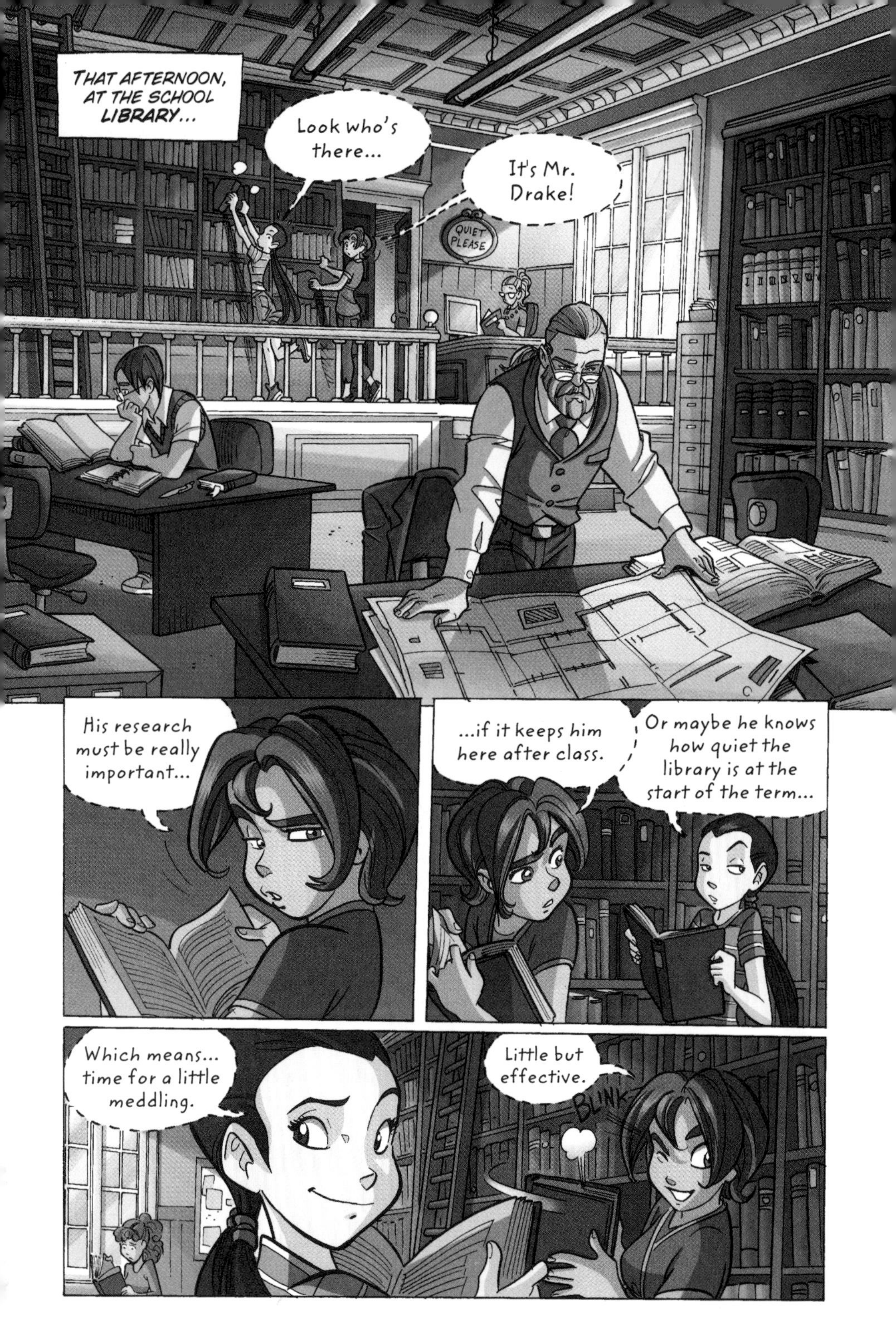
THAT AFTERNOON, AT THE SCHOOL LIBRARY...
Look who's there...
It's Mr. Drake!
QUIET PLEASE
His research must be really important...
...if it keeps him here after class.
Or maybe he knows how quiet the library is at the start of the term...
Which means... time for a little meddling.
Little but effective.
BLINK

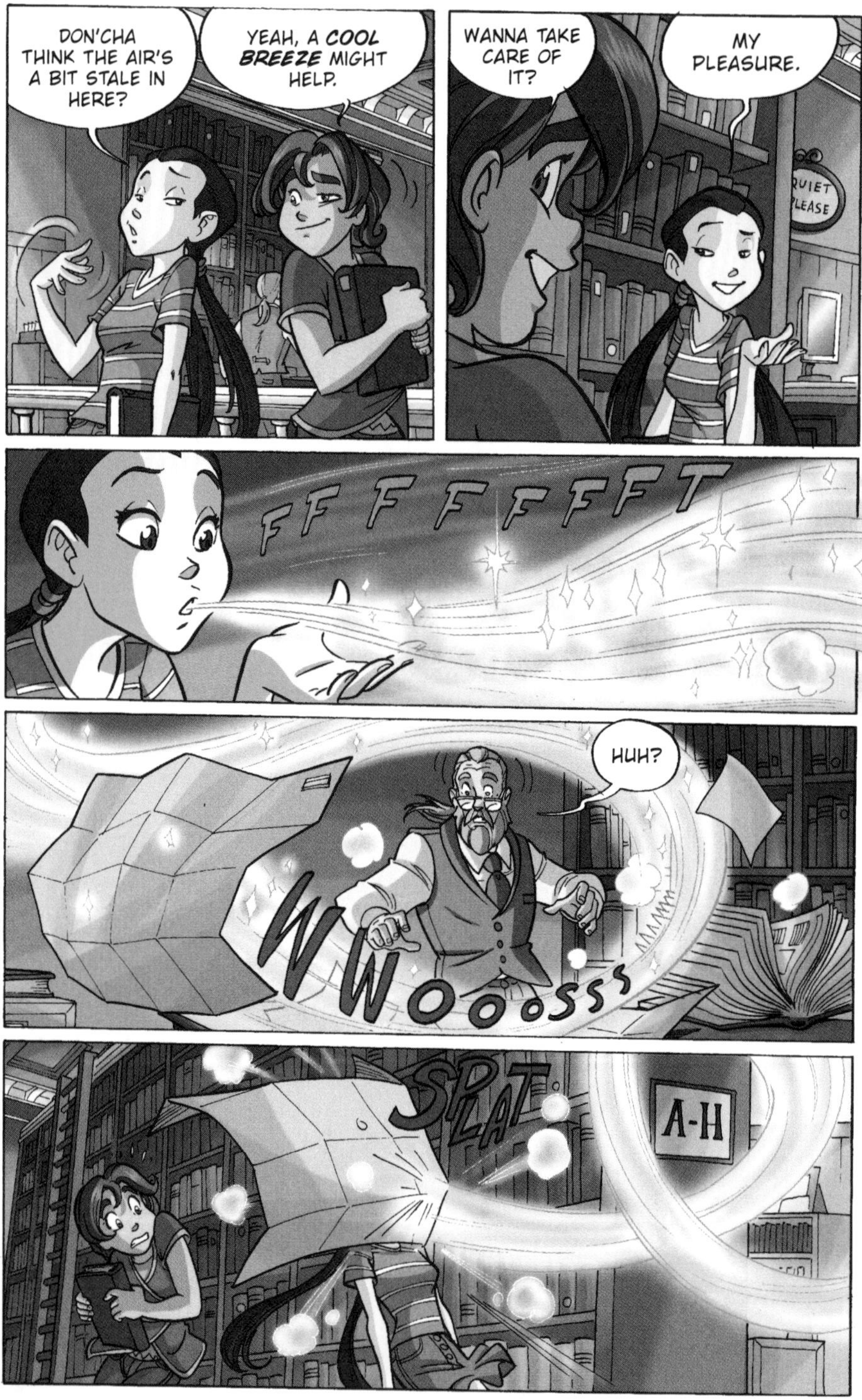
DON'CHA THINK THE AIR'S A BIT STALE IN HERE?
YEAH, A COOL BREEZE MIGHT HELP.
WANNA TAKE CARE OF IT?
MY PLEASURE.
QUIET PLEASE
FF F F F F F F T
HUH?
WWOoosss
SPLAT
A-H

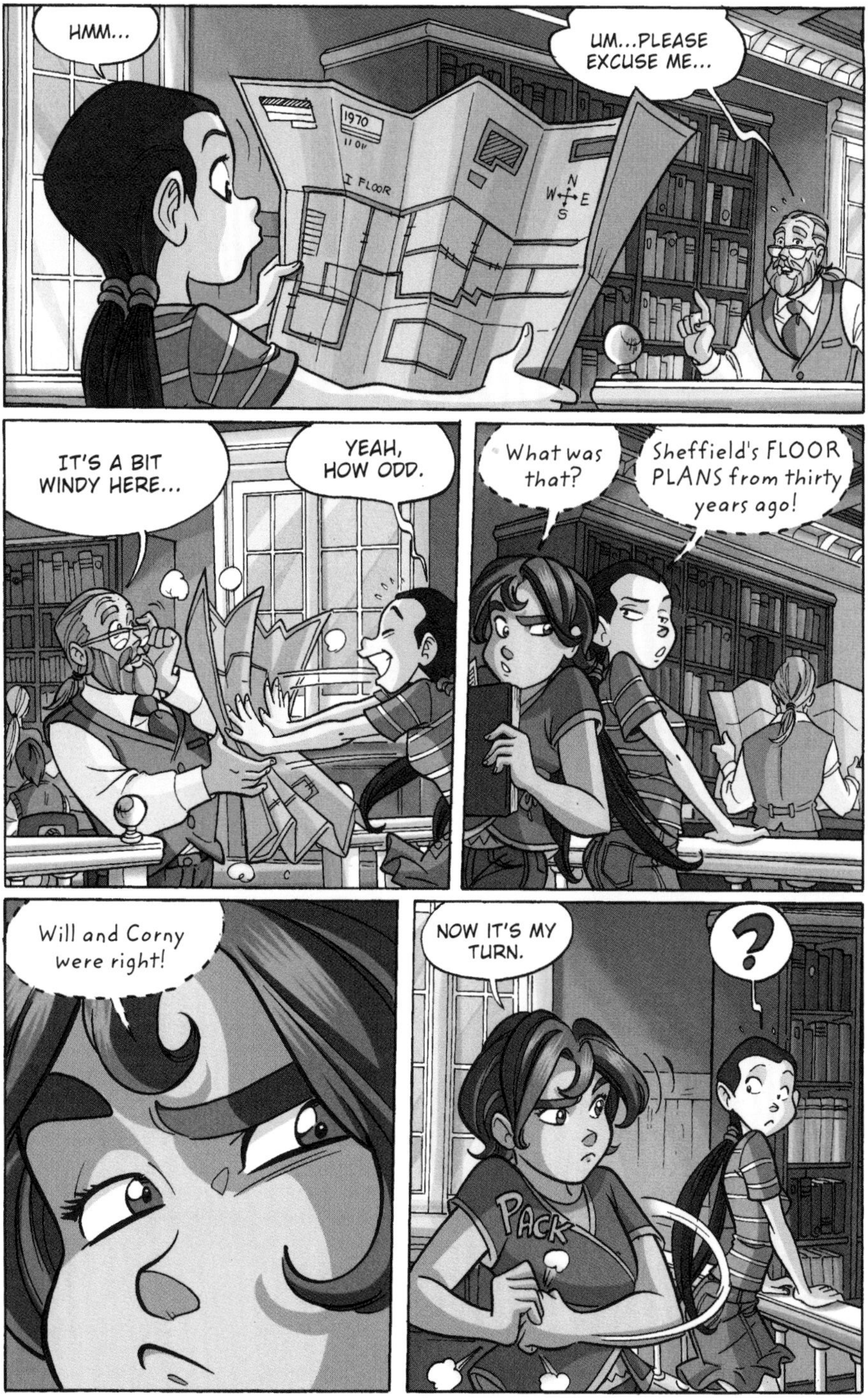
HMM...
UM...PLEASE EXCUSE ME...
1970
I FLOOR
N
W
E
S
IT'S A BIT WINDY HERE...
YEAH, HOW ODD.
What was that?
Sheffield's FLOOR PLANS from thirty years ago!
Will and Corny were right!
NOW IT'S MY TURN.
?
PACK

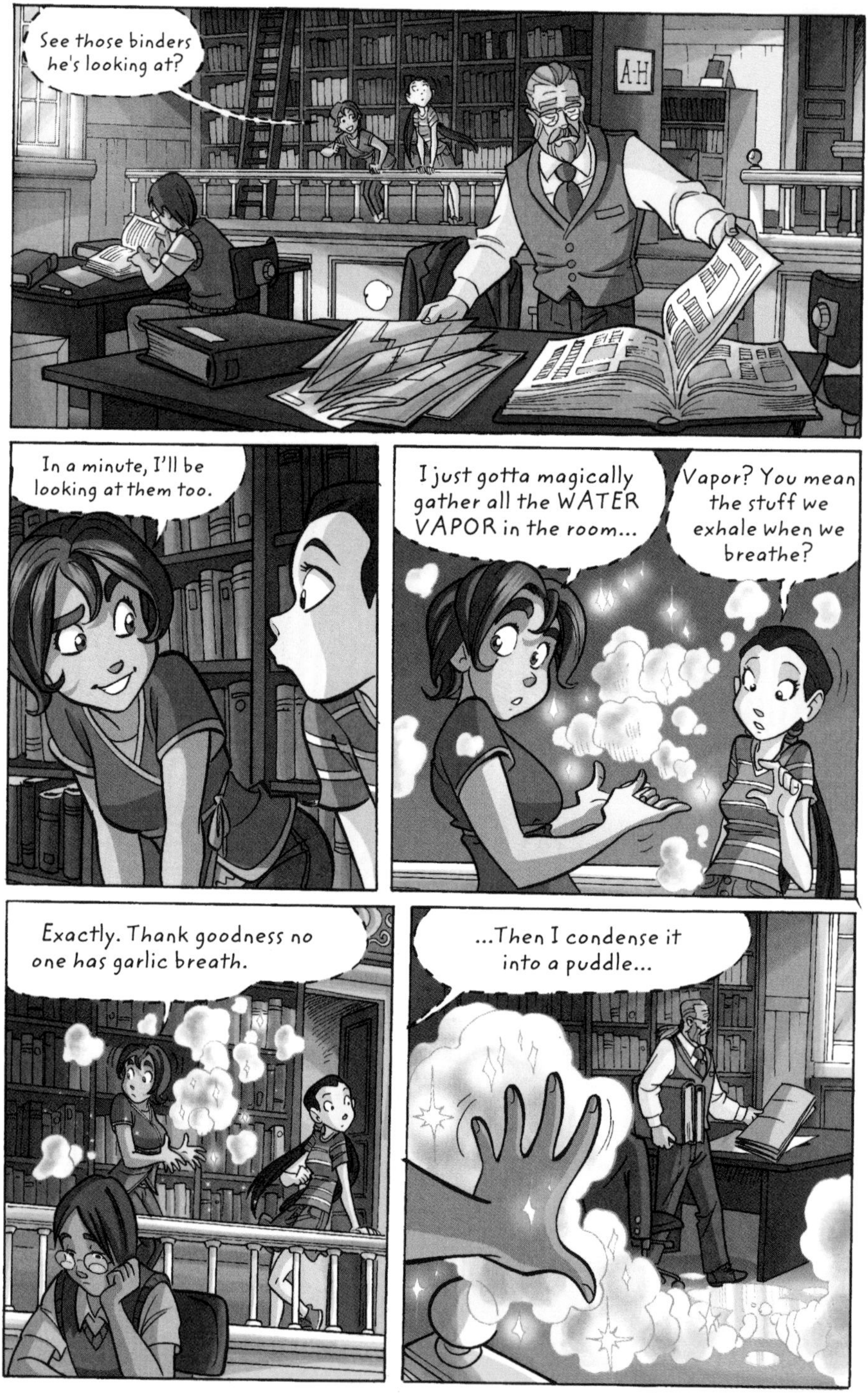
See those binders he's looking at?
A-H
In a minute, I'll be looking at them too.
I just gotta magically gather all the WATER VAPOR in the room...
Vapor? You mean the stuff we exhale when we breathe?
Exactly. Thank goodness no one has garlic breath.
...Then I condense it into a puddle...

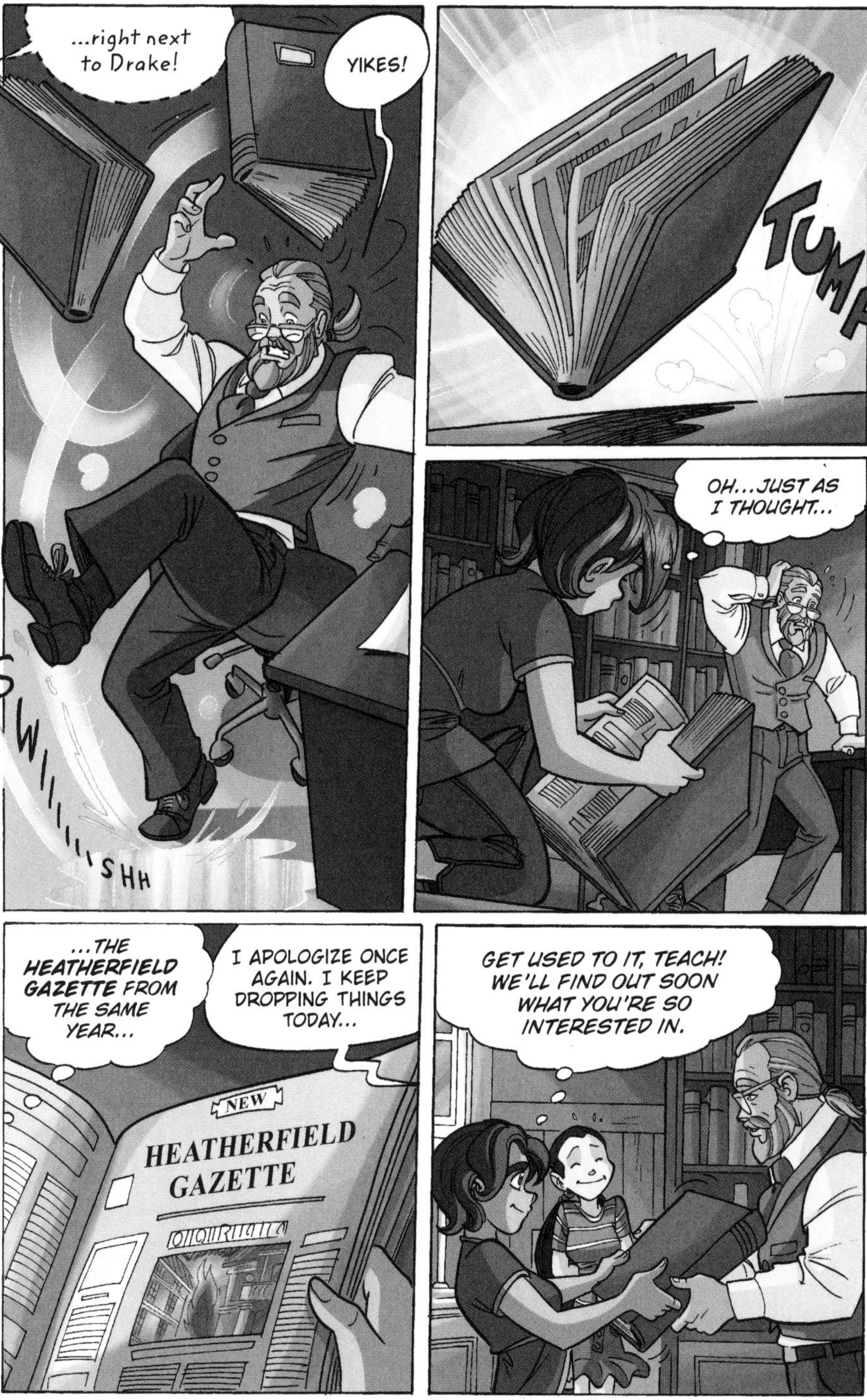
...right next to Drake!
YIKES!
SWIIIIIISHH
TUMP
OH...JUST AS I THOUGHT...
...THE HEATHERFIELD GAZETTE FROM THE SAME YEAR...
I APOLOGIZE ONCE AGAIN. I KEEP DROPPING THINGS TODAY...
NEW
HEATHERFIELD GAZETTE
GET USED TO IT, TEACH! WE'LL FIND OUT SOON WHAT YOU'RE SO INTERESTED IN.

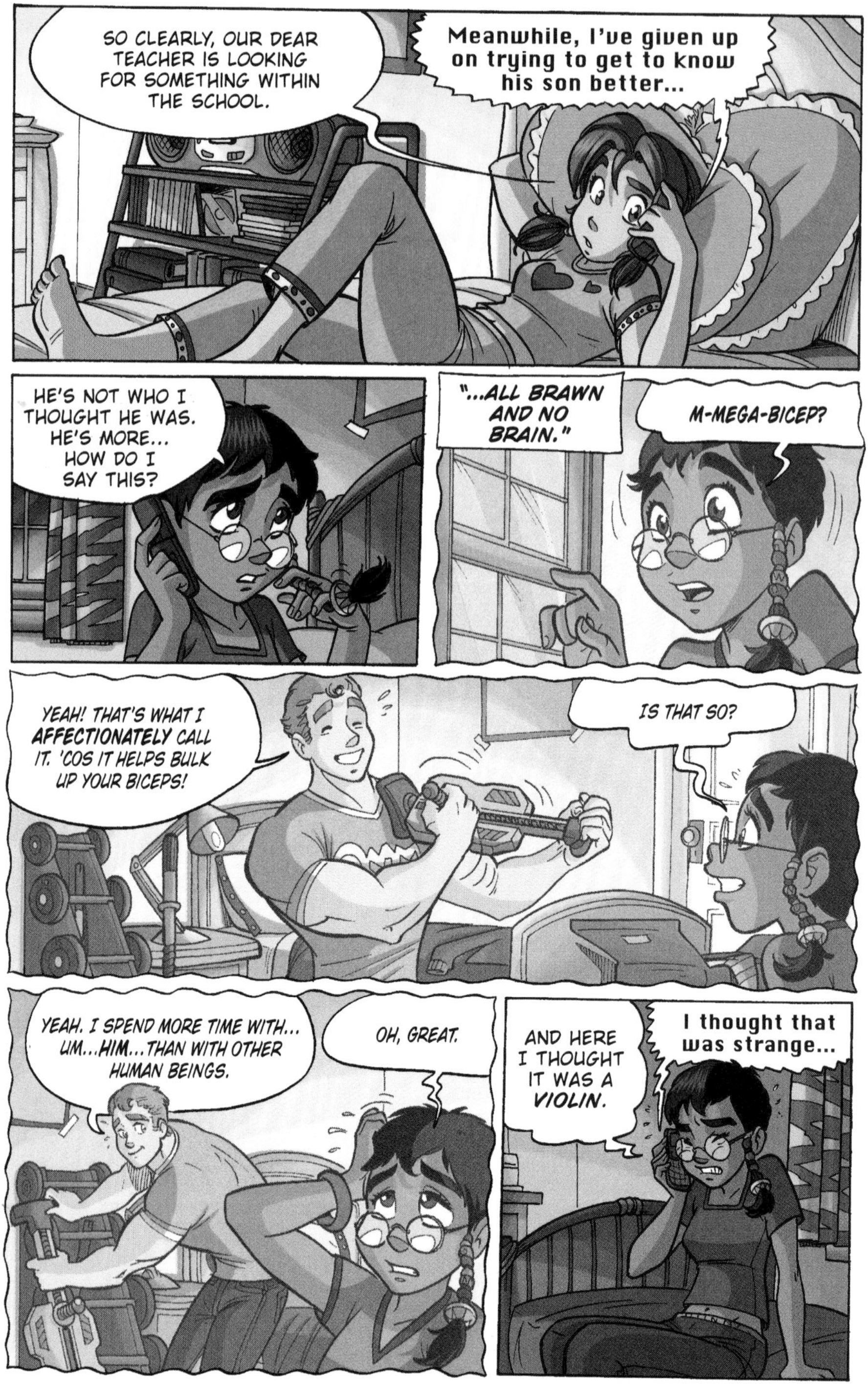
SO CLEARLY, OUR DEAR TEACHER IS LOOKING FOR SOMETHING WITHIN THE SCHOOL.
Meanwhile, I've given up on trying to get to know his son better...
HE'S NOT WHO I THOUGHT HE WAS. HE'S MORE... HOW DO I SAY THIS?
"...ALL BRAWN AND NO BRAIN."
M-MEGA-BICEP?
YEAH! THAT'S WHAT I AFFECTIONATELY CALL IT. 'COS IT HELPS BULK UP YOUR BICEPS!
IS THAT SO?
YEAH. I SPEND MORE TIME WITH... UM...HIM...THAN WITH OTHER HUMAN BEINGS.
OH, GREAT.
AND HERE I THOUGHT IT WAS A VIOLIN.
I thought that was strange...

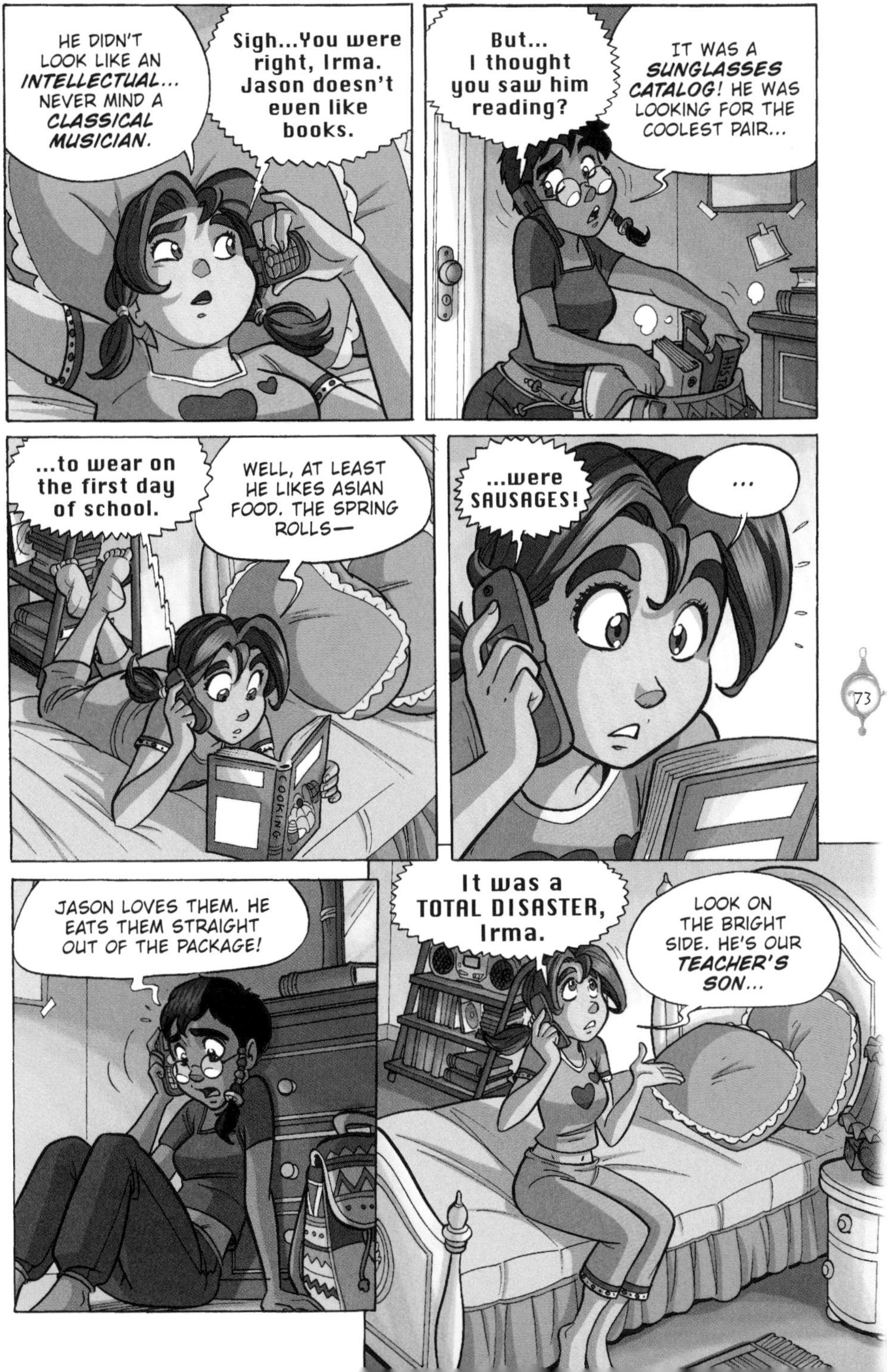
HE DIDN'T LOOK LIKE AN INTELLECTUAL... NEVER MIND A CLASSICAL MUSICIAN.
Sigh...You were right, Irma. Jason doesn't even like books.
But... I thought you saw him reading?
IT WAS A SUNGLASSES CATALOG! HE WAS LOOKING FOR THE COOLEST PAIR...
...to wear on the first day of school.
WELL, AT LEAST HE LIKES ASIAN FOOD. THE SPRING ROLLS—
...were SAUSAGES!
...
JASON LOVES THEM. HE EATS THEM STRAIGHT OUT OF THE PACKAGE!
It was a TOTAL DISASTER, Irma.
LOOK ON THE BRIGHT SIDE. HE'S OUR TEACHER'S SON...

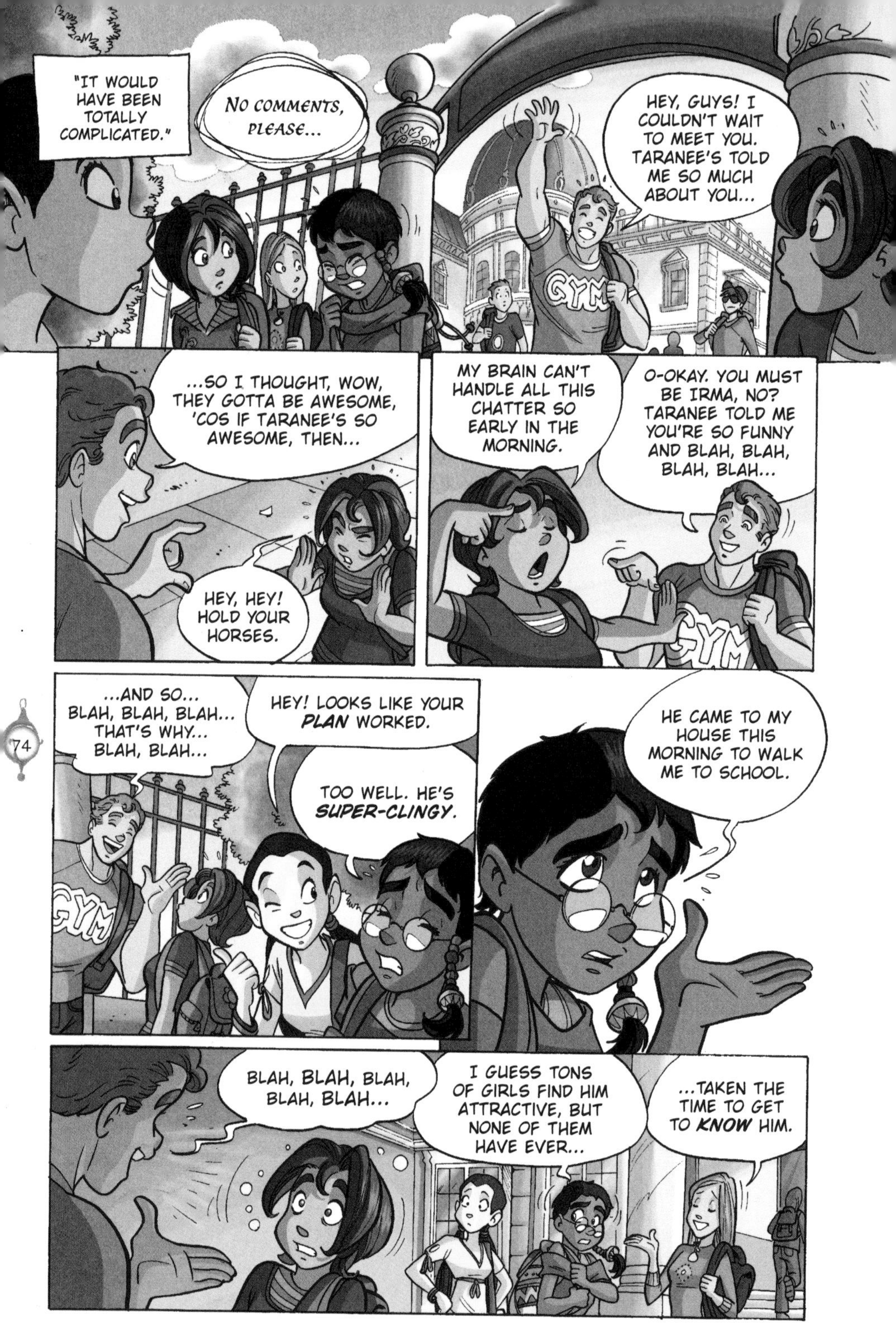
"IT WOULD HAVE BEEN TOTALLY COMPLICATED."
NO COMMENTS, PLEASE...
HEY, GUYS! I COULDN'T WAIT TO MEET YOU. TARANEE'S TOLD ME SO MUCH ABOUT YOU...
GYM
...SO I THOUGHT, WOW, THEY GOTTA BE AWESOME, 'COS IF TARANEE'S SO AWESOME, THEN...
HEY, HEY! HOLD YOUR HORSES.
MY BRAIN CAN'T HANDLE ALL THIS CHATTER SO EARLY IN THE MORNING.
O-OKAY. YOU MUST BE IRMA, NO? TARANEE TOLD ME YOU'RE SO FUNNY AND BLAH, BLAH, BLAH, BLAH...
GYM
...AND SO... BLAH, BLAH, BLAH... THAT'S WHY... BLAH, BLAH...
HEY! LOOKS LIKE YOUR ***PLAN*** WORKED.
TOO WELL. HE'S ***SUPER-CLINGY***.
GYM
HE CAME TO MY HOUSE THIS MORNING TO WALK ME TO SCHOOL.
BLAH, BLAH, BLAH, BLAH, BLAH...
I GUESS TONS OF GIRLS FIND HIM ATTRACTIVE, BUT NONE OF THEM HAVE EVER...
...TAKEN THE TIME TO GET TO ***KNOW*** HIM.

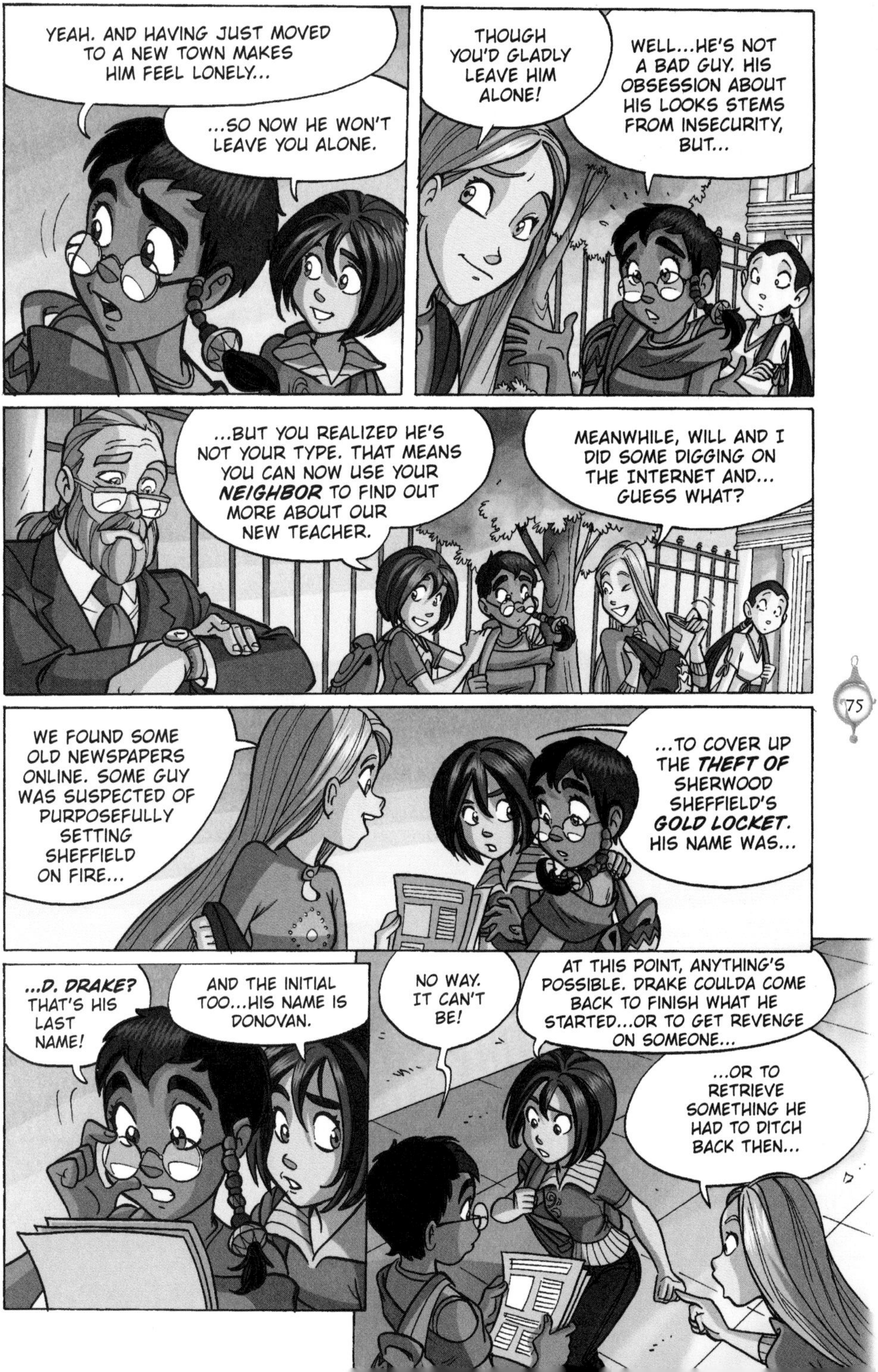
YEAH. AND HAVING JUST MOVED TO A NEW TOWN MAKES HIM FEEL LONELY...
...SO NOW HE WON'T LEAVE YOU ALONE.
THOUGH YOU'D GLADLY LEAVE HIM ALONE!
WELL...HE'S NOT A BAD GUY. HIS OBSESSION ABOUT HIS LOOKS STEMS FROM INSECURITY, BUT...
...BUT YOU REALIZED HE'S NOT YOUR TYPE. THAT MEANS YOU CAN NOW USE YOUR *NEIGHBOR* TO FIND OUT MORE ABOUT OUR NEW TEACHER.
MEANWHILE, WILL AND I DID SOME DIGGING ON THE INTERNET AND... GUESS WHAT?
WE FOUND SOME OLD NEWSPAPERS ONLINE. SOME GUY WAS SUSPECTED OF PURPOSEFULLY SETTING SHEFFIELD ON FIRE...
...TO COVER UP THE *THEFT OF* SHERWOOD SHEFFIELD'S *GOLD LOCKET*. HIS NAME WAS...
...D. DRAKE? THAT'S HIS LAST NAME!
AND THE INITIAL TOO...HIS NAME IS DONOVAN.
NO WAY. IT CAN'T BE!
AT THIS POINT, ANYTHING'S POSSIBLE. DRAKE COULDA COME BACK TO FINISH WHAT HE STARTED...OR TO GET REVENGE ON SOMEONE...
...OR TO RETRIEVE SOMETHING HE HAD TO DITCH BACK THEN...

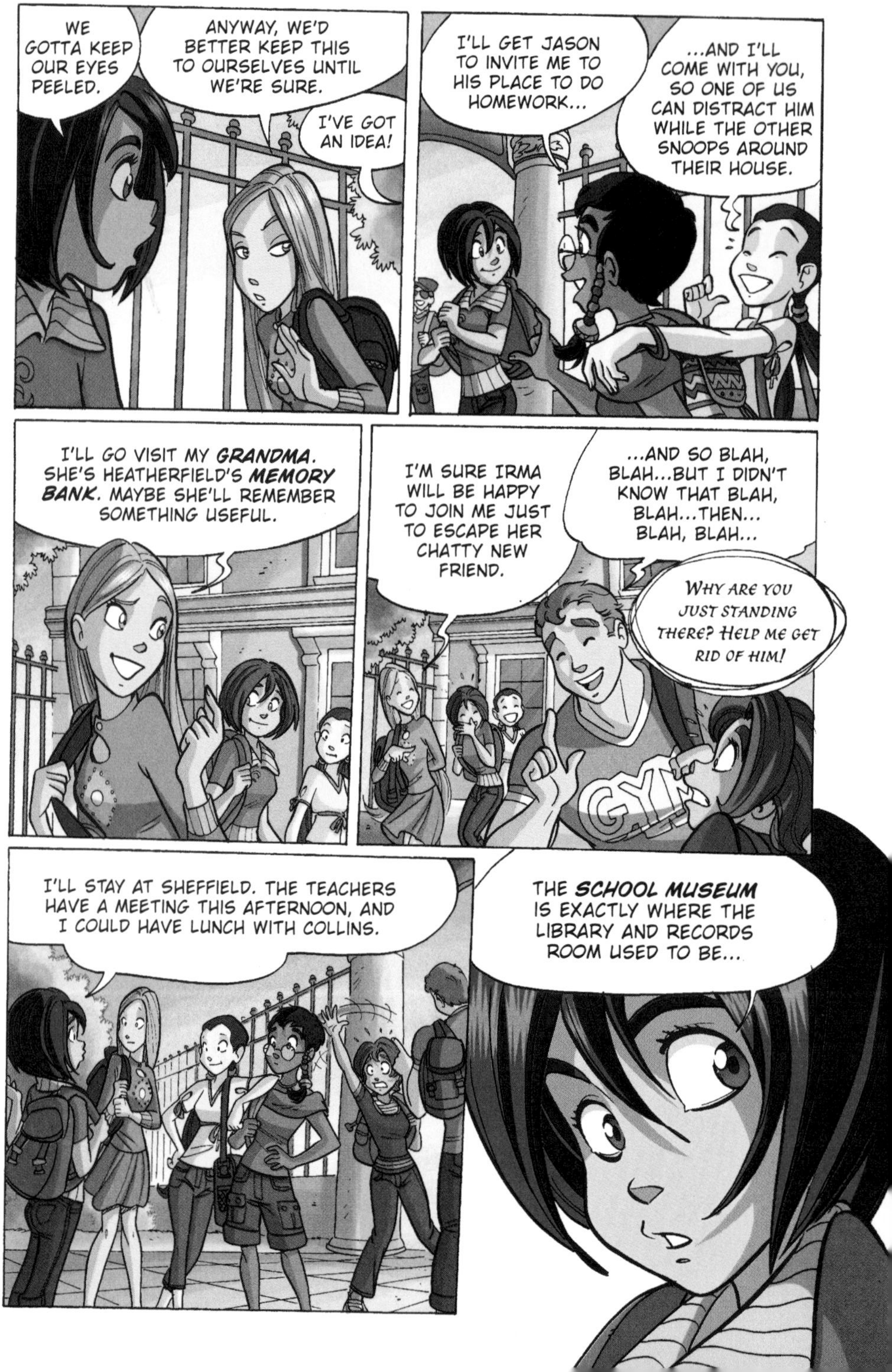
WE GOTTA KEEP OUR EYES PEELED.
ANYWAY, WE'D BETTER KEEP THIS TO OURSELVES UNTIL WE'RE SURE.
I'VE GOT AN IDEA!
I'LL GET JASON TO INVITE ME TO HIS PLACE TO DO HOMEWORK...
...AND I'LL COME WITH YOU, SO ONE OF US CAN DISTRACT HIM WHILE THE OTHER SNOOPS AROUND THEIR HOUSE.
I'LL GO VISIT MY GRANDMA. SHE'S HEATHERFIELD'S MEMORY BANK. MAYBE SHE'LL REMEMBER SOMETHING USEFUL.
I'M SURE IRMA WILL BE HAPPY TO JOIN ME JUST TO ESCAPE HER CHATTY NEW FRIEND.
...AND SO BLAH, BLAH...BUT I DIDN'T KNOW THAT BLAH, BLAH...THEN... BLAH, BLAH...
WHY ARE YOU JUST STANDING THERE? HELP ME GET RID OF HIM!
GYM
I'LL STAY AT SHEFFIELD. THE TEACHERS HAVE A MEETING THIS AFTERNOON, AND I COULD HAVE LUNCH WITH COLLINS.
THE SCHOOL MUSEUM IS EXACTLY WHERE THE LIBRARY AND RECORDS ROOM USED TO BE...

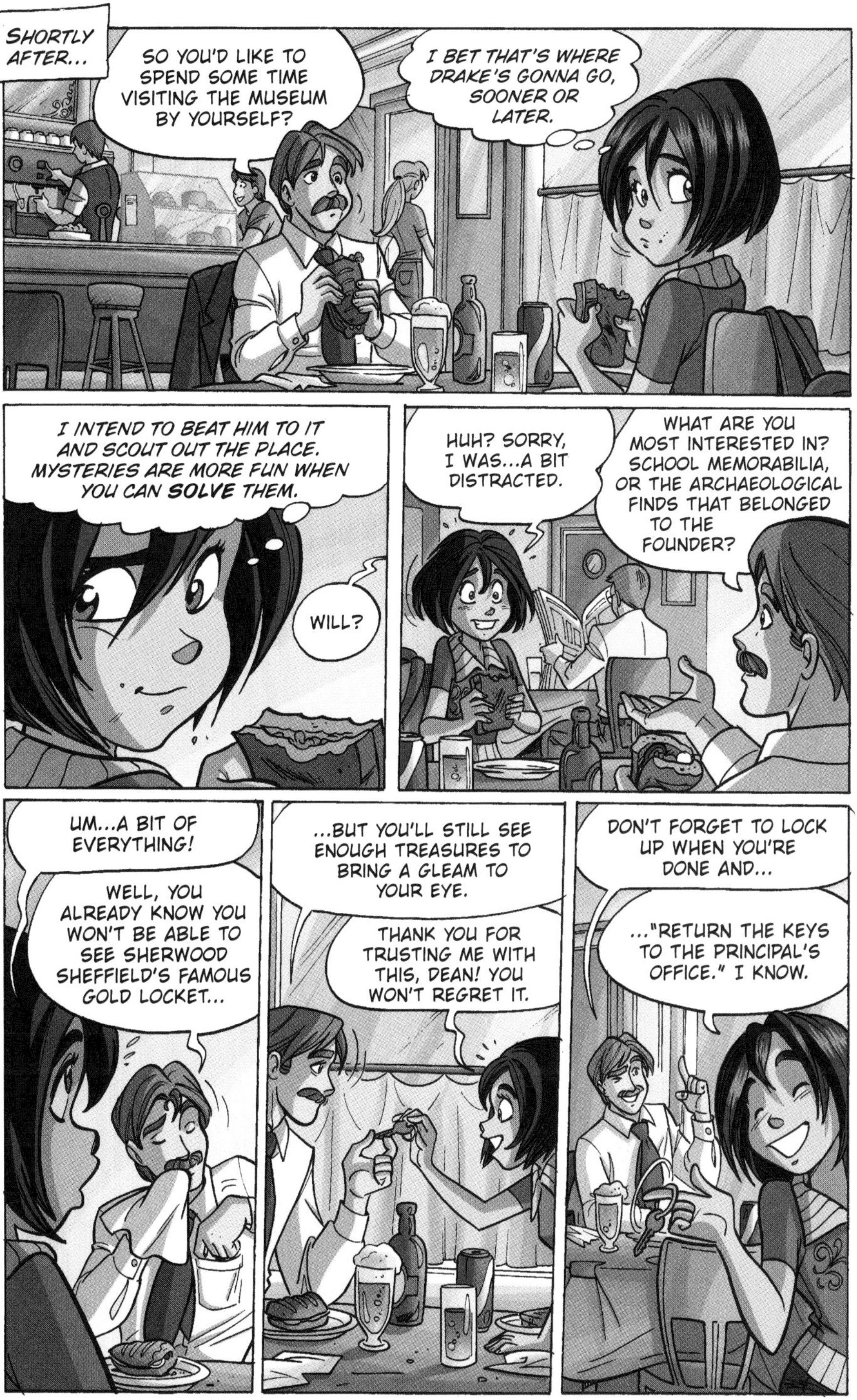
SHORTLY AFTER...
SO YOU'D LIKE TO SPEND SOME TIME VISITING THE MUSEUM BY YOURSELF?
I BET THAT'S WHERE DRAKE'S GONNA GO, SOONER OR LATER.
I INTEND TO BEAT HIM TO IT AND SCOUT OUT THE PLACE. MYSTERIES ARE MORE FUN WHEN YOU CAN SOLVE THEM.
WILL?
HUH? SORRY, I WAS...A BIT DISTRACTED.
WHAT ARE YOU MOST INTERESTED IN? SCHOOL MEMORABILIA, OR THE ARCHAEOLOGICAL FINDS THAT BELONGED TO THE FOUNDER?
UM...A BIT OF EVERYTHING!
WELL, YOU ALREADY KNOW YOU WON'T BE ABLE TO SEE SHERWOOD SHEFFIELD'S FAMOUS GOLD LOCKET...
...BUT YOU'LL STILL SEE ENOUGH TREASURES TO BRING A GLEAM TO YOUR EYE.
THANK YOU FOR TRUSTING ME WITH THIS, DEAN! YOU WON'T REGRET IT.
DON'T FORGET TO LOCK UP WHEN YOU'RE DONE AND...
..."RETURN THE KEYS TO THE PRINCIPAL'S OFFICE." I KNOW.

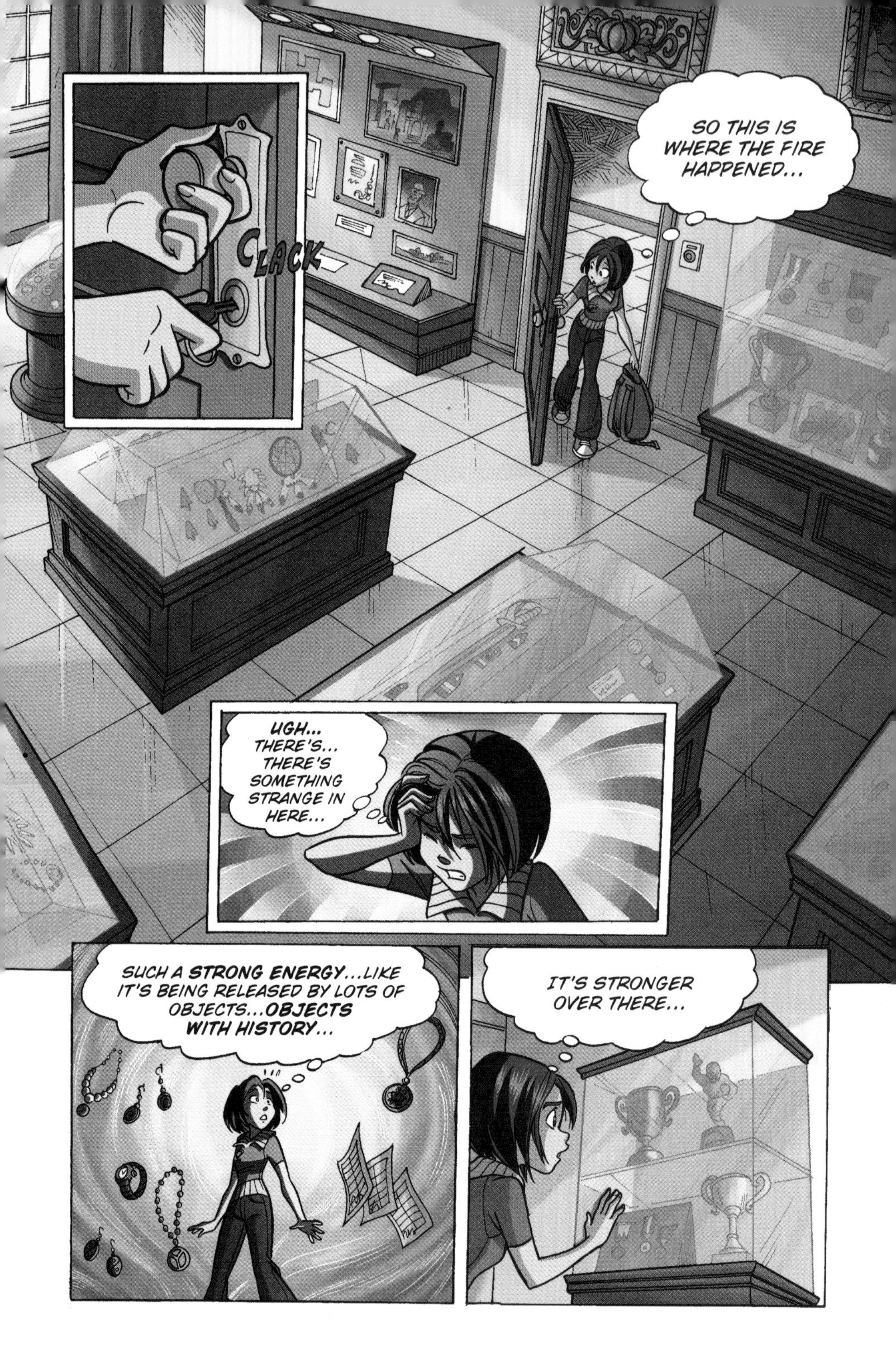
CLACK
SO THIS IS WHERE THE FIRE HAPPENED...
UGH... THERE'S... THERE'S SOMETHING STRANGE IN HERE...
SUCH A STRONG ENERGY...LIKE IT'S BEING RELEASED BY LOTS OF OBJECTS...OBJECTS WITH HISTORY...
IT'S STRONGER OVER THERE...

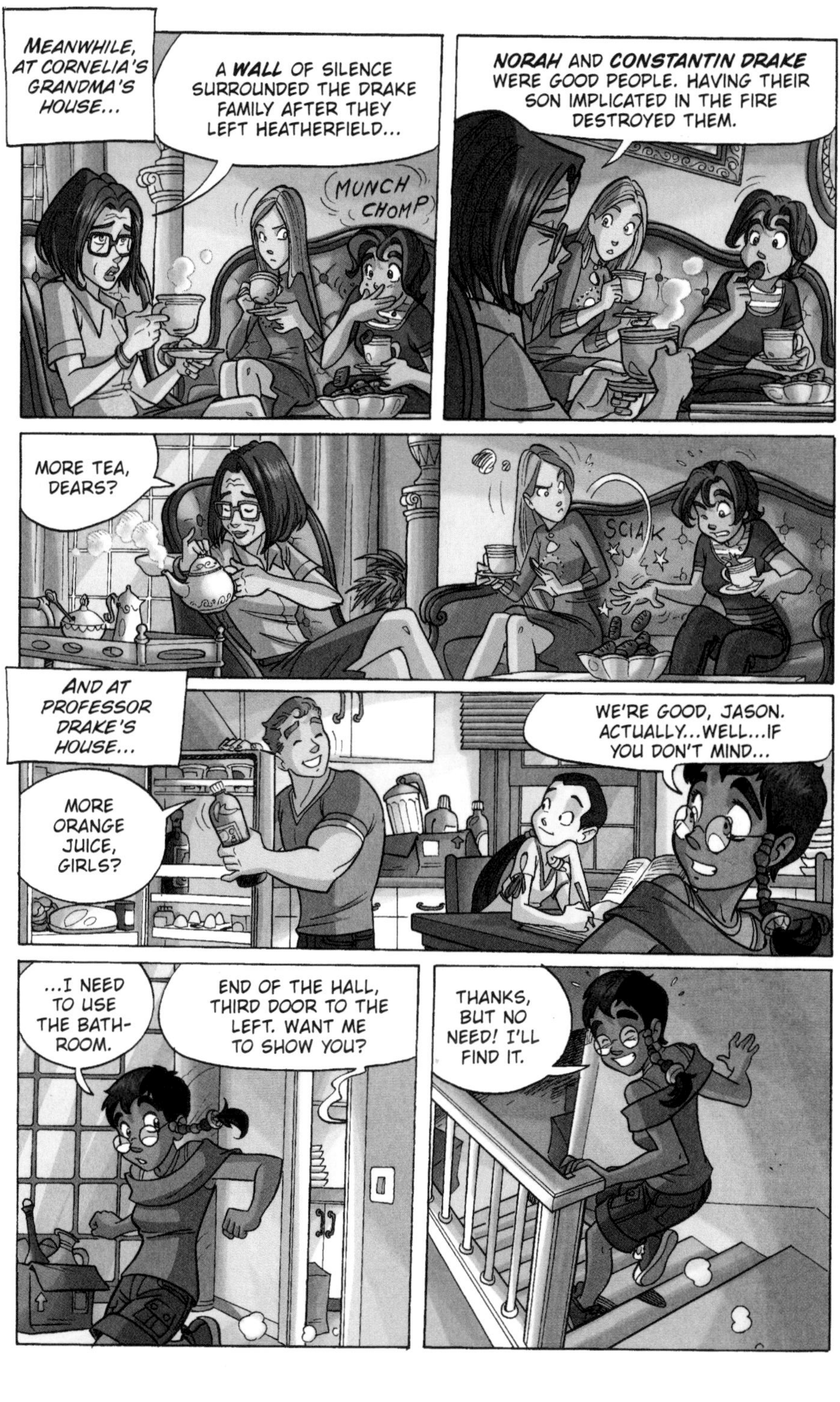
MEANWHILE, AT CORNELIA'S GRANDMA'S HOUSE...
A WALL OF SILENCE SURROUNDED THE DRAKE FAMILY AFTER THEY LEFT HEATHERFIELD...
MUNCH
CHOMP
NORAH AND CONSTANTIN DRAKE WERE GOOD PEOPLE. HAVING THEIR SON IMPLICATED IN THE FIRE DESTROYED THEM.
MORE TEA, DEARS?
SCIAK
AND AT PROFESSOR DRAKE'S HOUSE...
MORE ORANGE JUICE, GIRLS?
WE'RE GOOD, JASON. ACTUALLY...WELL...IF YOU DON'T MIND...
...I NEED TO USE THE BATH-ROOM.
END OF THE HALL, THIRD DOOR TO THE LEFT. WANT ME TO SHOW YOU?
THANKS, BUT NO NEED! I'LL FIND IT.

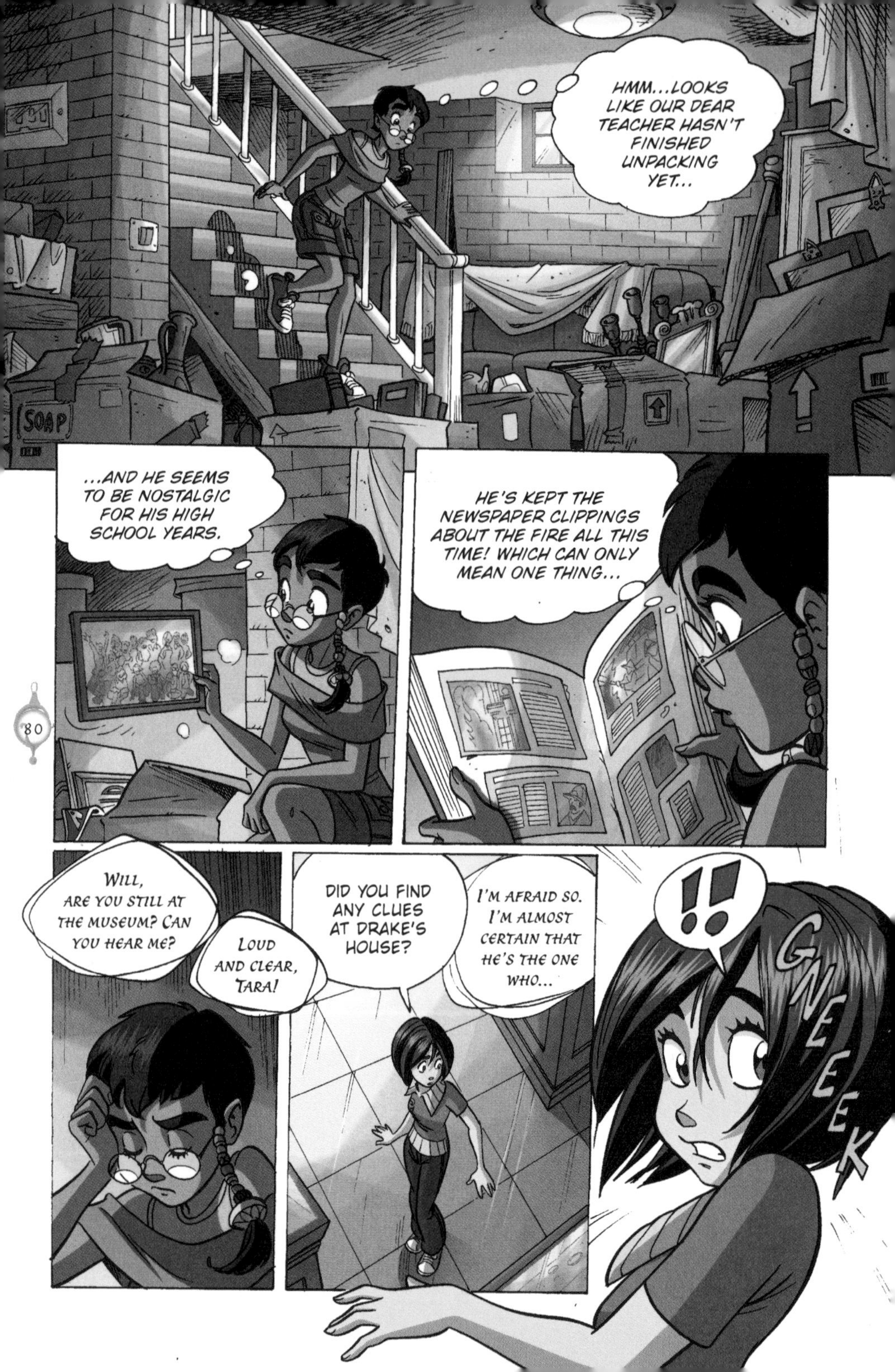
HMM...LOOKS LIKE OUR DEAR TEACHER HASN'T FINISHED UNPACKING YET...
SOAP
...AND HE SEEMS TO BE NOSTALGIC FOR HIS HIGH SCHOOL YEARS.
HE'S KEPT THE NEWSPAPER CLIPPINGS ABOUT THE FIRE ALL THIS TIME! WHICH CAN ONLY MEAN ONE THING...
WILL, ARE YOU STILL AT THE MUSEUM? CAN YOU HEAR ME?
LOUD AND CLEAR, TARA!
DID YOU FIND ANY CLUES AT DRAKE'S HOUSE?
I'M AFRAID SO. I'M ALMOST CERTAIN THAT HE'S THE ONE WHO...
!!
GNEEEK

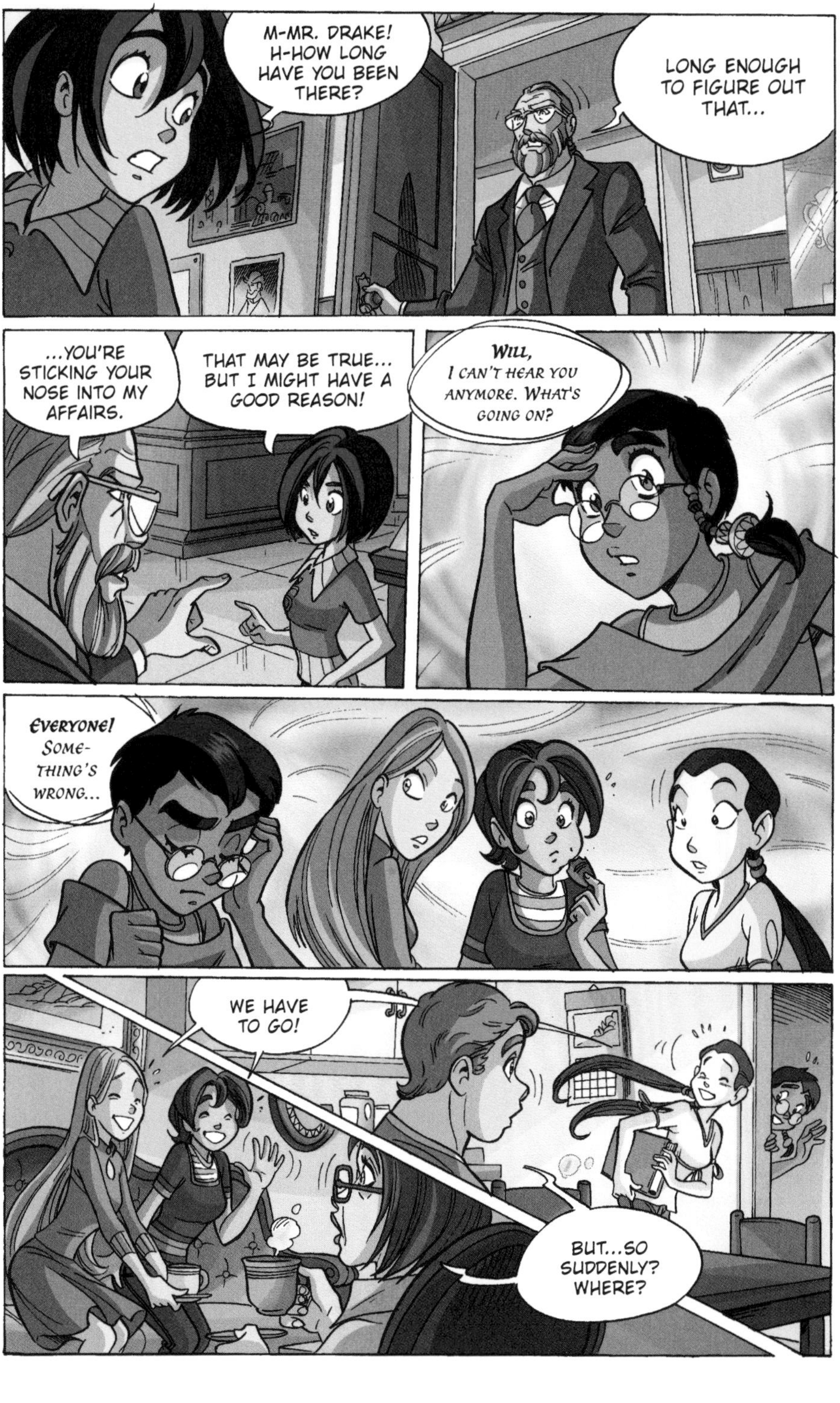
M-MR. DRAKE! H-HOW LONG HAVE YOU BEEN THERE?
LONG ENOUGH TO FIGURE OUT THAT...
...YOU'RE STICKING YOUR NOSE INTO MY AFFAIRS.
THAT MAY BE TRUE... BUT I MIGHT HAVE A GOOD REASON!
WILL, I CAN'T HEAR YOU ANYMORE. WHAT'S GOING ON?
EVERYONE! SOME-THING'S WRONG...
WE HAVE TO GO!
BUT...SO SUDDENLY? WHERE?

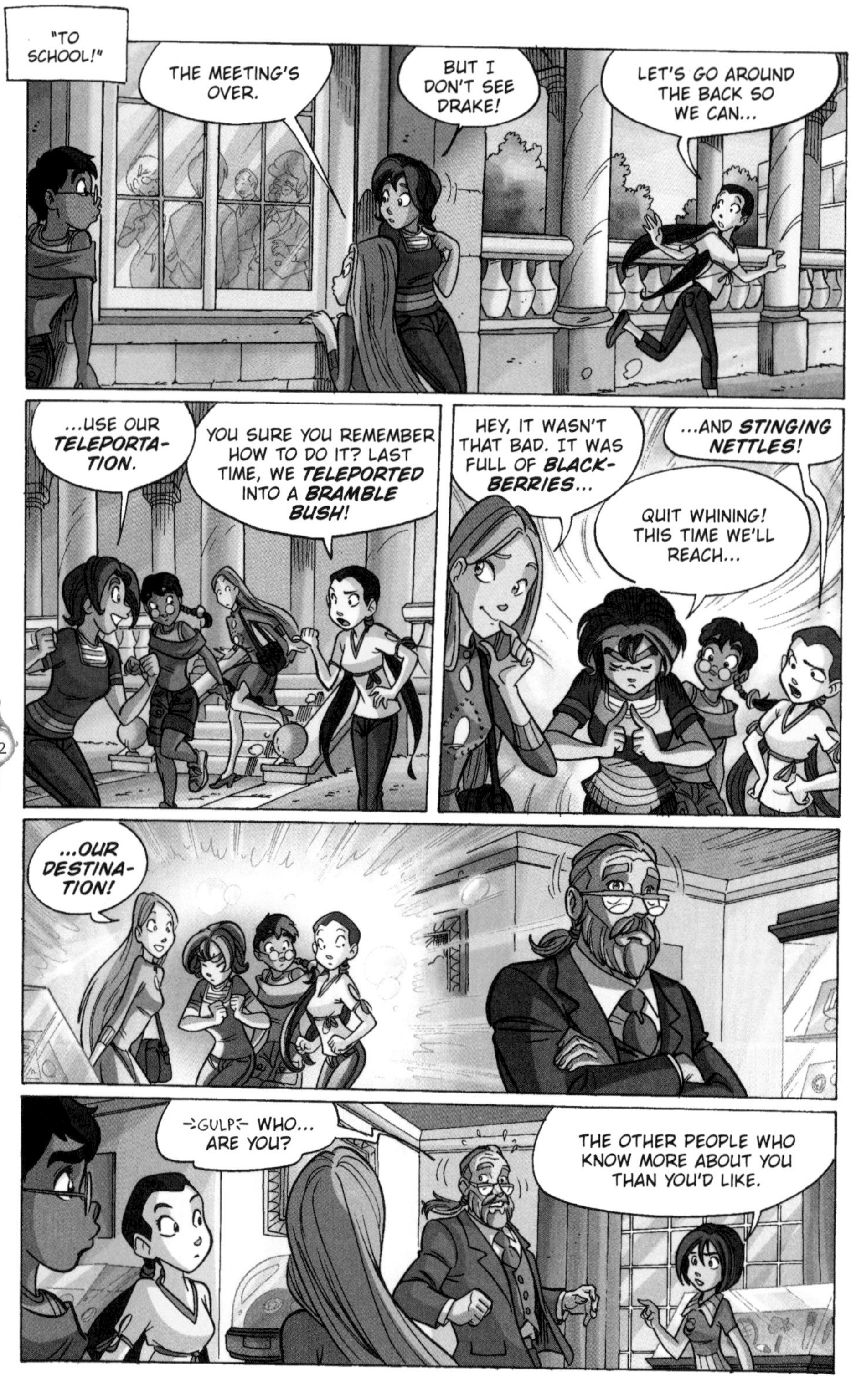

"TO SCHOOL!"
THE MEETING'S OVER.
BUT I DON'T SEE DRAKE!
LET'S GO AROUND THE BACK SO WE CAN...
...USE OUR TELEPORTATION.
YOU SURE YOU REMEMBER HOW TO DO IT? LAST TIME, WE TELEPORTED INTO A BRAMBLE BUSH!
HEY, IT WASN'T THAT BAD. IT WAS FULL OF BLACKBERRIES...
...AND STINGING NETTLES!
QUIT WHINING! THIS TIME WE'LL REACH...
...OUR DESTINATION!
-GULP- WHO... ARE YOU?
THE OTHER PEOPLE WHO KNOW MORE ABOUT YOU THAN YOU'D LIKE.

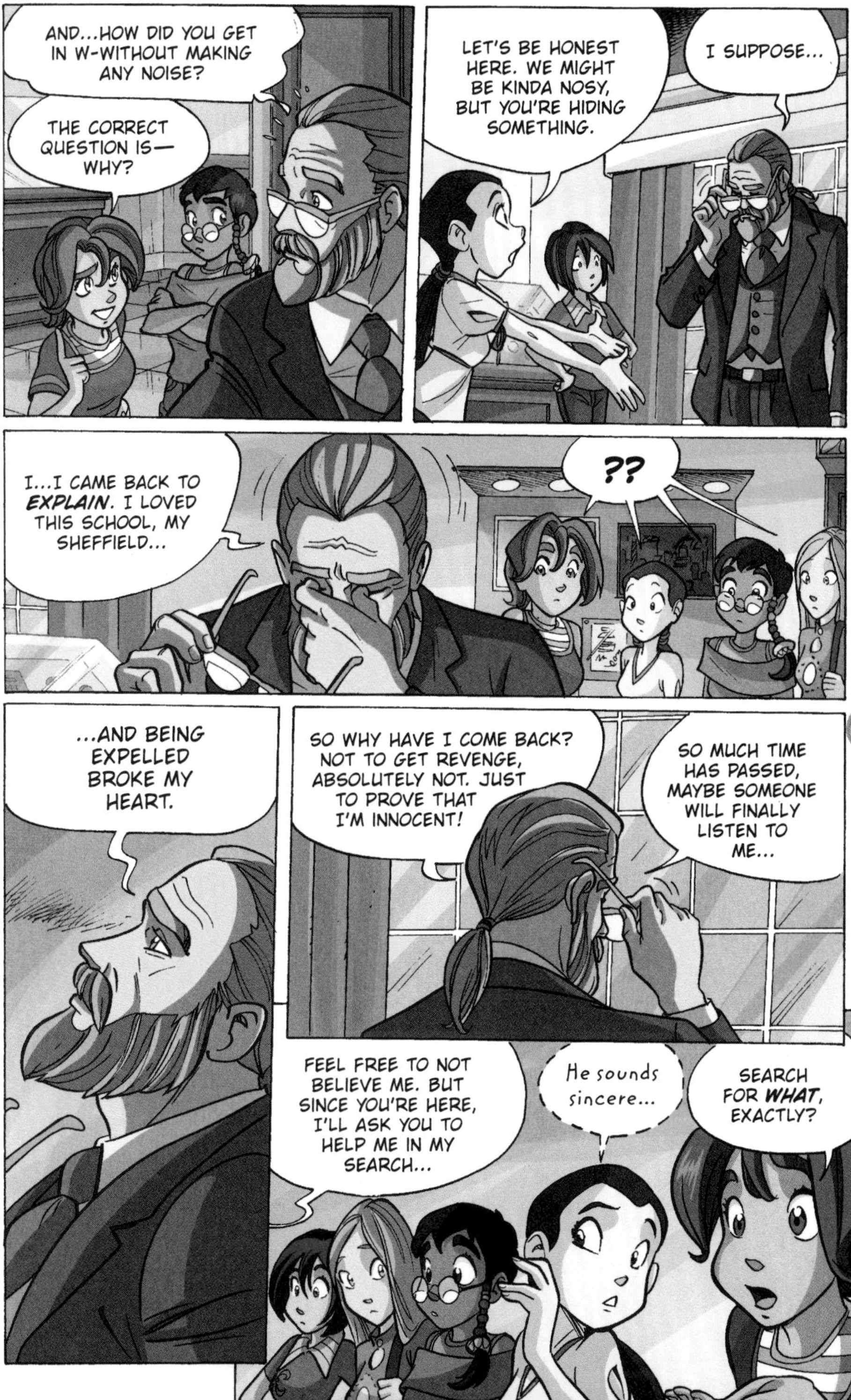
AND...HOW DID YOU GET IN W-WITHOUT MAKING ANY NOISE?
THE CORRECT QUESTION IS— WHY?
LET'S BE HONEST HERE. WE MIGHT BE KINDA NOSY, BUT YOU'RE HIDING SOMETHING.
I SUPPOSE...
I...I CAME BACK TO EXPLAIN. I LOVED THIS SCHOOL, MY SHEFFIELD...
??
...AND BEING EXPELLED BROKE MY HEART.
SO WHY HAVE I COME BACK? NOT TO GET REVENGE, ABSOLUTELY NOT. JUST TO PROVE THAT I'M INNOCENT!
SO MUCH TIME HAS PASSED, MAYBE SOMEONE WILL FINALLY LISTEN TO ME...
FEEL FREE TO NOT BELIEVE ME. BUT SINCE YOU'RE HERE, I'LL ASK YOU TO HELP ME IN MY SEARCH...
He sounds sincere...
SEARCH FOR WHAT, EXACTLY?

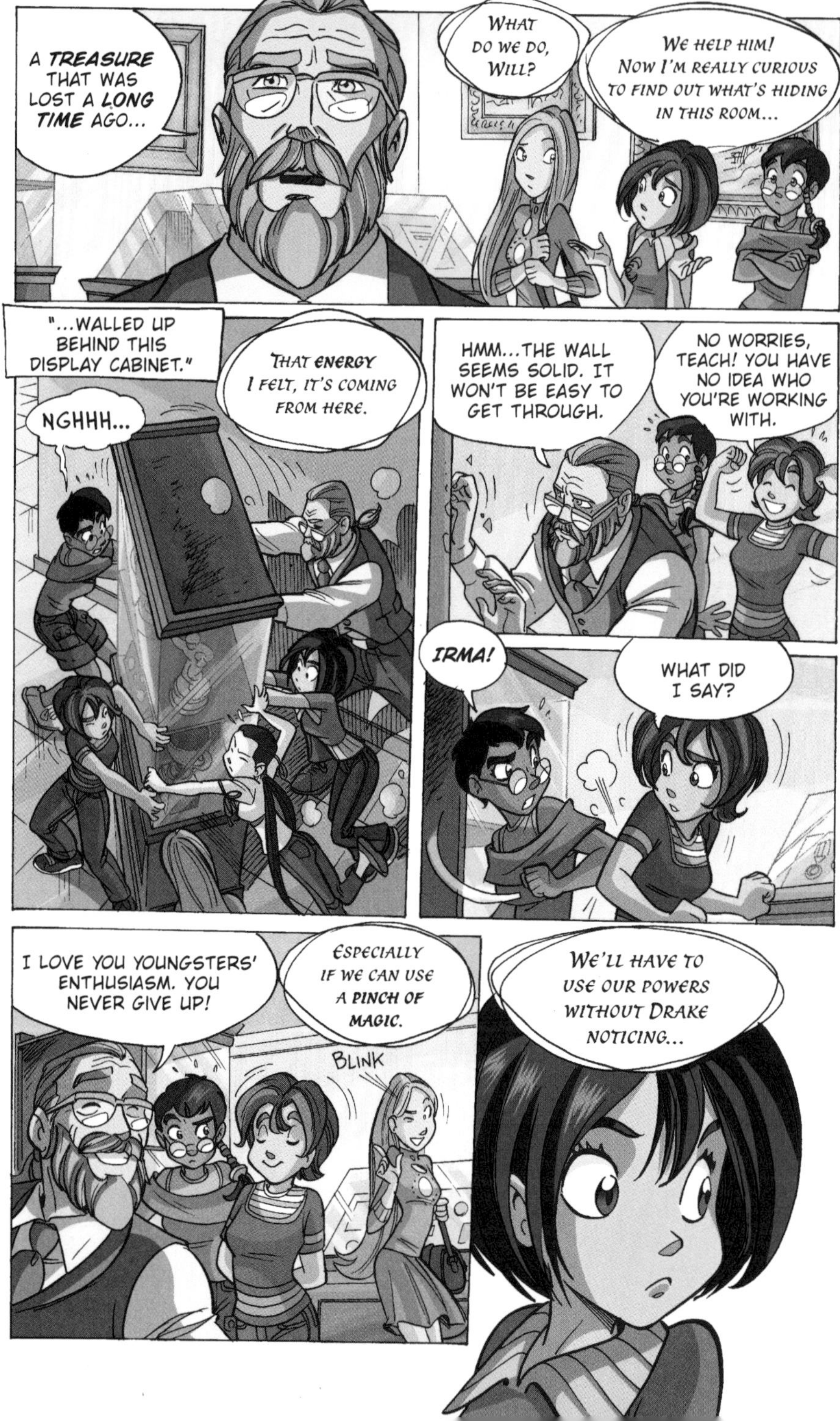

A TREASURE THAT WAS LOST A LONG TIME AGO...
WHAT DO WE DO, WILL?
WE HELP HIM! NOW I'M REALLY CURIOUS TO FIND OUT WHAT'S HIDING IN THIS ROOM...
"...WALLED UP BEHIND THIS DISPLAY CABINET."
NGHHH...
THAT ENERGY I FELT, IT'S COMING FROM HERE.
HMM...THE WALL SEEMS SOLID. IT WON'T BE EASY TO GET THROUGH.
NO WORRIES, TEACH! YOU HAVE NO IDEA WHO YOU'RE WORKING WITH.
IRMA!
WHAT DID I SAY?
I LOVE YOU YOUNGSTERS' ENTHUSIASM. YOU NEVER GIVE UP!
ESPECIALLY IF WE CAN USE A PINCH OF MAGIC.
BLINK
WE'LL HAVE TO USE OUR POWERS WITHOUT DRAKE NOTICING...

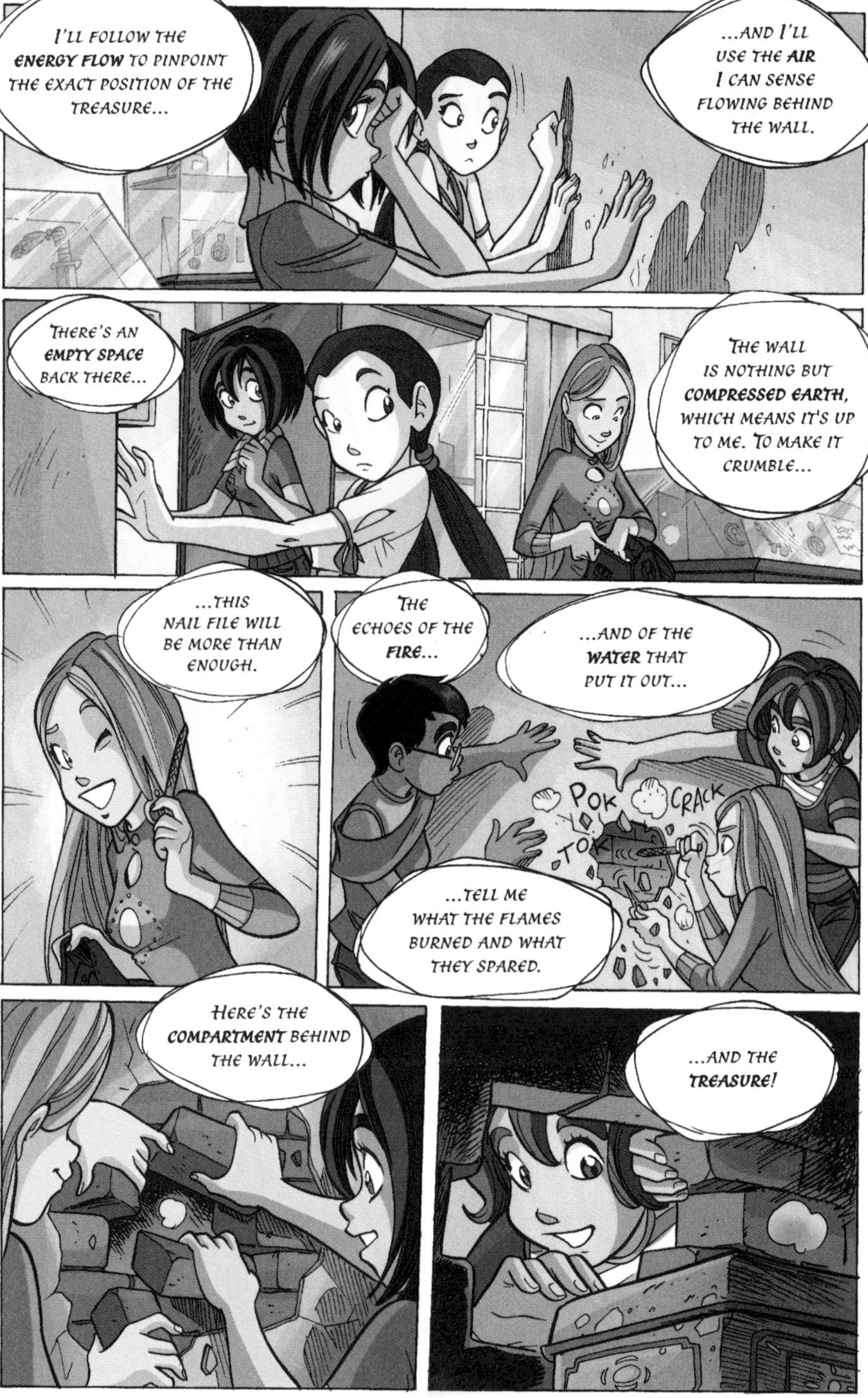
I'LL FOLLOW THE ENERGY FLOW TO PINPOINT THE EXACT POSITION OF THE TREASURE...
...AND I'LL USE THE AIR I CAN SENSE FLOWING BEHIND THE WALL.
THERE'S AN EMPTY SPACE BACK THERE...
THE WALL IS NOTHING BUT COMPRESSED EARTH, WHICH MEANS IT'S UP TO ME. TO MAKE IT CRUMBLE...
...THIS NAIL FILE WILL BE MORE THAN ENOUGH.
THE ECHOES OF THE FIRE...
...AND OF THE WATER THAT PUT IT OUT...
POK
CRACK
TOK
...TELL ME WHAT THE FLAMES BURNED AND WHAT THEY SPARED.
HERE'S THE COMPARTMENT BEHIND THE WALL...
...AND THE TREASURE!

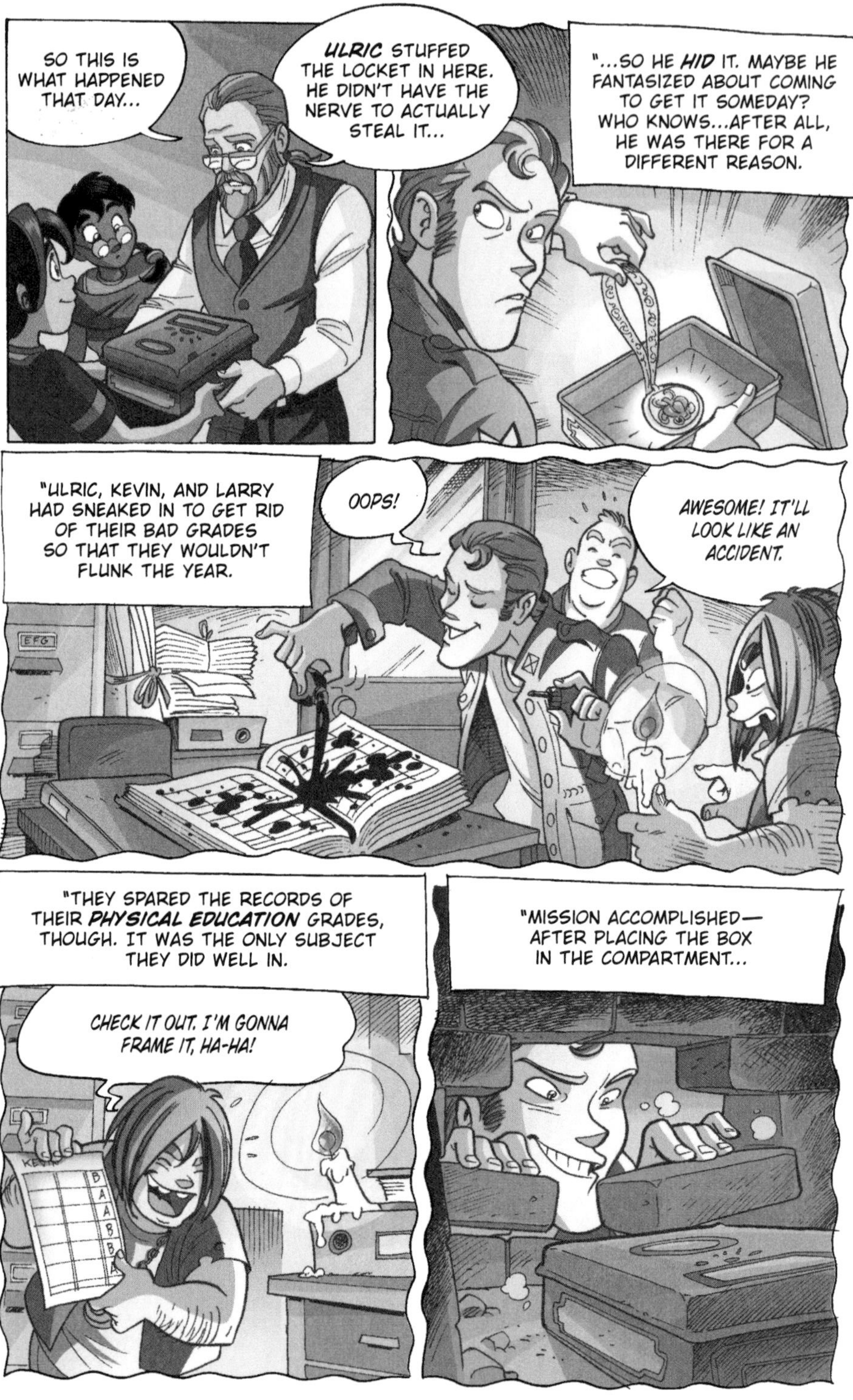

SO THIS IS WHAT HAPPENED THAT DAY...
ULRIC STUFFED THE LOCKET IN HERE. HE DIDN'T HAVE THE NERVE TO ACTUALLY STEAL IT...
"...SO HE HID IT. MAYBE HE FANTASIZED ABOUT COMING TO GET IT SOMEDAY? WHO KNOWS...AFTER ALL, HE WAS THERE FOR A DIFFERENT REASON.
"ULRIC, KEVIN, AND LARRY HAD SNEAKED IN TO GET RID OF THEIR BAD GRADES SO THAT THEY WOULDN'T FLUNK THE YEAR.
OOPS!
AWESOME! IT'LL LOOK LIKE AN ACCIDENT.
EFG
"THEY SPARED THE RECORDS OF THEIR PHYSICAL EDUCATION GRADES, THOUGH. IT WAS THE ONLY SUBJECT THEY DID WELL IN.
CHECK IT OUT. I'M GONNA FRAME IT, HA-HA!
"MISSION ACCOMPLISHED— AFTER PLACING THE BOX IN THE COMPARTMENT...

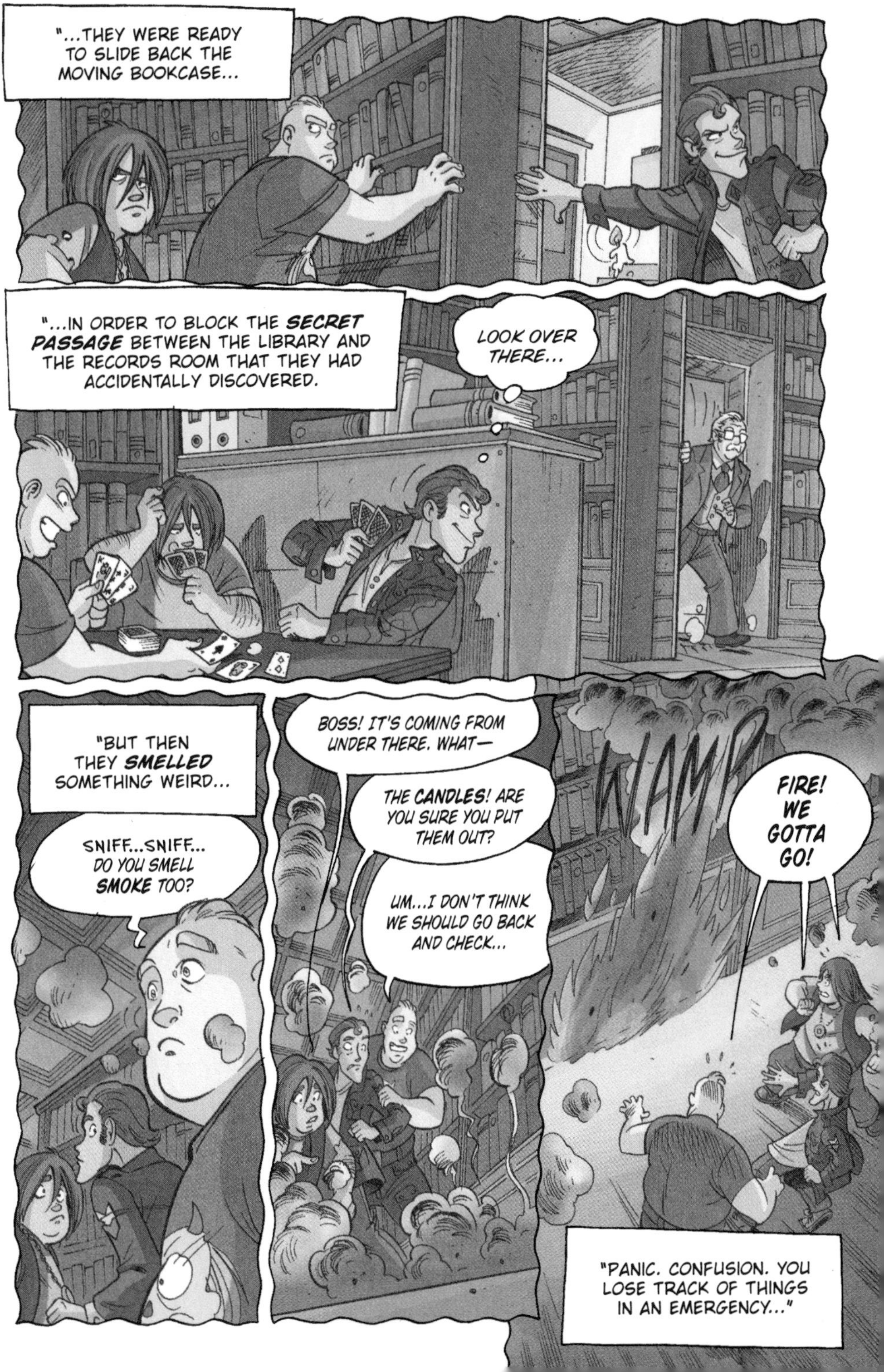
"...THEY WERE READY TO SLIDE BACK THE MOVING BOOKCASE...
"...IN ORDER TO BLOCK THE SECRET PASSAGE BETWEEN THE LIBRARY AND THE RECORDS ROOM THAT THEY HAD ACCIDENTALLY DISCOVERED.
LOOK OVER THERE...
"BUT THEN THEY SMELLED SOMETHING WEIRD...
SNIFF...SNIFF... DO YOU SMELL SMOKE TOO?
BOSS! IT'S COMING FROM UNDER THERE. WHAT—
THE CANDLES! ARE YOU SURE YOU PUT THEM OUT?
UM...I DON'T THINK WE SHOULD GO BACK AND CHECK...
WAMP
FIRE! WE GOTTA GO!
"PANIC. CONFUSION. YOU LOSE TRACK OF THINGS IN AN EMERGENCY..."

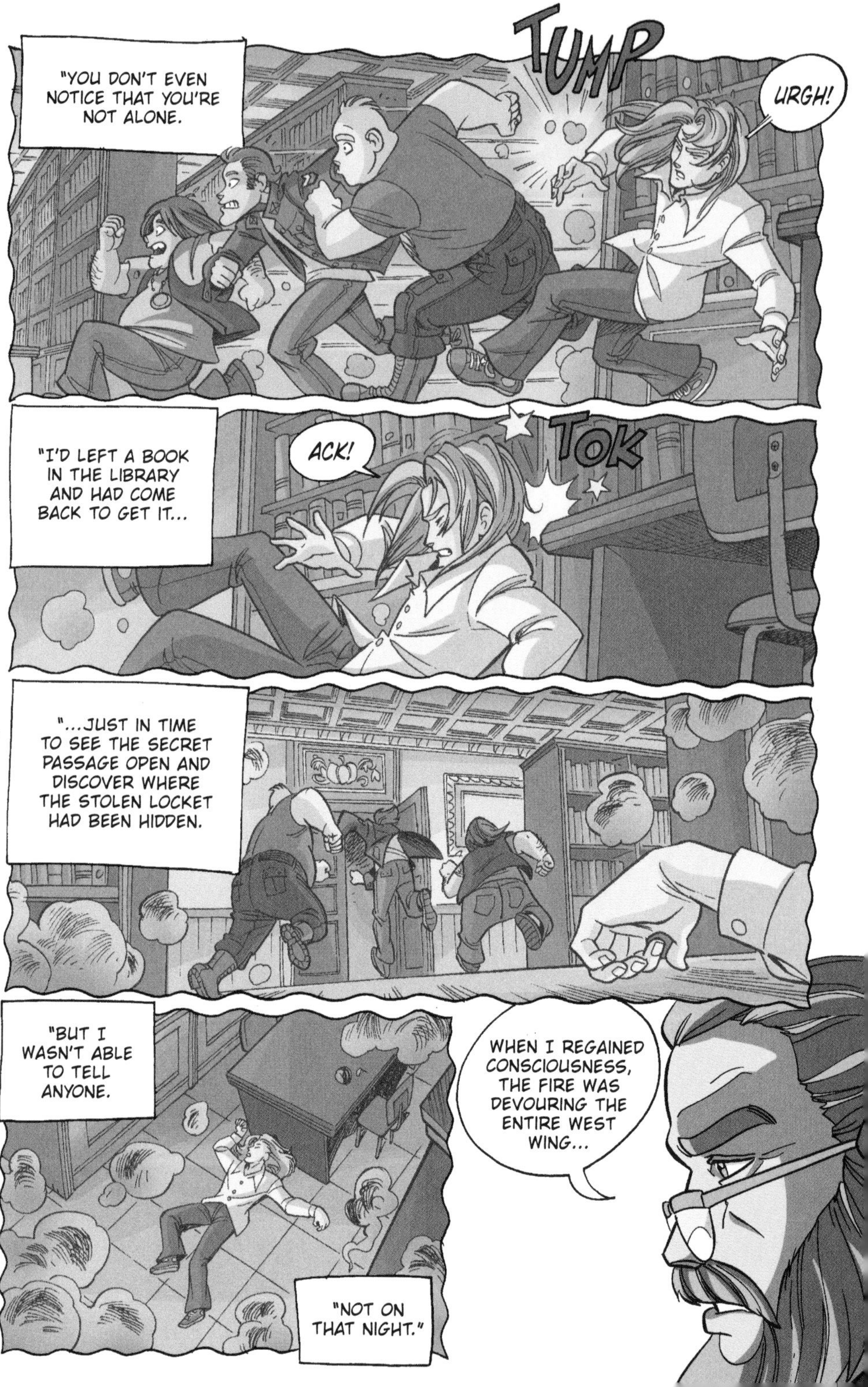
"YOU DON'T EVEN NOTICE THAT YOU'RE NOT ALONE.
TUMP
URGH!
"I'D LEFT A BOOK IN THE LIBRARY AND HAD COME BACK TO GET IT...
ACK!
TOK
"...JUST IN TIME TO SEE THE SECRET PASSAGE OPEN AND DISCOVER WHERE THE STOLEN LOCKET HAD BEEN HIDDEN.
"BUT I WASN'T ABLE TO TELL ANYONE.
WHEN I REGAINED CONSCIOUSNESS, THE FIRE WAS DEVOURING THE ENTIRE WEST WING...
"NOT ON THAT NIGHT."

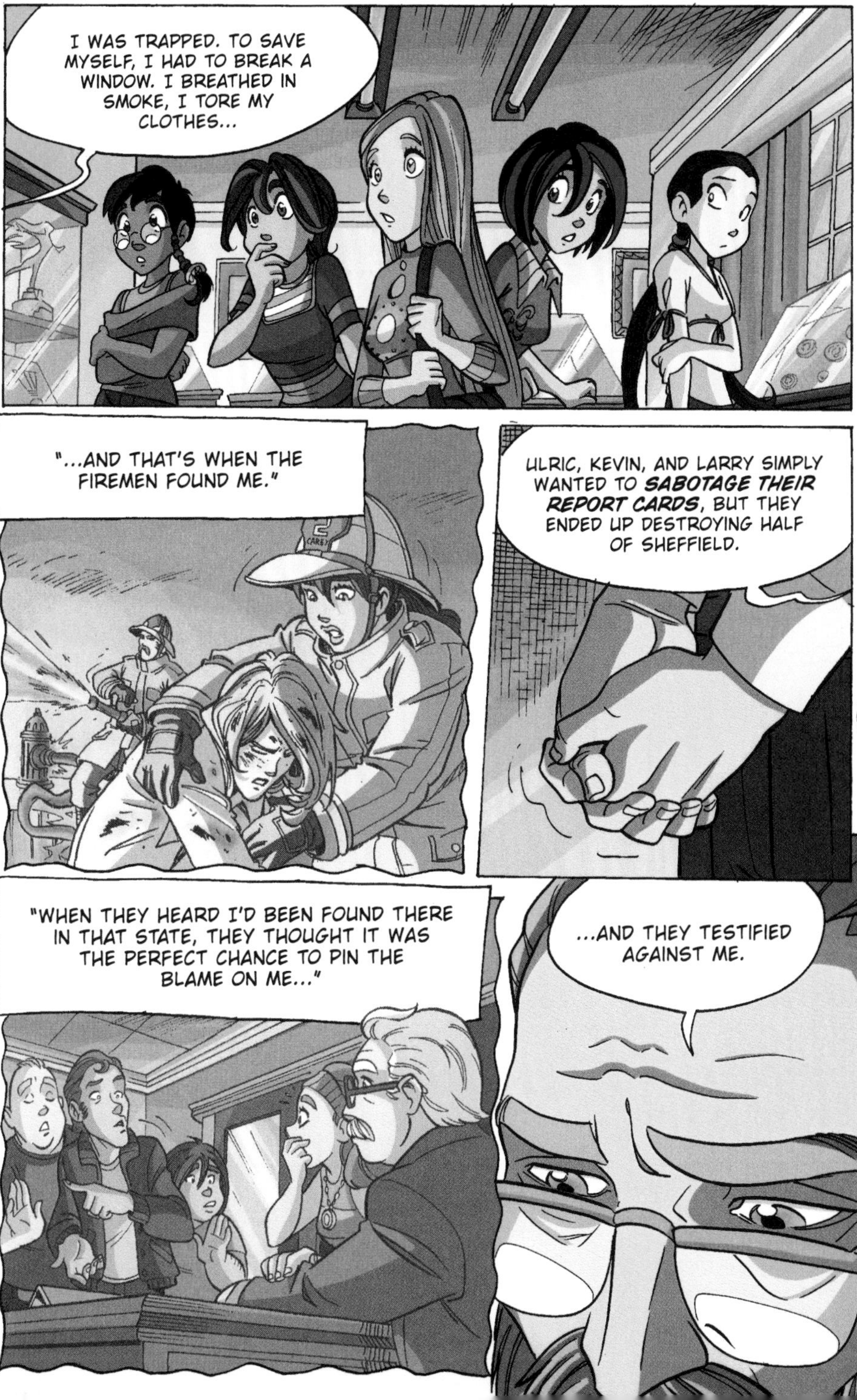

I WAS TRAPPED. TO SAVE MYSELF, I HAD TO BREAK A WINDOW. I BREATHED IN SMOKE, I TORE MY CLOTHES...
"...AND THAT'S WHEN THE FIREMEN FOUND ME."
ULRIC, KEVIN, AND LARRY SIMPLY WANTED TO ***SABOTAGE THEIR REPORT CARDS***, BUT THEY ENDED UP DESTROYING HALF OF SHEFFIELD.
"WHEN THEY HEARD I'D BEEN FOUND THERE IN THAT STATE, THEY THOUGHT IT WAS THE PERFECT CHANCE TO PIN THE BLAME ON ME..."
...AND THEY TESTIFIED AGAINST ME.

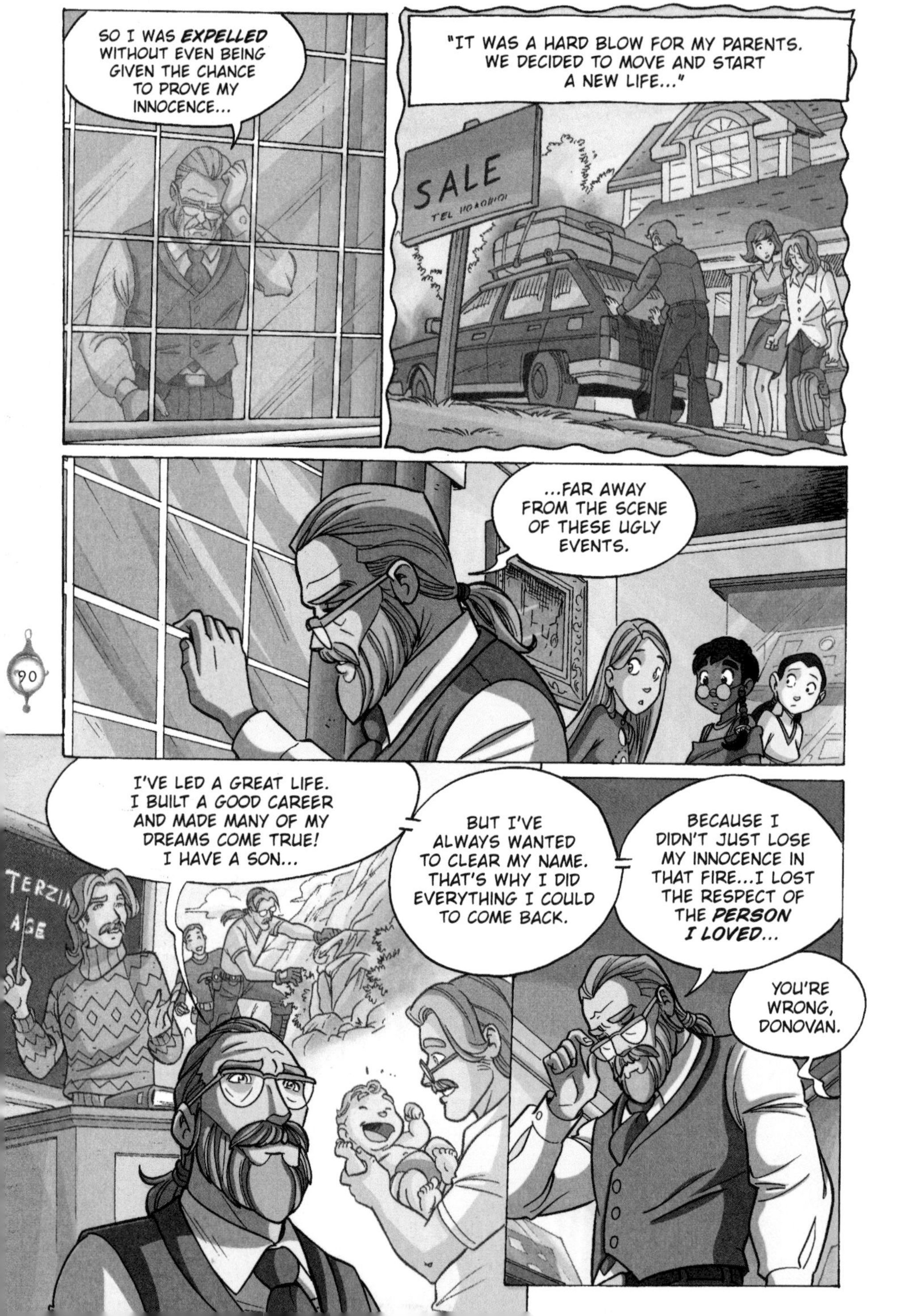
SO I WAS EXPELLED WITHOUT EVEN BEING GIVEN THE CHANCE TO PROVE MY INNOCENCE...
"IT WAS A HARD BLOW FOR MY PARENTS. WE DECIDED TO MOVE AND START A NEW LIFE..."
SALE
...FAR AWAY FROM THE SCENE OF THESE UGLY EVENTS.
I'VE LED A GREAT LIFE. I BUILT A GOOD CAREER AND MADE MANY OF MY DREAMS COME TRUE! I HAVE A SON...
BUT I'VE ALWAYS WANTED TO CLEAR MY NAME. THAT'S WHY I DID EVERYTHING I COULD TO COME BACK.
BECAUSE I DIDN'T JUST LOSE MY INNOCENCE IN THAT FIRE...I LOST THE RESPECT OF THE PERSON I LOVED...
YOU'RE WRONG, DONOVAN.

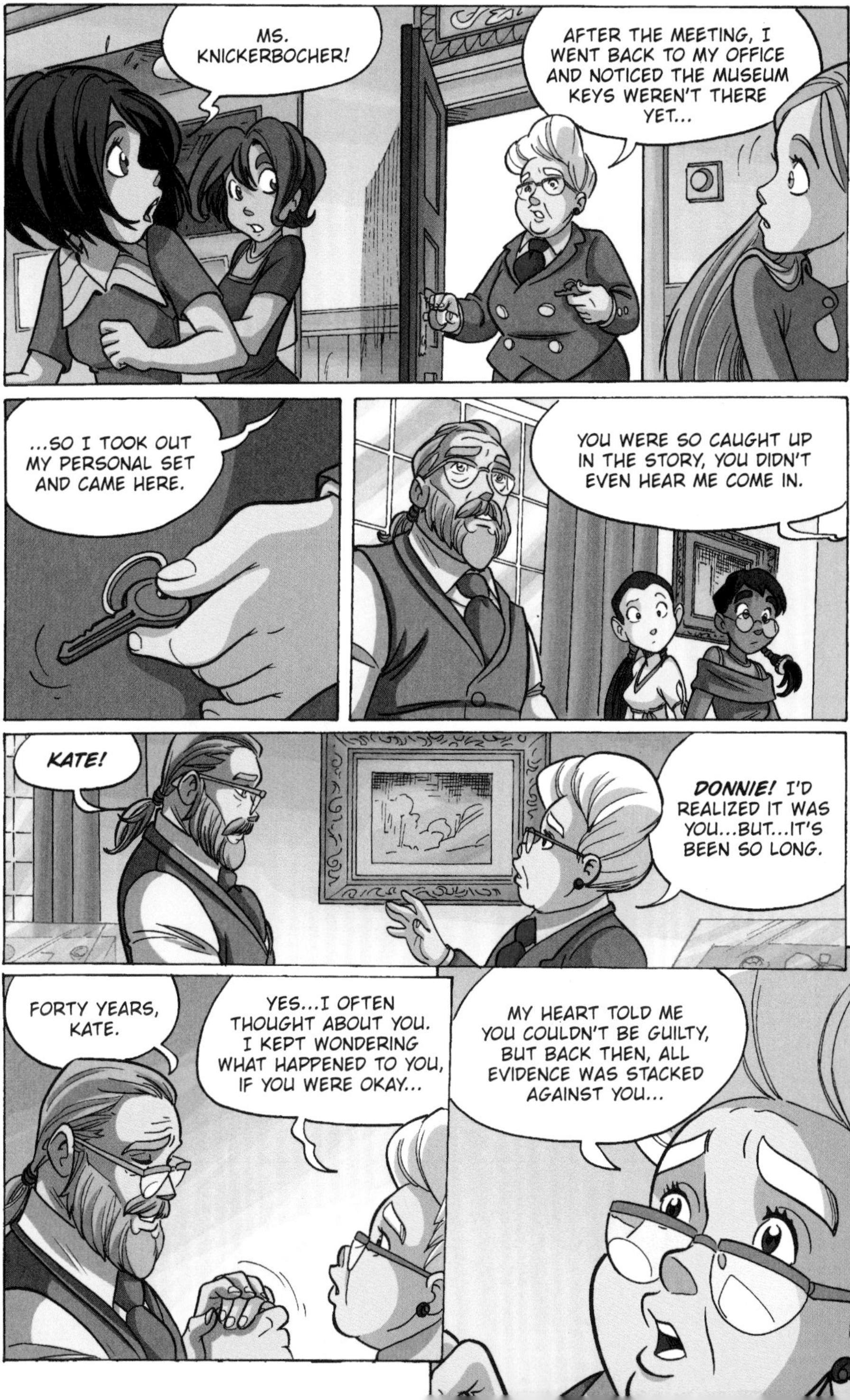
MS. KNICKERBOCHER!
AFTER THE MEETING, I WENT BACK TO MY OFFICE AND NOTICED THE MUSEUM KEYS WEREN'T THERE YET...
...SO I TOOK OUT MY PERSONAL SET AND CAME HERE.
YOU WERE SO CAUGHT UP IN THE STORY, YOU DIDN'T EVEN HEAR ME COME IN.
KATE!
DONNIE! I'D REALIZED IT WAS YOU...BUT...IT'S BEEN SO LONG.
FORTY YEARS, KATE.
YES...I OFTEN THOUGHT ABOUT YOU. I KEPT WONDERING WHAT HAPPENED TO YOU, IF YOU WERE OKAY...
MY HEART TOLD ME YOU COULDN'T BE GUILTY, BUT BACK THEN, ALL EVIDENCE WAS STACKED AGAINST YOU...

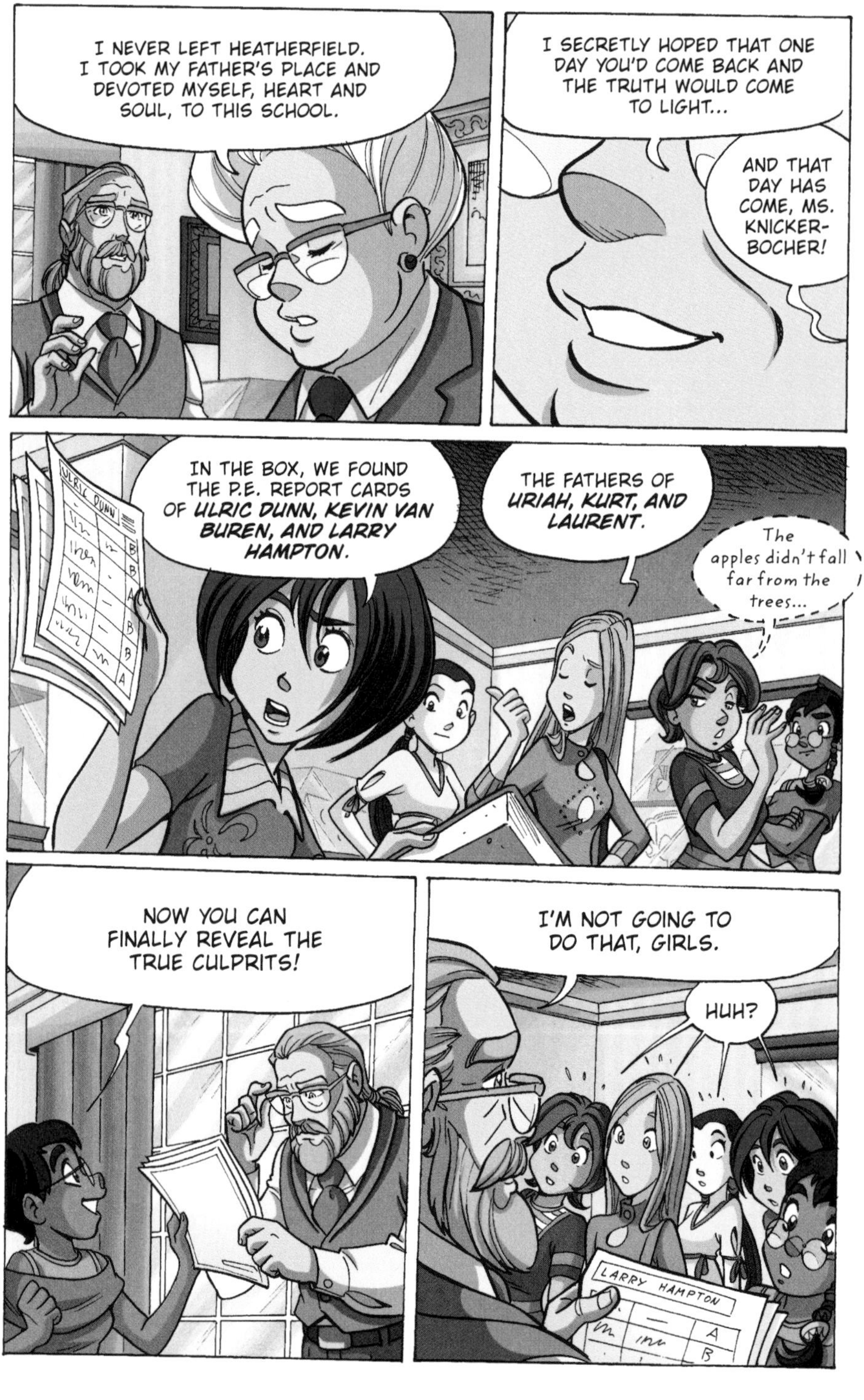
I NEVER LEFT HEATHERFIELD. I TOOK MY FATHER'S PLACE AND DEVOTED MYSELF, HEART AND SOUL, TO THIS SCHOOL.
I SECRETLY HOPED THAT ONE DAY YOU'D COME BACK AND THE TRUTH WOULD COME TO LIGHT...
AND THAT DAY HAS COME, MS. KNICKER-BOCHER!
ULRIC DUNN
IN THE BOX, WE FOUND THE P.E. REPORT CARDS OF ULRIC DUNN, KEVIN VAN BUREN, AND LARRY HAMPTON.
THE FATHERS OF URIAH, KURT, AND LAURENT.
The apples didn't fall far from the trees...
NOW YOU CAN FINALLY REVEAL THE TRUE CULPRITS!
I'M NOT GOING TO DO THAT, GIRLS.
HUH?
LARRY HAMPTON

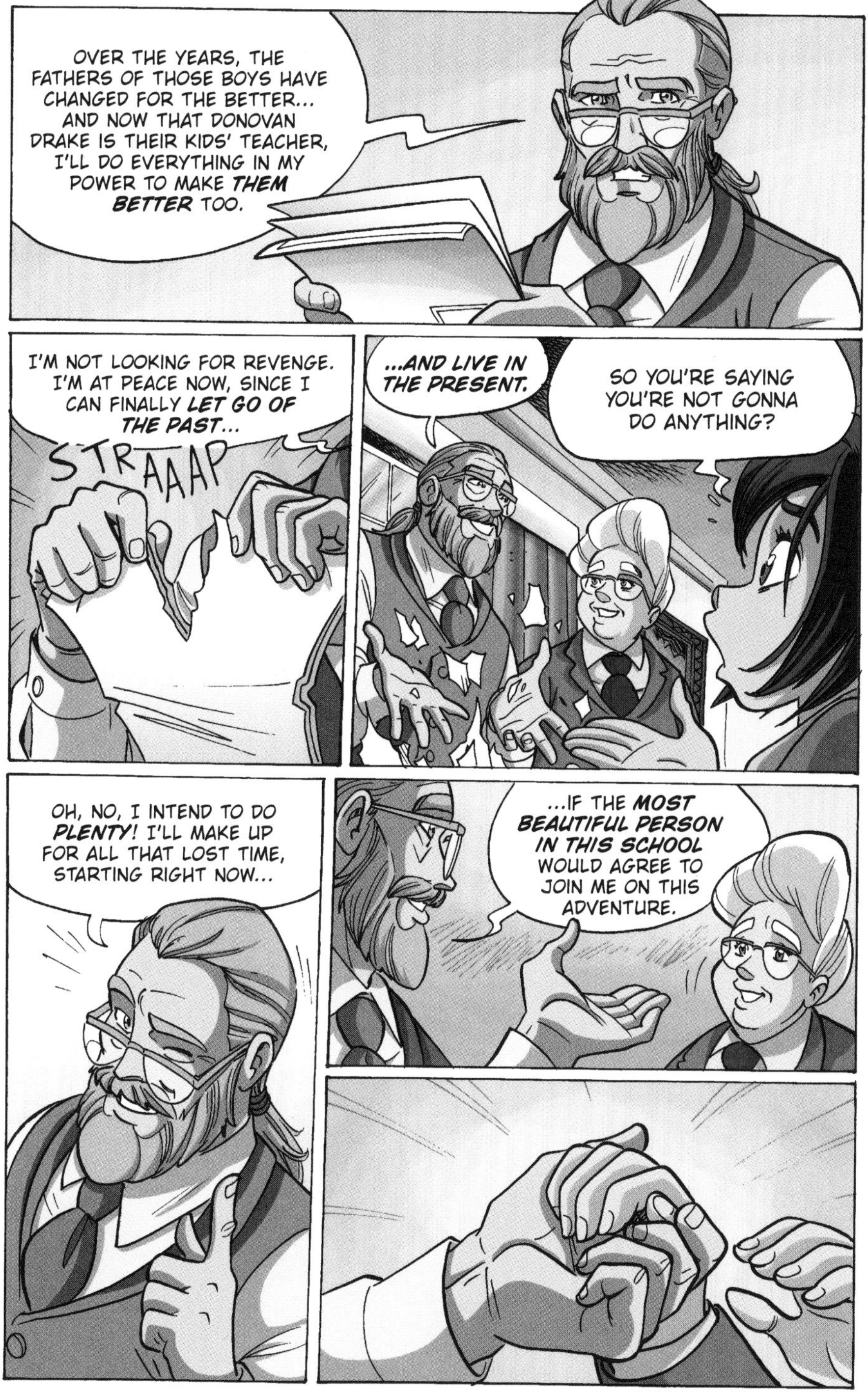
OVER THE YEARS, THE FATHERS OF THOSE BOYS HAVE CHANGED FOR THE BETTER... AND NOW THAT DONOVAN DRAKE IS THEIR KIDS' TEACHER, I'LL DO EVERYTHING IN MY POWER TO MAKE THEM BETTER TOO.
I'M NOT LOOKING FOR REVENGE. I'M AT PEACE NOW, SINCE I CAN FINALLY LET GO OF THE PAST...
STRAAAP
...AND LIVE IN THE PRESENT.
SO YOU'RE SAYING YOU'RE NOT GONNA DO ANYTHING?
OH, NO, I INTEND TO DO PLENTY! I'LL MAKE UP FOR ALL THAT LOST TIME, STARTING RIGHT NOW...
...IF THE MOST BEAUTIFUL PERSON IN THIS SCHOOL WOULD AGREE TO JOIN ME ON THIS ADVENTURE.

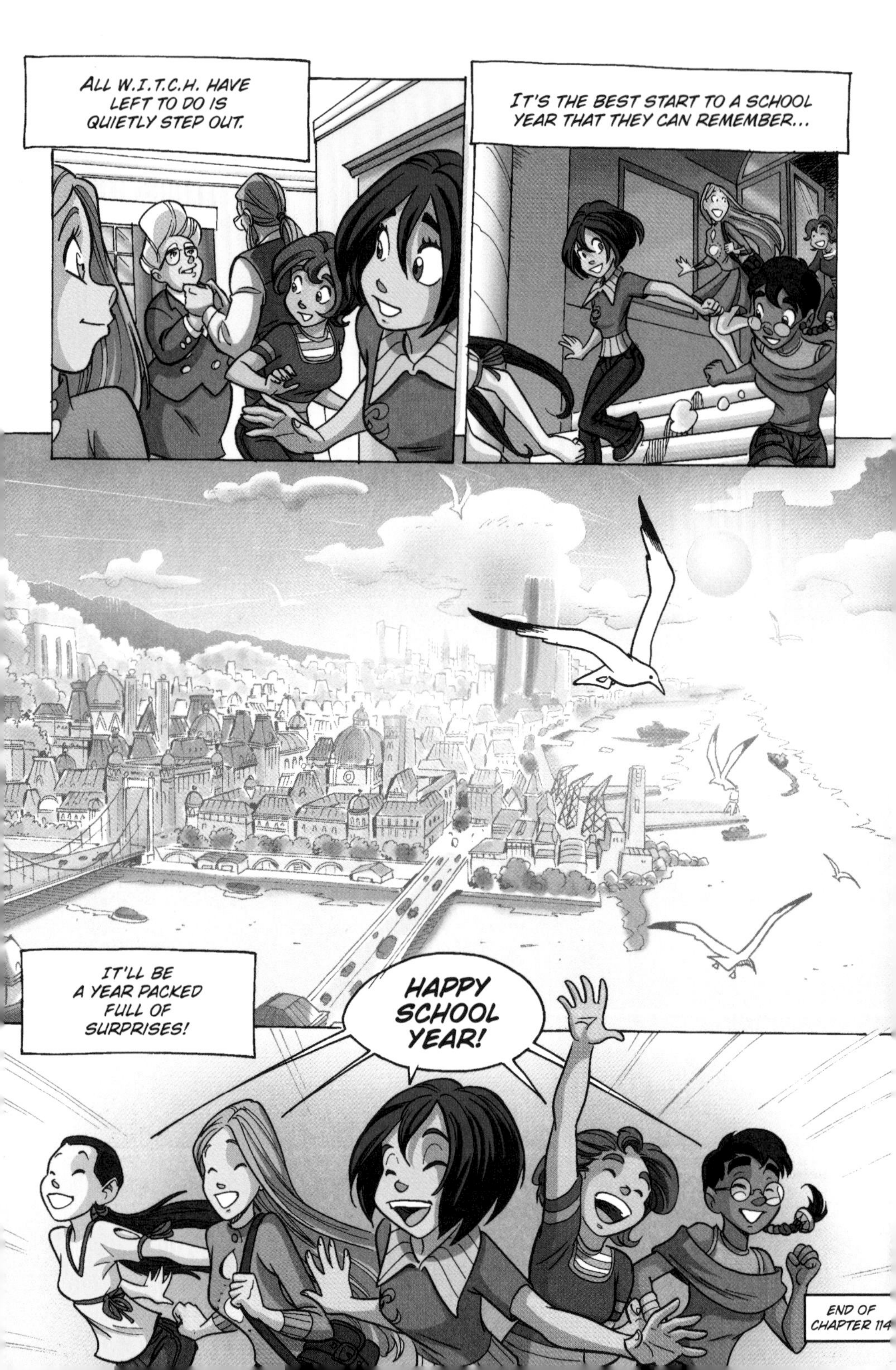
ALL W.I.T.C.H. HAVE LEFT TO DO IS QUIETLY STEP OUT.
IT'S THE BEST START TO A SCHOOL YEAR THAT THEY CAN REMEMBER...
IT'LL BE A YEAR PACKED FULL OF SURPRISES!
HAPPY SCHOOL YEAR!
END OF CHAPTER 114

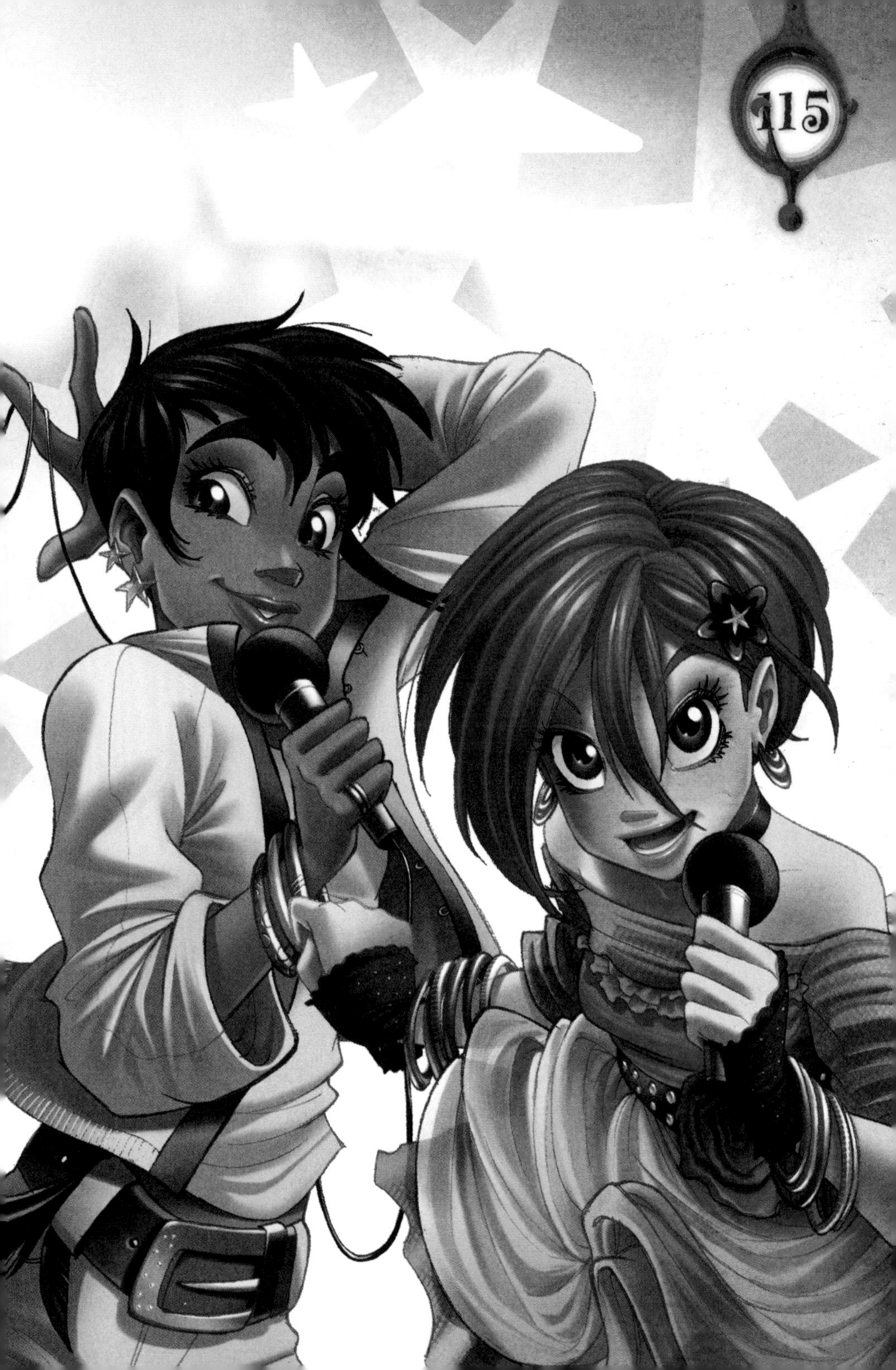

Will Irma Taranee Cornelia Hay Lin

A Special Journey

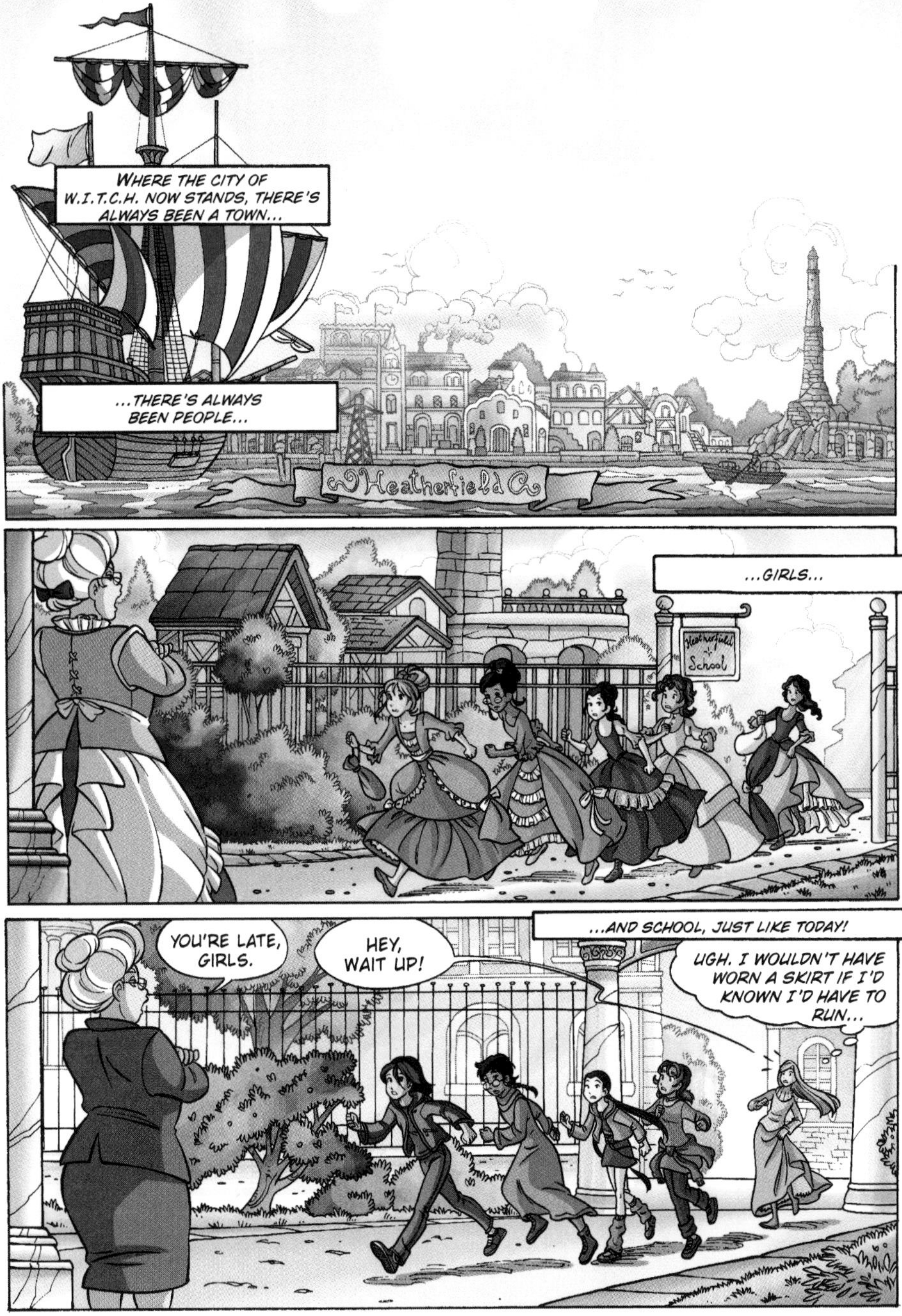
WHERE THE CITY OF W.I.T.C.H. NOW STANDS, THERE'S ALWAYS BEEN A TOWN...
...THERE'S ALWAYS BEEN PEOPLE...
Heatherfield
...GIRLS...
Heatherfield School
YOU'RE LATE, GIRLS.
HEY, WAIT UP!
...AND SCHOOL, JUST LIKE TODAY!
UGH. I WOULDN'T HAVE WORN A SKIRT IF I'D KNOWN I'D HAVE TO RUN...

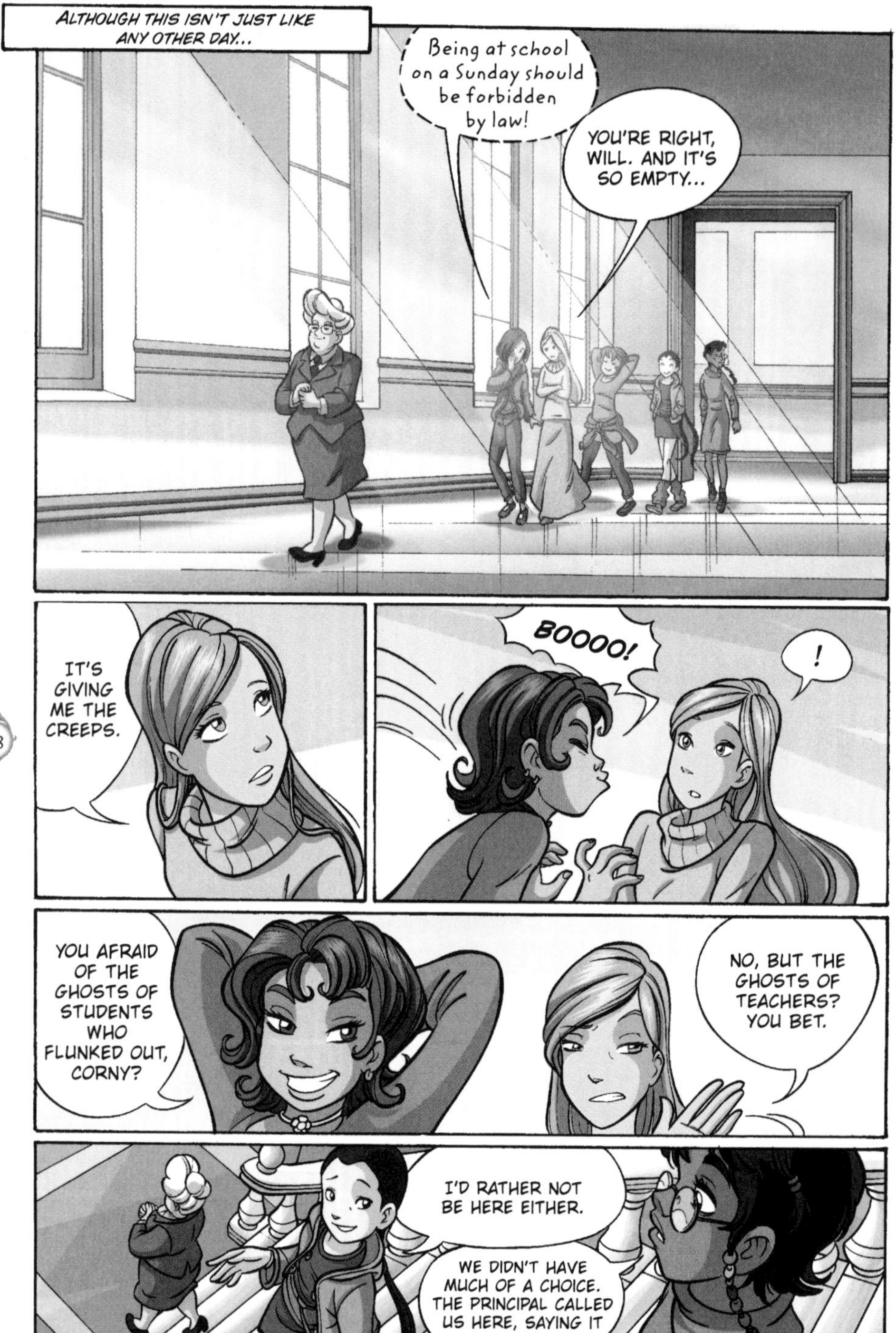
ALTHOUGH THIS ISN'T JUST LIKE ANY OTHER DAY...
Being at school on a Sunday should be forbidden by law!
YOU'RE RIGHT, WILL. AND IT'S SO EMPTY...
IT'S GIVING ME THE CREEPS.
BOOOO!
!
YOU AFRAID OF THE GHOSTS OF STUDENTS WHO FLUNKED OUT, CORNY?
NO, BUT THE GHOSTS OF TEACHERS? YOU BET.
I'D RATHER NOT BE HERE EITHER.
WE DIDN'T HAVE MUCH OF A CHOICE. THE PRINCIPAL CALLED US HERE, SAYING IT WAS URGENT...

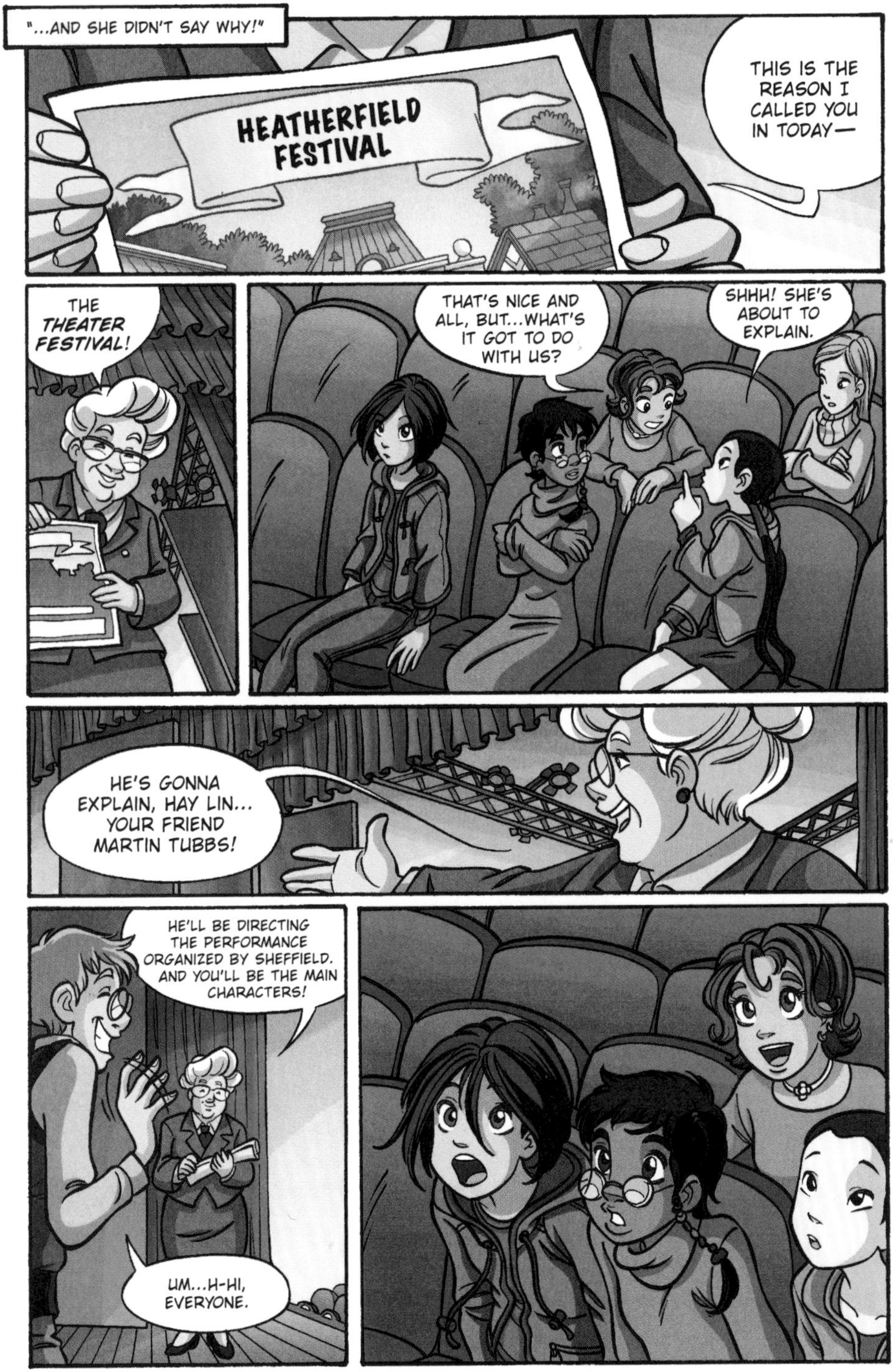
"...AND SHE DIDN'T SAY WHY!"
HEATHERFIELD FESTIVAL
THIS IS THE REASON I CALLED YOU IN TODAY—
THE *THEATER FESTIVAL!*
THAT'S NICE AND ALL, BUT...WHAT'S IT GOT TO DO WITH US?
SHHH! SHE'S ABOUT TO EXPLAIN.
HE'S GONNA EXPLAIN, HAY LIN... YOUR FRIEND MARTIN TUBBS!
HE'LL BE DIRECTING THE PERFORMANCE ORGANIZED BY SHEFFIELD. AND YOU'LL BE THE MAIN CHARACTERS!
UM...H-HI, EVERYONE.

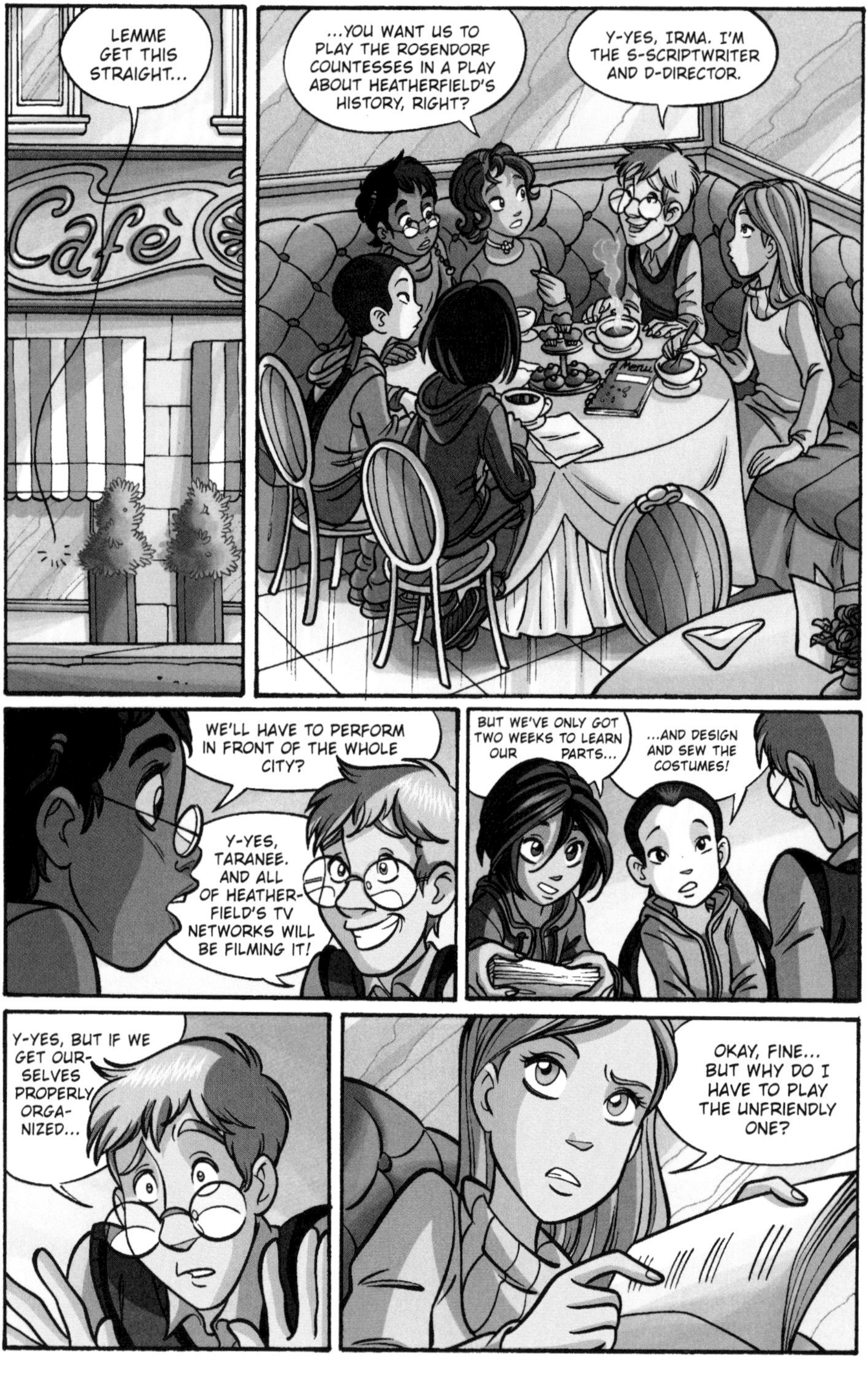
LEMME GET THIS STRAIGHT...
...YOU WANT US TO PLAY THE ROSENDORF COUNTESSES IN A PLAY ABOUT HEATHERFIELD'S HISTORY, RIGHT?
Y-YES, IRMA. I'M THE S-SCRIPTWRITER AND D-DIRECTOR.
WE'LL HAVE TO PERFORM IN FRONT OF THE WHOLE CITY?
Y-YES, TARANEE. AND ALL OF HEATHER-FIELD'S TV NETWORKS WILL BE FILMING IT!
BUT WE'VE ONLY GOT TWO WEEKS TO LEARN OUR PARTS...
...AND DESIGN AND SEW THE COSTUMES!
Y-YES, BUT IF WE GET OUR-SELVES PROPERLY ORGA-NIZED...
OKAY, FINE... BUT WHY DO I HAVE TO PLAY THE UNFRIENDLY ONE?

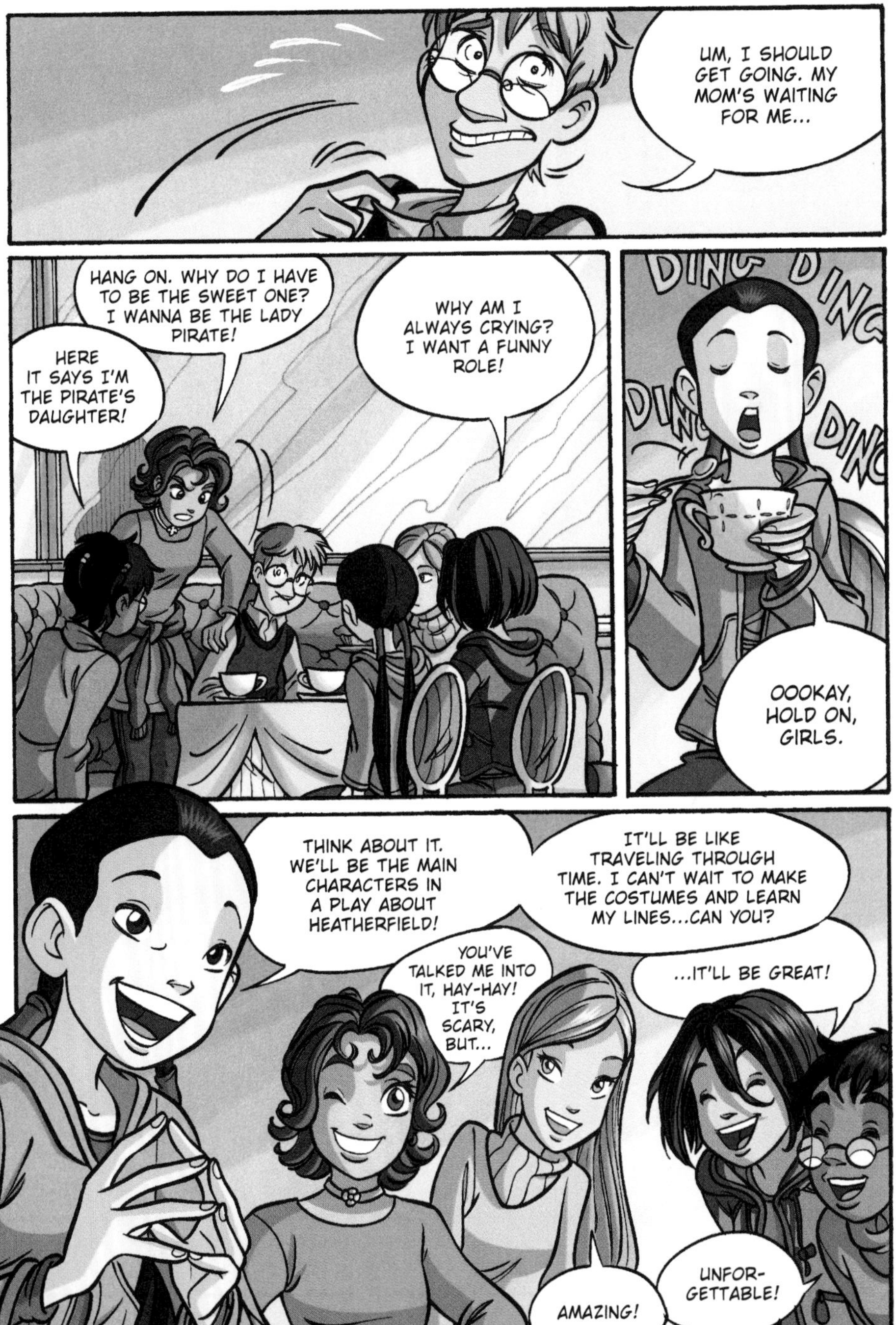
UM, I SHOULD GET GOING. MY MOM'S WAITING FOR ME...
HANG ON. WHY DO I HAVE TO BE THE SWEET ONE? I WANNA BE THE LADY PIRATE!
HERE IT SAYS I'M THE PIRATE'S DAUGHTER!
WHY AM I ALWAYS CRYING? I WANT A FUNNY ROLE!
DING DING
DING DING
OOOKAY, HOLD ON, GIRLS.
THINK ABOUT IT. WE'LL BE THE MAIN CHARACTERS IN A PLAY ABOUT HEATHERFIELD!
IT'LL BE LIKE TRAVELING THROUGH TIME. I CAN'T WAIT TO MAKE THE COSTUMES AND LEARN MY LINES...CAN YOU?
YOU'VE TALKED ME INTO IT, HAY-HAY! IT'S SCARY, BUT...
...IT'LL BE GREAT!
AMAZING!
UNFOR-GETTABLE!

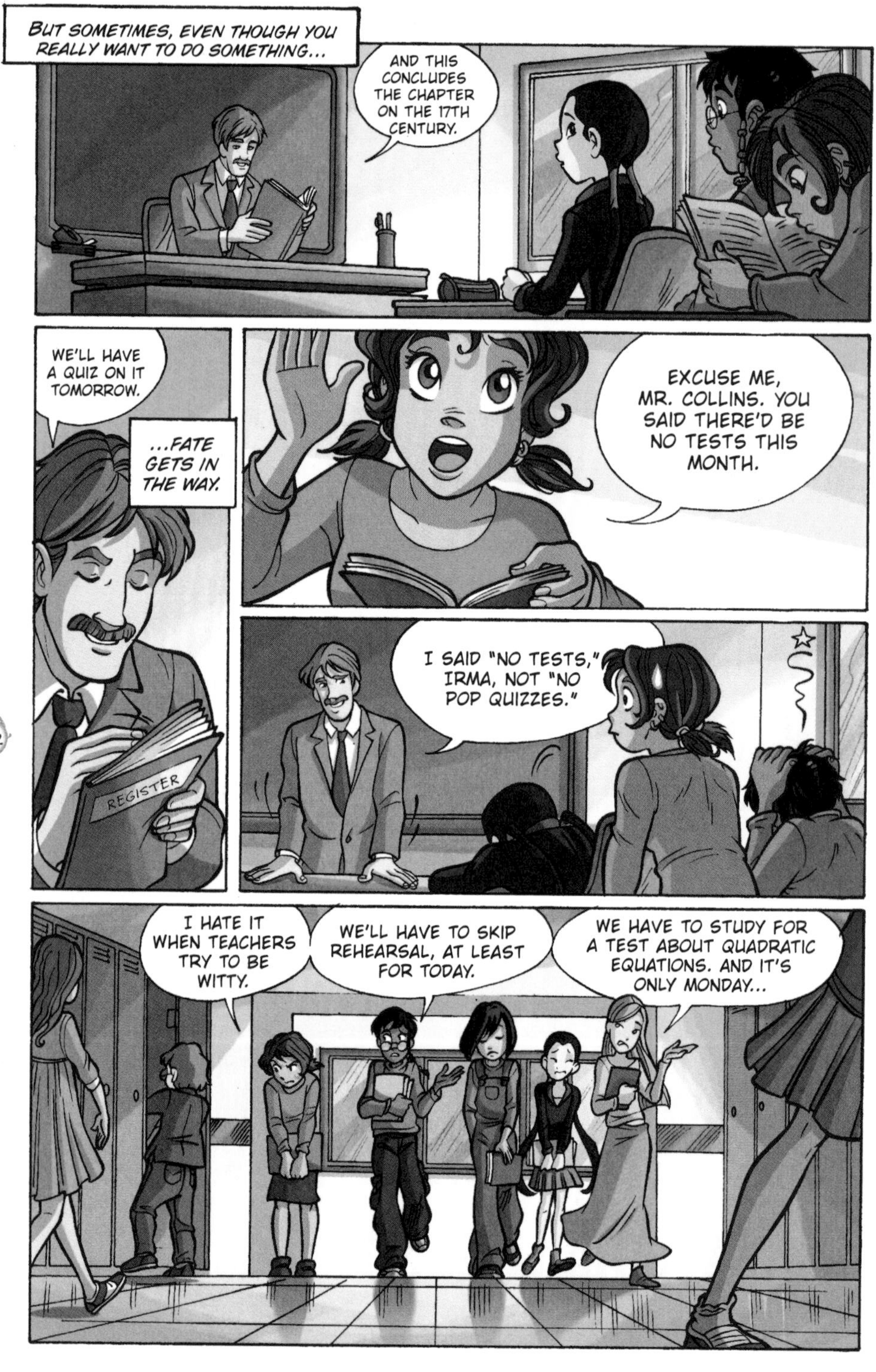

BUT SOMETIMES, EVEN THOUGH YOU REALLY WANT TO DO SOMETHING...
AND THIS CONCLUDES THE CHAPTER ON THE 17TH CENTURY.
WE'LL HAVE A QUIZ ON IT TOMORROW.
...FATE GETS IN THE WAY.
REGISTER
EXCUSE ME, MR. COLLINS. YOU SAID THERE'D BE NO TESTS THIS MONTH.
I SAID "NO TESTS," IRMA, NOT "NO POP QUIZZES."
I HATE IT WHEN TEACHERS TRY TO BE WITTY.
WE'LL HAVE TO SKIP REHEARSAL, AT LEAST FOR TODAY.
WE HAVE TO STUDY FOR A TEST ABOUT QUADRATIC EQUATIONS. AND IT'S ONLY MONDAY...

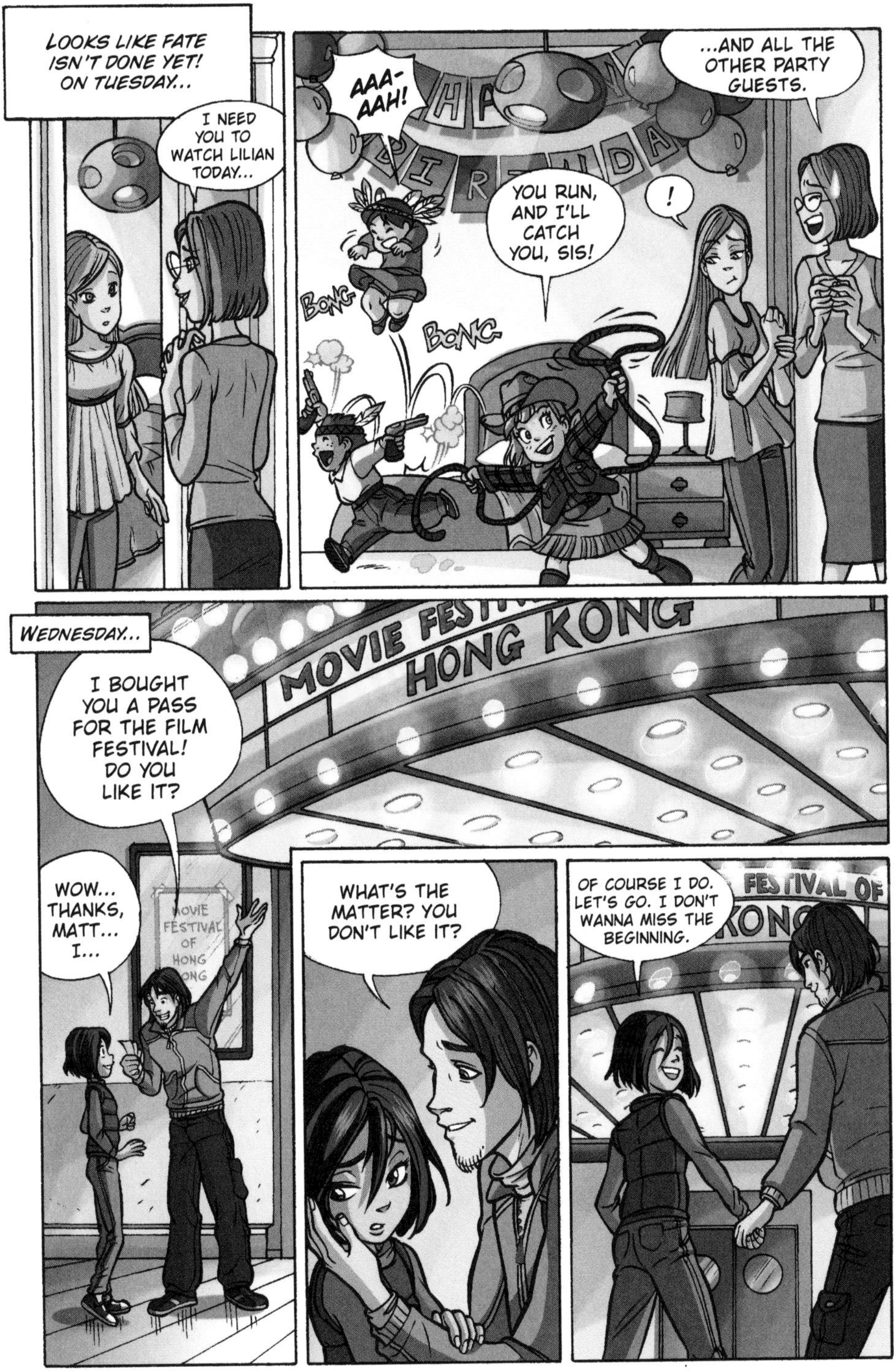
LOOKS LIKE FATE ISN'T DONE YET! ON TUESDAY...
I NEED YOU TO WATCH LILIAN TODAY...
AAA-AAAH!
...AND ALL THE OTHER PARTY GUESTS.
YOU RUN, AND I'LL CATCH YOU, SIS!
!
BONG
BONG
WEDNESDAY...
MOVIE FESTIV
HONG KONG
I BOUGHT YOU A PASS FOR THE FILM FESTIVAL! DO YOU LIKE IT?
WOW... THANKS, MATT... I...
MOVIE FESTIVAL OF HONG ONG
WHAT'S THE MATTER? YOU DON'T LIKE IT?
OF COURSE I DO. LET'S GO. I DON'T WANNA MISS THE BEGINNING.
FESTIVAL OF
KONG

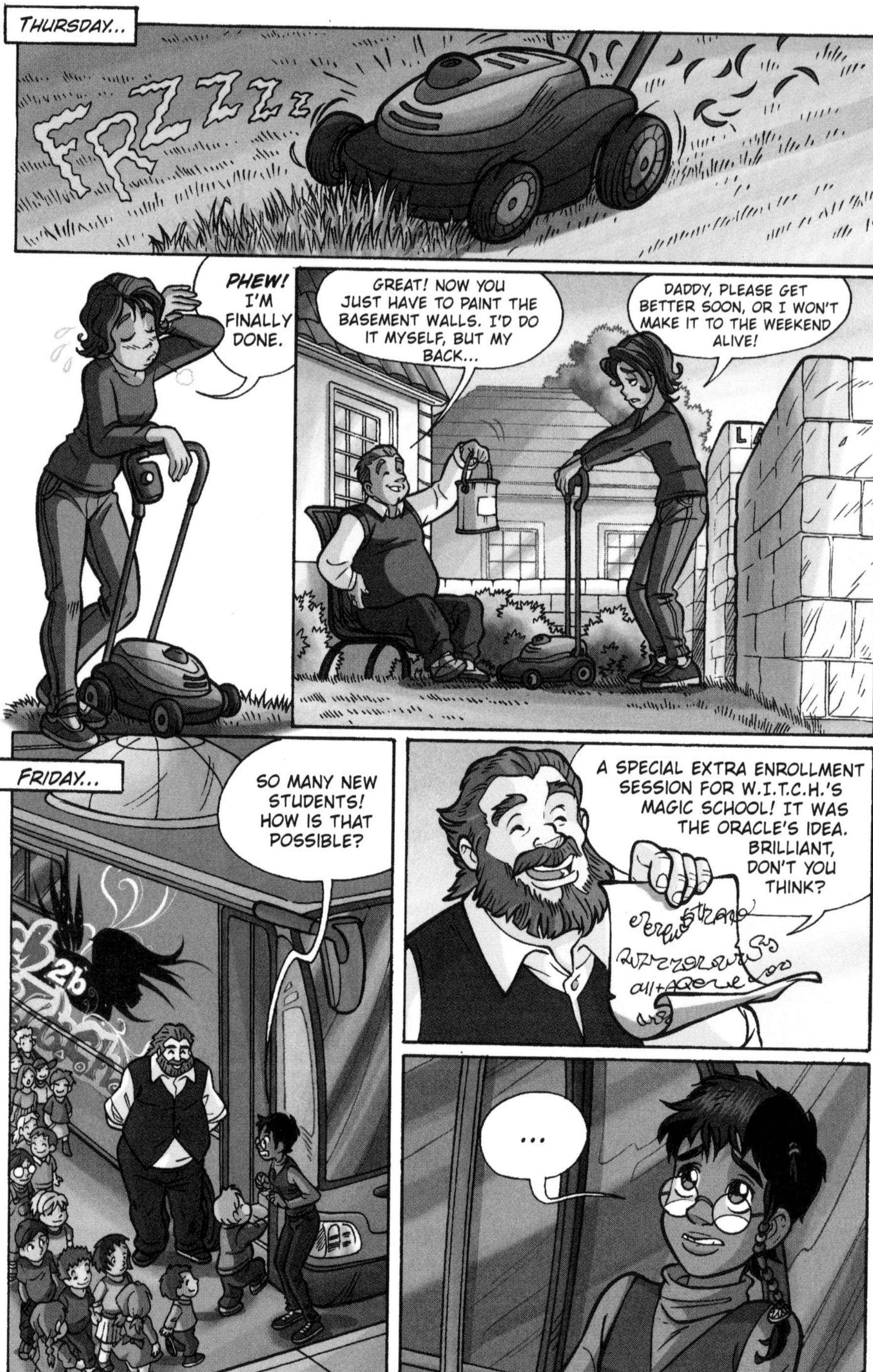
THURSDAY...
FRZZZz
PHEW! I'M FINALLY DONE.
GREAT! NOW YOU JUST HAVE TO PAINT THE BASEMENT WALLS. I'D DO IT MYSELF, BUT MY BACK...
DADDY, PLEASE GET BETTER SOON, OR I WON'T MAKE IT TO THE WEEKEND ALIVE!
FRIDAY...
SO MANY NEW STUDENTS! HOW IS THAT POSSIBLE?
A SPECIAL EXTRA ENROLLMENT SESSION FOR W.I.T.C.H.'S MAGIC SCHOOL! IT WAS THE ORACLE'S IDEA. BRILLIANT, DON'T YOU THINK?
...

SATURDAY...
ALMOST DONE.
THE SILVER DRAGON
CINESE RESTAURANT
THESE COSTUMES WILL BE MY MASTER-PIECE.
IT TOOK ME A WEEK...
...JUST TO PREPARE THE SKETCHES. I CAN'T WAIT TO SHOW THE OTHERS—
KRA-BOOM
OH NO... NONONONO!
...
ALL MY SKETCHES... THEY'RE LOST!
THE SILVER DRAGON

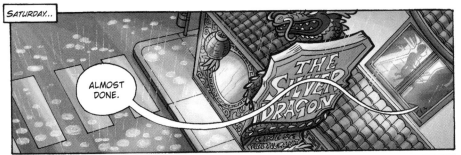

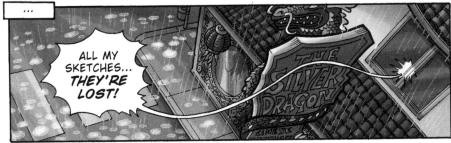

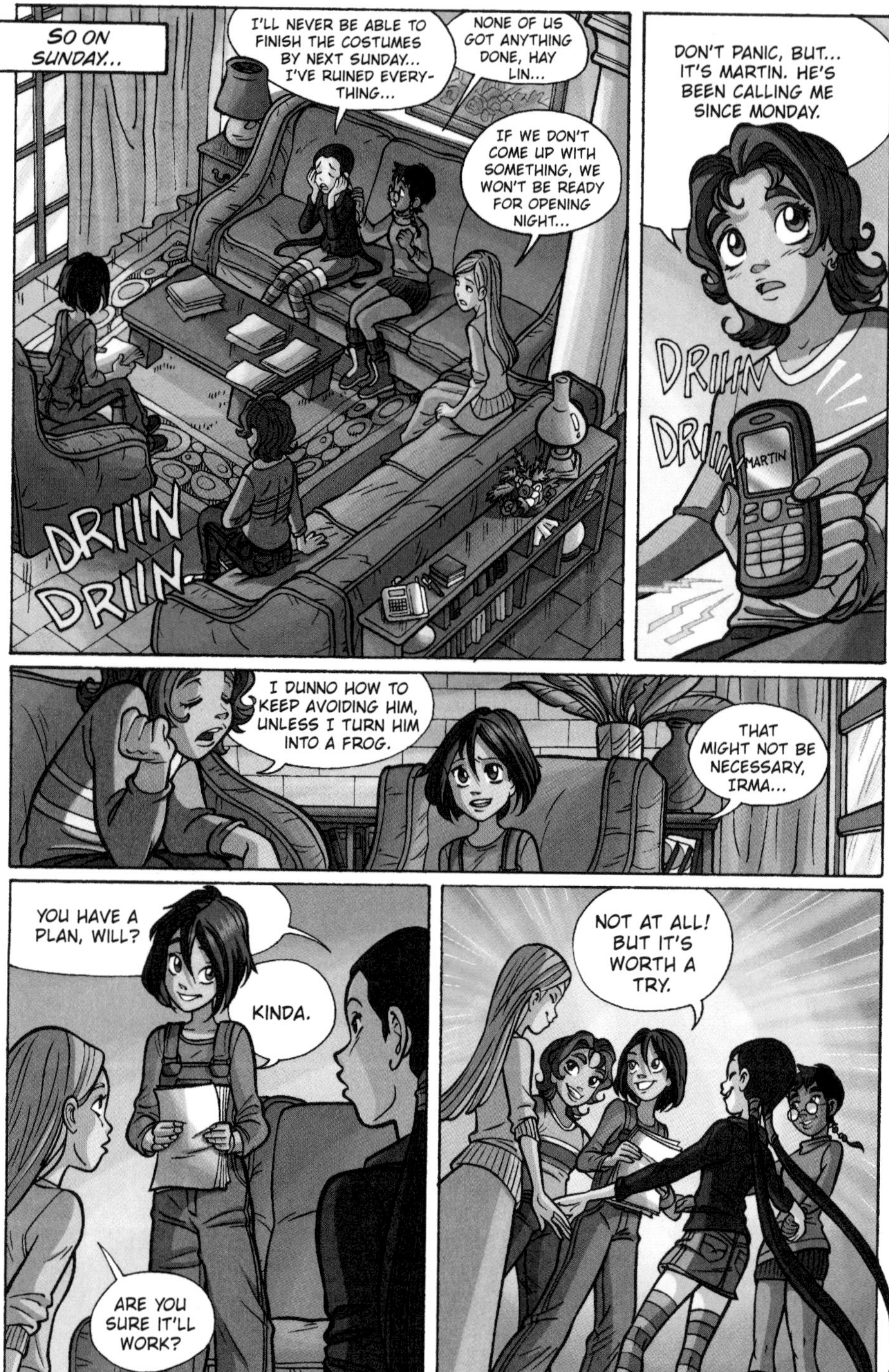
SO ON SUNDAY...
I'LL NEVER BE ABLE TO FINISH THE COSTUMES BY NEXT SUNDAY... I'VE RUINED EVERY-THING...
NONE OF US GOT ANYTHING DONE, HAY LIN...
IF WE DON'T COME UP WITH SOMETHING, WE WON'T BE READY FOR OPENING NIGHT...
DRIIN DRIIN
DON'T PANIC, BUT... IT'S MARTIN. HE'S BEEN CALLING ME SINCE MONDAY.
DRIIN DRIIN
MARTIN
I DUNNO HOW TO KEEP AVOIDING HIM, UNLESS I TURN HIM INTO A FROG.
THAT MIGHT NOT BE NECESSARY, IRMA...
YOU HAVE A PLAN, WILL?
KINDA.
ARE YOU SURE IT'LL WORK?
NOT AT ALL! BUT IT'S WORTH A TRY.

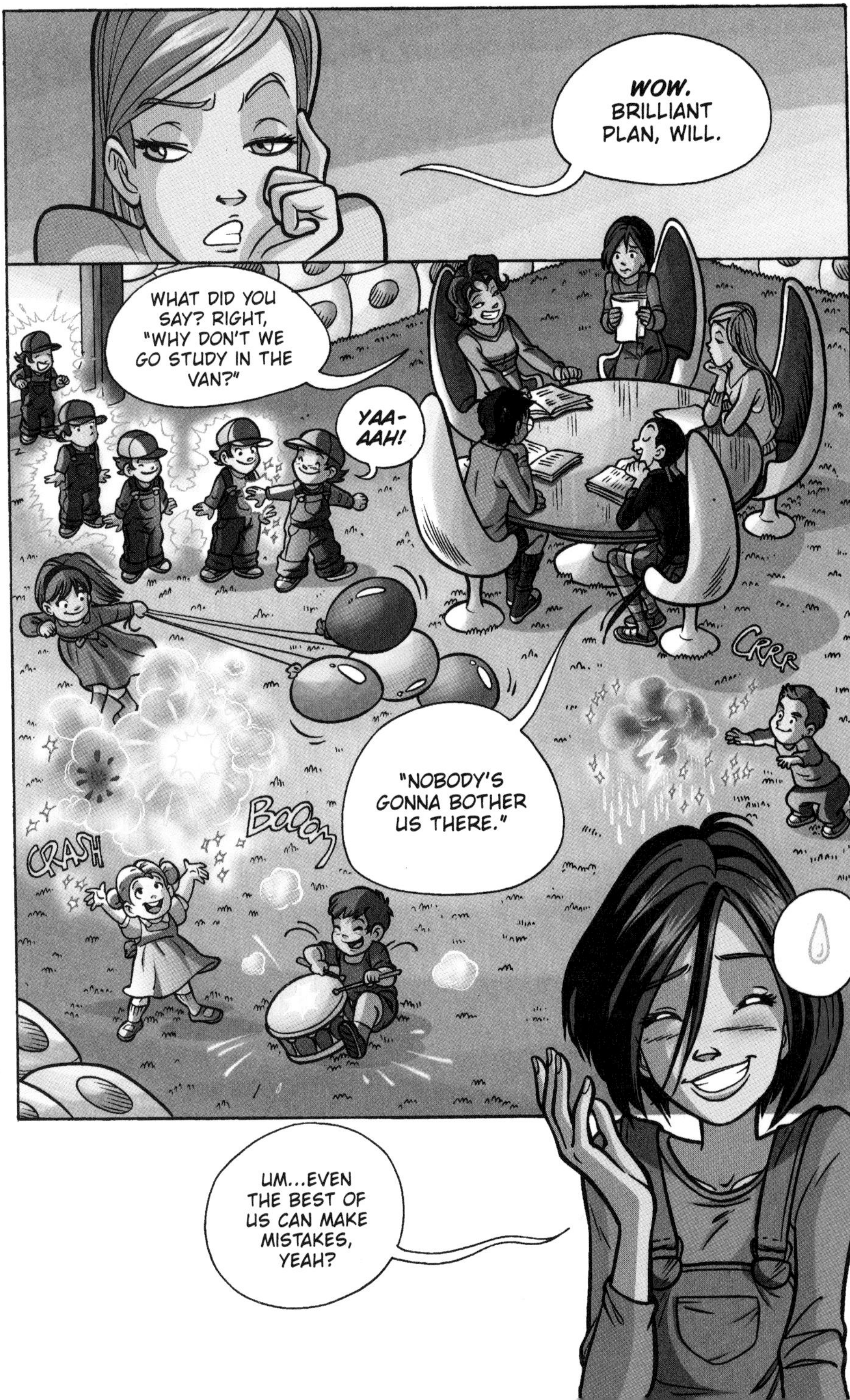
WOW. BRILLIANT PLAN, WILL.
WHAT DID YOU SAY? RIGHT, "WHY DON'T WE GO STUDY IN THE VAN?"
YAA-AAH!
CRRR
"NOBODY'S GONNA BOTHER US THERE."
BOOOM
CRASH
UM...EVEN THE BEST OF US CAN MAKE MISTAKES, YEAH?

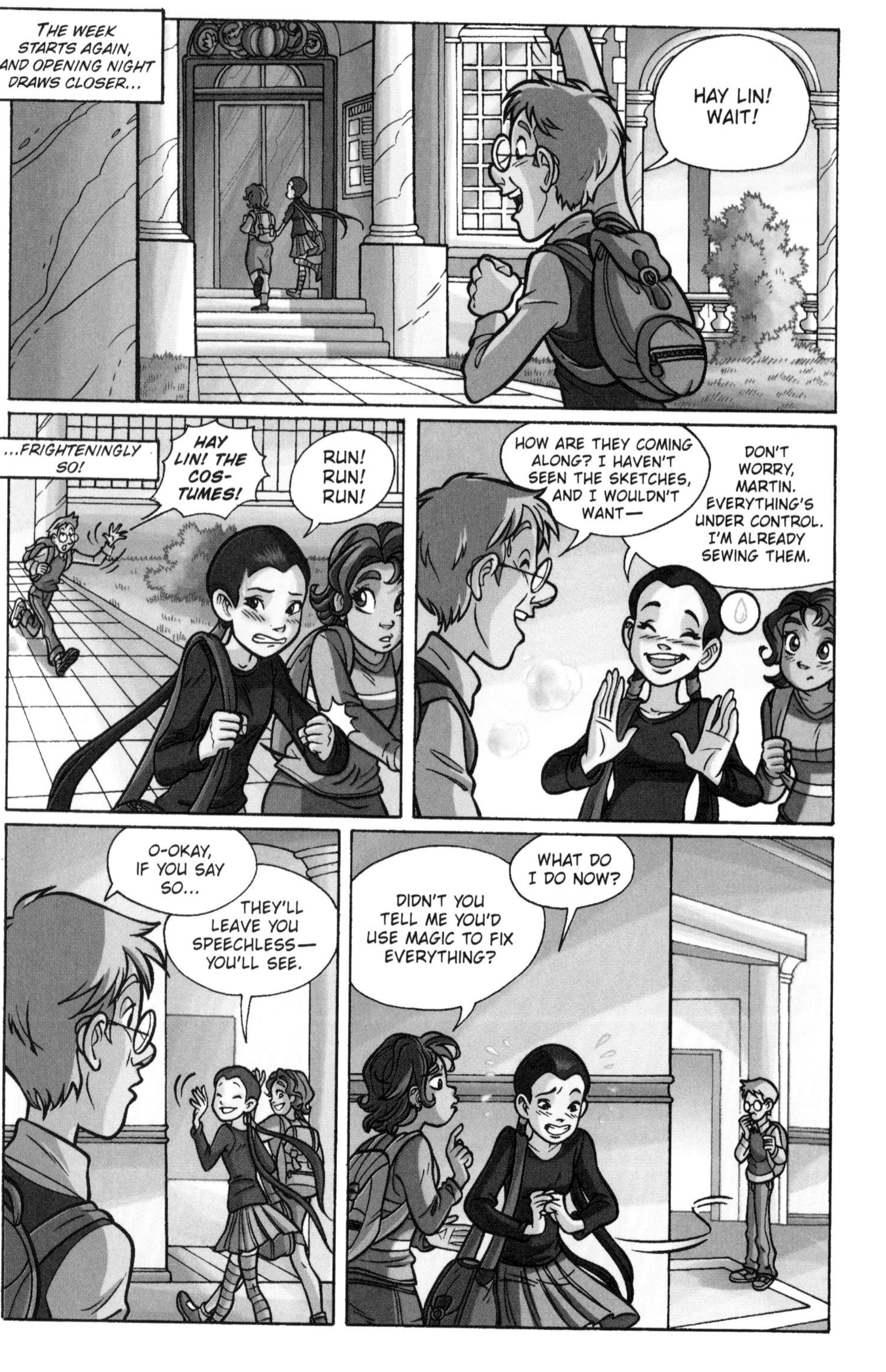
THE WEEK STARTS AGAIN, AND OPENING NIGHT DRAWS CLOSER...
HAY LIN! WAIT!
...FRIGHTENINGLY SO!
HAY LIN! THE COS-TUMES!
RUN! RUN! RUN!
HOW ARE THEY COMING ALONG? I HAVEN'T SEEN THE SKETCHES, AND I WOULDN'T WANT—
DON'T WORRY, MARTIN. EVERYTHING'S UNDER CONTROL. I'M ALREADY SEWING THEM.
O-OKAY, IF YOU SAY SO...
THEY'LL LEAVE YOU SPEECHLESS— YOU'LL SEE.
WHAT DO I DO NOW?
DIDN'T YOU TELL ME YOU'D USE MAGIC TO FIX EVERYTHING?

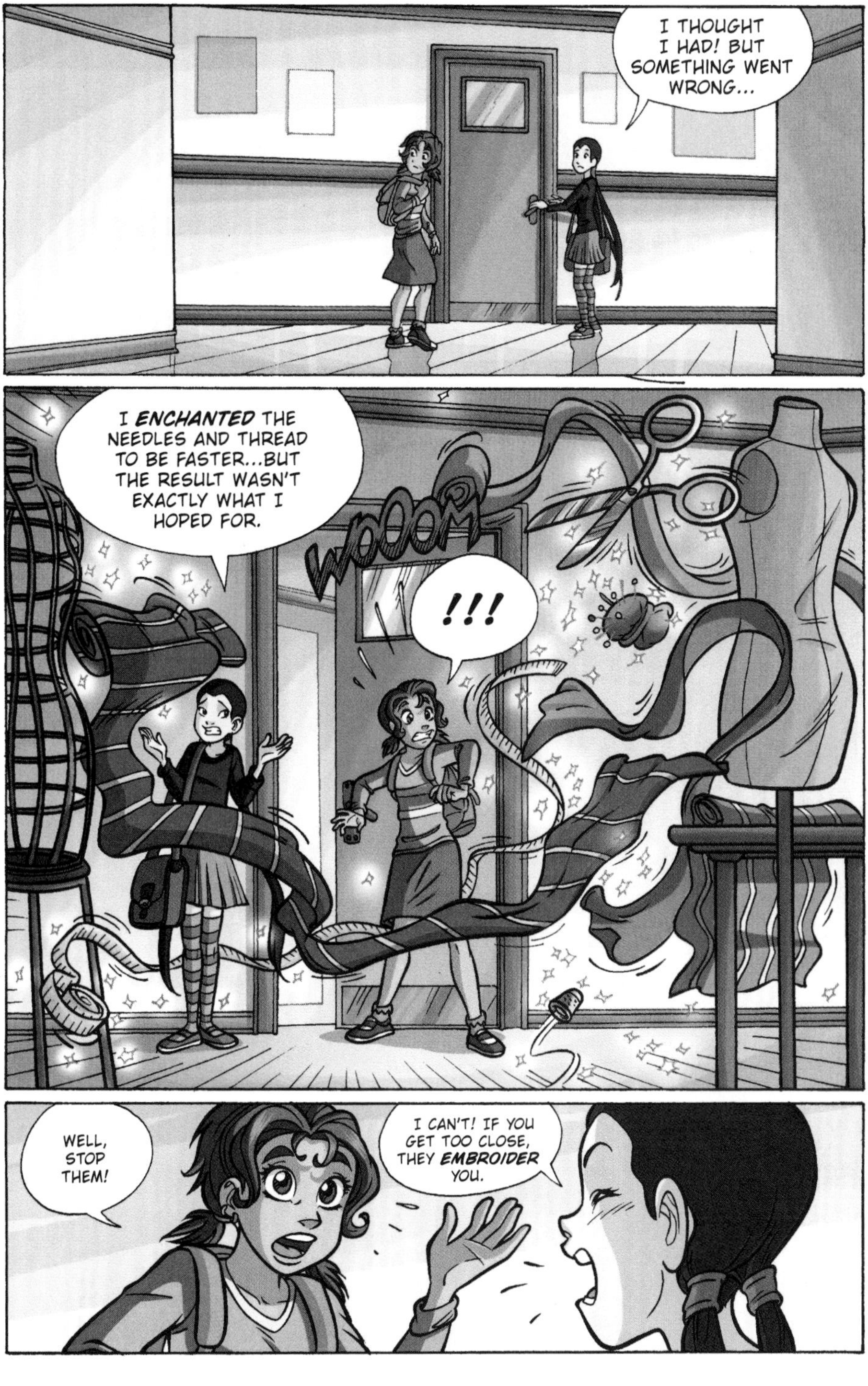
I THOUGHT I HAD! BUT SOMETHING WENT WRONG...
I *ENCHANTED* THE NEEDLES AND THREAD TO BE FASTER...BUT THE RESULT WASN'T EXACTLY WHAT I HOPED FOR.
WOOOM
!!!
WELL, STOP THEM!
I CAN'T! IF YOU GET TOO CLOSE, THEY *EMBROIDER* YOU.

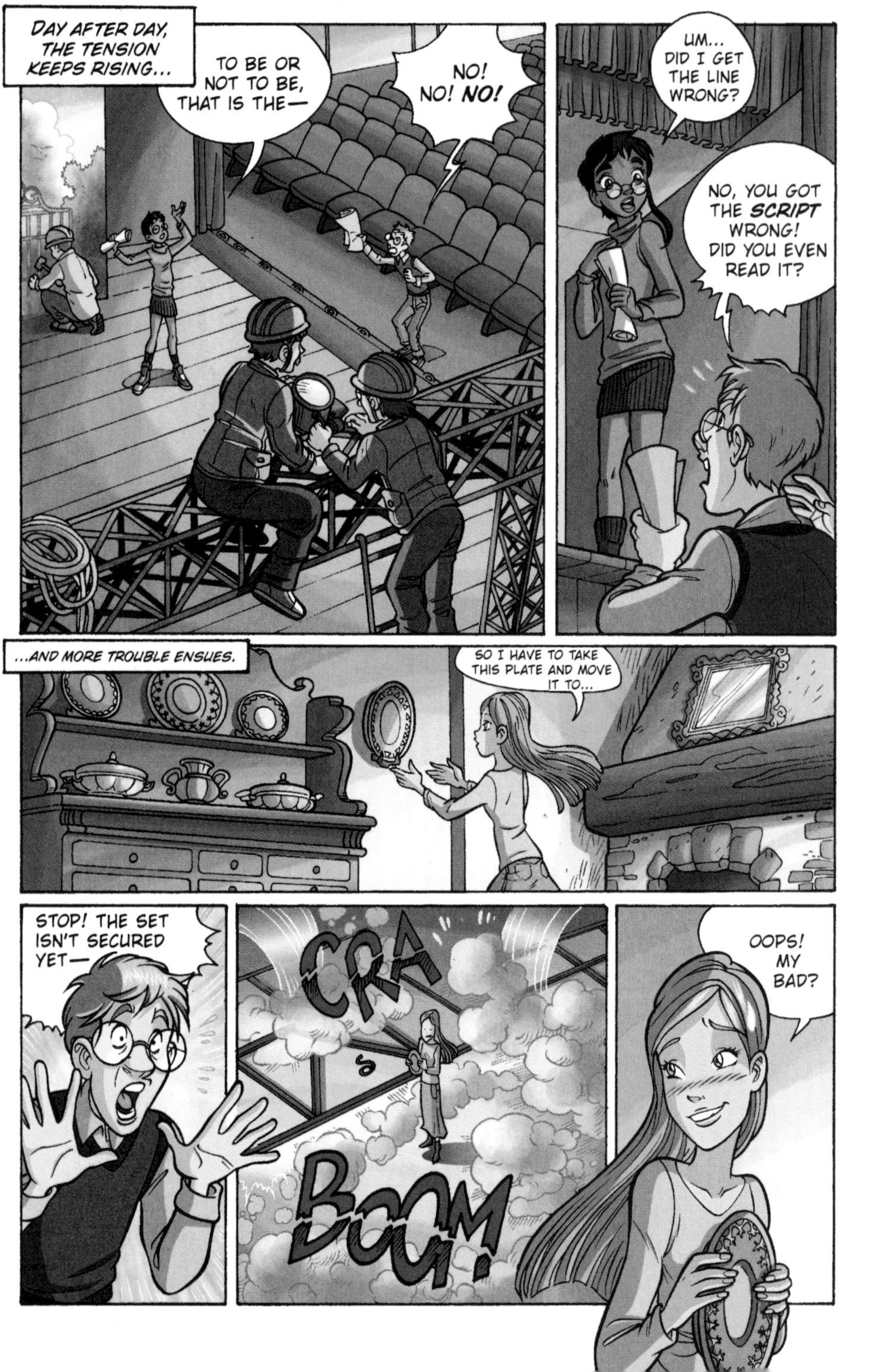
DAY AFTER DAY, THE TENSION KEEPS RISING...
TO BE OR NOT TO BE, THAT IS THE—
NO! NO! NO!
UM... DID I GET THE LINE WRONG?
NO, YOU GOT THE SCRIPT WRONG! DID YOU EVEN READ IT?
...AND MORE TROUBLE ENSUES.
SO I HAVE TO TAKE THIS PLATE AND MOVE IT TO...
STOP! THE SET ISN'T SECURED YET—
CRAS
BOOM!
OOPS! MY BAD?

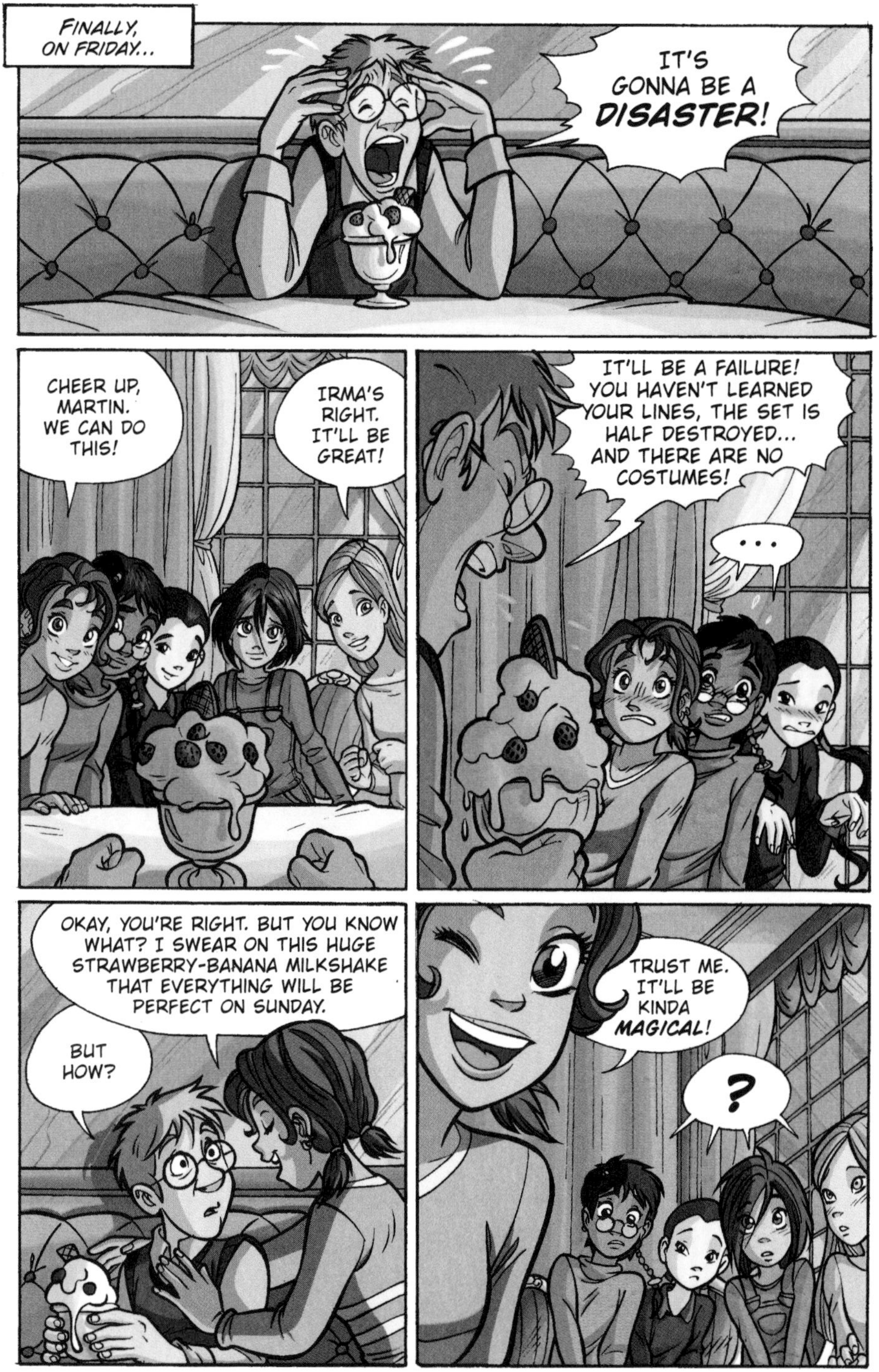
FINALLY, ON FRIDAY...
IT'S GONNA BE A DISASTER!
CHEER UP, MARTIN. WE CAN DO THIS!
IRMA'S RIGHT. IT'LL BE GREAT!
IT'LL BE A FAILURE! YOU HAVEN'T LEARNED YOUR LINES, THE SET IS HALF DESTROYED... AND THERE ARE NO COSTUMES!
...
OKAY, YOU'RE RIGHT. BUT YOU KNOW WHAT? I SWEAR ON THIS HUGE STRAWBERRY-BANANA MILKSHAKE THAT EVERYTHING WILL BE PERFECT ON SUNDAY.
BUT HOW?
TRUST ME. IT'LL BE KINDA MAGICAL!
?

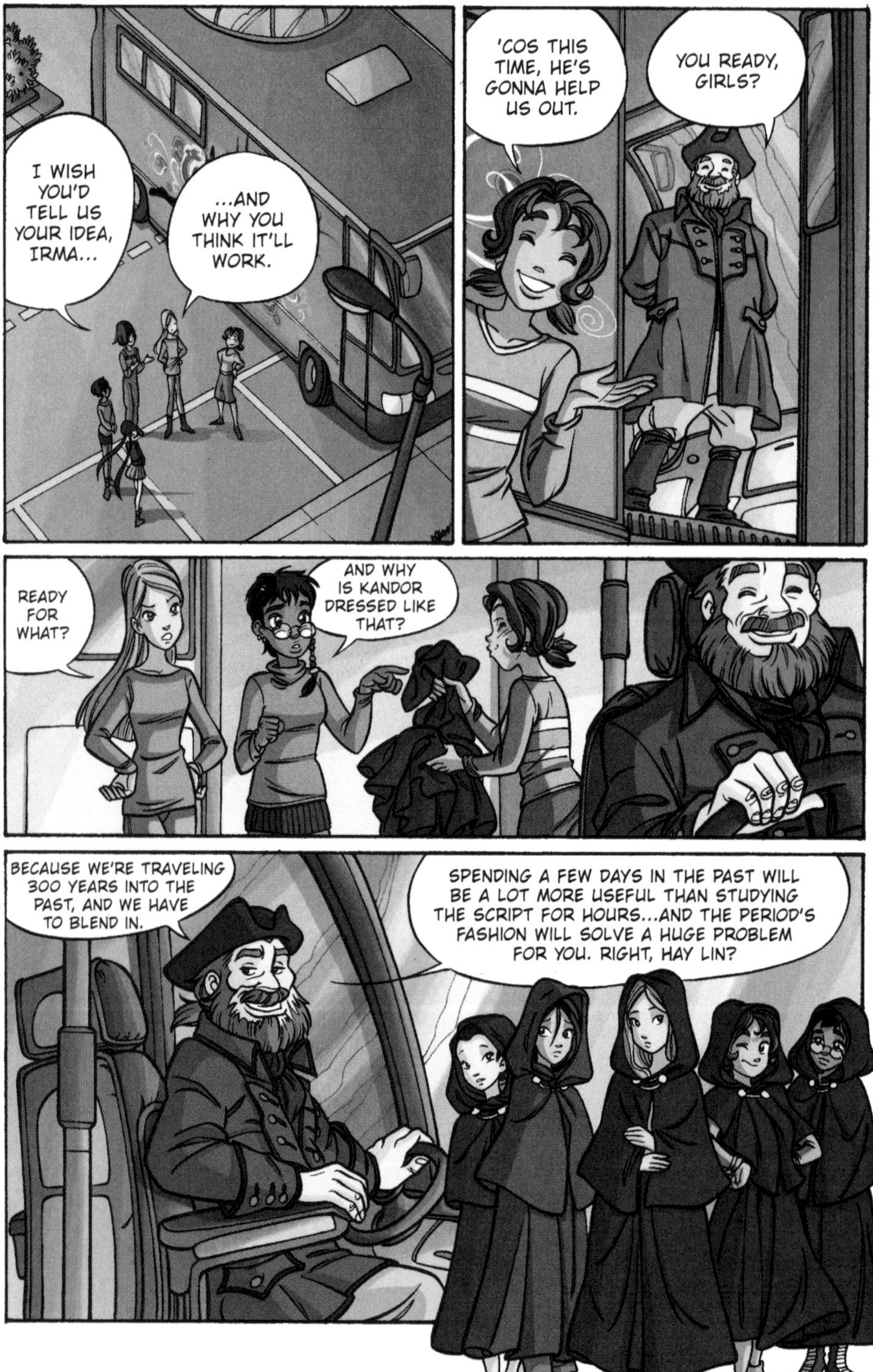
I WISH YOU'D TELL US YOUR IDEA, IRMA...
...AND WHY YOU THINK IT'LL WORK.
'COS THIS TIME, HE'S GONNA HELP US OUT.
YOU READY, GIRLS?
READY FOR WHAT?
AND WHY IS KANDOR DRESSED LIKE THAT?
BECAUSE WE'RE TRAVELING 300 YEARS INTO THE PAST, AND WE HAVE TO BLEND IN.
SPENDING A FEW DAYS IN THE PAST WILL BE A LOT MORE USEFUL THAN STUDYING THE SCRIPT FOR HOURS...AND THE PERIOD'S FASHION WILL SOLVE A HUGE PROBLEM FOR YOU. RIGHT, HAY LIN?

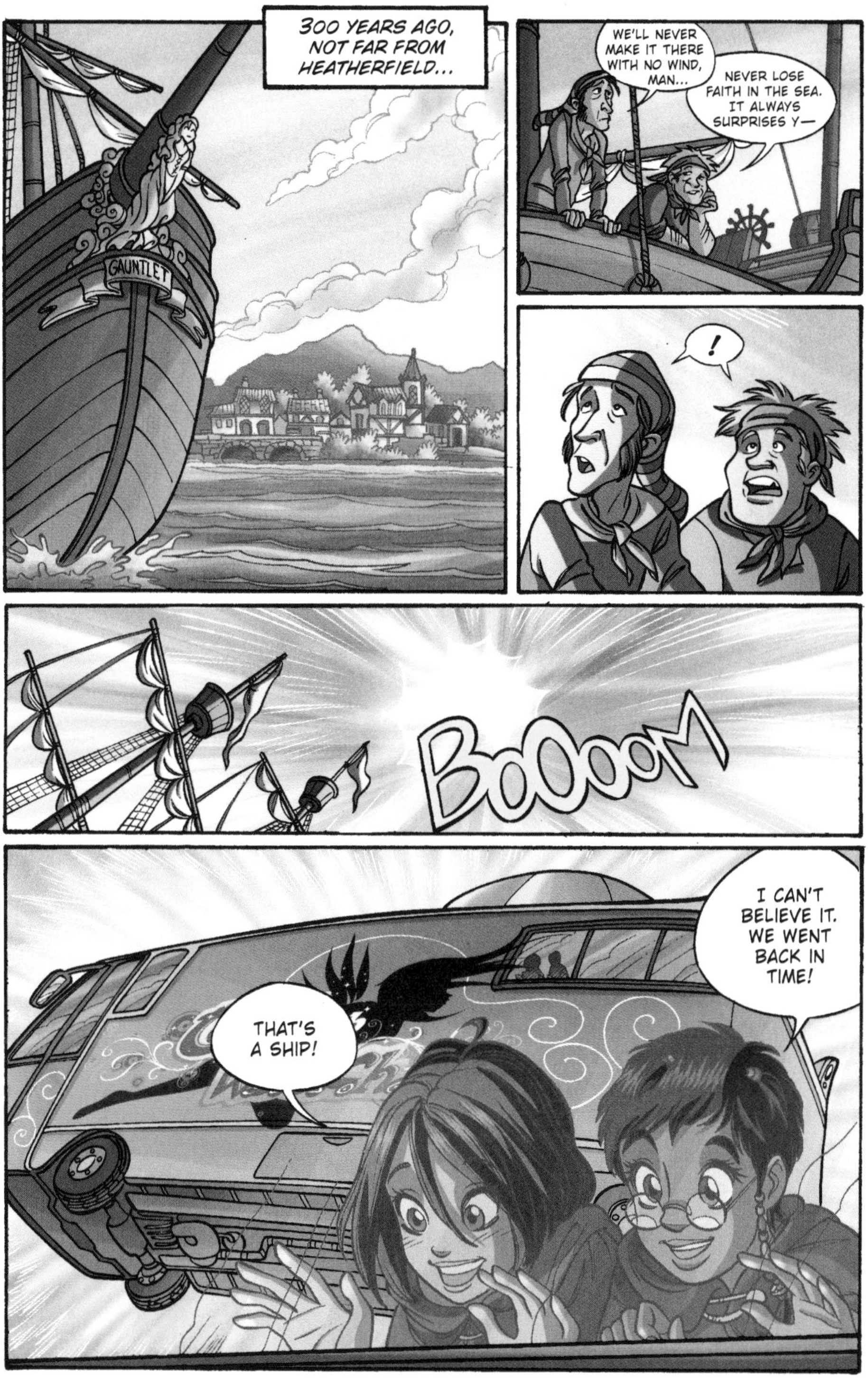

300 YEARS AGO, NOT FAR FROM HEATHERFIELD...
GAUNTLET
WE'LL NEVER MAKE IT THERE WITH NO WIND, MAN...
NEVER LOSE FAITH IN THE SEA. IT ALWAYS SURPRISES Y—
!
BoOOooM
I CAN'T BELIEVE IT. WE WENT BACK IN TIME!
THAT'S A SHIP!

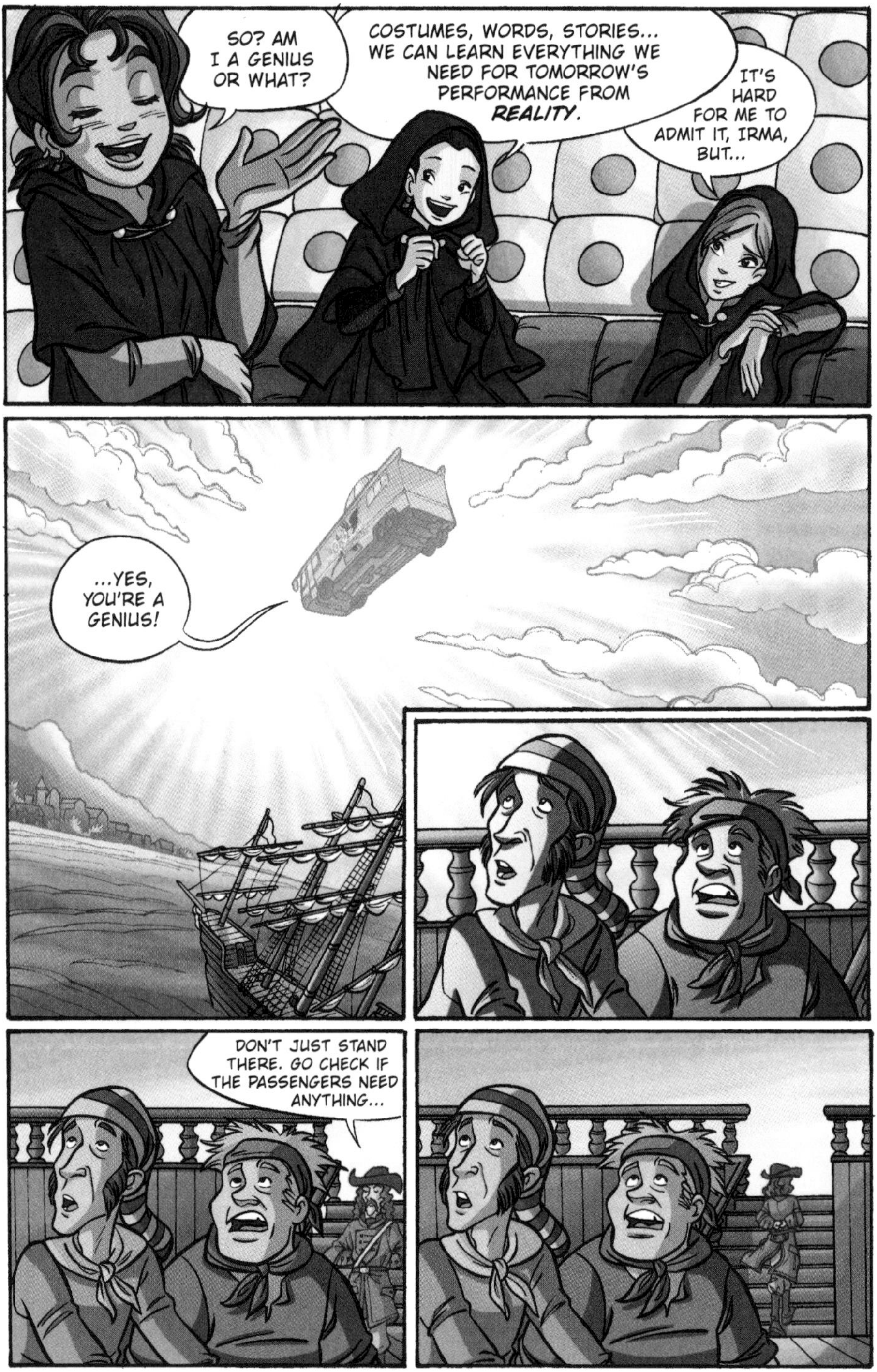
SO? AM I A GENIUS OR WHAT?
COSTUMES, WORDS, STORIES... WE CAN LEARN EVERYTHING WE NEED FOR TOMORROW'S PERFORMANCE FROM ***REALITY***.
IT'S HARD FOR ME TO ADMIT IT, IRMA, BUT...
...YES, YOU'RE A GENIUS!
DON'T JUST STAND THERE. GO CHECK IF THE PASSENGERS NEED ANYTHING...

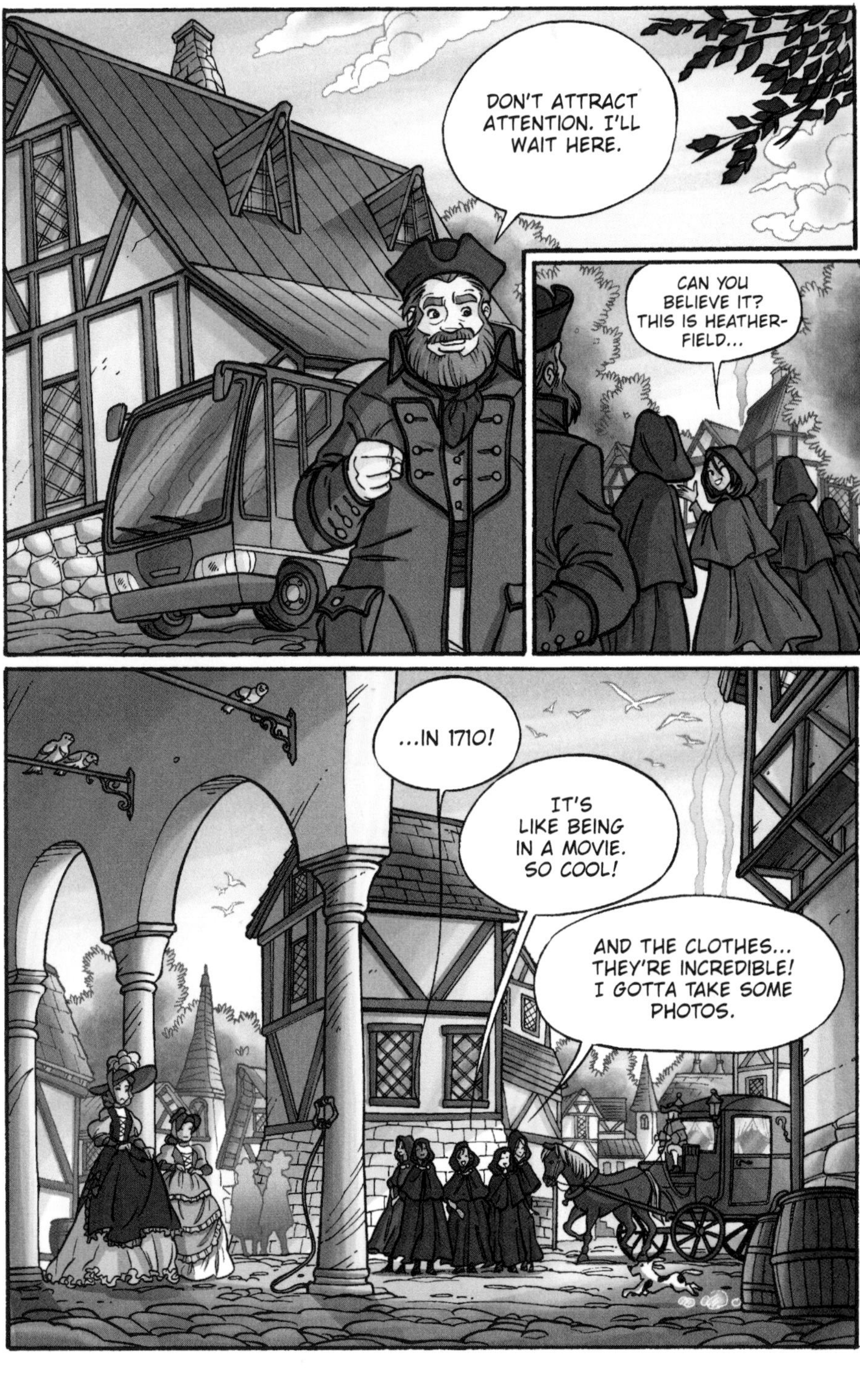
DON'T ATTRACT ATTENTION. I'LL WAIT HERE.
CAN YOU BELIEVE IT? THIS IS HEATHER-FIELD...
...IN 1710!
IT'S LIKE BEING IN A MOVIE. SO COOL!
AND THE CLOTHES... THEY'RE INCREDIBLE! I GOTTA TAKE SOME PHOTOS.

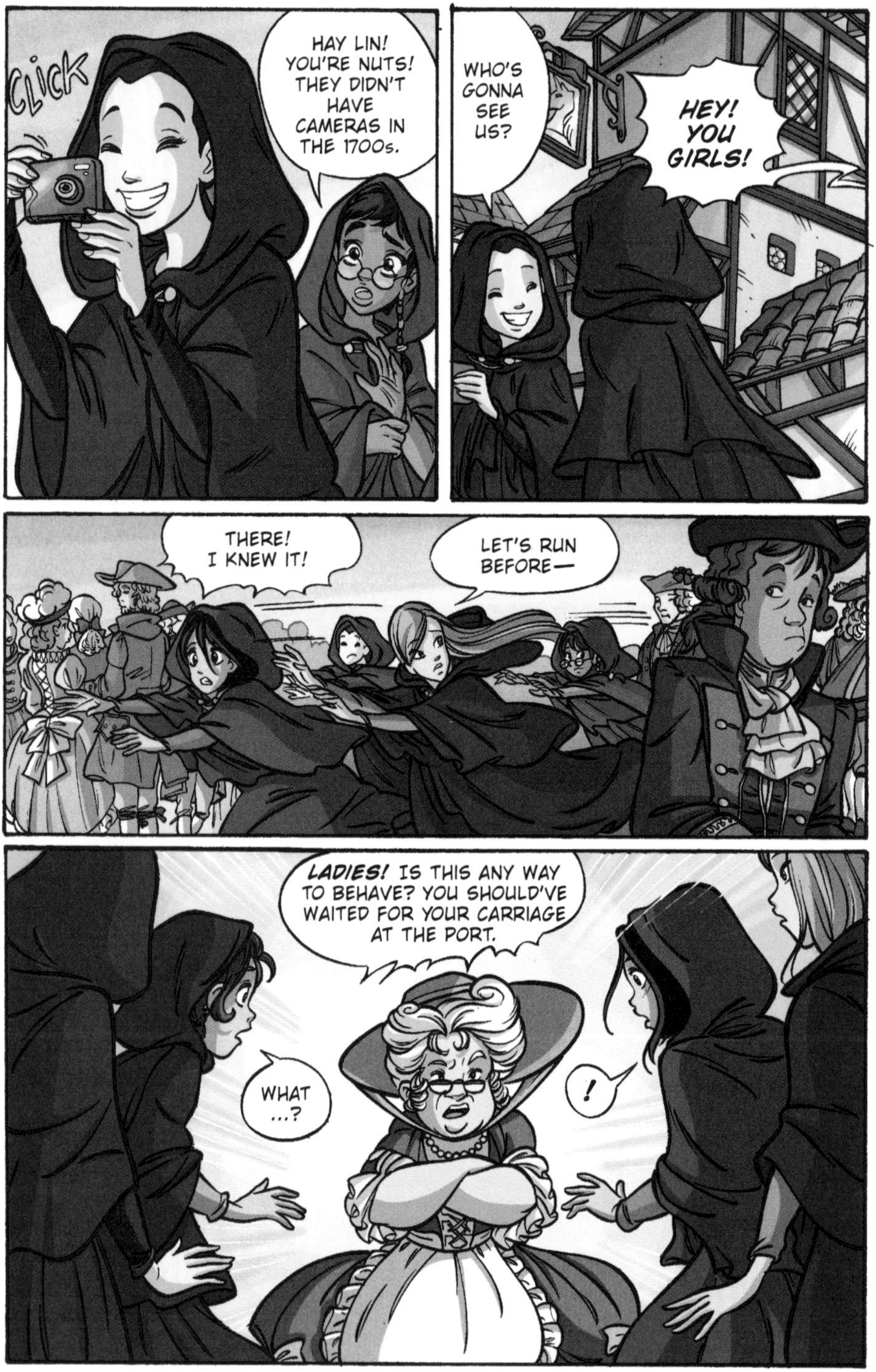
CLICK
HAY LIN! YOU'RE NUTS! THEY DIDN'T HAVE CAMERAS IN THE 1700s.
WHO'S GONNA SEE US?
HEY! YOU GIRLS!
THERE! I KNEW IT!
LET'S RUN BEFORE—
LADIES! IS THIS ANY WAY TO BEHAVE? YOU SHOULD'VE WAITED FOR YOUR CARRIAGE AT THE PORT.
WHAT ...?
!

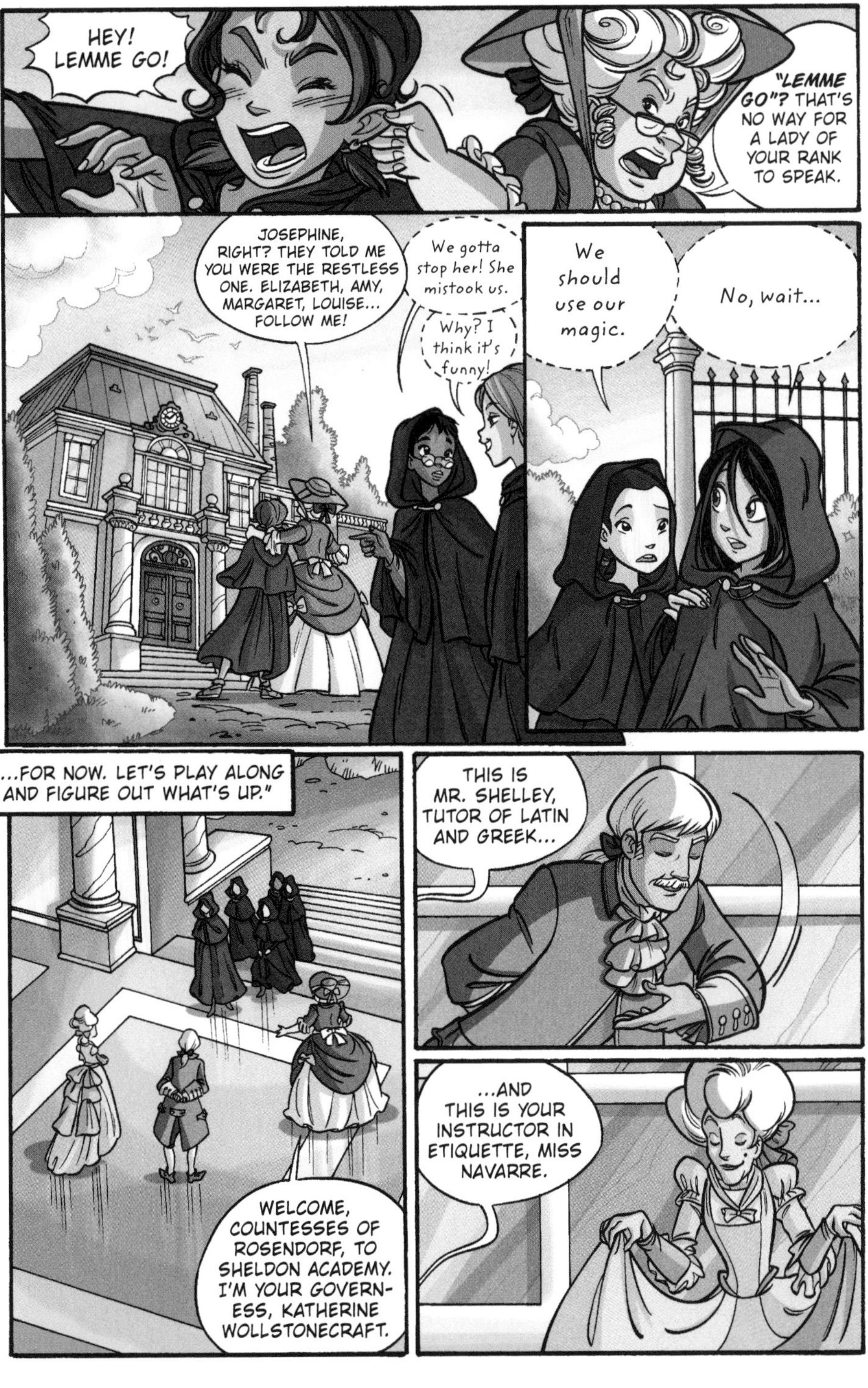
HEY! LEMME GO!
"LEMME GO"? THAT'S NO WAY FOR A LADY OF YOUR RANK TO SPEAK.
JOSEPHINE, RIGHT? THEY TOLD ME YOU WERE THE RESTLESS ONE. ELIZABETH, AMY, MARGARET, LOUISE... FOLLOW ME!
We gotta stop her! She mistook us.
Why? I think it's funny!
We should use our magic.
No, wait...
"...FOR NOW. LET'S PLAY ALONG AND FIGURE OUT WHAT'S UP."
WELCOME, COUNTESSES OF ROSENDORF, TO SHELDON ACADEMY. I'M YOUR GOVERN-ESS, KATHERINE WOLLSTONECRAFT.
THIS IS MR. SHELLEY, TUTOR OF LATIN AND GREEK...
...AND THIS IS YOUR INSTRUCTOR IN ETIQUETTE, MISS NAVARRE.

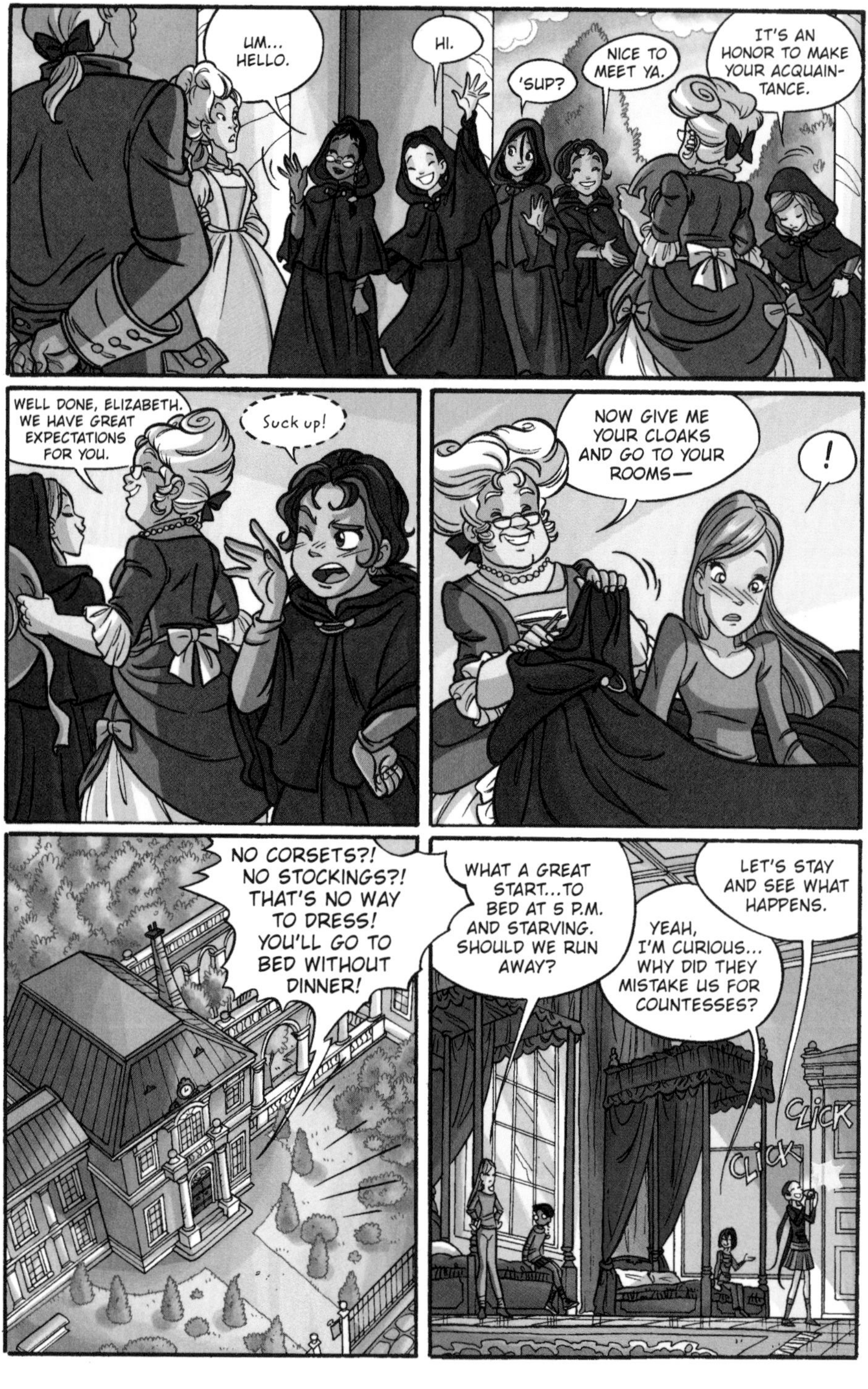
UM... HELLO.
HI.
'SUP?
NICE TO MEET YA.
IT'S AN HONOR TO MAKE YOUR ACQUAINTANCE.
WELL DONE, ELIZABETH. WE HAVE GREAT EXPECTATIONS FOR YOU.
Suck up!
NOW GIVE ME YOUR CLOAKS AND GO TO YOUR ROOMS—
!
NO CORSETS?! NO STOCKINGS?! THAT'S NO WAY TO DRESS! YOU'LL GO TO BED WITHOUT DINNER!
WHAT A GREAT START...TO BED AT 5 P.M. AND STARVING. SHOULD WE RUN AWAY?
LET'S STAY AND SEE WHAT HAPPENS.
YEAH, I'M CURIOUS... WHY DID THEY MISTAKE US FOR COUNTESSES?
CLICK
CLICK

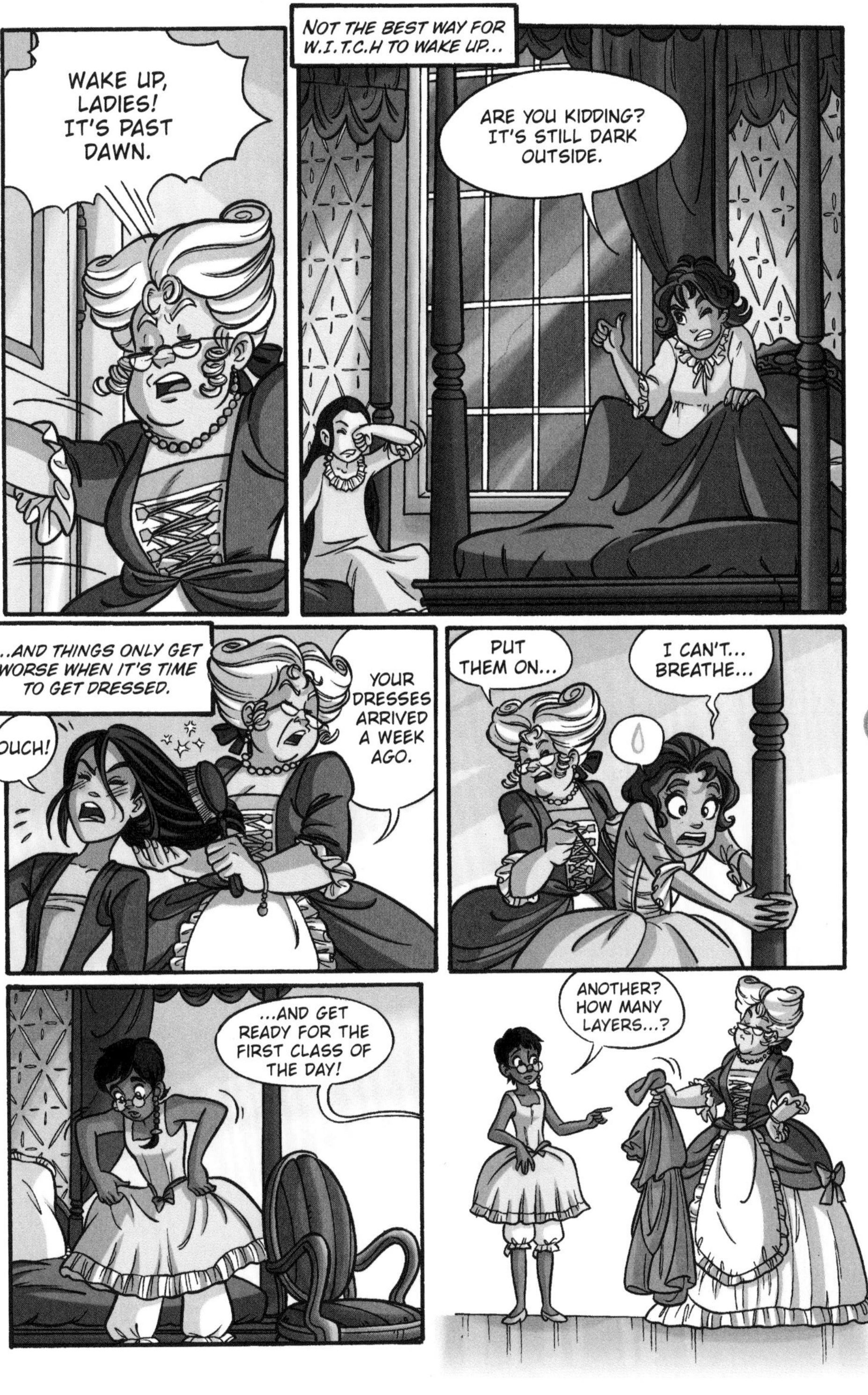

WAKE UP, LADIES! IT'S PAST DAWN.
NOT THE BEST WAY FOR W.I.T.C.H TO WAKE UP...
ARE YOU KIDDING? IT'S STILL DARK OUTSIDE.
...AND THINGS ONLY GET WORSE WHEN IT'S TIME TO GET DRESSED.
YOUR DRESSES ARRIVED A WEEK AGO.
OUCH!
PUT THEM ON...
I CAN'T... BREATHE...
...AND GET READY FOR THE FIRST CLASS OF THE DAY!
ANOTHER? HOW MANY LAYERS...?

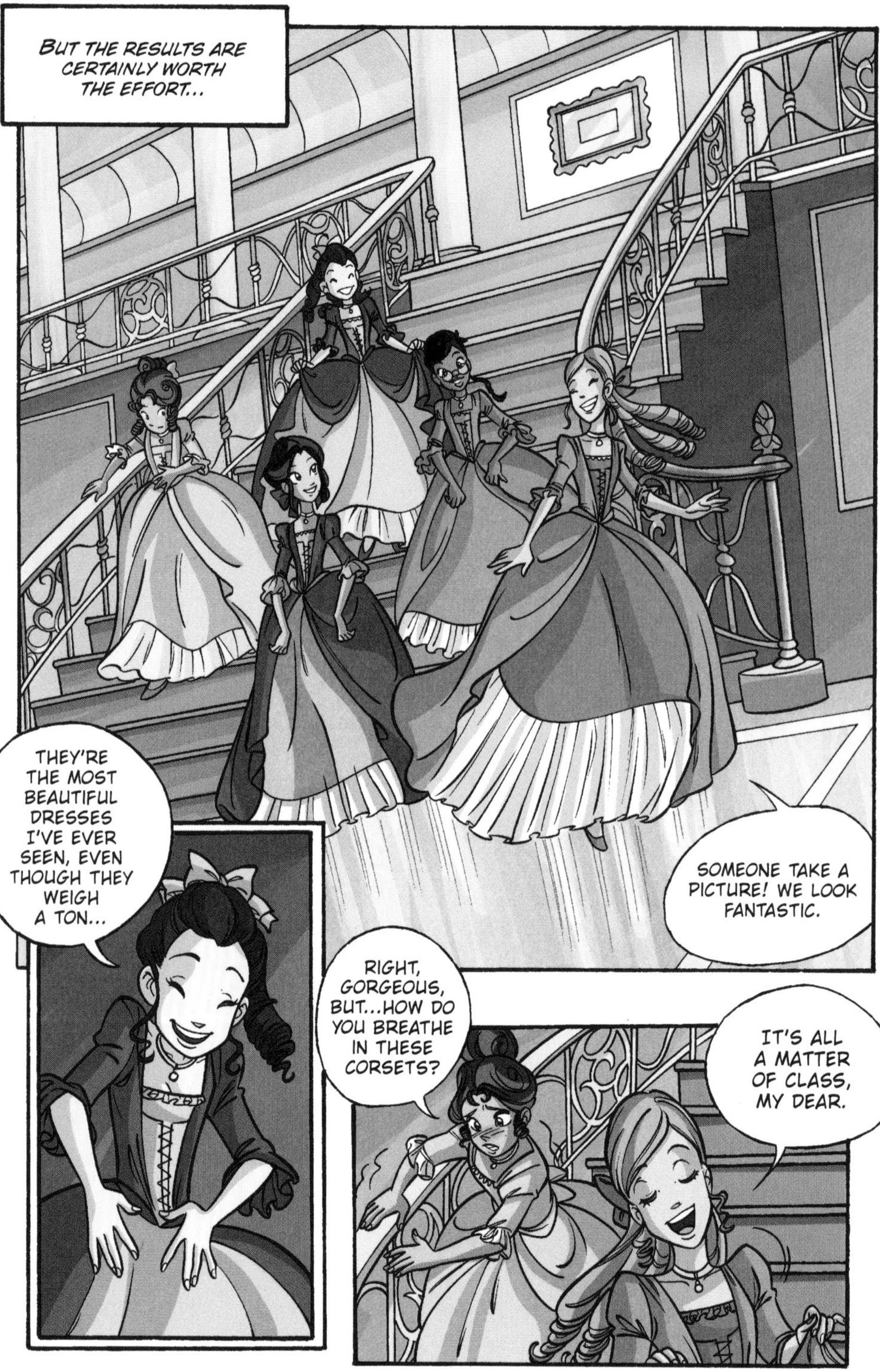

BUT THE RESULTS ARE CERTAINLY WORTH THE EFFORT...
THEY'RE THE MOST BEAUTIFUL DRESSES I'VE EVER SEEN, EVEN THOUGH THEY WEIGH A TON...
SOMEONE TAKE A PICTURE! WE LOOK FANTASTIC.
RIGHT, GORGEOUS, BUT...HOW DO YOU BREATHE IN THESE CORSETS?
IT'S ALL A MATTER OF CLASS, MY DEAR.

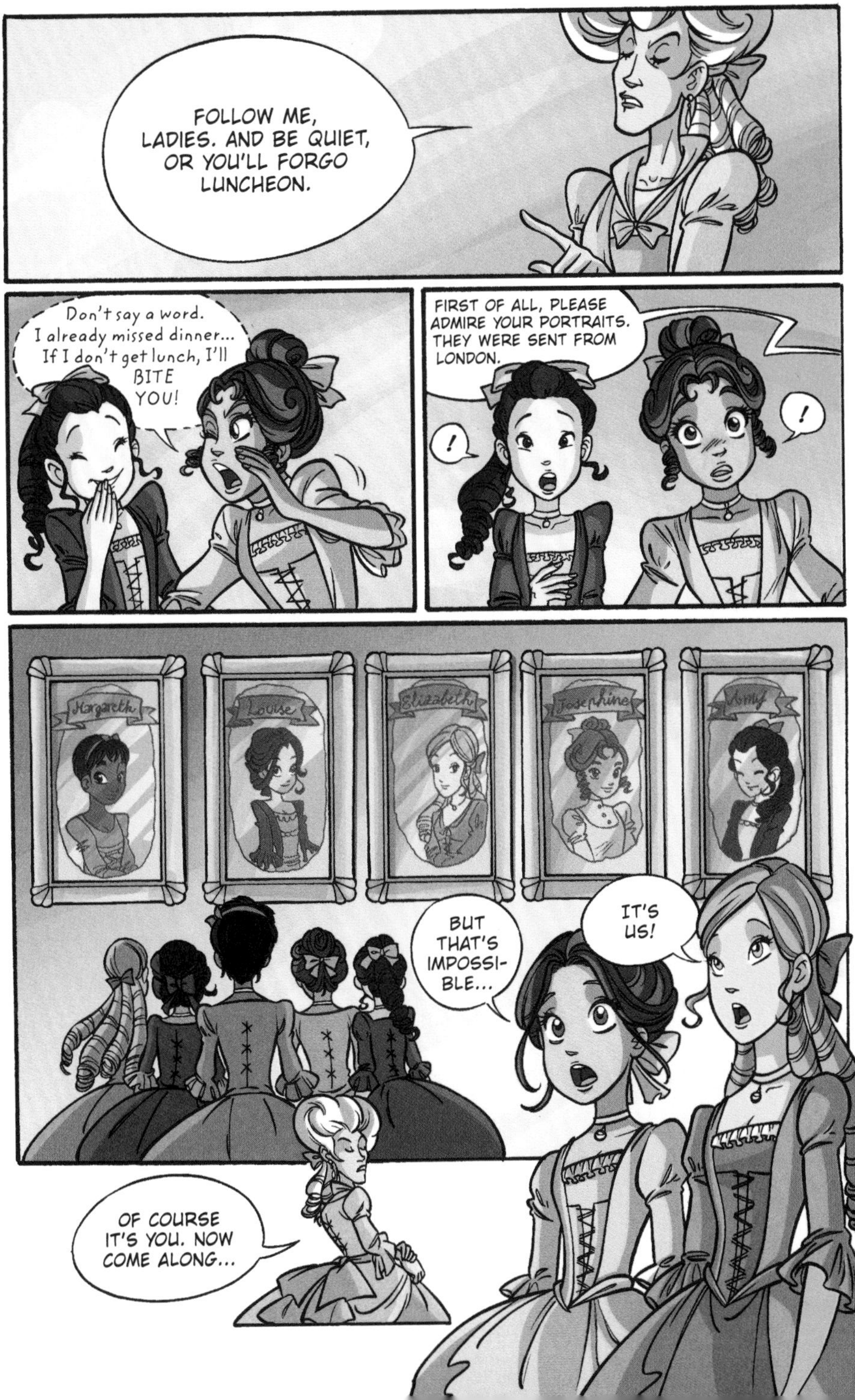
FOLLOW ME, LADIES. AND BE QUIET, OR YOU'LL FORGO LUNCHEON.
Don't say a word. I already missed dinner... If I don't get lunch, I'll BITE YOU!
FIRST OF ALL, PLEASE ADMIRE YOUR PORTRAITS. THEY WERE SENT FROM LONDON.
!
!
Margareth
Louise
Elizabeth
Josephine
Amy
BUT THAT'S IMPOSSI-BLE...
IT'S US!
OF COURSE IT'S YOU. NOW COME ALONG...

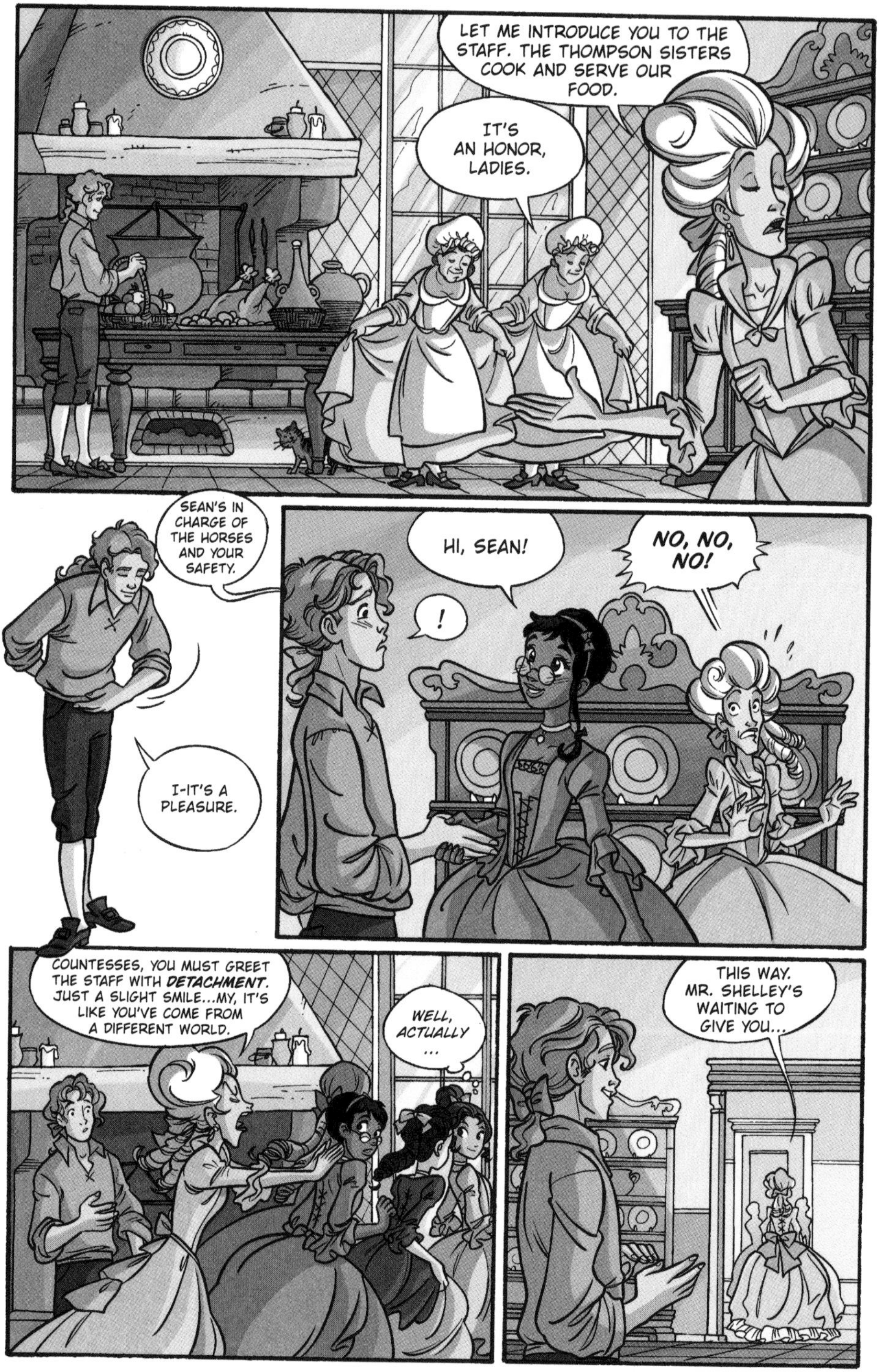
LET ME INTRODUCE YOU TO THE STAFF. THE THOMPSON SISTERS COOK AND SERVE OUR FOOD.
IT'S AN HONOR, LADIES.
SEAN'S IN CHARGE OF THE HORSES AND YOUR SAFETY.
I-IT'S A PLEASURE.
HI, SEAN!
!
NO, NO, NO!
COUNTESSES, YOU MUST GREET THE STAFF WITH DETACHMENT. JUST A SLIGHT SMILE...MY, IT'S LIKE YOU'VE COME FROM A DIFFERENT WORLD.
WELL, ACTUALLY ...
THIS WAY. MR. SHELLEY'S WAITING TO GIVE YOU...

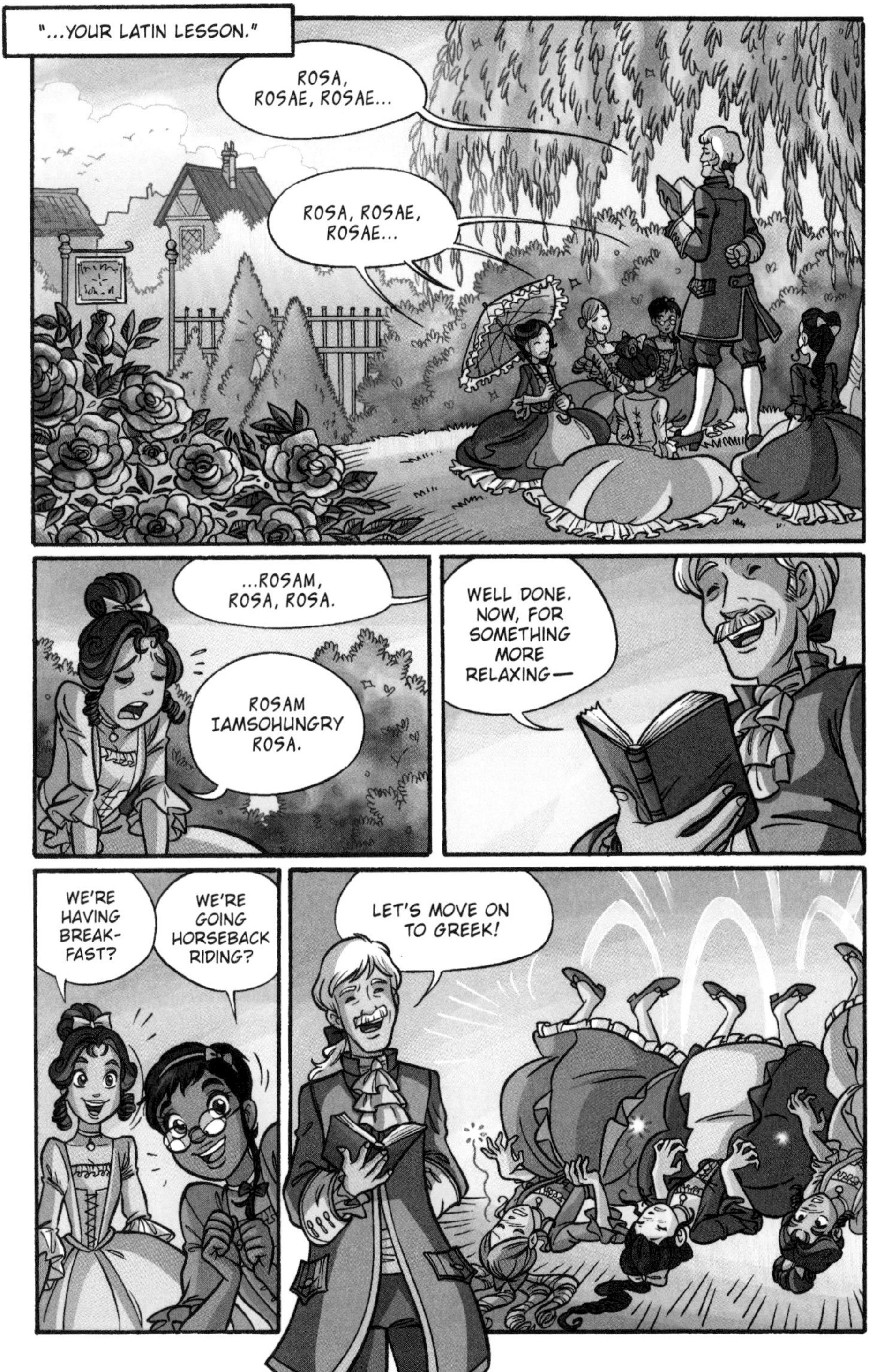

"...YOUR LATIN LESSON."
ROSA, ROSAE, ROSAE...
ROSA, ROSAE, ROSAE...
...ROSAM, ROSA, ROSA.
ROSAM IAMSOHUNGRY ROSA.
WELL DONE. NOW, FOR SOMETHING MORE RELAXING—
WE'RE HAVING BREAK-FAST?
WE'RE GOING HORSEBACK RIDING?
LET'S MOVE ON TO GREEK!

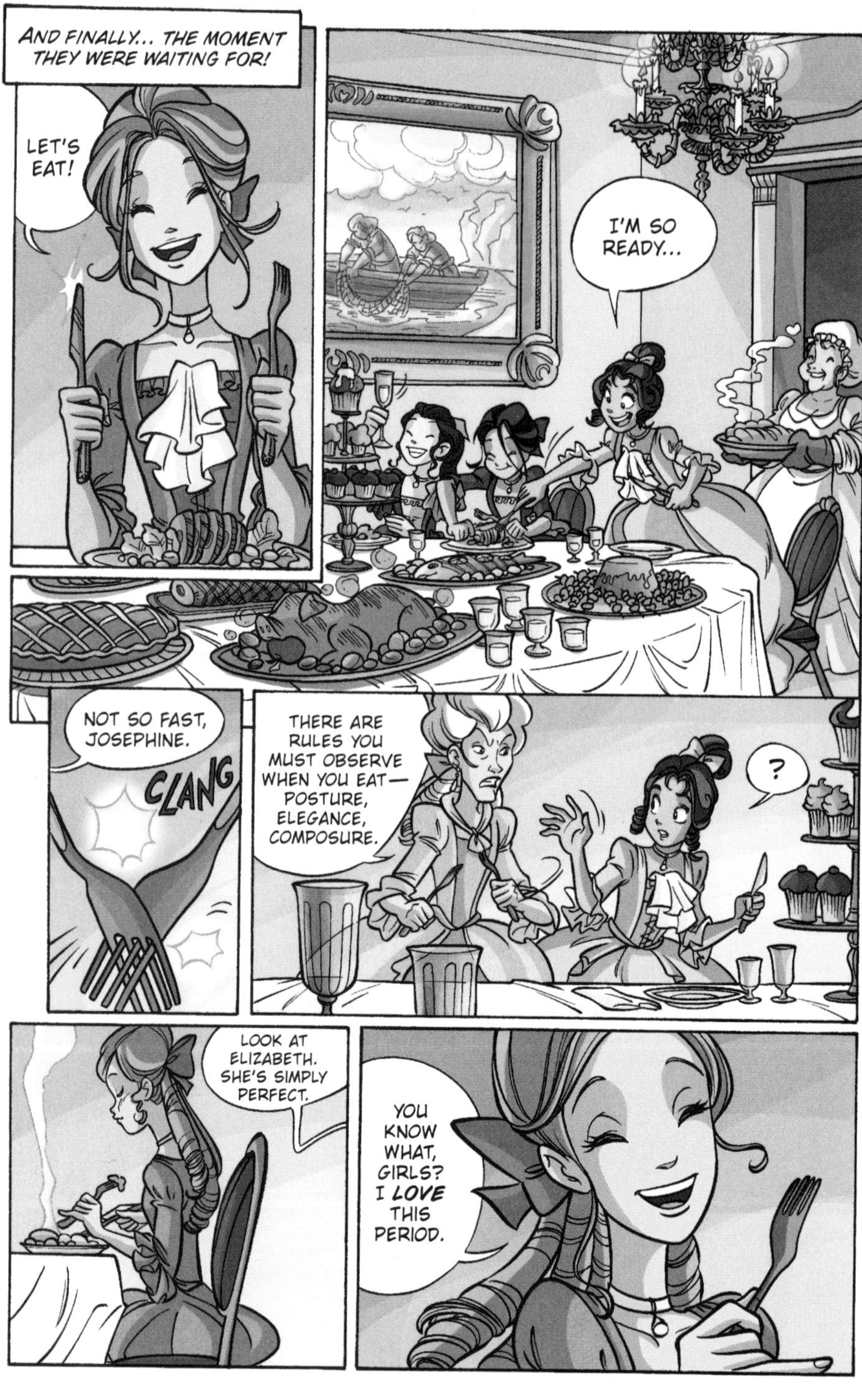
AND FINALLY... THE MOMENT THEY WERE WAITING FOR!
LET'S EAT!
I'M SO READY...
NOT SO FAST, JOSEPHINE.
CLANG
THERE ARE RULES YOU MUST OBSERVE WHEN YOU EAT—POSTURE, ELEGANCE, COMPOSURE.
?
LOOK AT ELIZABETH. SHE'S SIMPLY PERFECT.
YOU KNOW WHAT, GIRLS? I **LOVE** THIS PERIOD.

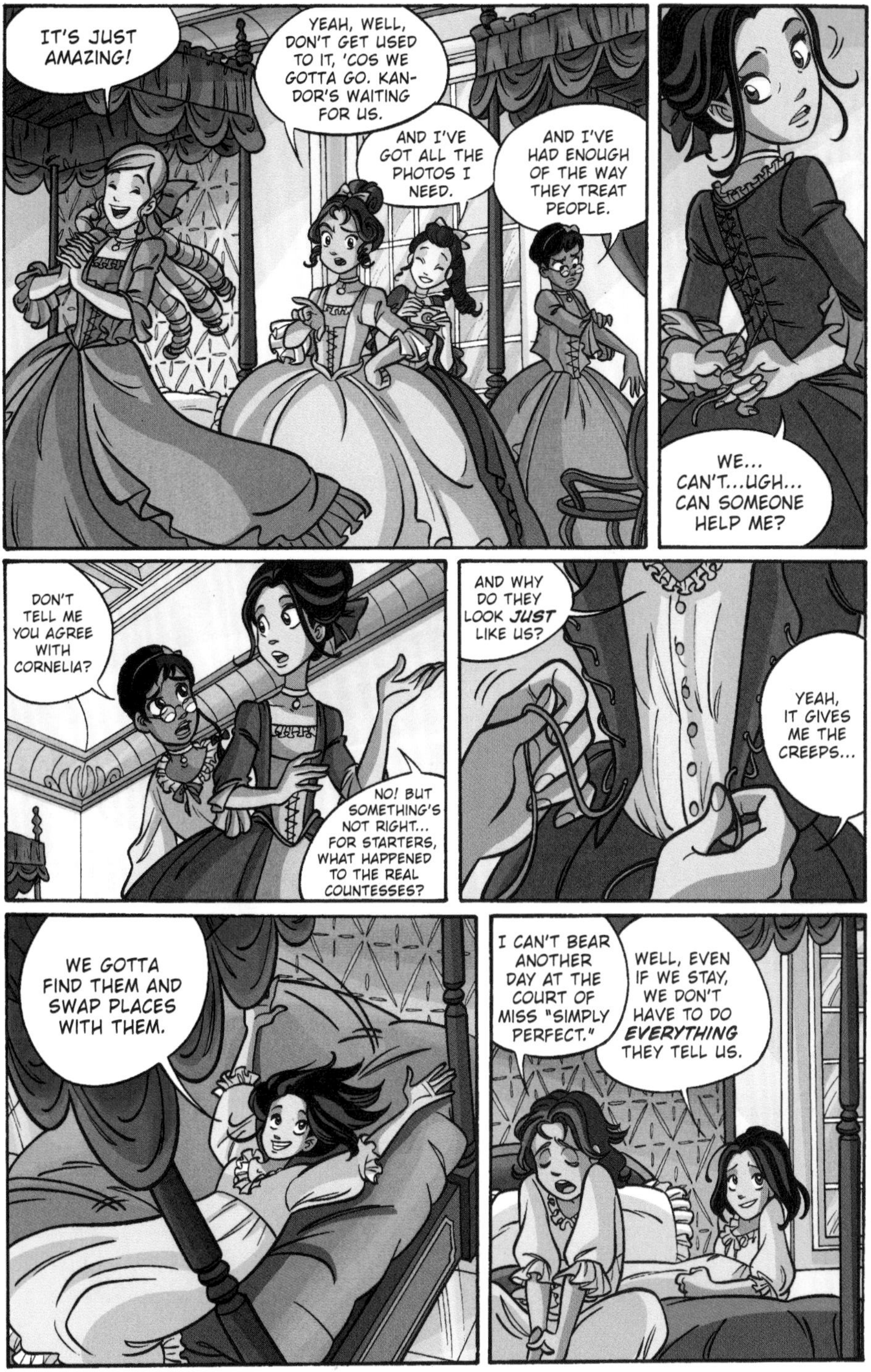
IT'S JUST AMAZING!
YEAH, WELL, DON'T GET USED TO IT, 'COS WE GOTTA GO. KAN-DOR'S WAITING FOR US.
AND I'VE GOT ALL THE PHOTOS I NEED.
AND I'VE HAD ENOUGH OF THE WAY THEY TREAT PEOPLE.
WE... CAN'T...UGH... CAN SOMEONE HELP ME?
DON'T TELL ME YOU AGREE WITH CORNELIA?
NO! BUT SOMETHING'S NOT RIGHT... FOR STARTERS, WHAT HAPPENED TO THE REAL COUNTESSES?
AND WHY DO THEY LOOK *JUST* LIKE US?
YEAH, IT GIVES ME THE CREEPS...
WE GOTTA FIND THEM AND SWAP PLACES WITH THEM.
I CAN'T BEAR ANOTHER DAY AT THE COURT OF MISS "SIMPLY PERFECT."
WELL, EVEN IF WE STAY, WE DON'T HAVE TO DO ***EVERYTHING*** THEY TELL US.

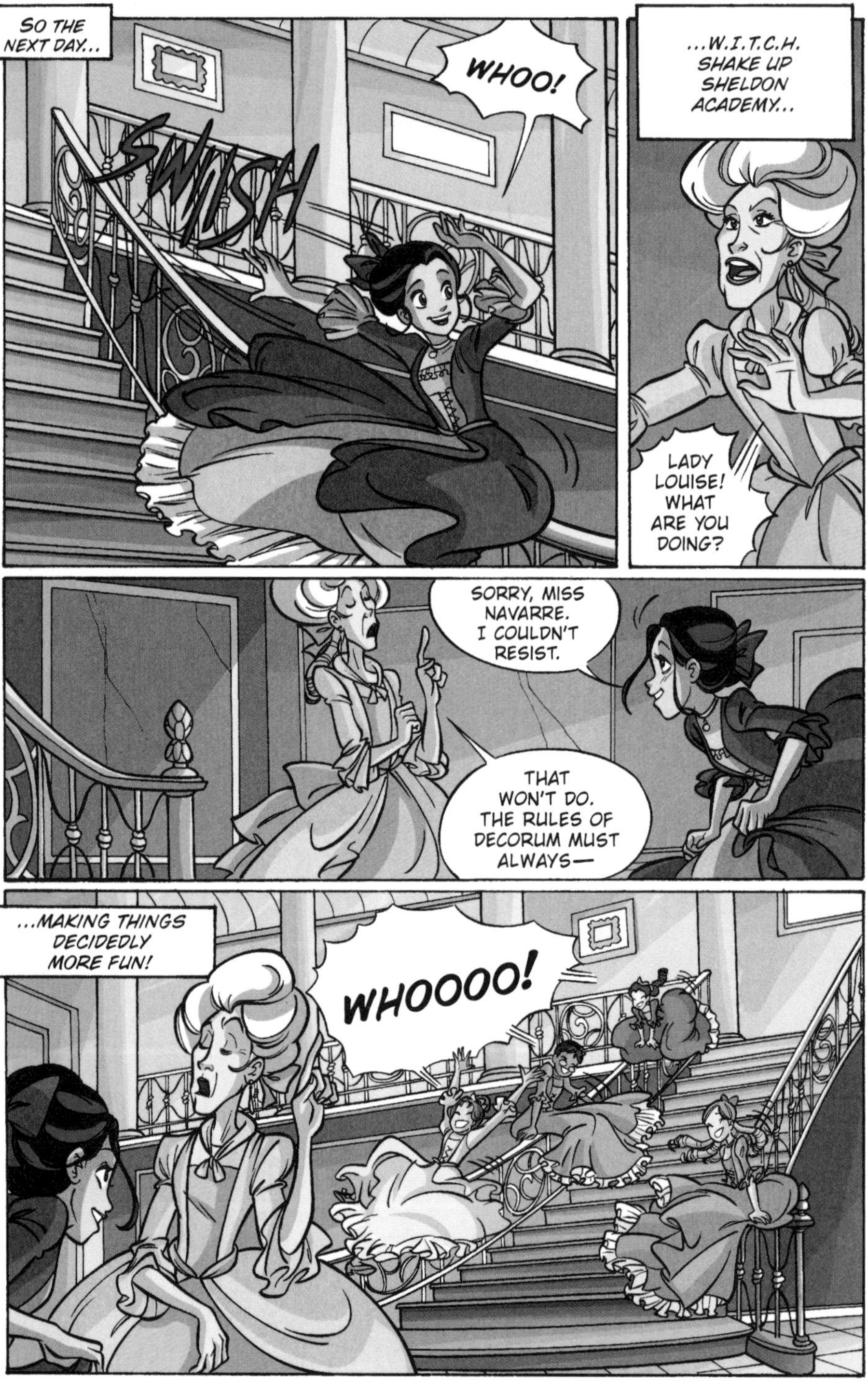
SO THE NEXT DAY...
SWISH
WHOO!
...W.I.T.C.H. SHAKE UP SHELDON ACADEMY...
LADY LOUISE! WHAT ARE YOU DOING?
SORRY, MISS NAVARRE. I COULDN'T RESIST.
THAT WON'T DO. THE RULES OF DECORUM MUST ALWAYS—
...MAKING THINGS DECIDEDLY MORE FUN!
WHOOOO!

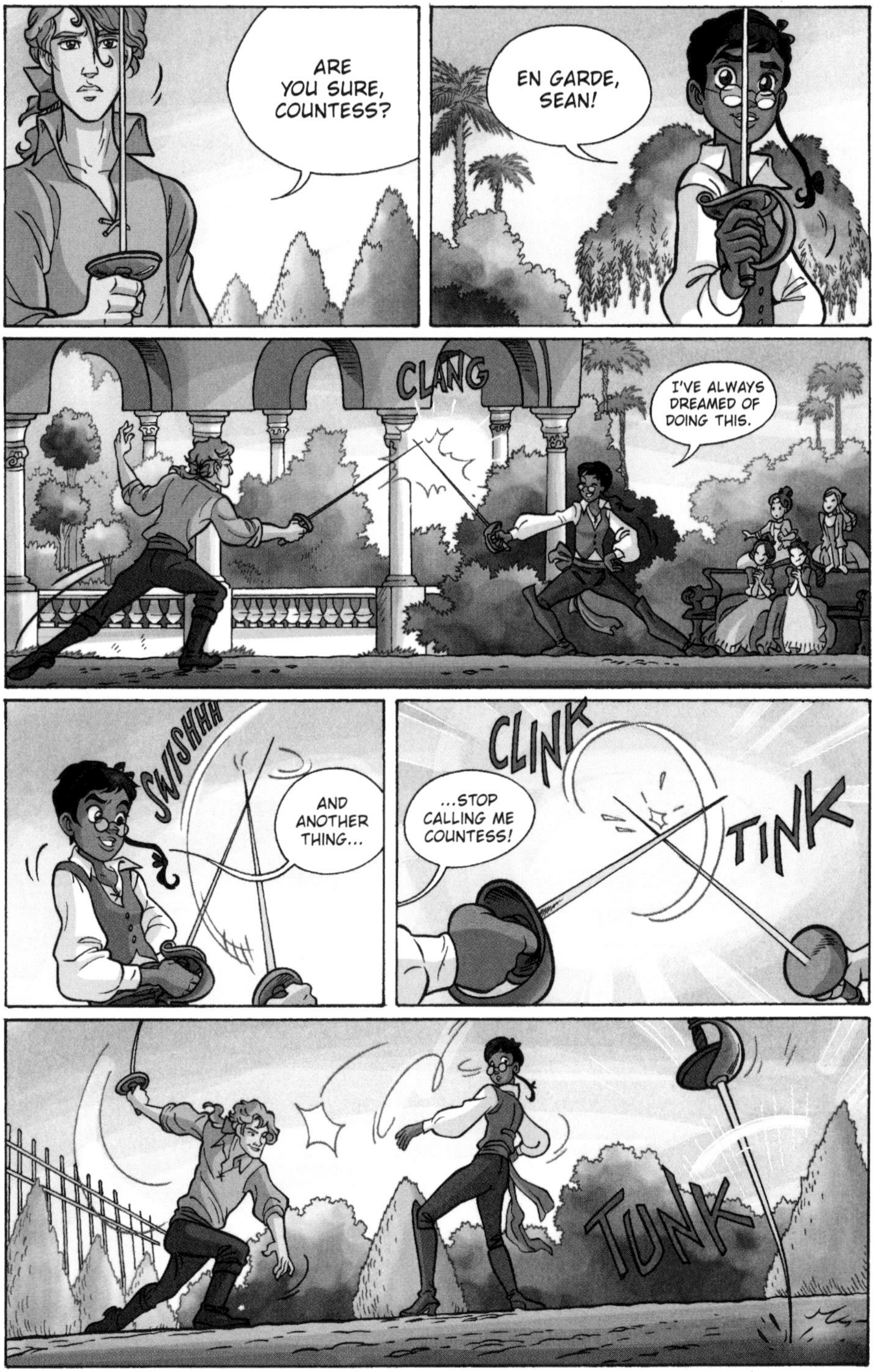

ARE YOU SURE, COUNTESS?
EN GARDE, SEAN!
CLANG
I'VE ALWAYS DREAMED OF DOING THIS.
SWISHHH
AND ANOTHER THING...
CLINK
...STOP CALLING ME COUNTESS!
TINK
TUNK

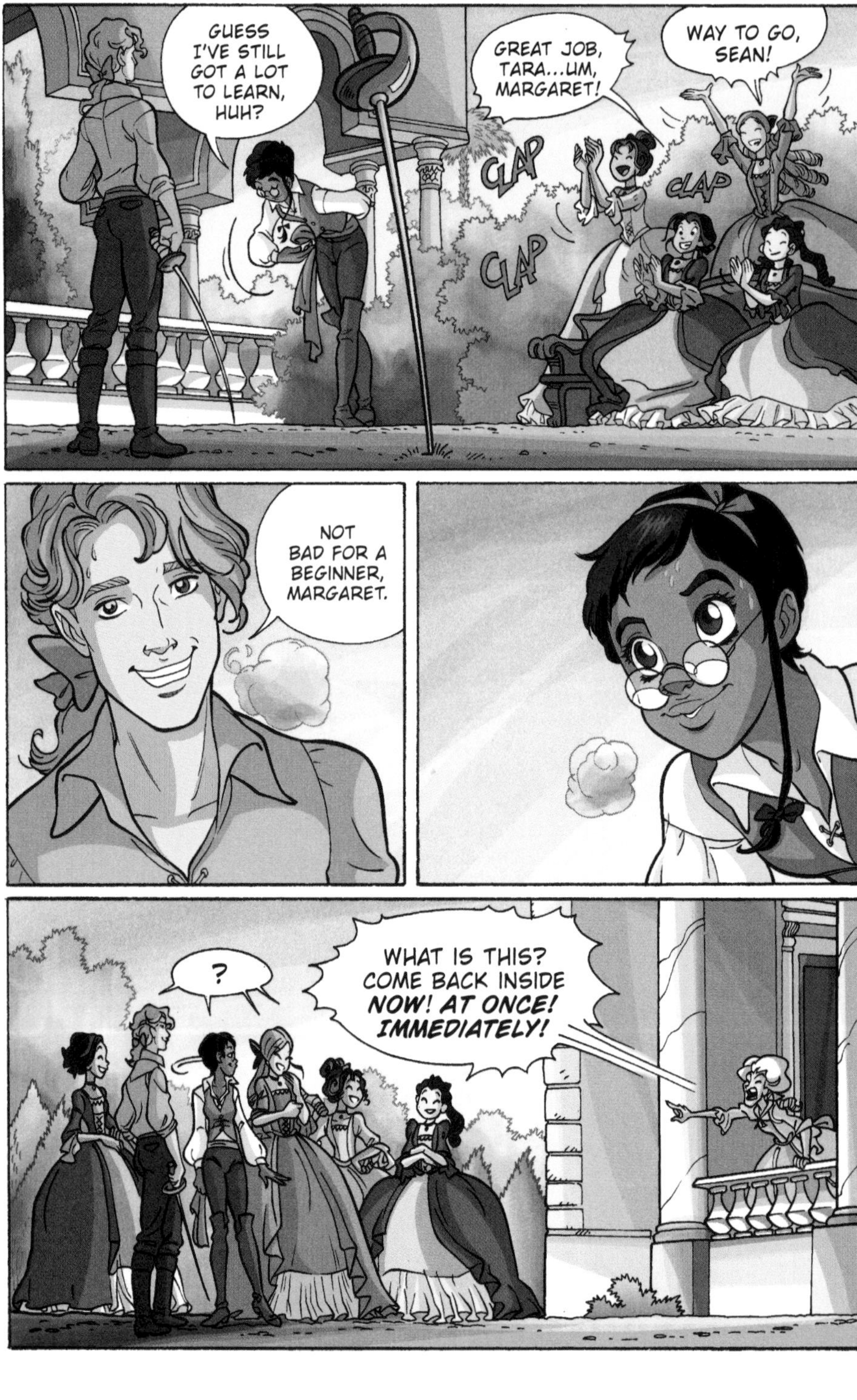
GUESS I'VE STILL GOT A LOT TO LEARN, HUH?
GREAT JOB, TARA...UM, MARGARET!
WAY TO GO, SEAN!
CLAP
CLAP
CLAP
NOT BAD FOR A BEGINNER, MARGARET.
?
WHAT IS THIS? COME BACK INSIDE NOW! AT ONCE! IMMEDIATELY!

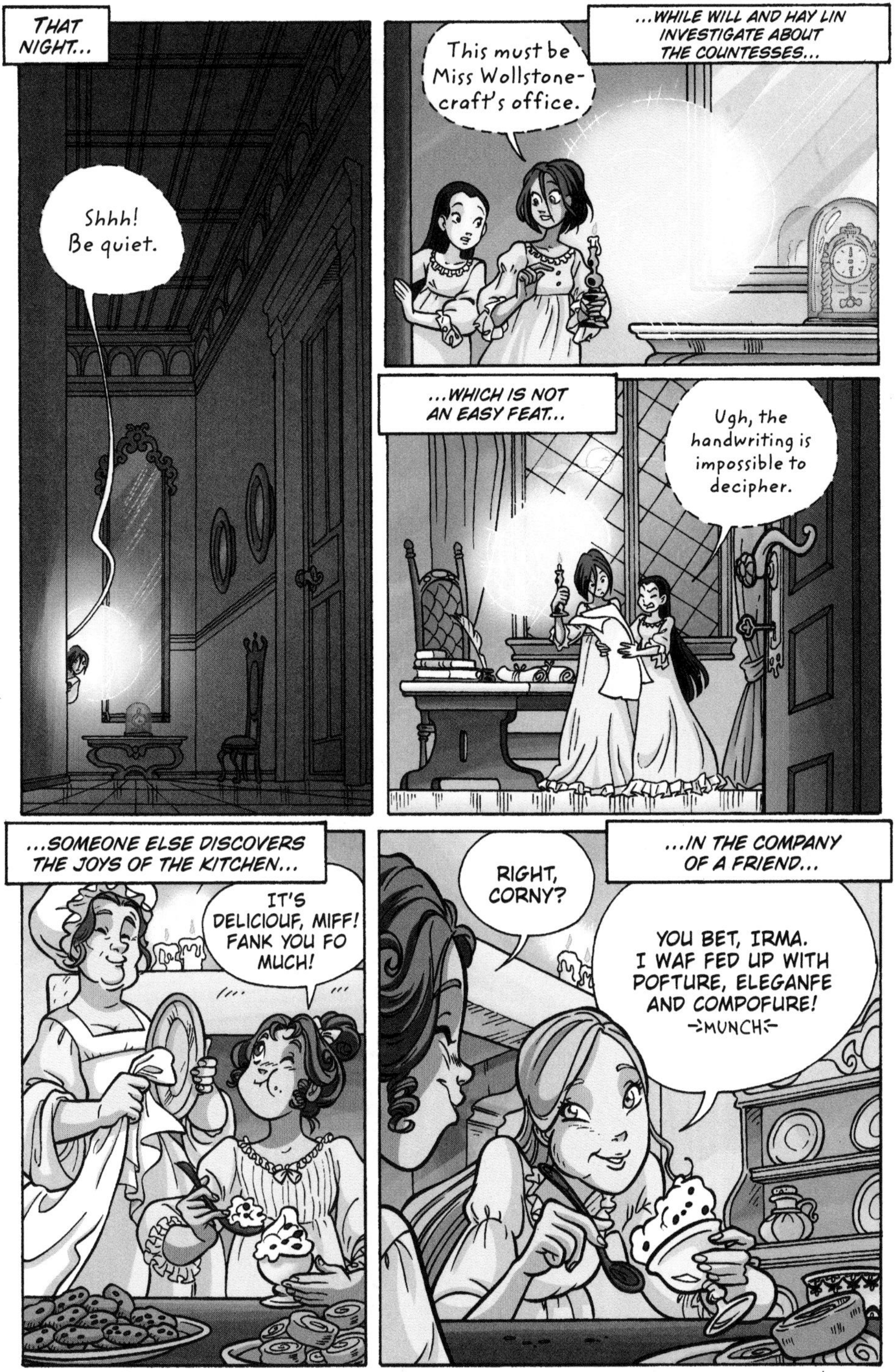
THAT NIGHT...
Shhh! Be quiet.
...WHILE WILL AND HAY LIN INVESTIGATE ABOUT THE COUNTESSES...
This must be Miss Wollstone-craft's office.
...WHICH IS NOT AN EASY FEAT...
Ugh, the handwriting is impossible to decipher.
...SOMEONE ELSE DISCOVERS THE JOYS OF THE KITCHEN...
IT'S DELICIOUF, MIFF! FANK YOU FO MUCH!
...IN THE COMPANY OF A FRIEND...
RIGHT, CORNY?
YOU BET, IRMA. I WAF FED UP WITH POFTURE, ELEGANFE AND COMPOFURE!
MUNCH

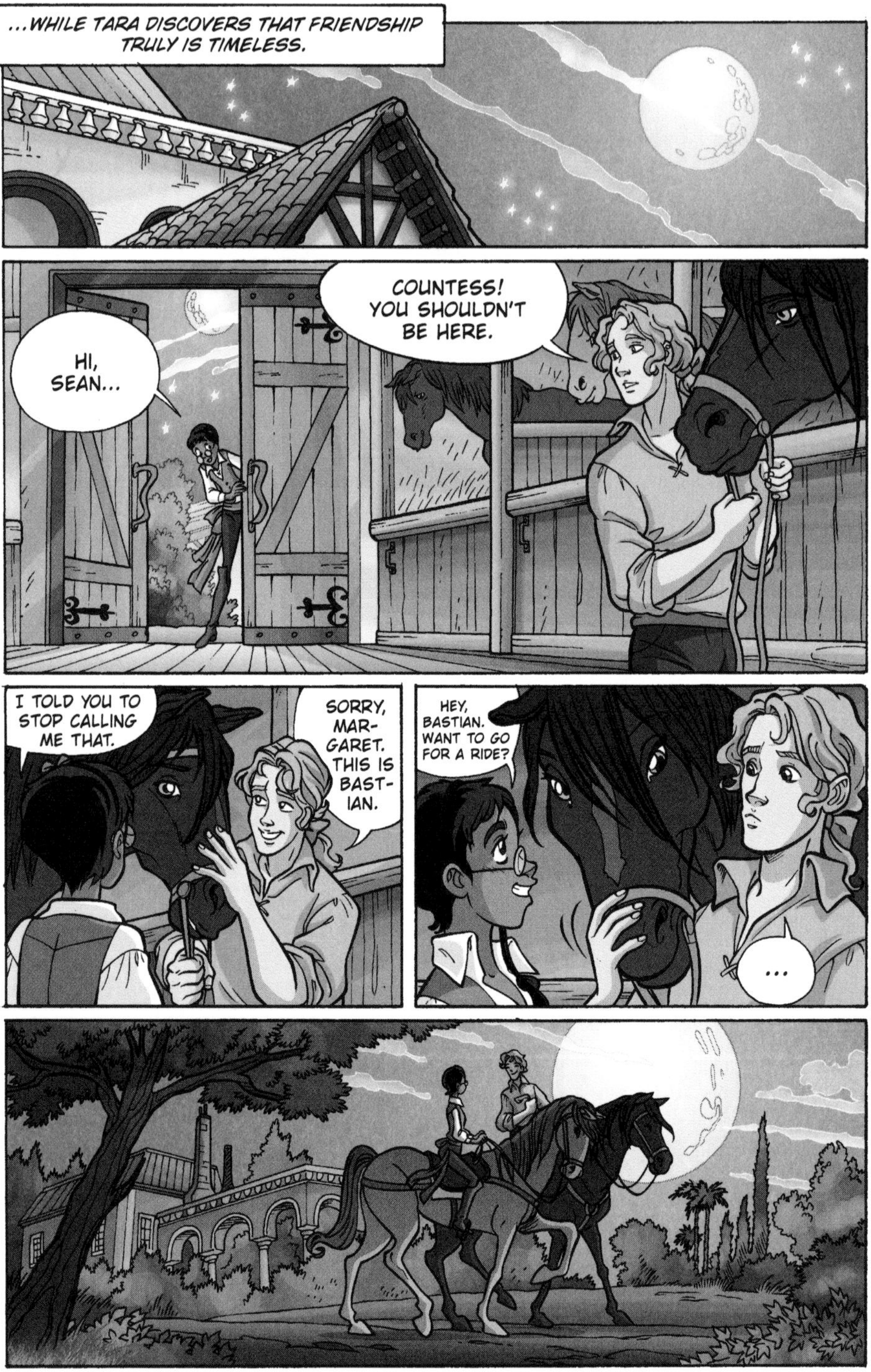
...WHILE TARA DISCOVERS THAT FRIENDSHIP TRULY IS TIMELESS.
COUNTESS! YOU SHOULDN'T BE HERE.
HI, SEAN...
I TOLD YOU TO STOP CALLING ME THAT.
SORRY, MARGARET. THIS IS BASTIAN.
HEY, BASTIAN. WANT TO GO FOR A RIDE?
...

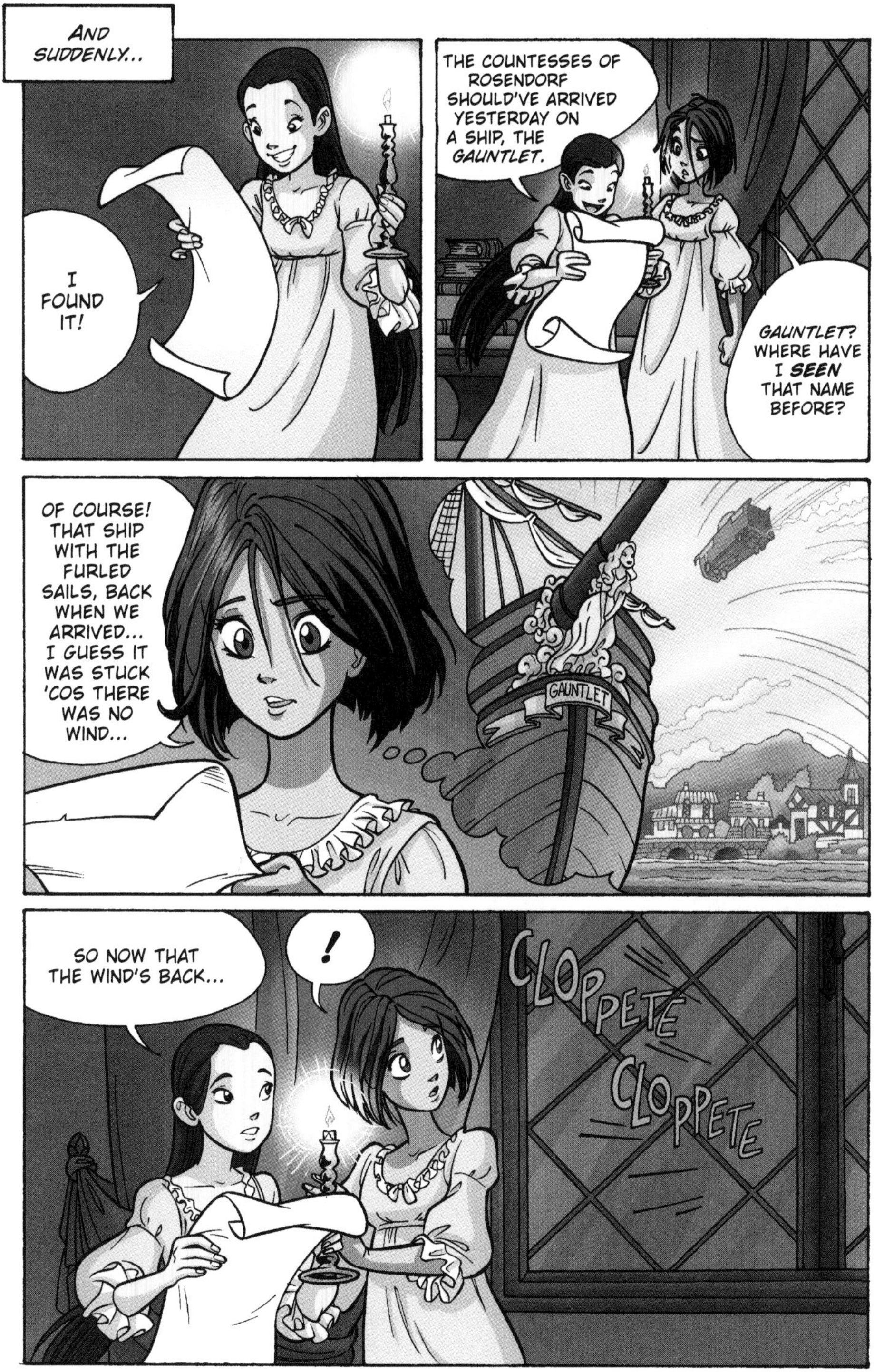
AND SUDDENLY...
I FOUND IT!
THE COUNTESSES OF ROSENDORF SHOULD'VE ARRIVED YESTERDAY ON A SHIP, THE GAUNTLET.
GAUNTLET? WHERE HAVE I SEEN THAT NAME BEFORE?
OF COURSE! THAT SHIP WITH THE FURLED SAILS, BACK WHEN WE ARRIVED... I GUESS IT WAS STUCK 'COS THERE WAS NO WIND...
GAUNTLET
SO NOW THAT THE WIND'S BACK...
!
CLOPPETE CLOPPETE

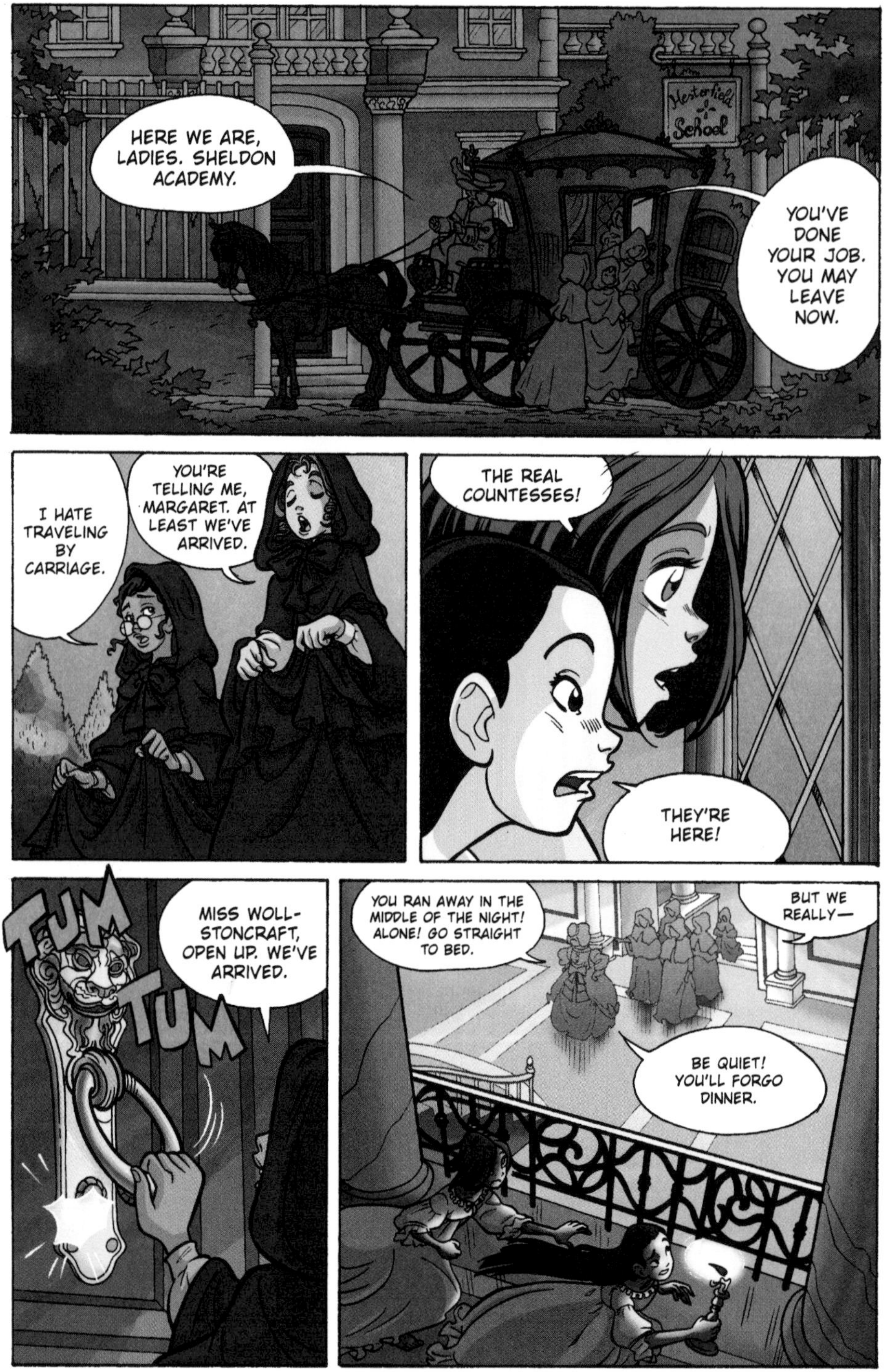

Hesterfield School
HERE WE ARE, LADIES. SHELDON ACADEMY.
YOU'VE DONE YOUR JOB. YOU MAY LEAVE NOW.
I HATE TRAVELING BY CARRIAGE.
YOU'RE TELLING ME, MARGARET. AT LEAST WE'VE ARRIVED.
THE REAL COUNTESSES!
THEY'RE HERE!
TUM
TUM
MISS WOLL-STONCRAFT, OPEN UP. WE'VE ARRIVED.
YOU RAN AWAY IN THE MIDDLE OF THE NIGHT! ALONE! GO STRAIGHT TO BED.
BUT WE REALLY—
BE QUIET! YOU'LL FORGO DINNER.

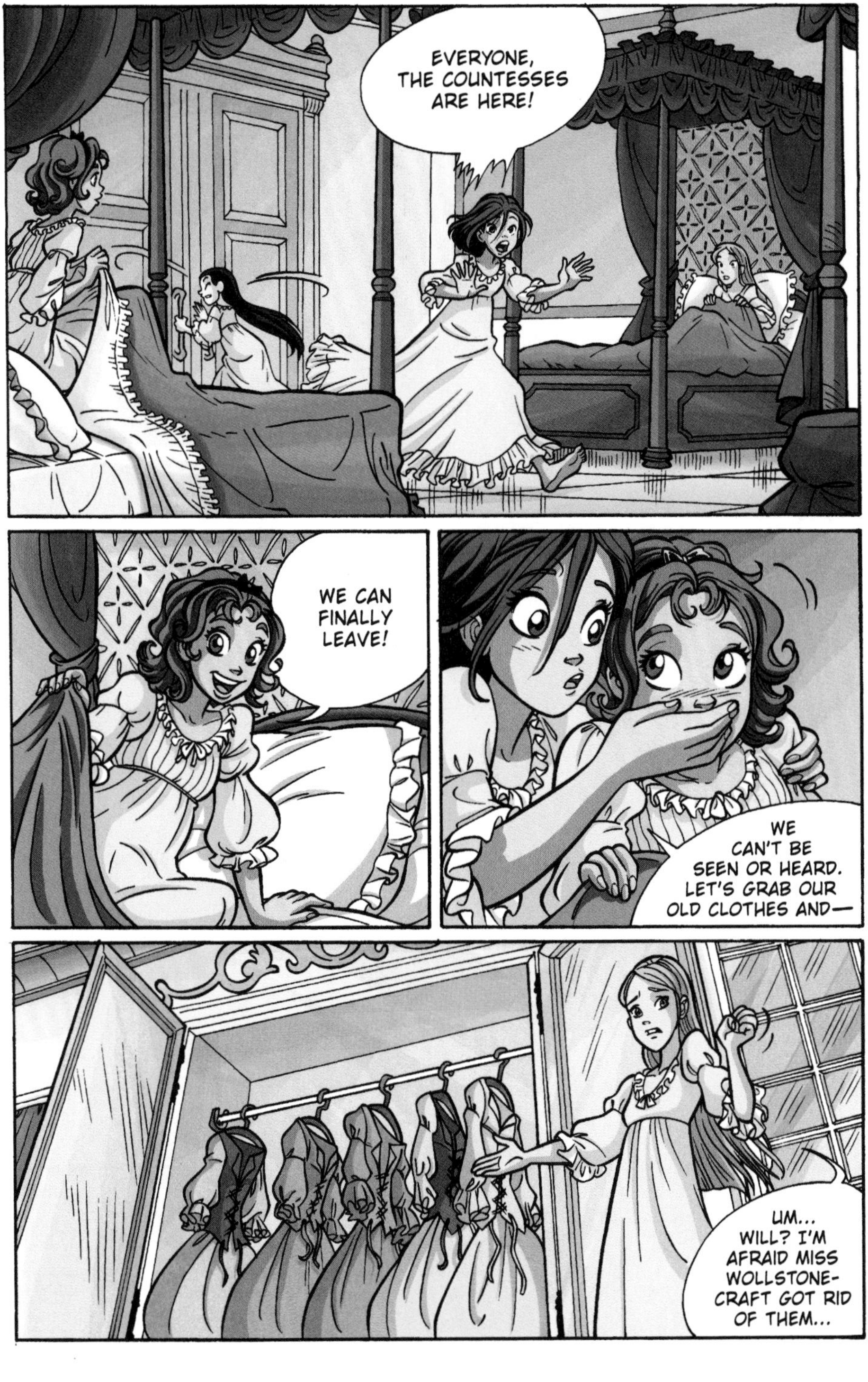
EVERYONE, THE COUNTESSES ARE HERE!
WE CAN FINALLY LEAVE!
WE CAN'T BE SEEN OR HEARD. LET'S GRAB OUR OLD CLOTHES AND—
UM... WILL? I'M AFRAID MISS WOLLSTONE-CRAFT GOT RID OF THEM...

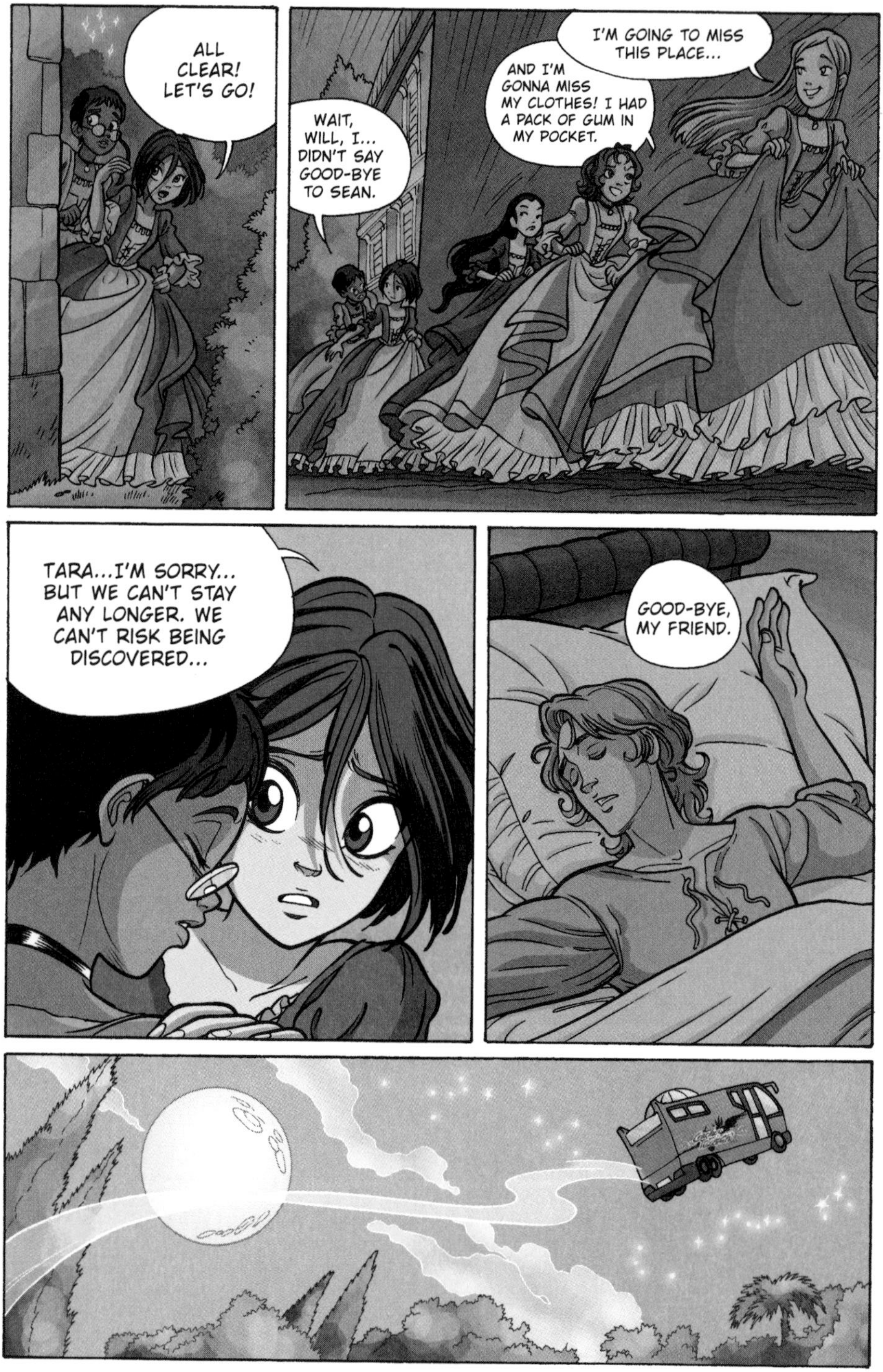
ALL CLEAR! LET'S GO!
WAIT, WILL, I... DIDN'T SAY GOOD-BYE TO SEAN.
I'M GOING TO MISS THIS PLACE...
AND I'M GONNA MISS MY CLOTHES! I HAD A PACK OF GUM IN MY POCKET.
TARA...I'M SORRY... BUT WE CAN'T STAY ANY LONGER. WE CAN'T RISK BEING DISCOVERED...
GOOD-BYE, MY FRIEND.

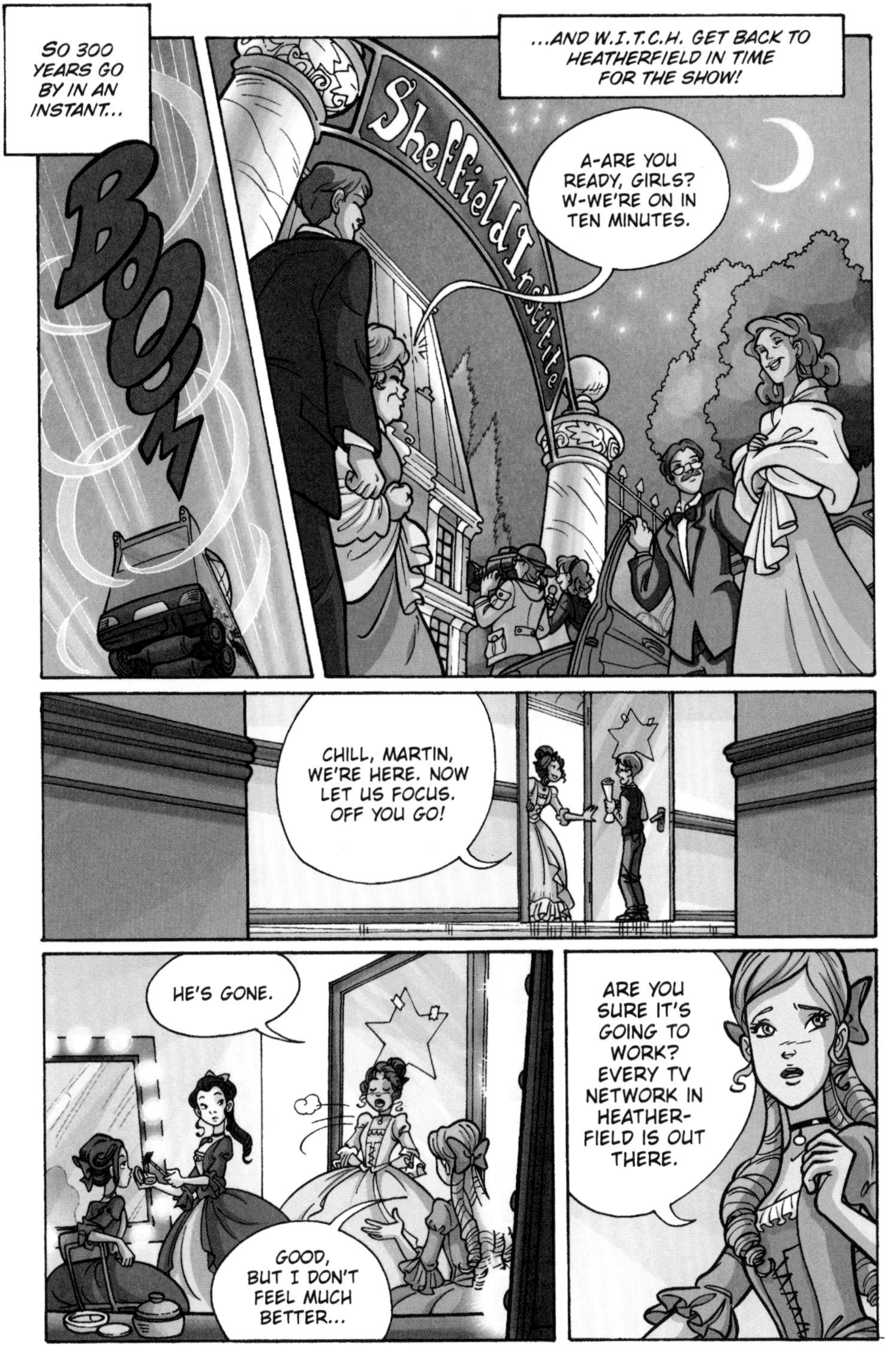
SO 300 YEARS GO BY IN AN INSTANT...
BOOM
...AND W.I.T.C.H. GET BACK TO HEATHERFIELD IN TIME FOR THE SHOW!
Sheffield Institute
A-ARE YOU READY, GIRLS? W-WE'RE ON IN TEN MINUTES.
CHILL, MARTIN, WE'RE HERE. NOW LET US FOCUS. OFF YOU GO!
HE'S GONE.
GOOD, BUT I DON'T FEEL MUCH BETTER...
ARE YOU SURE IT'S GOING TO WORK? EVERY TV NETWORK IN HEATHER-FIELD IS OUT THERE.

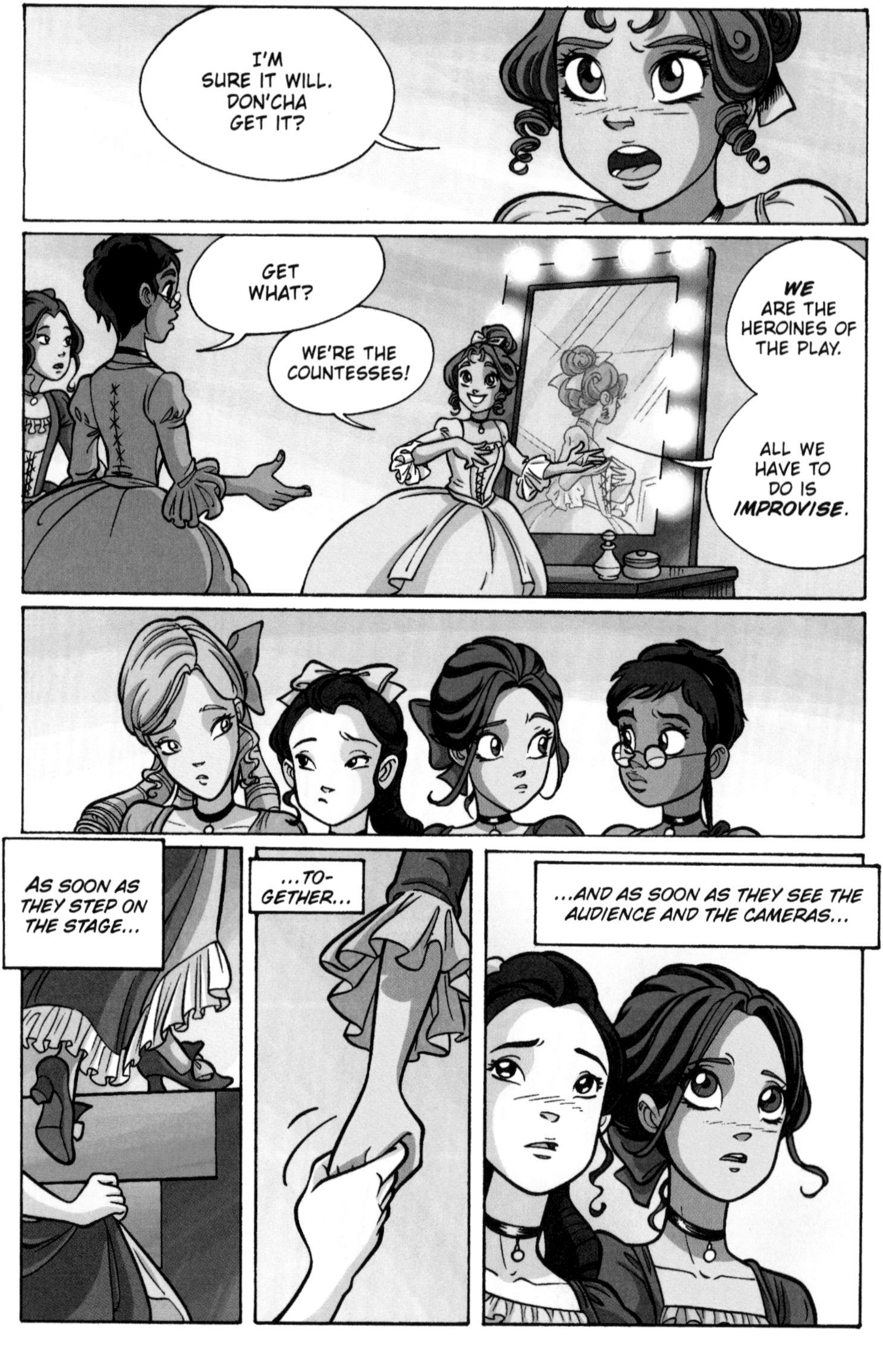
I'M SURE IT WILL. DON'CHA GET IT?
GET WHAT?
WE'RE THE COUNTESSES!
WE ARE THE HEROINES OF THE PLAY.
ALL WE HAVE TO DO IS IMPROVISE.
AS SOON AS THEY STEP ON THE STAGE...
...TO-GETHER...
...AND AS SOON AS THEY SEE THE AUDIENCE AND THE CAMERAS...

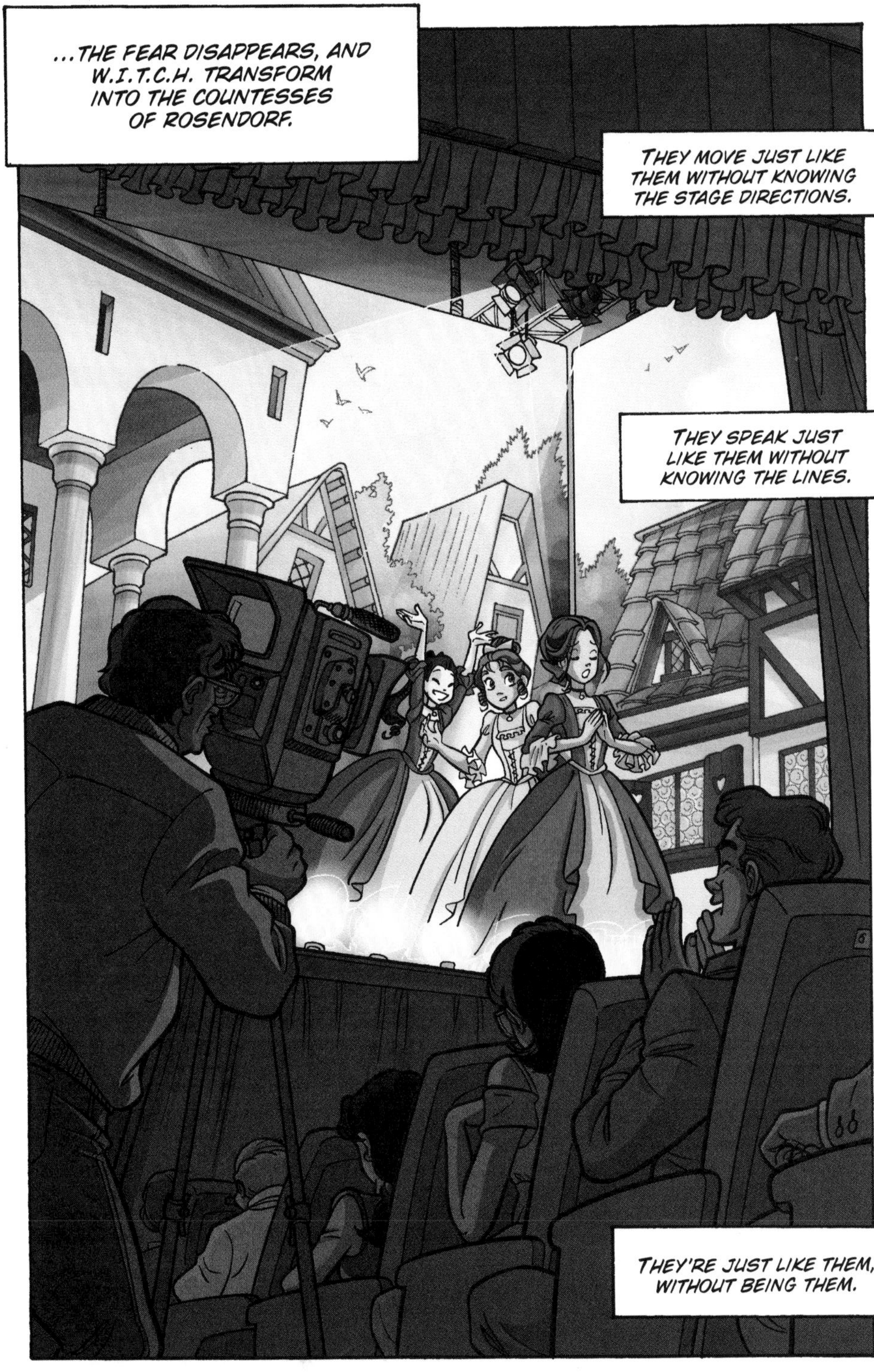
...THE FEAR DISAPPEARS, AND W.I.T.C.H. TRANSFORM INTO THE COUNTESSES OF ROSENDORF.
THEY MOVE JUST LIKE THEM WITHOUT KNOWING THE STAGE DIRECTIONS.
THEY SPEAK JUST LIKE THEM WITHOUT KNOWING THE LINES.
THEY'RE JUST LIKE THEM, WITHOUT BEING THEM.

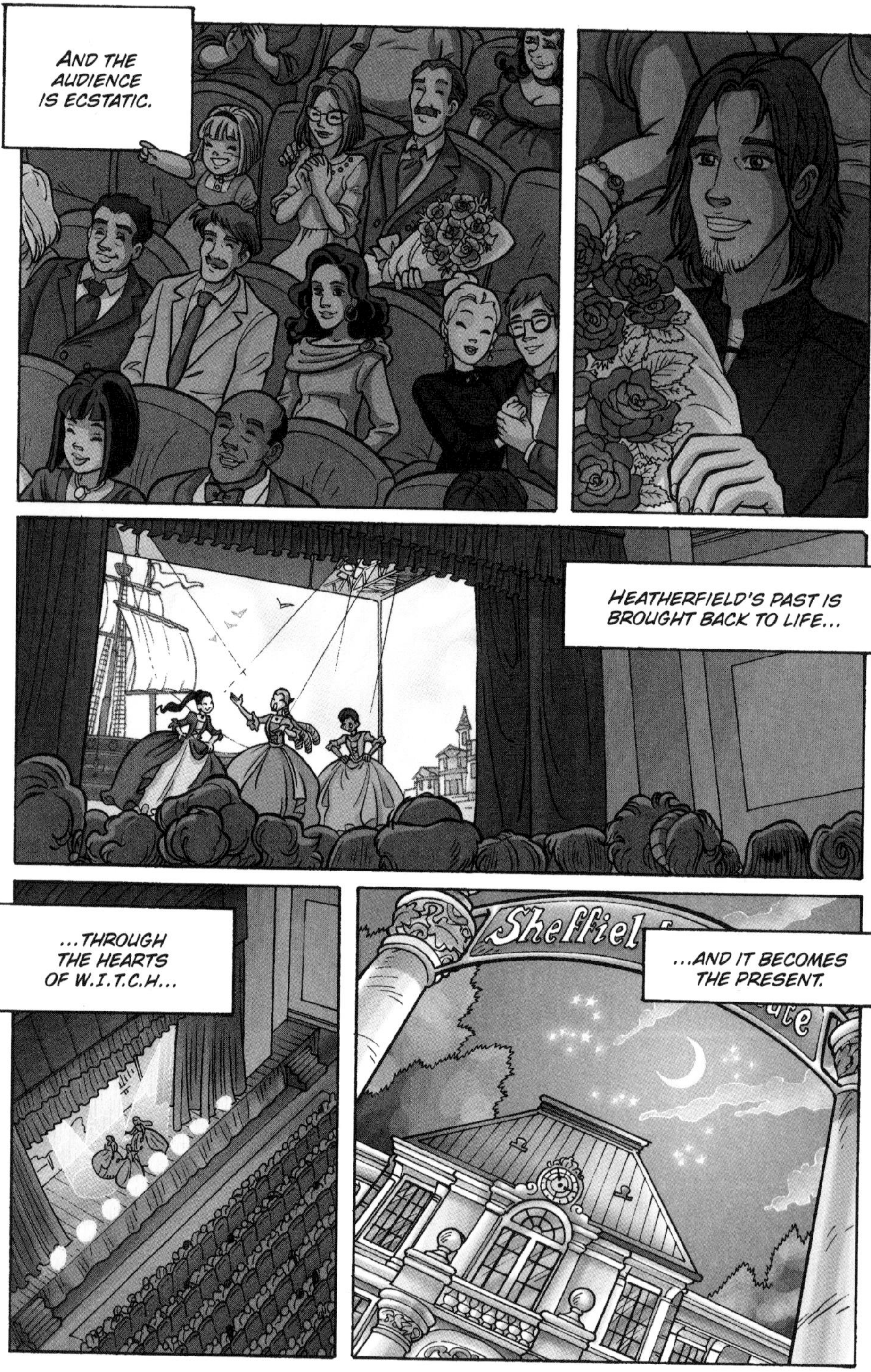
AND THE AUDIENCE IS ECSTATIC.
HEATHERFIELD'S PAST IS BROUGHT BACK TO LIFE...
...THROUGH THE HEARTS OF W.I.T.C.H...
...AND IT BECOMES THE PRESENT.

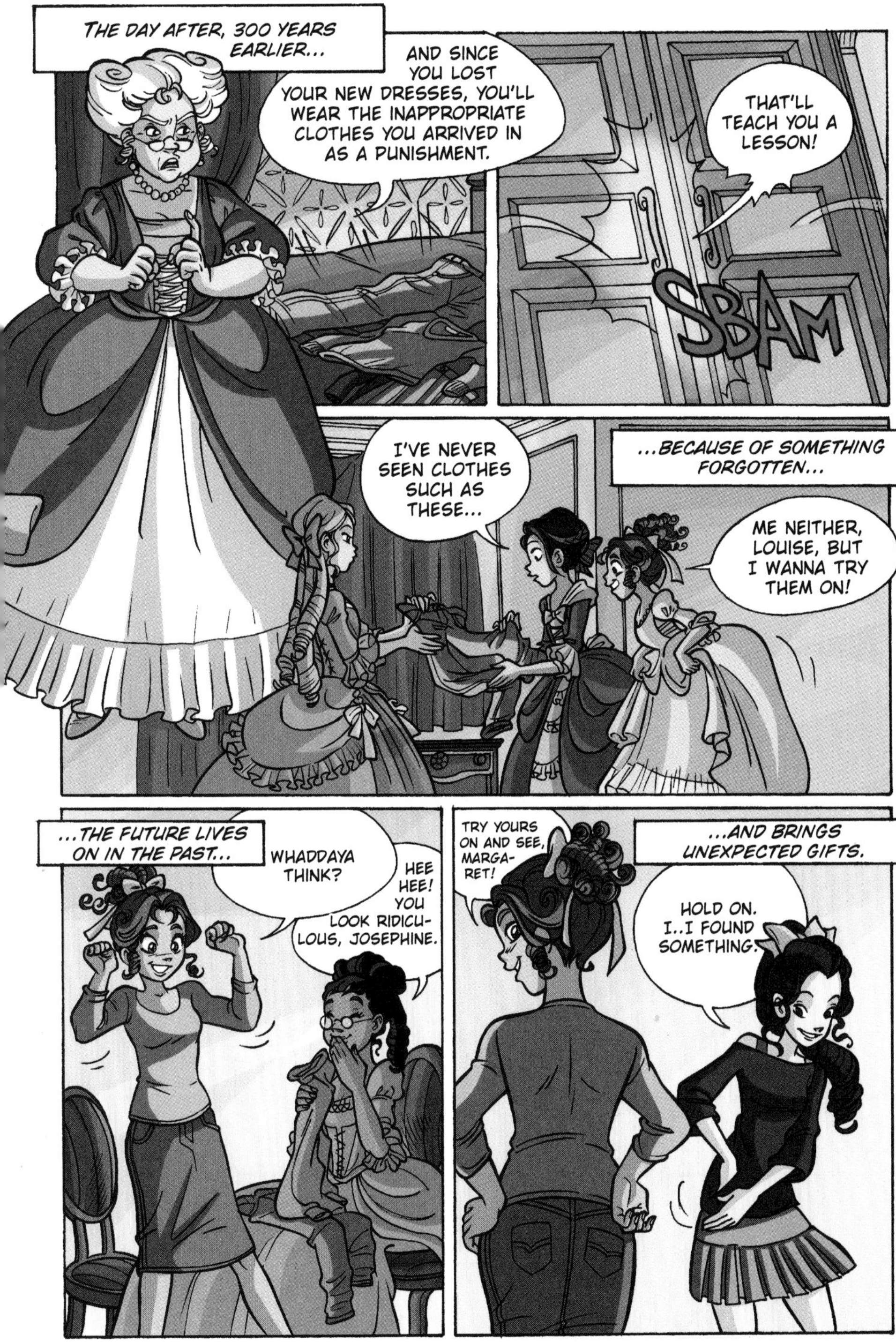
THE DAY AFTER, 300 YEARS EARLIER...
AND SINCE YOU LOST YOUR NEW DRESSES, YOU'LL WEAR THE INAPPROPRIATE CLOTHES YOU ARRIVED IN AS A PUNISHMENT.
THAT'LL TEACH YOU A LESSON!
SBAM
I'VE NEVER SEEN CLOTHES SUCH AS THESE...
...BECAUSE OF SOMETHING FORGOTTEN...
ME NEITHER, LOUISE, BUT I WANNA TRY THEM ON!
...THE FUTURE LIVES ON IN THE PAST...
WHADDAYA THINK?
HEE HEE! YOU LOOK RIDICU-LOUS, JOSEPHINE.
TRY YOURS ON AND SEE, MARGA-RET!
...AND BRINGS UNEXPECTED GIFTS.
HOLD ON. I..I FOUND SOMETHING.

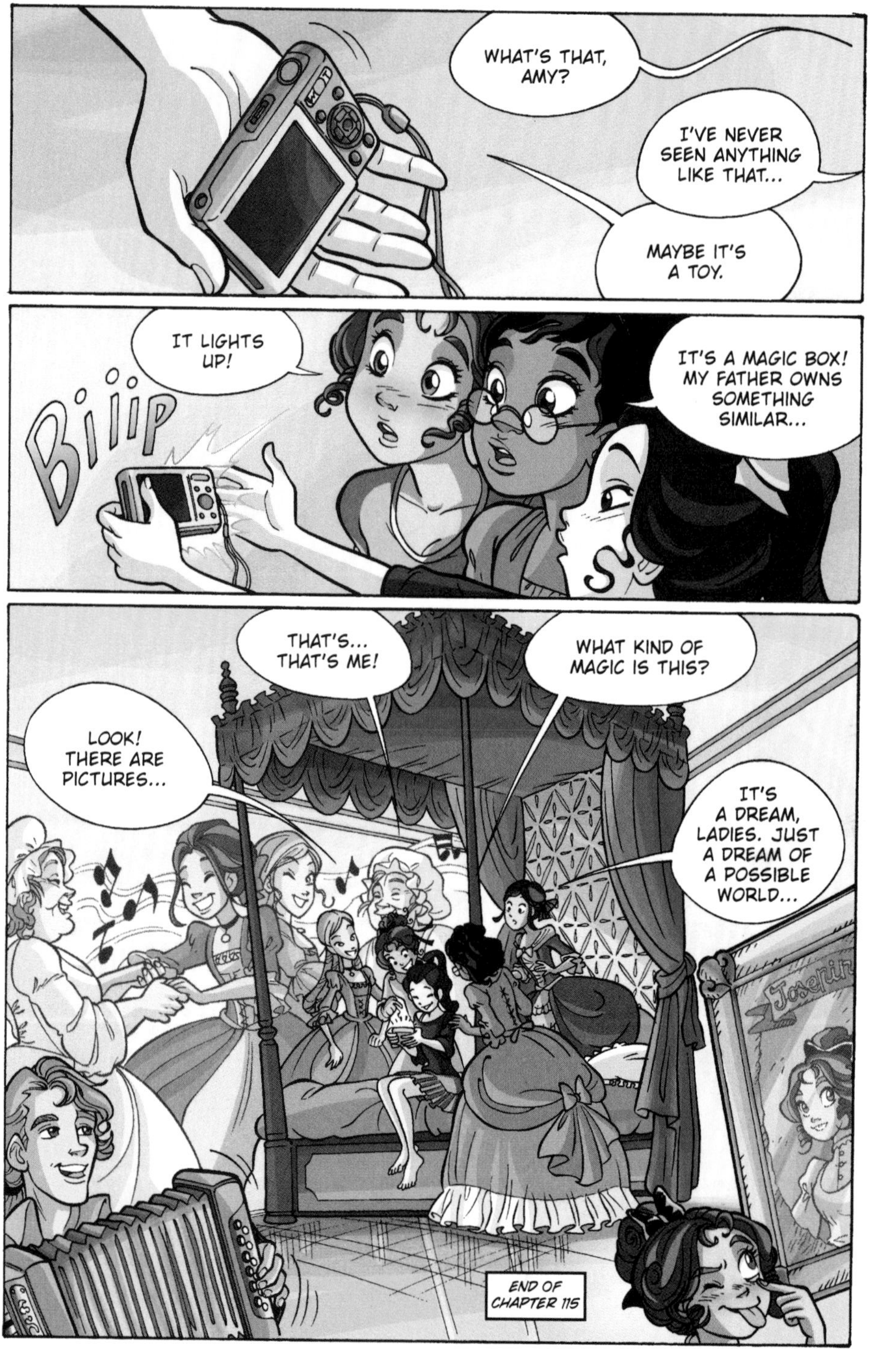
WHAT'S THAT, AMY?
I'VE NEVER SEEN ANYTHING LIKE THAT...
MAYBE IT'S A TOY.
IT LIGHTS UP!
BIIIP
IT'S A MAGIC BOX! MY FATHER OWNS SOMETHING SIMILAR...
LOOK! THERE ARE PICTURES...
THAT'S... THAT'S ME!
WHAT KIND OF MAGIC IS THIS?
IT'S A DREAM, LADIES. JUST A DREAM OF A POSSIBLE WORLD...
END OF CHAPTER 115

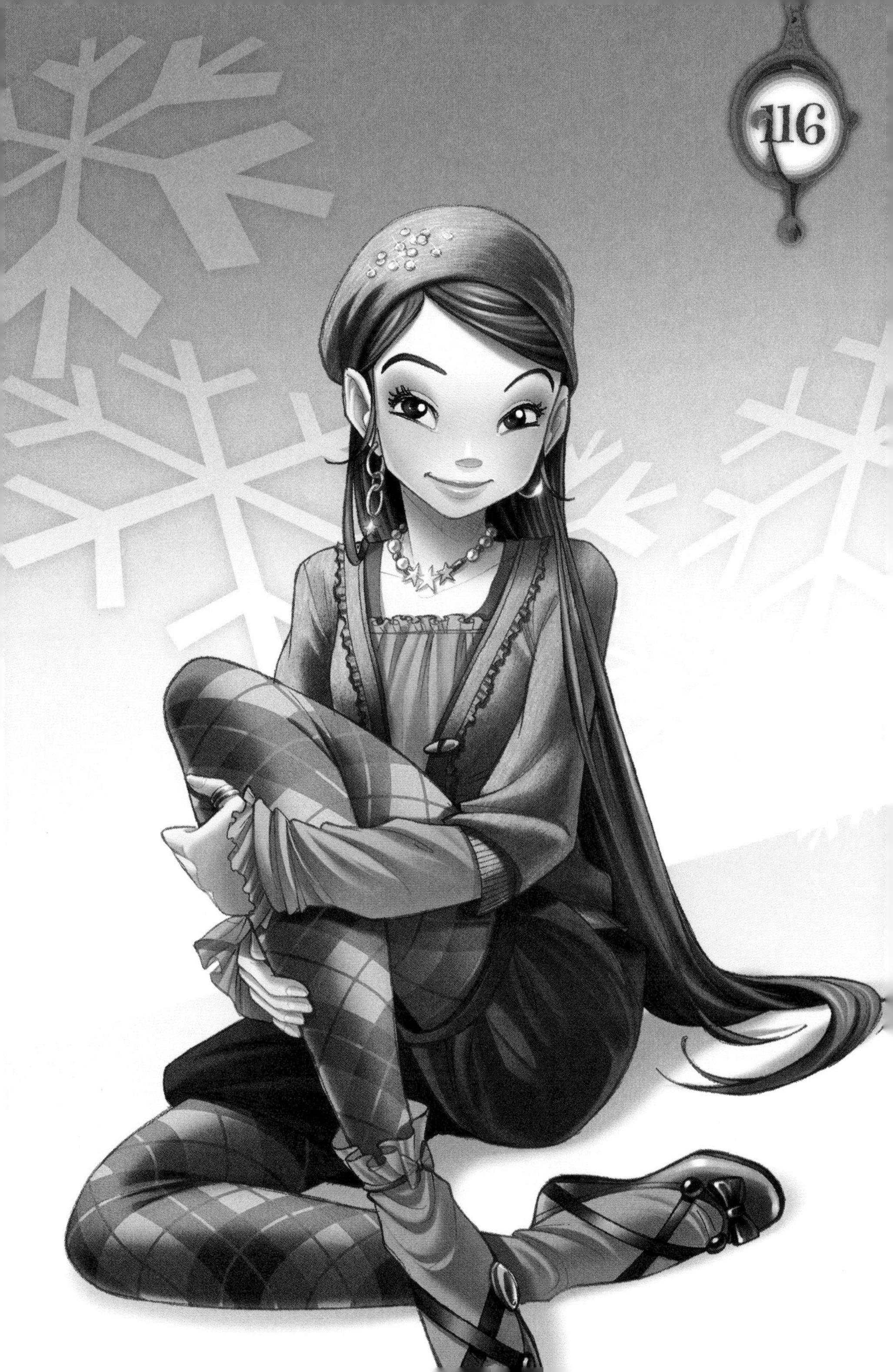

W.i.t.c.h.

Will Irma Taranee Cornelia Hay Lin

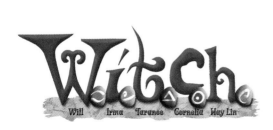

The Right Distance

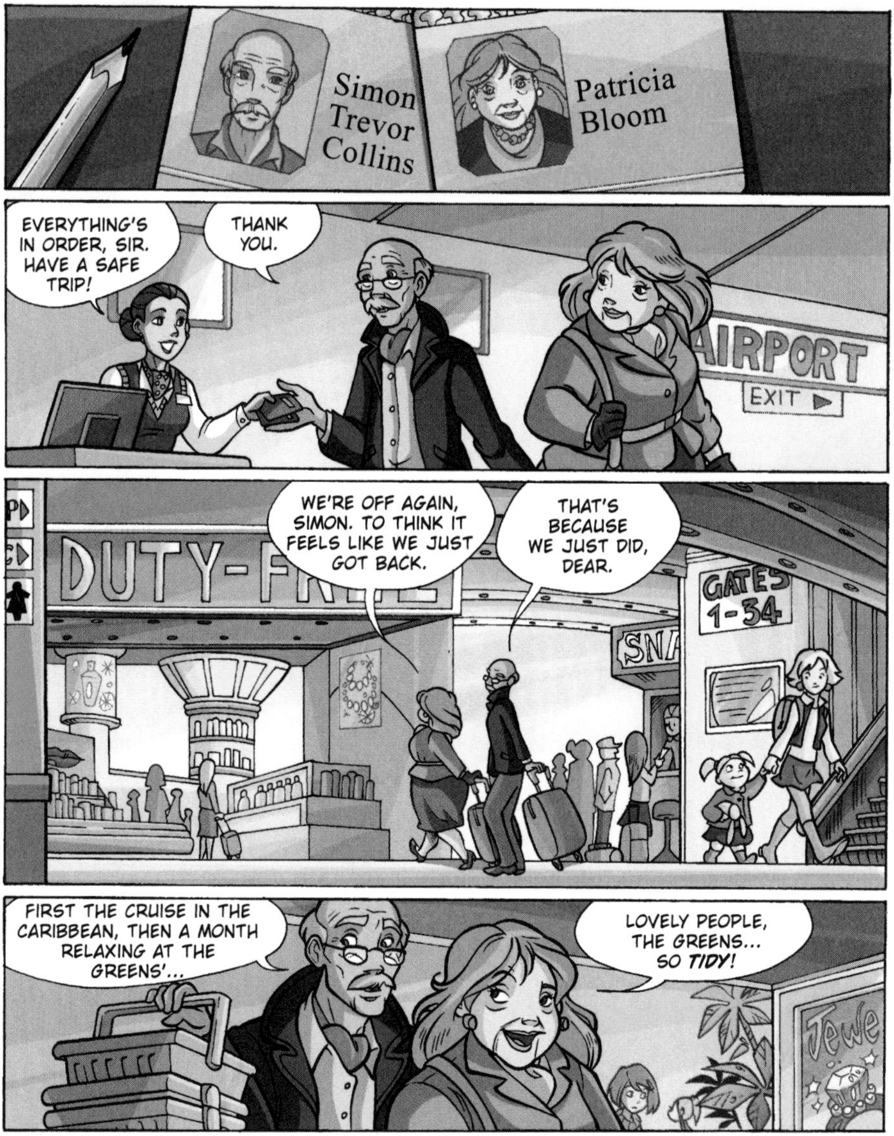
Simon
Trevor
Collins
Patricia
Bloom
EVERYTHING'S IN ORDER, SIR. HAVE A SAFE TRIP!
THANK YOU.
AIRPORT
EXIT
DUTY-FREE
GATES 1-34
WE'RE OFF AGAIN, SIMON. TO THINK IT FEELS LIKE WE JUST GOT BACK.
THAT'S BECAUSE WE JUST DID, DEAR.
FIRST THE CRUISE IN THE CARIBBEAN, THEN A MONTH RELAXING AT THE GREENS'...
LOVELY PEOPLE, THE GREENS... SO *TIDY*!

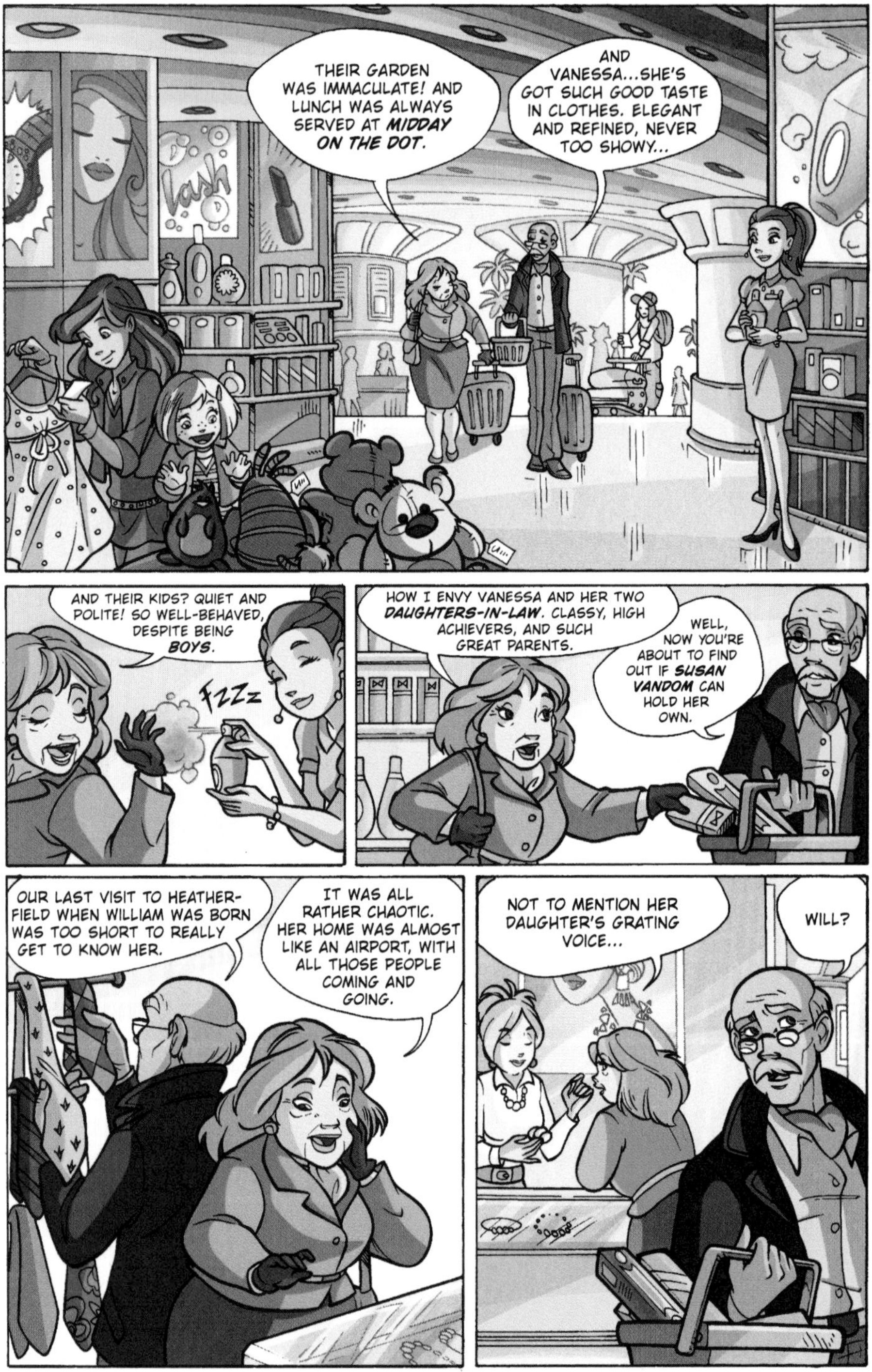
THEIR GARDEN WAS IMMACULATE! AND LUNCH WAS ALWAYS SERVED AT MIDDAY ON THE DOT.
AND VANESSA...SHE'S GOT SUCH GOOD TASTE IN CLOTHES. ELEGANT AND REFINED, NEVER TOO SHOWY...
AND THEIR KIDS? QUIET AND POLITE! SO WELL-BEHAVED, DESPITE BEING BOYS.
FZZz
HOW I ENVY VANESSA AND HER TWO DAUGHTERS-IN-LAW. CLASSY, HIGH ACHIEVERS, AND SUCH GREAT PARENTS.
WELL, NOW YOU'RE ABOUT TO FIND OUT IF SUSAN VANDOM CAN HOLD HER OWN.
OUR LAST VISIT TO HEATHER-FIELD WHEN WILLIAM WAS BORN WAS TOO SHORT TO REALLY GET TO KNOW HER.
IT WAS ALL RATHER CHAOTIC. HER HOME WAS ALMOST LIKE AN AIRPORT, WITH ALL THOSE PEOPLE COMING AND GOING.
NOT TO MENTION HER DAUGHTER'S GRATING VOICE...
WILL?

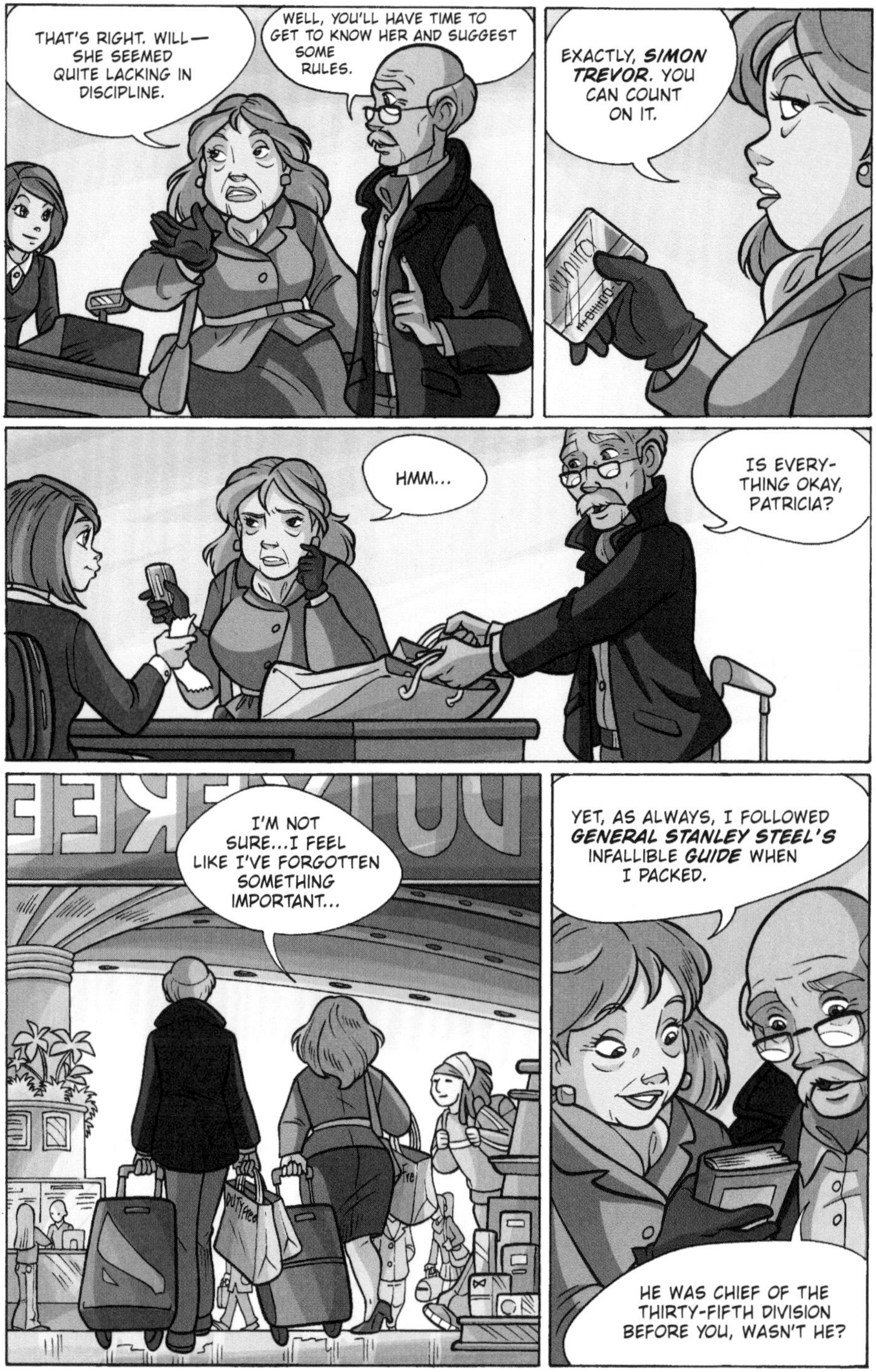
THAT'S RIGHT. WILL— SHE SEEMED QUITE LACKING IN DISCIPLINE.
WELL, YOU'LL HAVE TIME TO GET TO KNOW HER AND SUGGEST SOME RULES.
EXACTLY, **SIMON TREVOR**. YOU CAN COUNT ON IT.
HMM...
IS EVERYTHING OKAY, PATRICIA?
I'M NOT SURE...I FEEL LIKE I'VE FORGOTTEN SOMETHING IMPORTANT...
YET, AS ALWAYS, I FOLLOWED **GENERAL STANLEY STEEL'S** INFALLIBLE **GUIDE** WHEN I PACKED.
HE WAS CHIEF OF THE THIRTY-FIFTH DIVISION BEFORE YOU, WASN'T HE?

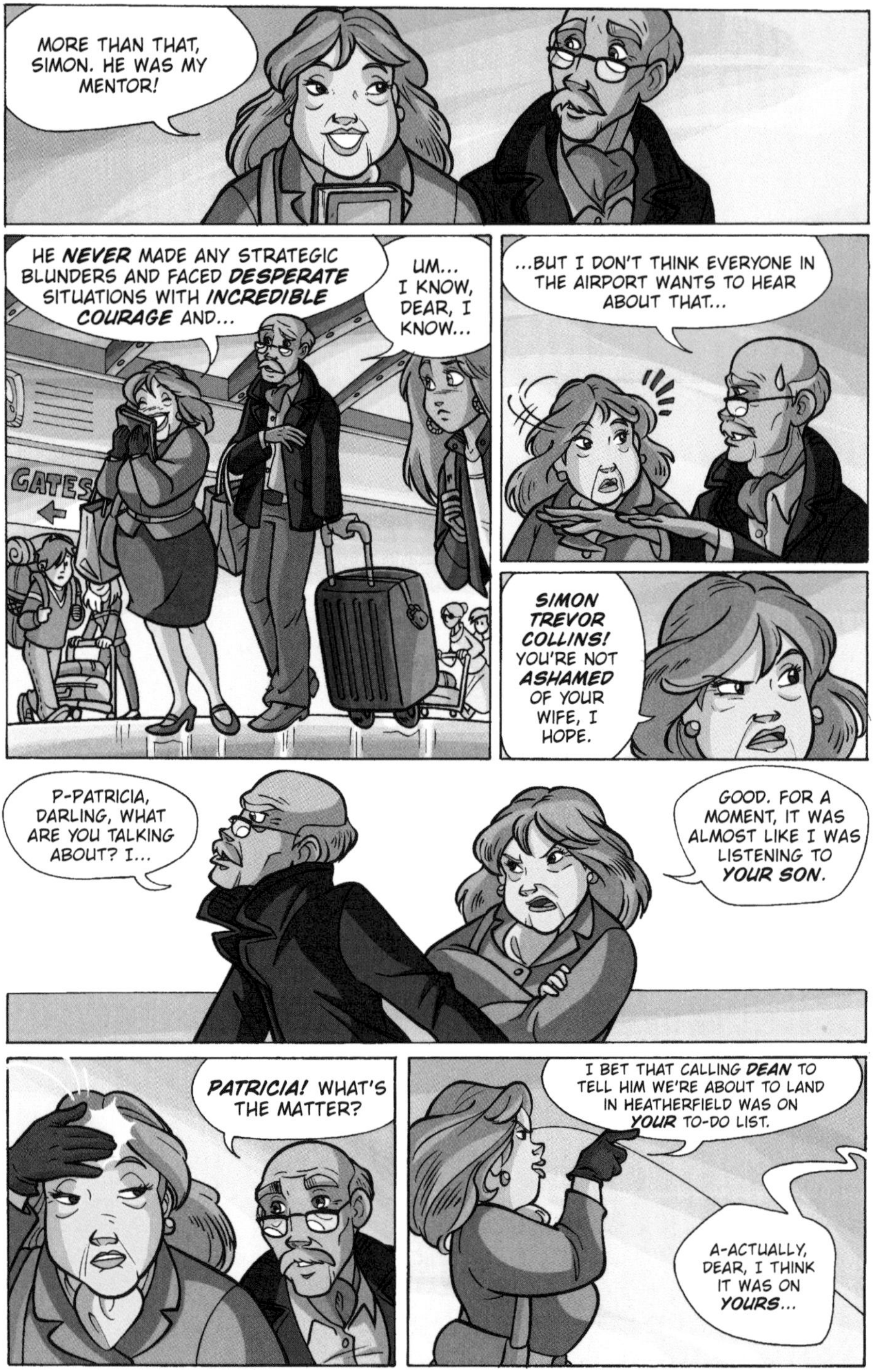
MORE THAN THAT, SIMON. HE WAS MY MENTOR!
HE NEVER MADE ANY STRATEGIC BLUNDERS AND FACED DESPERATE SITUATIONS WITH INCREDIBLE COURAGE AND...
UM... I KNOW, DEAR, I KNOW...
GATES
...BUT I DON'T THINK EVERYONE IN THE AIRPORT WANTS TO HEAR ABOUT THAT...
SIMON TREVOR COLLINS! YOU'RE NOT ASHAMED OF YOUR WIFE, I HOPE.
P-PATRICIA, DARLING, WHAT ARE YOU TALKING ABOUT? I...
GOOD. FOR A MOMENT, IT WAS ALMOST LIKE I WAS LISTENING TO YOUR SON.
PATRICIA! WHAT'S THE MATTER?
I BET THAT CALLING DEAN TO TELL HIM WE'RE ABOUT TO LAND IN HEATHERFIELD WAS ON YOUR TO-DO LIST.
A-ACTUALLY, DEAR, I THINK IT WAS ON YOURS...

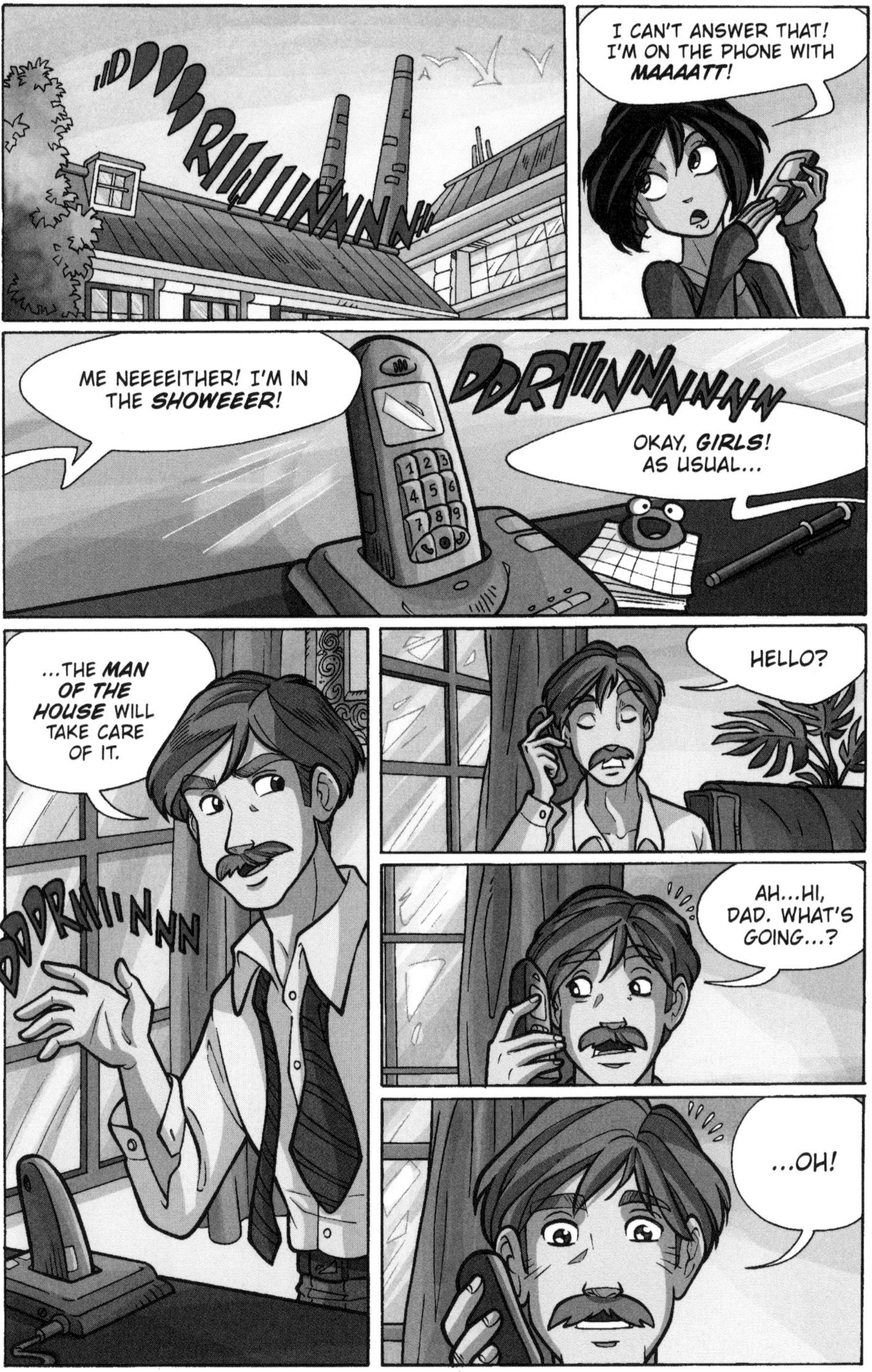
DDDRIIIIINNNNN
I CAN'T ANSWER THAT! I'M ON THE PHONE WITH MAAAATT!
ME NEEEEITHER! I'M IN THE SHOWEEER!
DDRIIIINNNNNNN
OKAY, GIRLS! AS USUAL...
...THE MAN OF THE HOUSE WILL TAKE CARE OF IT.
DDDRIIIINNN
HELLO?
AH...HI, DAD. WHAT'S GOING...?
...OH!

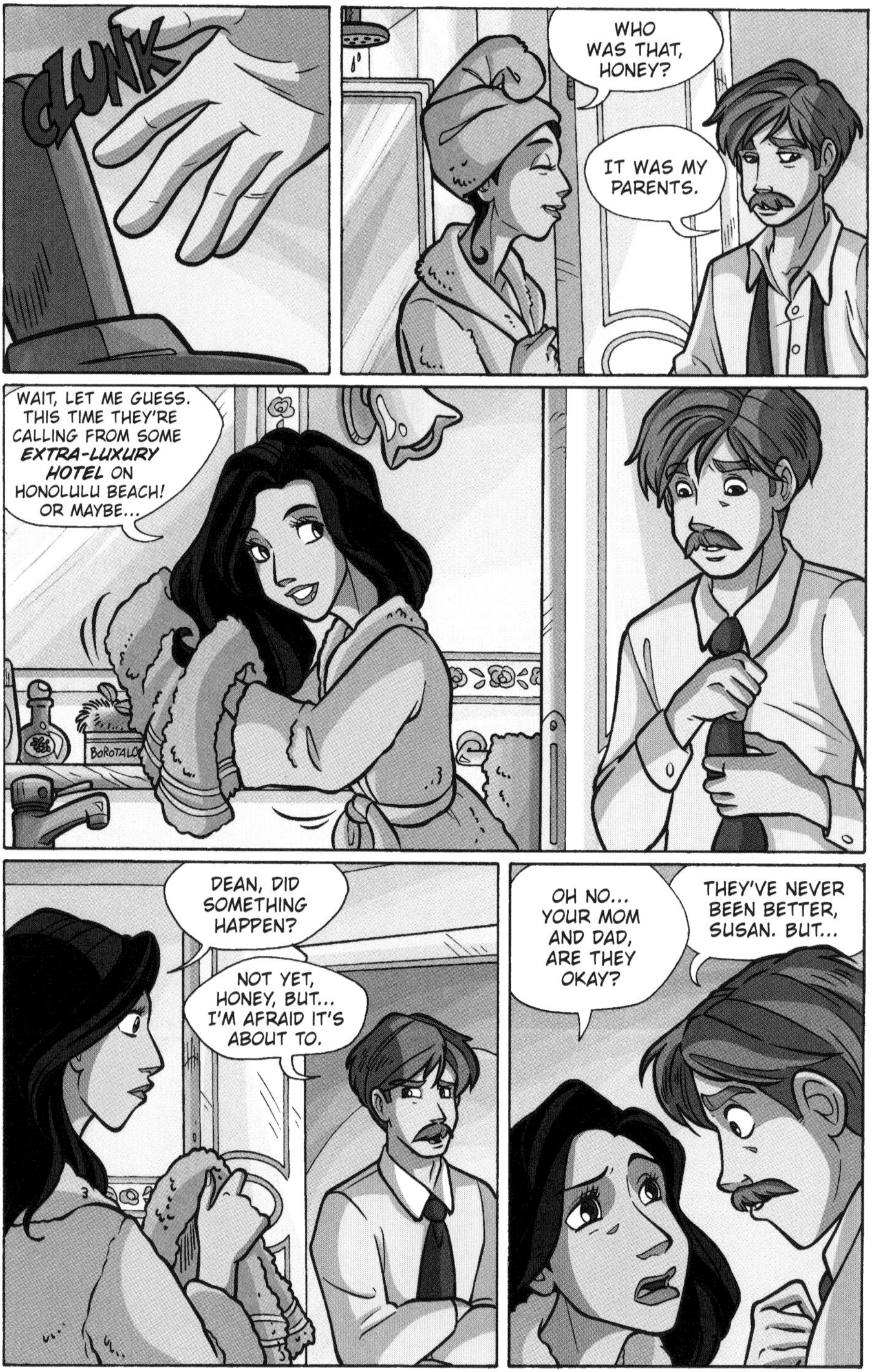
CLUNK
WHO WAS THAT, HONEY?
IT WAS MY PARENTS.
WAIT, LET ME GUESS. THIS TIME THEY'RE CALLING FROM SOME EXTRA-LUXURY HOTEL ON HONOLULU BEACH! OR MAYBE...
BOROTALC
DEAN, DID SOMETHING HAPPEN?
NOT YET, HONEY, BUT... I'M AFRAID IT'S ABOUT TO.
OH NO... YOUR MOM AND DAD, ARE THEY OKAY?
THEY'VE NEVER BEEN BETTER, SUSAN. BUT...

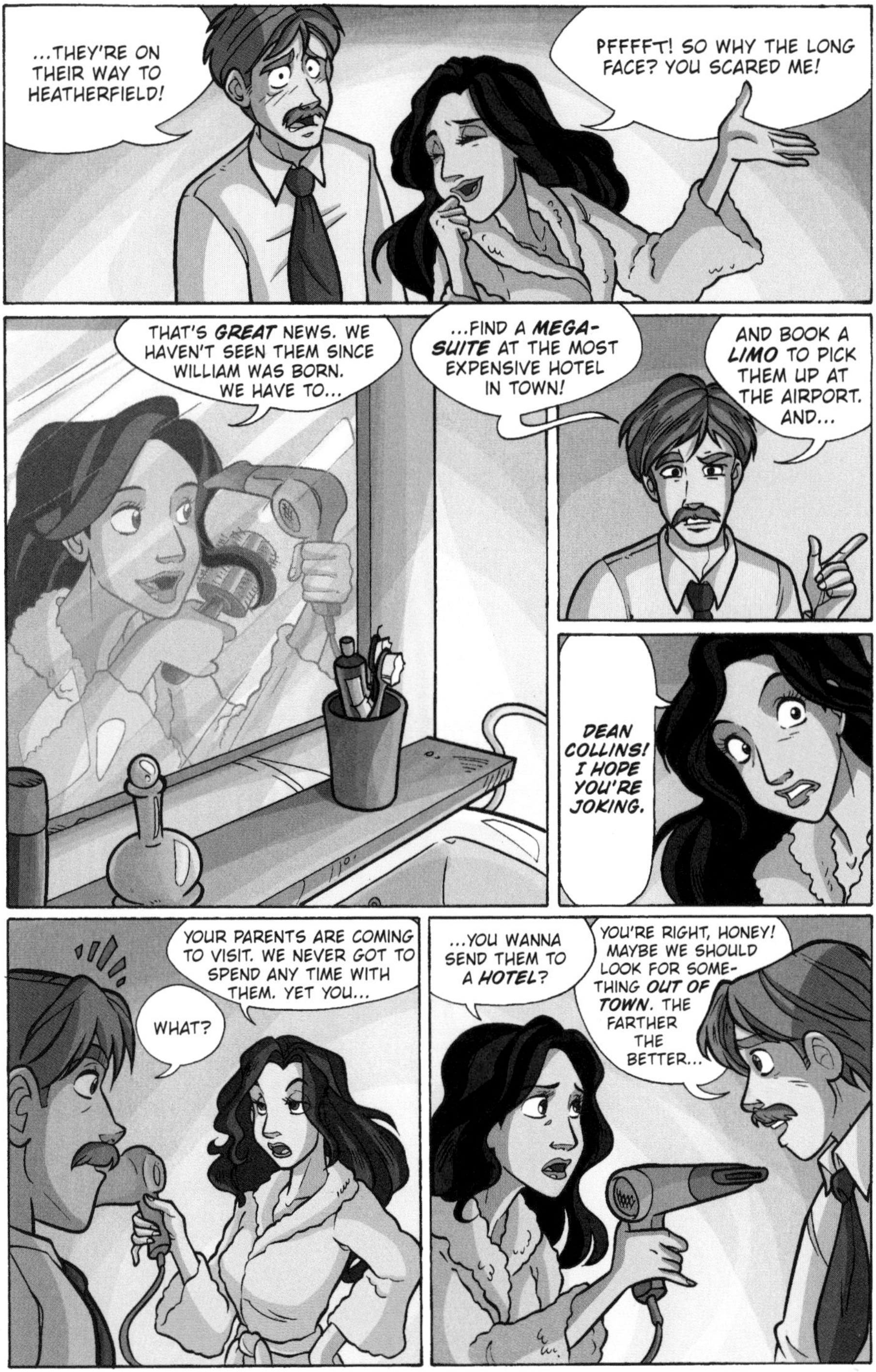
...THEY'RE ON THEIR WAY TO HEATHERFIELD!
PFFFFT! SO WHY THE LONG FACE? YOU SCARED ME!
THAT'S **GREAT** NEWS. WE HAVEN'T SEEN THEM SINCE WILLIAM WAS BORN. WE HAVE TO...
...FIND A **MEGA-SUITE** AT THE MOST EXPENSIVE HOTEL IN TOWN!
AND BOOK A **LIMO** TO PICK THEM UP AT THE AIRPORT. AND...
DEAN COLLINS! I HOPE YOU'RE JOKING.
YOUR PARENTS ARE COMING TO VISIT. WE NEVER GOT TO SPEND ANY TIME WITH THEM. YET YOU...
WHAT?
...YOU WANNA SEND THEM TO A **HOTEL**?
YOU'RE RIGHT, HONEY! MAYBE WE SHOULD LOOK FOR SOMETHING **OUT OF TOWN**. THE FARTHER THE BETTER...

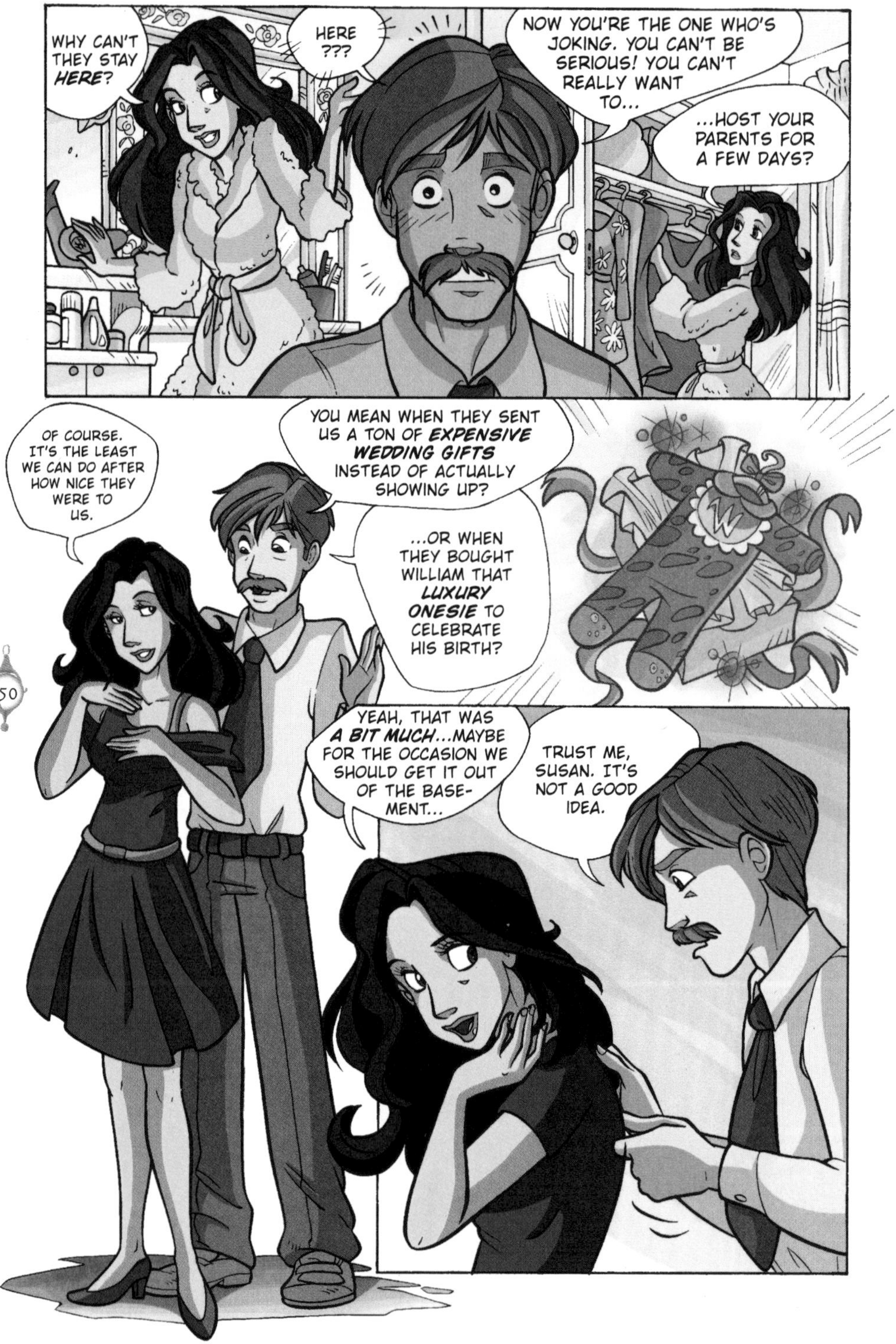
WHY CAN'T THEY STAY *HERE*?
HERE ???
NOW YOU'RE THE ONE WHO'S JOKING. YOU CAN'T BE SERIOUS! YOU CAN'T REALLY WANT TO...
...HOST YOUR PARENTS FOR A FEW DAYS?
OF COURSE. IT'S THE LEAST WE CAN DO AFTER HOW NICE THEY WERE TO US.
YOU MEAN WHEN THEY SENT US A TON OF ***EXPENSIVE WEDDING GIFTS*** INSTEAD OF ACTUALLY SHOWING UP?
...OR WHEN THEY BOUGHT WILLIAM THAT ***LUXURY ONESIE*** TO CELEBRATE HIS BIRTH?
YEAH, THAT WAS ***A BIT MUCH***...MAYBE FOR THE OCCASION WE SHOULD GET IT OUT OF THE BASE- MENT...
TRUST ME, SUSAN. IT'S NOT A GOOD IDEA.

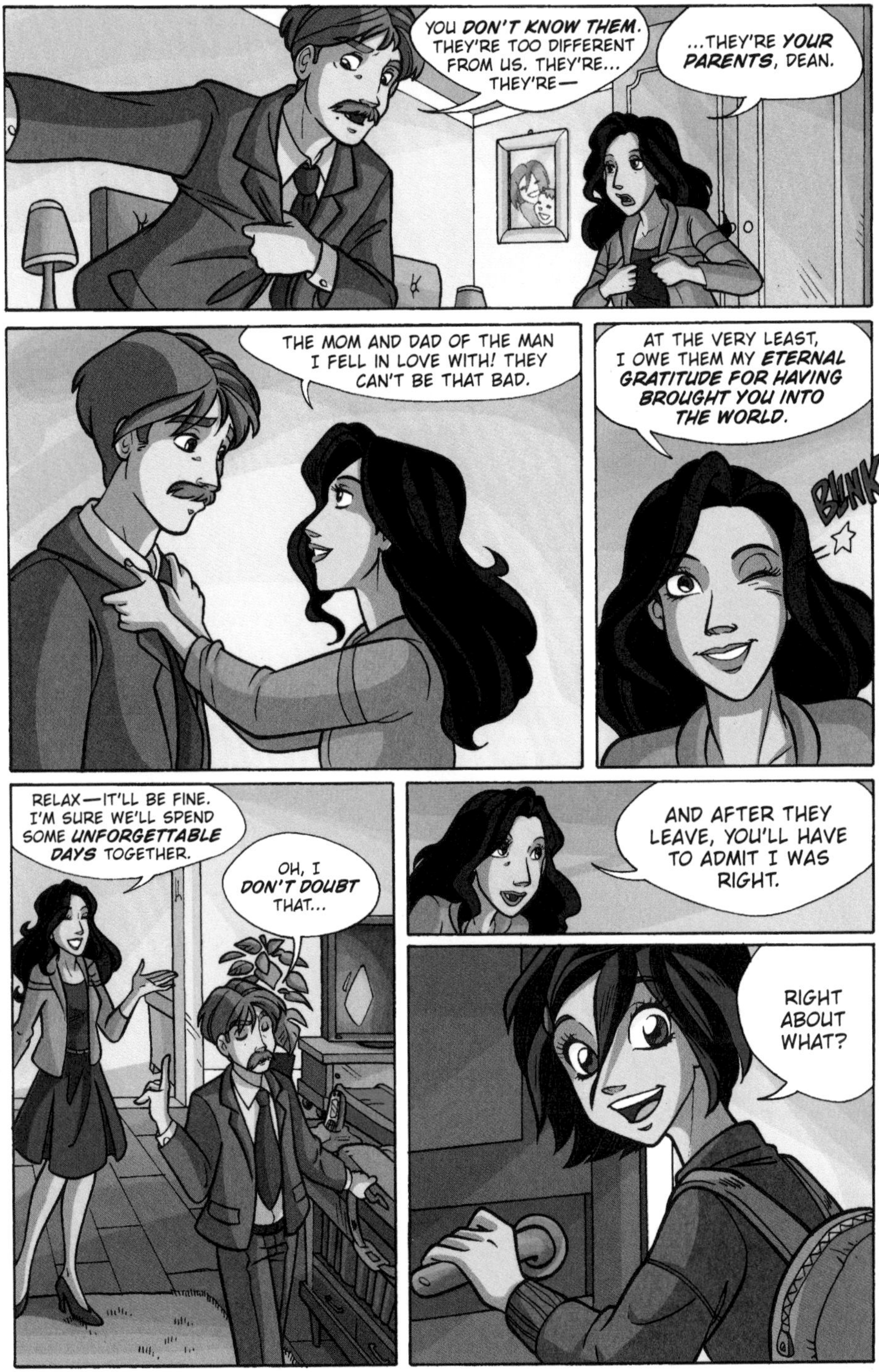
YOU **DON'T KNOW THEM.** THEY'RE TOO DIFFERENT FROM US. THEY'RE... THEY'RE—
...THEY'RE **YOUR PARENTS**, DEAN.
THE MOM AND DAD OF THE MAN I FELL IN LOVE WITH! THEY CAN'T BE THAT BAD.
AT THE VERY LEAST, I OWE THEM MY **ETERNAL GRATITUDE FOR HAVING BROUGHT YOU INTO THE WORLD.**
BLINK
RELAX—IT'LL BE FINE. I'M SURE WE'LL SPEND SOME **UNFORGETTABLE DAYS** TOGETHER.
OH, I **DON'T DOUBT** THAT...
AND AFTER THEY LEAVE, YOU'LL HAVE TO ADMIT I WAS RIGHT.
RIGHT ABOUT WHAT?

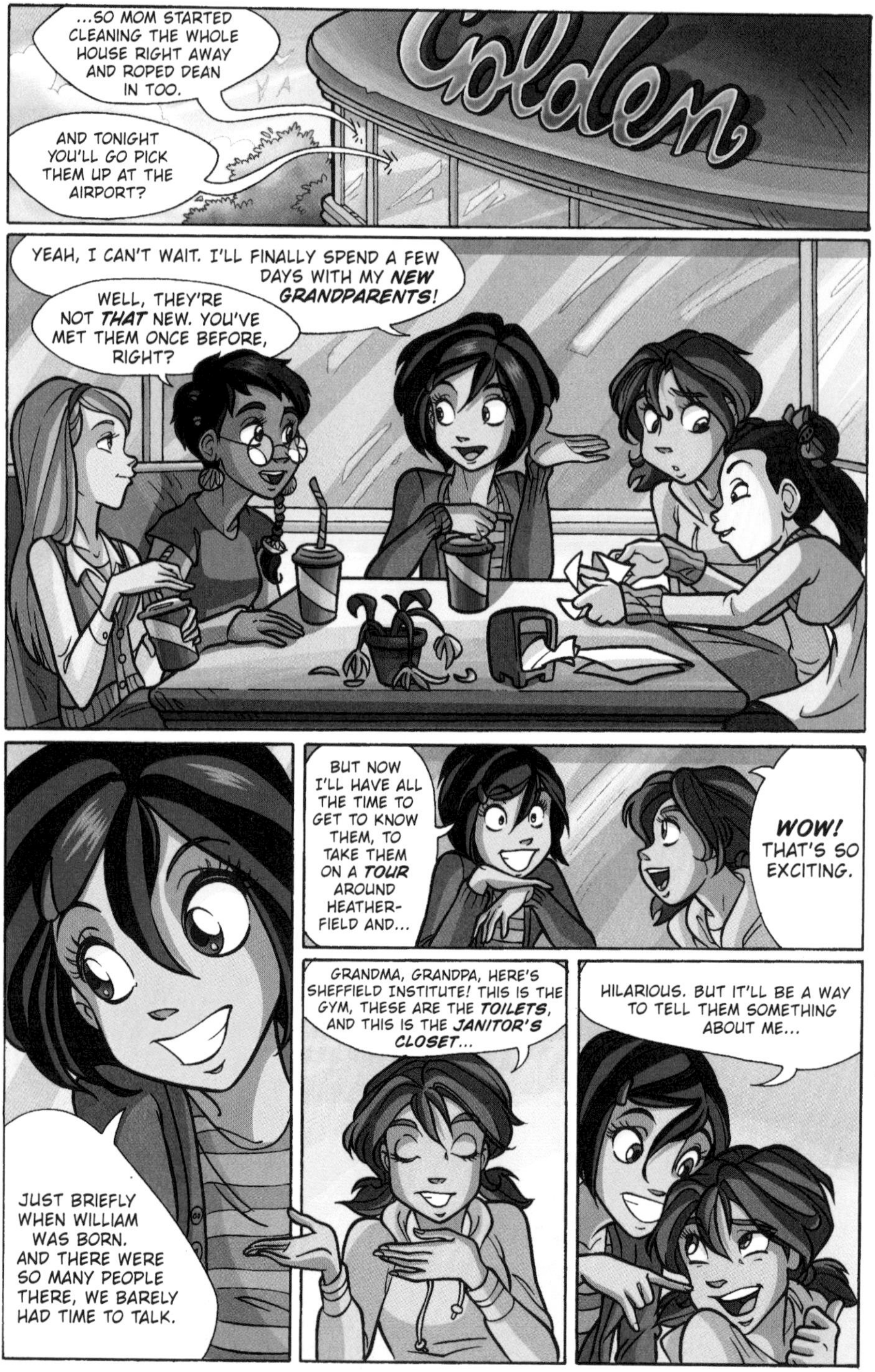

GOLDEN
...SO MOM STARTED CLEANING THE WHOLE HOUSE RIGHT AWAY AND ROPED DEAN IN TOO.
AND TONIGHT YOU'LL GO PICK THEM UP AT THE AIRPORT?
YEAH, I CAN'T WAIT. I'LL FINALLY SPEND A FEW DAYS WITH MY *NEW GRANDPARENTS*!
WELL, THEY'RE NOT *THAT* NEW. YOU'VE MET THEM ONCE BEFORE, RIGHT?
JUST BRIEFLY WHEN WILLIAM WAS BORN. AND THERE WERE SO MANY PEOPLE THERE, WE BARELY HAD TIME TO TALK.
BUT NOW I'LL HAVE ALL THE TIME TO GET TO KNOW THEM, TO TAKE THEM ON A *TOUR* AROUND HEATHER-FIELD AND...
WOW! THAT'S SO EXCITING.
GRANDMA, GRANDPA, HERE'S SHEFFIELD INSTITUTE! THIS IS THE GYM, THESE ARE THE *TOILETS*, AND THIS IS THE *JANITOR'S CLOSET*...
HILARIOUS. BUT IT'LL BE A WAY TO TELL THEM SOMETHING ABOUT ME...

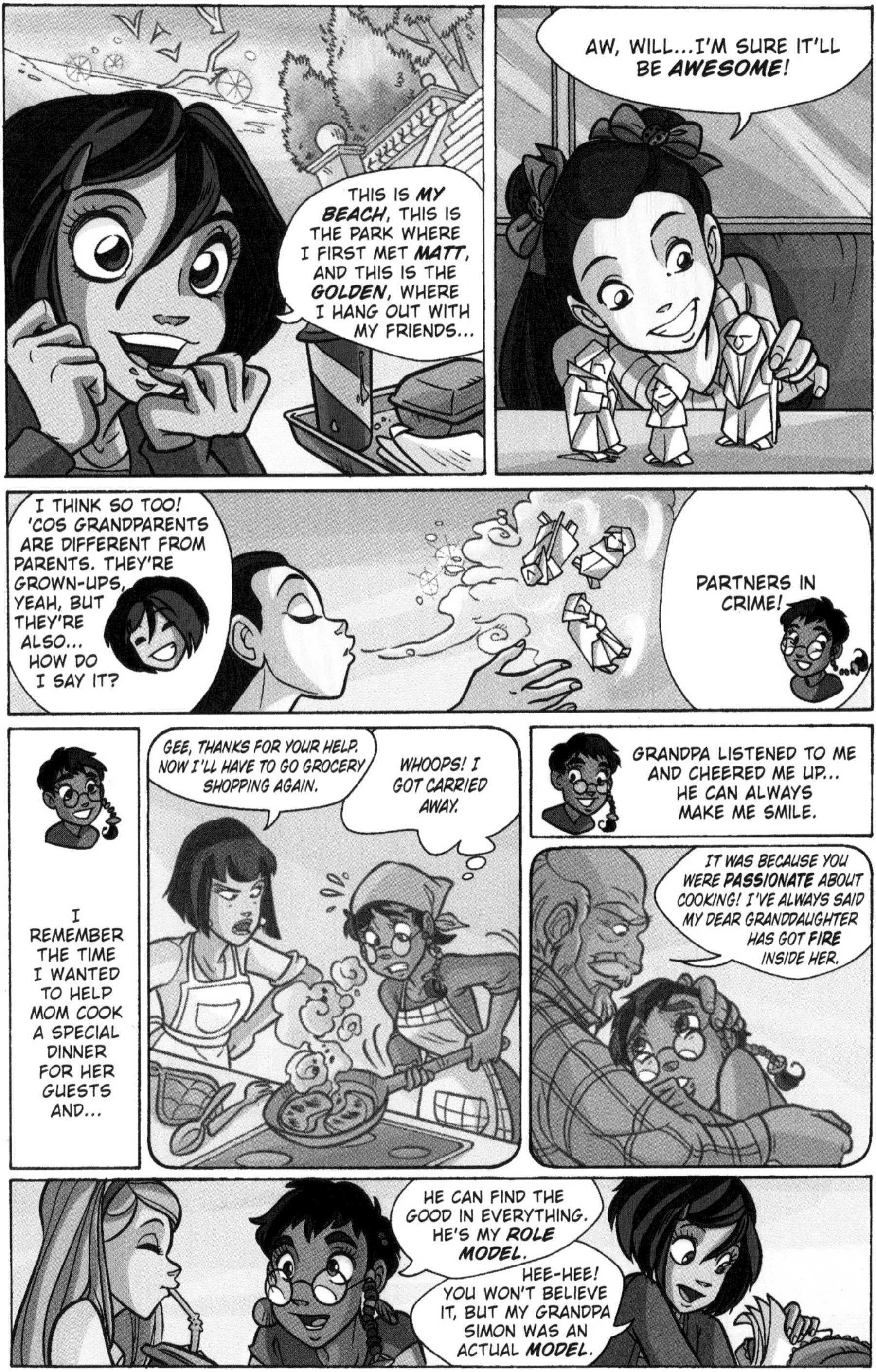
THIS IS MY BEACH, THIS IS THE PARK WHERE I FIRST MET MATT, AND THIS IS THE GOLDEN, WHERE I HANG OUT WITH MY FRIENDS...
AW, WILL...I'M SURE IT'LL BE AWESOME!
I THINK SO TOO! 'COS GRANDPARENTS ARE DIFFERENT FROM PARENTS. THEY'RE GROWN-UPS, YEAH, BUT THEY'RE ALSO... HOW DO I SAY IT?
PARTNERS IN CRIME!
I REMEMBER THE TIME I WANTED TO HELP MOM COOK A SPECIAL DINNER FOR HER GUESTS AND...
GEE, THANKS FOR YOUR HELP. NOW I'LL HAVE TO GO GROCERY SHOPPING AGAIN.
WHOOPS! I GOT CARRIED AWAY.
GRANDPA LISTENED TO ME AND CHEERED ME UP... HE CAN ALWAYS MAKE ME SMILE.
IT WAS BECAUSE YOU WERE PASSIONATE ABOUT COOKING! I'VE ALWAYS SAID MY DEAR GRANDDAUGHTER HAS GOT FIRE INSIDE HER.
HE CAN FIND THE GOOD IN EVERYTHING. HE'S MY ROLE MODEL.
HEE-HEE! YOU WON'T BELIEVE IT, BUT MY GRANDPA SIMON WAS AN ACTUAL MODEL.

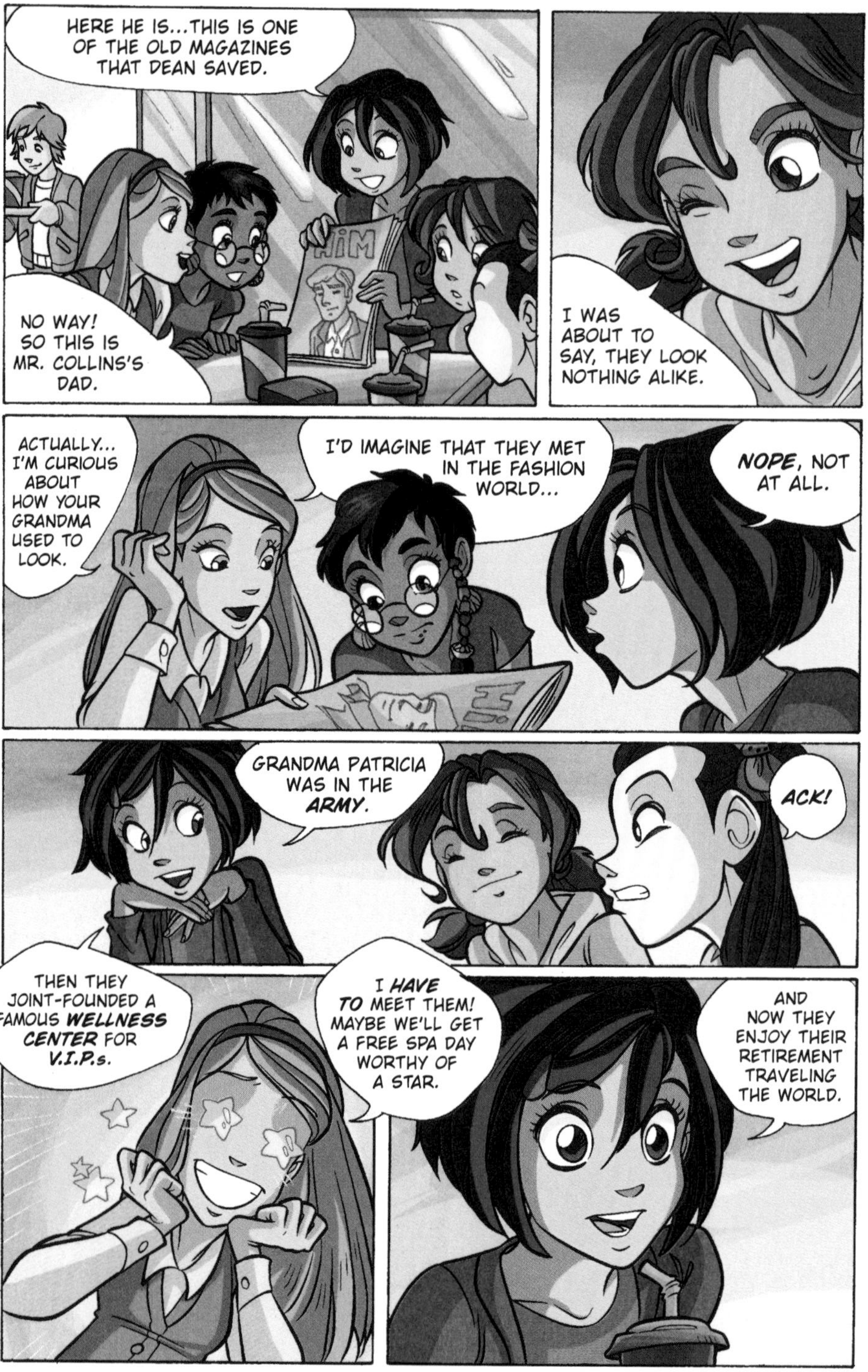
HERE HE IS...THIS IS ONE OF THE OLD MAGAZINES THAT DEAN SAVED.
HIM
NO WAY! SO THIS IS MR. COLLINS'S DAD.
I WAS ABOUT TO SAY, THEY LOOK NOTHING ALIKE.
ACTUALLY... I'M CURIOUS ABOUT HOW YOUR GRANDMA USED TO LOOK.
I'D IMAGINE THAT THEY MET IN THE FASHION WORLD...
NOPE, NOT AT ALL.
GRANDMA PATRICIA WAS IN THE ARMY.
ACK!
THEN THEY JOINT-FOUNDED A FAMOUS WELLNESS CENTER FOR V.I.P.s.
I HAVE TO MEET THEM! MAYBE WE'LL GET A FREE SPA DAY WORTHY OF A STAR.
AND NOW THEY ENJOY THEIR RETIREMENT TRAVELING THE WORLD.

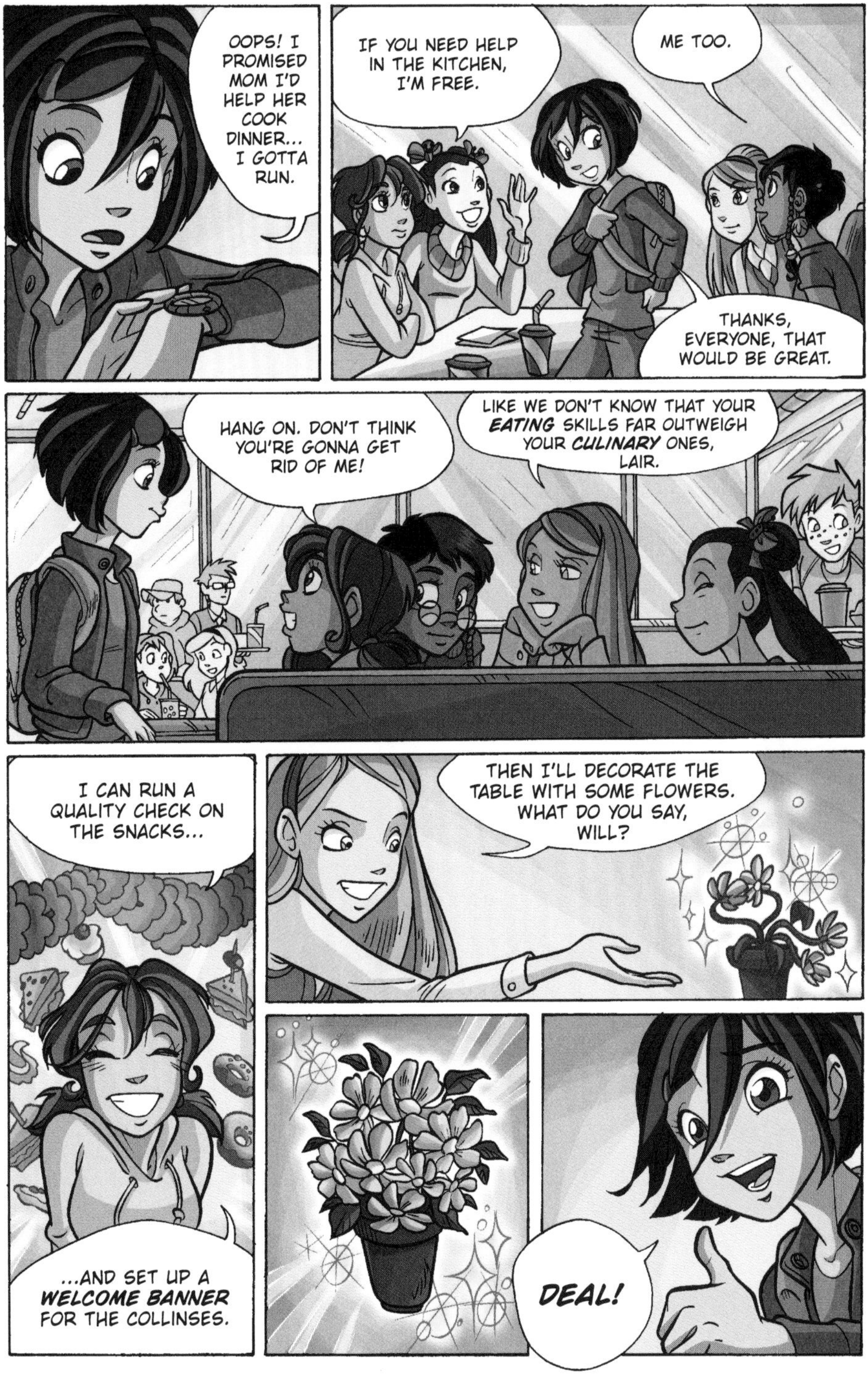
OOPS! I PROMISED MOM I'D HELP HER COOK DINNER... I GOTTA RUN.
IF YOU NEED HELP IN THE KITCHEN, I'M FREE.
ME TOO.
THANKS, EVERYONE, THAT WOULD BE GREAT.
HANG ON. DON'T THINK YOU'RE GONNA GET RID OF ME!
LIKE WE DON'T KNOW THAT YOUR EATING SKILLS FAR OUTWEIGH YOUR CULINARY ONES, LAIR.
I CAN RUN A QUALITY CHECK ON THE SNACKS...
...AND SET UP A WELCOME BANNER FOR THE COLLINSES.
THEN I'LL DECORATE THE TABLE WITH SOME FLOWERS. WHAT DO YOU SAY, WILL?
DEAL!

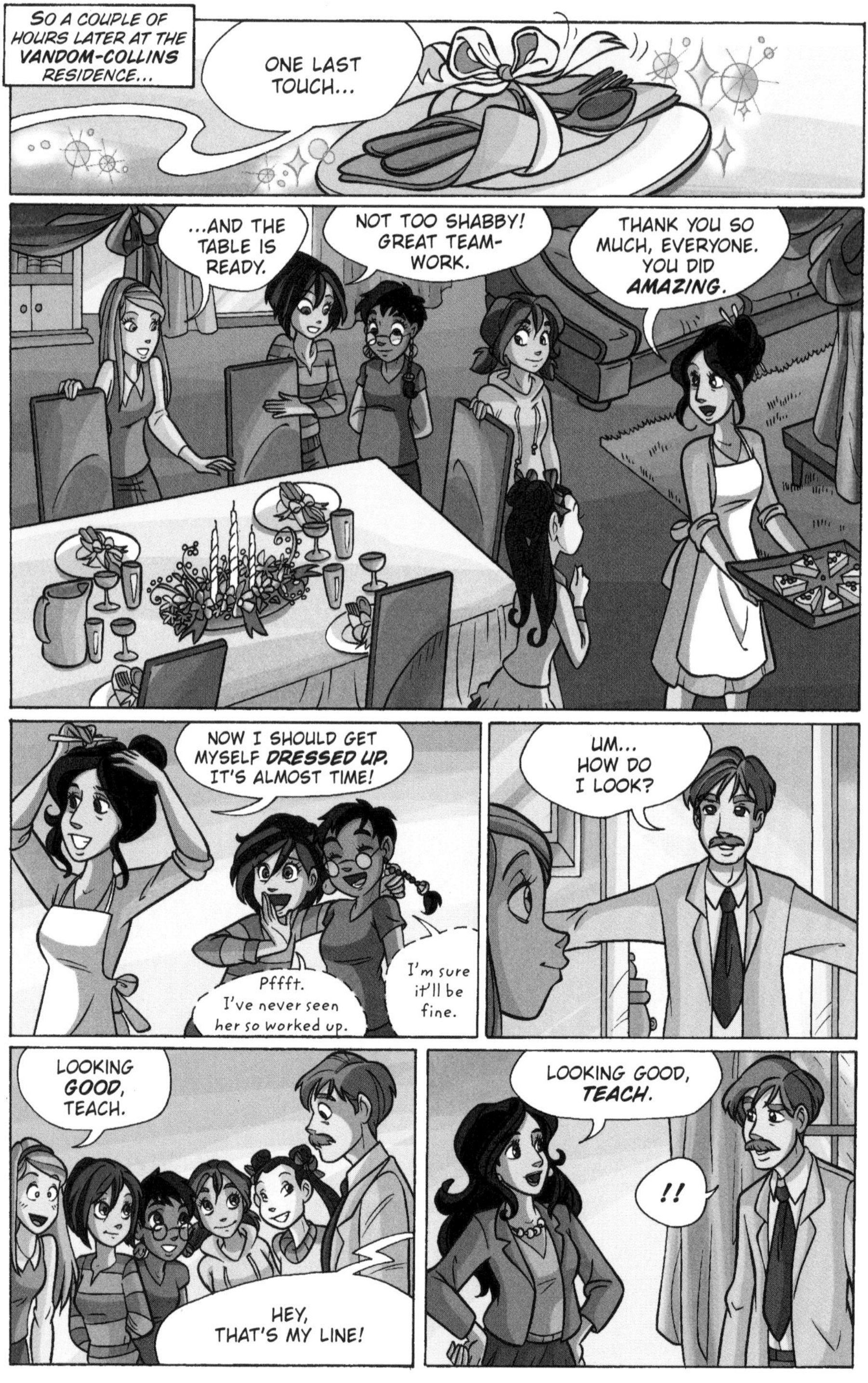
SO A COUPLE OF HOURS LATER AT THE VANDOM-COLLINS RESIDENCE...
ONE LAST TOUCH...
...AND THE TABLE IS READY.
NOT TOO SHABBY! GREAT TEAM-WORK.
THANK YOU SO MUCH, EVERYONE. YOU DID AMAZING.
NOW I SHOULD GET MYSELF DRESSED UP. IT'S ALMOST TIME!
Pffft. I've never seen her so worked up.
I'm sure it'll be fine.
UM... HOW DO I LOOK?
LOOKING GOOD, TEACH.
HEY, THAT'S MY LINE!
LOOKING GOOD, TEACH.
!!

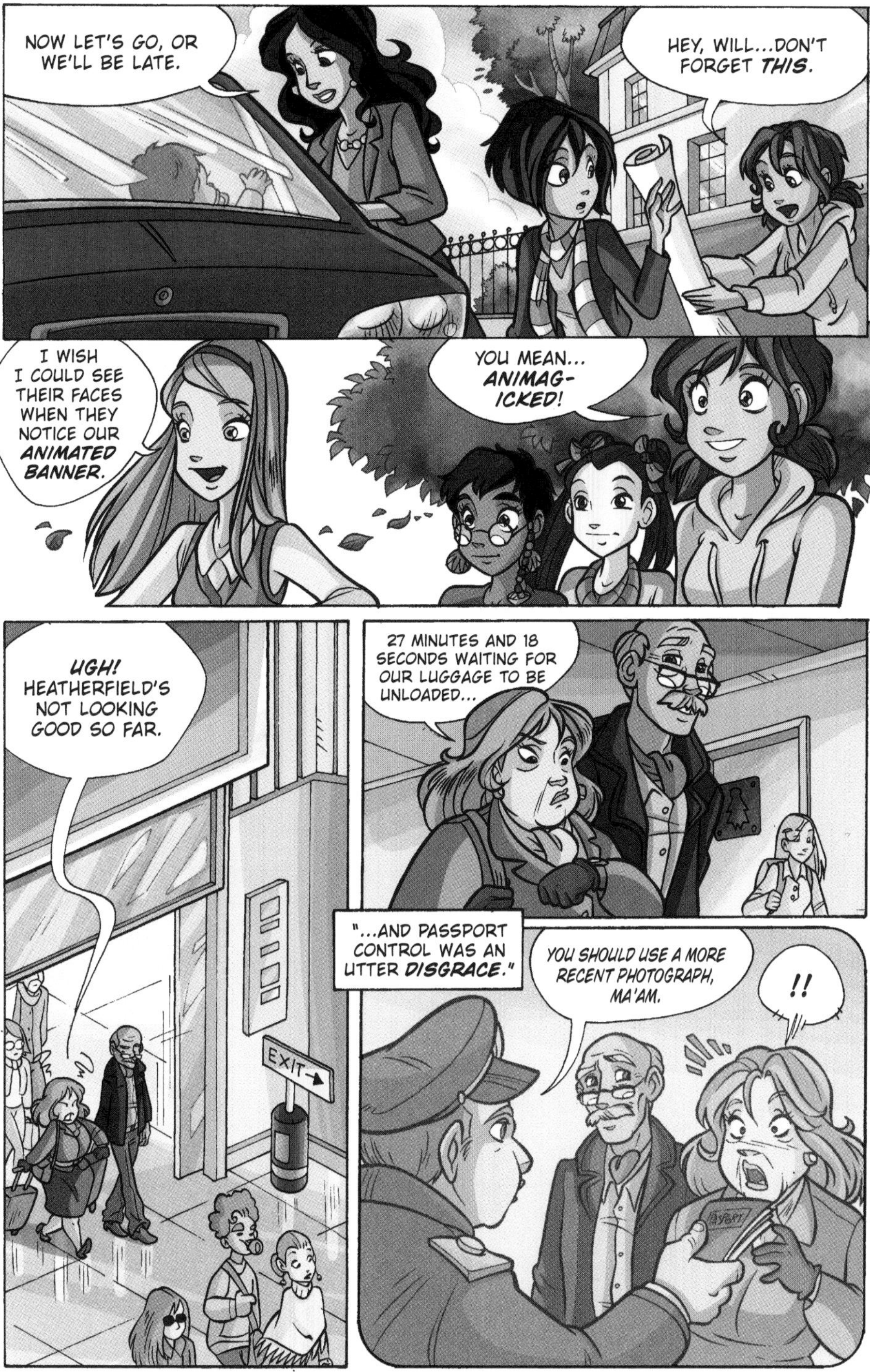
NOW LET'S GO, OR WE'LL BE LATE.
HEY, WILL...DON'T FORGET *THIS*.
I WISH I COULD SEE THEIR FACES WHEN THEY NOTICE OUR *ANIMATED BANNER*.
YOU MEAN... *ANIMAG-ICKED!*
UGH! HEATHERFIELD'S NOT LOOKING GOOD SO FAR.
27 MINUTES AND 18 SECONDS WAITING FOR OUR LUGGAGE TO BE UNLOADED...
EXIT
"...AND PASSPORT CONTROL WAS AN UTTER *DISGRACE*."
YOU SHOULD USE A MORE RECENT PHOTOGRAPH, MA'AM.
!!

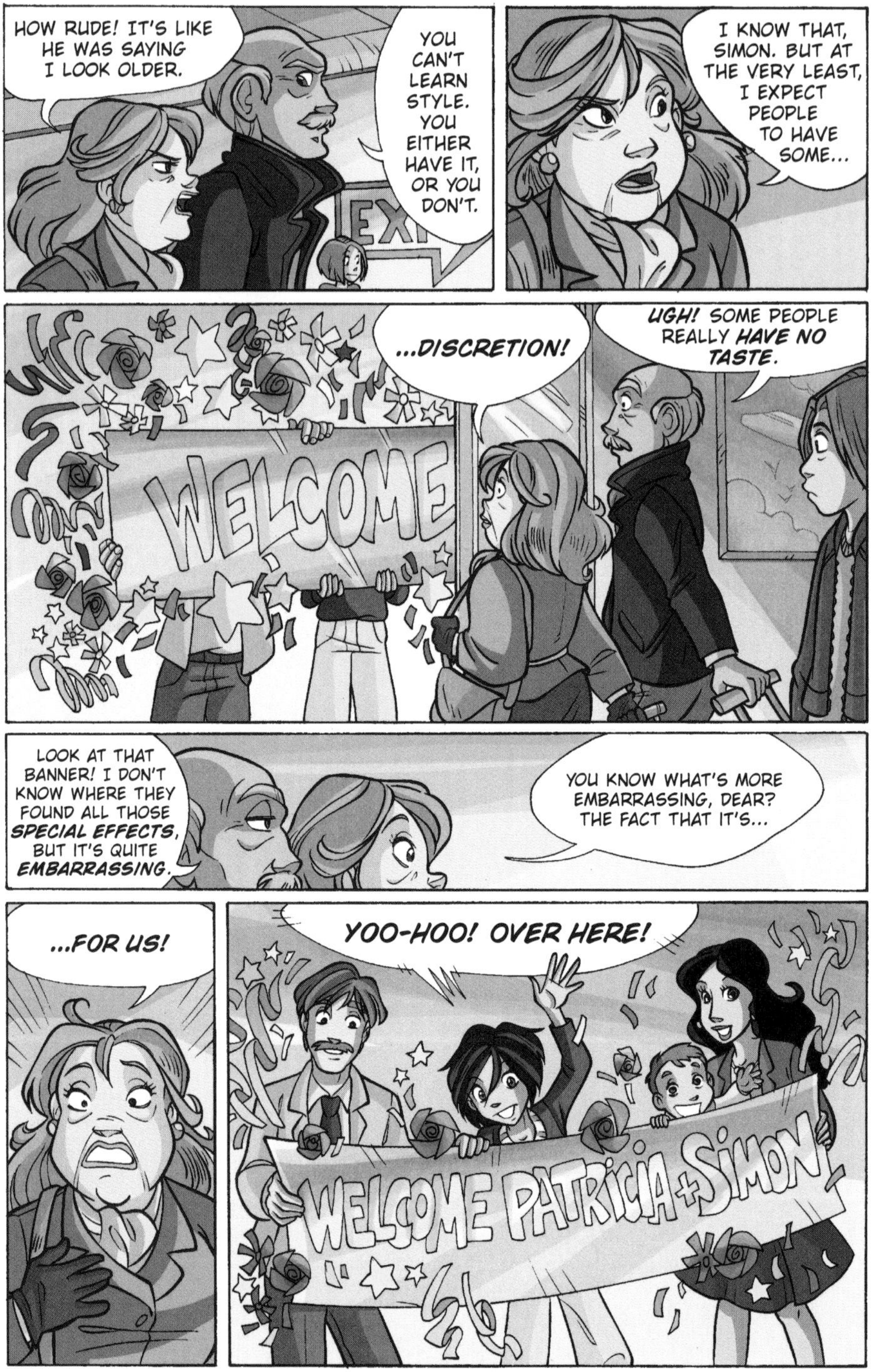
HOW RUDE! IT'S LIKE HE WAS SAYING I LOOK OLDER.
YOU CAN'T LEARN STYLE. YOU EITHER HAVE IT, OR YOU DON'T.
I KNOW THAT, SIMON. BUT AT THE VERY LEAST, I EXPECT PEOPLE TO HAVE SOME...
...DISCRETION!
UGH! SOME PEOPLE REALLY HAVE NO TASTE.
WELCOME
LOOK AT THAT BANNER! I DON'T KNOW WHERE THEY FOUND ALL THOSE SPECIAL EFFECTS, BUT IT'S QUITE EMBARRASSING.
YOU KNOW WHAT'S MORE EMBARRASSING, DEAR? THE FACT THAT IT'S...
...FOR US!
YOO-HOO! OVER HERE!
WELCOME PATRICIA + SIMON

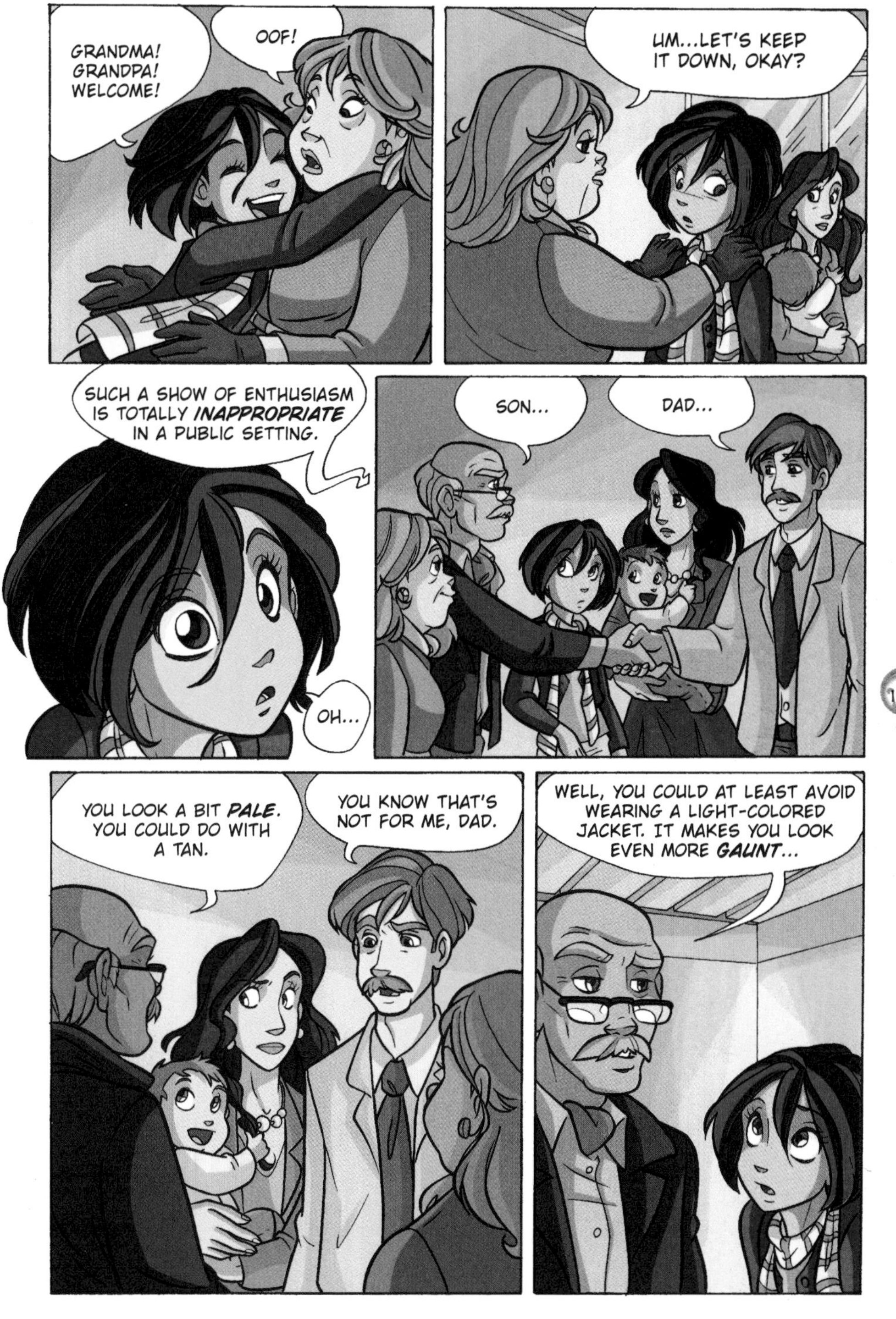
GRANDMA! GRANDPA! WELCOME!
OOF!
UM...LET'S KEEP IT DOWN, OKAY?
SUCH A SHOW OF ENTHUSIASM IS TOTALLY *INAPPROPRIATE* IN A PUBLIC SETTING.
OH...
SON...
DAD...
YOU LOOK A BIT *PALE*. YOU COULD DO WITH A TAN.
YOU KNOW THAT'S NOT FOR ME, DAD.
WELL, YOU COULD AT LEAST AVOID WEARING A LIGHT-COLORED JACKET. IT MAKES YOU LOOK EVEN MORE *GAUNT*...

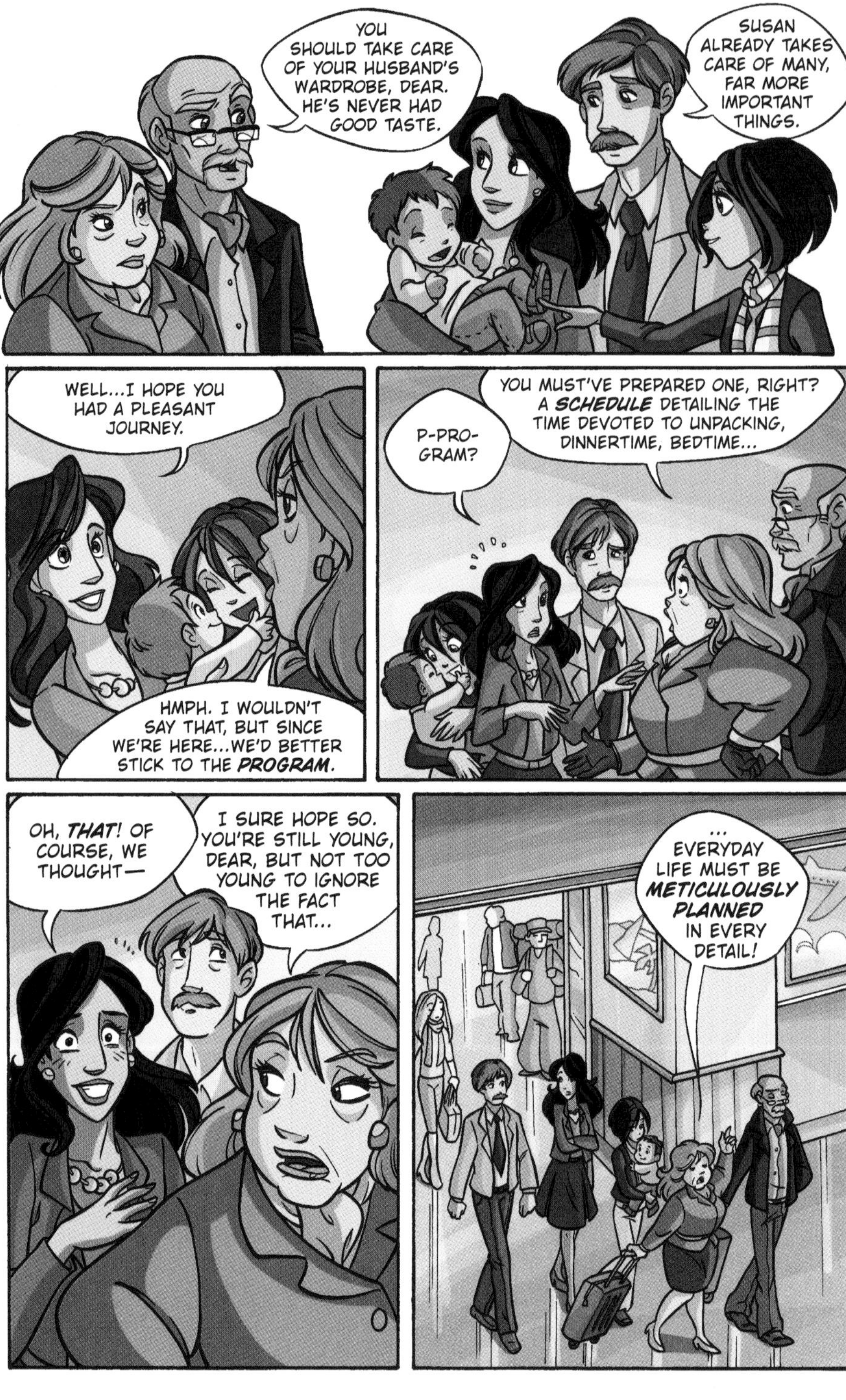

YOU SHOULD TAKE CARE OF YOUR HUSBAND'S WARDROBE, DEAR. HE'S NEVER HAD GOOD TASTE.
SUSAN ALREADY TAKES CARE OF MANY, FAR MORE IMPORTANT THINGS.
WELL...I HOPE YOU HAD A PLEASANT JOURNEY.
HMPH. I WOULDN'T SAY THAT, BUT SINCE WE'RE HERE...WE'D BETTER STICK TO THE ***PROGRAM***.
P-PRO-GRAM?
YOU MUST'VE PREPARED ONE, RIGHT? A ***SCHEDULE*** DETAILING THE TIME DEVOTED TO UNPACKING, DINNERTIME, BEDTIME...
OH, ***THAT***! OF COURSE, WE THOUGHT—
I SURE HOPE SO. YOU'RE STILL YOUNG, DEAR, BUT NOT TOO YOUNG TO IGNORE THE FACT THAT...
...EVERYDAY LIFE MUST BE ***METICULOUSLY PLANNED*** IN EVERY DETAIL!

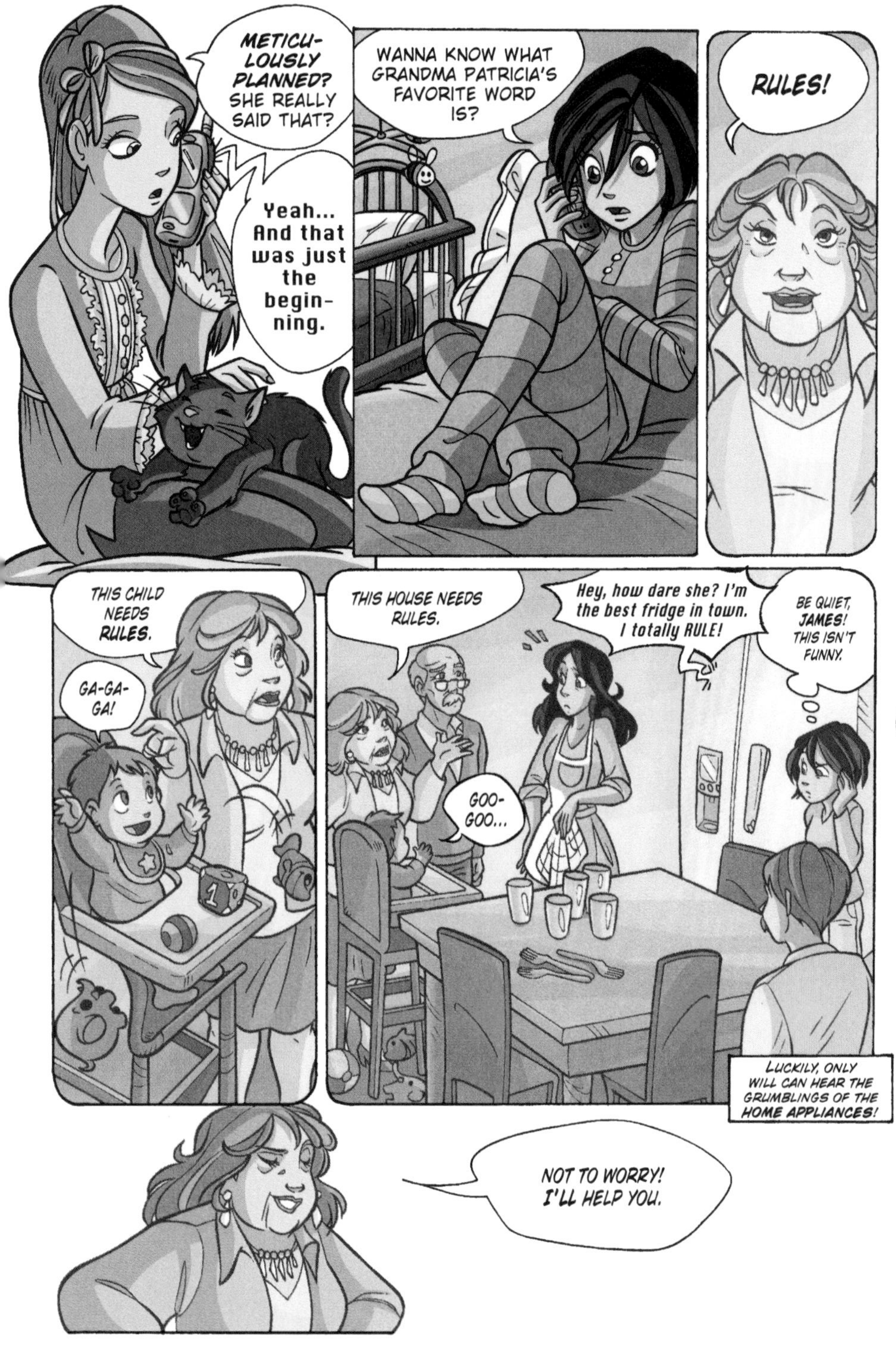
METICULOUSLY PLANNED? SHE REALLY SAID THAT?
Yeah... And that was just the beginning.
WANNA KNOW WHAT GRANDMA PATRICIA'S FAVORITE WORD IS?
RULES!
THIS CHILD NEEDS RULES.
GA-GA-GA!
THIS HOUSE NEEDS RULES.
Hey, how dare she? I'm the best fridge in town. I totally RULE!
BE QUIET, JAMES! THIS ISN'T FUNNY.
GOO-GOO...
LUCKILY, ONLY WILL CAN HEAR THE GRUMBLINGS OF THE HOME APPLIANCES!
NOT TO WORRY! I'LL HELP YOU.

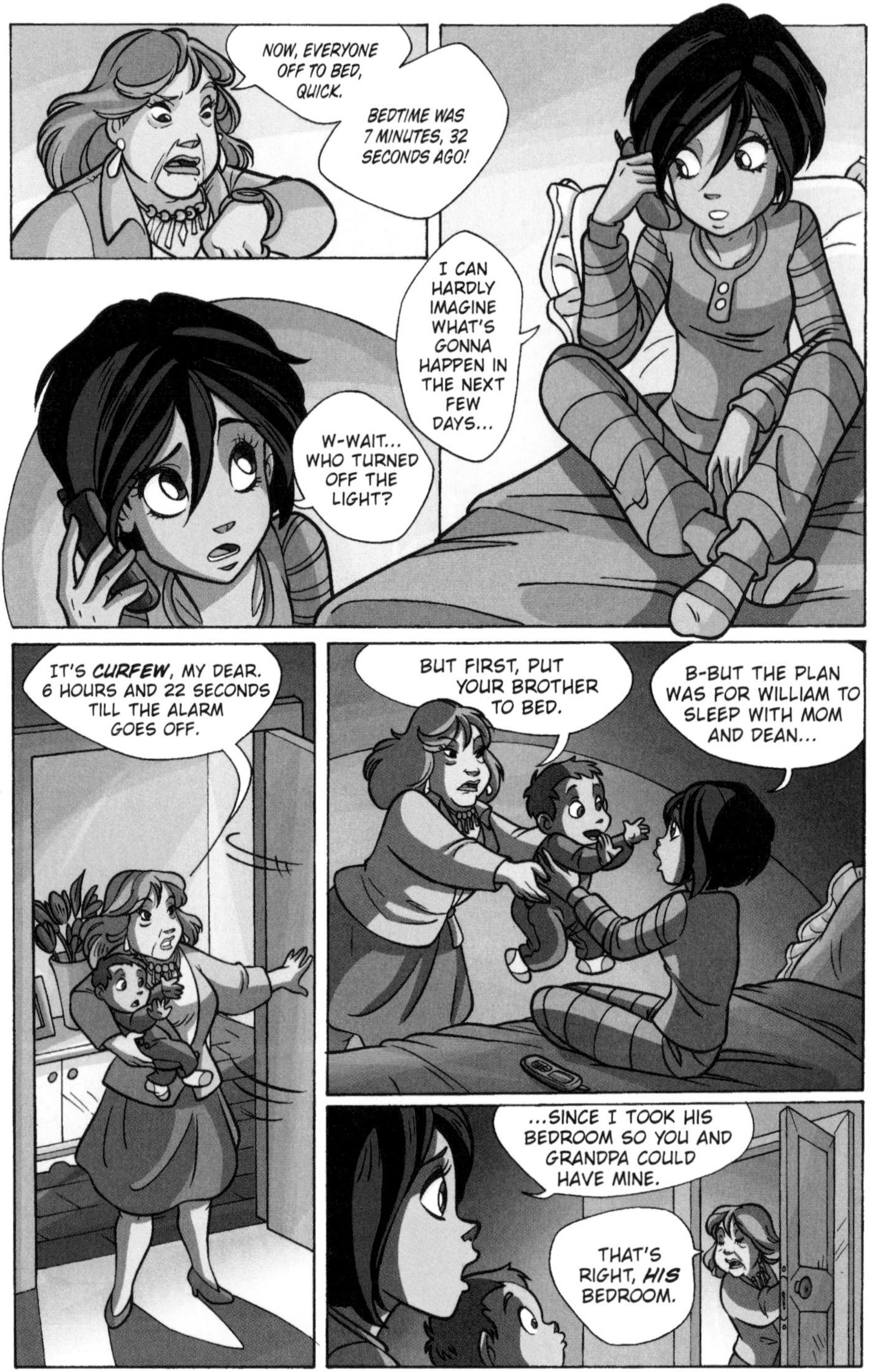
NOW, EVERYONE OFF TO BED, QUICK.
BEDTIME WAS 7 MINUTES, 32 SECONDS AGO!
I CAN HARDLY IMAGINE WHAT'S GONNA HAPPEN IN THE NEXT FEW DAYS...
W-WAIT... WHO TURNED OFF THE LIGHT?
IT'S **CURFEW**, MY DEAR. 6 HOURS AND 22 SECONDS TILL THE ALARM GOES OFF.
BUT FIRST, PUT YOUR BROTHER TO BED.
B-BUT THE PLAN WAS FOR WILLIAM TO SLEEP WITH MOM AND DEAN...
...SINCE I TOOK HIS BEDROOM SO YOU AND GRANDPA COULD HAVE MINE.
THAT'S RIGHT, ***HIS*** BEDROOM.

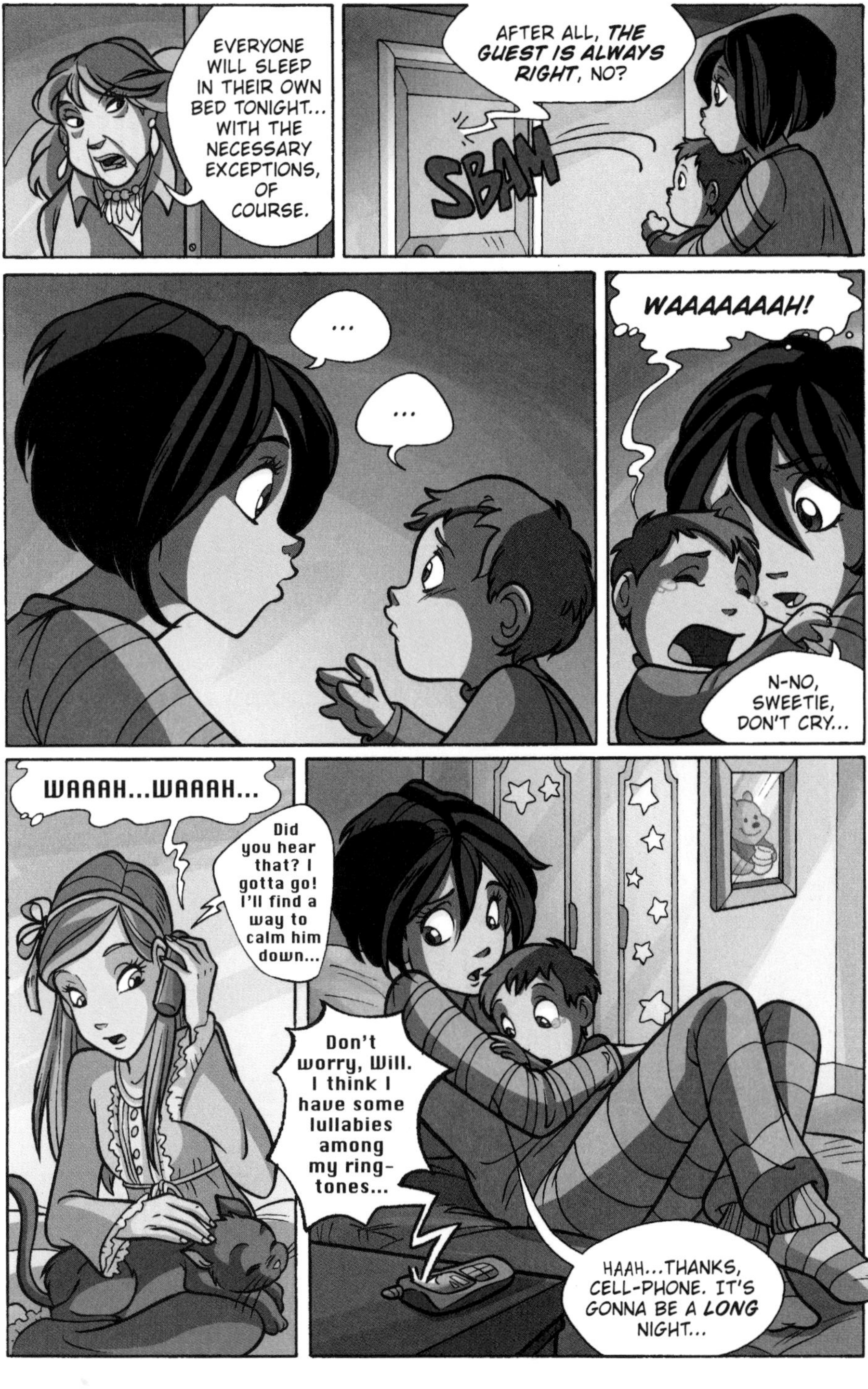
EVERYONE WILL SLEEP IN THEIR OWN BED TONIGHT... WITH THE NECESSARY EXCEPTIONS, OF COURSE.
AFTER ALL, THE GUEST IS ALWAYS RIGHT, NO?
SBAM
...
...
WAAAAAAAH!
N-NO, SWEETIE, DON'T CRY...
WAAAH...WAAAH...
Did you hear that? I gotta go! I'll find a way to calm him down...
Don't worry, Will. I think I have some lullabies among my ring-tones...
HAAH...THANKS, CELL-PHONE. IT'S GONNA BE A LONG NIGHT...

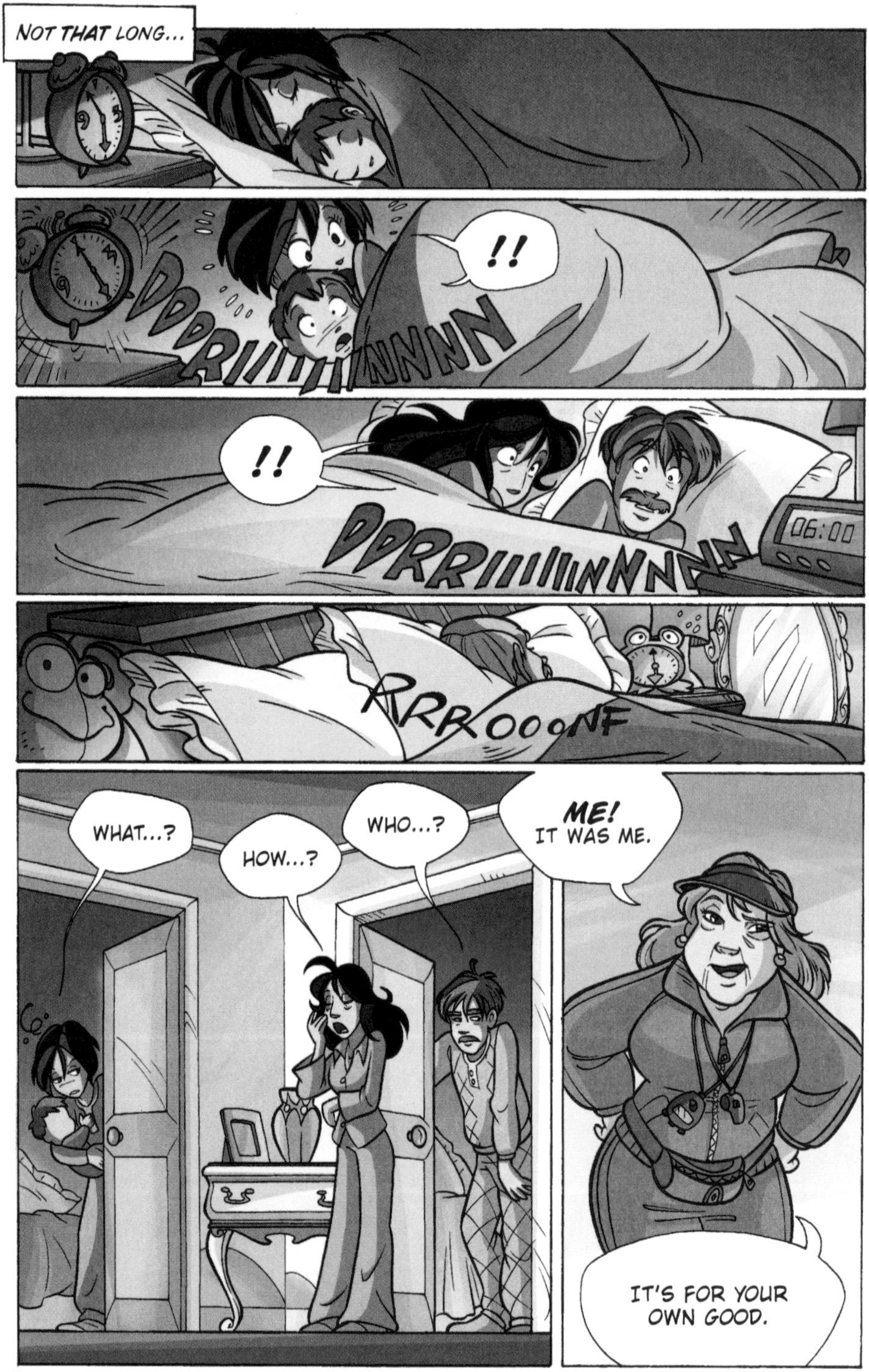
NOT THAT LONG...
!!
DDRIIIIIIINNNNN
!!
06:00
DDRRIIIIIIINNNNN
RRRROOOONF
WHAT...?
HOW...?
WHO...?
ME! IT WAS ME.
IT'S FOR YOUR OWN GOOD.

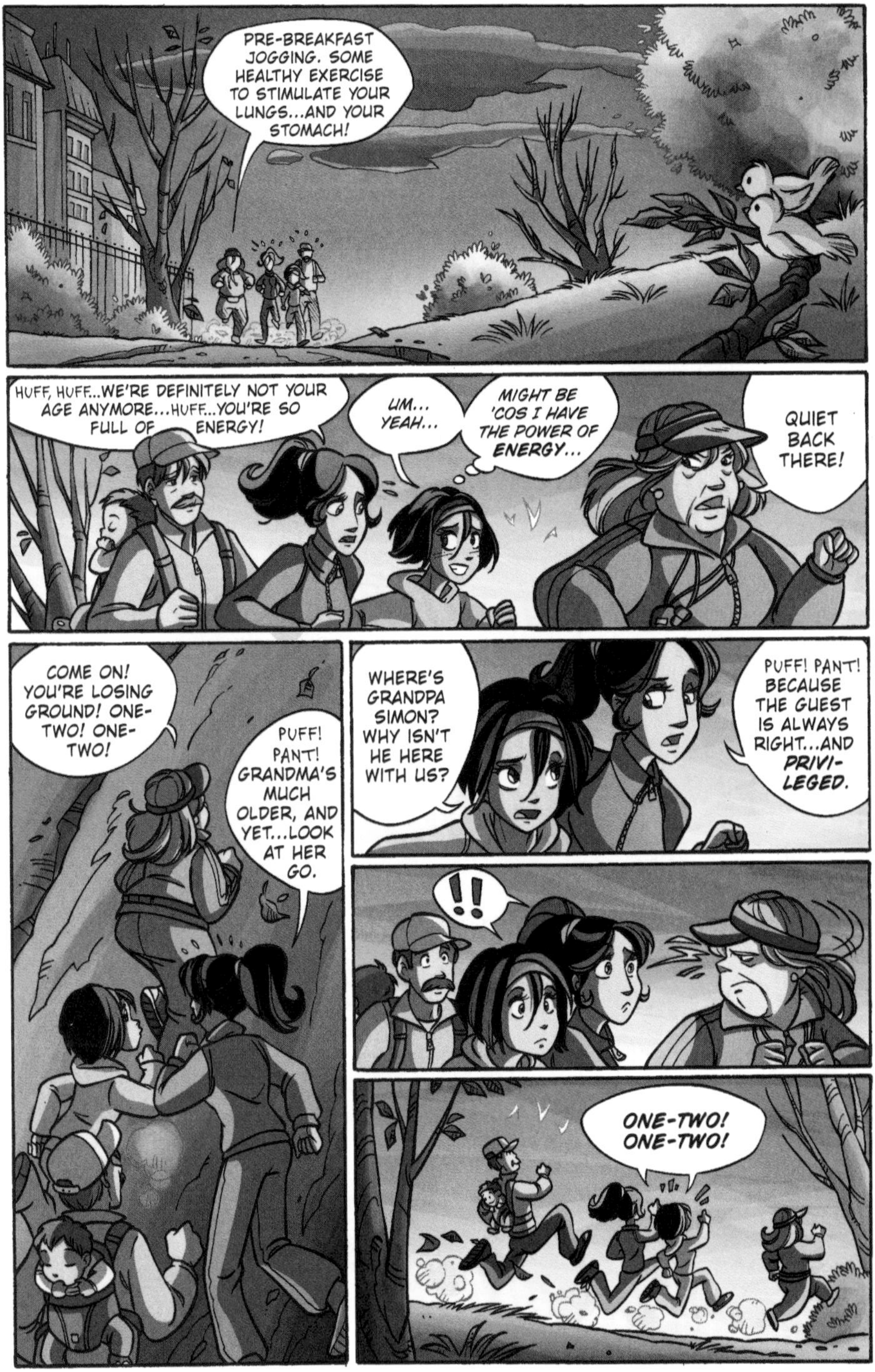
PRE-BREAKFAST JOGGING. SOME HEALTHY EXERCISE TO STIMULATE YOUR LUNGS...AND YOUR STOMACH!
HUFF, HUFF...WE'RE DEFINITELY NOT YOUR AGE ANYMORE...HUFF...YOU'RE SO FULL OF ENERGY!
UM... YEAH...
MIGHT BE 'COS I HAVE THE POWER OF ENERGY...
QUIET BACK THERE!
COME ON! YOU'RE LOSING GROUND! ONE-TWO! ONE-TWO!
PUFF! PANT! GRANDMA'S MUCH OLDER, AND YET...LOOK AT HER GO.
WHERE'S GRANDPA SIMON? WHY ISN'T HE HERE WITH US?
PUFF! PANT! BECAUSE THE GUEST IS ALWAYS RIGHT...AND PRIVI-LEGED.
!!
ONE-TWO! ONE-TWO!

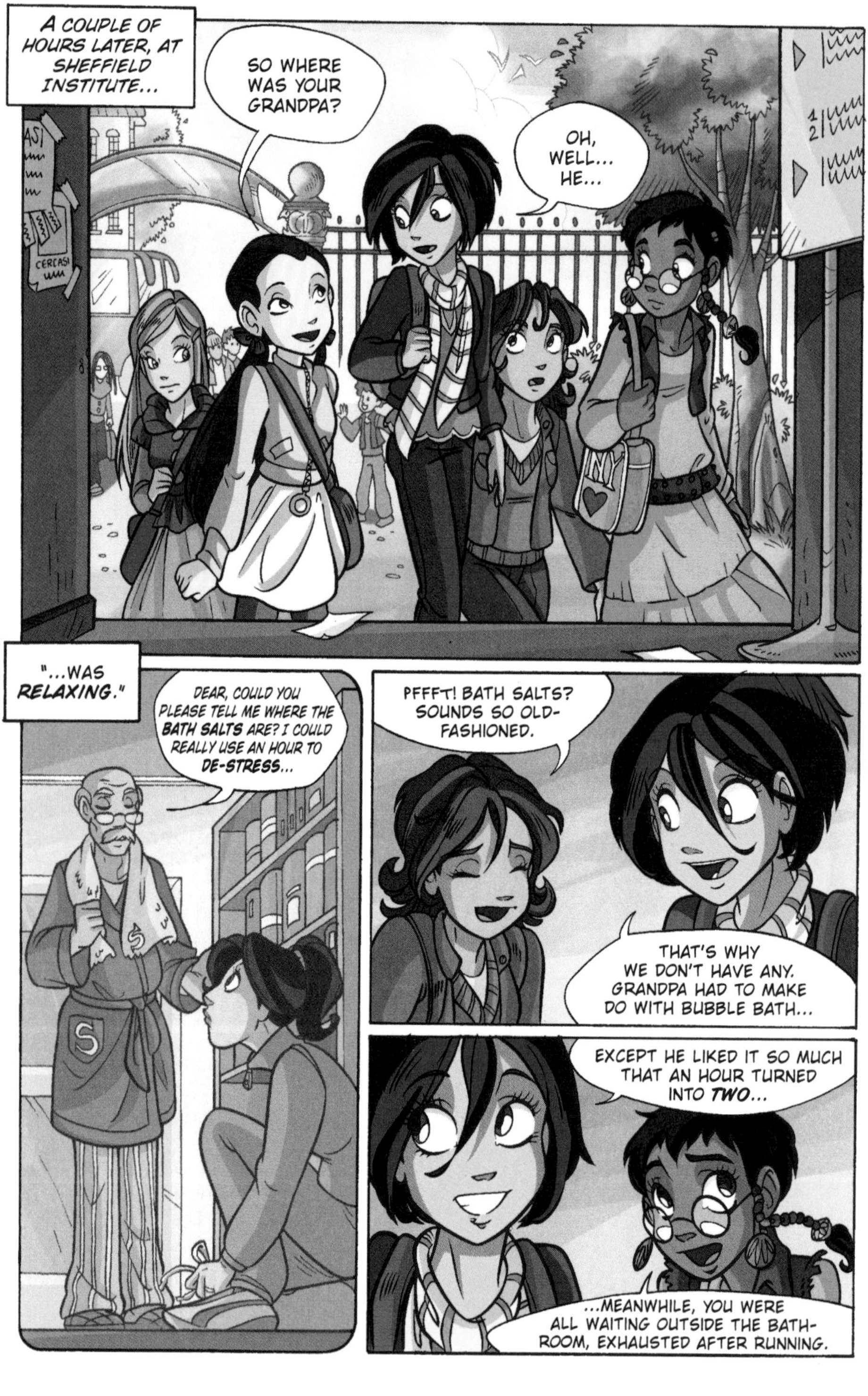
A COUPLE OF HOURS LATER, AT SHEFFIELD INSTITUTE...
SO WHERE WAS YOUR GRANDPA?
OH, WELL... HE...
"...WAS RELAXING."
DEAR, COULD YOU PLEASE TELL ME WHERE THE BATH SALTS ARE? I COULD REALLY USE AN HOUR TO DE-STRESS...
PFFFT! BATH SALTS? SOUNDS SO OLD-FASHIONED.
THAT'S WHY WE DON'T HAVE ANY. GRANDPA HAD TO MAKE DO WITH BUBBLE BATH...
EXCEPT HE LIKED IT SO MUCH THAT AN HOUR TURNED INTO TWO...
...MEANWHILE, YOU WERE ALL WAITING OUTSIDE THE BATH-ROOM, EXHAUSTED AFTER RUNNING.

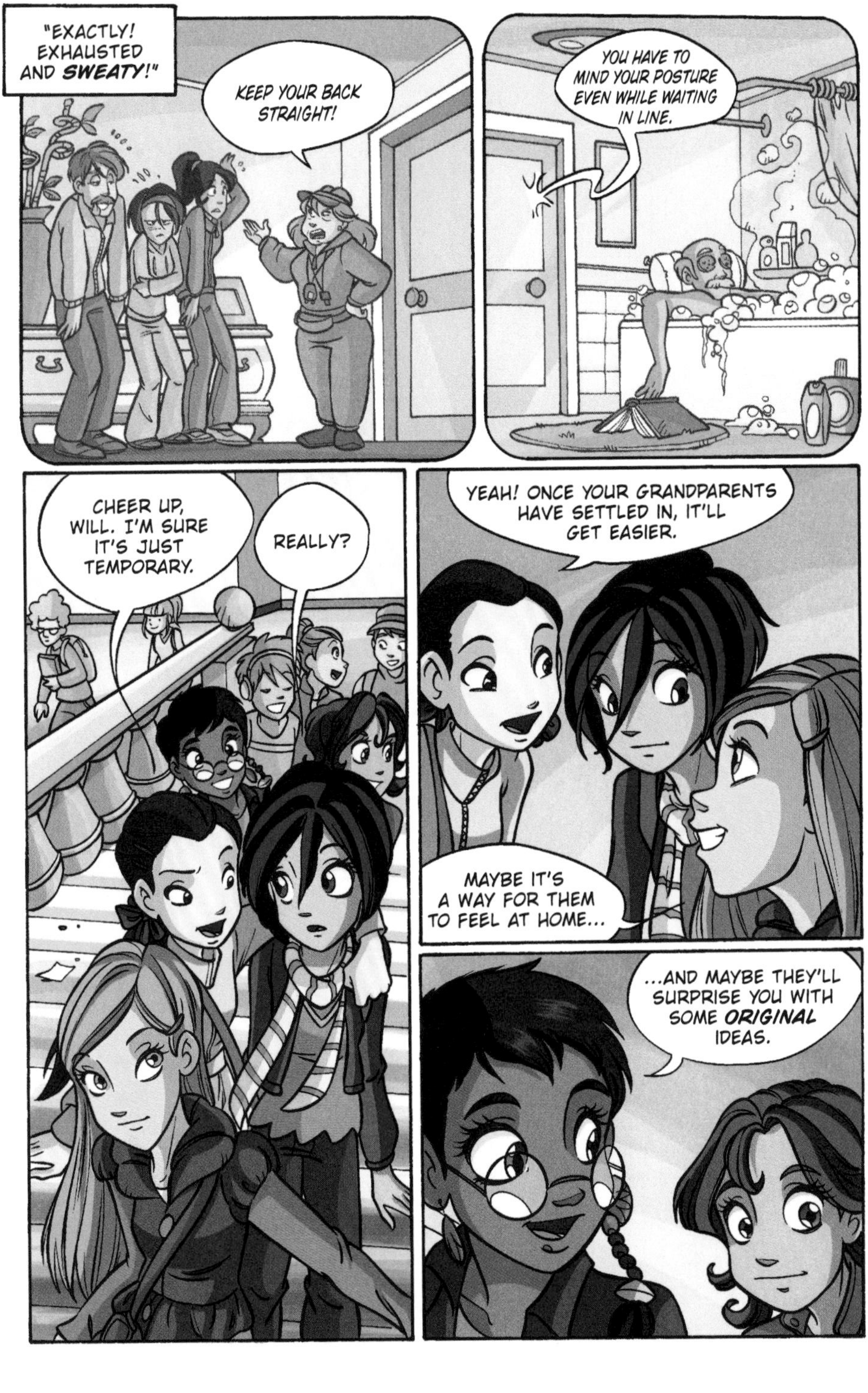
"EXACTLY! EXHAUSTED AND **SWEATY**!"
KEEP YOUR BACK STRAIGHT!
YOU HAVE TO MIND YOUR POSTURE EVEN WHILE WAITING IN LINE.
CHEER UP, WILL. I'M SURE IT'S JUST TEMPORARY.
REALLY?
YEAH! ONCE YOUR GRANDPARENTS HAVE SETTLED IN, IT'LL GET EASIER.
MAYBE IT'S A WAY FOR THEM TO FEEL AT HOME...
...AND MAYBE THEY'LL SURPRISE YOU WITH SOME **ORIGINAL** IDEAS.

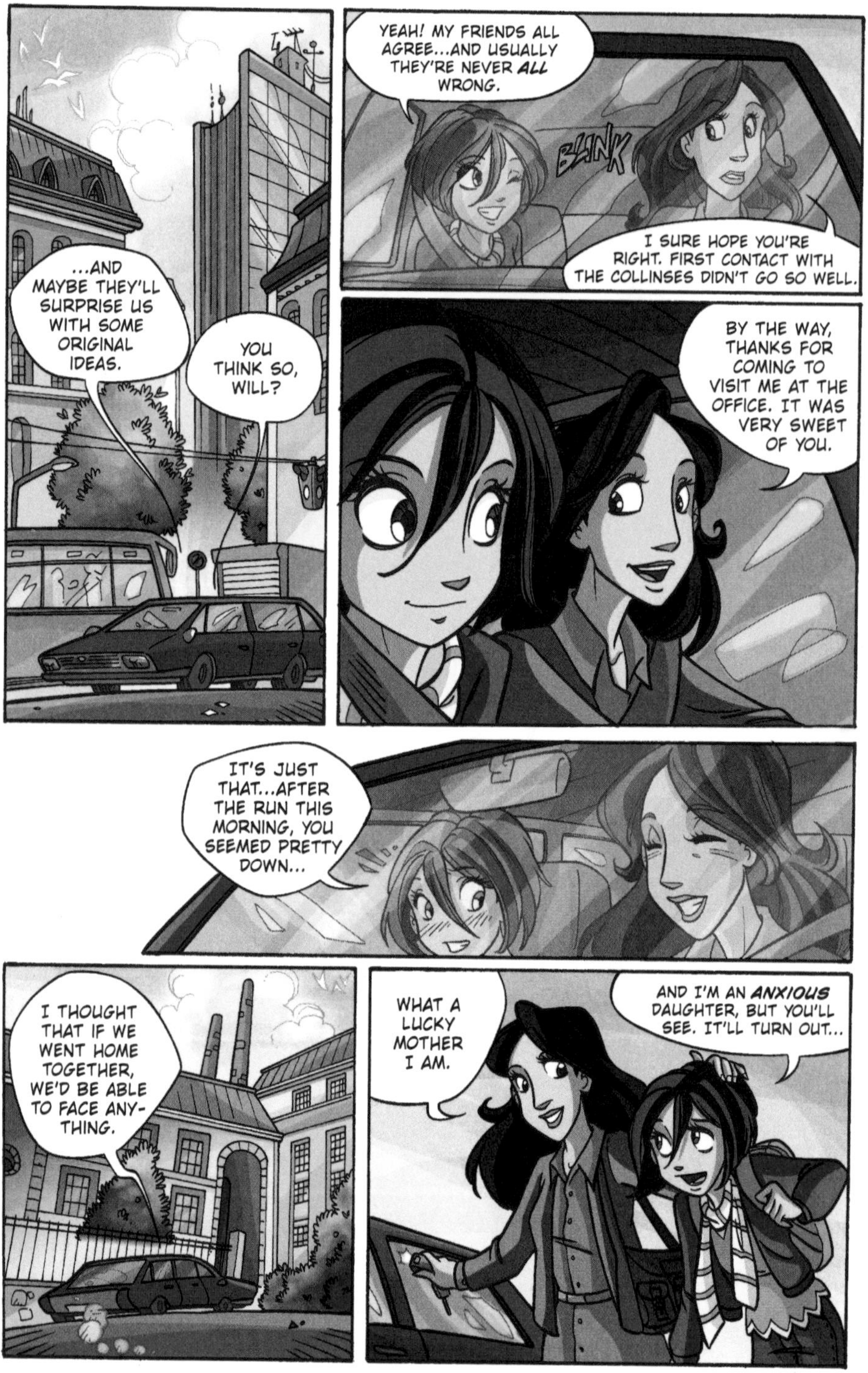
...AND MAYBE THEY'LL SURPRISE US WITH SOME ORIGINAL IDEAS.
YOU THINK SO, WILL?
YEAH! MY FRIENDS ALL AGREE...AND USUALLY THEY'RE NEVER ***ALL*** WRONG.
BLINK
I SURE HOPE YOU'RE RIGHT. FIRST CONTACT WITH THE COLLINSES DIDN'T GO SO WELL.
BY THE WAY, THANKS FOR COMING TO VISIT ME AT THE OFFICE. IT WAS VERY SWEET OF YOU.
IT'S JUST THAT...AFTER THE RUN THIS MORNING, YOU SEEMED PRETTY DOWN...
I THOUGHT THAT IF WE WENT HOME TOGETHER, WE'D BE ABLE TO FACE ANY-THING.
WHAT A LUCKY MOTHER I AM.
AND I'M AN ***ANXIOUS*** DAUGHTER, BUT YOU'LL SEE. IT'LL TURN OUT...

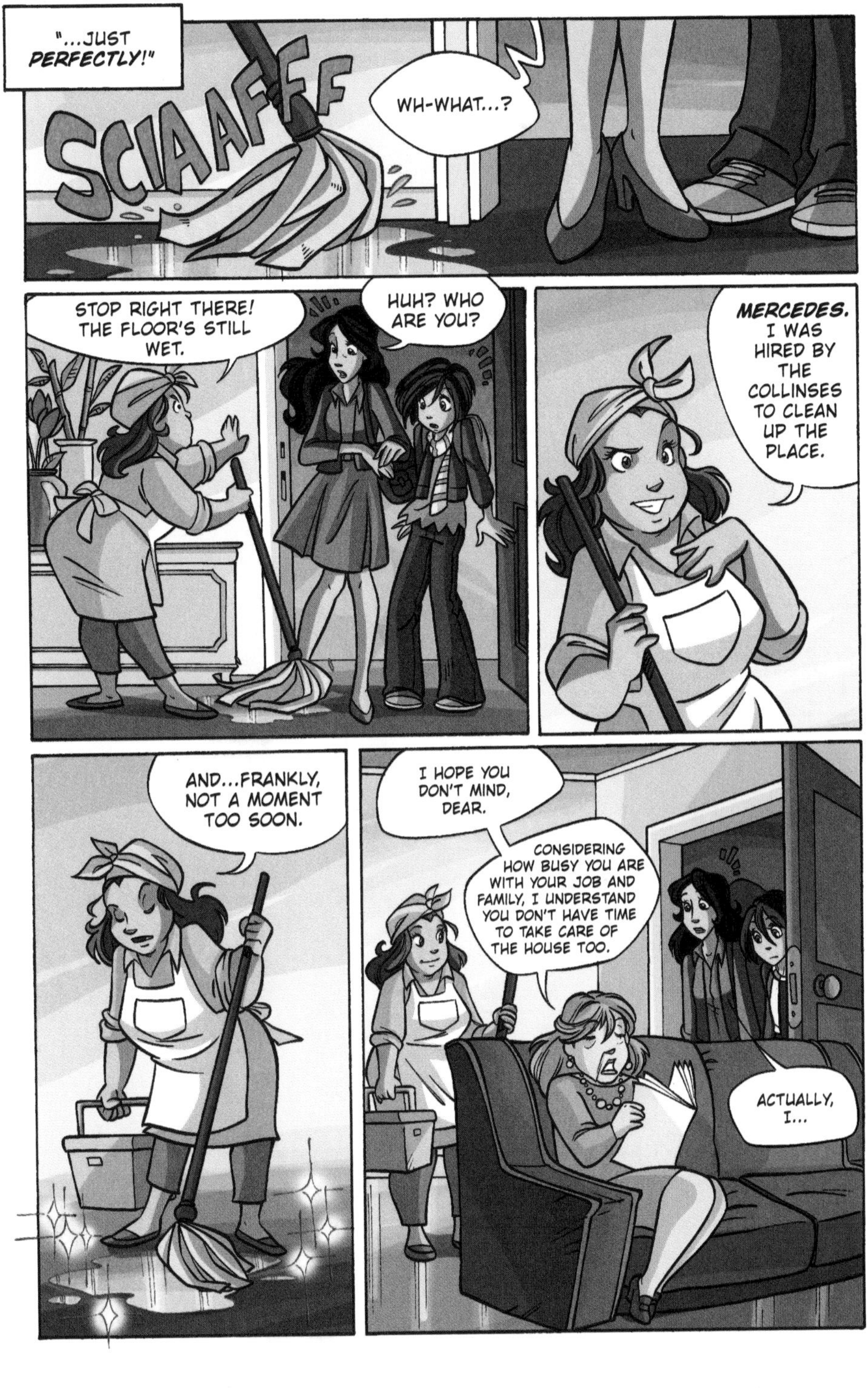
"...JUST *PERFECTLY!*"
SCIAAFFF
WH-WHAT...?
STOP RIGHT THERE! THE FLOOR'S STILL WET.
HUH? WHO ARE YOU?
MERCEDES. I WAS HIRED BY THE COLLINSES TO CLEAN UP THE PLACE.
AND...FRANKLY, NOT A MOMENT TOO SOON.
I HOPE YOU DON'T MIND, DEAR.
CONSIDERING HOW BUSY YOU ARE WITH YOUR JOB AND FAMILY, I UNDERSTAND YOU DON'T HAVE TIME TO TAKE CARE OF THE HOUSE TOO.
ACTUALLY, I...

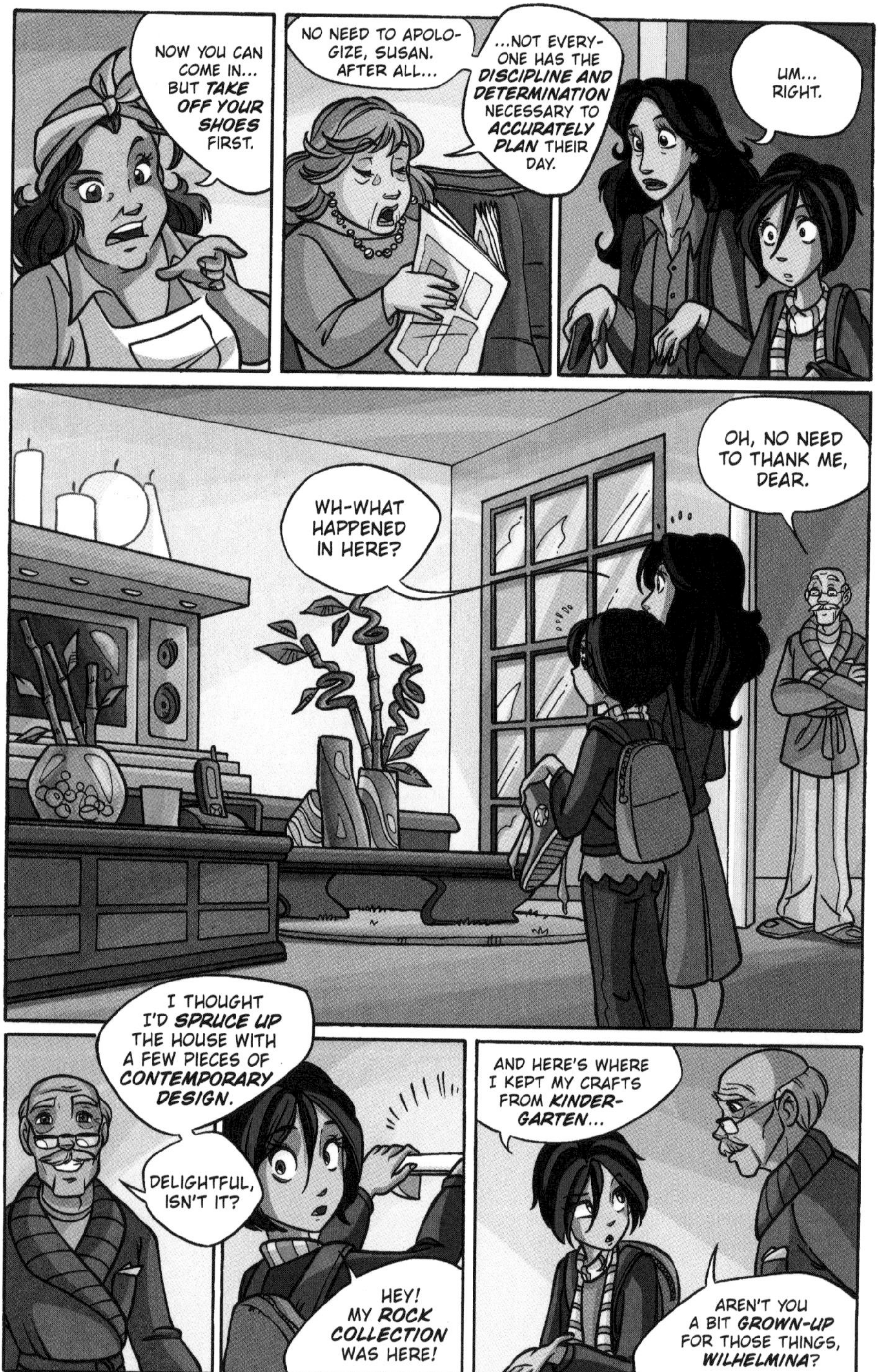
NOW YOU CAN COME IN... BUT TAKE OFF YOUR SHOES FIRST.
NO NEED TO APOLOGIZE, SUSAN. AFTER ALL...
...NOT EVERYONE HAS THE DISCIPLINE AND DETERMINATION NECESSARY TO ACCURATELY PLAN THEIR DAY.
UM... RIGHT.
WH-WHAT HAPPENED IN HERE?
OH, NO NEED TO THANK ME, DEAR.
I THOUGHT I'D SPRUCE UP THE HOUSE WITH A FEW PIECES OF CONTEMPORARY DESIGN.
DELIGHTFUL, ISN'T IT?
HEY! MY ROCK COLLECTION WAS HERE!
AND HERE'S WHERE I KEPT MY CRAFTS FROM KINDERGARTEN...
AREN'T YOU A BIT GROWN-UP FOR THOSE THINGS, WILHELMINA?

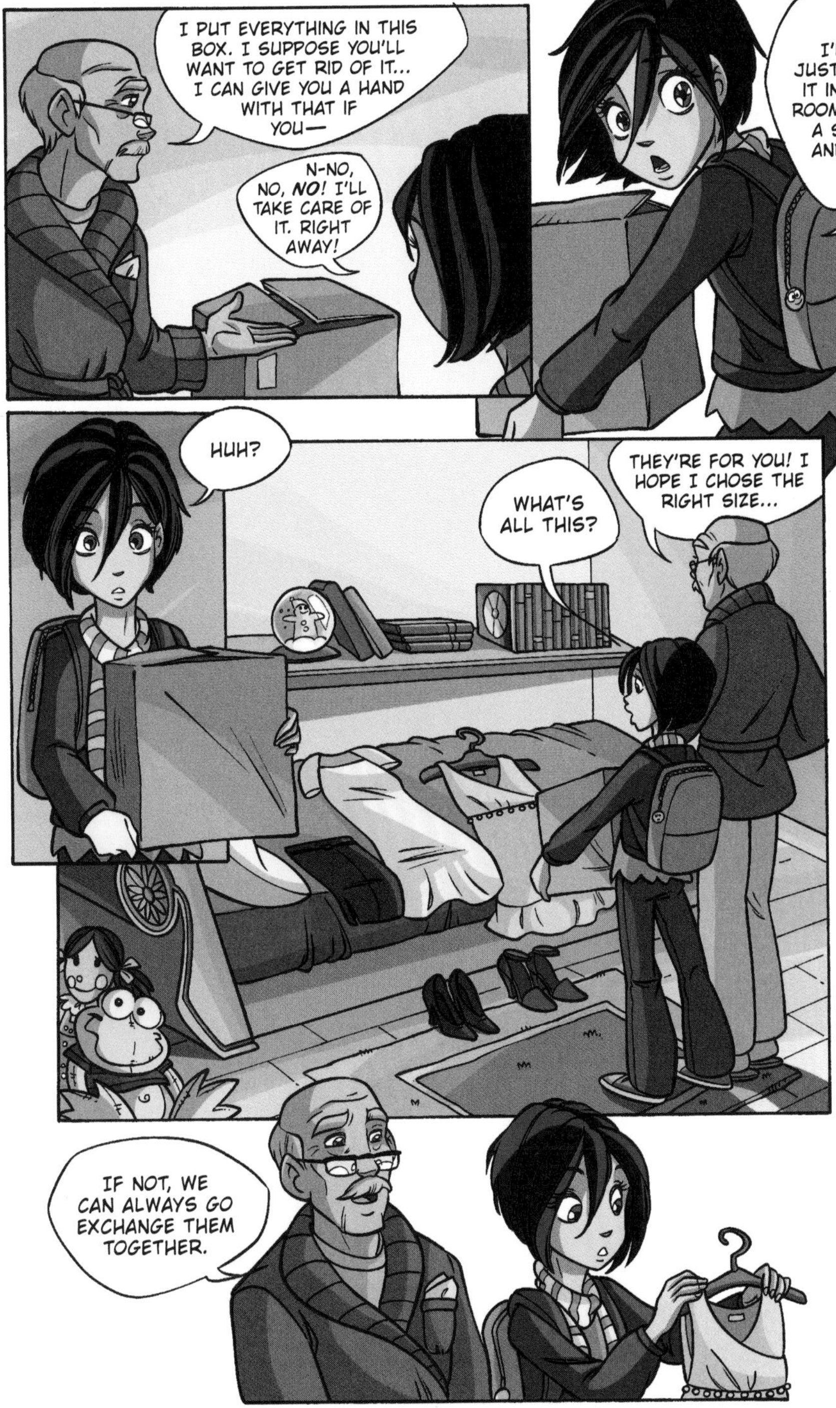
I PUT EVERYTHING IN THIS BOX. I SUPPOSE YOU'LL WANT TO GET RID OF IT... I CAN GIVE YOU A HAND WITH THAT IF YOU—
N-NO, NO, *NO*! I'LL TAKE CARE OF IT. RIGHT AWAY!
I'LL JUST PUT IT IN MY ROOM FOR A SEC AND...
HUH?
WHAT'S ALL THIS?
THEY'RE FOR YOU! I HOPE I CHOSE THE RIGHT SIZE...
IF NOT, WE CAN ALWAYS GO EXCHANGE THEM TOGETHER.

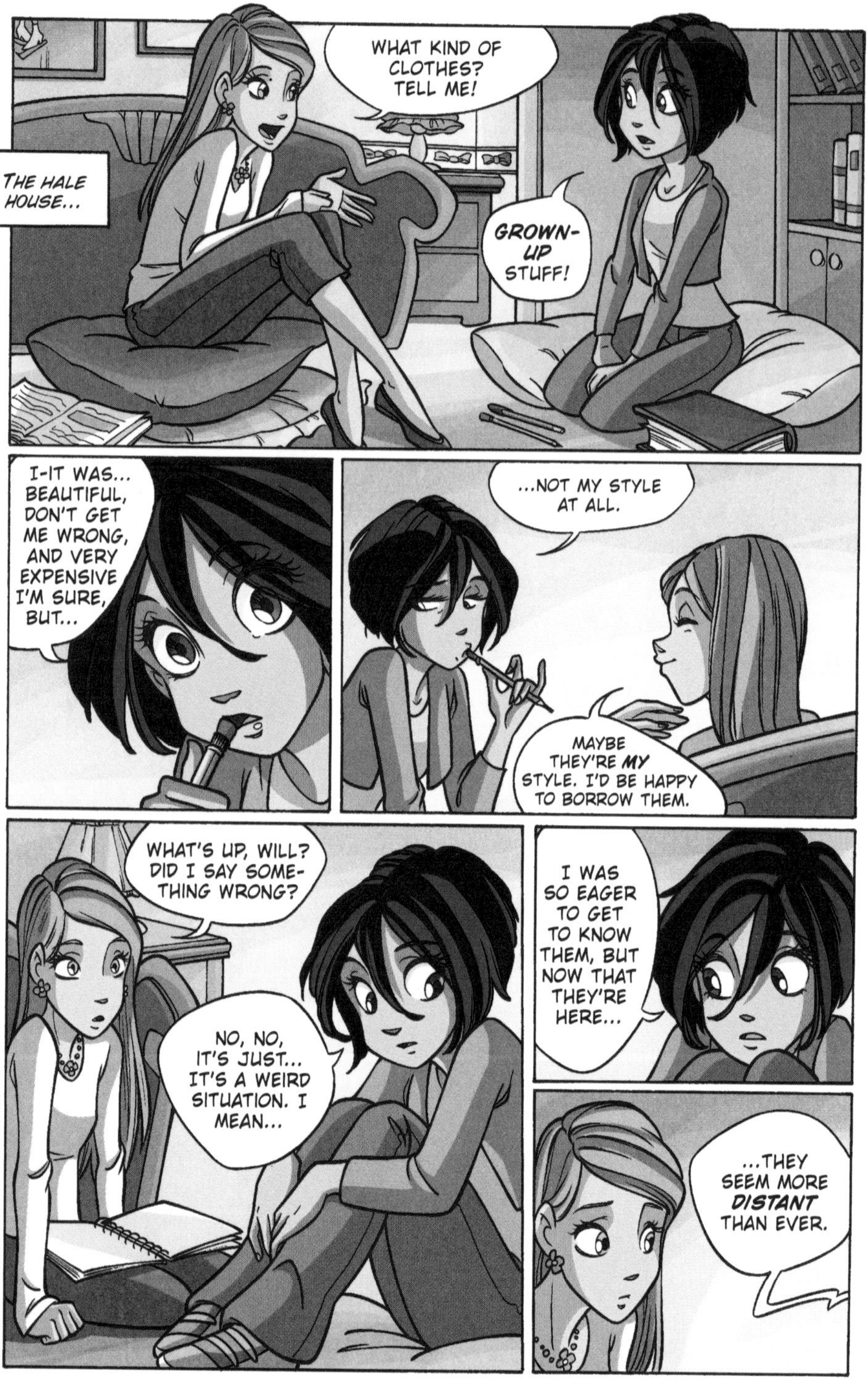

THE HALE HOUSE...
WHAT KIND OF CLOTHES? TELL ME!
GROWN-UP STUFF!
I-IT WAS... BEAUTIFUL, DON'T GET ME WRONG, AND VERY EXPENSIVE I'M SURE, BUT...
...NOT MY STYLE AT ALL.
MAYBE THEY'RE MY STYLE. I'D BE HAPPY TO BORROW THEM.
WHAT'S UP, WILL? DID I SAY SOME-THING WRONG?
NO, NO, IT'S JUST... IT'S A WEIRD SITUATION. I MEAN...
I WAS SO EAGER TO GET TO KNOW THEM, BUT NOW THAT THEY'RE HERE...
...THEY SEEM MORE DISTANT THAN EVER.

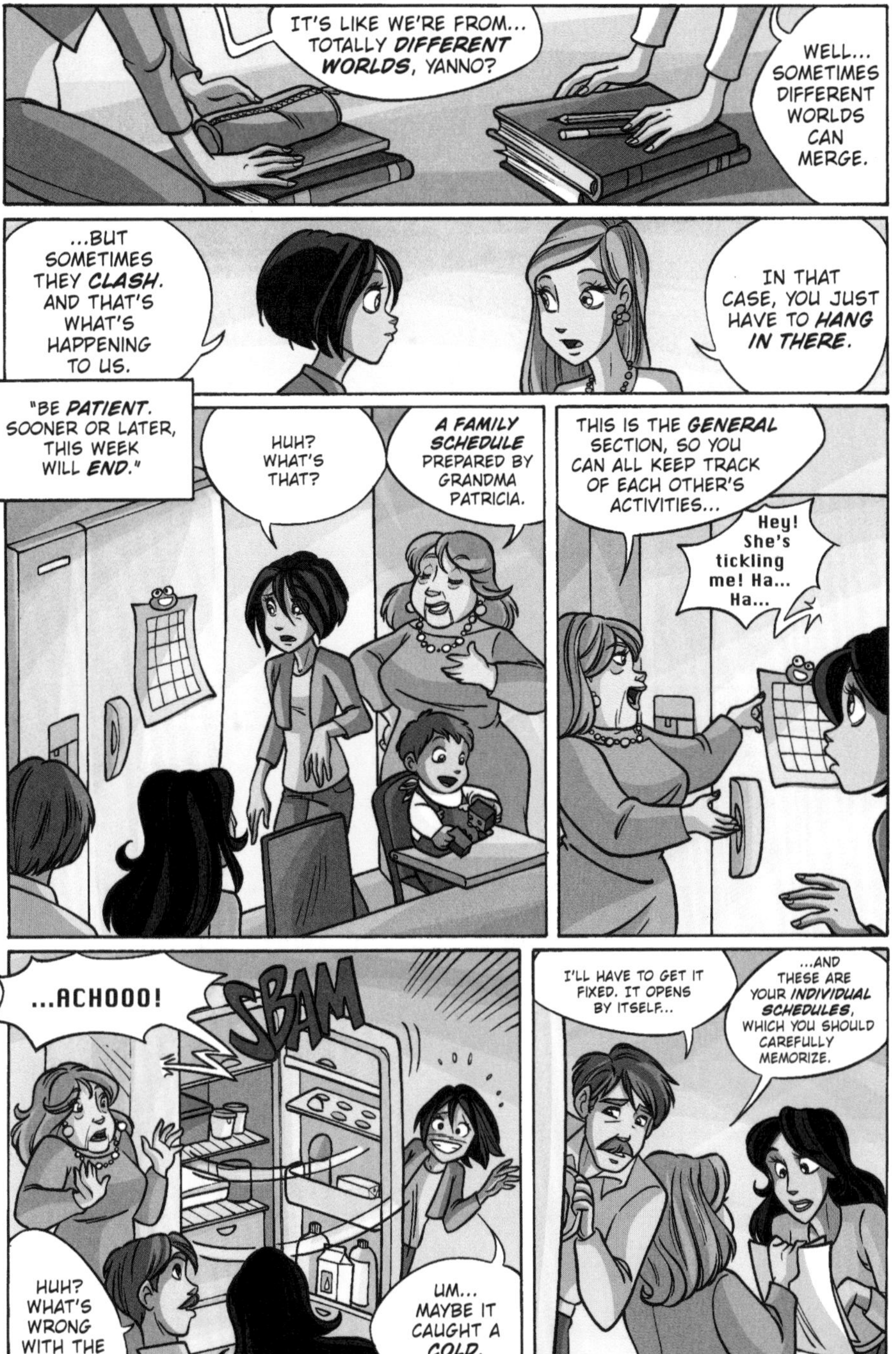

IT'S LIKE WE'RE FROM... TOTALLY DIFFERENT WORLDS, YANNO?
WELL... SOMETIMES DIFFERENT WORLDS CAN MERGE.
...BUT SOMETIMES THEY CLASH. AND THAT'S WHAT'S HAPPENING TO US.
IN THAT CASE, YOU JUST HAVE TO HANG IN THERE.
"BE PATIENT. SOONER OR LATER, THIS WEEK WILL END."
HUH? WHAT'S THAT?
A FAMILY SCHEDULE PREPARED BY GRANDMA PATRICIA.
THIS IS THE GENERAL SECTION, SO YOU CAN ALL KEEP TRACK OF EACH OTHER'S ACTIVITIES...
Hey! She's tickling me! Ha... Ha...
...ACHOOO!
SBAM
HUH? WHAT'S WRONG WITH THE FRIDGE?
UM... MAYBE IT CAUGHT A COLD.
I'LL HAVE TO GET IT FIXED. IT OPENS BY ITSELF...
...AND THESE ARE YOUR INDIVIDUAL SCHEDULES, WHICH YOU SHOULD CAREFULLY MEMORIZE.

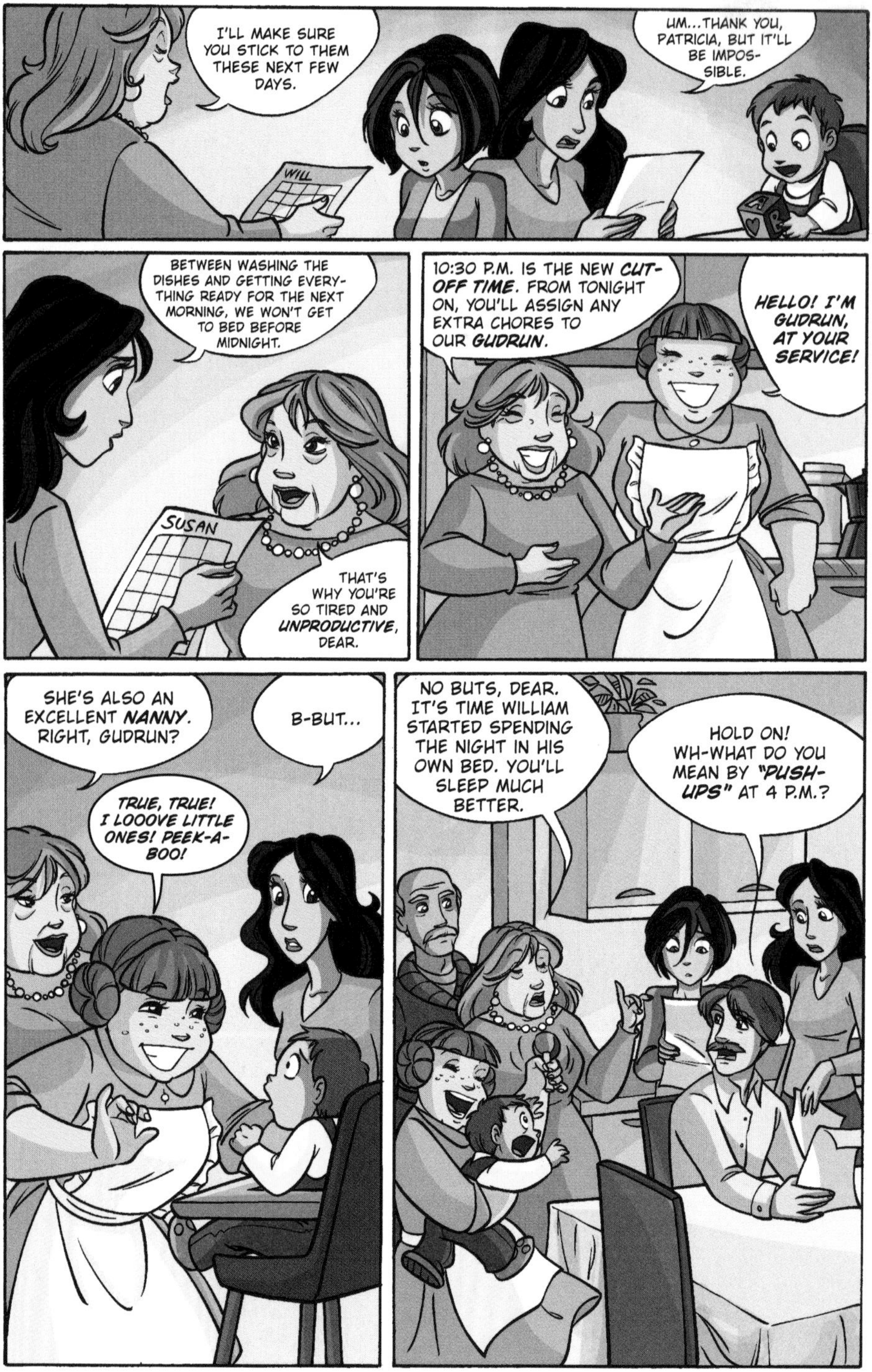
I'LL MAKE SURE YOU STICK TO THEM THESE NEXT FEW DAYS.
UM...THANK YOU, PATRICIA, BUT IT'LL BE IMPOSSIBLE.
WILL
BETWEEN WASHING THE DISHES AND GETTING EVERYTHING READY FOR THE NEXT MORNING, WE WON'T GET TO BED BEFORE MIDNIGHT.
SUSAN
THAT'S WHY YOU'RE SO TIRED AND UNPRODUCTIVE, DEAR.
10:30 P.M. IS THE NEW CUT-OFF TIME. FROM TONIGHT ON, YOU'LL ASSIGN ANY EXTRA CHORES TO OUR GUDRUN.
HELLO! I'M GUDRUN, AT YOUR SERVICE!
SHE'S ALSO AN EXCELLENT NANNY. RIGHT, GUDRUN?
B-BUT...
TRUE, TRUE! I LOOOVE LITTLE ONES! PEEK-A-BOO!
NO BUTS, DEAR. IT'S TIME WILLIAM STARTED SPENDING THE NIGHT IN HIS OWN BED. YOU'LL SLEEP MUCH BETTER.
HOLD ON! WH-WHAT DO YOU MEAN BY "PUSH-UPS" AT 4 P.M.?

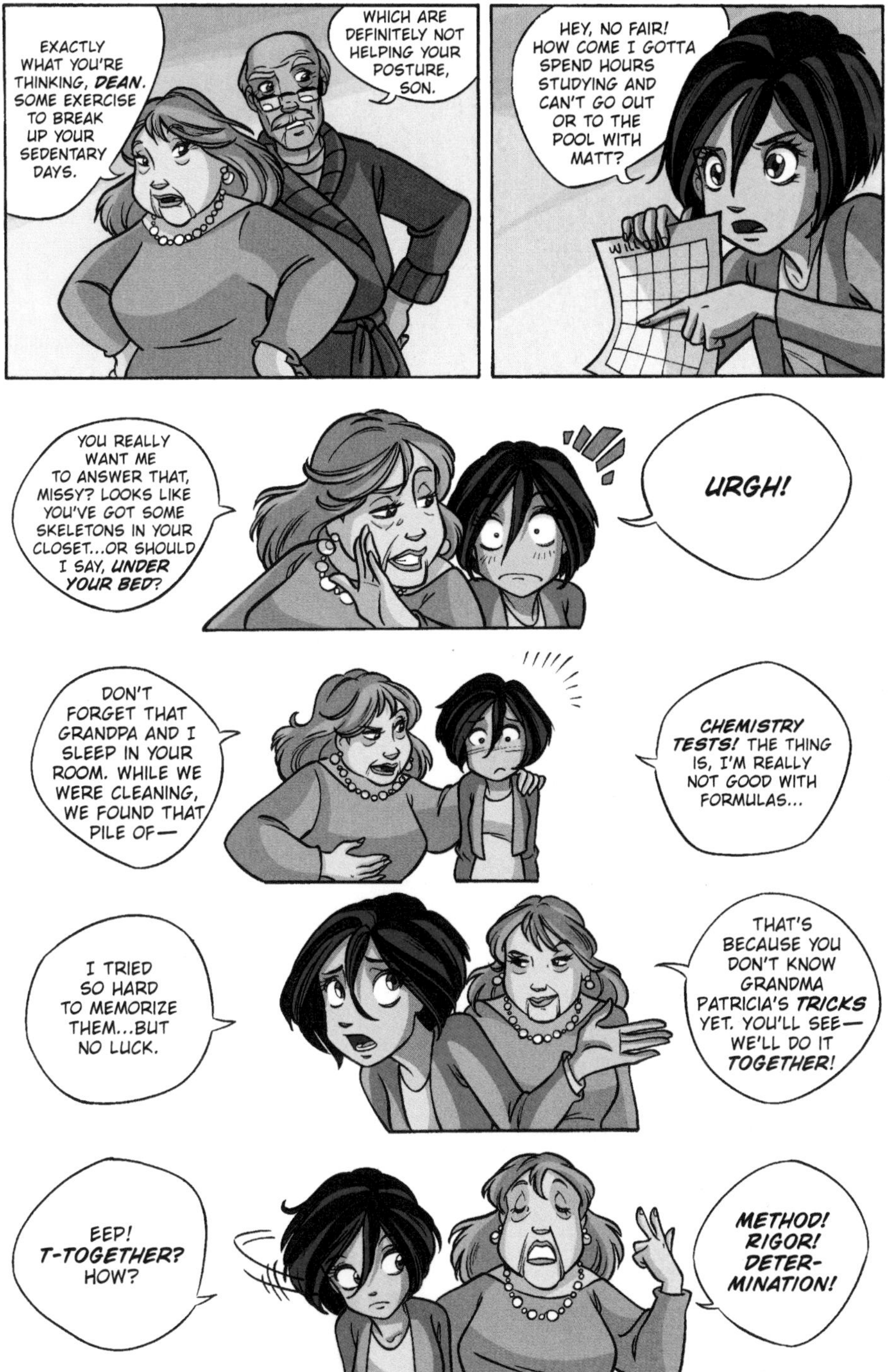
EXACTLY WHAT YOU'RE THINKING, DEAN. SOME EXERCISE TO BREAK UP YOUR SEDENTARY DAYS.
WHICH ARE DEFINITELY NOT HELPING YOUR POSTURE, SON.
HEY, NO FAIR! HOW COME I GOTTA SPEND HOURS STUDYING AND CAN'T GO OUT OR TO THE POOL WITH MATT?
YOU REALLY WANT ME TO ANSWER THAT, MISSY? LOOKS LIKE YOU'VE GOT SOME SKELETONS IN YOUR CLOSET...OR SHOULD I SAY, UNDER YOUR BED?
URGH!
DON'T FORGET THAT GRANDPA AND I SLEEP IN YOUR ROOM. WHILE WE WERE CLEANING, WE FOUND THAT PILE OF—
CHEMISTRY TESTS! THE THING IS, I'M REALLY NOT GOOD WITH FORMULAS...
I TRIED SO HARD TO MEMORIZE THEM...BUT NO LUCK.
THAT'S BECAUSE YOU DON'T KNOW GRANDMA PATRICIA'S TRICKS YET. YOU'LL SEE—WE'LL DO IT TOGETHER!
EEP! T-TOGETHER? HOW?
METHOD! RIGOR! DETER-MINATION!

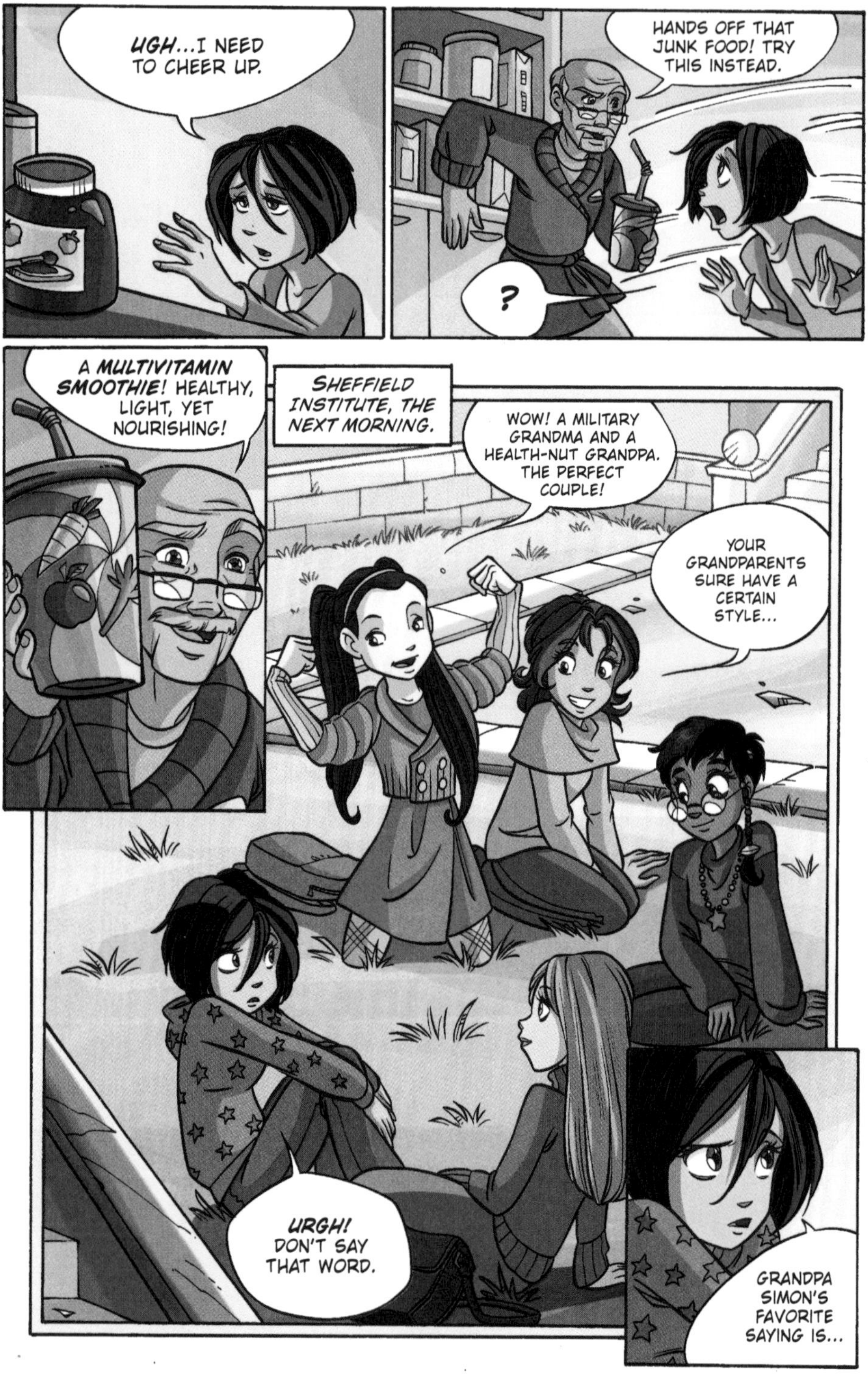
UGH...I NEED TO CHEER UP.
HANDS OFF THAT JUNK FOOD! TRY THIS INSTEAD.
?
A MULTIVITAMIN SMOOTHIE! HEALTHY, LIGHT, YET NOURISHING!
SHEFFIELD INSTITUTE, THE NEXT MORNING.
WOW! A MILITARY GRANDMA AND A HEALTH-NUT GRANDPA. THE PERFECT COUPLE!
YOUR GRANDPARENTS SURE HAVE A CERTAIN STYLE...
URGH! DON'T SAY THAT WORD.
GRANDPA SIMON'S FAVORITE SAYING IS...

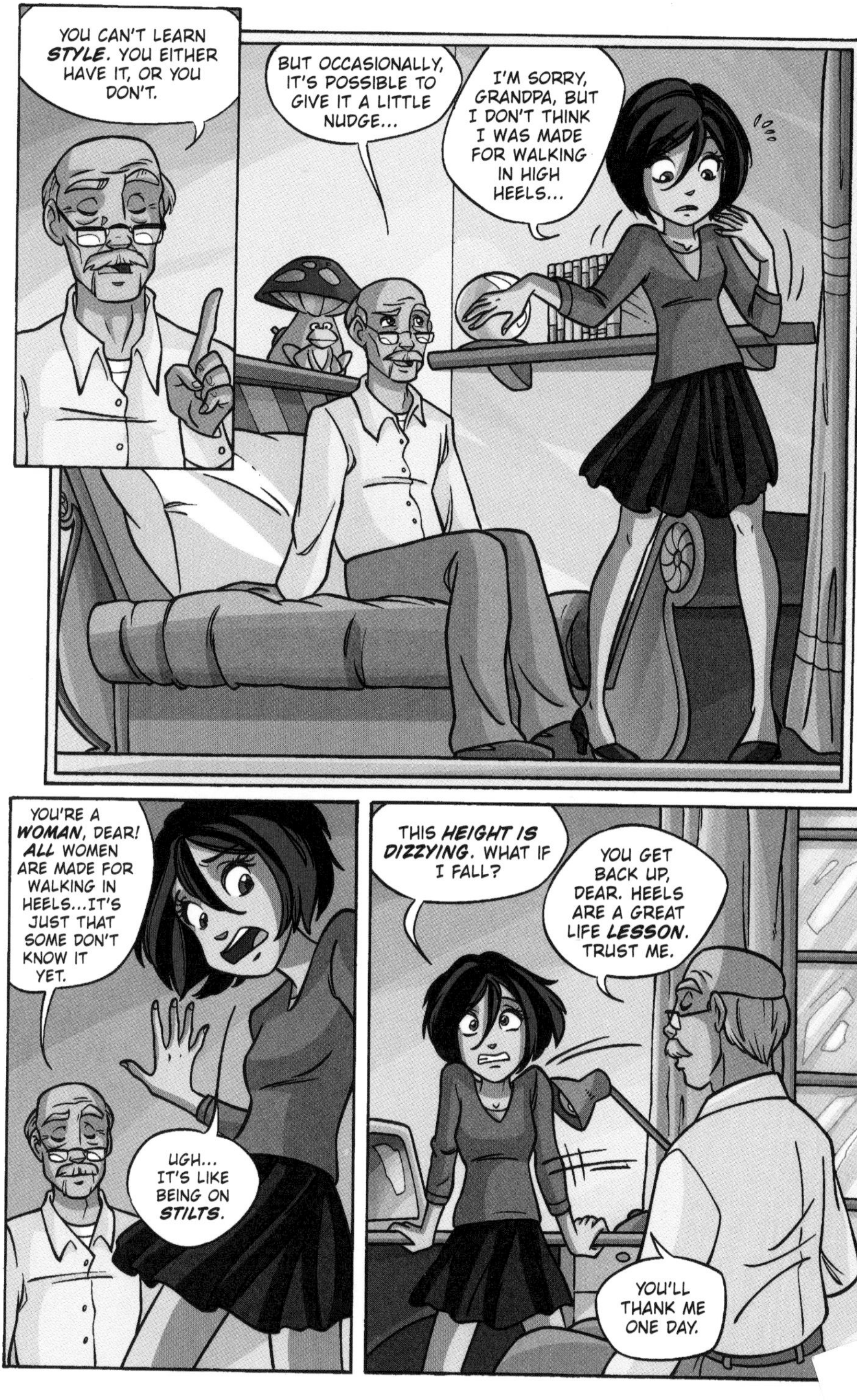
YOU CAN'T LEARN STYLE. YOU EITHER HAVE IT, OR YOU DON'T.
BUT OCCASIONALLY, IT'S POSSIBLE TO GIVE IT A LITTLE NUDGE...
I'M SORRY, GRANDPA, BUT I DON'T THINK I WAS MADE FOR WALKING IN HIGH HEELS...
YOU'RE A WOMAN, DEAR! ALL WOMEN ARE MADE FOR WALKING IN HEELS...IT'S JUST THAT SOME DON'T KNOW IT YET.
UGH... IT'S LIKE BEING ON STILTS.
THIS HEIGHT IS DIZZYING. WHAT IF I FALL?
YOU GET BACK UP, DEAR. HEELS ARE A GREAT LIFE LESSON. TRUST ME.
YOU'LL THANK ME ONE DAY.

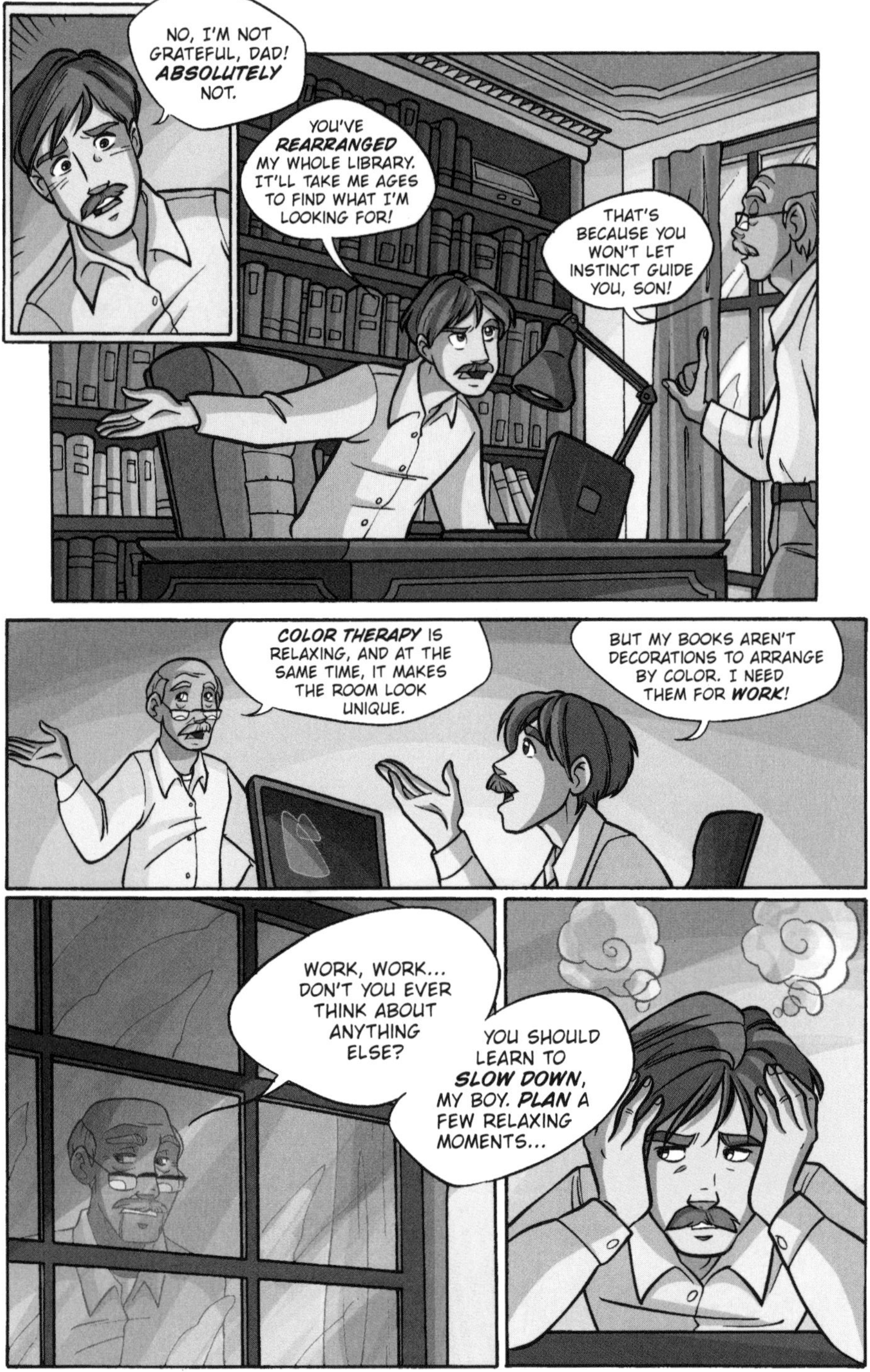

NO, I'M NOT GRATEFUL, DAD! **ABSOLUTELY** NOT.
YOU'VE **REARRANGED** MY WHOLE LIBRARY. IT'LL TAKE ME AGES TO FIND WHAT I'M LOOKING FOR!
THAT'S BECAUSE YOU WON'T LET INSTINCT GUIDE YOU, SON!
COLOR THERAPY IS RELAXING, AND AT THE SAME TIME, IT MAKES THE ROOM LOOK UNIQUE.
BUT MY BOOKS AREN'T DECORATIONS TO ARRANGE BY COLOR. I NEED THEM FOR **WORK**!
WORK, WORK... DON'T YOU EVER THINK ABOUT ANYTHING ELSE?
YOU SHOULD LEARN TO **SLOW DOWN**, MY BOY. **PLAN** A FEW RELAXING MOMENTS...

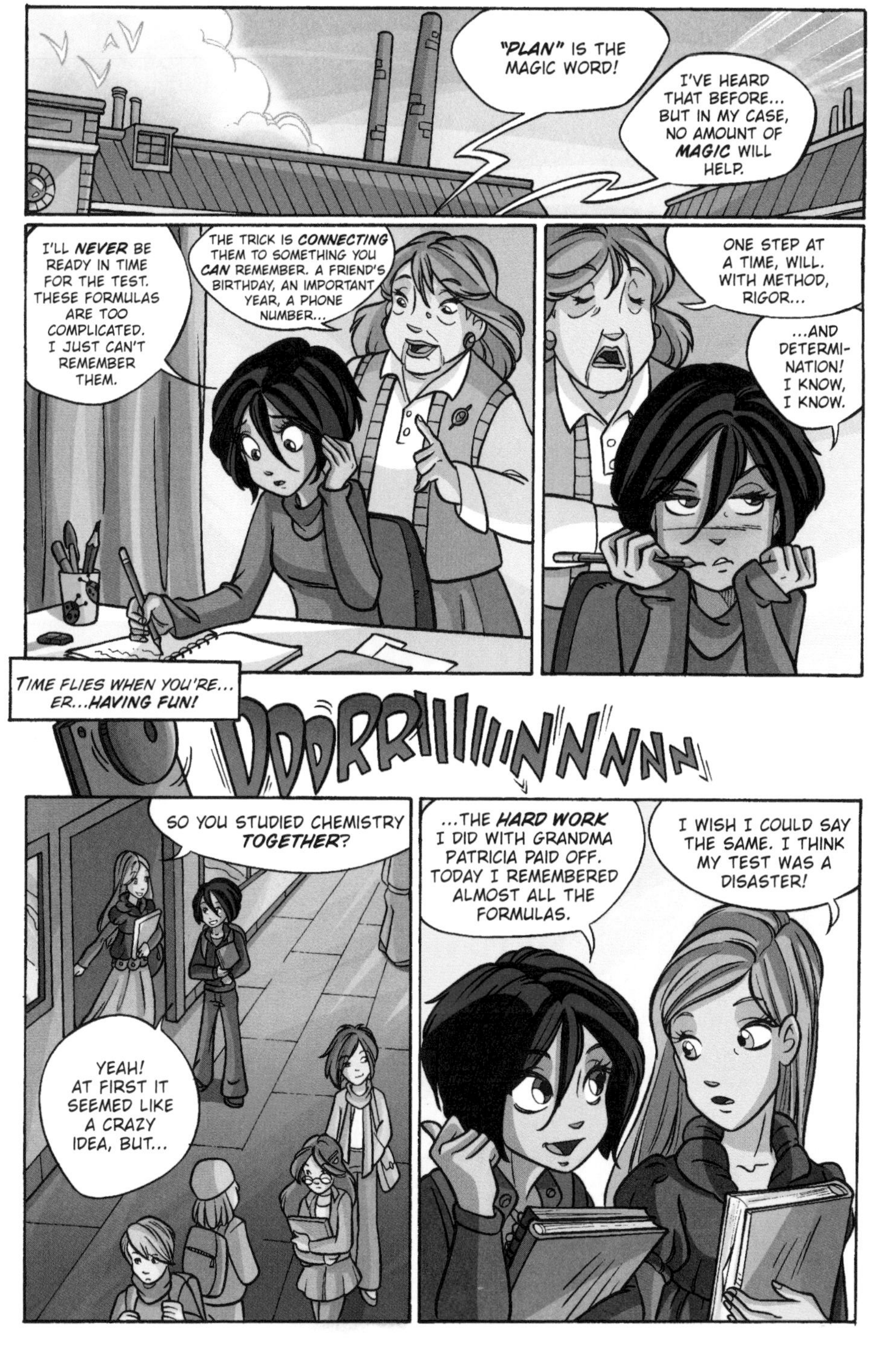
"PLAN" IS THE MAGIC WORD!
I'VE HEARD THAT BEFORE... BUT IN MY CASE, NO AMOUNT OF MAGIC WILL HELP.
I'LL NEVER BE READY IN TIME FOR THE TEST. THESE FORMULAS ARE TOO COMPLICATED. I JUST CAN'T REMEMBER THEM.
THE TRICK IS CONNECTING THEM TO SOMETHING YOU CAN REMEMBER. A FRIEND'S BIRTHDAY, AN IMPORTANT YEAR, A PHONE NUMBER...
ONE STEP AT A TIME, WILL. WITH METHOD, RIGOR...
...AND DETERMINATION! I KNOW, I KNOW.
TIME FLIES WHEN YOU'RE... ER...HAVING FUN!
DDDRRIIIIINNNNN
SO YOU STUDIED CHEMISTRY TOGETHER?
YEAH! AT FIRST IT SEEMED LIKE A CRAZY IDEA, BUT...
...THE HARD WORK I DID WITH GRANDMA PATRICIA PAID OFF. TODAY I REMEMBERED ALMOST ALL THE FORMULAS.
I WISH I COULD SAY THE SAME. I THINK MY TEST WAS A DISASTER!

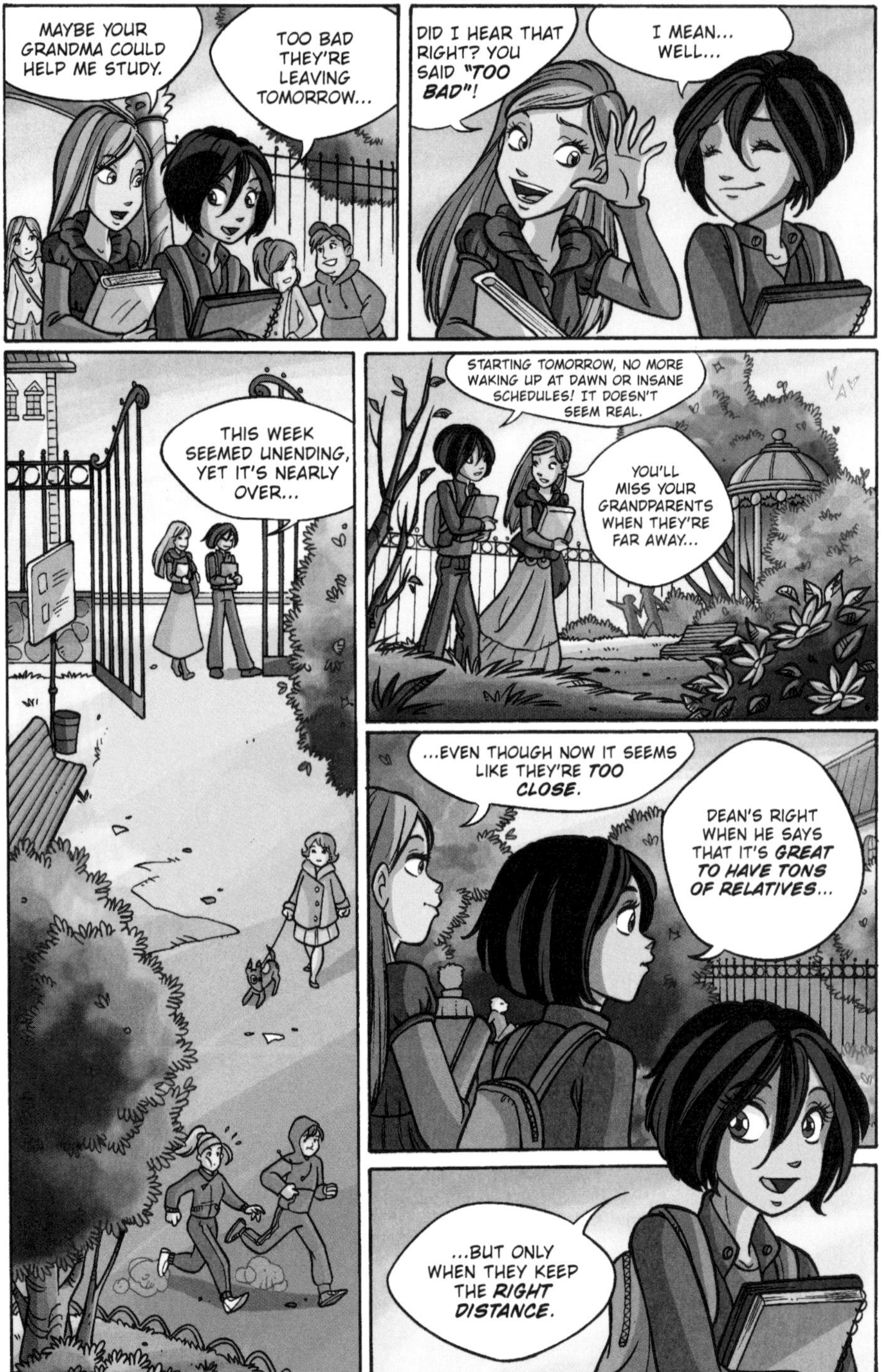
MAYBE YOUR GRANDMA COULD HELP ME STUDY.
TOO BAD THEY'RE LEAVING TOMORROW...
DID I HEAR THAT RIGHT? YOU SAID "TOO BAD"!
I MEAN... WELL...
THIS WEEK SEEMED UNENDING, YET IT'S NEARLY OVER...
STARTING TOMORROW, NO MORE WAKING UP AT DAWN OR INSANE SCHEDULES! IT DOESN'T SEEM REAL.
YOU'LL MISS YOUR GRANDPARENTS WHEN THEY'RE FAR AWAY...
...EVEN THOUGH NOW IT SEEMS LIKE THEY'RE TOO CLOSE.
DEAN'S RIGHT WHEN HE SAYS THAT IT'S GREAT TO HAVE TONS OF RELATIVES...
...BUT ONLY WHEN THEY KEEP THE RIGHT DISTANCE.

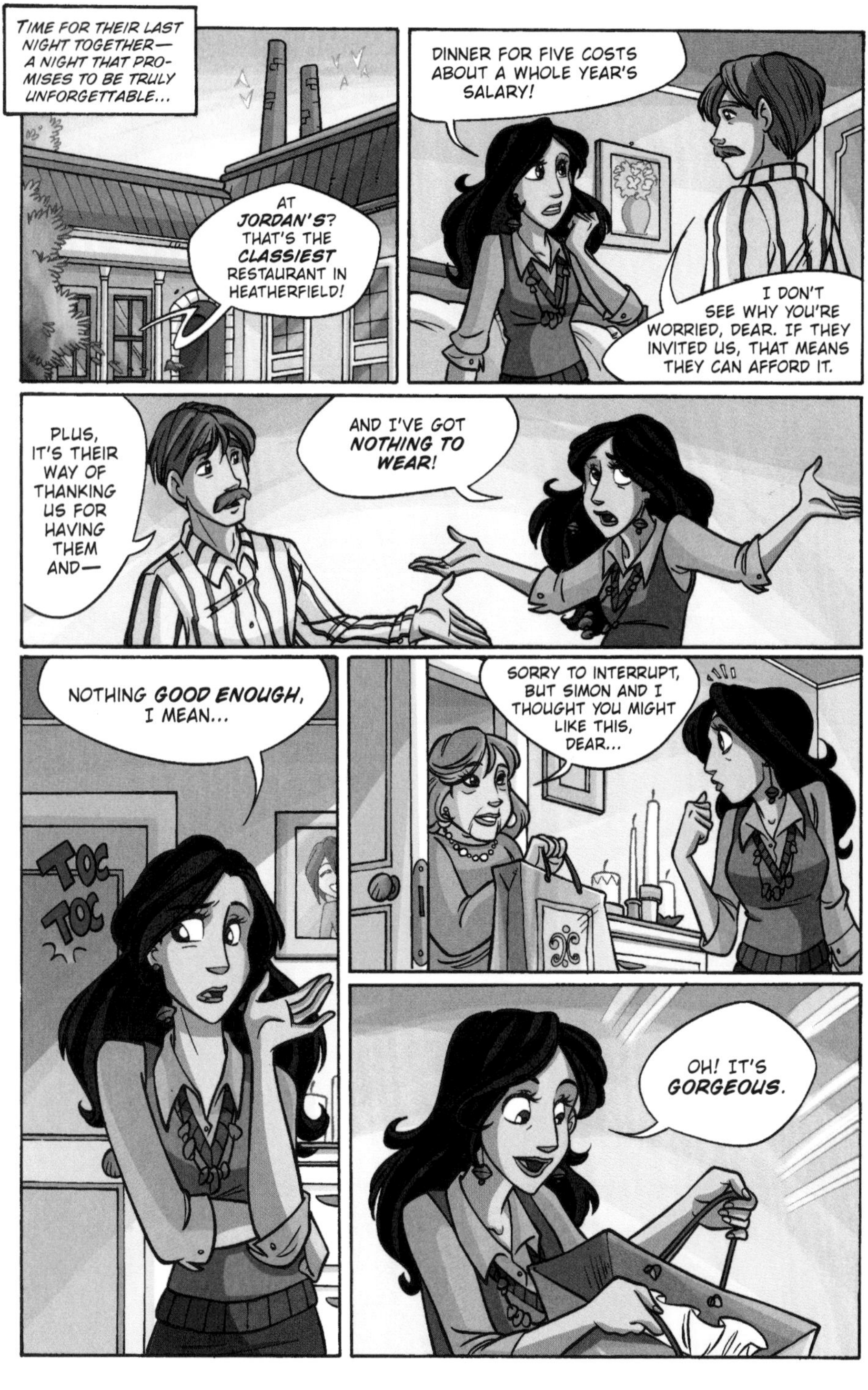
TIME FOR THEIR LAST NIGHT TOGETHER— A NIGHT THAT PROMISES TO BE TRULY UNFORGETTABLE...
AT JORDAN'S? THAT'S THE CLASSIEST RESTAURANT IN HEATHERFIELD!
DINNER FOR FIVE COSTS ABOUT A WHOLE YEAR'S SALARY!
I DON'T SEE WHY YOU'RE WORRIED, DEAR. IF THEY INVITED US, THAT MEANS THEY CAN AFFORD IT.
PLUS, IT'S THEIR WAY OF THANKING US FOR HAVING THEM AND—
AND I'VE GOT NOTHING TO WEAR!
NOTHING GOOD ENOUGH, I MEAN...
TOC TOC
SORRY TO INTERRUPT, BUT SIMON AND I THOUGHT YOU MIGHT LIKE THIS, DEAR...
OH! IT'S GORGEOUS.

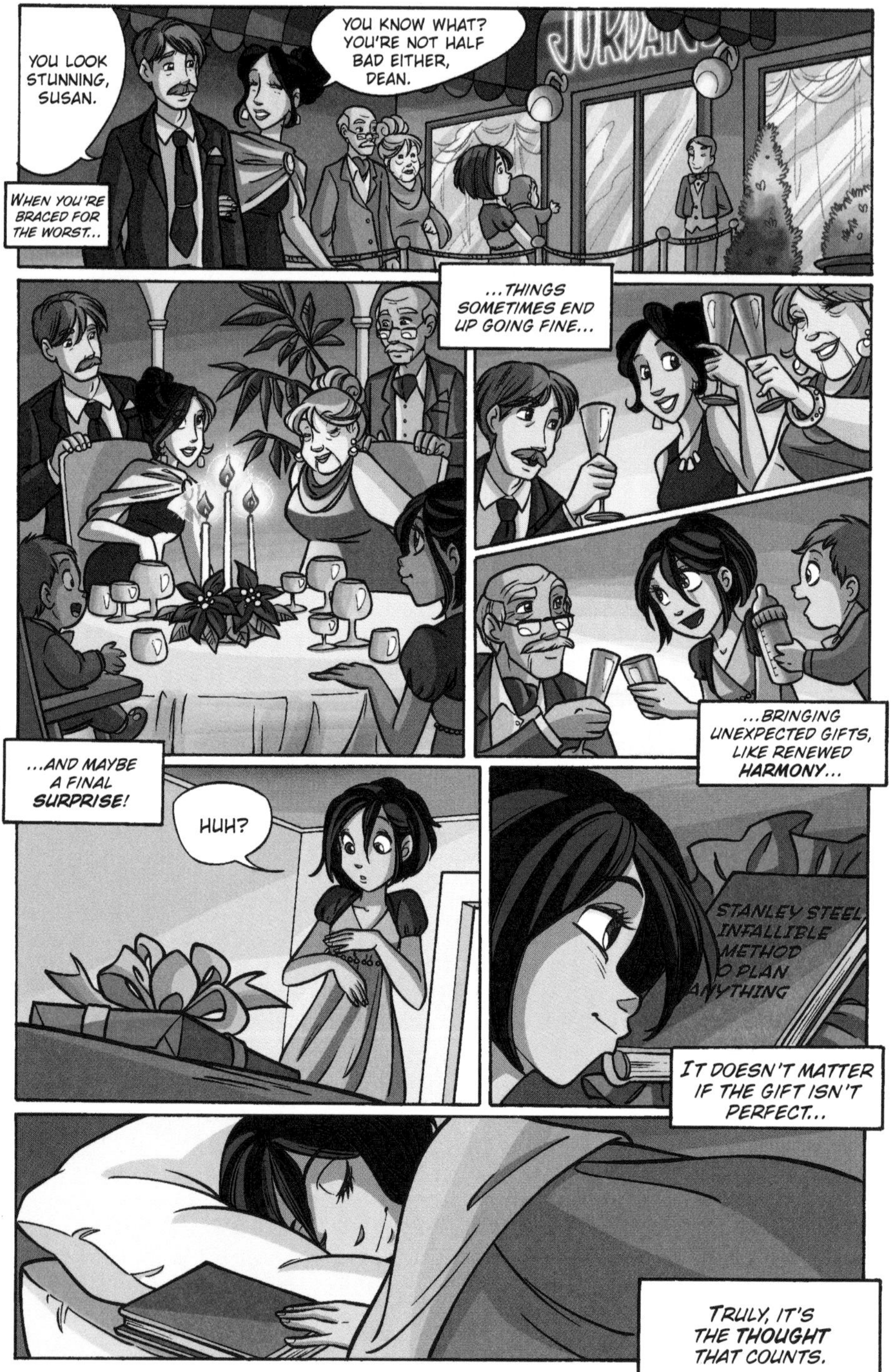
YOU LOOK STUNNING, SUSAN.
YOU KNOW WHAT? YOU'RE NOT HALF BAD EITHER, DEAN.
JORDAN'S
WHEN YOU'RE BRACED FOR THE WORST...
...THINGS SOMETIMES END UP GOING FINE...
...BRINGING UNEXPECTED GIFTS, LIKE RENEWED HARMONY...
...AND MAYBE A FINAL SURPRISE!
HUH?
STANLEY STEEL INFALLIBLE METHOD O PLAN NYTHING
IT DOESN'T MATTER IF THE GIFT ISN'T PERFECT...
TRULY, IT'S THE THOUGHT THAT COUNTS.

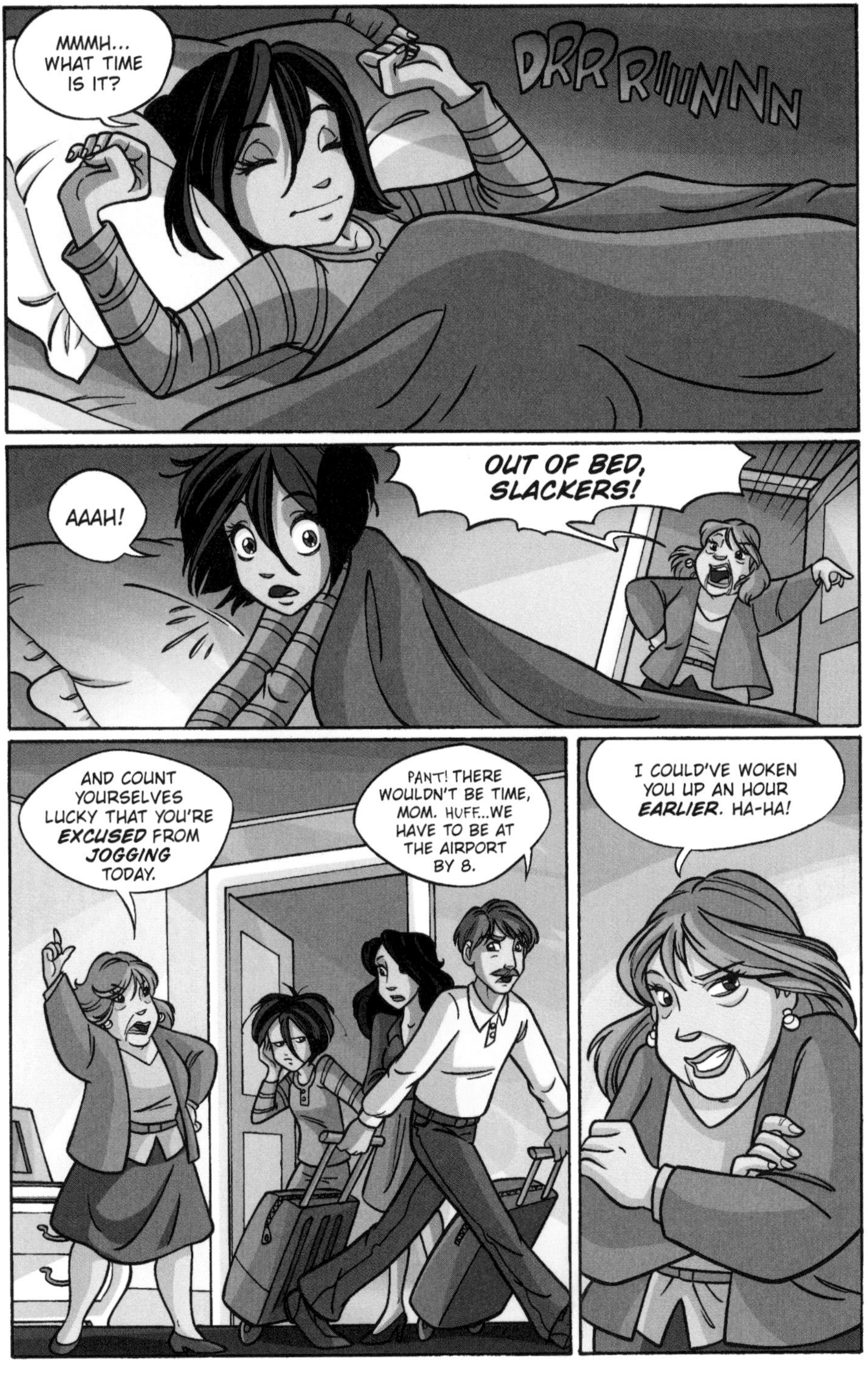
MMMH... WHAT TIME IS IT?
DRRRRIIIINNNN
AAAH!
OUT OF BED, SLACKERS!
AND COUNT YOURSELVES LUCKY THAT YOU'RE EXCUSED FROM JOGGING TODAY.
PANT! THERE WOULDN'T BE TIME, MOM. HUFF...WE HAVE TO BE AT THE AIRPORT BY 8.
I COULD'VE WOKEN YOU UP AN HOUR EARLIER. HA-HA!

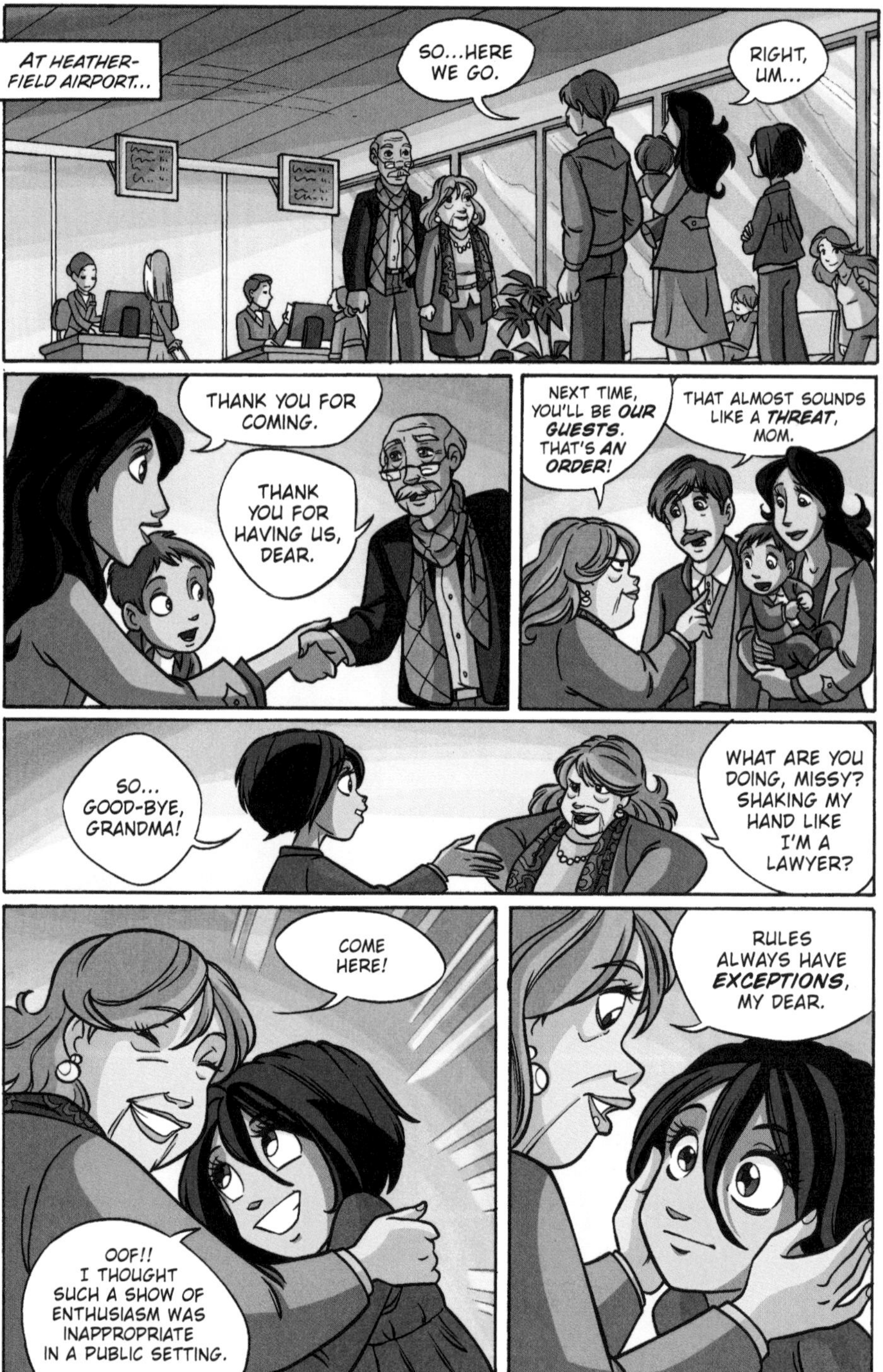
AT HEATHER-FIELD AIRPORT...
SO...HERE WE GO.
RIGHT, UM...
THANK YOU FOR COMING.
THANK YOU FOR HAVING US, DEAR.
NEXT TIME, YOU'LL BE ***OUR GUESTS***. THAT'S ***AN ORDER***!
THAT ALMOST SOUNDS LIKE A ***THREAT***, MOM.
SO... GOOD-BYE, GRANDMA!
WHAT ARE YOU DOING, MISSY? SHAKING MY HAND LIKE I'M A LAWYER?
COME HERE!
OOF!! I THOUGHT SUCH A SHOW OF ENTHUSIASM WAS INAPPROPRIATE IN A PUBLIC SETTING.
RULES ALWAYS HAVE ***EXCEPTIONS***, MY DEAR.

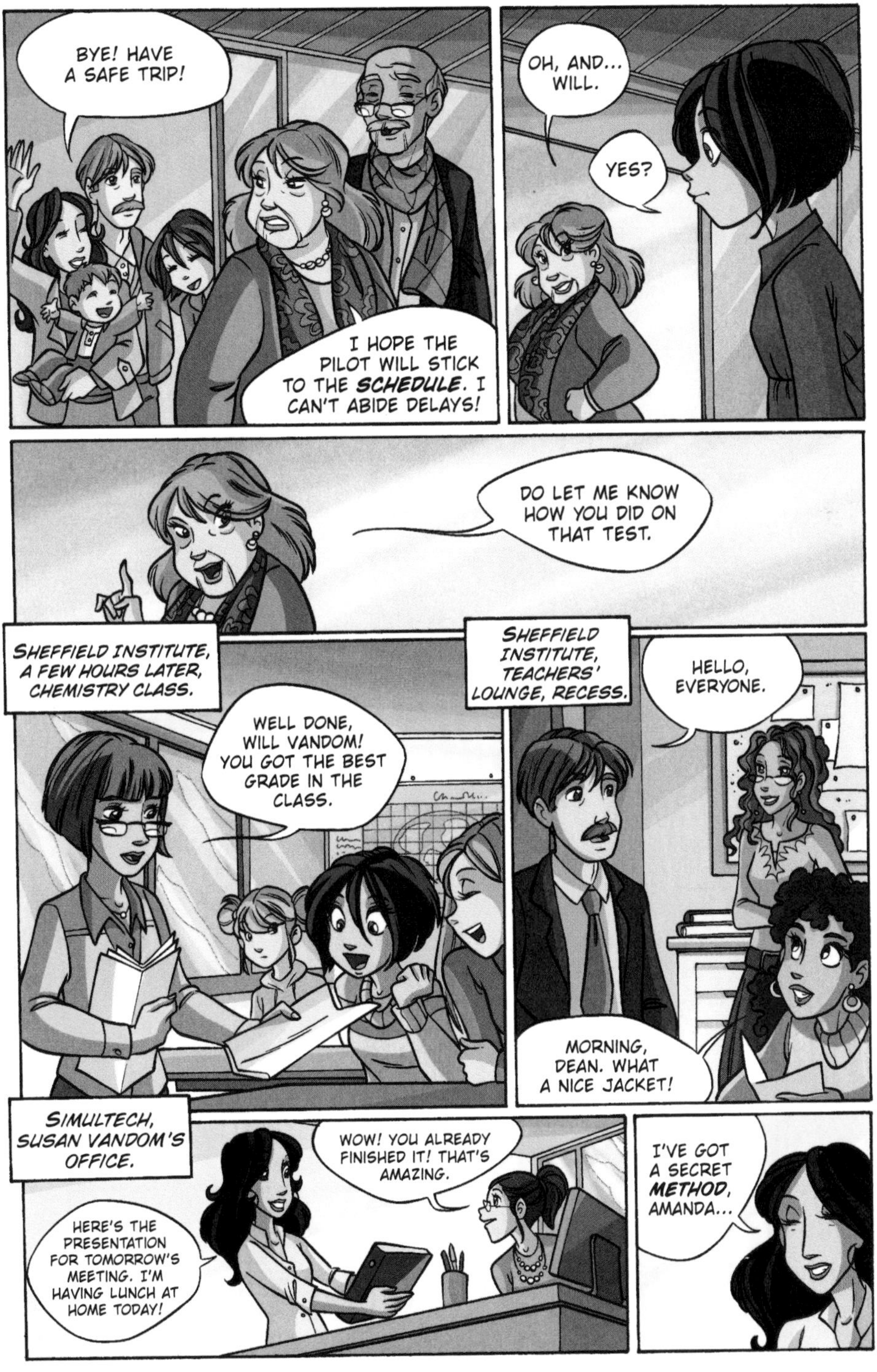
BYE! HAVE A SAFE TRIP!
I HOPE THE PILOT WILL STICK TO THE SCHEDULE. I CAN'T ABIDE DELAYS!
OH, AND... WILL.
YES?
DO LET ME KNOW HOW YOU DID ON THAT TEST.
SHEFFIELD INSTITUTE, A FEW HOURS LATER, CHEMISTRY CLASS.
WELL DONE, WILL VANDOM! YOU GOT THE BEST GRADE IN THE CLASS.
SHEFFIELD INSTITUTE, TEACHERS' LOUNGE, RECESS.
HELLO, EVERYONE.
MORNING, DEAN. WHAT A NICE JACKET!
SIMULTECH, SUSAN VANDOM'S OFFICE.
HERE'S THE PRESENTATION FOR TOMORROW'S MEETING. I'M HAVING LUNCH AT HOME TODAY!
WOW! YOU ALREADY FINISHED IT! THAT'S AMAZING.
I'VE GOT A SECRET METHOD, AMANDA...

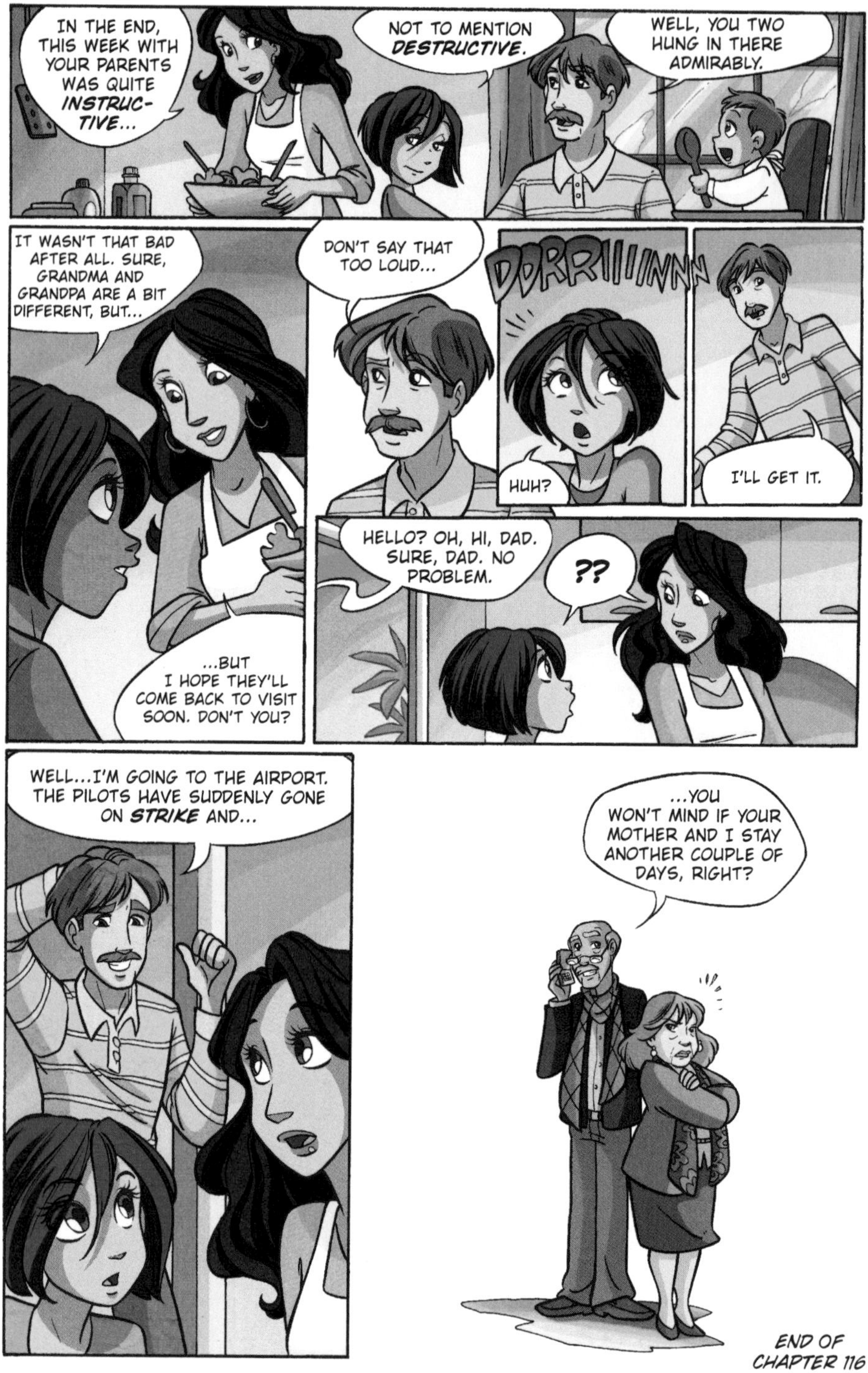

IN THE END, THIS WEEK WITH YOUR PARENTS WAS QUITE INSTRUCTIVE...
NOT TO MENTION DESTRUCTIVE.
WELL, YOU TWO HUNG IN THERE ADMIRABLY.
IT WASN'T THAT BAD AFTER ALL. SURE, GRANDMA AND GRANDPA ARE A BIT DIFFERENT, BUT...
...BUT I HOPE THEY'LL COME BACK TO VISIT SOON. DON'T YOU?
DON'T SAY THAT TOO LOUD...
DDRRIIIINNN
HUH?
I'LL GET IT.
HELLO? OH, HI, DAD. SURE, DAD. NO PROBLEM.
??
WELL...I'M GOING TO THE AIRPORT. THE PILOTS HAVE SUDDENLY GONE ON STRIKE AND...
...YOU WON'T MIND IF YOUR MOTHER AND I STAY ANOTHER COUPLE OF DAYS, RIGHT?
END OF CHAPTER 116

117

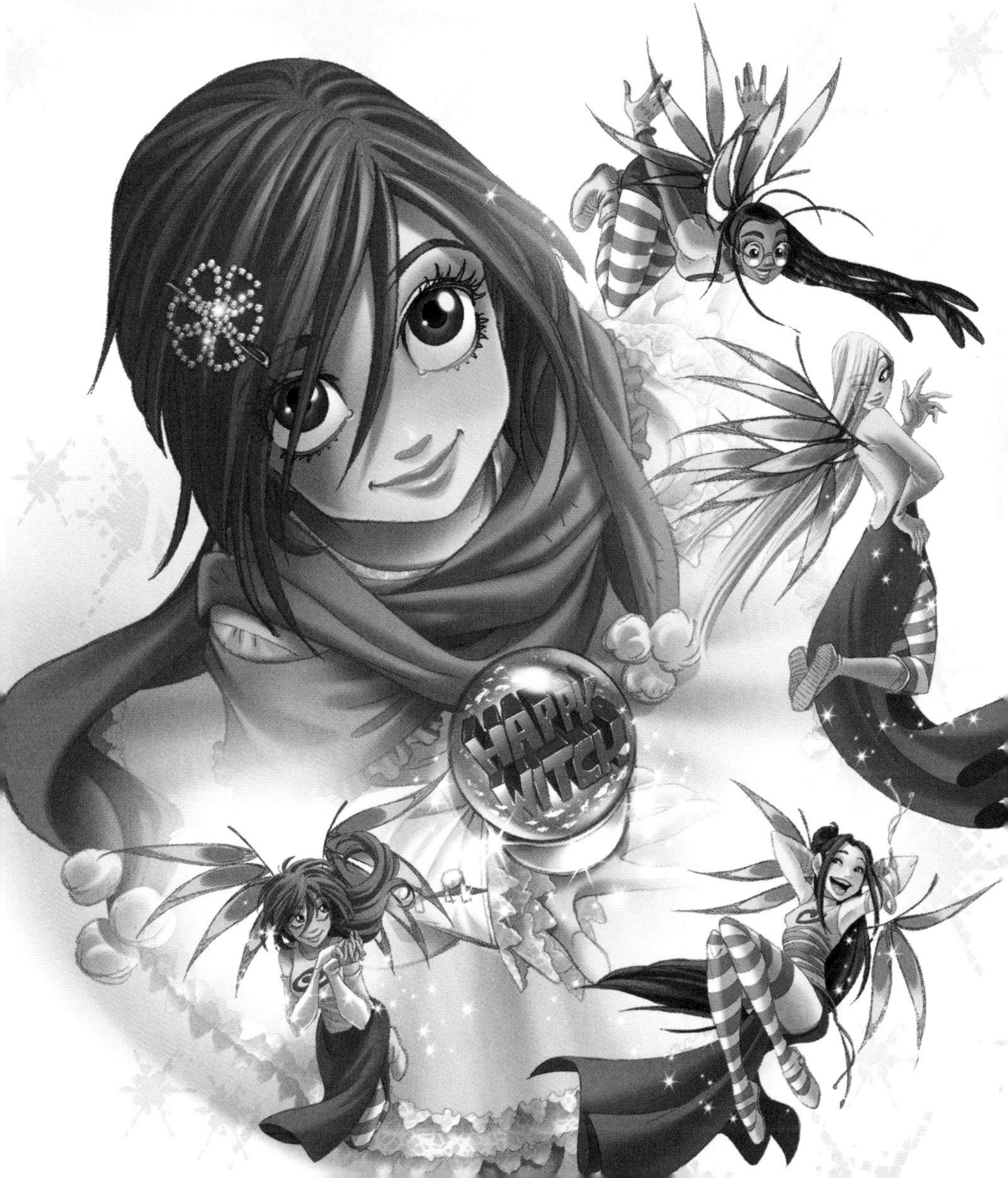

W.i.t.c.h.

Will Irma Taranee Cornelia Hay Lin

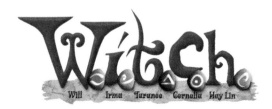

The Best Party

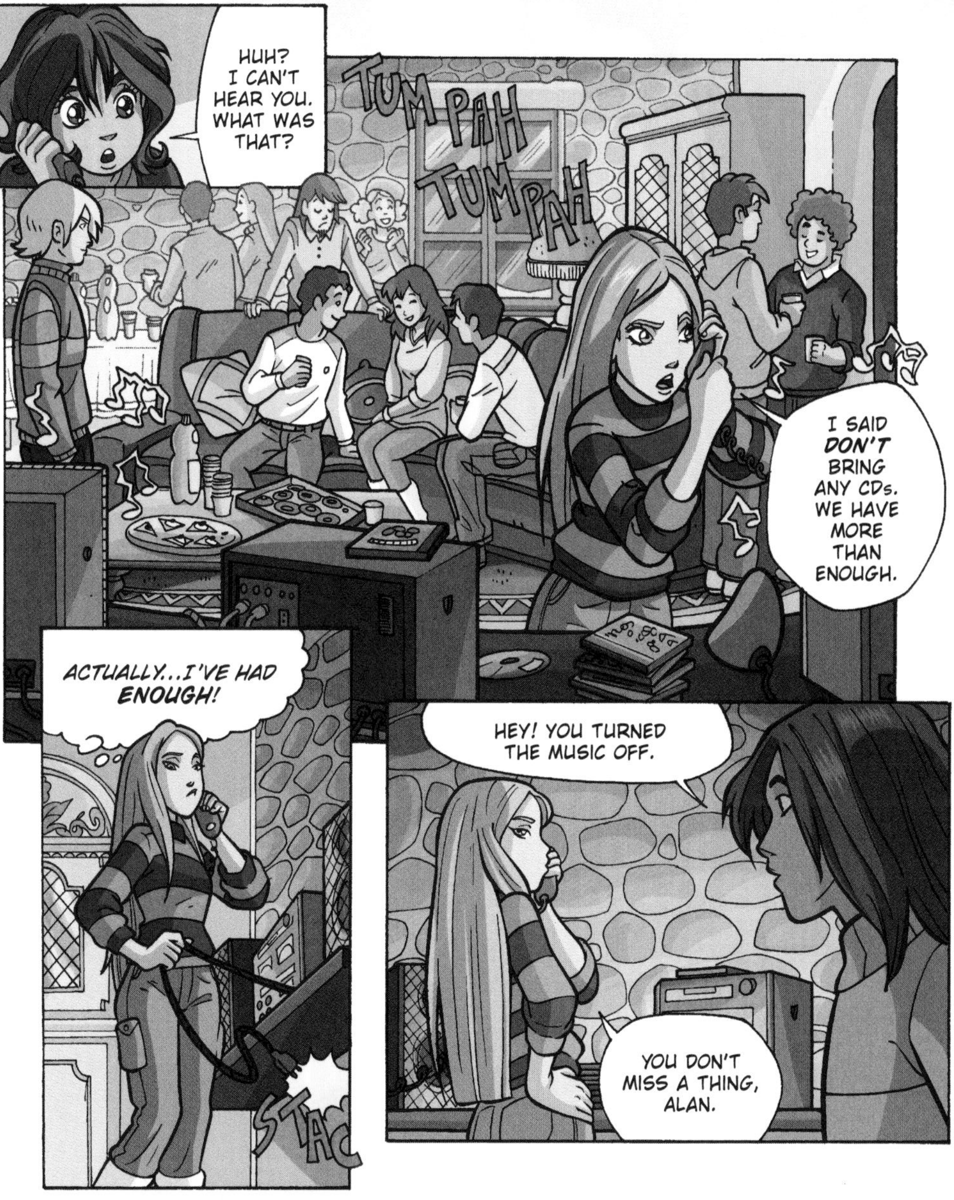
HUH? I CAN'T HEAR YOU. WHAT WAS THAT?
TUM PAH TUM PAH
I SAID DON'T BRING ANY CDs. WE HAVE MORE THAN ENOUGH.
ACTUALLY...I'VE HAD ENOUGH!
STAC
HEY! YOU TURNED THE MUSIC OFF.
YOU DON'T MISS A THING, ALAN.

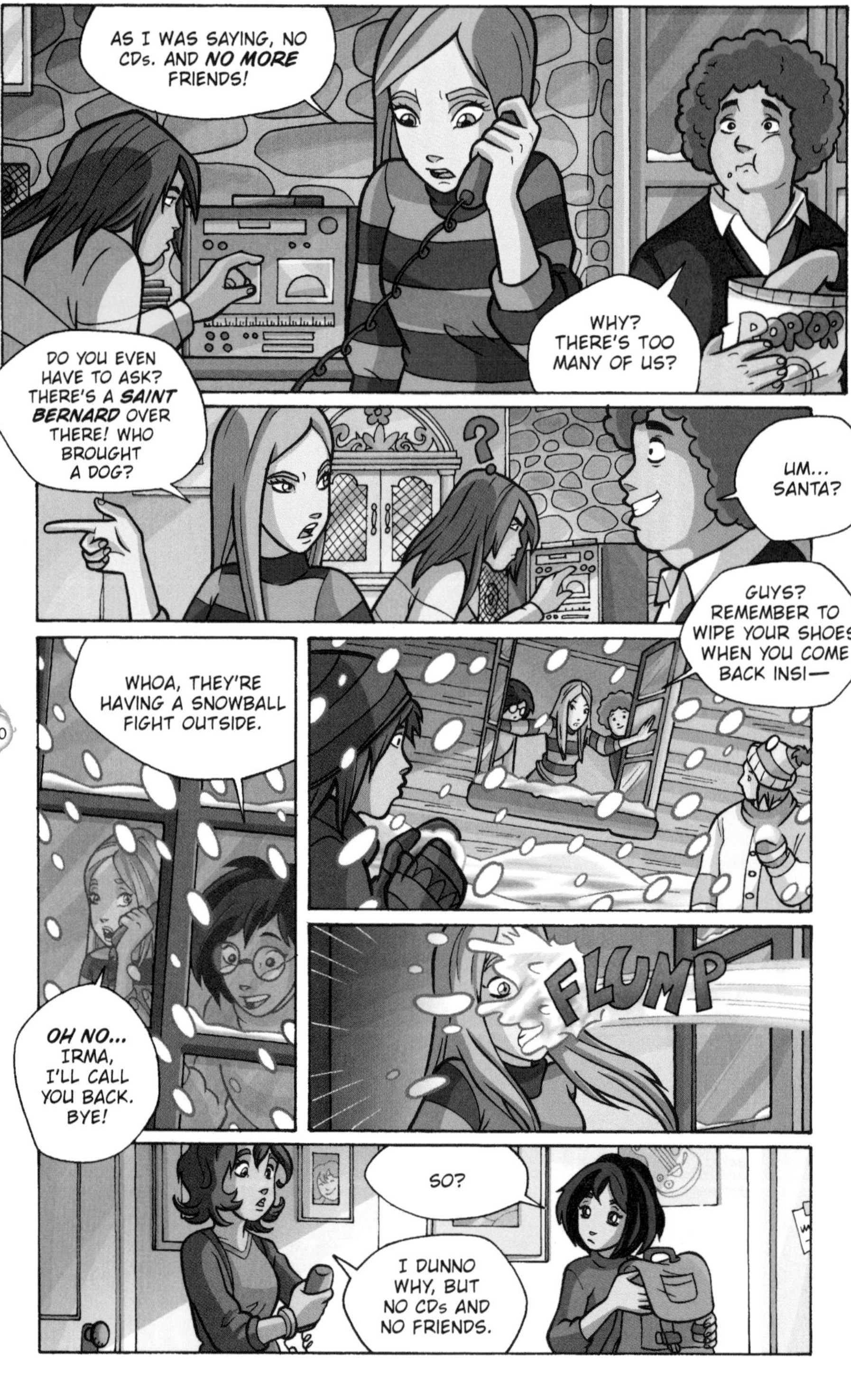
AS I WAS SAYING, NO CDs. AND NO MORE FRIENDS!
WHY? THERE'S TOO MANY OF US?
POPCOR
DO YOU EVEN HAVE TO ASK? THERE'S A SAINT BERNARD OVER THERE! WHO BROUGHT A DOG?
?
UM... SANTA?
GUYS? REMEMBER TO WIPE YOUR SHOES WHEN YOU COME BACK INSI—
WHOA, THEY'RE HAVING A SNOWBALL FIGHT OUTSIDE.
OH NO... IRMA, I'LL CALL YOU BACK. BYE!
FLUMP
SO?
I DUNNO WHY, BUT NO CDs AND NO FRIENDS.

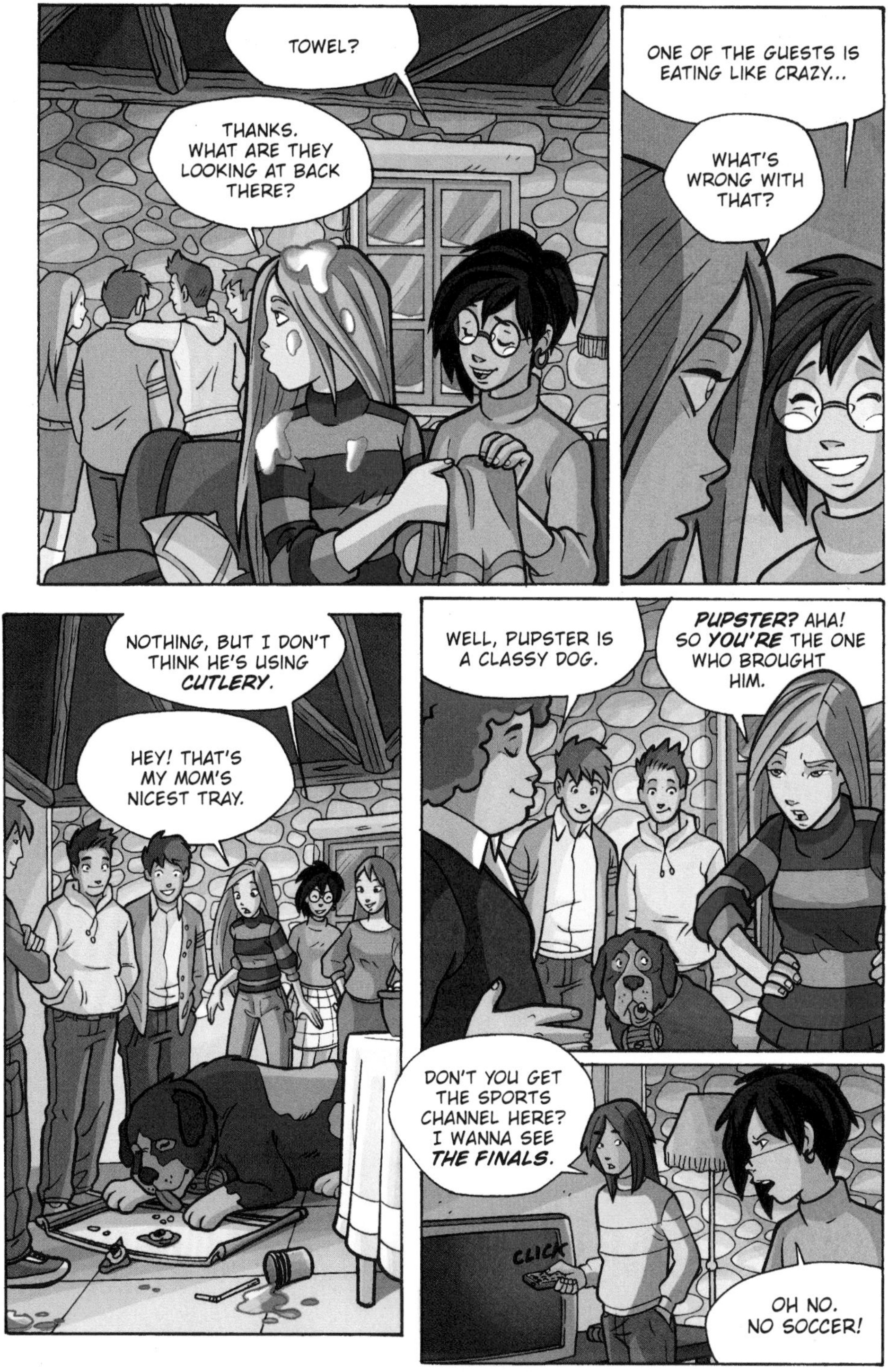
TOWEL?
THANKS. WHAT ARE THEY LOOKING AT BACK THERE?
ONE OF THE GUESTS IS EATING LIKE CRAZY...
WHAT'S WRONG WITH THAT?
NOTHING, BUT I DON'T THINK HE'S USING *CUTLERY*.
HEY! THAT'S MY MOM'S NICEST TRAY.
WELL, PUPSTER IS A CLASSY DOG.
PUPSTER? AHA! SO *YOU'RE* THE ONE WHO BROUGHT HIM.
DON'T YOU GET THE SPORTS CHANNEL HERE? I WANNA SEE *THE FINALS*.
CLICK
OH NO. NO SOCCER!

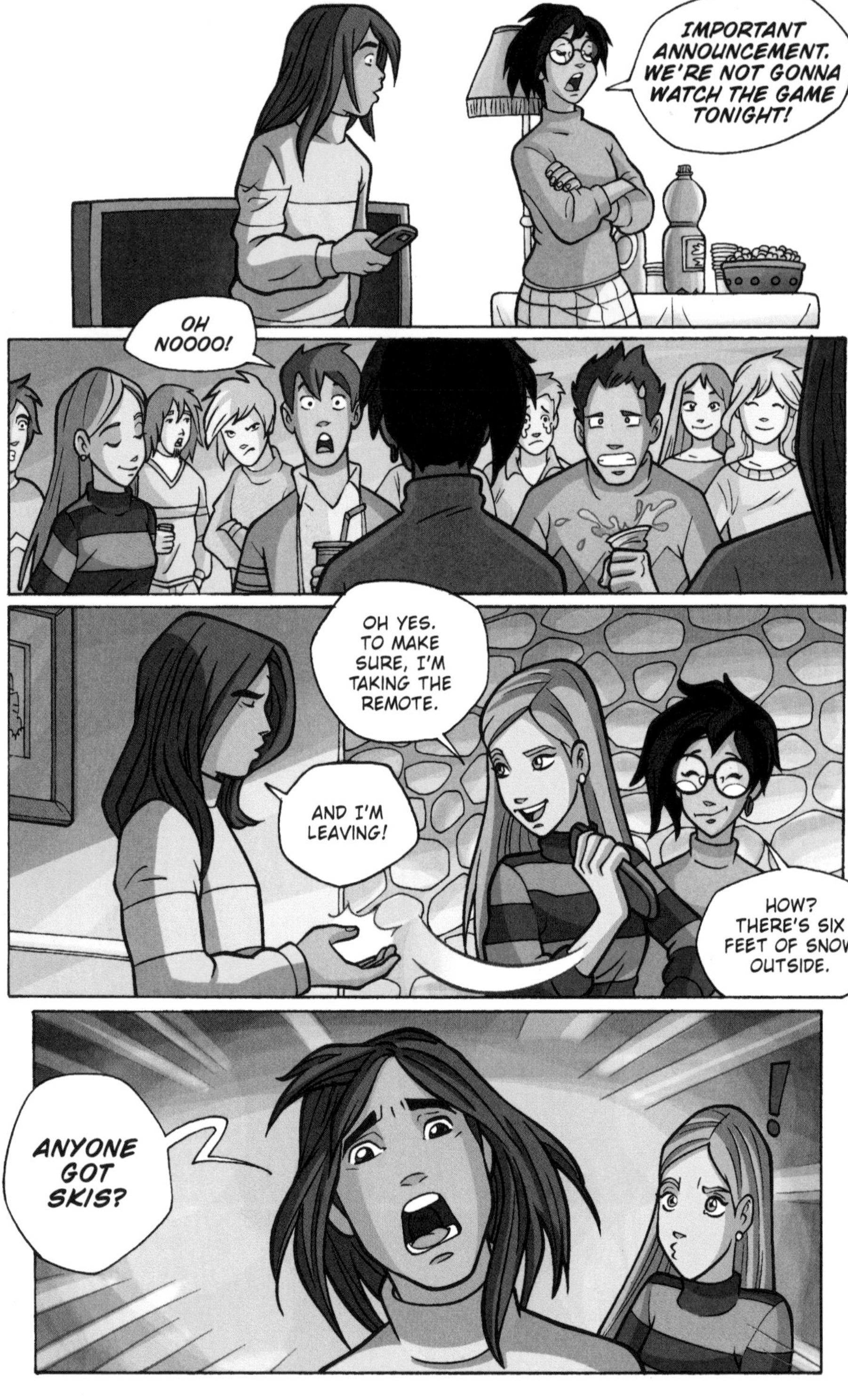
IMPORTANT ANNOUNCEMENT. WE'RE NOT GONNA WATCH THE GAME TONIGHT!
OH NOOOO!
OH YES. TO MAKE SURE, I'M TAKING THE REMOTE.
AND I'M LEAVING!
HOW? THERE'S SIX FEET OF SNOW OUTSIDE.
ANYONE GOT SKIS?
!

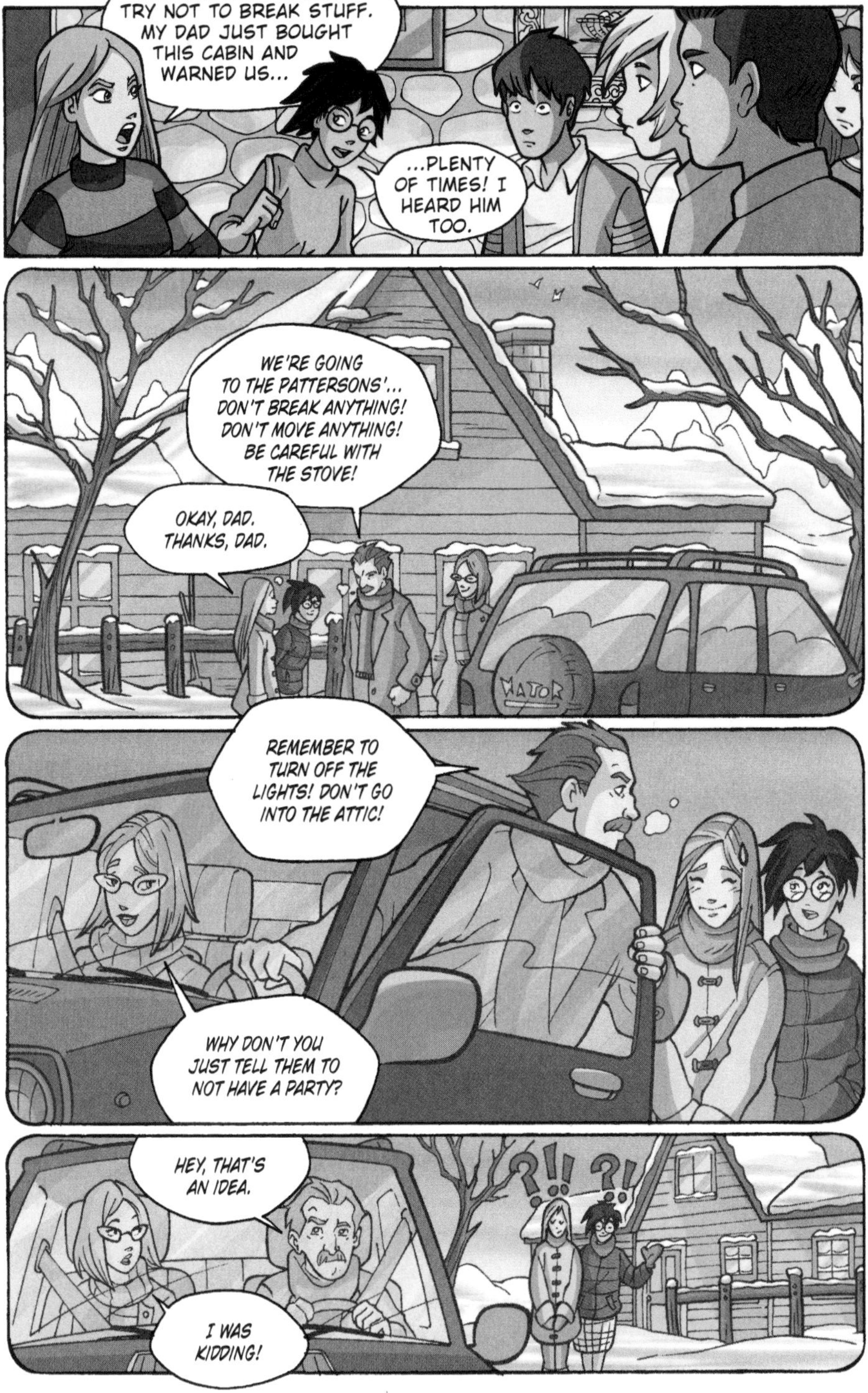
AND ANOTHER THING... TRY NOT TO BREAK STUFF. MY DAD JUST BOUGHT THIS CABIN AND WARNED US...
...PLENTY OF TIMES! I HEARD HIM TOO.
WE'RE GOING TO THE PATTERSONS'... DON'T BREAK ANYTHING! DON'T MOVE ANYTHING! BE CAREFUL WITH THE STOVE!
OKAY, DAD. THANKS, DAD.
REMEMBER TO TURN OFF THE LIGHTS! DON'T GO INTO THE ATTIC!
WHY DON'T YOU JUST TELL THEM TO NOT HAVE A PARTY?
HEY, THAT'S AN IDEA.
?!! ?!
I WAS KIDDING!

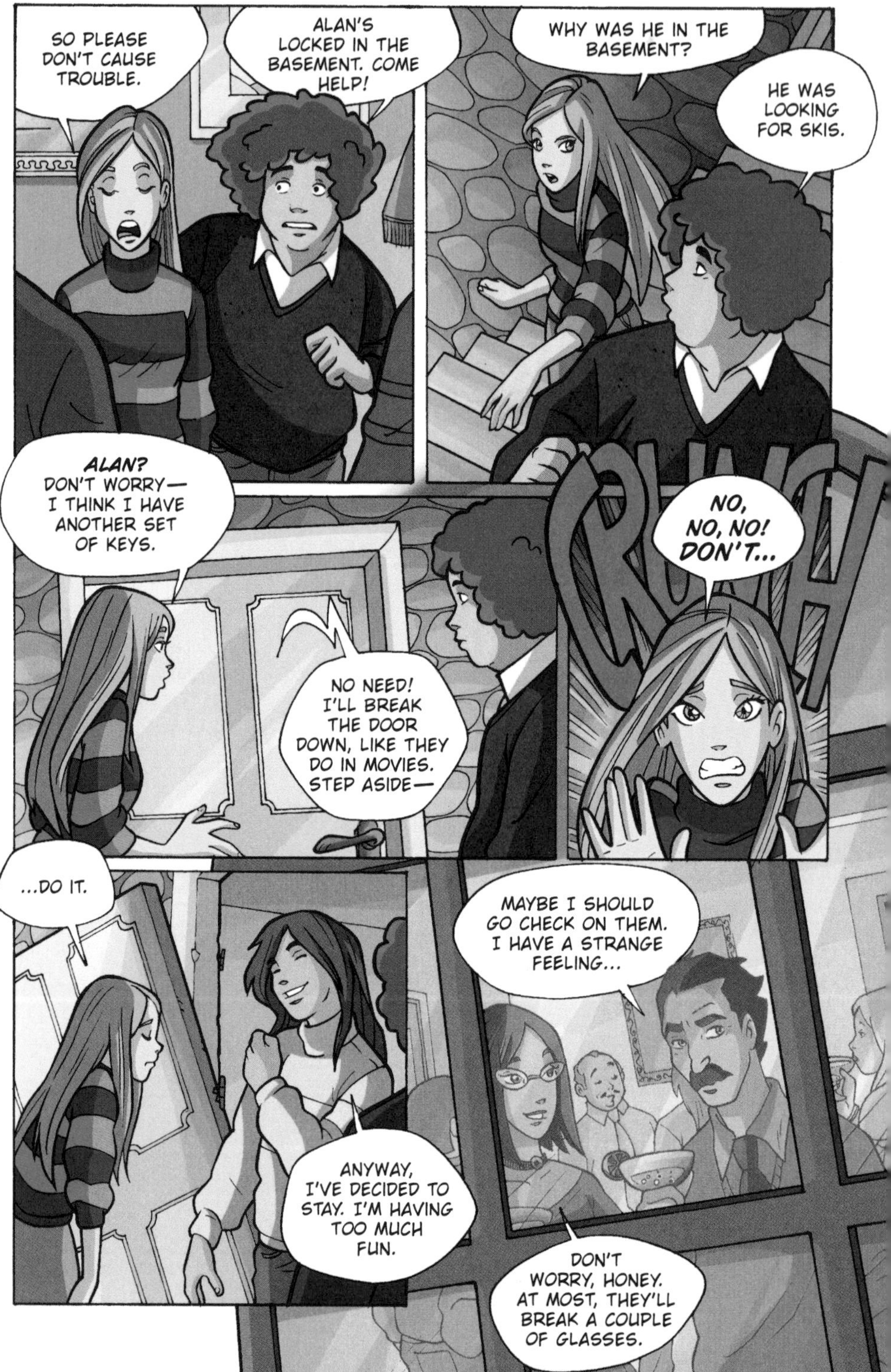
SO PLEASE DON'T CAUSE TROUBLE.
ALAN'S LOCKED IN THE BASEMENT. COME HELP!
WHY WAS HE IN THE BASEMENT?
HE WAS LOOKING FOR SKIS.
ALAN? DON'T WORRY— I THINK I HAVE ANOTHER SET OF KEYS.
NO NEED! I'LL BREAK THE DOOR DOWN, LIKE THEY DO IN MOVIES. STEP ASIDE—
CRUNCH
NO, NO, NO! DON'T...
...DO IT.
ANYWAY, I'VE DECIDED TO STAY. I'M HAVING TOO MUCH FUN.
MAYBE I SHOULD GO CHECK ON THEM. I HAVE A STRANGE FEELING...
DON'T WORRY, HONEY. AT MOST, THEY'LL BREAK A COUPLE OF GLASSES.

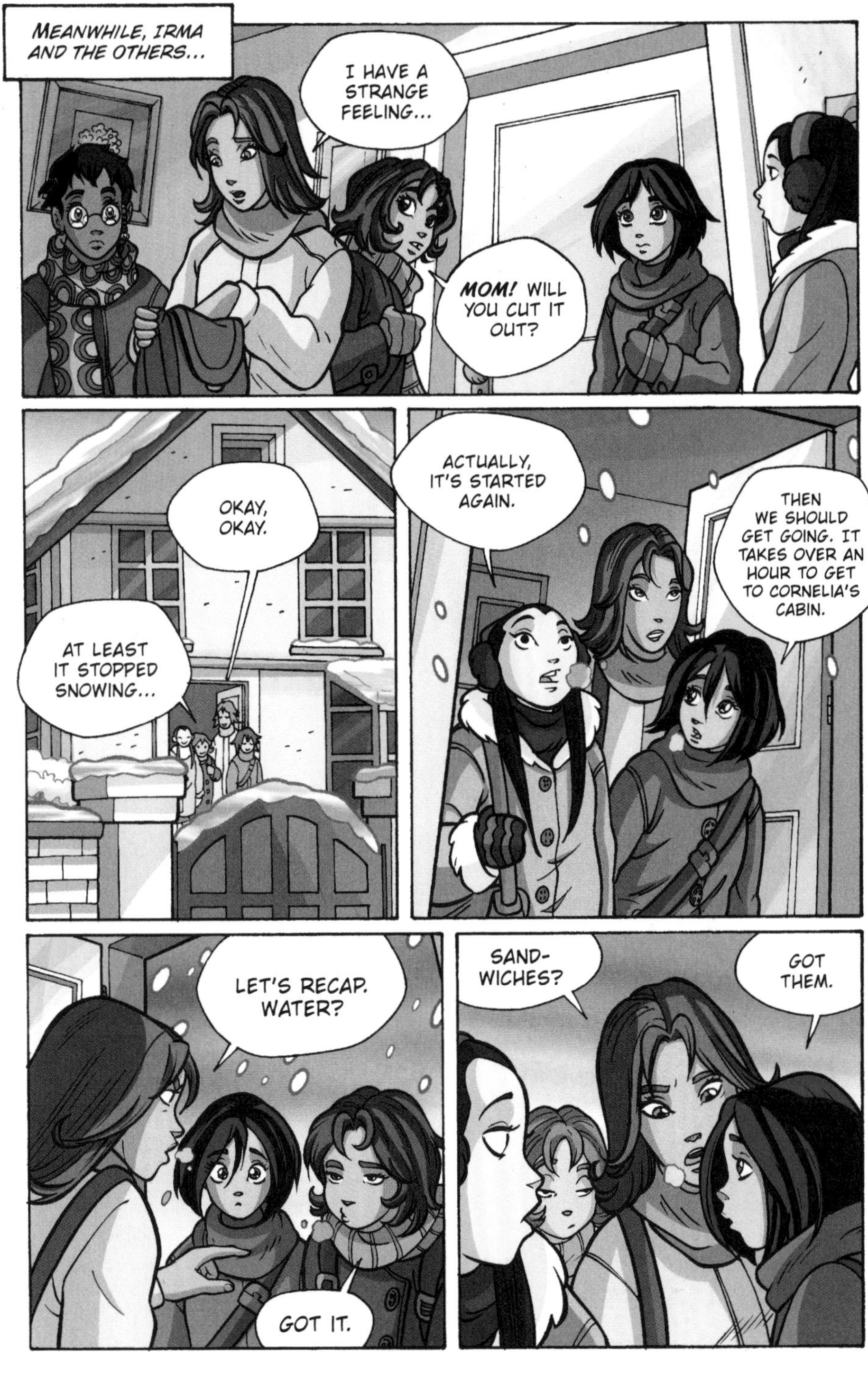
MEANWHILE, IRMA AND THE OTHERS...
I HAVE A STRANGE FEELING...
MOM! WILL YOU CUT IT OUT?
AT LEAST IT STOPPED SNOWING...
OKAY, OKAY.
ACTUALLY, IT'S STARTED AGAIN.
THEN WE SHOULD GET GOING. IT TAKES OVER AN HOUR TO GET TO CORNELIA'S CABIN.
LET'S RECAP. WATER?
GOT IT.
SAND-WICHES?
GOT THEM.

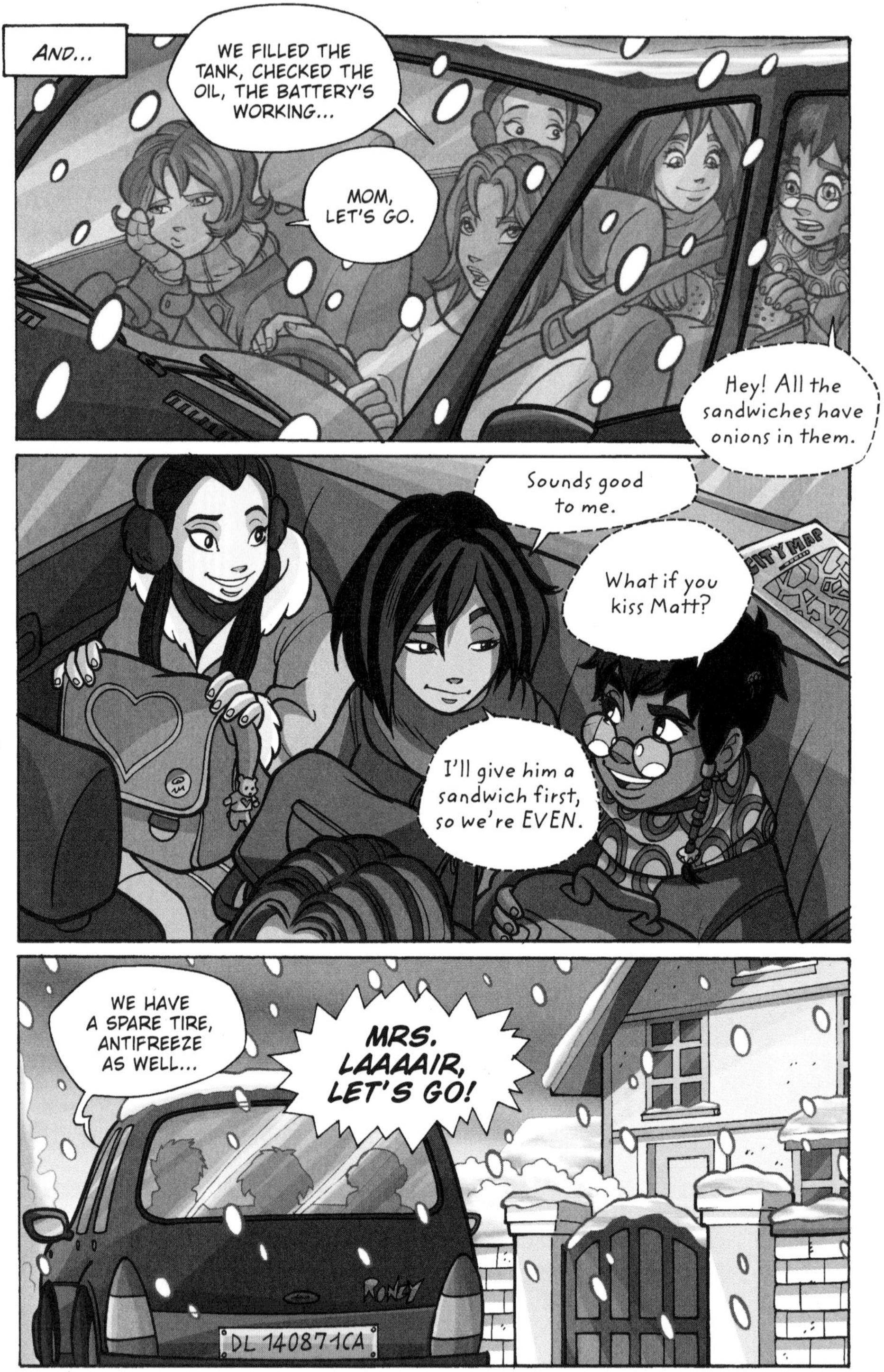
AND...
WE FILLED THE TANK, CHECKED THE OIL, THE BATTERY'S WORKING...
MOM, LET'S GO.
Hey! All the sandwiches have onions in them.
Sounds good to me.
What if you kiss Matt?
I'll give him a sandwich first, so we're EVEN.
WE HAVE A SPARE TIRE, ANTIFREEZE AS WELL...
MRS. LAAAAIR, LET'S GO!
CITY MAP
DL 140871CA

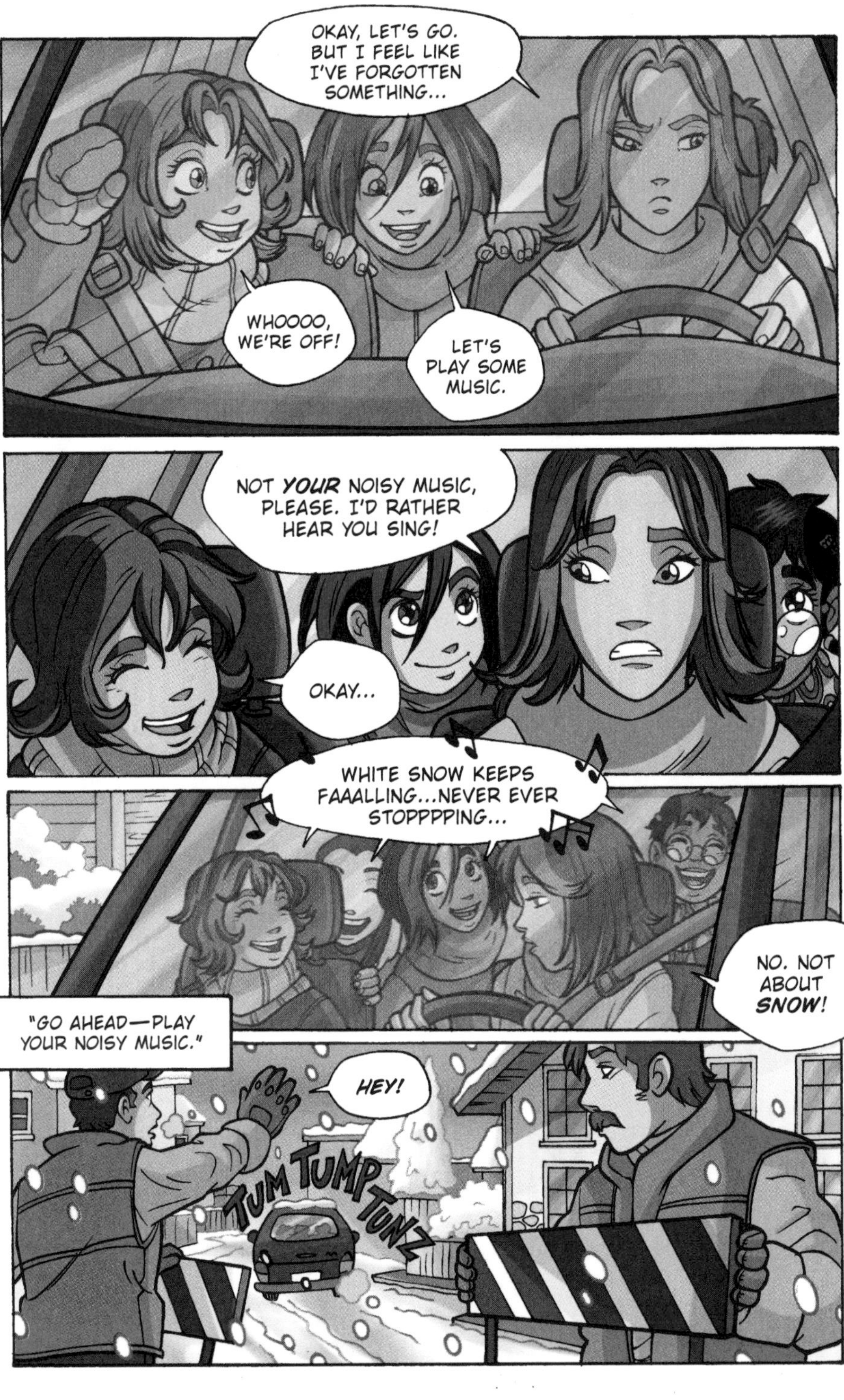
OKAY, LET'S GO. BUT I FEEL LIKE I'VE FORGOTTEN SOMETHING...
WHOOOO, WE'RE OFF!
LET'S PLAY SOME MUSIC.
NOT *YOUR* NOISY MUSIC, PLEASE. I'D RATHER HEAR YOU SING!
OKAY...
WHITE SNOW KEEPS FAAALLING...NEVER EVER STOPPPPING...
NO. NOT ABOUT *SNOW*!
"GO AHEAD—PLAY YOUR NOISY MUSIC."
HEY!
TUM TUMP TUNZ

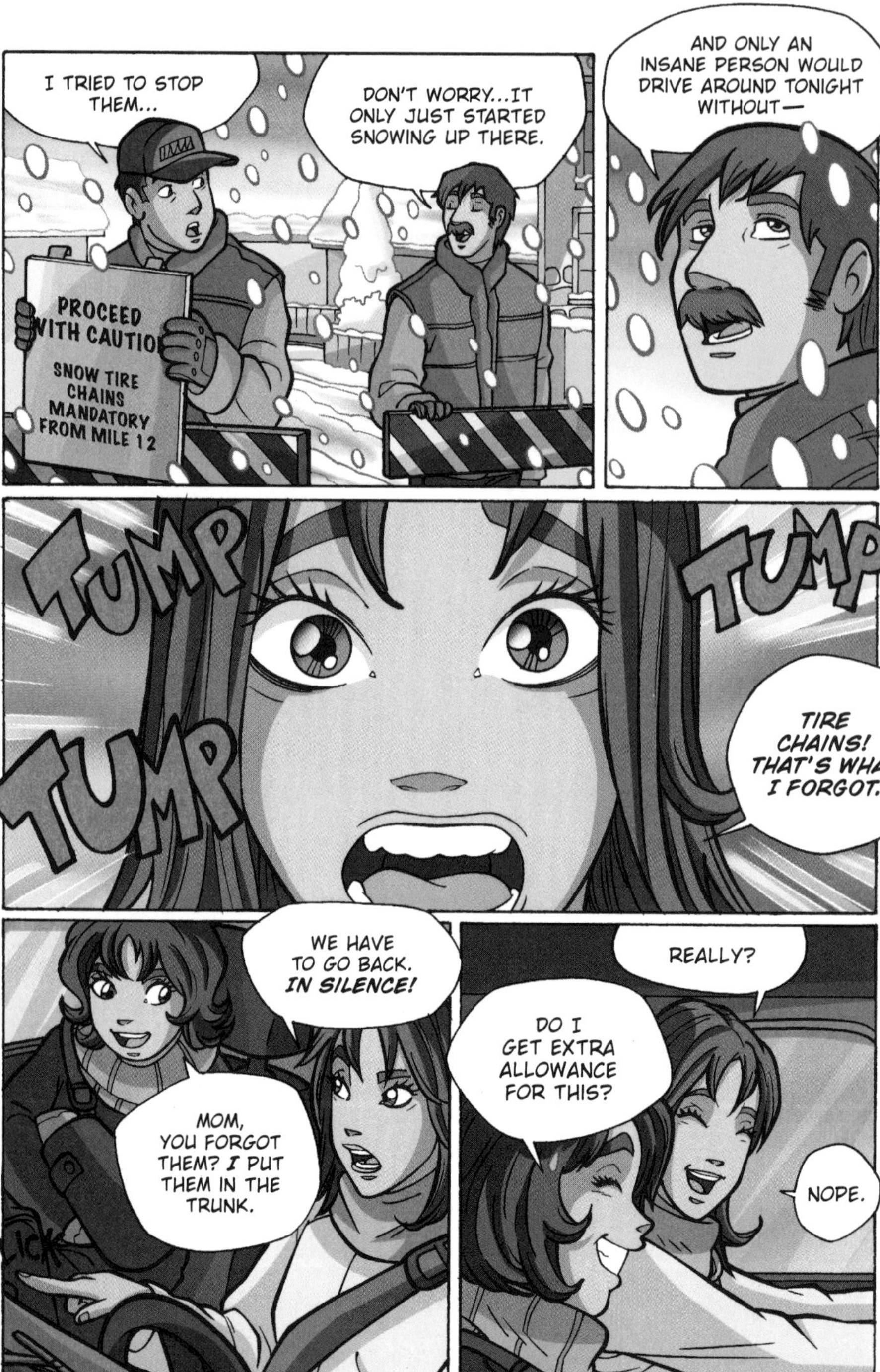
I TRIED TO STOP THEM...
PROCEED WITH CAUTIO
SNOW TIRE CHAINS MANDATORY FROM MILE 12
DON'T WORRY...IT ONLY JUST STARTED SNOWING UP THERE.
AND ONLY AN INSANE PERSON WOULD DRIVE AROUND TONIGHT WITHOUT—
TUMP
TUMP
TUMP
TIRE CHAINS! THAT'S WHAT I FORGOT.
WE HAVE TO GO BACK. IN SILENCE!
MOM, YOU FORGOT THEM? I PUT THEM IN THE TRUNK.
CLICK
REALLY?
DO I GET EXTRA ALLOWANCE FOR THIS?
NOPE.

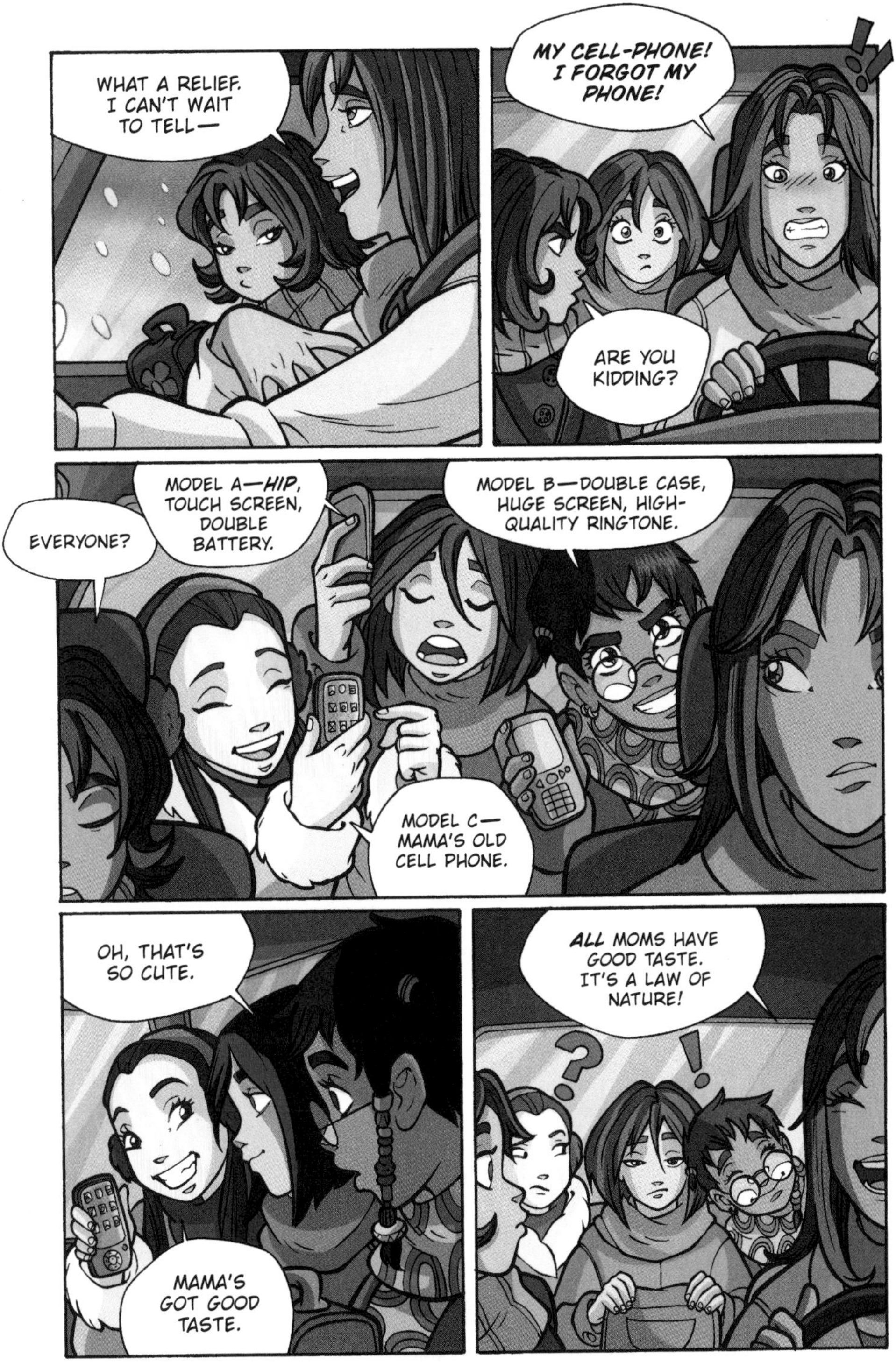
WHAT A RELIEF. I CAN'T WAIT TO TELL—
MY CELL-PHONE! I FORGOT MY PHONE!
ARE YOU KIDDING?
EVERYONE?
MODEL A—HIP, TOUCH SCREEN, DOUBLE BATTERY.
MODEL B—DOUBLE CASE, HUGE SCREEN, HIGH-QUALITY RINGTONE.
MODEL C—MAMA'S OLD CELL PHONE.
OH, THAT'S SO CUTE.
MAMA'S GOT GOOD TASTE.
ALL MOMS HAVE GOOD TASTE. IT'S A LAW OF NATURE!

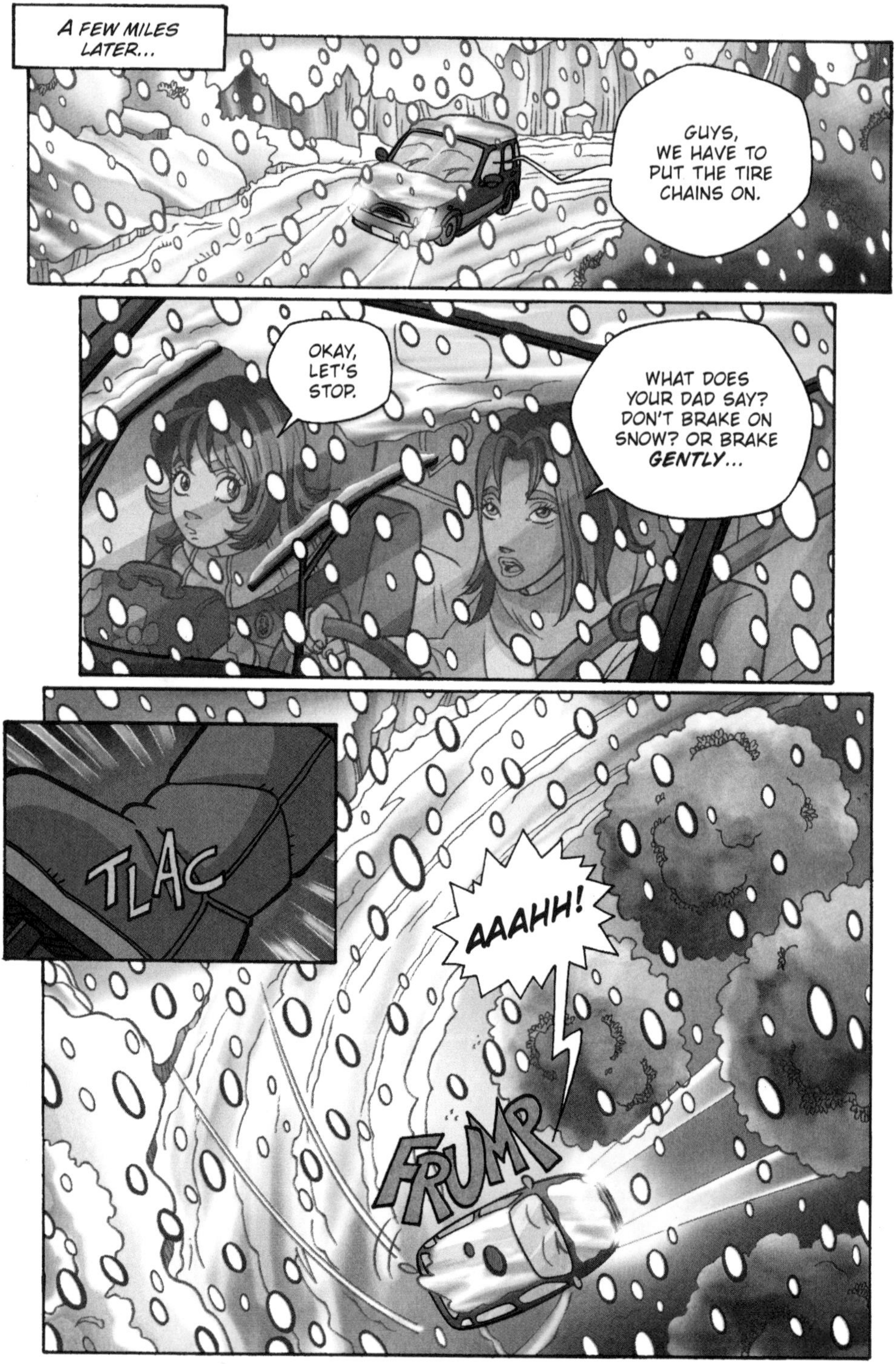
A FEW MILES LATER...
GUYS, WE HAVE TO PUT THE TIRE CHAINS ON.
OKAY, LET'S STOP.
WHAT DOES YOUR DAD SAY? DON'T BRAKE ON SNOW? OR BRAKE GENTLY...
TLAC
AAAHH!
FRUMP

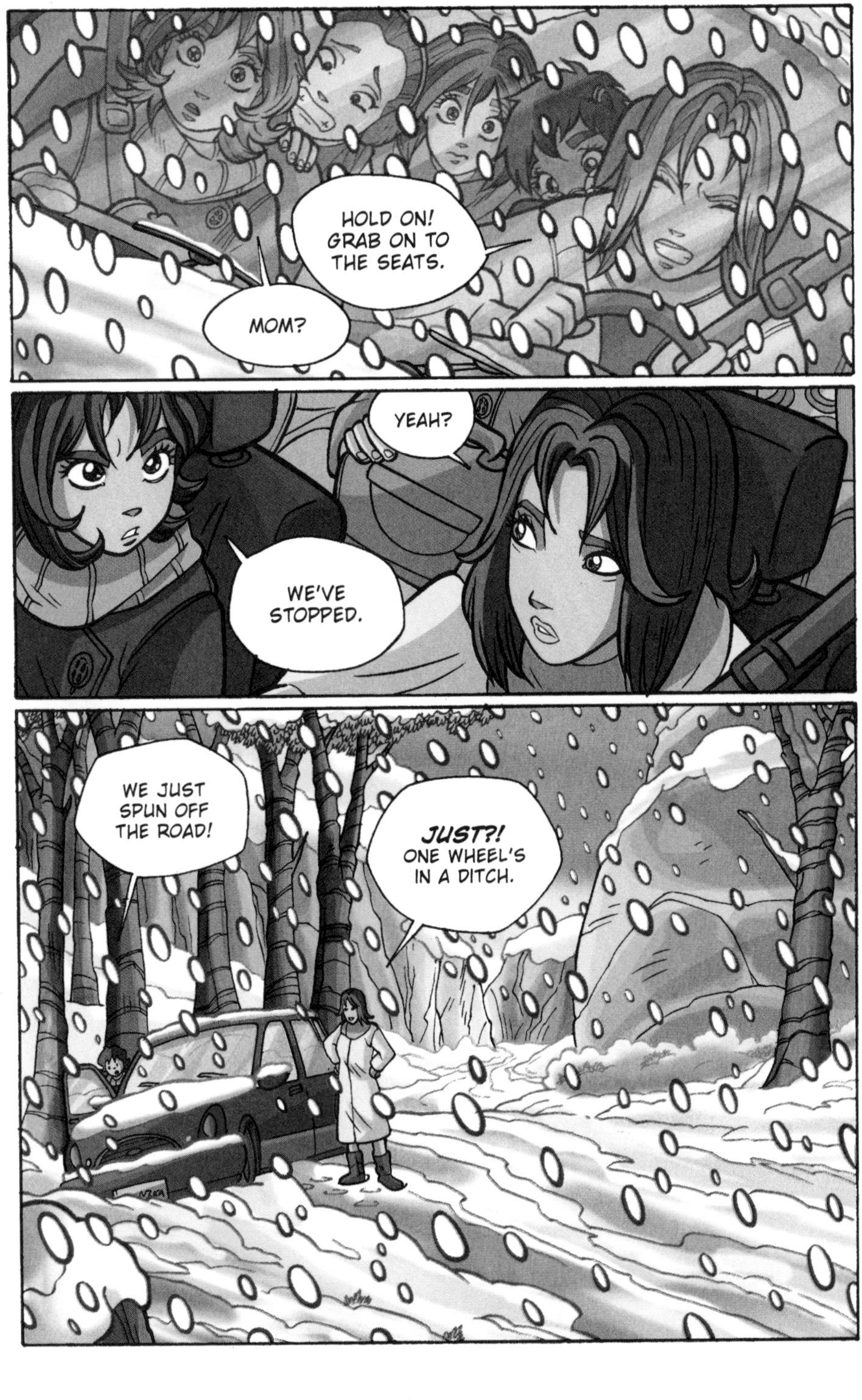
HOLD ON! GRAB ON TO THE SEATS.
MOM?
YEAH?
WE'VE STOPPED.
WE JUST SPUN OFF THE ROAD!
JUST?! ONE WHEEL'S IN A DITCH.

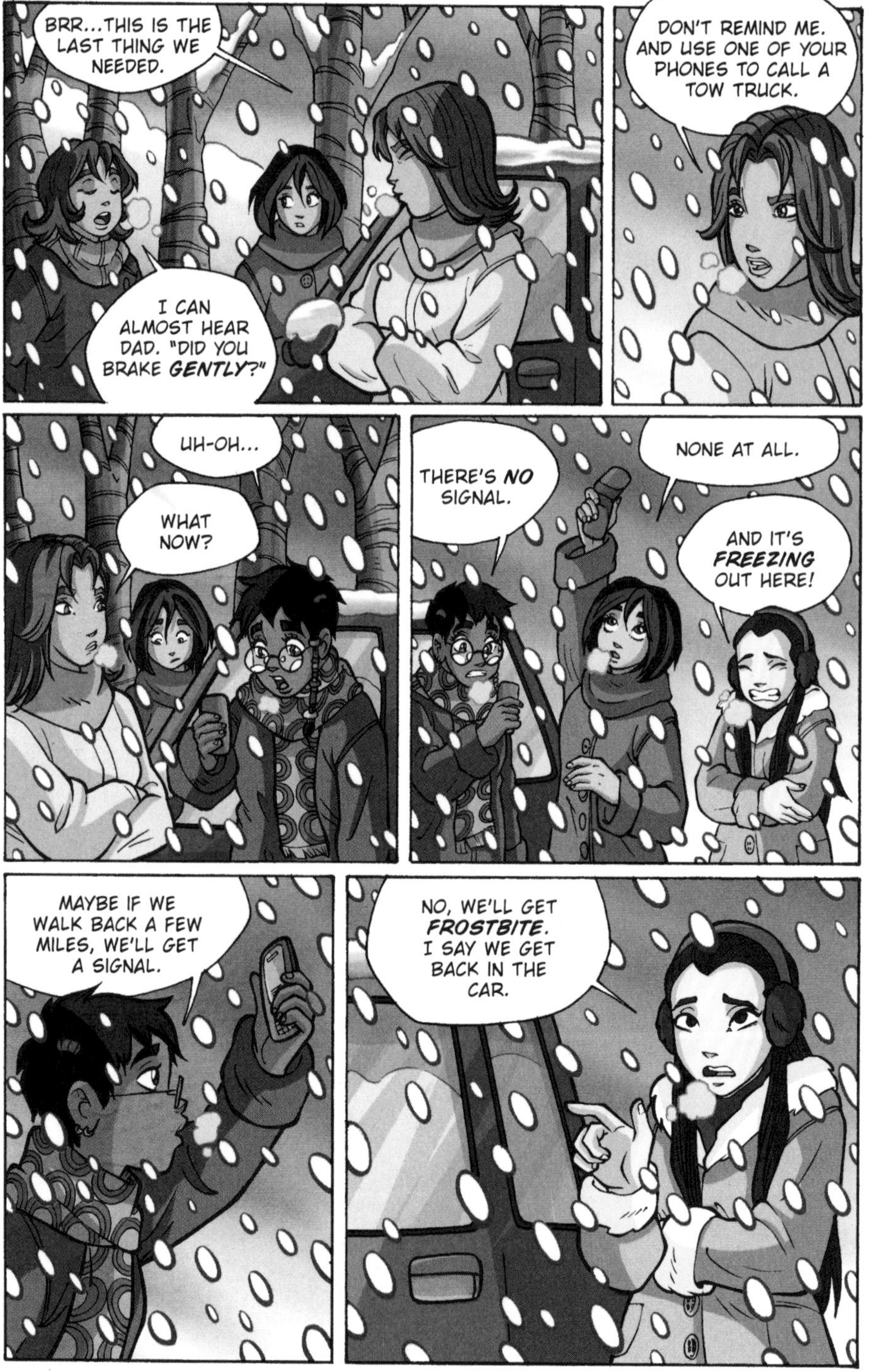
BRR...THIS IS THE LAST THING WE NEEDED.
I CAN ALMOST HEAR DAD. "DID YOU BRAKE GENTLY?"
DON'T REMIND ME. AND USE ONE OF YOUR PHONES TO CALL A TOW TRUCK.
UH-OH...
WHAT NOW?
THERE'S NO SIGNAL.
NONE AT ALL.
AND IT'S FREEZING OUT HERE!
MAYBE IF WE WALK BACK A FEW MILES, WE'LL GET A SIGNAL.
NO, WE'LL GET FROSTBITE. I SAY WE GET BACK IN THE CAR.

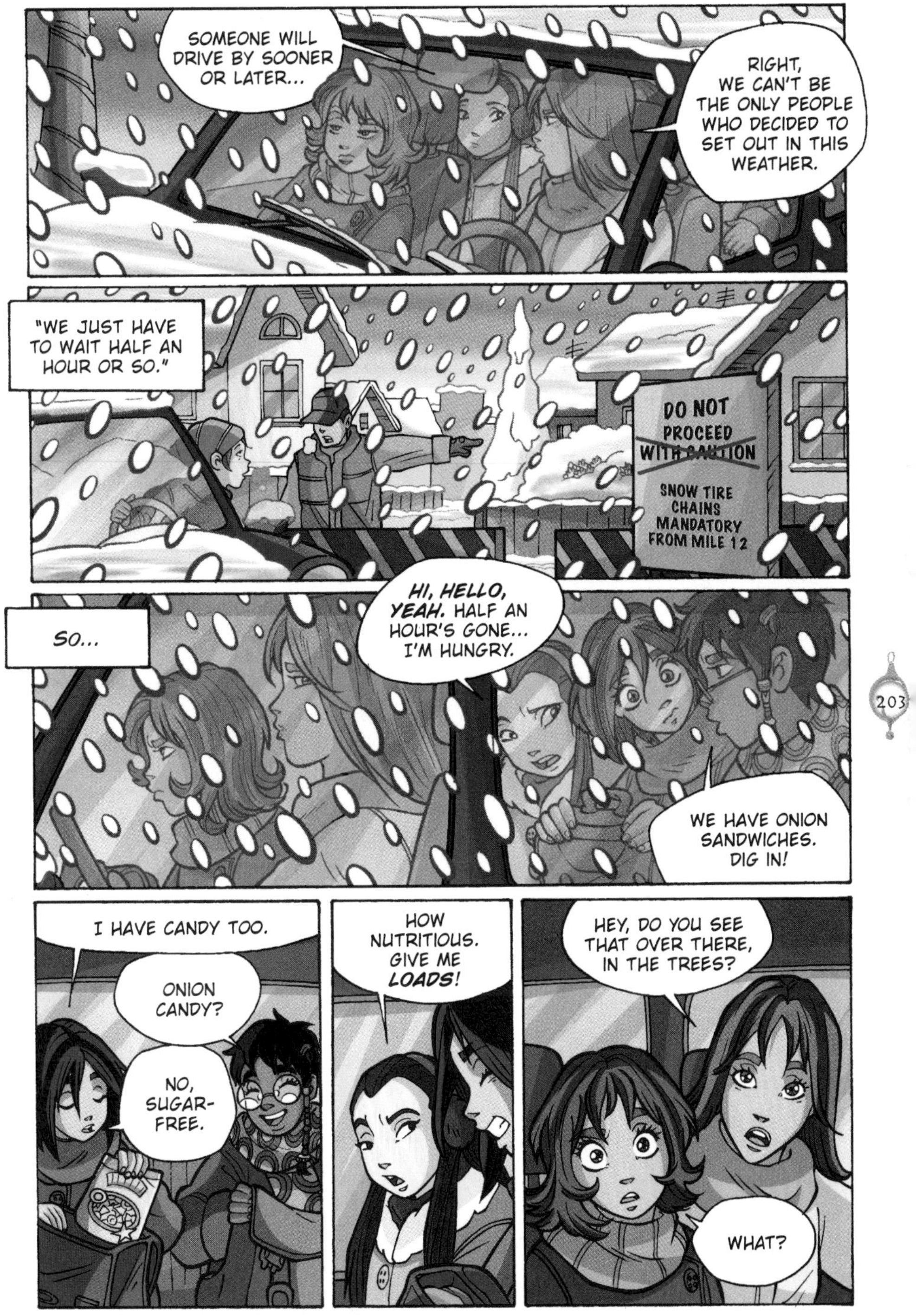
SOMEONE WILL DRIVE BY SOONER OR LATER...
RIGHT, WE CAN'T BE THE ONLY PEOPLE WHO DECIDED TO SET OUT IN THIS WEATHER.
"WE JUST HAVE TO WAIT HALF AN HOUR OR SO."
DO NOT PROCEED WITH CAUTION
SNOW TIRE CHAINS MANDATORY FROM MILE 12
SO...
HI, HELLO, YEAH. HALF AN HOUR'S GONE... I'M HUNGRY.
WE HAVE ONION SANDWICHES. DIG IN!
I HAVE CANDY TOO.
ONION CANDY?
NO, SUGAR-FREE.
HOW NUTRITIOUS. GIVE ME LOADS!
HEY, DO YOU SEE THAT OVER THERE, IN THE TREES?
WHAT?

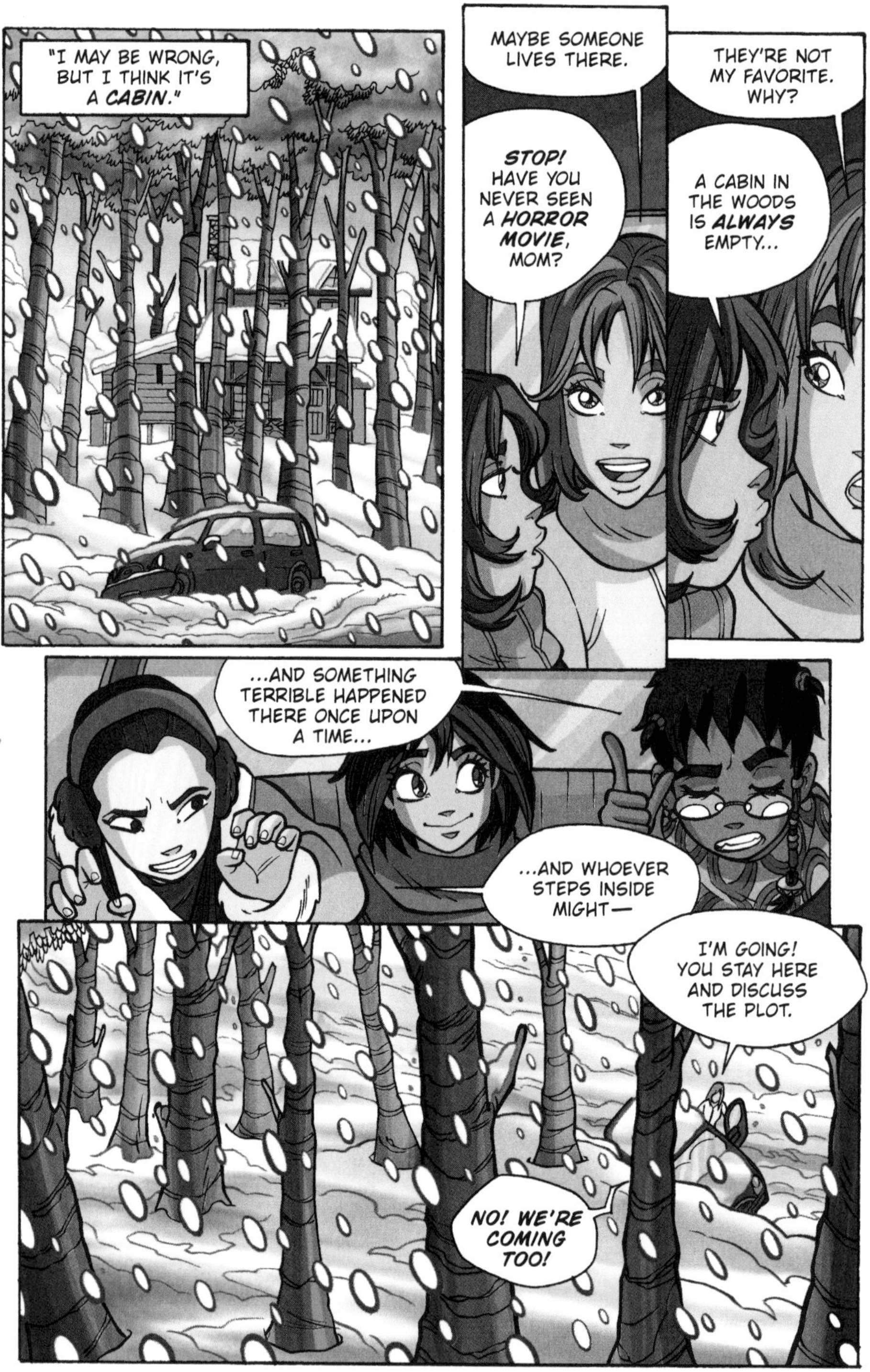
"I MAY BE WRONG, BUT I THINK IT'S A *CABIN*."
MAYBE SOMEONE LIVES THERE.
STOP! HAVE YOU NEVER SEEN A *HORROR MOVIE*, MOM?
THEY'RE NOT MY FAVORITE. WHY?
A CABIN IN THE WOODS IS *ALWAYS* EMPTY...
...AND SOMETHING TERRIBLE HAPPENED THERE ONCE UPON A TIME...
...AND WHOEVER STEPS INSIDE MIGHT—
I'M GOING! YOU STAY HERE AND DISCUSS THE PLOT.
NO! WE'RE COMING TOO!

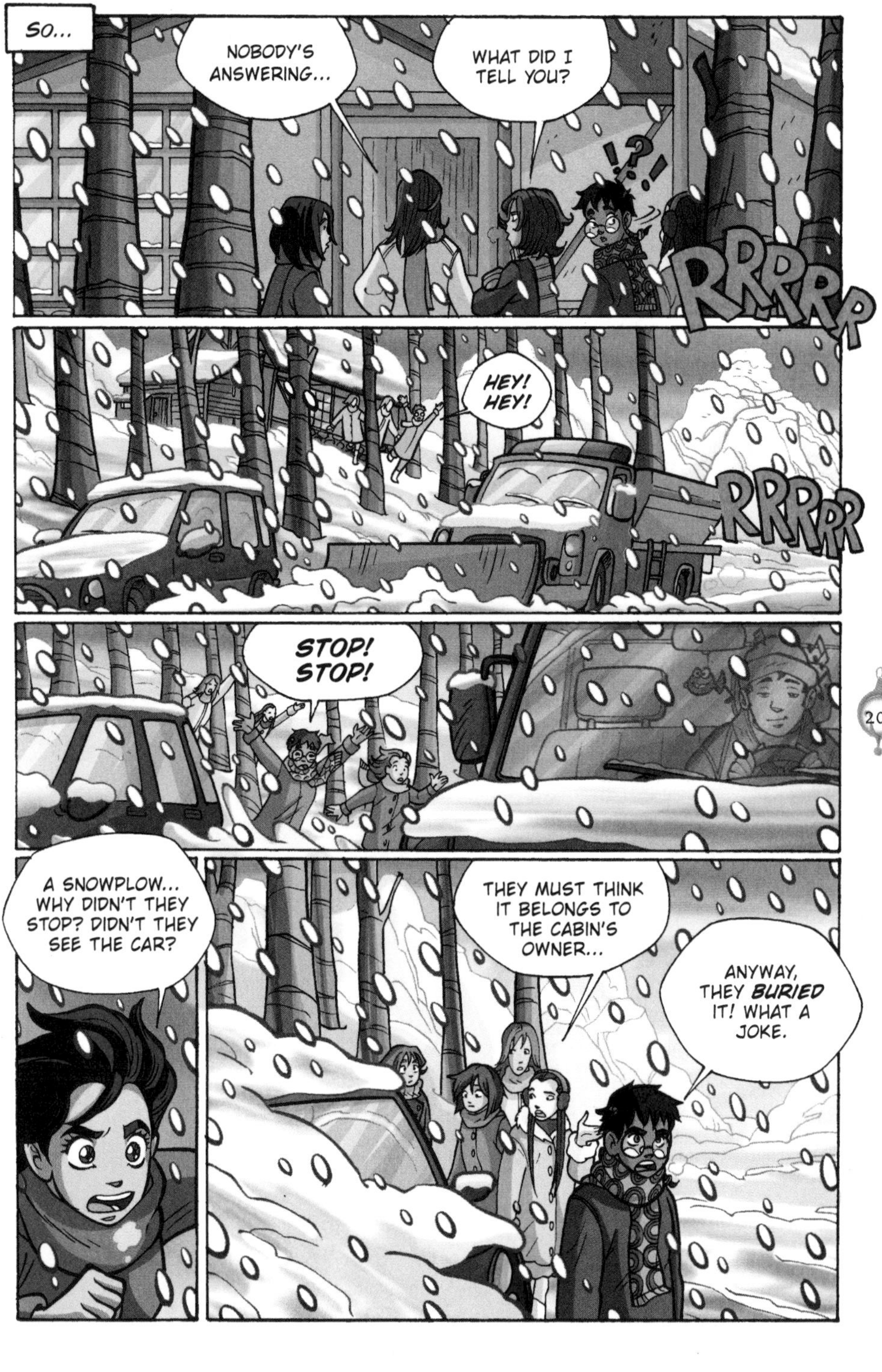
SO...
NOBODY'S ANSWERING...
WHAT DID I TELL YOU?
!?!
RRRRRR
HEY! HEY!
RRRRR
STOP! STOP!
A SNOWPLOW... WHY DIDN'T THEY STOP? DIDN'T THEY SEE THE CAR?
THEY MUST THINK IT BELONGS TO THE CABIN'S OWNER...
ANYWAY, THEY **BURIED** IT! WHAT A JOKE.

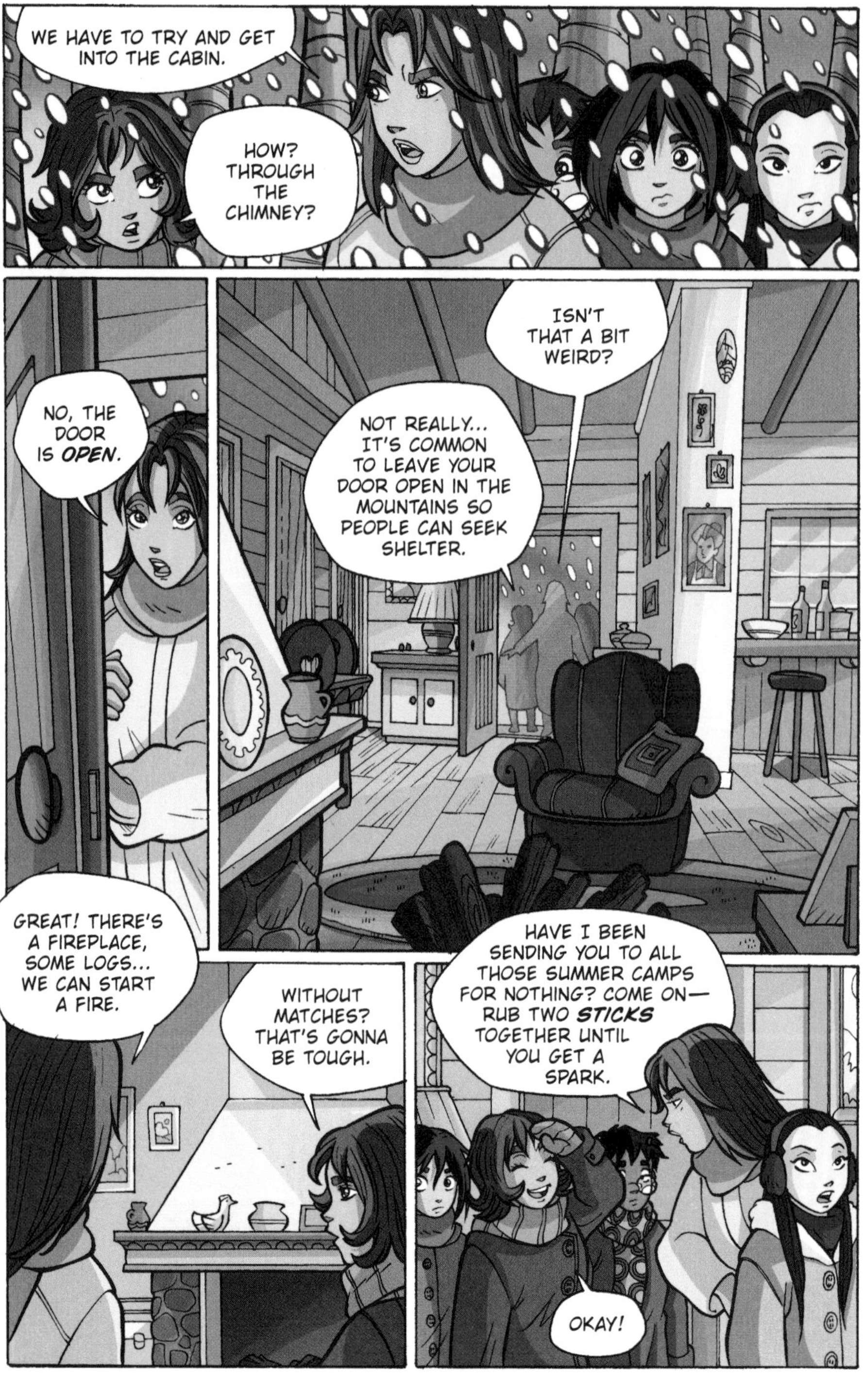
WE HAVE TO TRY AND GET INTO THE CABIN.
HOW? THROUGH THE CHIMNEY?
NO, THE DOOR IS OPEN.
ISN'T THAT A BIT WEIRD?
NOT REALLY... IT'S COMMON TO LEAVE YOUR DOOR OPEN IN THE MOUNTAINS SO PEOPLE CAN SEEK SHELTER.
GREAT! THERE'S A FIREPLACE, SOME LOGS... WE CAN START A FIRE.
WITHOUT MATCHES? THAT'S GONNA BE TOUGH.
HAVE I BEEN SENDING YOU TO ALL THOSE SUMMER CAMPS FOR NOTHING? COME ON— RUB TWO STICKS TOGETHER UNTIL YOU GET A SPARK.
OKAY!

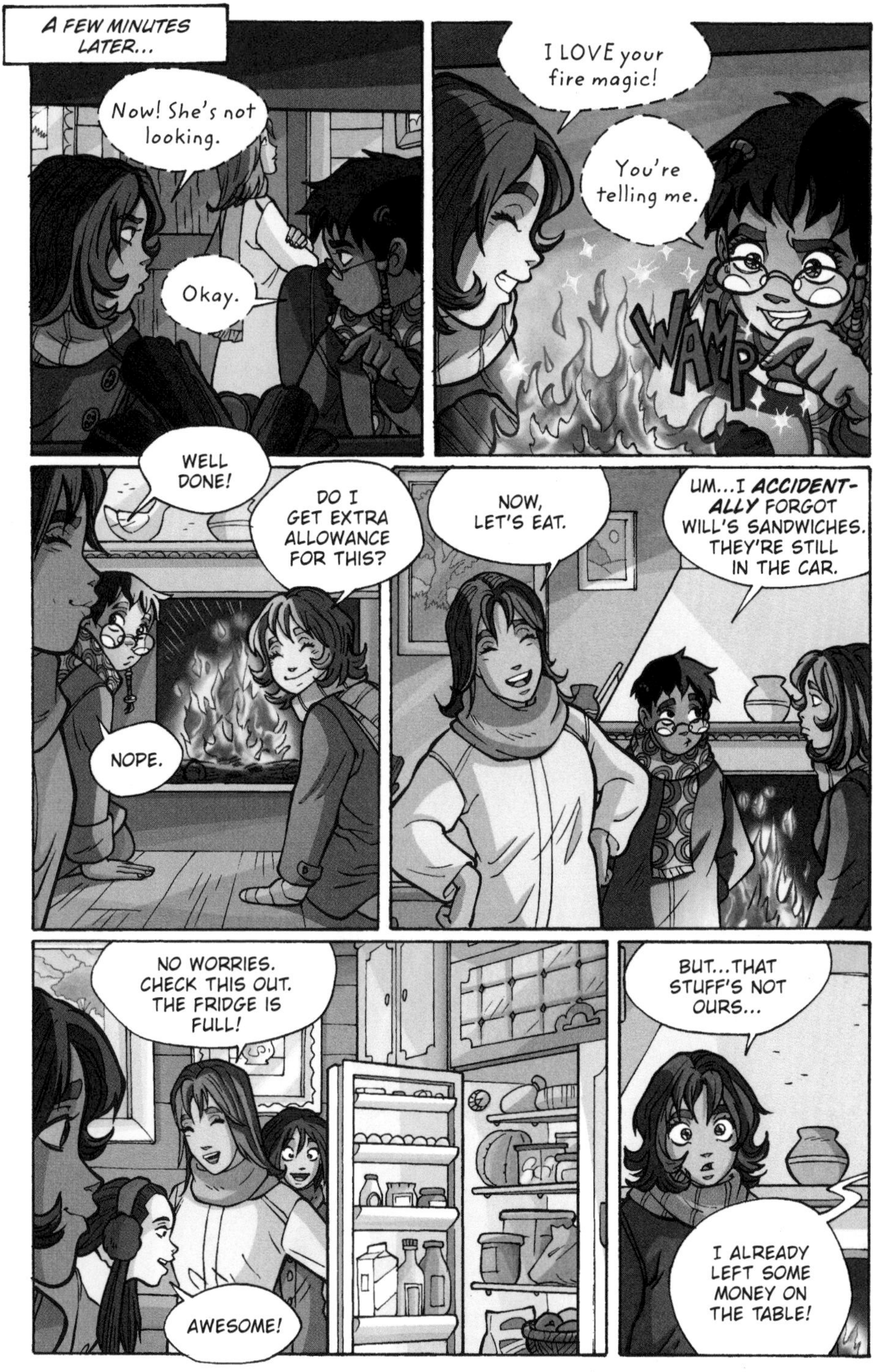
A FEW MINUTES LATER...
Now! She's not looking.
Okay.
I LOVE your fire magic!
You're telling me.
WAMP
WELL DONE!
DO I GET EXTRA ALLOWANCE FOR THIS?
NOPE.
NOW, LET'S EAT.
UM...I ACCIDENTALLY FORGOT WILL'S SANDWICHES. THEY'RE STILL IN THE CAR.
NO WORRIES. CHECK THIS OUT. THE FRIDGE IS FULL!
AWESOME!
BUT...THAT STUFF'S NOT OURS...
I ALREADY LEFT SOME MONEY ON THE TABLE!

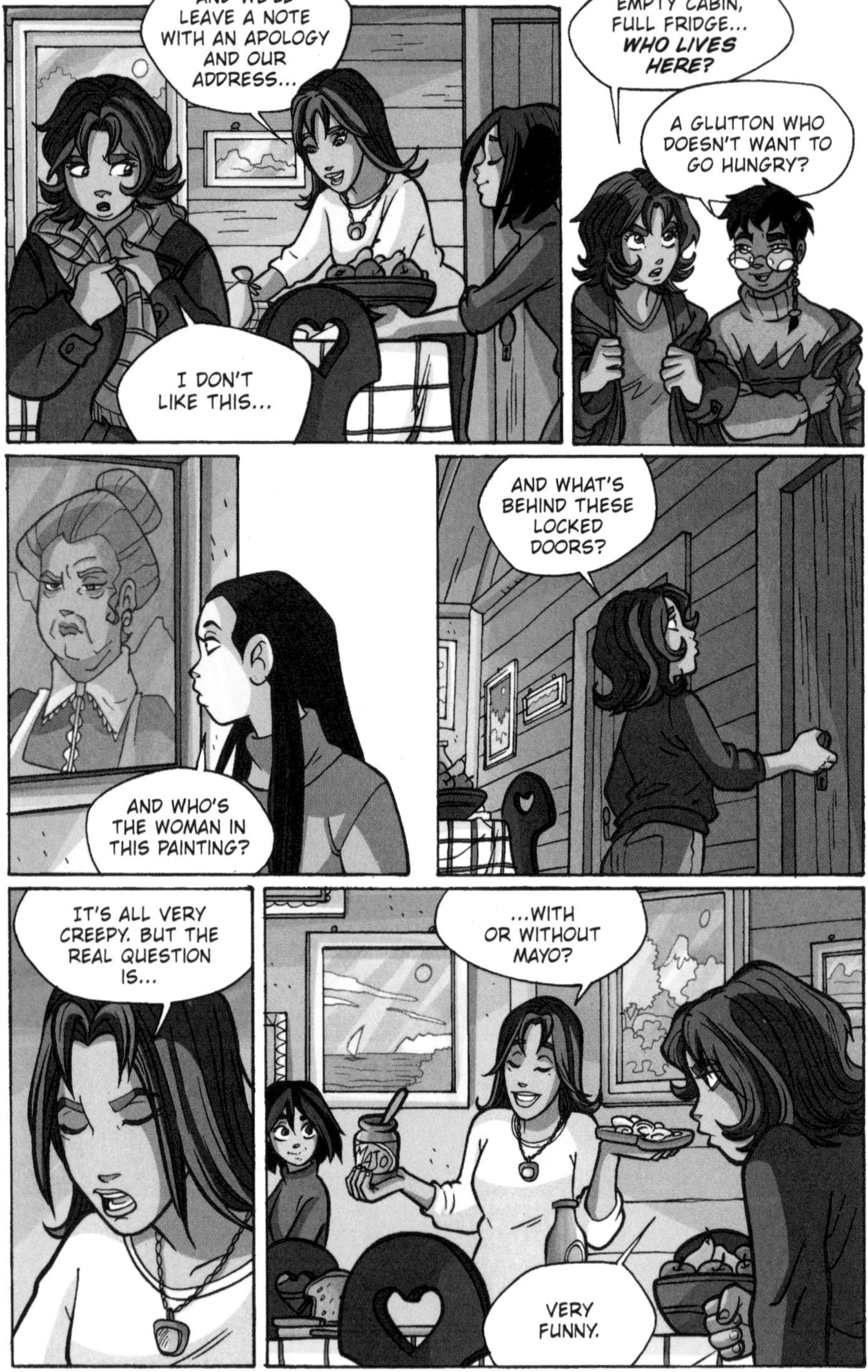
AND WE'LL LEAVE A NOTE WITH AN APOLOGY AND OUR ADDRESS...
I DON'T LIKE THIS...
EMPTY CABIN, FULL FRIDGE... ***WHO LIVES HERE?***
A GLUTTON WHO DOESN'T WANT TO GO HUNGRY?
AND WHO'S THE WOMAN IN THIS PAINTING?
AND WHAT'S BEHIND THESE LOCKED DOORS?
IT'S ALL VERY CREEPY. BUT THE REAL QUESTION IS...
...WITH OR WITHOUT MAYO?
MAJO
VERY FUNNY.

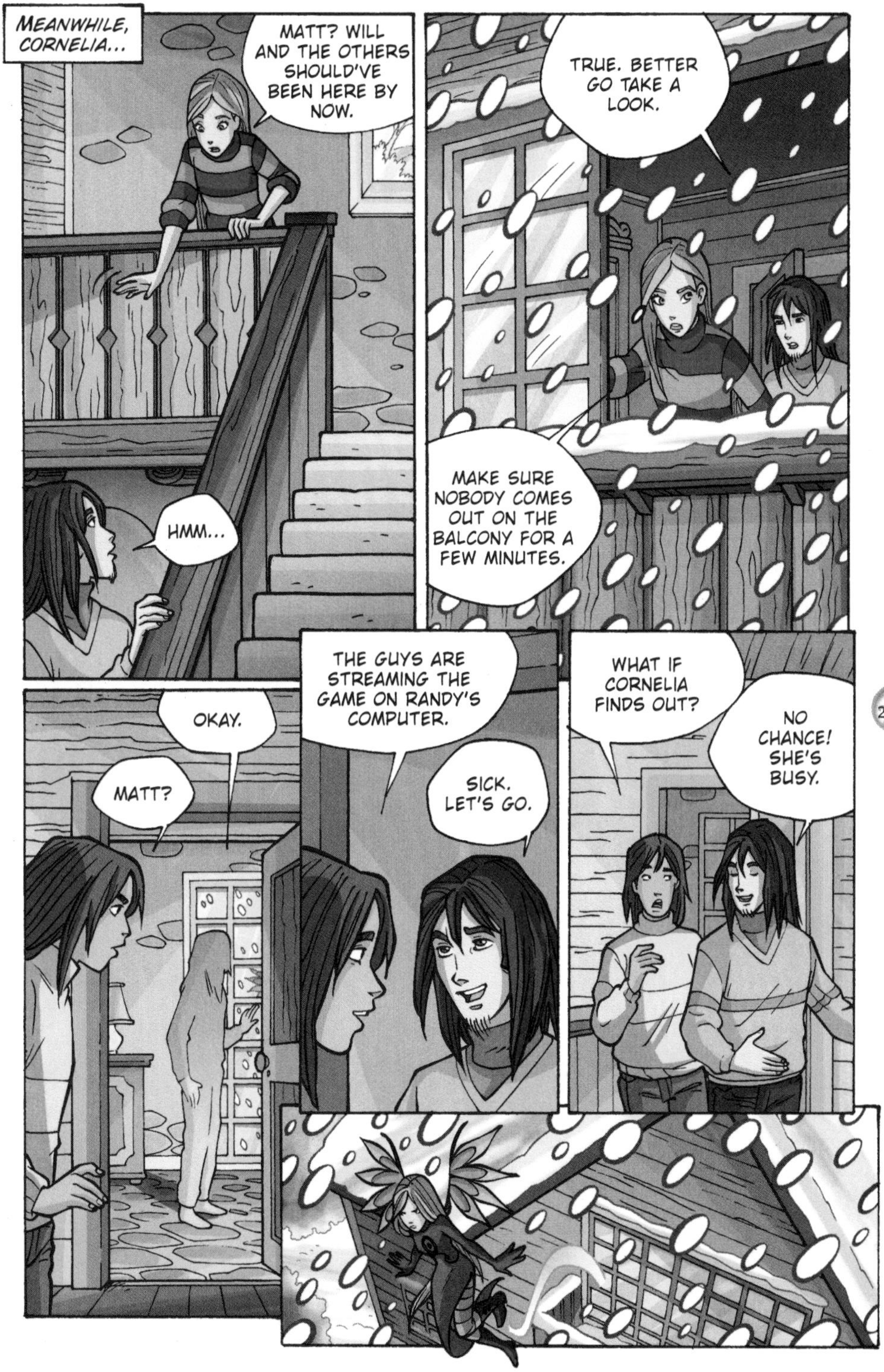
MEANWHILE, CORNELIA...
MATT? WILL AND THE OTHERS SHOULD'VE BEEN HERE BY NOW.
HMM...
TRUE. BETTER GO TAKE A LOOK.
MAKE SURE NOBODY COMES OUT ON THE BALCONY FOR A FEW MINUTES.
OKAY.
MATT?
THE GUYS ARE STREAMING THE GAME ON RANDY'S COMPUTER.
SICK. LET'S GO.
WHAT IF CORNELIA FINDS OUT?
NO CHANCE! SHE'S BUSY.

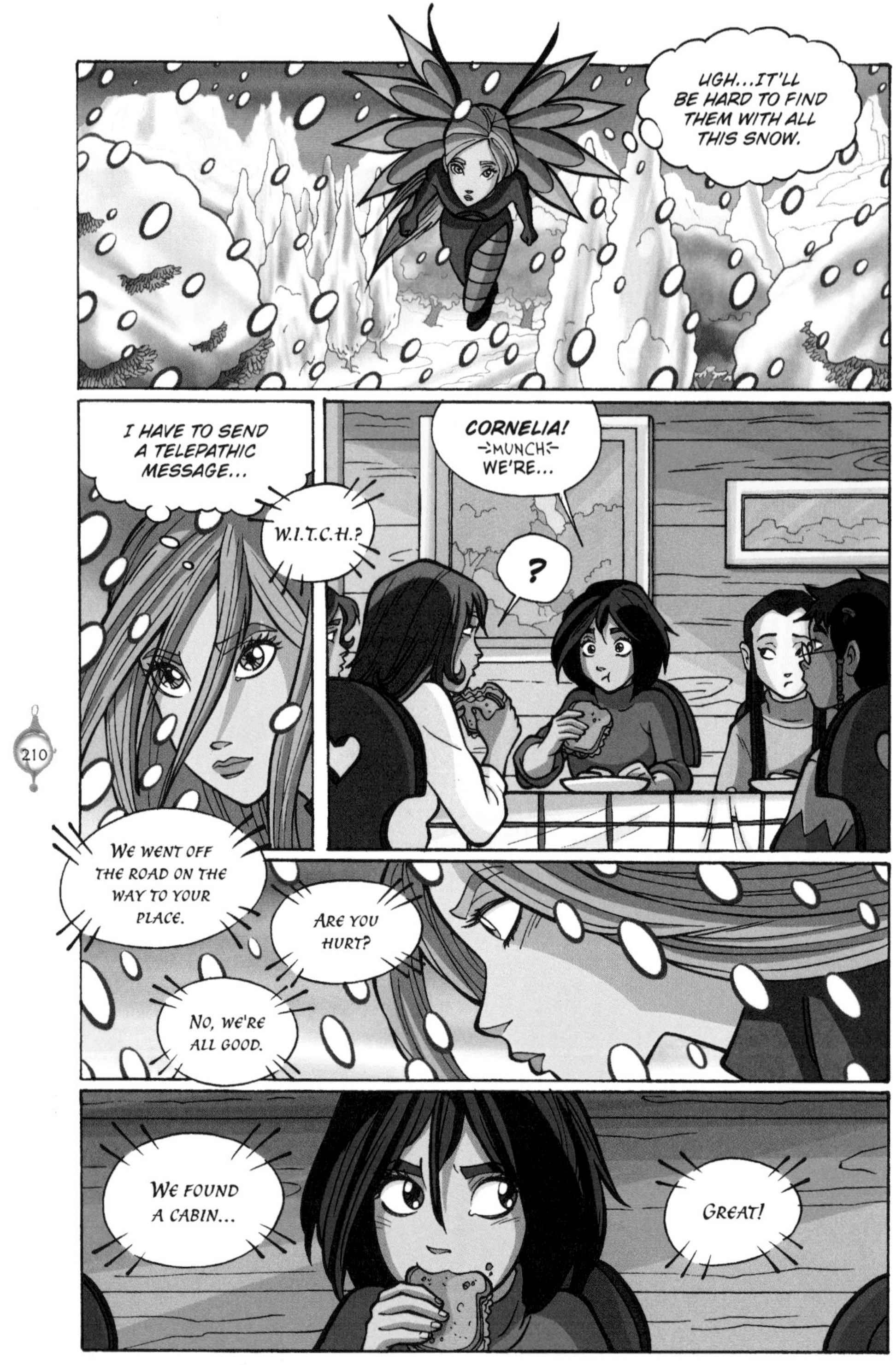
UGH...IT'LL BE HARD TO FIND THEM WITH ALL THIS SNOW.
I HAVE TO SEND A TELEPATHIC MESSAGE...
W.I.T.C.H.?
CORNELIA! MUNCH WE'RE...
?
WE WENT OFF THE ROAD ON THE WAY TO YOUR PLACE.
ARE YOU HURT?
NO, WE'RE ALL GOOD.
WE FOUND A CABIN...
GREAT!

210

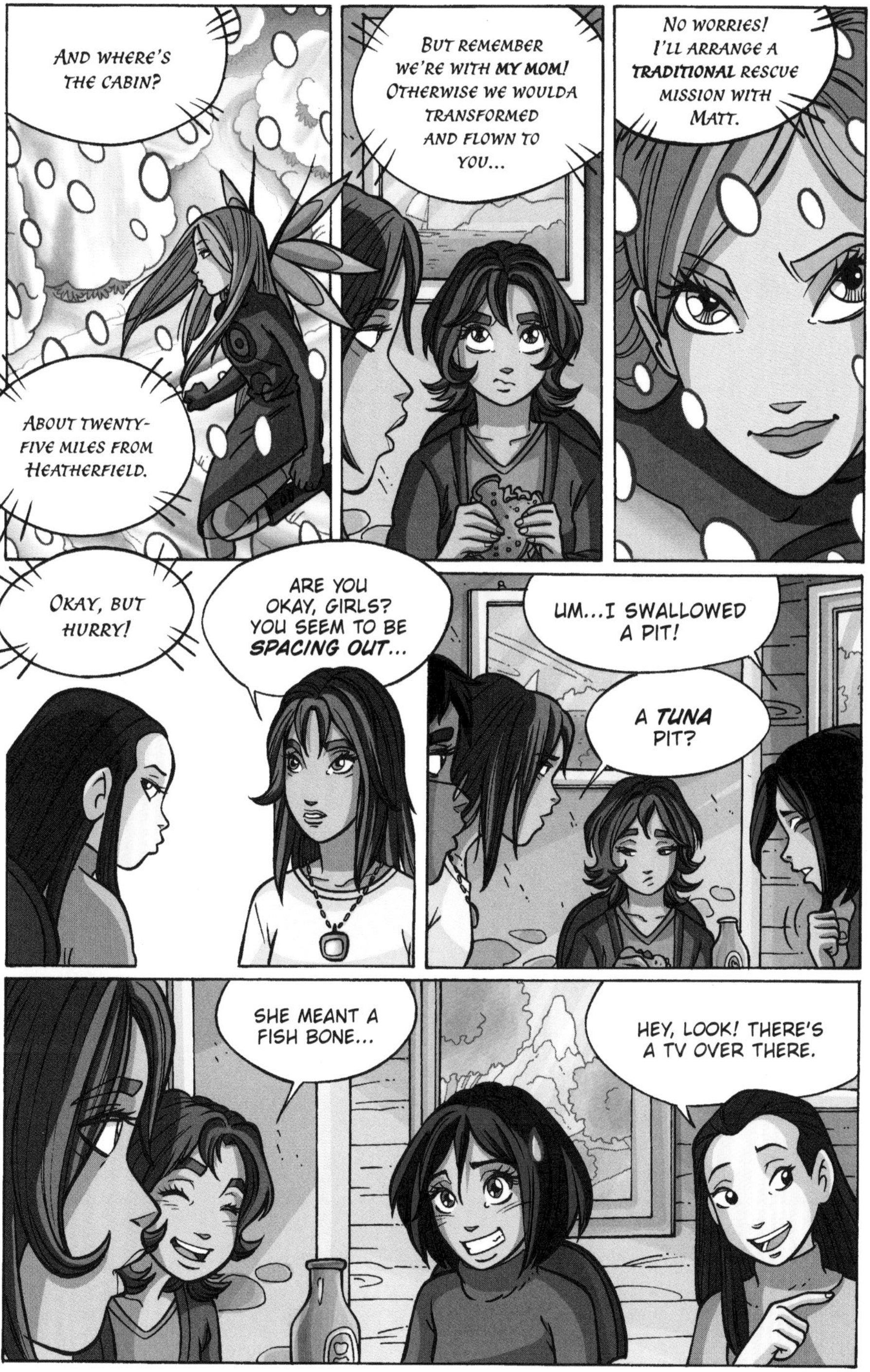
And where's the cabin?
About twenty-five miles from Heatherfield.
But remember we're with **my mom!** Otherwise we woulda transformed and flown to you...
No worries! I'll arrange a **traditional** rescue mission with Matt.
Okay, but hurry!
Are you okay, girls? You seem to be ***spacing out***...
Um...I swallowed a pit!
A ***tuna*** pit?
She meant a fish bone...
Hey, look! There's a TV over there.

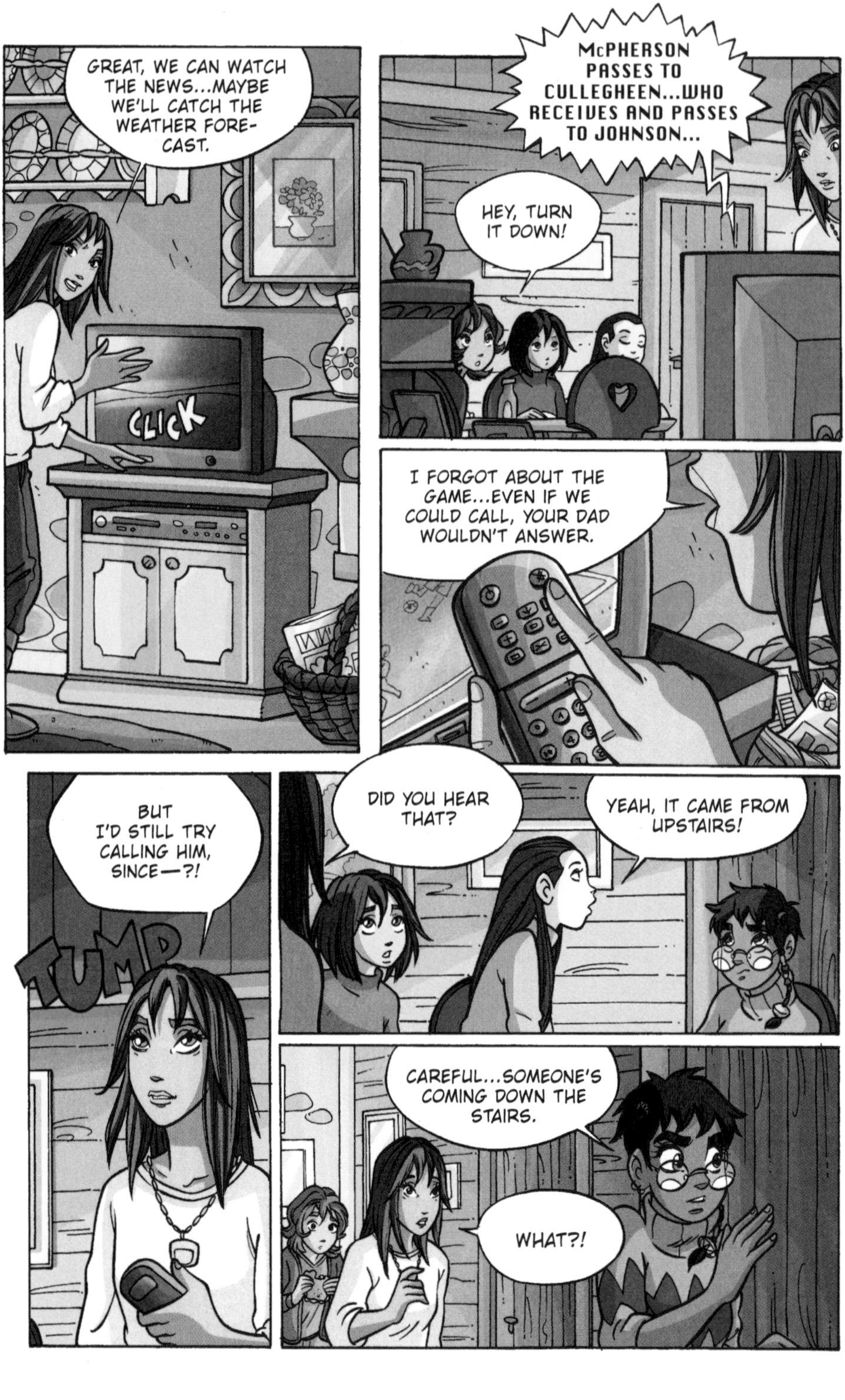
GREAT, WE CAN WATCH THE NEWS...MAYBE WE'LL CATCH THE WEATHER FORE-CAST.
CLICK
McPHERSON PASSES TO CULLEGHEEN...WHO RECEIVES AND PASSES TO JOHNSON...
HEY, TURN IT DOWN!
I FORGOT ABOUT THE GAME...EVEN IF WE COULD CALL, YOUR DAD WOULDN'T ANSWER.
BUT I'D STILL TRY CALLING HIM, SINCE—?!
TUMP
DID YOU HEAR THAT?
YEAH, IT CAME FROM UPSTAIRS!
CAREFUL...SOMEONE'S COMING DOWN THE STAIRS.
WHAT?!

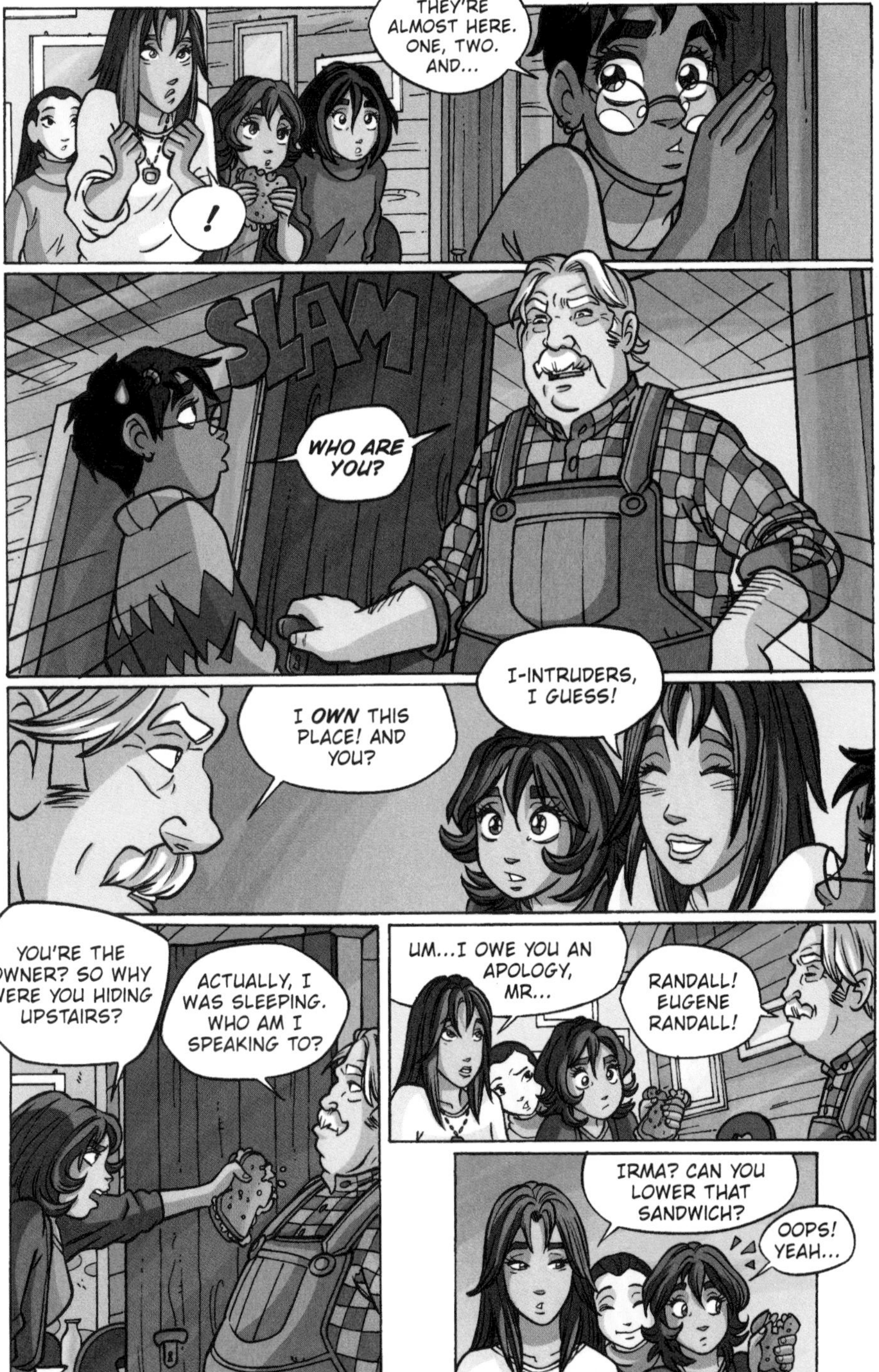
THEY'RE ALMOST HERE. ONE, TWO. AND...
!
SLAM
WHO ARE YOU?
I OWN THIS PLACE! AND YOU?
I-INTRUDERS, I GUESS!
YOU'RE THE OWNER? SO WHY WERE YOU HIDING UPSTAIRS?
ACTUALLY, I WAS SLEEPING. WHO AM I SPEAKING TO?
UM...I OWE YOU AN APOLOGY, MR...
RANDALL! EUGENE RANDALL!
IRMA? CAN YOU LOWER THAT SANDWICH?
OOPS! YEAH...

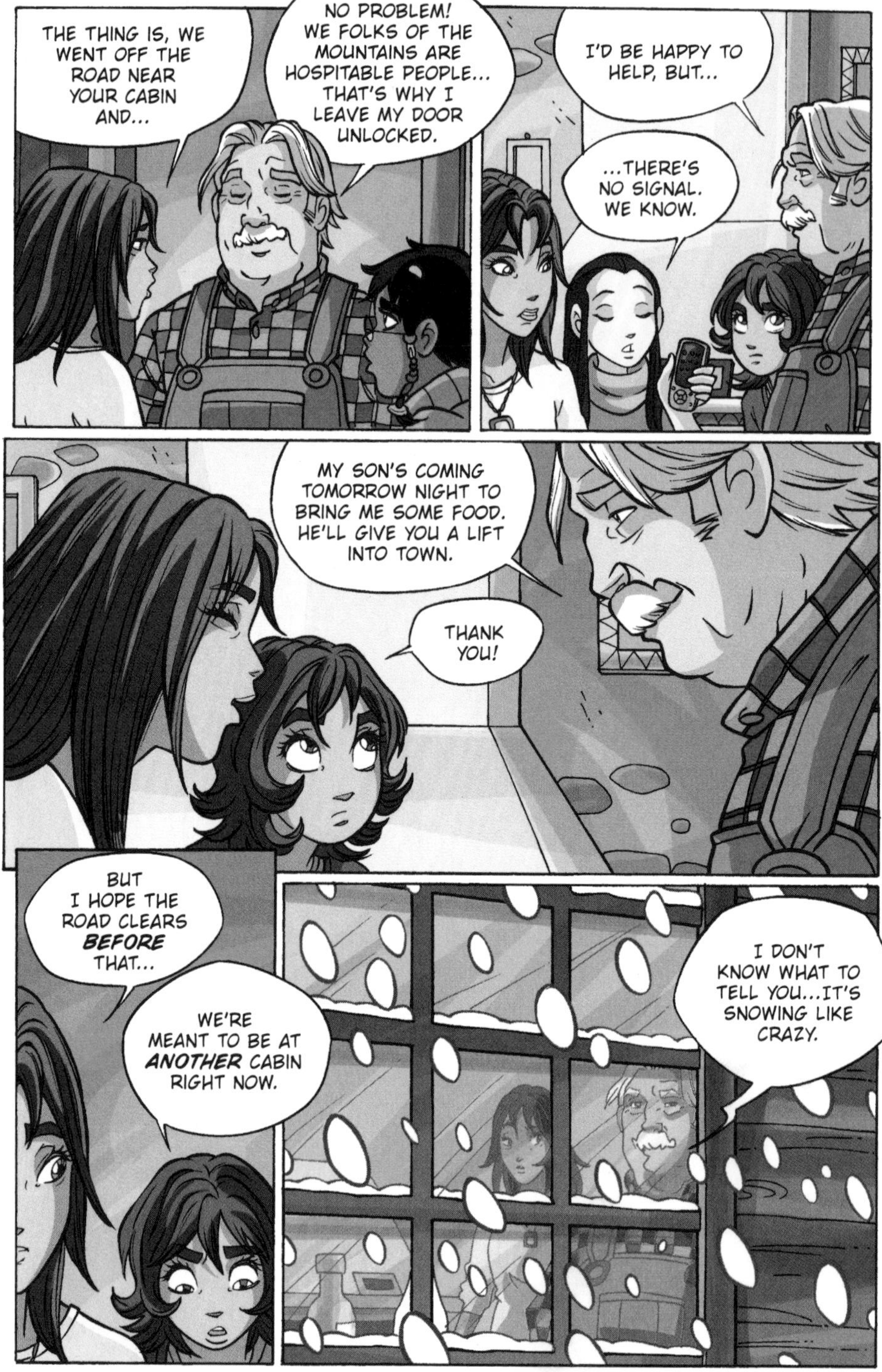
THE THING IS, WE WENT OFF THE ROAD NEAR YOUR CABIN AND...
NO PROBLEM! WE FOLKS OF THE MOUNTAINS ARE HOSPITABLE PEOPLE... THAT'S WHY I LEAVE MY DOOR UNLOCKED.
I'D BE HAPPY TO HELP, BUT...
...THERE'S NO SIGNAL. WE KNOW.
MY SON'S COMING TOMORROW NIGHT TO BRING ME SOME FOOD. HE'LL GIVE YOU A LIFT INTO TOWN.
THANK YOU!
BUT I HOPE THE ROAD CLEARS ***BEFORE*** THAT...
WE'RE MEANT TO BE AT ***ANOTHER*** CABIN RIGHT NOW.
I DON'T KNOW WHAT TO TELL YOU...IT'S SNOWING LIKE CRAZY.

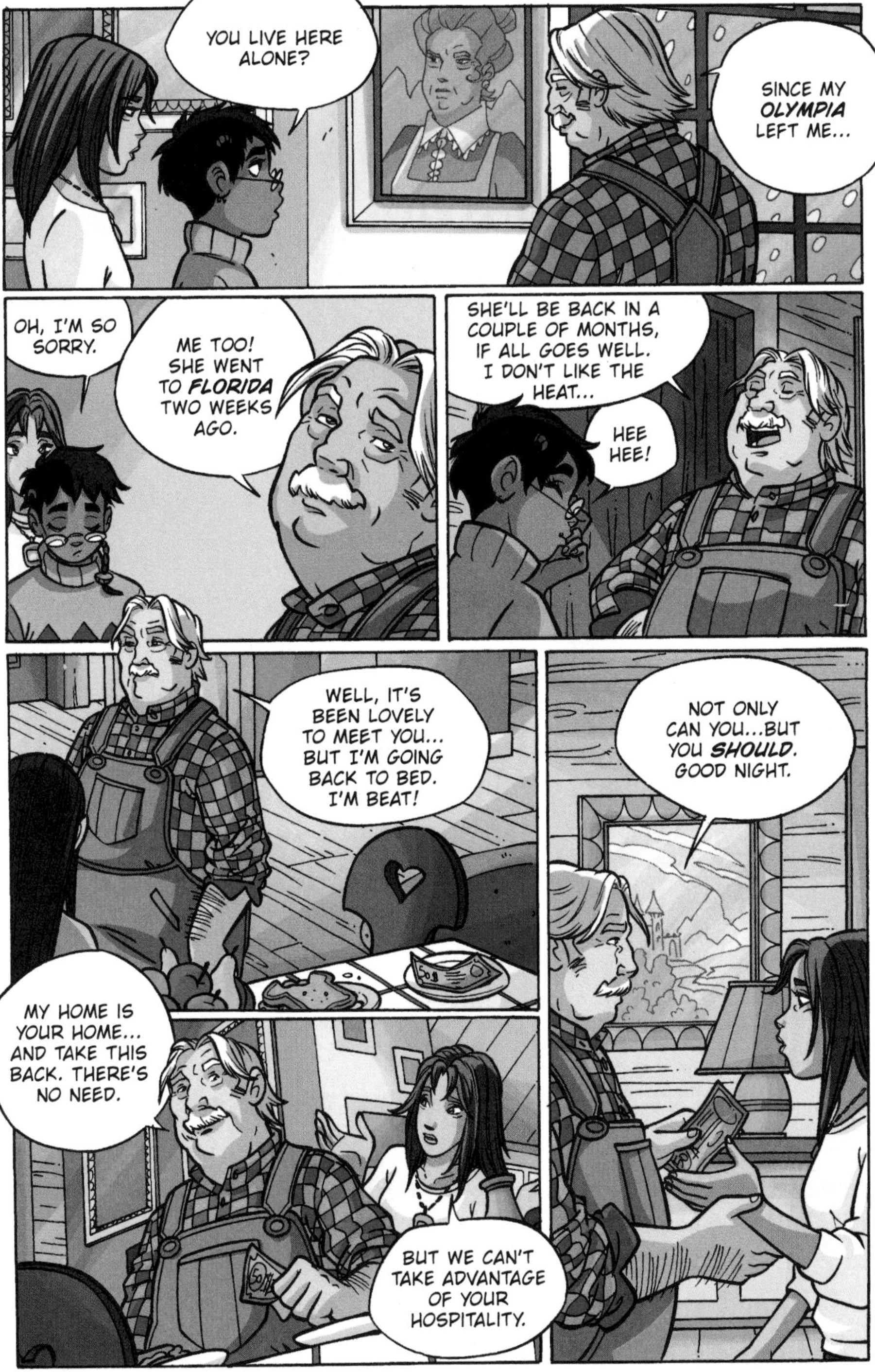
YOU LIVE HERE ALONE?
SINCE MY *OLYMPIA* LEFT ME...
OH, I'M SO SORRY.
ME TOO! SHE WENT TO *FLORIDA* TWO WEEKS AGO.
SHE'LL BE BACK IN A COUPLE OF MONTHS, IF ALL GOES WELL. I DON'T LIKE THE HEAT...
HEE HEE!
WELL, IT'S BEEN LOVELY TO MEET YOU... BUT I'M GOING BACK TO BED. I'M BEAT!
MY HOME IS YOUR HOME... AND TAKE THIS BACK. THERE'S NO NEED.
BUT WE CAN'T TAKE ADVANTAGE OF YOUR HOSPITALITY.
NOT ONLY CAN YOU...BUT YOU *SHOULD*. GOOD NIGHT.

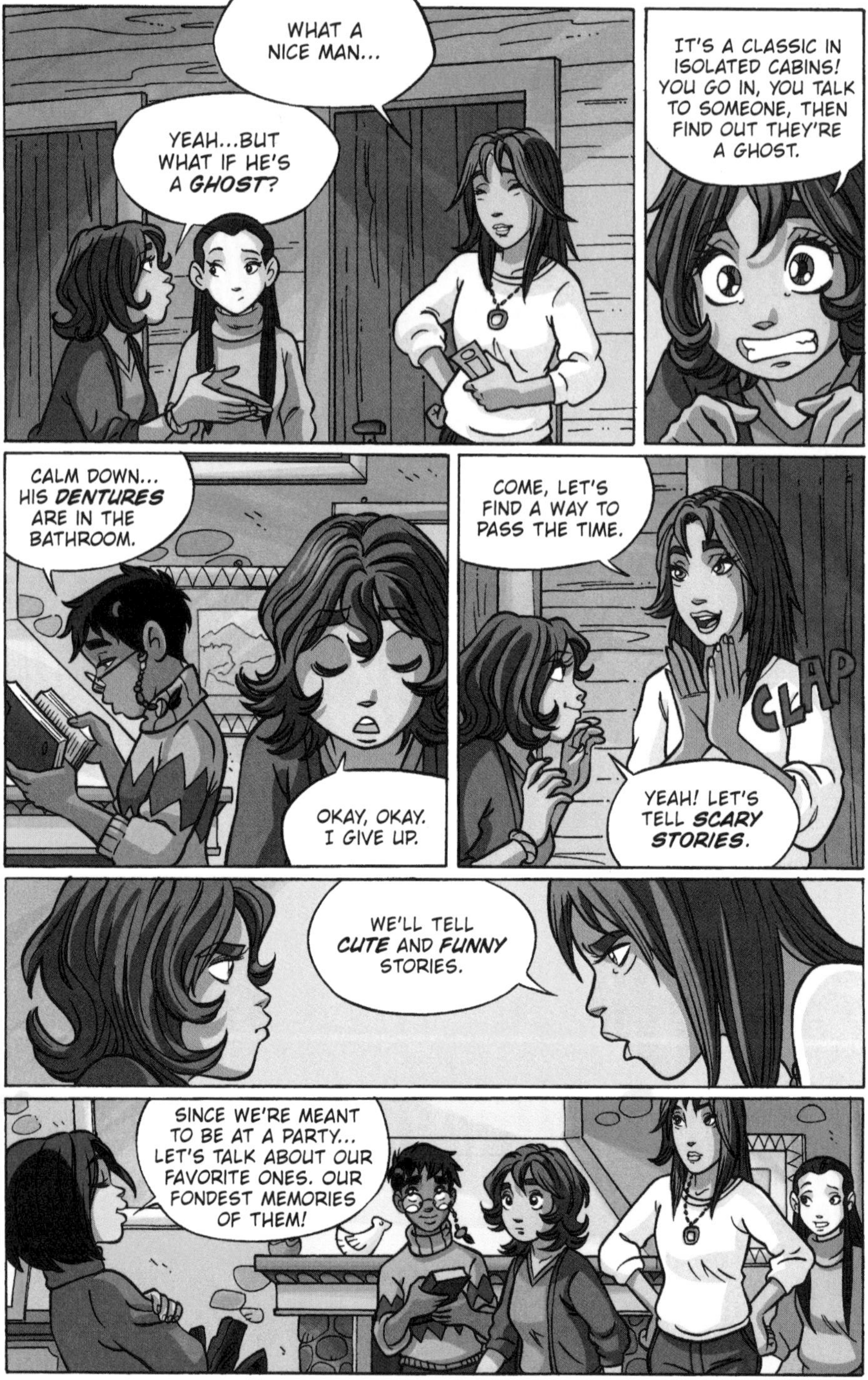

WHAT A NICE MAN...
YEAH...BUT WHAT IF HE'S A GHOST?
IT'S A CLASSIC IN ISOLATED CABINS! YOU GO IN, YOU TALK TO SOMEONE, THEN FIND OUT THEY'RE A GHOST.
CALM DOWN... HIS DENTURES ARE IN THE BATHROOM.
OKAY, OKAY. I GIVE UP.
COME, LET'S FIND A WAY TO PASS THE TIME.
CLAP
YEAH! LET'S TELL SCARY STORIES.
WE'LL TELL CUTE AND FUNNY STORIES.
SINCE WE'RE MEANT TO BE AT A PARTY... LET'S TALK ABOUT OUR FAVORITE ONES. OUR FONDEST MEMORIES OF THEM!

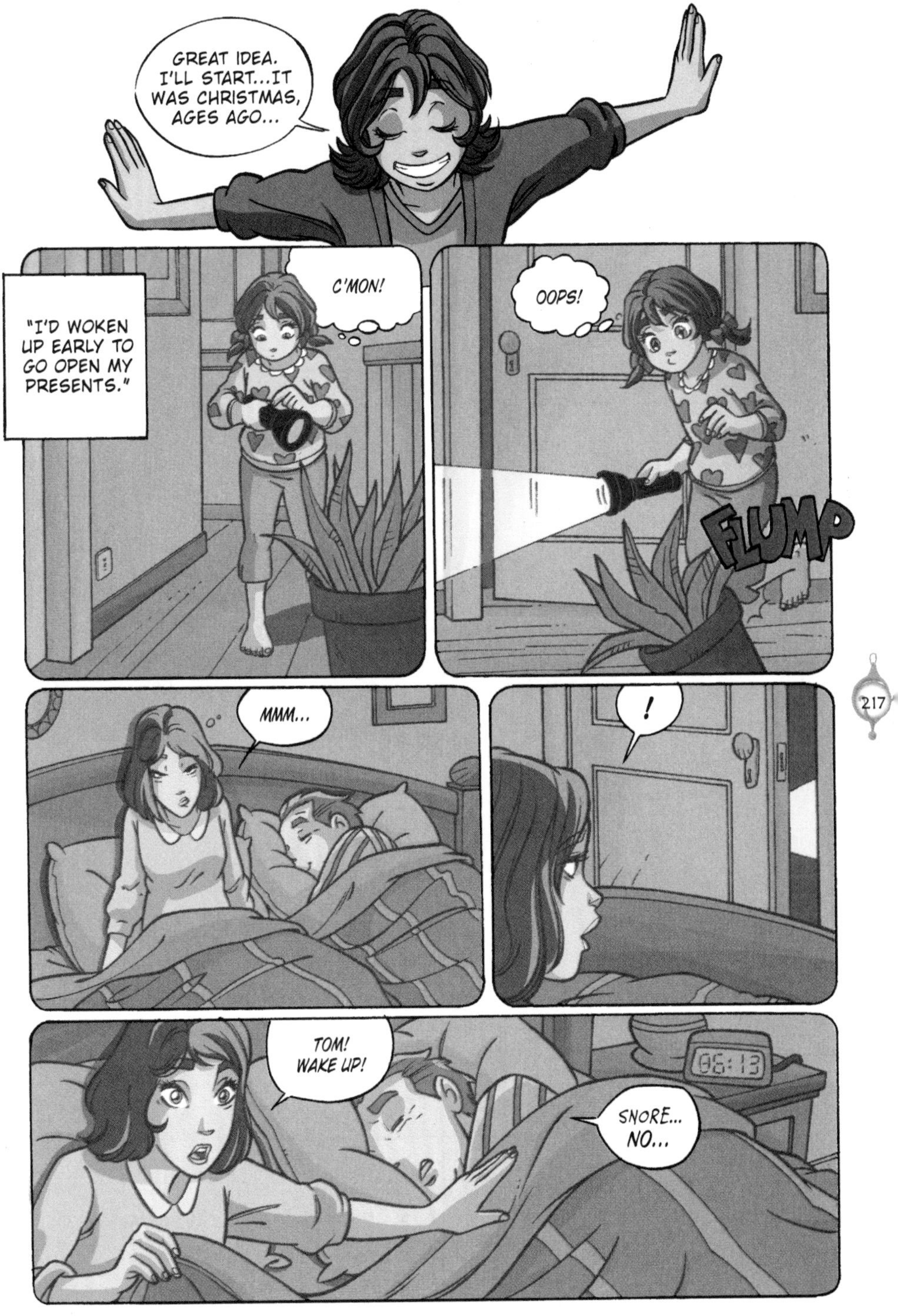
GREAT IDEA. I'LL START...IT WAS CHRISTMAS, AGES AGO...
"I'D WOKEN UP EARLY TO GO OPEN MY PRESENTS."
C'MON!
OOPS!
FLUMP
MMM...
!
TOM! WAKE UP!
06:13
SNORE... NO...

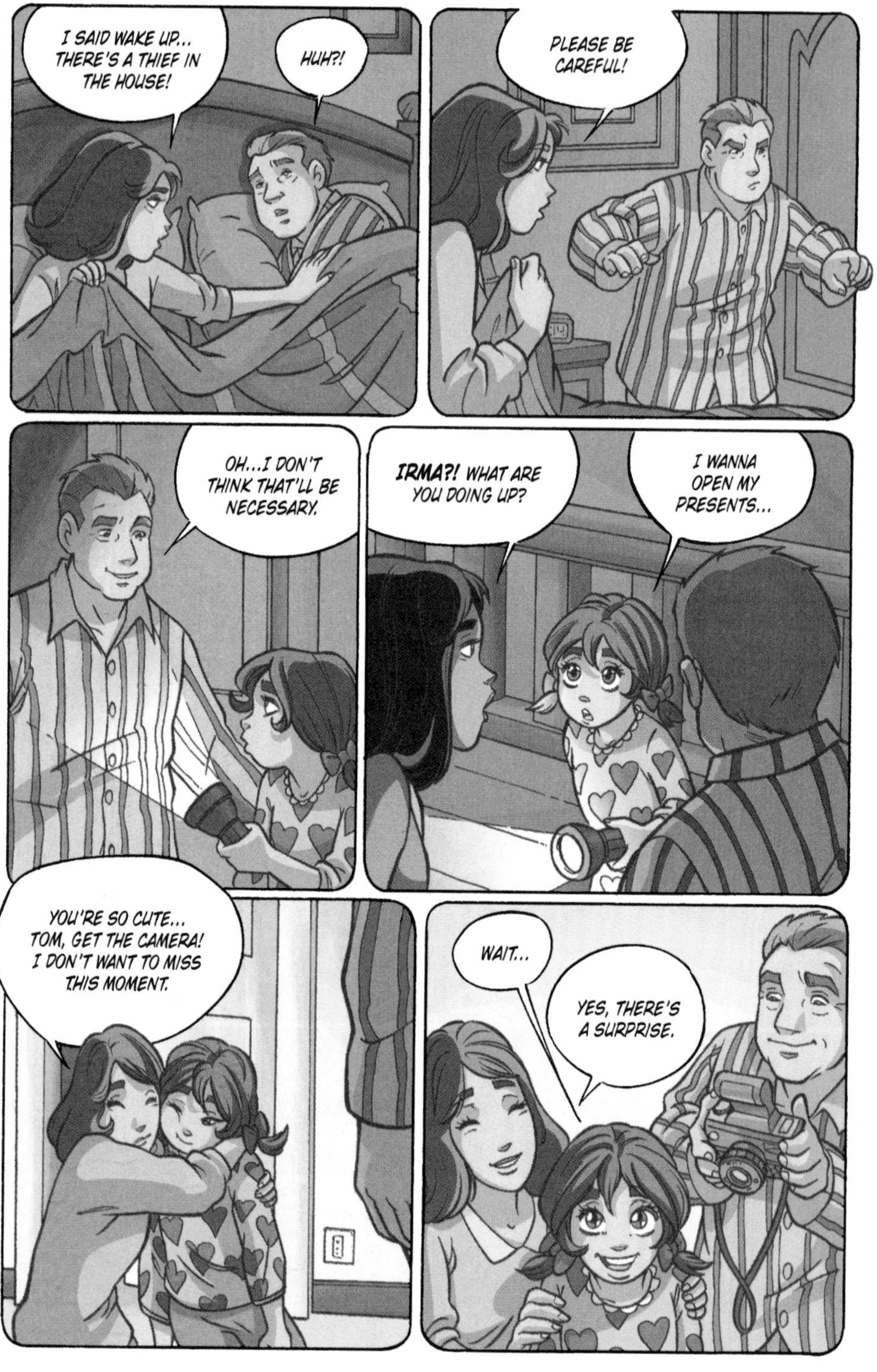
I SAID WAKE UP... THERE'S A THIEF IN THE HOUSE!
HUH?!
PLEASE BE CAREFUL!
OH...I DON'T THINK THAT'LL BE NECESSARY.
IRMA?! WHAT ARE YOU DOING UP?
I WANNA OPEN MY PRESENTS...
YOU'RE SO CUTE... TOM, GET THE CAMERA! I DON'T WANT TO MISS THIS MOMENT.
WAIT...
YES, THERE'S A SURPRISE.

218

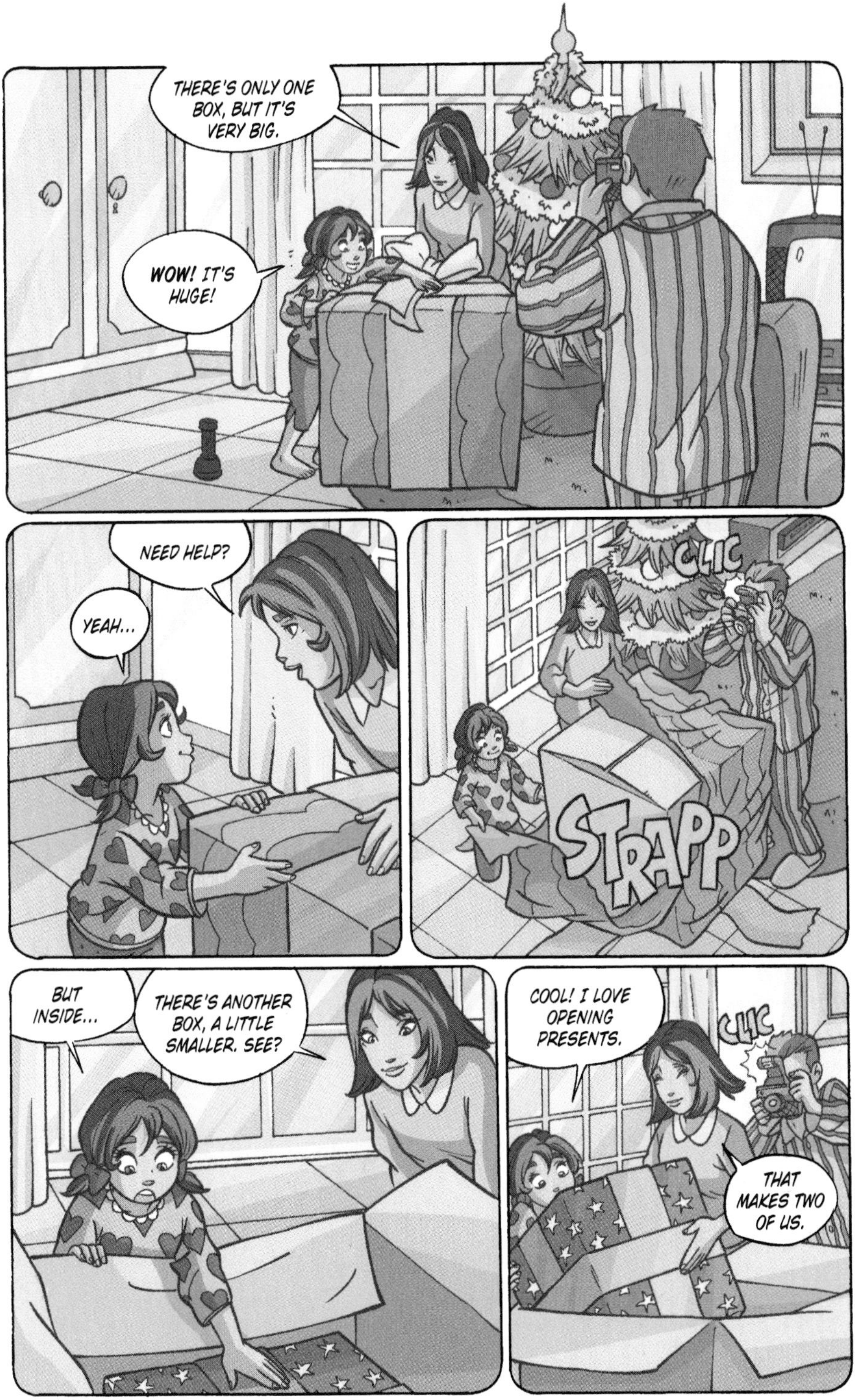
THERE'S ONLY ONE BOX, BUT IT'S VERY BIG.
WOW! IT'S HUGE!
NEED HELP?
YEAH...
CLIC
STRAPP
BUT INSIDE...
THERE'S ANOTHER BOX, A LITTLE SMALLER. SEE?
COOL! I LOVE OPENING PRESENTS.
CLIC
THAT MAKES TWO OF US.

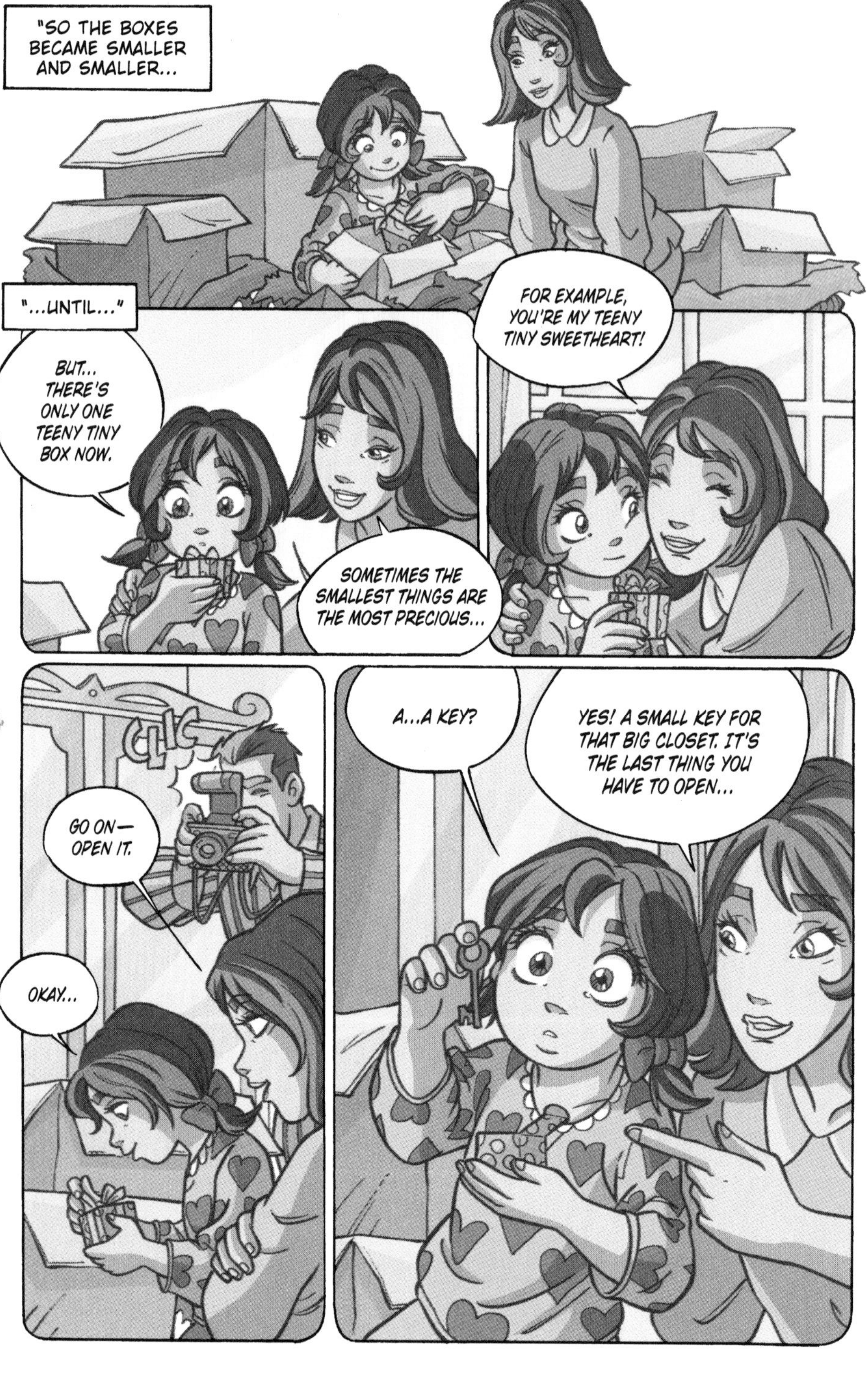
"SO THE BOXES BECAME SMALLER AND SMALLER...
"...UNTIL..."
BUT... THERE'S ONLY ONE TEENY TINY BOX NOW.
SOMETIMES THE SMALLEST THINGS ARE THE MOST PRECIOUS...
FOR EXAMPLE, YOU'RE MY TEENY TINY SWEETHEART!
CLIC
GO ON— OPEN IT.
OKAY...
A...A KEY?
YES! A SMALL KEY FOR THAT BIG CLOSET. IT'S THE LAST THING YOU HAVE TO OPEN...

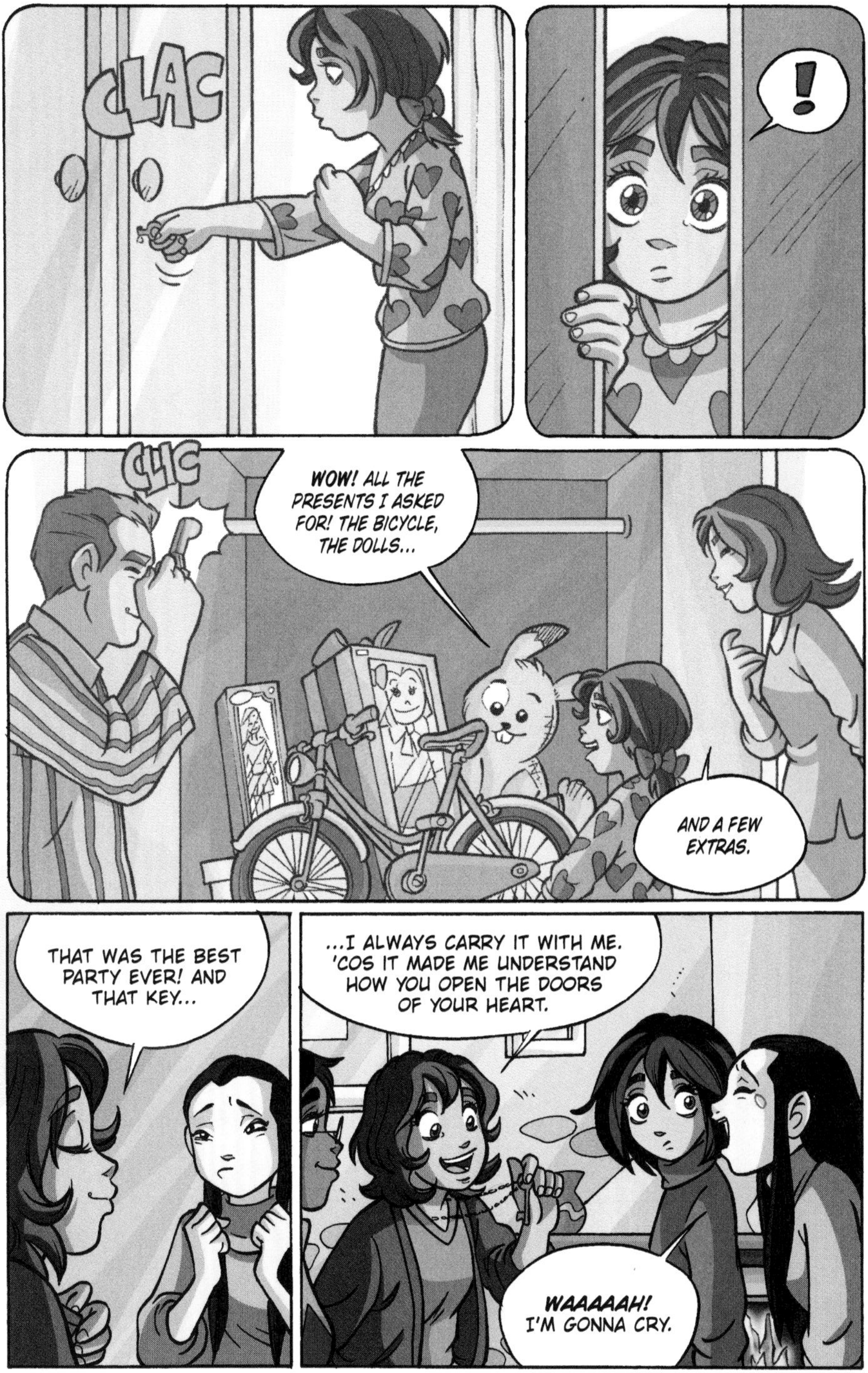
CLAC
!
CLIC
WOW! ALL THE PRESENTS I ASKED FOR! THE BICYCLE, THE DOLLS...
AND A FEW EXTRAS.
THAT WAS THE BEST PARTY EVER! AND THAT KEY...
...I ALWAYS CARRY IT WITH ME. 'COS IT MADE ME UNDERSTAND HOW YOU OPEN THE DOORS OF YOUR HEART.
WAAAAAH! I'M GONNA CRY.

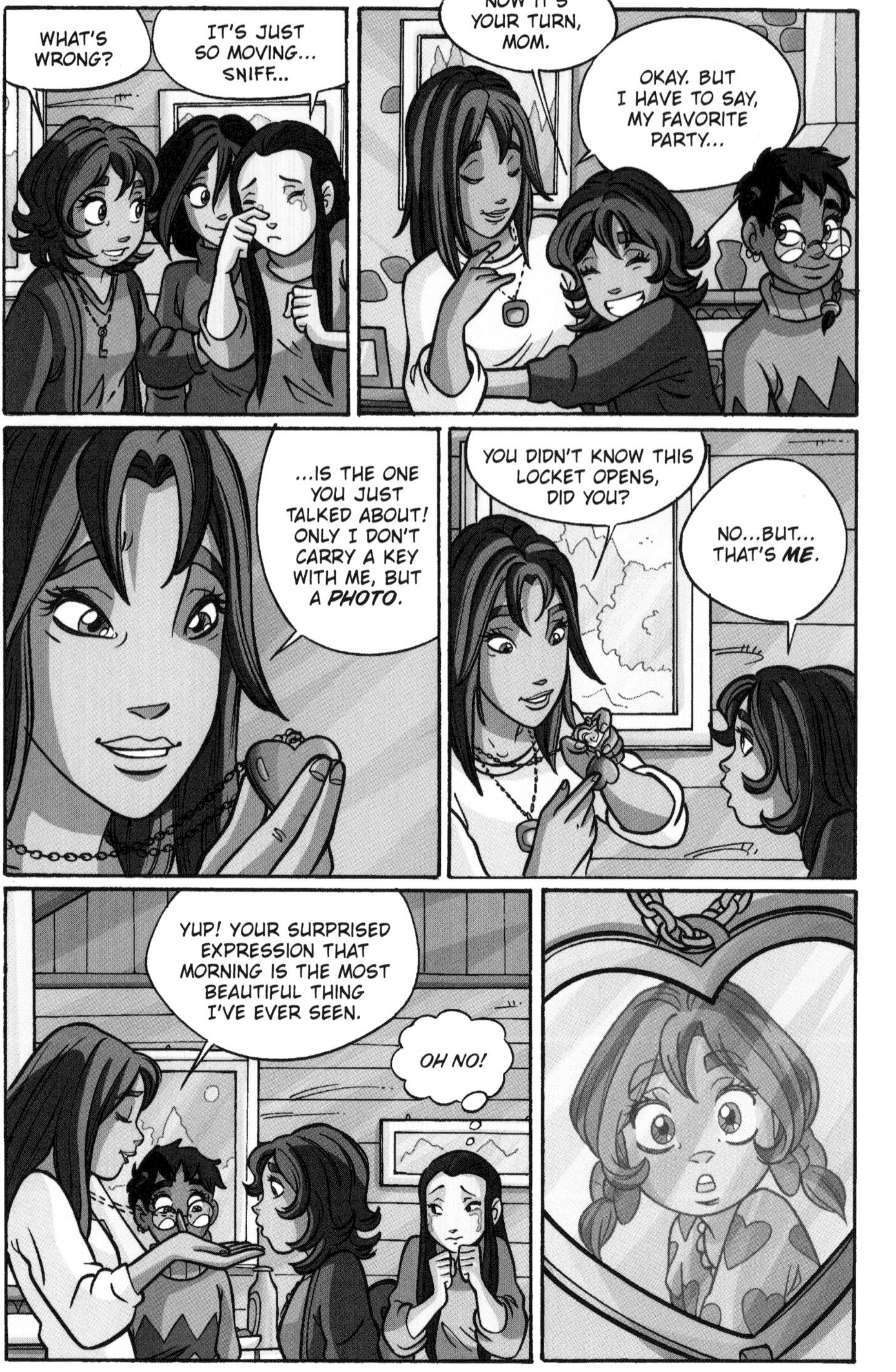
WHAT'S WRONG?
IT'S JUST SO MOVING... SNIFF...
NOW IT'S YOUR TURN, MOM.
OKAY. BUT I HAVE TO SAY, MY FAVORITE PARTY...
...IS THE ONE YOU JUST TALKED ABOUT! ONLY I DON'T CARRY A KEY WITH ME, BUT A *PHOTO*.
YOU DIDN'T KNOW THIS LOCKET OPENS, DID YOU?
NO...BUT... THAT'S *ME*.
YUP! YOUR SURPRISED EXPRESSION THAT MORNING IS THE MOST BEAUTIFUL THING I'VE EVER SEEN.
OH NO!

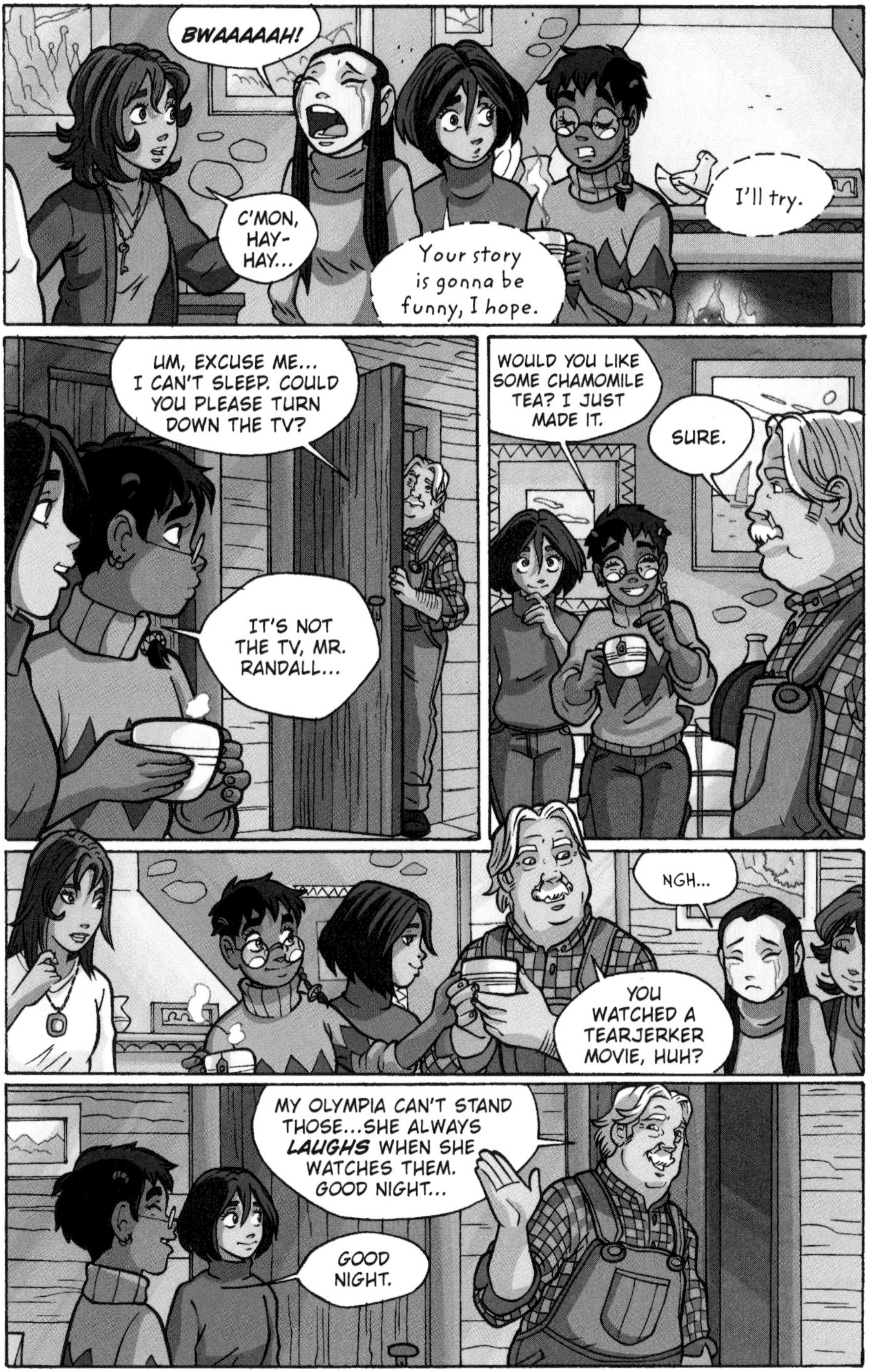
BWAAAAAH!
C'MON, HAY-HAY...
Your story is gonna be funny, I hope.
I'll try.
UM, EXCUSE ME... I CAN'T SLEEP. COULD YOU PLEASE TURN DOWN THE TV?
IT'S NOT THE TV, MR. RANDALL...
WOULD YOU LIKE SOME CHAMOMILE TEA? I JUST MADE IT.
SURE.
NGH...
YOU WATCHED A TEARJERKER MOVIE, HUH?
MY OLYMPIA CAN'T STAND THOSE...SHE ALWAYS LAUGHS WHEN SHE WATCHES THEM. GOOD NIGHT...
GOOD NIGHT.

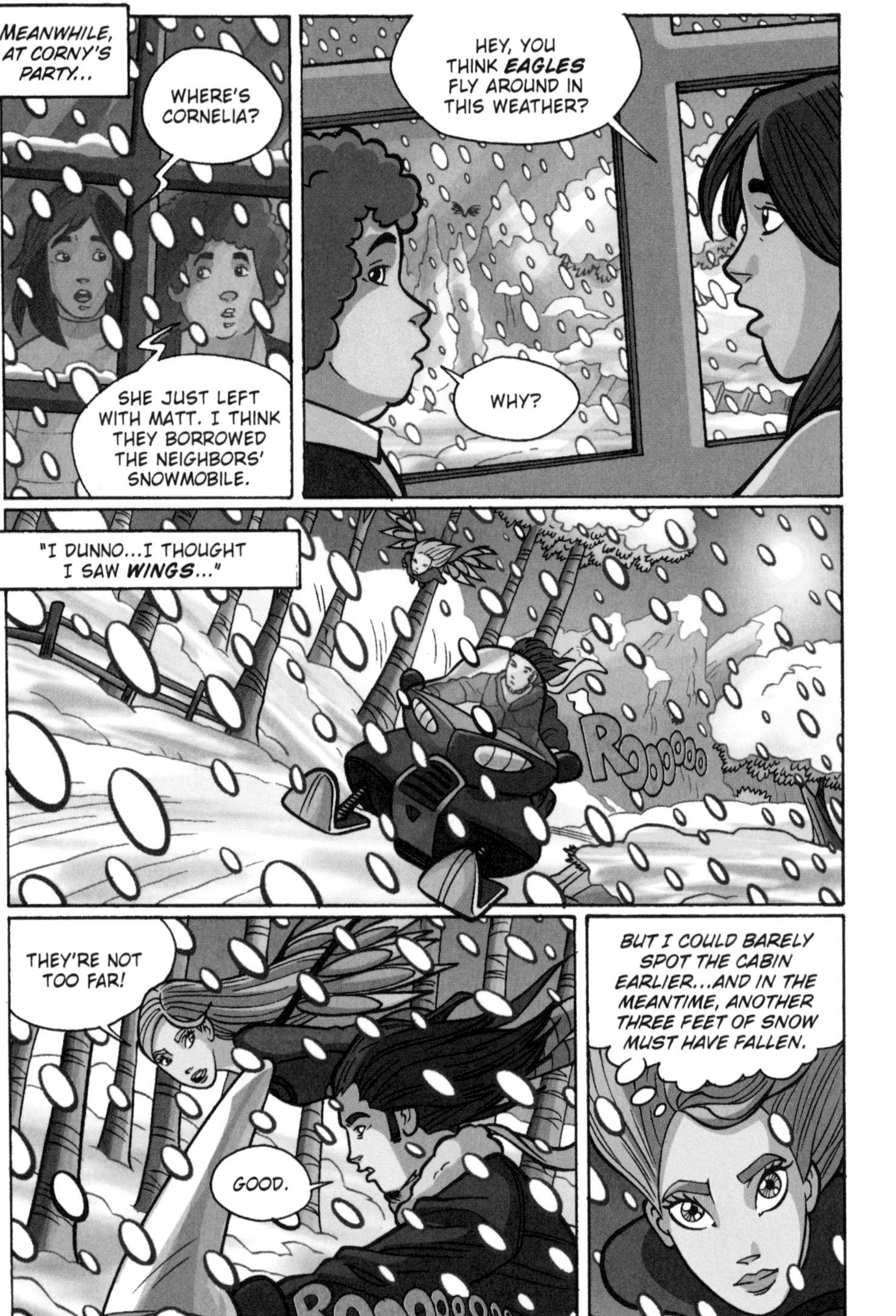
MEANWHILE, AT CORNY'S PARTY...
WHERE'S CORNELIA?
SHE JUST LEFT WITH MATT. I THINK THEY BORROWED THE NEIGHBORS' SNOWMOBILE.
HEY, YOU THINK EAGLES FLY AROUND IN THIS WEATHER?
WHY?
"I DUNNO...I THOUGHT I SAW WINGS..."
ROOOOOO
THEY'RE NOT TOO FAR!
GOOD.
ROOOOOOOOO
BUT I COULD BARELY SPOT THE CABIN EARLIER...AND IN THE MEANTIME, ANOTHER THREE FEET OF SNOW MUST HAVE FALLEN.

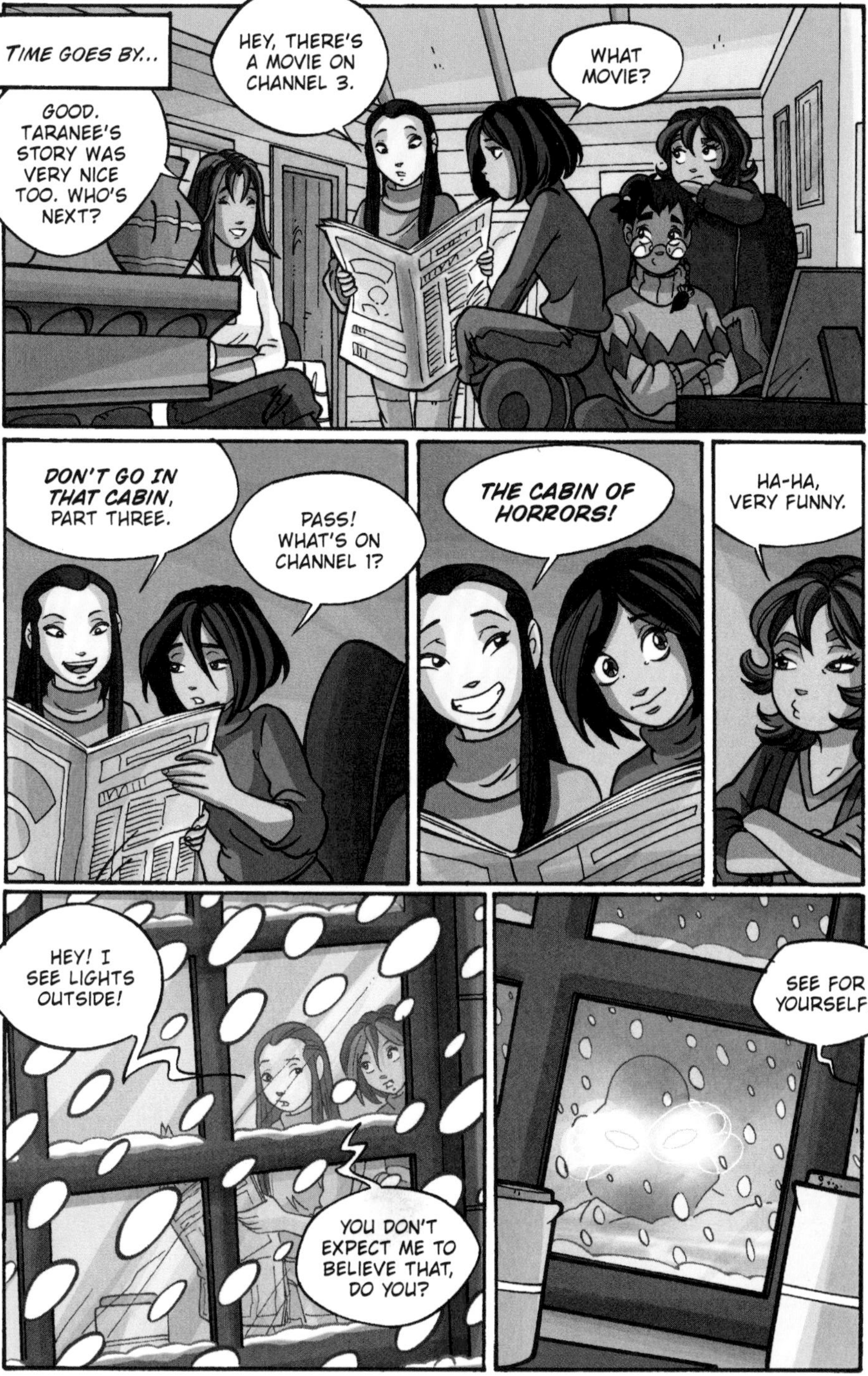
TIME GOES BY...
GOOD. TARANEE'S STORY WAS VERY NICE TOO. WHO'S NEXT?
HEY, THERE'S A MOVIE ON CHANNEL 3.
WHAT MOVIE?
DON'T GO IN THAT CABIN, PART THREE.
PASS! WHAT'S ON CHANNEL 1?
THE CABIN OF HORRORS!
HA-HA, VERY FUNNY.
HEY! I SEE LIGHTS OUTSIDE!
YOU DON'T EXPECT ME TO BELIEVE THAT, DO YOU?
SEE FOR YOURSELF!

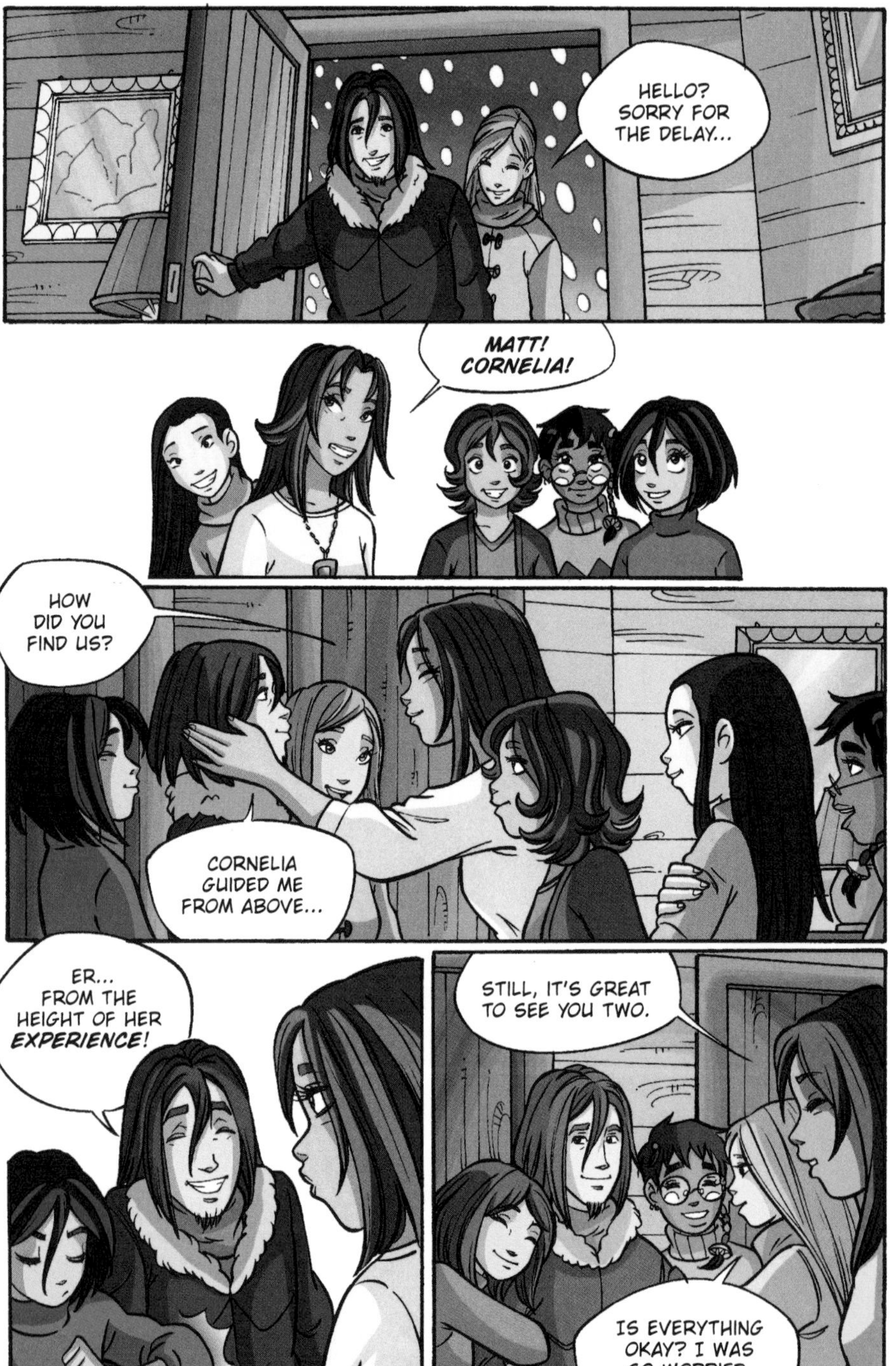
HELLO? SORRY FOR THE DELAY...
MATT! CORNELIA!
HOW DID YOU FIND US?
CORNELIA GUIDED ME FROM ABOVE...
ER... FROM THE HEIGHT OF HER *EXPERIENCE!*
STILL, IT'S GREAT TO SEE YOU TWO.
IS EVERYTHING OKAY? I WAS SO WORRIED.

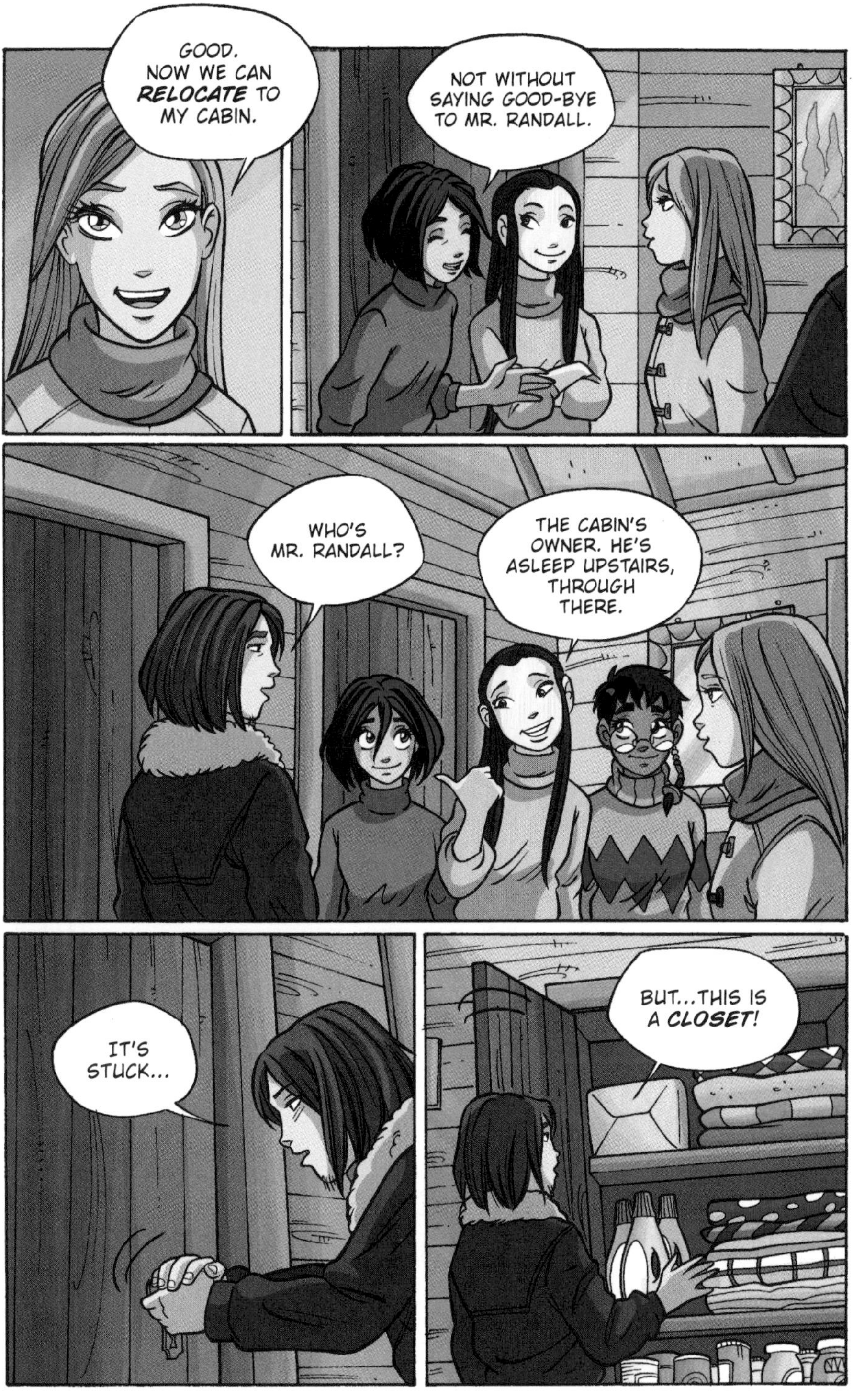
GOOD. NOW WE CAN RELOCATE TO MY CABIN.
NOT WITHOUT SAYING GOOD-BYE TO MR. RANDALL.
WHO'S MR. RANDALL?
THE CABIN'S OWNER. HE'S ASLEEP UPSTAIRS, THROUGH THERE.
IT'S STUCK...
BUT...THIS IS A CLOSET!

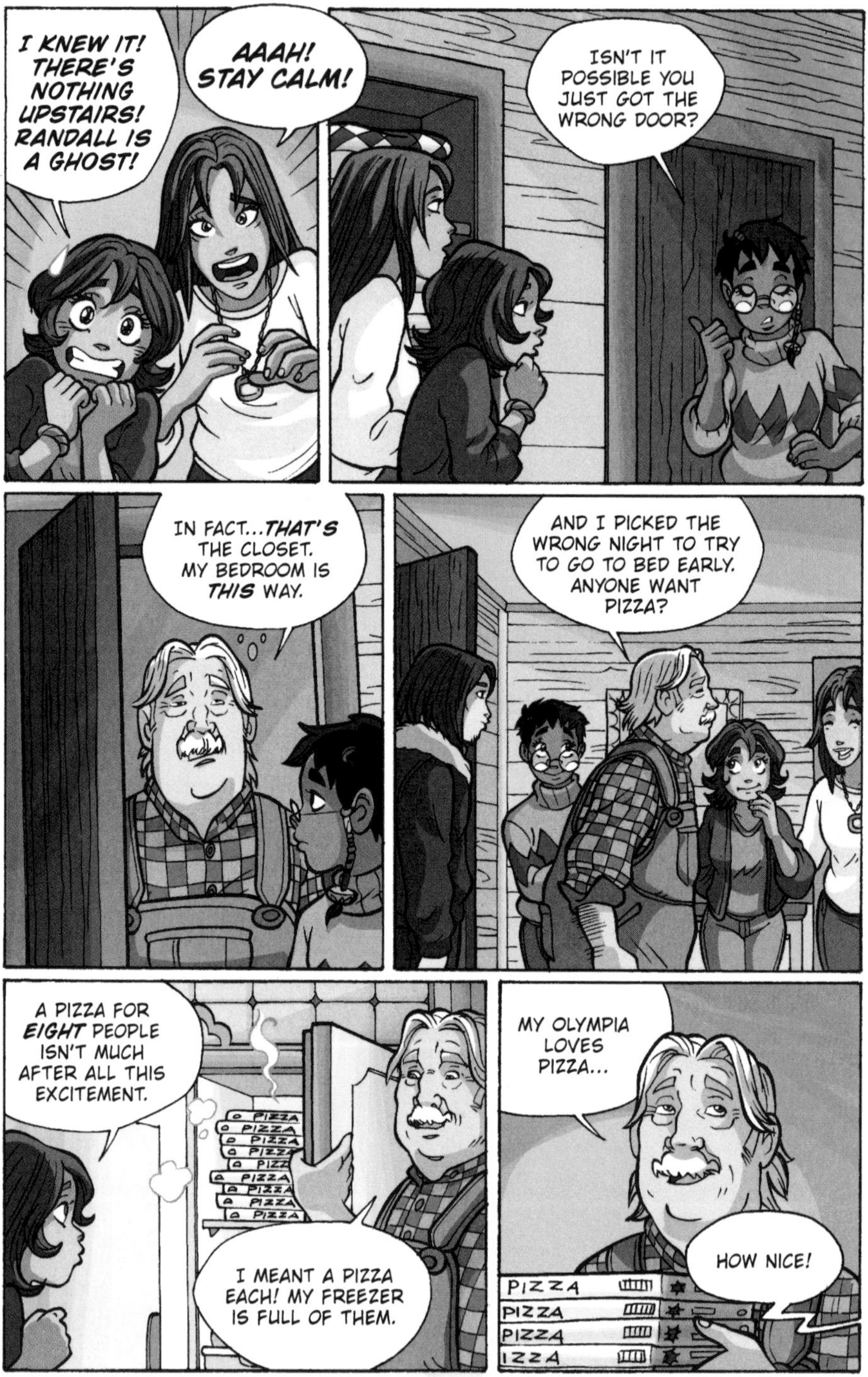
I KNEW IT! THERE'S NOTHING UPSTAIRS! RANDALL IS A GHOST!
AAAH! STAY CALM!
ISN'T IT POSSIBLE YOU JUST GOT THE WRONG DOOR?
IN FACT...THAT'S THE CLOSET. MY BEDROOM IS THIS WAY.
AND I PICKED THE WRONG NIGHT TO TRY TO GO TO BED EARLY. ANYONE WANT PIZZA?
A PIZZA FOR EIGHT PEOPLE ISN'T MUCH AFTER ALL THIS EXCITEMENT.
PIZZA
PIZZA
PIZZA
PIZZA
PIZZA
PIZZA
PIZZA
PIZZA
PIZZA
I MEANT A PIZZA EACH! MY FREEZER IS FULL OF THEM.
MY OLYMPIA LOVES PIZZA...
HOW NICE!
PIZZA
PIZZA
PIZZA
IZZA

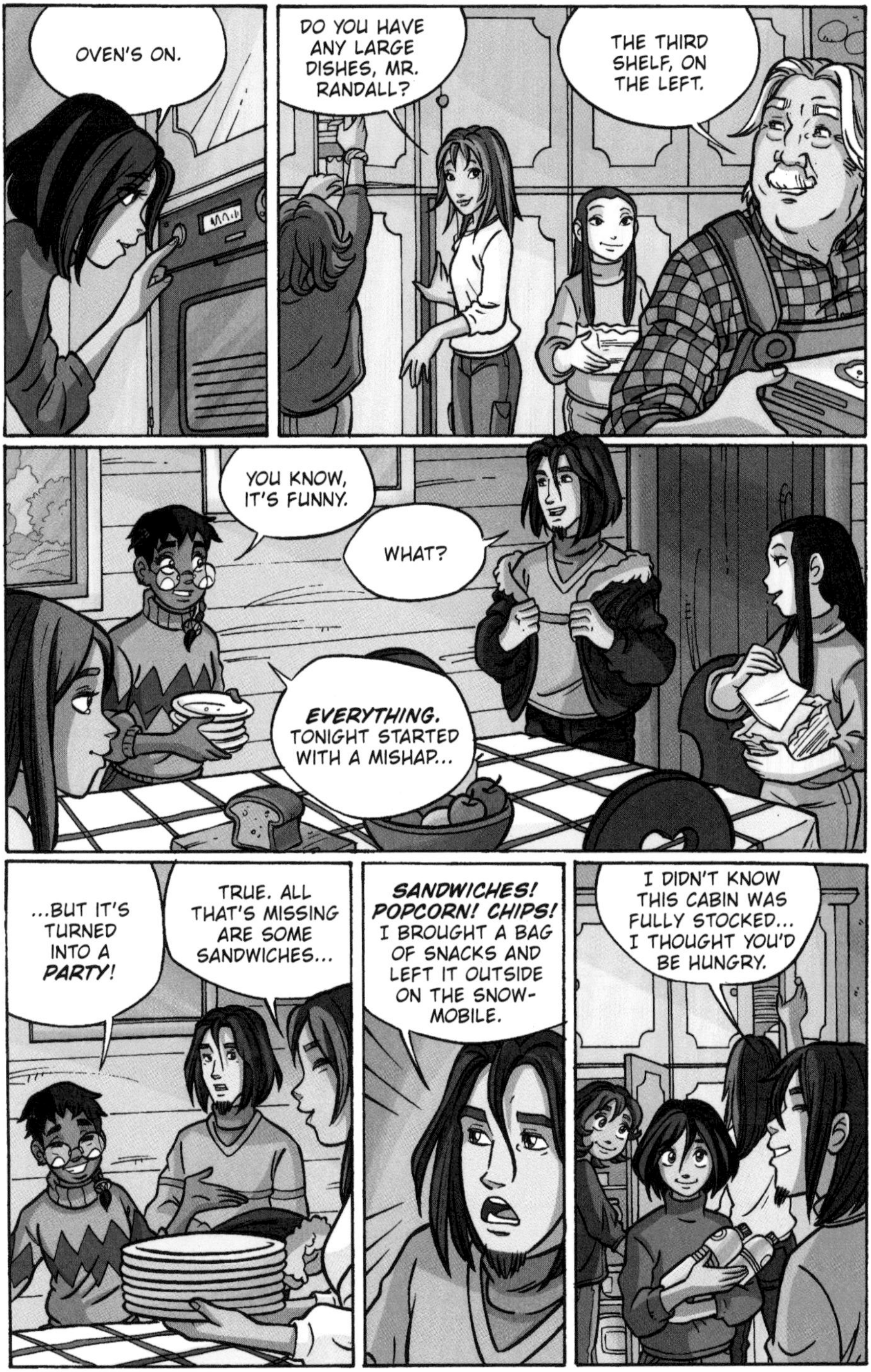
OVEN'S ON.
DO YOU HAVE ANY LARGE DISHES, MR. RANDALL?
THE THIRD SHELF, ON THE LEFT.
YOU KNOW, IT'S FUNNY.
WHAT?
EVERYTHING. TONIGHT STARTED WITH A MISHAP...
...BUT IT'S TURNED INTO A PARTY!
TRUE. ALL THAT'S MISSING ARE SOME SANDWICHES...
SANDWICHES! POPCORN! CHIPS! I BROUGHT A BAG OF SNACKS AND LEFT IT OUTSIDE ON THE SNOW-MOBILE.
I DIDN'T KNOW THIS CABIN WAS FULLY STOCKED... I THOUGHT YOU'D BE HUNGRY.

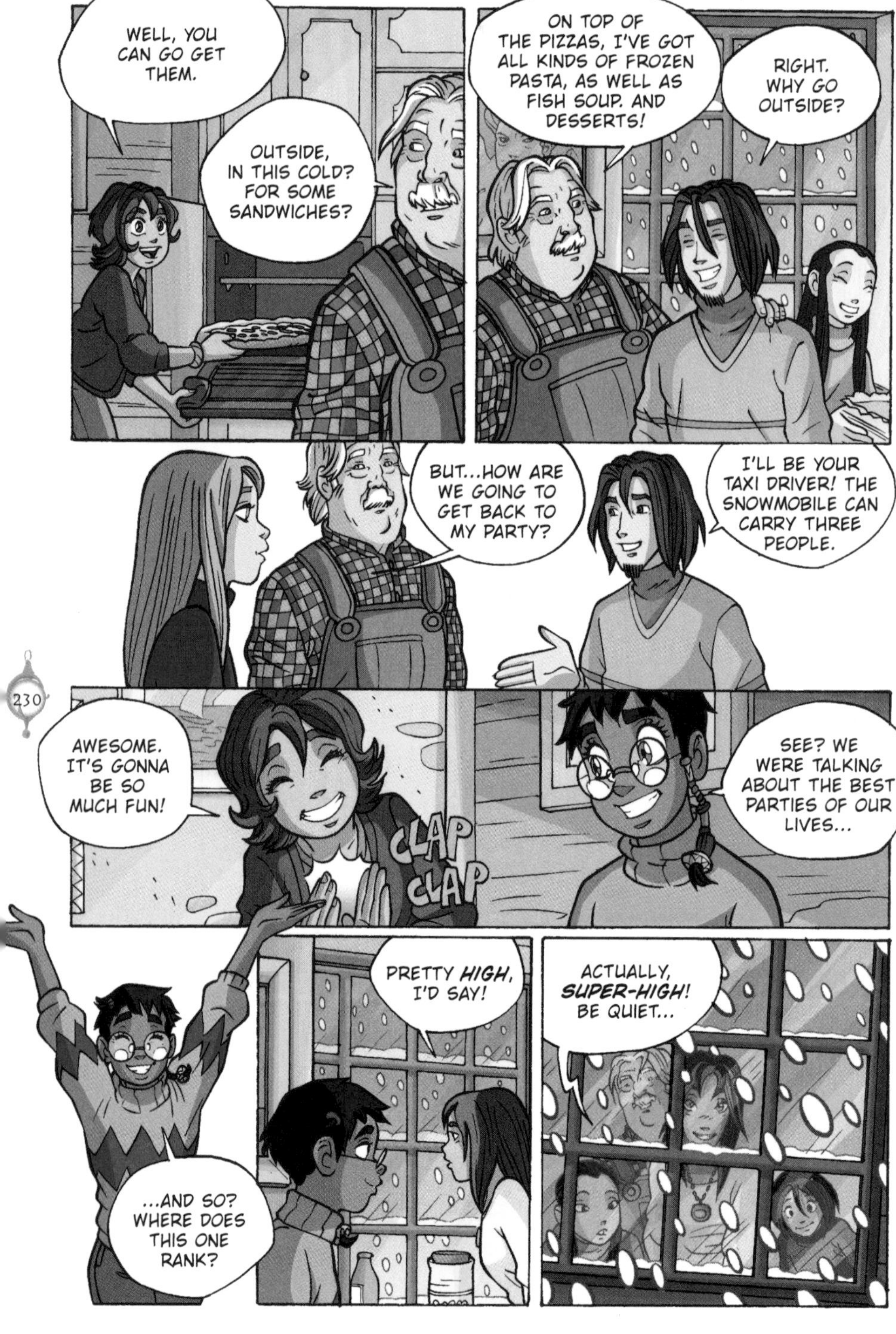
WELL, YOU CAN GO GET THEM.
OUTSIDE, IN THIS COLD? FOR SOME SANDWICHES?
ON TOP OF THE PIZZAS, I'VE GOT ALL KINDS OF FROZEN PASTA, AS WELL AS FISH SOUP. AND DESSERTS!
RIGHT. WHY GO OUTSIDE?
BUT...HOW ARE WE GOING TO GET BACK TO MY PARTY?
I'LL BE YOUR TAXI DRIVER! THE SNOWMOBILE CAN CARRY THREE PEOPLE.
AWESOME. IT'S GONNA BE SO MUCH FUN!
CLAP CLAP
SEE? WE WERE TALKING ABOUT THE BEST PARTIES OF OUR LIVES...
...AND SO? WHERE DOES THIS ONE RANK?
PRETTY HIGH, I'D SAY!
ACTUALLY, SUPER-HIGH! BE QUIET...

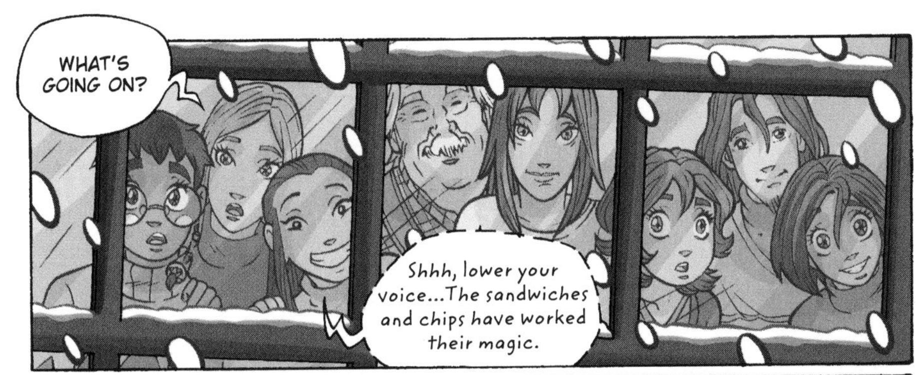
WHAT'S GOING ON?
Shhh, lower your voice...The sandwiches and chips have worked their magic.

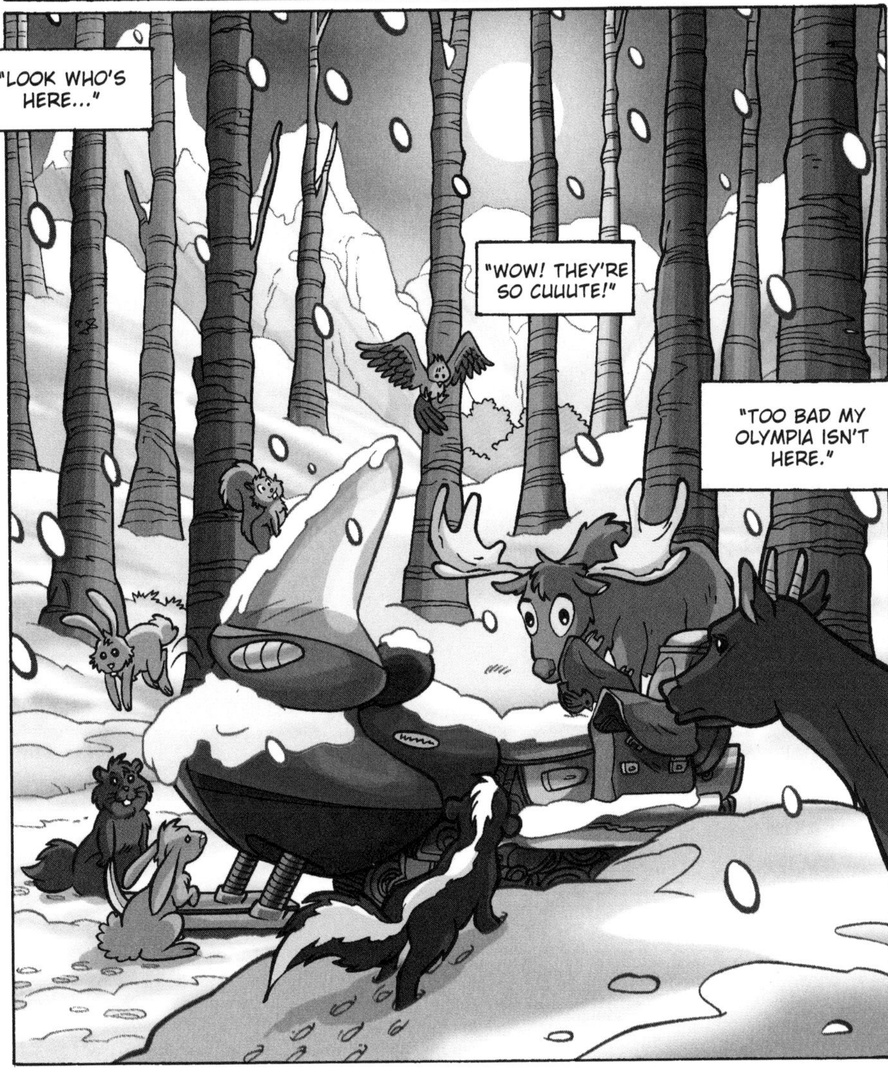
"LOOK WHO'S HERE..."
"WOW! THEY'RE SO CUUUTE!"
"TOO BAD MY OLYMPIA ISN'T HERE."

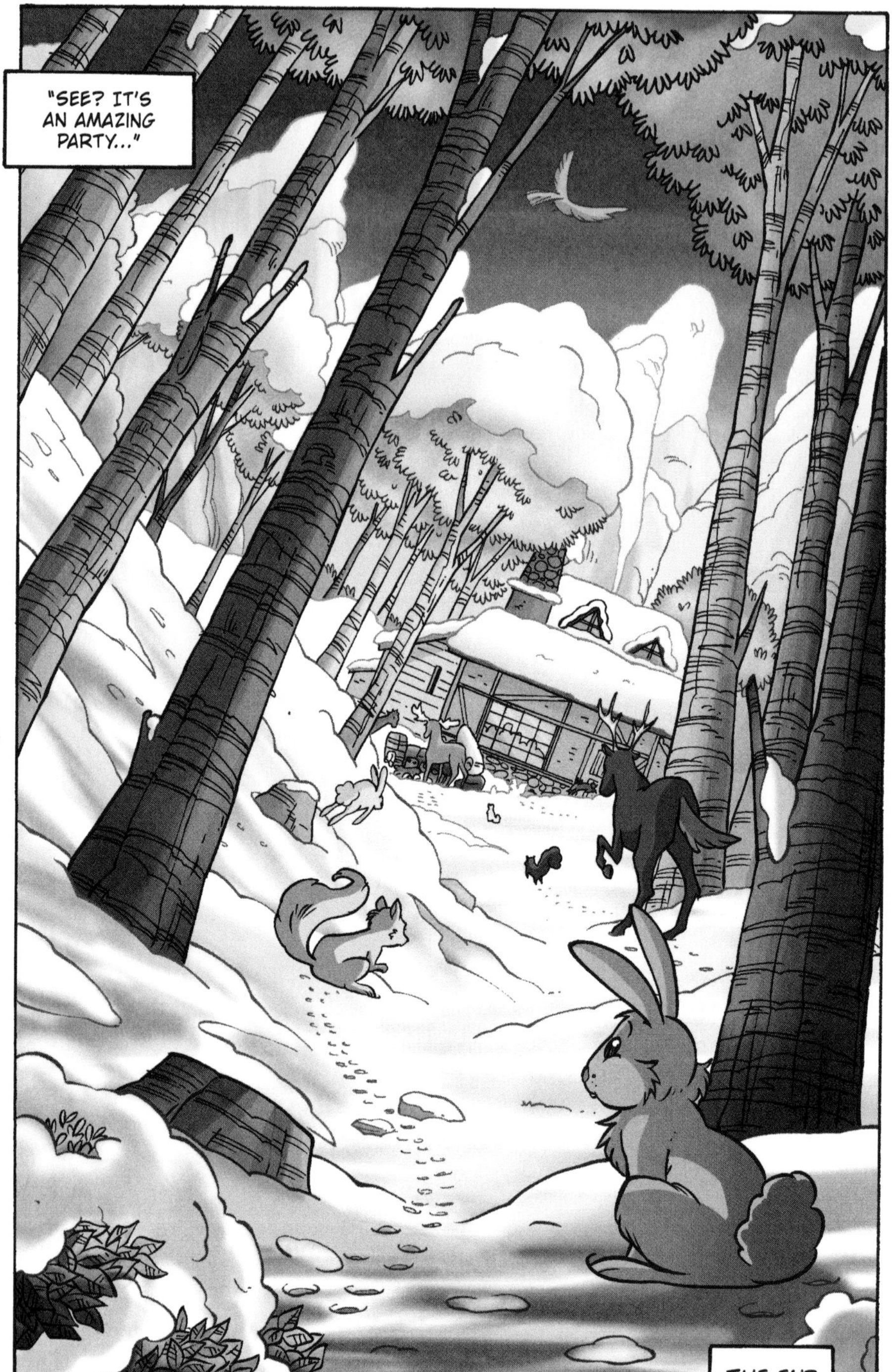
"SEE? IT'S AN AMAZING PARTY..."
THE END

Read on in Volume 30!

W.i.t.c.h.

Will Irma Taranee Cornelia Hay Lin

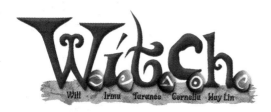

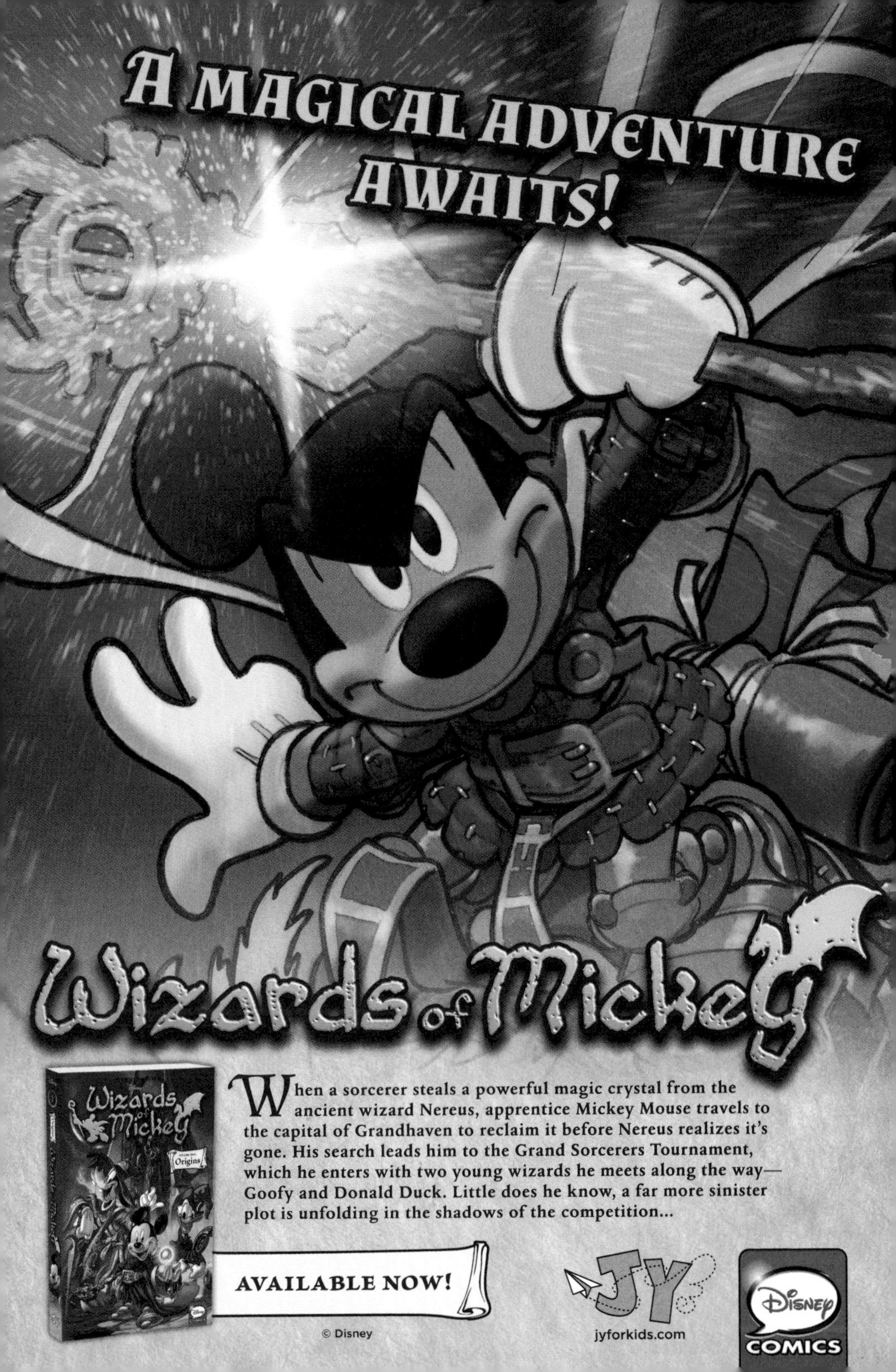
A MAGICAL ADVENTURE AWAITS!
Wizards of Mickey
Wizards of Mickey
Origins
When a sorcerer steals a powerful magic crystal from the ancient wizard Nereus, apprentice Mickey Mouse travels to the capital of Grandhaven to reclaim it before Nereus realizes it's gone. His search leads him to the Grand Sorcerers Tournament, which he enters with two young wizards he meets along the way—Goofy and Donald Duck. Little does he know, a far more sinister plot is unfolding in the shadows of the competition...
AVAILABLE NOW!
JY
© Disney
jyforkids.com
Disney COMICS

W.i.t.c.h.

Will Irma Taranee Cornelia Hay Lin

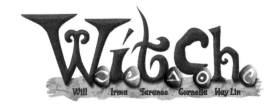

W.i.t.c.h.

Will Irma Taranee Cornelia Hay Lin

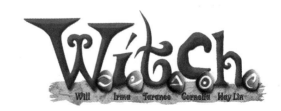

Part IX. 100% W.I.T.C.H. • Volume 4

Series Created by Elisabetta Gnone
Comic Art Direction: Alessandro Barbucci, Barbara Canepa

W.I.T.C.H.: The Graphic Novel,
Part IX: 100% W.I.T.C.H.
© Disney Enterprises, Inc.

English translation © 2022 by Disney Enterprises, Inc.

JY
150 West 30th Street, 19th Floor
New York, NY 10001

Visit us at jyforkids.com
facebook.com/jyforkids
twitter.com/jyforkids
jyforkids.tumblr.com
instagram.com/jyforkids

First JY Edition: June 2022
Edited by Yen Press Editorial: Liz Marbach, Won Young Seo
Designed by Yen Press Design: Liz Parlett

JY is an imprint of Yen Press, LLC.
The JY name and logo are trademarks of Yen Press, LLC.

The publisher is not responsible for websites (or their content) that are not owned by the publisher.

Library of Congress Control Number: 2017950917

ISBNs:
978-1-9753-2327-1 (paperback)
978-1-9753-2328-8 (ebook)

10 9 8 7 6 5 4 3 2 1

LSC-C

Printed in the United States of America

Cover Art by Giada Perissinotto
Colors by Andrea Cagol

Translation by Linda Ghio and
Stephanie Dagg at Editing Zone
Lettering by Katie Blakeslee

THE LONG KISS

Script by Augusto Macchetto
Layout and Pencils by Giada Perissinotto
Inks by Marina Baggio and Roberta Zanotta

BACK TO SCHOOL

Script by Teresa Radice
Layout, Pencils, and Inks by Lucio Leoni

A SPECIAL JOURNEY

Concept and Script by Alessandro Ferrari
Layout by Daniela Vetro
Pencils by Davide Baldoni
Inks by Marina Baggio and Roberta Zanotta

THE RIGHT DISTANCE

Concept and Script by Teresa Radice
Layout by Paolo Campinoti
Pencils by Federica Salfo
Inks by Marina Baggio and Roberta Zanotta

THE BEST PARTY

Concept and Script by Augusto Macchetto
Layout by Alberto Zanon
Pencils by Danilo Loizedda
Inks by Marina Baggio and Roberta Zanotta